A horrifying sound came from the ranks of the Yellow Knives and the soldiers. It was a long, howling cry. It must have struck terror, too, into the hearts of the foe. The sound was unmistakable. I had heard it on the rocky slopes of Torvaldsland, on the sands of the Tahari, in the jungles of the Ua.

Emerging then from the ranks of the enemy came a gigantic Kur, some nine feet in height, some nine hundred pounds in weight. It carried a huge shield and lance, the accounterments of a man. Behind it, on each side similarly armed, came others.

The lines, men screaming, mounts wheeling about, were shattered. Fear became flight, and flight rout, and rout slaughter. Yellow Knives and soldiers pressed on. Women and children screamed.

I lowered my lance. I trained it on the heart of the gigantic Kur. It was Sardak, the leader of the death squad from the steel worlds. . . .

JOHN NORMAN

books available from DAW:

HUNTERS OF GOR
MARAUDERS OF GOR
TRIBESMEN OF GOR
SLAVE GIRL OF GOR
BEASTS OF GOR
EXPLORERS OF GOR
FIGHTING SLAVE OF GOR (Jason Marshall I)
ROGUE OF GOR (Jason Marshall II)
GUARDSMAN OF GOR (Jason Marshall III)
SAVAGES OF GOR
BLOOD BROTHERS OF GOR

GHOST DANCE
TIME SLAVE
IMAGINATIVE SEX

Blood Brothers of Gor

John Norman

DAW BOOKS, INC.
DONALD A. WOLLHEIM, PUBLISHER
1633 Broadway, New York, N.Y. 10019

Cover art by Ken W. Kelly.

FIRST PRINTING, NOVEMBER 1982

1 2 3 4 5 6 7 8 9

DAW TRADEMARK REGISTERED
U.S. PAT. OFF. MARCA
REGISTRADA. HECHO EN U.S.A.

PRINTED IN U.S.A.

1

THE PTE

"There it is," said Grunt, pointing ahead and to our right. "Do you see it?"

"Yes," I said. "Too, I feel it." I could feel the tremor in the earth, even through the paws and legs of the lofty, silken kaiila.

"I have seen it only once before," he said.

I rose in the stirrups. The vibration, clearly, was registered in the narrow, flat-based rings. Earlier, dismounted, we had placed the palms of our hands to the earth. It was then that we had first felt it, earlier this morning, from as faraway as perhaps twenty pasangs.

"They are coming," had said Cuwignaka, happily.

"I am puzzled," said Grunt. "It is early, is it not?"

I sat back on the saddle.

"Yes," said Cuwignaka, astride his kaiila, to my left.

The current moon was Takiyuhawi, the moon in which the tabuk rut. It is sometimes known also as Canpasapawi, or the moon when the chokecherries are ripe.

"I do not understand," said Grunt. "It is not due until Kantasawi." This was the moon in which the plums become red. It is generally the hottest time of the year in the Barrens. It occurs in the latter portion of the summer.

"Why is it early?" asked Grunt.

"I do not know," said Cuwignaka.

Our kaiila shifted beneath us, on the grassy rise. The grass here came to the knees of the kaiila. It would have come to the thighs of a girl.

"Perhaps there is some mistake," I suggested. "Perhaps it is not what you think."

"There is no mistaking it," said Grunt.

"No," said Cuwignaka, happily.

"Could it not be another?" I asked.

"No," said Cuwignaka.

"These things are like the summer and the winter," said Grunt, "like the phases of the moons, like day and night."

"Why then is it early?" I asked.

"Has it been early before?" asked Grunt of Cuwignaka.

"Not in my lifetime," said Cuwignaka. "In the old stories it has sometimes been late, but never, as far as I know, has it been early."

"Think," I said. "Can you recall nothing of such a sort?"

Cuwignaka shrugged. "I can think of nothing of that sort," he said.

"Can there be no mistake?" I asked Grunt.

"No," said Grunt. "It is here."

"It looks like it is raining there," I said.

"That is dust, in the wind," said Cuwignaka. "It is raised by the hoofs."

"It is here," said Grunt. "There is no doubt about it."

I looked into the distance. It was like a Vosk of horn and hide.

"How long is it?" I asked. I could not even see the end of it.

"It is probably about fifteen pasangs in length," said Grunt. "It is some four or five pasangs in width."

"It can take the better part of a day to ride around it," said Cuwignaka.

"How many beasts are numbered in such a group?" I asked.

"Who has counted the stars, who has numbered the blades of grass," said Cuwignaka.

"It is estimated," said Grunt, "that there are between some two and three million beasts there."

"Surely it is the largest such group in the Barrens," I said.

"No," said Grunt, "there are larger. Boswell claims to have seen one such group which took five days to swim a river."

"How long would it take a group like this to swim a river?" I asked.

"Two to three days," said Grunt.

"I see," I said. The Boswell he had referred to, incidentally, was the same fellow for whom the Boswell Pass through the Thentis Mountains had been named. He was an early explorer in the Barrens. Others were such men as Diaz, Hogarthe and Bento.

"It is an awesome and splendid sight," I said. "Let us ride closer."

"But let us be careful," said Cuwignaka. Then, with a cry of pleasure, kicking his heels back into the flanks of his kaiila, he urged his beast down the slope.

Grunt and I looked at one another, and grinned. "He is still a boy," said Grunt.

We then followed Cuwignaka. It was toward noon when we reined up beside him on another rise. The animals were now some three to four pasangs away, below us.

"It is the Pte!" called out Cuwignaka happily to us, turning to look at us.

"Yes," said Grunt.

We could now smell the animals clearly. My mount, a lofty black kaiila, silken and swift, shifted nervously beneath me. Its nostrils were flared. Its storm lids were drawn, giving its large round eyes a distinctive yellowish cast. I did not think that it, a kaiila purchased some months ago in the town of Kailiauk, near the perimeter, had ever smelled such beasts before, and certainly not in such numbers. Too, I supposed that there were many among such beasts, perhaps most, in fact, who had never smelled a man, or a kaiila, before. Grit and dust settled about us. I blinked my eyes against it. It was very impressive to be so close to such beasts. I scarcely dared to conjecture what it might be like to be even closer, say, within a few hundred yards of them. Individual kills on such animals, incidentally, are commonly made from distances where one can almost reach out and touch the beast. One must be that close for the lance thrust to be made or for the arrow, from the small bow, to strike with sufficient depth, to the feathers, either into the intestinal cavity behind the last rib, resulting in large-scale internal hemorrhaging, or behind the left shoulder blade, into the heart.

"Is there always this much dust?" I asked. I raised my voice somewhat, against the sounds of the beasts, their bellowing and the thud of the hoofs.

"No," said Cuwignaka, raising his voice. "It is moving now, not drifting and grazing."

"Sometimes, for no clear reason," said Grunt, "it will move, and more or less swiftly. Then, at other times, for similarly no apparent reason, it will halt and graze, or move slowly, gently grazing along the way."

"It is early," I said.

"Yes," said Grunt. "That is interesting. It must have been moving more than is usual."

"I will inspect the animals," said Cuwignaka.

"Be careful," said Grunt.

We watched Cuwignaka move his kaiila down the slope and toward the animals. He would not approach them too closely. There were tribal reasons for this.

"It is like a flood," I said, "or a movement of the earth; it is like wind, or thunder; it is like a natural phenomenon."

"Yes," said Grunt.

"In its way," I said, "I suppose it is a natural phenomenon."

"Yes, in its way, it is," said Grunt.

The movement of this group of animals had been reported in the camp of the Isbu Kaiila, or the Little-Stones band of the Kaiila, for more than ten days now, in a rough map drawn to the east of the camp, with notched sticks, the notching indicating the first and second day, and so on, of the animals' progress, and the placement of the sticks indicating the position of the animals on the day in question. Scouts of the Sleen Soldiers, a warrior society of the Isbu, had been keeping track of the animals since they had entered the country of the Kaiila more than two weeks ago. This was a moon in which the Sleen Soldiers held police powers in the camp, and so it was to their lot that numerous details, such as scouting and guarding, supervising the camp and settling minor disputes, now fell. Among their other duties, of course, would come the planning, organization and policing of the great Wanasapi, the hunt or chase.

In a few Ehn Cuwignaka, sweating, elated, his braided hair behind him, returned his lathered kaiila to our side.

"It is glorious!" he said.

"Good," said Grunt, pleased at the young man's pleasure.

It is difficult to make clear to those who are not intimately acquainted with such things the meaning of the Pte, or Kailiauk, to the red savages. It is regarded by them with reverence and affection. It is a central phenomenon in their life, and much of their life revolves around it. The mere thought of the kailiauk can inspire awe in them, and pleasure and excitement. More to them than meat for the stomach and clothes for the back is the kailiauk to them; too, it is mystery and meaning for them; it is heavy with medicine; it is a danger; it is a sport; it is a challenge; and, at dawn, with a lance or bow in one's hand, and a swift, eager kaiila between one's knees, it is a joy to the heart.

"Look," said Grunt, pointing to the right.

A rider, a red savage, was approaching rapidly. He wore a breechclout and moccasins. About his neck was a string of sleen claws. There were no feathers in his hair and neither he nor his animal wore paint. Too, he did not carry lance and shield. He was not on the business of war. He did have a bow case and quiver, and at the thong on his waist was a beaded sheath, from which protruded the hilt of a trade knife.

"It is Hci," said Cuwignaka. There is no exact translation of the expression 'Hci' from Kaiila, into either Gorean or English. This is not all that unusual, incidentally. One cannot expect identical regularities in meaning and usage to obtain in diverse linguistic communities. The expression, for most practical purposes, signifies a certain type of gap, such as, for example, might occur in the edge of a trade ax, or hatchet, for use in drawing nails, an occupation for which red savages, of course, have little use. It is also used more broadly for a gash, such as an ax might cut in a tree, or for a cut or scar. It seems to be clearly in the latter range of meanings that the name belonged. At the left side of Hci's face, at the chin, there was an irregular, jagged scar, some two inches in length. This dated from several years ago, when he had been seventeen, from the second time he had set the paws of his kaiila on the warpath. It had been given to him by a Yellow Knife in mounted combat, the result of a stroke by a long-handled, stone-bladed tomahawk, or canhpi. Before that time, as a stalwart, handsome lad, he had been affectionately known as Ihdazicaka, or One-Who-Counts-Himself-Rich. Afterwards he had become, by his own wish, only Hci. He had become morose and cruel. Immersing himself in the comraderie, and the rituals and ceremonies of the Sleen Soldiers, it seemed he lived then for little other than the concerns of raiding and war. There were members of his own society who feared to ride with him, so swift, so fierce, so careless of danger he was. Once, in a fight with Fleer, he had leaped to the ground and thrust his lance through the long, trailing end of the society's war sash, which, on that occasion, he had been wearing. He thus fastened himself in place, on foot, among the charging Fleer. "I will not yield this ground!" he had cried. The fleeing members of his society, seeing this, and knowing that he wore the war sash, had then rallied and, though outnumbered, had charged the Fleer. The Fleer, eventually, had left the scene of battle, feeling the cost of obtaining a victory over such men would be too high. As they left they had raised their lances in salute to the young warrior. Such courage is acknowledged in the Barrens, even though it be in an enemy.

Hci reined in his kaiila, squealing, kicking dust, before us.

The disfigurement was indeed prominent. The blow of the canhpi had slashed through to the jawbone.

"What are you doing here?" demanded Hci, speaking in Kaiila. I could now, given my time with Grunt and Cuwignaka, and my time in the Isbu camp, follow much of what was said. I could now, too, to some extent, communicate in that expressive, sibilant language.

"We have come to see the Pte," said Cuwignaka. The expression 'Pte', literally, stands for the kailiauk cow, as 'Tatanka' stands for the kailiauk bull, but it is commonly used colloquially, more generally, to stand for the kailiauk in general. In a sense, the "Pte" may be considered the mother of the tribes, as it is through her that their nomadic life, in its richness and variety, becomes possible. More formally, of course, one speaks of the kailiauk. The expression 'kailiauk' is a Gorean word and, as far as I know, does not have an Earth origin.

I looked beyond Hci to the beasts, some two to three pasangs away. The kailiauk is a large, lumbering, shaggy, trident-horned ruminant. It has four stomachs and an eight-valved heart. It is dangerous, gregarious, small-eyed and short-tempered. Adult males can stand as high as twenty or twenty-five hands at the shoulder and weigh as much as four thousand pounds.

"You have no right here," said Hci, angrily.

"We are causing no harm," said Cuwignaka.

"No one will hunt until the great hunt," said Hci. "Then we will hunt. The Isbu will hunt. The Casmu will hunt! The Isanna will hunt! The Napoktan will hunt! The Wismahi will hunt! The Kaiila will hunt!"

The Isbu, or Little-Stones band; the Casmu, or Sand, band; the Isanna, the Little-Knife band; the Napoktan, or Bracelets, band; and the Wismahi, or Arrowhead band, are the five bands which constitute the Kaiila tribe. The origins of these names are not always clear. It seems probable that the Little-Stones and the Sand bands may have had their names from geographical features, perhaps those adjacent to riverside encampments. The Wismahi, or Arrowhead, band is said by some to have once made their winter camp at the confluence of two rivers, the joining of the rivers resembling the point of an arrowhead. Others claim that they once lived in a flint-rich area and, prior to the general availability of trade points, conducted a lively trade in flint with surrounding tribes. The Bracelets band, or the Napoktan, wear copper bracelets on the left wrist. This band, outside of the Kaiila, is often known as the Mazahuhu band, which is the Dust-Leg word for bracelets. I do not know the origin of the name for the Isanna, or the Little-Knife, band. Sometimes, as I suspect was the case with the Napoktan, these names may owe their origin to the idiosyncrasies of given leaders, to unique historical events or perhaps, even, to dreams. Dreams, and dreaming on matters of importance, are taken very seriously by the red savages. Indeed, is it not that in dreams one may even enter the medicine world itself? In dreams is it not the case that one might sit about the fires of the dead, conversing with them? Is it not the case that in dreams one may understand the speech of animals? And is it not the case that in dreams one may find oneself in distant lands and countries, moons away, and yet, in a single night, find oneself, awakening, returned to one's lodge, to the embers of one's fire and the familiar poles and skins about one?

"We are here to see the Pte," said Cuwignaka, "not to hunt."

"It is well for you," said Hci, angrily. "You well know the penalties for illicit hunting."

Cuwignaka did not even deign to respond. To be sure, the penalties were not light. One might be publicly denounced and abuse, even beaten, in the village. One's weapons could be broken. One's lodge, and robes, and possessions could be taken away or cut to pieces with knives and scattered to the winds. In the beliefs of the red savages the welfare of the whole, that of the tribe, takes precedence over the welfare of the individual. In the thinking of the red savages the right to diminish and jeopardize the community does not lie within the prerogatives of the individual.

"Go away!" said Hci, with an angry wave of his arm.

Cuwignaka stiffened on the back of his kaiila.

Hci angrily gestured to the string of sleen claws about his neck, the sign of the Sleen Soldiers.

"It is an order," said Grunt to Cuwignaka, in Gorean. "He is well within his authority, as you know. He is a Sleen Soldier, and it is among his duties to track and protect the kailiauk. Do not think of it as a personal thing. He is a Sleen Soldier, doing his work. In his place you would doubtless do much the same."

Cuwignaka nodded, recognizing the justice of this view. It was not Hci, so to speak, who was being obeyed, but rather a duly constituted authority, an officer, a constable or warden in such matters.

We turned our kaiila about, to take our way from the place.

"Women, slaves and white men are not to ride forth to look upon the Pte," called Hci after us.

Cuwignaka wheeled his kaiila about, angrily. I, wheeling about, too, caught his arm.

"I am not a woman!" said Cuwignaka.

Hci laughed.

"I am not a woman," said Cuwignaka.

"You are a woman," said Hci. "You should please warriors."

"I am not a woman," said Cuwignaka.

"You do not wear the breechclout," said Hci. "You did not take the warpath."

"I am not a woman," said Cuwignaka.

"You wear the dress of a woman," said Hci. "You do the work of a woman. I think I will give you the name of a woman. I think I will call you Siptopto."

Cuwignaka's fists clenched on the reins of his kaiila. The expression 'Siptopto' is a common expression for beads.

"You should please warriors," said Hci.

"No," said Cuwignaka.

"You did not take the warpath," said Hci.

"I had no quarrel with the Fleer," said Cuwignaka.

"You are not welcome among the Isbu," said Hci. "You shame them. You cannot mate among us. Why do you not go away?"

"I am Isbu," said Cuwignaka. "I am Isbu Kaiila!"

My hand on his arm restrained Cuwignaka from charging Hci. Had he attempted to do so he would have been, without a saddle, dragged literally from the back of the kaiila.

"You should have been left staked out," said Hci. "It would have been better for the Kaiila."

Cuwignaka shrugged. "Perhaps," he said. "I do not know."

Cuwignaka, on the back of his kaiila, wore the remains of a white dress, a portion of the loot of a destroyed wagon train. He had been a slave of soldiers traveling with the train. Originally he had been Isbu Kaiila. He had twice refused to go on the warpath against the Fleer, hereditary enemies of the Kaiila. The first time he had been put in the dress of a woman and forced to live as a woman, performing the work of a woman and being referred to in the feminine gender. It was from that time that he had been called Cuwignaka, which means "Woman's Dress." It is, moreover, the word for the dress of a white woman and, in this, given the contempt in which the proud red savages hold white females, commonly reducing them to fearful, groveling slaves, utilizing them as little more than beasts of burden and ministrants to their will, in all respects, it possesses to the Kaiila an additional subtle and delicious irony.

The second time Cuwignaka had refused to go on the warpath he had been bound in his dress and traded to Dust Legs, from whom, eventually, he was purchased as a slave by whites, in the vicinity of the Ihanke, the border between the lands of farmers and ranchers and the lands of the red savages. Near the perimeter, as a slave, he had learned to speak Gorean. Later he was acquired by soldiers and brought again into the Barrens, their intention being to use him as an interpreter. When the wagon train had been destroyed, that with which the soldiers were then traveling, he had fallen into the hands of the victors. He had returned to the Barrens. He had been the slave of the hated enemy. He was staked out, to die. A lance, unbroken, had been placed by him, butt down, in the earth, in token of respect, at least, by Canka, Fire-Steel, his brother. Canka had also taken the dress which Hci had thrown contemptuously beside him, taken from the loot of one of the wagons, and wrapped it about the lance. In this fashion Canka had conspicuously marked the place, as though with a flag.

It has been my considered judgment that Canka, in doing this, had hoped to draw attention to the location, that he hoped by this device to attract others to the spot, who might free the lad, or perhaps to mark it for himself, that he might later, accepting exile and outlawry at the hands of the Isbu, free his brother. As it turned out Grunt and I, traversing the Barrens, had come on the lad and freed him. Shortly thereafter we were apprehended by a mixed group of unlikely allies, representatives of Sleen, Yellow Knives and Kaiila, who, in virtue of the Memory, as it is called, had joined forces to attack the wagon train and soldiers.

Grunt had brought a coffle of white slave girls into the Barrens with him, as pack animals and trade goods. He had also acquired two prisoners, two former enemies of his, Max and Kyle Hobart, in effect as gifts from Dust Legs. The Sleen took two of his girls, Ginger and Evelyn, former tavern girls from the town of Kailiauk, near the Ihanke, and the Hobarts, from him. Four other girls were led away from him naked and bound, their necks in tethers, by a Yellow-Knife warrior.

These were two American girls, Lois and Inez, an English girl, named Priscilla, and a short, dark-haired French girl, named Corinne.

The Kaiila were mostly members of the All Comrades, a warrior society, like the Sleen Soldiers, of the Isbu Kaiila. They were under the command of Canka, Cuwignaka's brother. One other was with the party, too, an older warrior, Kahintokapa, One-Who-Walks-Before, of the prestigious Yellow-Kaiila Riders. He was of the Casmu, or Sand, band.

Grunt's prize on the coffle, a beautiful red-haired girl, a former debutante from Pennsylvania, once Miss Millicent Aubrey-Welles, was selected out by Canka as a personal slave, one to run at the left flank of his own kaiila and wear her leather, beaded collar, placed on her by his command, for him alone. Grunt's last slave, the dark-haired beauty, Wasnapohdi, or Pimples, whom he had acquired in trade for three hatchets from Dust Legs, he was permitted to keep. This was probably because Canka truly bore us no ill will. Indeed, he was probably pleased, as I now understand, that we had freed Cuwignaka. He may also have permitted Grunt to keep Wasnapohdi, of course, because she was conversant in Kaiila. He would have respected her for that.

"Slave," said Hci, regarding me, scornfully.

I did not meet his eyes. It was I, of course, who had actually freed Cuwignaka. It had been my knife which had cut the thongs. This was something which Canka, as Blotanhunka, or war-party leader, of the All Comrades, had, of course, not been able to overlook. Regardless of his own feelings in the matter or even, possibly, of his own intentions with respect to the future, such an act could not be allowed to pass unnoticed. A prisoner of the Kaiila, one duly dealt with, so to speak, had been freed. There was a payment to be made. I, on foot, had looked at the mounted warriors, the Kaiila left then in the place. There were some seventeen of them, including Canka. Each was an All Comrade; each was skilled; all had counted coup.

"I am ready to fight," I had said.

"Do not be a fool," had said Grunt.

"I am ready ," I had said to Canka.

"There is an alternative," had said Grunt. "Can't you see? He is waiting."

"What?" I asked.

"The collar," said Grunt.

"Never," I said.

"Please, Tatankasa," had said Canka. This was what he had called me, when he had learned that I was willing to fight with his men, no quarter given or taken. It means, in effect, "Red Bull." 'Tatanka' designates the kailiauk bull, and the suffix 'sa' means red. In Kaiila, as in most of the languages of the Barrens, the adjective commonly succeeds the noun. The name was one in which respect was conveyed.

"Please," had said Cuwignaka.

"Please," had said Grunt.

Numbly I had unbuckled my sword belt. I had wrapped the belt about the sword and knife sheath, and had given the belt, and these objects, to Grunt. I had disarmed myself. In moments Canka's beaded collar had been tied on my neck. I had become his slave.

"Slave," sneered Hci.

I did not respond to him.

"White men," said Hci, scornfully, gesturing to myself and Grunt.

"Yes," said Grunt, pleasantly.

"How is it that a slave," asked Hci of Cuwignaka, "wears moccasins and rides a kaiila?"

"It is permitted by Canka," said Cuwignaka.

"Dismount," said Hci to me. "Remove your moccasins and your garments, completely."

"He is not your slave," said Cuwignaka.

"Nor is he yours," said Hci.

I dismounted and stripped, removing also the moccasins which Canka had given me. I handed the clothing, and the moccasins, to Grunt. I then stood before Hci's kaiila. I wore now only the beaded leather collar which had been placed on me some two weeks ago. It was about an inch and a half high. It had a distinctive pattern of beading. The colors and design of the beading marked it as Canka's. It is common among red savages to use such designs, such devices, to mark their possessions. A collar of identical design, back in the village, was worn by the lovely, red-haired girl, the former Miss Millicent Aubrey-Welles, who had so taken the fancy of the young warrior. Both of our collars were tied shut. The knots on them had been retied personally by Canka after our arrival at his camp. This is done, in effect, with a signature knot, in a given tribal style, known only to the tier. This gives him a way of telling if the knot has been untied and retied in his absence. It is death, incidentally, for a slave to remove such a collar without permission. It can be understood then that slaves of the red savages do not tamper with their collars. They keep them on.

"Slave," said Hci, contemptuously.

One difference, of course, was clear between the collars of the girl and myself. Hers was the collar of a true slave, in the fullness of that meaning, whereas mine, in effect, though identical, functioned almost as a badge of protection. In being Canka's slave I had a status and place in the Isbu camp which, in its way, sheltered me from the type of sportive attack to which a lone, free white man might be otherwise exposed. In another way, Grunt's familiarity to the Kaiila, for he had visited them last year, and was close to Mahpiyasapa, Black Clouds, the civil chieftain of the Isbu, and his knowledge of their language, which closely resembles Dust Leg, garnered him a similar protection. His value as a trader, too, was clear to the Kaiila. They prized many of the things of value which he might bring into the Barrens, the men relishing trinkets such as trade points and knife blades, and the women welcoming trade cloth, chemical dyes and drilled glass beads. Too, Grunt was an honest man, and likable. This pleased the Kaiila, as it also did the Dust Legs and the Fleer.

The collar of Canka which I wore, as I had come to realize in the past several days, was, all things considered, as he did not intend to enforce its significance upon me, a valuable accouterment. Canka was a respected and important young warrior; indeed, in the recent action to the west, he had even served as Blotanhunka of the All Comrades. This gave me, as his property, a certain prestige, particularly as Canka himself treated me with obvious respect. He called me Tatankasa, or Red Bull, which was a noble name from the point of view of the Kaiila. He gave me moccasins. He permitted me my clothing. He let me have, even, the use of my former kaiila. I did not even stay in his lodge, or have to sleep near it. I stayed with Cuwignaka in a tattered lodge, donated by Akihoka, One-Who-Is-Skillful, a close friend of Canka. For most practical purposes I was free in the village.

"Kneel," said Hci.

I knelt, naked, save for the collar of Canka, in the tall, dry grass.

"Put your head down," said Hci.

I did so.

"This is not necessary," said Cuwignaka.

"Be quiet, Siptopto," said Hci, "lest I consign you to the pleasure of warriors."

"I do not fear you," said Cuwignaka.

"You speak boldly for a female," said Hci.

"I am a man," said Cuwignaka. Bold speech, incidentally, is commonly accepted from free females of their own people by the red savages. If she grows too irritating, of course, she may, like any other woman, be beaten. Bold speech, on the other hand, is not accepted from female slaves among the red savages. Female slaves among such peoples quickly learn their place, a place in which they are kept with perfection.

"I did not know that," said Hci, as though interested.

"Yes," said Cuwignaka.

"On your belly," said Hci to me.

"Do not do this," said Cuwignaka.

"Crawl to the paws of my kaiila," said Hci to me.

"No," said Cuwignaka.

"Is he not a slave?" asked Hci.

"Yes," said Cuwignaka, uncertainly.

I moved to the paws of the kaiila, on my belly, my head down.

"Kiss the paws of my kaiila," said Hci to me, imperiously.

I did so. I had been commanded, as though I might have been a girl.

"Canka will hear of this," said Cuwignaka.

"See that he does," said Hci, angrily, and then pulled the kaiila away. The dust from the paws of the kaiila was in my mouth. "And now, get away from here! Return to the camp!" Little love was lost, I gathered, between Hci and Canka. Hci doubtless held Canka responsible, in some fashion, for Cuwignaka's freedom, and his presence among the Isbu, a presence which many among the Isbu, including Hci, found infuriating and shameful. In humiliating me, whom Canka treated with respect and honor, he was, in effect, demeaning Canka. On Canka's part, similarly, there was little affection borne toward Hci, largely because of the latter's hostility towards his brother, Cuwignaka. In Canka's view Hci's contempt for Cuwignaka was more unbending, more extreme and rigid, than was called for. Cuwignaka lived and dressed as a woman; he was referred to as a woman and performed the labors of a woman. He was not to be permitted to mate among the Kaiila. What more did Hci want?

I myself suspected that the matter went deeper than Hci's tribal pride and sense of propriety. Already Canka was a rising young warrior in the tribe. Already, once, he had served as Blotanhunka, or the leader of a war party. Hci, in spite of his skills and courage, had not yet received such an honor. This may have stung Hci even more as he was the son of Mahpiyasapa, the civil chief of the Isbu. Such leadership might have seemed almost owed to one in his position. Yet it had been denied him. I suspected that the reason that Hci had never been given the command of a raiding party was not because he was not admired and liked among the Isbu, nor because his trail and war skills were not respected, but because his judgment was not trusted. The recklessness with which he conducted himself and his insouciant disregard of personal danger did not augur well for his capacity to discharge the duties of a responsible leadership.

I did not think, incidentally, that Hci's hostility toward Canka had anything to do with Canka's acquisition of, and ownership of, Winyela, the lovely, white, red-haired female slave, the former Miss Millicent Aubrey-Welles, of Pennsylvania, whom Grunt had brought into the Barrens for Mahpiyasapa, his father. Hci had little use for such slaves, except occasionally to rape and quirt them. Mahpiyasapa, on the other hand, had been extremely displeased that Canka, despite being informed of the intended disposition of the white female, had asserted his war rights of slave capture, and, desiring her mightily, had taken her for himself. Mahpiyasapa, incidentally, as I have mentioned, was the civil chief of the Isbu.

Among the red savages there are various sorts of chief. The primary types of chief are the war chief, the medicine chief and the civil chief. One may be, interestingly, only one sort of chief at a time. This, like the rotation of police powers among warrior societies, is a portion of the checks and balances, so to speak, which tend to characterize tribal governance. Other checks and balances are such things as tradition and custom, the closeness of the governed and the governors, multiple-family interrelatednesses, the election of chiefs, the submission of significant matters to a council, and, ultimately, the feasibility of simply leaving the group, in greater or lesser numbers. Despotism, then, in virtue of the institutions of the red savages, is impractical for them; this impracticality is a much surer guarantee of its absence in a society than the most fervid of negative rhetorics.

"Go," ordered Hci.

"Do you command me as Hci, or as a Sleen Soldier?" asked Cuwignaka, angrily.

"Go," said Hci, menacingly.

"I obey you as a Sleen Soldier," said Cuwignaka. "I will go."

"When the hunt is mounted," said Hci to Cuwignaka, "you may not hunt. You will cut meat with the women."

"That is known to me," said Cuwignaka.

"For you are a woman," said Hci, sneeringly.

"No," said Cuwignaka. "I am a man."

"She is pretty, isn't she?" asked Hci of Grunt.

Grunt did not respond.

"If she does not please you," said Hci to Grunt, "beat her, as you would any other woman." He then turned his mount abruptly about. I heard its paws, suddenly, striking the turf, the sound rapidly diminishing.

"Do not pursue him," said Grunt to Cuwignaka.

"I am a man," said Cuwignaka, angrily.

"That is known to me," said Grunt.

"I must fight him," said Cuwignaka.

"No," said Grunt. "That would not be wise. He is one of the finest of the warriors of the Isbu."

"Rise up, Mitakola, my friend," said Cuwignaka to me. "He is gone."

I rose to my feet, wiping my face with my right forearm. Grunt handed me my clothing and moccasins. I donned them. I again mounted my kaiila.

Hci was now better than two pasangs away, at the fringe of the kailiauk.

"Do you not wish to kill him?" asked Cuwignaka, bitterly.

I shrugged. "He was not attacking me," I said. "He was attacking Canka." Too, I had accepted the collar. In doing this, I had understood what I was doing. Hci, as would have been any other free person, had been fully within his rights. I had no delusions concerning my status. I was a slave.

"Do you not want to kill him?" asked Cuwignaka.

"No," I said.

"I want to kill him," said Cuwignaka, bitterly.

"No, you do not," said Grunt. "He is of the Isbu, he is of your own band."

"But I do not have to like him," said Cuwignaka, suddenly, laughing.

"That is true," grinned Grunt.

I looked after Hci. He seemed to be a bitter, driven young man. This had come about, I gathered, after his disfigurement. From that time on he had seemed to live for little more than killing and vengeance, not only against the Yellow

Knives but against any enemy, or reputed enemy, of the Kaiila.

"He is mad," said Cuwignaka.

"He is bitter," I said.

It interested me that Hci had taken the attitude he had towards his disfigurement. Many warriors would have been little concerned about such a mark, particularly as it did not impair them in any significant fashion. Others might have welcomed it as a sign of bravery, a revelatory token of courage in close combat. Still others might have welcomed it as a savage, brutal enhancement to their appearance. But not so Hci. He, like not a few of the red savages, had been excessively vain about his appearance. Indeed, sometimes a young fellow will have his hair greased and braided, and will dress himself in finery and paint, and simply ride about the camp, parading, in effect, before his fellow villagers, and, in particular, the maidens. This perhaps somewhat vain but surely splendid sight is not unusual in a camp. But no longer, now, would Hci venture forth in such a fashion, displaying himself, and his kaiila and regalia, in the impressive glory of such a primitive promenade. It seemed now he would scarcely show his face but to the men of the tribe, and, in particular, to his brothers of the Sleen Soldiers. The canhpi of the Yellow Knife had done more than strike flesh and bone; it had cut, too, deeply, perhaps unaccountably, or mysteriously, into the vanity, the pride and self-image of a man. The difficulty of relating to the disfigurement had perhaps been particularly cruel in Hci's case because he had been, apparently, extremely good-looking before this. Too, of course, he had had fine prospects, and had been rich and highly placed in the tribe. He was even the son of Mahpiyasapa, the civil chief of the Isbu. Then it seemed he found himself, at least to his own mind, marred, irrevocably, in one bloody moment.

I could no longer see Hci now, in the dust from the kailiauk. Indeed, I could not even, yet, see the end of the great, long, moving mass of animals. Even at the speed at which the animals were traveling, it could take them between four and five Ahn to pass a given point.

The vanity of human beings is interesting. From my own point of view it seemed that Hci retained a great deal of what must once have been an unusual degree of savage handsomeness. The marking of his countenance, though surely not what a fellow would be likely to elect for cosmetic purposes, did not seem to me sufficiently serious to warrant his reaction to it. It might even have been regarded by some, as I have suggested, in the rude heraldry of the plains, as an enhancement to their appearance. Surely the maidens of the Isbu did not seem to find the mark objectionable. Many of them would have been much pleased had Hci, such a splendid warrior, deigned to pay them court. But no longer did Hci come to sit cross-legged outside their lodges, playing the love flute, to lure them forth under the Gorean moons.

"Do not have trouble with Hci," said Grunt to Cuwignaka. "Your brother, Canka, already has difficulties enough with Mahpiyasapa."

"You are right," said Cuwignaka.

I thought of the slender, lovely, red-haired Winyela, the former debutante from Pennsylvania, Canka's slave. She had been brought into the Barrens by Grunt, chained in his coffle, all the way from Kailiauk, near the Ihanke. She was to have been sold to Mahpiyasapa, who was interested in such a woman, white and red-haired, for five hides of the yellow kailiauk. Last year he had, in effect, put in an order for such a woman, an order which Grunt had agreed, to the best of his ability, to fill.

Cuwignaka and I, and Grunt, then turned our attention to survey the Pte, the kailiauk.

"It seems there is no end to them," I said.

"They are glorious," said Cuwignaka.

"Yes," said Grunt, "glorious." Grunt, short-bodied, thick and muscular, still wore the broad-brimmed hat I remembered so well. Indeed, interestingly, I had never seen him without it.

"We must be going," said Cuwignaka. "We must return to camp."

I looked again in the direction in which Hci had disappeared. He had killed the man who had struck him.

"They are glorious!" exclaimed Cuwignaka, and then he turned his kaiila and descended the small rise, moving towards the camp.

Grunt and I remained for a moment on the rise, gazing on the awesome sight in the distance.

"You are sure?" I asked him.

"Yes," he said, "it is the Bento herd."

"It is early," I said. It was not due in the country of the Kaiila until Kantasawi, the moon in which the plums become red. This was only Takiyuhawi, the moon in which the tabuk rut, or, as some call it, Canpasapawi, the moon in which the chokecherries are ripe.

"Yes," he said. "It is early."

"Why?" I asked.

"I do not know," he said.

We then brought our kaiila about and, descending the rise, followed Cuwignaka toward the camp.

2

THE PROCESSION OF THE ISANNA

Wasnapohdi, or Pimples, naked, her dark hair loose and wild behind her, strings of glass beads about her throat, put there by Grunt, marking her as his, in the tattered lodge I shared with Cuwignaka, clutched me, gasping, half rearing under me.

"Do not bite," I warned her, "or you will be beaten."

She moaned. I felt her fingernails in my arms.

She sobbed, helplessly, begging wordlessly in my arms for a new thrust.

She had the helpless passion of a woman broken to slavery. I was pleased that Grunt, her master, let me use her. Canka, too, had encouraged me, Grunt being willing, to please myself with her. The desperate tensions of the strong male must be relieved, and well, else health must be replaced with illness, eccentricity or neurosis. Perhaps the cruelest deprivation which a master or mistress can inflict on a male slave is to deny him access to soft, warm, yielding female flesh. Every strong man needs one or more slaves.

"Finish with her, quickly," said Cuwignaka, entering the lodge. "There is much to see. The Isanna, already, have come to the camp. They are in long lines. You must see them! Too, in moments, the medicine party will go forth to cut the pole. Many are going to accompany them. Hurry!"

Pimples looked at me, wildly, clutching me.

"Hurry! Finish with her!" said Cuwignaka.

My hands were hard on the upper arms of Pimples. I made as though to thrust her from me. Tears sprang into her eyes. She whimpered.

"Hurry!" said Cuwignaka, happily.

Then ruthlessly, with power, I did master rites upon the

helpless slave, and she lay sobbing, and shuddering, her legs then drawn up, on the robes on the floor of the lodge. I drew on my tunic and slipped into the moccasins. Cuwignaka thrust back the flap at the entrance to the lodge, on its wooden frame. I glanced back into the lodge. The hides, in places, were worn. Here and there tiny pinpricklike holes admitted spots of light. Light, too, came through the smoke hole at the apex of the lodge. Later in the day we might roll up the sides of the lodge, some four or five feet. The lodge then, open and airy, becomes transformed into little more than a summery canopy. In the winter it can be insulated with a kailiauk-hide liner. I looked back at the girl. Her skin was mottled deeply with red blotches. Her nipples were in lovely erection. The five strands of heavy, cheap glass beads about her throat glinted. They took the light nicely.

"Get dressed, if you wish," I said, "and come with us."

"If master is through with the slave," she said, angrily, "the slave must report back to her master."

"On your hands and knees," I said. I had not cared for her tone of voice.

Frightened, she got on her hands and knees, and looked at me. Would she be lashed? Her breasts depended, beautifully.

I smiled. It is pleasant to see a woman in such a position. It is also a position which is commonly used for neck-chaining them.

She smiled at me.

I returned to the interior of the lodge and lifted her up, to her knees. Our lips met. She kissed me avidly, twice. I pressed her back.

Our eyes met. "A slave is grateful that a master deigned to touch her," she whispered.

"You may come with us, if you wish," I assured her.

"Perhaps," she smiled.

"Hurry!" said Cuwignaka, impatiently. "You know she is yours whenever you wish. Grunt has told you as much. Now hurry. There are important things to do!"

I kissed the girl then, and left her behind me. She would get dressed, donning the brief, simple shirtdress of hide she had been given, and report back, head down and kneeling, to Grunt, her master.

"Throw the hoop, throw the hoop, Tatankasa!" cried out a lad.

I took the hoop and, after two false starts, suddenly flung it to my left. The lad turned swiftly, seeing the movement with his peripheral vision, and fired a small arrow expertly through the rolling object.

"Eca! Well done!" I cried. I was truly amazed at the little devil's expertise.

"Again! Again, Tatankasa!" cried the little fellow. Such games, of course, have their role to play in honing skills and sharpening reflexes that may be of great importance in adulthood.

"I cannot," I told him.

"Please, Tatankasa!" cried the lad.

"I am a slave," I told him. "I must accompany Cuwignaka."

"Yes," said Cuwignaka, firmly.

"I understand," said the lad. "You are a slave. You must obey."

"Yes," I said.

I then hurried after Cuwignaka, who was almost darting between lodges.

A domestic sleen snarled at me. I gave it a wide berth.

"There!" said Cuwignaka. "There, you see!"

"They are the Isanna?" I asked.

"Yes!" said Cuwignaka.

The Isanna was the Little-Knife Band of the Kaiila. They came from the countries around Council Rock, north of the northern fork of the Kaiila River and west of the Snake, a tributary to the Northern Kaiila. The normal distributions, given food supply and such, of the bands of the Kaiila are usually rather as follows. First, understand that there exists the Kaiila River, flowing generally in a southwestward direction. At a given point, high in the territory of the Kaiila tribe, it branches into two rivers, which are normally spoken of as the Northern Kaiila and the Southern Kaiila. The Snake, flowing in an almost southern direction, is a tributary to the Northern Kaiila. The land of the Napoktan, or Bracelets band of the Kaiila, is east of the Snake, and north of the Northern Kaiila, and the Kaiila proper. The Wismahi, or Arrowhead band of the Kaiila, holds the more northern lands in and below, to some extent, the fork of the Kaiila. The Isbu's lands are the more southern lands between the Northern and Southern branches of the Kaiila. The lands of the Casmu, or Sand band of the Kaiila, lie to the west of the Isanna, and to the north and west of the Isbu, above the descending northern branch of the Northern Kaiila. It is not clear, historically, whether the river is named for the red savages through whose territories it tends to flow, or whether the savages have taken their name from the river system. My own suspicion in this matter, borne out by tribal stories, is that the early savages in this area found large herds of wild kaiila roaming the plains. They took, then, probably for medicine reasons, the name of the Kaiila for themselves. Subsequently, one supposes, watercourses originally understood to be, say, the rivers of the Kaiila people, or the rivers in the country of the Kaiila people, came to be known more simply as the Kaiila River, or Rivers.

"It is a splendid sight!" said Cuwignaka.

"It is," I granted him.

The Isanna Kaiila number between some seven and eight hundred. They were now entering the camp, from the east, in long lines, in their full regalia. The Casmu, the Wismahi and the Napoktan had already joined the Isbu in the summer gathering. The Casmu numbered in the neighborhood of one thousand; the Wismahi, one of the smaller bands, numbered about five or six hundred. The Isbu was the largest band, containing between sixteen and seventeen hundred members. The Napoktan, which had arrived at the camp only yesterday, was the smallest of the bands of the Kaiila, numbering between some three and four hundred members. These bands, within their own territories, are often divided into separate villages or encampments. In a given encampment, usually under a minor chief, there is seldom more than two or three hundred individuals. Indeed, sometimes an encampment contains only seven or eight families.

"Splendid! Splendid!" said Cuwignaka.

Three or four abreast, in long lines, led by their civil chief, Watonka, One-Who-Is-Rich, and subchiefs and high warriors, the Isanna entered the camp of the Isbu. They carried feathered lances, and war shields and medicine shields, in decorated cases. They carried bow cases and quivers. They were resplendent in finery and paint. Feathers, each one significant and meaningful, in the codes of the Kaiila, recounting their deeds and honors, adorned their hair. Necklaces and rude bracelets glinted in the sun. High-pommeled saddles were polished. Coins and beads hung from the reins. Exploit markings and luck signs were painted on the flanks and forequarters of their animals, and ribbons and feathers were fixed in the braided, silken manes. Women, too, in their shirt-dresses and knee-length leggings, and beads, bracelets and armbands, and colorful blankets and capes, astride their kaiila, riding as red savages ride, participated in this barbaric parade.

Some of these rode kaiila to which travois were attached. Some had cradles slung about the pommels of their saddles. These cradles, most of them, are essentially wooden frames on which are fixed leather, open-fronted enclosures, opened and closed by lacings, for the infant. The wooden frame projects both above and below the enclosure for the infant. In particular it contains two sharpened projections at the top, like picket spikes, extending several inches above the point where the baby's head will be located. This is to protect the infant's head in the event of the cradle falling, say, from the back of a running kaiila. Such a cradle will often, in such a case, literally stick upside down in the earth. The child, then, laced in the enclosure, protected and supported by it, is seldom injured.

Such cradles, too, vertically, are often hung from a lodge pole or in the branches of a tree. In the tree, of course, the wind, in its rocking motion, can lull the infant to sleep. Older children often ride on the skins stretched between travois poles. Sometimes their fathers or mothers carry them before them, on the kaiila. When a child is about six, if his family is well-fixed, he will commonly have his own kaiila. The red savage, particularly the males, will usually be a skilled rider by the age of seven. Bareback riding, incidentally, is common in war and the hunt. In trading and visiting, interestingly, saddles are commonly used. This is perhaps because they can be decorated lavishly, adding to one's appearance, and may serve, in virtue of the pommel, primarily, as a support for provisions, gifts and trade articles.

"It is simply splendid," said Cuwignaka, happily.

"Yes," I said.

Children, too, I noted, those not in cradles, greased, their hair braided, their bodies and clothing ornamented, in splendid finery, like miniature versions of the adults, some riding, some sitting on the skins stretched between travois poles, participated happily and proudly, or bewilderedly, in this handsome procession.

"They are bringing their goods with them," I said. The travois with them were heavily laden, with bundles, and lodge skins and poles. Indeed, the travois poles themselves, when untied and freed from the kaiila, would be used as lodge poles.

"It is the way our peoples move," said Cuwignaka. Goods would not be left behind, save occasionally in hidden caches.

At the flanks of some of the warriors' kaiila marched stripped white women, in beaded collars. Their wrists were tied behind them. About their throats, on thong loops, below the collars, dangling between their breasts, hung leather, braided kaiila quirts. There was little doubt as to what such women were. I met the eyes of one, and she looked away, tossing her head, disdainfully, in her bonds and collar, the quirt about her neck. She was the property of a red master. I then met the eyes of another. This one, too, looked away, but she did so quickly, fearfully. She was very frightened. I gathered that she was terribly afraid of her master. She did not so much as dare to look at another man. These girls had both been blond. So, too, I noted, were most of the other such women.

"The two-legged, female animals here are mostly blond," I said to Cuwignaka.

"Yes," he said. "They are being displayed."

I nodded. Such a hair color is a rarity in the Barrens. I supposed the women understood clearly that they, like the silver pendants tied in the manes, like the coins fastened on the reins, like the saddles inlaid with gold, with golden wire wrapped about the pommels, were being displayed as portions of the wealth of the Isanna.

"The others," said Cuwignaka, "stripped, are kept in small herds, with the kaiila, outside the camp, watched over by boys."

"I understand," I said. The Isanna would probably see little point in marching more familiar types, more common women, before the Isbu.

I saw another blonde moving by. She was half stumbling, half being dragged along, weeping, on a short neck tether, not more than five feet long. She was, I would guess, about seventeen. The tether was in the fist of a red master. I did not think he was more than eighteen years of age. He was moving his kaiila quickly, along the side of the lines, probably hurrying to occupy his designated place in the procession. He was not gentle with his lovely property. She was crying. She seemed new to her collar. I suspected she had not been a slave long. She was a survivor, perhaps, of the wagon train which had been attacked several days ago. She was doubtless still in the process of learning her new purposes in life. I saw no woman with the Isanna, incidentally, who had a hair color remotely like that of the slender, lovely Winyela, Canka's slave. I wondered if she knew the extent to which she was a prize in the Barrens.

"Mahpiyasapa is going to greet Watonka," said Cuwignaka. "Let us hurry forward, that we may see."

I was not at all certain that this was a good idea, but I accompanied Cuwignaka. He was so young, so insuppressible, so elated to be again with the Isbu, his people, that, I think, he did not soberly consider whether or not he would be likely to be welcome at such an encounter, even as a bystander.

Mahpiyasapa, Black Clouds, civil chief of the Isbu, greeted Watonka, One-Who-Is-Rich, on foot, welcoming him officially to the Isbu camp. This honor accorded him, Watonka dismounted. The two men embraced. About them were gathered medicine men and high warriors. With Mahpiyasapa were his son, Hci, and members of the Sleen Soldiers. Canka, too, was there, and several of the All Comrades. Chiefs and representatives of the Casmu, Napoktan and Wismahi, too, were present. Among them I saw Kahintokapa, One-Who-Walks-Before, of the Casmu, and two other members, as well, of the prestigious Yellow-Kaiila Riders.

"Greetings, Iwoso," said Cuwignaka. "How beautiful you have become."

He had spoken to a girl who was standing near the stirrup of another girl, mounted on a kaiila. The standing girl, to whom Cuwignaka had spoken, had come with the Isanna. She had come walking at the stirrup of the mounted girl. She wore a rather plain shirtdress, with knee-length leggings and moccasins. Her braided hair was tied with red cloth. There were glass beads about her neck. She was quite lovely. The girl on the kaiila, too, was very lovely, indeed, perhaps even more lovely than she afoot. But her beauty, in any event, was much enhanced by her finery. Her dress was of soft-tanned hide, almost white, fringed, into which, about the breasts and shoulders, were worked intricate patterns of yellow and red beading. Her leggings and moccasins were similarly decorated. Her braided hair, glossy and long, was bound with silver string. Two golden bracelets adorned her left wrist. She wore two necklaces of beads, and another on which were threaded tiny, heavy tubes and pendants, spaced intermittently, of silver and gold. Across her forehead hung a tiny silver chain on which were tiny silver droplets.

"You, too, Bloketu," said Cuwignaka, looking up at the mounted girl.

"Do not speak to my maiden," said the girl on the kaiila.

"Iwoso is a Yellow Knife," said Cuwignaka. "She was taken when she was twelve. Bloketu is the daughter of Watonka."

"I see," I said. The girl, Iwoso, did not wear a collar. I had suspected, however, from the plainness of her dress, the fact that she was on foot, with the Isanna, and seemed clearly in attendance on the girl astride the kaiila, that she was not of the Isanna, but was, rather, one owned by them, or, at least, living with them.

"Iwoso has high status with the Isanna," said Cuwignaka. "You can see that she is not even collared."

"Yes," I said. The name 'Iwoso', incidentally, means "Pouting Lips." Her lips, on the other hand, were not protrusive. The name, thusly, I conjectured, might once have been given to her for other than anatomical reasons. Probably she had once been sullen or petulant. She had then discovered that, by the decision of her master or mistress, she was "Pouting Lips." The expression 'Bloketu', incidentally, the name of the girl on the kaiila, the daughter of the Isanna chieftain, Watonka, means "Summer" or "Summertime."

"What have we here?" asked Watonka, chieftain of the Isanna.

"I do not know her," said Bloketu, not deigning to look upon Cuwignaka.

"From the summer dances, long ago," said Cuwignaka. "You remember me, surely. I was Petuste. I found flowers for you. We rode kaiila together."

"Perhaps my maiden remembers you," said the girl. 'Petuste' means "Firebrand." More broadly, of course, it can refer to any piece of burning wood. He was the brother of Canka, of course, Fire-Steel. This was the first time I had ever heard the former name of Cuwignaka.

"Do you remember her, Iwoso?" asked the girl on the kaiila of the girl at her stirrup.

"No," said Iwoso.

"Iwoso!" protested Cuwignaka.

"You see," said Bloketu, from the height of the saddle, "you are not remembered."

"Who is she?" inquired Watonka.

"A shame of the Isbu," said Mahpiyasapa. He was still furious with Canka, who had seen fit, in virtue of capture rights, muchly desiring her, to put his collar on the lovely Winyela.

"Obviously she is only a female of the Isbu," said one of the men with Watonka.

"Go away," said Canka to Cuwignaka, angrily. "You do us shame."

"That is her brother," said Hci to one of the Isanna. "He has such a one for a sister, and yet was permitted to serve as Blotanhunka for the All Comrades."

"Oh?" said the man.

"Yes," said Hci.

"Beware, Hci!" said Canka.

"Of what?" asked Hci. "Do I not speak the truth?"

Canka clenched his fists, in fury.

"What do you think of one who takes a woman brought into our country to be sold to his chieftain?" asked Mahpiyasapa of Watonka.

"I think such a one should be punished," said Watonka. "Then the woman should be given to the chief."

"I was within my rights," said Canka.

"Let me, and the Sleen Soldiers, punish him," said Hci. "Let us destroy his lodge and break his weapons. Then we will bring you the woman naked, and tied in leather."

"I will think on it," said Mahpiyasapa.

"I was within my rights," said Canka.

"Deliver the woman to me," said Mahpiyasapa.

"No," said Canka. "She is mine."

"Perhaps I will take her," said Mahpiyasapa. "I will think on it."

"She is mine," said Canka.

Mahpiyasapa shrugged. "If I want," he said, "I will take her."

Canka, in fury, turned about and strode from the group.

"Beware of an angry young man," said Watonka to Mahpiyasapa. Hci looked after Canka.

"Perhaps you will come sew with us sometime," said Bloketu, lofty and beautiful on the kaiila, to Cuwignaka.

Cuwignaka did not respond to her.

"Isn't she pretty, Iwoso?" asked Bloketu.

"Yes," said Iwoso.

"I wonder if she is the sort of woman who must please warriors," said Bloketu.

Cuwignaka regarded her with fury. I saw that he would not have minded teaching the lofty Bloketu something about the pleasing of men.

"Perhaps," laughed Iwoso.

This, too, stung Cuwignaka. He, Kaiila, did not care to be the butt of the humor of one who, when all was said and done, was naught but a slave.

"You were told to go away," said Hci to Cuwignaka. "Does a sister not obey her brother?"

"He is my older brother," said Cuwignaka. "I will go away." He then turned and left. I followed him. Behind us we heard the laughter of the two girls.

"It was a mistake," I told him, when we were between the lodges, "to intrude yourself so closely upon the meeting of the Isanna and Isbu."

"Not at all," said Cuwignaka. "How often does such a meeting take place? Who would wish to miss it? Too, I wanted to see the white slaves, and Bloketu and Iwoso."

"You have feelings toward such women?" I asked.

"Yes," said Cuwignaka. "I would like to own them. In my lodge I would have them naked and I would then, with my quirt, if necessary, teach them to obey me well."

"What of Bloketu and Iwoso?" I asked.

"If they were slaves," said Cuwignaka, "I would strip them and teach them, like the slaves they would then be, no different from others, to obey me well."

"Would you quirt them?" I asked.

"Of course," said Cuwignaka. "If they were even the least bit displeasing they, like the others, would be well quirted."

"Iwoso is already a slave," I said.

"Yes," said Cuwignaka, "in a sense. But she is really almost free. She is a girl's maiden."

"That is true," I said. Iwoso did not even wear a collar.

"Where are you going?" I asked.

"After the hunt," said Cuwignaka, "the great dance will be held."

I had to walk quickly to keep up with Cuwignaka.

"Where are you going now?" I asked Cuwignaka.

"To see the cutting of the pole," he said.

"Where does this take place?" I asked. I did not understand what was going on.

"This year it is only three pasangs from camp," he said.

"I do not understand," I said.

"This year," Cuwignaka, "I am going to dance. I am going to show them I am a man."

"The pole," I said, "is used in this dance?"

"Of course," said Cuwignaka.

"Should we not get the kaiila?" I asked.

"It is better for such as us to go afoot," said Cuwignaka.

"But others will be mounted?" I asked.

"Yes," said Cuwignaka.

"Who will be coming?" I asked.

"The Isanna are now here," said Cuwignaka. "Many will come, from the Isbu, from the Casmu, from the Wismahi, from the Napoktan, from the Isanna."

"Who will select this pole?" I asked.

"The medicine chief of the dance," said Cuwignaka. "This year it is Cancega, of the Casmu." 'Cancega', here, I think, would be best translated as "Drum." More literally, it is a skin stretched over a hoop. The expression 'cega', itself, may refer to a kettle, a pot, a pail, a bucket, or so on. 'Cancega', then, in a sense, could be taken to mean such things as "Kettle Skin," or "Pot Skin." The translation "Drum," all things considered, seems to be best in this context.

"Who will cut down this pole," I asked, "chieftains?"

"No," laughed Cuwignaka. "How little you understand these things!"

I shrugged.

"Do you not understand the meaning of the pole?"

"No," I said.

"It is a pole," said Cuwignaka, "a great pole."

"Yes?" I said.

"Who, then, must begin its preparation for the great manhood dance?" asked Cuwignaka.

"I do not know," I said.

"A captive female," said Cuwignaka.

"Would a slave do?" I asked.

"That is ideal," said Cuwignaka, "provided she is not Kaiila."

"Has it been decided," I asked, "who will perform this crucial role in the ceremony?"

"Yes," said Cuwignaka. "A suitable slave has been selected."

In a few moments we had left the vicinity of the lodges and were making our way across the fields. We passed some kaiila herds. Too, we passed some small herds of stripped white women, huddled together. Each wore a beaded collar. These women were mostly brunets. They had been brought in by the Isanna, with their kaiila. They had not been regarded as being desirable enough to be displayed in the procession of the Isanna. Boys, mounted on kaiila, watched out over these herds, including those of the women. The boys carried rawhide ropes, and whips.

3

THE POLE

"How beautiful she is," said Cuwignaka.

"Yes," I said.

My breath was almost taken away by the incredible beauty of the former Miss Millicent Aubrey-Welles, once a debutante from Pennsylvania. She was slender and lovely. She was fairly complexioned and had delicately beautiful and sensitive features. She was exquisitely feminine. The slavers who had originally selected her to wear a Gorean collar had known their business. She was dressed, and adorned, in all the colorful, glittering, striking barbaric richness, in all the impressiveness and splendor, in all the festive display, fit for feasts and dances, of a red-savage female. Even the daughters of chieftains, such as Bloketu, the daughter of Watonka, might have envied her the sumptuousness and glory of her raiment. Her long shirtdress of soft-tanned tabuk hide was almost white. So, too, were her knee-length leggings and moccasins. These things, too, were painted with designs, and fringed. Her hair, red, radiant in the sun, had been braided in the fashion of the red savages. It was tied with golden string. Necklaces of shells and beads, and ornaments and trinkets, and pierced coins, of gold and silver, hung about her neck. On her wrists, visible within the capelike sleeves of the shirtdress, were silver bracelets. To look at her one might not have thought she was a slave. To be sure, her wrists were tied behind her back, and on her throat, leading to riders on each side of her, were two rawhide tethers. Detectable, but inconspicuous among all this finery, thrust up under her chin, above the tethers, was a beaded collar. It was Canka's. It was to him that she, in the final analysis, belonged.

"That is Cancega," whispered Cuwignaka to me.

A man was now riding slowly forward, alone, toward some trees a few hundred yards away. Lines of such trees, in the Barrens, and low, sloping geodesics, watersheds, tend to mark, often, the location of the tiny streams which occur in the country. Such streams, in this area, would be tributary to the Lower, or Southern, Kaiila. At this time of year, of course, they would be little more than trickles of water.

Indeed, at this time of year, a man could wade the Southern Kaiila. Later in the year, in Kantasawi, many small streams would be dry altogether and even major rivers, like the Southern Kaiila itself, would seem little more than pools of water in a riverbed. The body of Cancega, clad in little more than a breechclout and a roach of feathers, was covered with medicine paint. In his hand he carried a long, feathered medicine wand.

"The five high coups have already been taken," said Cuwignaka.

"What are they?" I asked.

"The young men, more than a hundred of them, selected from the bands, sent ahead days ago, as soon as the Pte were sighted, have ridden for the tree."

"I do not understand," I said.

"It is a race," said Cuwignaka. "They are lined up. The first five men who strike the tree, with their hand, or with a canhpi, a lance or coup stick, obtain high coups."

"Did Canka or Hci participate in this race?" I asked.

"No," said Cuwignaka. "Both of them, in former years, have obtained such a coup."

"The group is advancing," I said.

"We shall accompany them," said Cuwignaka.

We then walked along with the group, some mounted and some, like ourselves, on foot, who, in effect, were following Cancega.

"Cancega seems to be a very important fellow," I said.

"He is more important than you understand," said Cuwignaka. "At this time, during the festivals, he is in charge of the whole camp. We listen to him. We do what he says."

"He is, then," I said, "at this time, in effect, the chief of all the Kaiila."

"I do not think I would put it just that way," said Cuwignaka, somewhat defensively. "The civil chiefs, in deferring to him, are not really relinquishing their power."

"I see the distinction," I said. "Do all the Kaiila ever have but one chief?"

"Sometimes a war chief is elected," said Cuwignaka. "In a sense, then, he is the high chief."

"But a war chief cannot be a civil chief," I said.

"No," said Cuwignaka. "It is better, we think, to keep those things apart."

"That is interesting," I said.

"One may, of course, at different times, be a war chief and a civil chief," said Cuwignaka.

"I understand," I said.

"Sometimes a man is good at both," said Cuwignaka, "but they are still different things."

"I understand," I said.

"And, generally, I think," said Cuwignaka, "that it would be only a very unusual man who would be good at both."

"Perhaps," I said.

"They are very different sorts of things," said Cuwignaka.

"That seems to me right," I said.

In moments we, with the others, were splashing across a narrow, shallow stream. I could see pebbles in the bottom of this stream. The Southern, or Lower, Kaiila, like the other larger rivers in the Barrens, however, bearing witness to the accumulation of silts, would be brown and muddy.

On the other side of the stream Cancega, and most of his fellows, dismounted, their kaiila being held to the side.

Cancega, then, began a slow, shuffling dance. Two others, near him, also with roaches of feathers, shaking rattles, joined him. The focal point of this dance, which wove back and forth, in a fanlike motion, before it, was a high, white-barked tree. Cancega repeated, over and over, carrying the medicine wand, and dancing, "It is the tree." The other two fellows, who had joined him, with the rattles, would add a refrain, "It is tall and straight." This refrain, too, was sometimes echoed by those about us.

Winyela, her hands bound behind her, and her neck in the tethers, in her finery, watched.

I could see the marks of various weapons in the bark of the tree where, perhaps two or three days ago, the young men had charged to it, to be the first to reach it, in their race for coups.

"It is the tree!" suddenly cried Cancega, rushing to the tree and striking it with the medicine wand.

"It is tall and straight!" shouted the two seconds, in the dance, and most of the others, as well, including my friend, Cuwignaka.

Two men rushed to Winyela and untied her hands. She was pushed forward, the tethers still on her neck, but now rather behind her.

A long-handled, single-bladed ax was pressed into her hands. It was a trade ax. Its back was blunted, for the driving of pegs, stakes and wedges. It was heavy for her.

"You should not be here," said a man to Cuwignaka. "This is no place for free women."

"I am a man," said Cuwignaka.

The man shrugged.

I looked about. To be sure, there were no women present, with the exception of the lovely Winyela.

She began, under the direction of Cancega, and others, to strike at the lower portions of the tree.

I wondered why there were no free women present. Could it be that something was to occur which was regarded as not being suitable, perhaps, for the sensibilities of free women?

Winyela continued to chop at the tree.

It was some twenty-five to thirty feet in height, but it was not, really, a large tree. Its trunk was slim and polelike, and surely only some eight to ten inches in width. A man, working with such a tool, would have felled it in a matter of moments. Winyela, of course, was neither a man nor a woodsman. She was only a lovely slave. Her hands were widely spaced on the ax handle, and her blows were short. Cancega and the others, interestingly, in spite of the fact that she was a slave, were patient with her. To be sure, she had enough sense not to beg to rest. The necklaces and ornaments she wore rustled and shimmered, making tiny sounds, as she labored. I supposed it was the first time in her life she had had such an implement in her hands. They are seldom used by debutantes from Pennsylvania nor, of course, by Gorean slave girls.

I saw Canka ride up, on his kaiila. He had come, apparently, from the camp. She looked at him, the tethers on her neck. He indicated that she should continue to work.

In a moment there was a cracking noise, and then, after a few more blows, a splintering, rending sound as the tree tipped, and then, its branches striking the earth, fell. Five last blows were struck, cutting the last fibers and wood, and the trunk, freed, laid level, a yard above the ground, held in place by branches and foliage.

The men grunted with approval. The ax was removed from Winyela's hands and she was dragged back and knelt, her knees closely together, on the ground. The two men who held her tethers now stood beside her, the slack in the tethers, looped, now taken up, the rawhide loops in their fists.

"What occurs now?" I asked Cuwignaka.

"Watch," said he to me.

Several of the men, now, under the direction of Cancega,

began to remove the branches and bark from the felled tree. Two forks were left, one about eighteen feet high and the other about twenty-three feet high. This was to allow for the pole later being set in the earth, within the enclosure of the dance, set among its supporting stakes, to a depth of some seven or eight feet. These forks would then be, respectively, about ten and fifteen feet high.

The slim trunk of the tree, with its forks, stripped of its bark, was now long, smooth and white.

It was set in two stout tripods of branches, about a yard above the ground.

Paint was brought forth, in a small clay vessel. The girl, too, was again brought forward.

It was she, herself, with the paint, the slave, who must proclaim that the pole was Kaiila. In this type of application of paint, on wood, over a large surface, or bands of a large surface, a brush of chopped, twisted grass is used. The paint itself was red. This red was probably obtained from powdered earths or clays. It may also, of course, have been obtained from crushed rock, containing oxides of iron. Some reds, too, may be obtained from boiled roots.

Winyela, in her finery, the beautiful, delicate, red-haired, white slave girl, under the direction of Cancega, medicine chief of the summer camp of all the Kaiila, carefully, obediently, frightened, applied the red paint. "It is Kaiila," chanted many of the men about, as she did this. Thrice did Winyela, with the brush, as the pole was turned in the tripods, scarletly band the rotated surface. "It is Kaiila," chanted the men. She was then drawn back, the paint and brush removed from her, and again knelt, her knees closely together, the two tethers on her throat.

The three scarlet bands of paint were bright on the white pole. Scarlet bands, in number from one to five, are commonly used by Kaiila warriors to mark their weapons, in particular their lances and arrows. To this mark, or marks, then, will be added the personal design, or pattern, of the individual warrior. An arrow then, say, may be identified not only as Kaiila, but, within the tribe, or band, as the arrow of a particular warrior.

The Kaiila, incidentally, in the Barrens, are generally known as the "Cutthroat tribe." The bands, then, generally by outsiders, and usually even among the Kaiila themselves, are supposed to have this sort of significance. I have met Kaiila, however, who have denied this entire line of interpretation.

They call my attention to the fact that the Kaiila themselves seldom, among themselves, think of themselves as the "Cut-throat tribe." They think of themselves as being the Kaiila, or the people of the Kaiila. Similarly they point out that a symbolic representation of a cut throat should surely be a single slash, not one or more encircling bands. The true origin, then, of the encircling bands, I suppose, is lost in history. The bands, incidentally, are usually three in number. This suggests to me that they might originally have been thought to be phallic in significance. The number three, as is well known, is often thought to be a very special number. This probably has to do, of course, with the triune nature of the male genitals.

The paint was bright on the pole.

The three bands, each about four or five inches in width, and separated also by such distances, were painted in such a way that the bottom ring, or band, was about seven and a half to eight and a half feet from the base of the pole. Thus, when the pole was set in the ground, amidst its supporting stakes, these circles would be at the visible base, or root, of the pole. Too, they would be beneath the belt of an encircling dancer.

"It is Kaiila!" shouted the men.

The neck tethers were then removed from Winyela. I gathered that her part in the ceremony was now concluded.

Suddenly the girl screamed.

I tensed.

"Do not interfere," said Cuwignaka.

The hands of men, then, were at the necklaces about her throat, the ornaments. Her moccasins and leggings were removed. The golden strings were untied, and taken, which had bound her hair. Her hair was rapidly and deftly unbraided. The silver bracelets were slipped from her wrists. The soft-tanned shirtdress, with its designs, and beading and fringe, was then thrust over her head and pulled away. She now knelt absolutely naked, save for Canka's collar, among the men. Her knees were clenched closely together. Her hair, now loose, radiant in the sun, was spread and smoothed down her back. She was very white. She almost shone in the sun. Not only was she quite fairly complexioned but, prior to her being adorned in her finery, now removed from her, she had been washed, and clipped, and groomed and scrubbed, apparently, as thoroughly and carefully as a prize kaiila.

"She is quite beautiful," said Cuwignaka.

"Yes," I said.

The girl whimpered as the two rawhide tethers were now, again, tied on her throat, below Canka's collar.

"What is to be done with her now?" I asked.

"Observe," said Cuwignaka.

"Oh," cried the girl. One of the men, behind her, had thrown dust upon her. "Oh!" she sobbed, as two men, rather in front of her, one on each side, tossed, each, a double handful of dust upon her. She closed her eyes, blinking against the grit of the dust. Then she opened her eyes, and shrank back, for Cancega, with a shallow, rounded box, was crouching before her. The box contained some sort of black paste, or grease. She shuddered as Cancega, taking the material on his fingertips, applied it to her cheeks. He made three dark lines, about a finger's width each, on each cheek. These were signs, I supposed, for the Kaiila. Then he rubbed the material elsewhere, in smudges, upon her body, on her arms, and back, and breasts and belly, and on the tops of her thighs, on her calves, and, then, thrusting his hand between them, on the interior of her thighs.

The girl regarded him, frightened, as he, intent, did this work.

He then stood up.

She knelt at his feet, looking up at him, frightened, her knees now again pressed closely together.

Two men, with kaiila quirts, now stood behind the girl. She was not aware of their presence.

I then realized what the men, doubtless, had in mind.

I smiled.

"Oh!" cried the girl, frightened, dismayed, as Cancega suddenly, with his foot, forced her knees widely apart. She did not dare close them. She now, for the first time in the afternoon, knelt as a slave.

Then, suddenly, the two men with the kaiila quirts struck her across the back and, before she could do more than cry out, she was, too, pulled to her feet and forward, on the two tethers.

She then stood, held by the tethers, wildly, before the pole.

Cancega pointed to the pole.

She looked at him, bewildered. Then the quirts, again, struck her, and she cried out in pain.

Cancega again pointed to the pole.

Winyela then put her head down and took the pole in her small hands, and kissed it, humbly.

"Yes," said Cancega, encouraging her. "Yes."

Again Winyela kissed the pole.

"Yes," said Cancega.

Winyela then heard the rattles behind her, giving her her rhythm. These rattles were then joined by the fifing of whistles, shrill and high, formed from the wing bones of the taloned Herlit. A small drum, too, then began to sound. Its more accented beats, approached subtly but predictably, instructed the helpless, lovely dancer as to the placement and timing of the more dramatic of her demonstrations and motions.

"It is the Kaiila," chanted the men.

Winyela danced. There was dust upon her hair and on her body. On her cheeks were the three bars of grease that marked her as the property of the Kaiila. Grease, too, had been smeared liberally upon her body. No longer was she a shining beauty. She was now only a filthy slave, an ignoble animal, something of no account, something worthless, obviously, but nonetheless permitted, in the kindness of the Kaiila, a woman of another people, to attempt to please the pole.

I smiled.

Was this not suitable? Was this not appropriate for her, a slave?

Winyela, kissing the pole, and caressing it, and moving about it, and rubbing her body against it, under the directions of Cancega, and guided sometimes by the tethers on her neck, continued to dance.

I whistled softly to myself.

"Ah," said Cuwignaka.

"It is the Kaiila!" chanted the men.

"I think the pole will be pleased," I said.

"I think a rock would be pleased," said Cuwignaka.

"I agree," I said.

Winyela, by the neck tethers, was pulled against the pole. She seized it, and writhed against it, and licked at it.

"It is the Kaiila!" chanted the men.

"It is the Kaiila!" shouted Cuwignaka.

A transformation seemed suddenly to come over Winyela. This was evinced in her dance.

"She is aroused," said Cuwignaka.

"Yes," I said.

She began, then, helplessly, to dance her servitude, her submission, her slavery. The dance, then, came helplessly from the depths of her. The tethers pulled her back from the pole and she reached forth for it. She struggled to reach it, writhing. Bit by bit she was permitted to near it, and then she embraced it. She climbed, then, upon the pole. There her dance, on her knees, her belly and back, squirming and clutching, continued.

I looked to Canka. He was a few yards away, astride his kaiila. He rode bareback. This is common in short rides about the village, or in going out to check kaiila. The prestige of the saddle, and its dressiness, is not required in local errands or short jaunts. Similarly, in such trips its inconvenience may be dispensed with. He watched Winyela dance. His dark eyes shone. He knew he was her master.

Winyela now knelt on the pole and bent backwards, until her hair fell about the wood, and then she slipped her legs down about the pole and lay back on it, her hands holding to the pole behind her head. She reared helplessly on the pole, and writhed upon it, almost as though she might have been chained to it, and then, she turned about and lay on the pole, on her stomach, her thighs gripping it, her hands pushing her body up, and away from the pole, and then, suddenly, moving down about the trunk, bringing her head and shoulders down. Her red hair hung about the smooth, white wood. Her lips, again and again, pressed down upon it, in helpless kisses.

"She is quite good, the slave," said Cuwignaka.

"Yes," I said.

"She has not been trained to do this, has she?" asked Cuwignaka.

"Not to my knowledge," I said. It seemed to me rather unlikely that debutantes from high society would be trained to perform the supplication and passion dances of slave girls.

"It is instinctual in a woman," said Cuwignaka.

"I think so," I said. It seemed to me not unlikely, for many reasons, having to do with sexual selection, in particular, that such behaviors were, at least in broad outlines, genetically coded. Behaviors can be selected for, of course, and tendencies to behaviors, as well as such things as the color of hair and eyes. This is evident from the data of ethology. A woman's acquisition of the skills of erotic dance, incidentally, like those of a child's linguistic skills, follows an unusually sharp learning curve. This suggests that the rudiments of such dance, or the readiness for it, like the capacity, at least, for the rapid and efficient acquisition of language, is genetically coded. Sex, and human nature, may not be irrelevant to biology.

"Superb," said Cuwignaka.

"Yes," I said.

Winyela, helplessly, piteously, danced her obeisance to the great pole, and, in this, to her masters, and to men.

"Look," said Cuwignaka.

"Yes," I said. "Yes!"

I well understood, now, why free women could not be permitted to see such a dance. It was the dance of a slave. How horrified, how scandalized, they would have been. Better that they not even know such things could exist. Such dances, that such things could be, are doubtless best kept as the secrets of masters and slaves. Too, how furious, how outraged, they would be, to see how beautiful, how exciting and desirable another woman could be, a thousand times more beautiful, exciting and desirable than themselves, and one who was naught but a slave. But then how could any free woman compete with a slave, one who is truly mastered and owned?

I watched Winyela dance.

It was easy to see how free women could be almost insanely jealous of slaves, and how they could hate them so, so inordinately and deeply. Too, it was little wonder that slaves, helpless in their collars, so feared and dreaded free women.

"The slave dances well," said Cuwignaka.

"Yes," I said.

In her dance, of course, Winyela was understood to be dancing not only her personal slavery, which she surely was, but, from the point of view of the Kaiila, in the symbolism of the dance, in the medicine of the dance, that the women of enemies were fit to be no more than the slaves of the Kaiila. I did not doubt but what the Fleer and the Yellow Knives, and other peoples, too, might have similar ceremonies, in which, in one way or another, a similar profession might take place, there being danced or enacted also by a woman of another group, perhaps even, in those cases, by a maiden of the Kaiila. I, myself, saw the symbolism of the dance, and, I think, so, too, did Winyela, in a pattern far deeper than that of an ethnocentric idiosyncrasy. I saw the symbolism as being in accord with what is certainly one of the deepest and most pervasive themes of organic nature, that of dominance and submission. In the dance, as I chose to understand it, Winyela danced the glory of life and the natural order; in it she danced her submission to the might of men and the fulfillment of her own femaleness; in it she danced her desire to be owned, to feel passion, to give of herself, unstintingly, to surrender herself, rejoicing, to service and love.

"It is the Kaiila!" shouted the men.

"It is the Kaiila!" shouted Cuwignaka.

Winyela was dragged back, toward the bottom of the pole, on its tripods. There she was knelt down. The two men holding her neck tethers slipped the rawhide, between their fist and the girl's neck, under their feet, the man on her left under his right foot, and the man on her right under his left foot. But already Winyela, of her own accord, breathing deeply from the exertions of her dance, and trembling, had put her head to the dirt, humbly, before the pole. Then the tension on the two tethers was increased, the rawhide on her neck being drawn tight under the feet of her keepers. I do not think Winyela desired to raise her head. But now, of course, she could not have done so had she wished. It was held in place. I think this is the way she would have wanted it. This is what she would have chosen, to be owned, to serve, to be deprived of choice.

The men about slapped their thighs and grunted their approval. The music stopped. The tethers were removed from Winyela's neck. She then, tentatively, lifted her head. It seemed now she was forgotten. Her garments and jewelry, rolled in a bundle, were tied in what would be the lower fork of the pole. Two other objects, on long thongs, which were wrapped about the higher fork, were placed in the higher fork. Later, when the pole was set in the enclosure of the dance, the thongs would be unwrapped and the two objects would hang beside the pole. Both were of leather. One was an image of a kailiauk. The other was an image of a man. The image of the man had an exaggerated phallus, thrust forth and nearly as long as an arm, of a sort common in primitive art. I was reminded by these things of the medicine of the pole, and of the great forthcoming dance, projected to take place about it. The medicine of the pole and dance had intimately to do, obviously, with such things as hunting, fertility and manhood. To the red savage the medicine world is very real.

"You may get up," said Cuwignaka to Winyela. She was looking about herself, bewildered, apparently forgotten. She rose up and went to the side of Canka, astride his kaiila, her master. Men were lowering the medicine pole to the ground and breaking apart the tripods. Ropes had been put on the pole. Then, preceded by Cancega, with his medicine wand, uttering formulas, followed by his two seconds, with their rattles, the pole, pulled on its ropes, being drawn by several kaiila, was dragged toward the camp.

"You were very beautiful, Winyela," said Canka.

"Thank you, Master," she said.

He put down his hand and drew her up, before him, both her legs to the left side, to the back of the Kaiila. He then held her in place, before him. He wore only his breechclout, moccasins and knife.

"I am so dirty," she said. "Surely you will not want me to touch your body."

But he held her to him, possessively. One arm was about her shoulders, the other beneath her thighs. She looked small in his arms, on the kaiila.

"I am so ashamed," she said, "how I must have looked, how I acted."

I remembered that she was from Earth, with its foolish, irrational negativistic conditionings, largely a heritage from the teachings of celibate lunatics. How pernicious can be the infected, poisonous heirlooms of madmen.

"In your dance," said Canka, "you were not ashamed."

"No," she said. "It was almost as though I were another. I was sensuous, brazen, bold and free."

"Free?" asked Canka, smiling.

"Surely Master knows that of all women it is only a total slave who can be truly free."

Canka smiled. In one sense, of course, the slave has no freedom whatsoever. She has no rights, and is totally and absolutely owned. In another sense, of course, she is the most free of women.

"I am not truly ashamed," said the girl.

"I know," said Canka.

"Rather, I am shamelessly proud and happy," she said.

"Good," said Canka. "That is how it should be."

"I am only a slave," she said.

"That is true," said Canka.

"It is your collar which is on my neck, Master," she said.

"Yes," said Canka.

"I am your slave," she said.

"Yes," said Canka.

"I love you, Master," she said. "Do you care for me, perhaps, just a little?"

"Perhaps," said Canka.

She nestled back, in his arms.

"What are you going to do with me now, Master?" she asked.

"I am going to take you to my lodge," said Canka. "There I will use you, many times."

"Ho, Itancanka," she said. "Yes, Master."

Canka then moved his heels back into the flanks of the kaiila and, guiding it with his knees, turned it back towards the village.

4

THE KAIILA WILL GO FORTH FOR THE HUNT

"It is nearly time. Awaken!" said Cuwignaka, shaking my shoulder. "Soon we will be going out."

I rolled over in the robes and opened my eyes. I could see the poles sloping together over my head, the encircling hides. The sky was still almost dark, visible through the smoke hole.

"Hurry," said Cuwignaka.

I thrust back the robes, and sat up. In the half darkness I saw Cuwignaka pull his dress over his head. He stood up, then, and straightened it on his body, and pulled down the hem. He had, a few days ago, torn away the sleeves. Prior to that, even on the field of battle, weeks ago, he had shortened it, and ripped it at the left thigh, to give himself greater freedom of movement. Males of the red savages, incidentally, commonly sleep naked. I, too, was naked, save that I wore Canka's collar. As a slave I was not permitted to remove it. It must stay on me. Collars are, of course, sometimes removed from slaves. This is often the case, for example, when they are sold or given away. Too, however, they may be removed at other times, for other purposes. It can be done, of course, solely on the decision, and will, of free persons. A given individual may, for example, for one reason or another, not want others to know that a given woman is his slave. Accordingly, she may wear her collar only in his lodge.

This is analogous to the secret slaveries which sometimes exist on Earth, where a woman, returning home, kneels and waits to be collared. How startled would be the fellows in the office to discover that that trimly figured, luscious coworker of theirs, to them seemingly so cool, aloof and inaccessible, is at home another man's slave. Too, how startled would be the women in certain neighborhoods, or in certain organizations and groups, to discover that one of their most popular neighbors, or prominent members, is, in the privacy of her own dwelling, a slave. Alerted by a code word in a seemingly innocent phone call, she prepares herself for her master. She bathes herself and combs herself. She makes herself up. She applies perfume. When he arrives home she is awaiting him, naked, kneeling, on the slave mat, at the foot of his bed, her collar before her. "Greetings, Master," she says. She then lifts the collar in her teeth, that he may put it on her.

"Wakapapi," said Cuwignaka to me. This is the Kaiila word for pemmican. A soft cake of this substance was pressed into my hands. I crumbled it. In the winter, of course, such cakes can be frozen solid. One then breaks them into smaller pieces, warms them in one's hands and mouth, and eats them bit by bit. I lifted the crumbled pemmican to my mouth and ate of it. There are various ways in which pemmican may be prepared, depending primarily on what one adds into the mixture, in the way of herbs, seasonings and fruit. A common way of preparing it is as follows. Strips of kailiauk meat, thinly sliced and dried on poles in the sun, are pounded fine, almost to a powder. Crushed fruit, usually chokecherries, is then added to the meat. The whole, then, is mixed with, and fixed by, kailiauk fat, subsequently, usually, being divided into small, flattish, rounded cakes. The fruit sugars make this, in its way, a quick-energy food, while the meat, of course, supplies valuable, long-lasting stamina protein. This, like the dried meat, or jerky, from which it is made, can be eaten either raw or cooked. It is not uncommon for both to be carried in hunting or on war parties. Children will also carry it in their play. The thin slicing of the meat not only abets its preservation, effected by time, the wind and sun, but makes it impractical for flies to lay their eggs in it. Jerky and pemmican, which is usually eaten cooked in the villages, is generally boiled. In these days a trade pot or kettle is normally used. In the old days it was prepared by stone-boiling. In this technique a hole is used. This hole, dug either within the lodge or outside of it, is lined with hide and filled with water. Fire-heated stones would then be placed in the water, heating it, eventually, to boiling. As the stones cooled, of course, they would be removed from the hide pot and replaced with hot stones, the first stones meanwhile, if needed, being reheated.

"I am going to check the kaiila," said Cuwignaka. "I am going to hitch up the travois."

I nodded.

He wiped his mouth with the back of his forearm. He had been crouching near me, in the half darkness, the white dress marking his position, partaking, too, of the pemmican.

I smiled to myself. Both kaiila, one given to him by his brother, Canka, and the black kaiila, which had been mine, put at my disposal, with the permission of Canka, my master, by my friend, Grunt, the trader, were picketed but a few feet from the threshold of the lodge. Similarly the two travois, fashioned for the morning, were not more than feet away. Cuwignaka was eager.

I sat on the robes, in the half darkness, eating of the pemmican, in Canka's collar.

Outside I could hear the stirrings of the camp. I thought of various slaves I had owned, when I was free, wenches such as Constance, Arlene and Sandra, and Vella and Elicia. They were all hot and looked well in their collars. There was not one there whose lips and tongue, in eager, submissive obedience, a man would not have welcomed on his body. All now knew that on Gor they were naught, and could be naught, but slaves. Too I thought of another woman, olive-skinned, green-eyed, black-haired Talena, once, until disowned, the daughter of Marlenus, the Ubar of Ar. How proud she had been. How she had scorned me when she had thought me helpless! Anger, even in the lodge of Cuwignaka, suffused me. I wondered what she would look like, stripped, in close chains, lying on her side, terrified, at my feet. The common Gorean slave whip has five soft, broad strands. It punishes a woman, terribly. On the other hand it does not mark her. It does not, thus, lower her value.

I sat on the robes, eating the crumbled cake of pemmican. I thought of Talena. Once she had been owned by Rask of Treve. Doubtless he had taught her her slavery well. I thought I might teach it to her better. She lived now, free, but sequestered and dishonored, in the city of Ar, in the Central Cylinder itself, perhaps the most fortified, best-defended tower or keep in that huge city. It would be impossible, or almost so, to even think of extracting her from such a place. No, I must put it from my mind. I recalled her vanity, her arrogance and pride. In the Central Cylinder, if nowhere else, she was surely safe from the bracelets and nooses of marauding tarnsmen. No one, surely, could get at her there. There she was surely safe. I recalled her scorn, her contempt.

One day, I thought, perhaps, I might try chain-luck in the city of Ar. It is said there are some good-looking women there. I wondered if a place for such a woman might be found in my own holding, say, in my kitchens. Too, of course, I could always give her, as a worthless trinket, one in which I was not personally interested, to one of the lowest and meanest of the taverners of Port Kar. This thought amused me. But I would have to choose the taverner and tavern well. The taverner must be harsh and exacting, petty, avaricious and uncompromising. And his place of business must be one of the worst in the city; it must be in the area of the lower canals; it must be stinking, dingy, squalid and cheap; and it must be busy, crowded often with boisterous ruffians, some in just from the sea, who are impatient with slaves. There, in such a place, let the proud Talena, once the daughter of a Ubar, wear the collar of her master. Let her there, stripped, or silked, as he might choose, serve and please his customers.

I chewed the last of the pemmican. Too, I thought I would, before giving her to such a taverner, have her ears pierced. This would, in effect, guarantee that she would remain always only a slave on Gor. Gorean men find pierced ears, as do many men of Earth, stimulatory. To the Gorean such ear-piercing speaks blatantly of bondage. Penetration of a woman's flesh is publicly symbolized, in her very body; the wounds inflicted on her were intended and deliberate; and her body has now been prepared to bear, fastened in its very flesh, barbaric ornamentation. These things all speak to the Gorean of the female slave. In a woman who is truly free such things, of course, would be unthinkable. Many free women, knowing how such things are viewed by Gorean men, fear them more than the brand and collar. Slave girls, of course, once they have begun to learn their collars, and once they have begun to learn that they are truly slaves, and what it might mean, become very vain and proud over the piercing of their ears. They know that it makes them more attractive to men, and significantly so, and, too, they relish being able, with earrings, to make themselves even more beautiful and exciting. Slave girls tend to be very proud and happy in their sexuality. This type of pleasure, commonly denied to the free woman, is probably an additional reason why they tend to hate their helplessly imbonded sisters.

"Are you not ready?" asked Cuwignaka, coming into the lodge. "Are you not dressed?"

"I am almost ready," I said.

I reached over and picked up my tunic, and drew it over my head. I then stood up and adjusted it on my body.

Cuwignaka, then, disappeared again through the threshold of the lodge.

Most Gorean males, and their slaves, incidentally, not merely the males of the red savages, commonly sleep naked. If the girl is permitted a sleeping garment it is commonly short, front-opening, and fastened with a single tie. In this way if the master, in the middle of the night, should light a lamp, he may reveal his slave, swiftly and conveniently, to himself. Similarly, even in the darkness, it provides little impedence to his hands or body.

I was thirsty from the pemmican.

"Make ready your arrows," I heard, a crying from outside the lodge. "Make ready your arrows! Make ready your knives! We are going to make meat! We are going to make meat!" This was a crier of the Sleen Soldiers, Agleskala, Striped Lizard. He was moving through the village.

I went to the side of the lodge and felt for the water bag. It was the one which I had once kept on my pack kaiila. Its presence, like that of certain other utensils and articles in the lodge, was due to Grunt. Several other things had been given to Cuwignaka by Canka, or other members of the Isbu, usually of the All Comrades. The lodge itself had been given to him by Akihoka, One-Who-Is-Skillful, an All Comrade, one of Canka's close friends. It is cultural for red savages to look out for one another. Our housekeeping paraphernalia, therefore, though somewhat modest, was adequate. One robe had even been donated by Mahpiyasapa, the civil chief of the Isbu. In doing this he had set an example to his people and, more importantly from Cuwignaka's point of view, acknowledged his right to remain with the Isbu.

I heard some kaiila moving past outside. These were probably scouts going out to make contact with the herd guards.

I wondered why the kailiauk were early this year.

I looked about the lodge. It was not untypical. The lodge poles were about twenty-five feet high. They were of tem wood which dries evenly and is long-lasting. The bark is removed from the poles and they are trimmed to an even thickness for most of their length. They are usually about twelve inches around. The top yard or so of their length is tapered, to facilitate their clustering, and being tied in position. In setting up the lodge three or four poles are tied together and raised to a standing position, rather resembling a tripod. The other poles, appropriately spaced, are laid against these. A long rawhide rope, then, from the ground, wound about several times, fastens the primary and secondary poles together. The end of this rope hangs near the lodge entrance, where it may, on a moment's notice, be conveniently utilized. The cover of the lodge consists of several kailiauk hides, sewn together. Depending on the size of the lodge and the size of the hides available, a lodge will usually require in the neighborhood of nineteen or twenty hides. Two long poles, lighter than the lodge poles, are tied to the cover. By means of these lighter poles the cover is put in its place. The two poles hang near the lodge entrance. They are used not only to lift the cover into place, to adjust it, and remove it, but also in the regulation of the flaps at the apex of the lodge, altering or adjusting the smoke hole, in effect, dependent on temperature and wind conditions. Pegs or tent-pins fasten the cover down. In the winter a hide liner may be placed inside the lodge. This will usually have a height of about five feet inside the lodge. A wall of brush, as a snow fence, in effect, may also be used. In the summer the walls of the lodge, as I have mentioned, may be rolled up, transforming it, in effect, into a sun canopy.

The outsides of the lodge may be painted, as the occupant pleases. Hunting and war exploits are common themes. The lodge, thus, is a very personal dwelling. Various tribes use different numbers of poles in setting up their lodges. The Fleer usually use twenty, the Sleen twenty-two and the Kaiila twenty-four. Similarly different encampment sites tend to be favored by different tribes. The Kaiila will usually camp near water but in the open, a pasang or so from timber. They seem unusually cognizant of the possibilities of ambush. The Fleer will usually camp in the open but near timber, probably for the convenience of firewood. Yellow Knives often camp in open timber. Sleen, interestingly, often make their camps in thick timber, and even in brush and thickets. What seems to one tribe to present a dangerous possibility of ambush may, to another, seem to provide cover and shelter.

Different tribes, too, incidentally, tend to use different moccasin designs. Accordingly, if a track is fresh it is often possible to tell if it was made by a foot wearing, say, a Kaiila or Fleer moccasin. War parties, of course, occasionally utilize this idiosyncrasy, donning moccasins of an enemy pattern when making intrusions into foreign territories. The hides used in the lodges are, of course, translucent. Thus, in the daylight, it is easy to see in the interior. Similarly, at night, one can see shadows within. The lodge at night, interestingly, illuminated from within by its fire, can be a quite lovely sight. This is even more impressive, of course, with a number of lodges.

A camp, at night, incidentally, is usually quite a noisy place. It would not form, for example, an ideal refuge for scholarship. The stereotype of the taciturn red savage is one based, usually, on encountering him in guarded situations, where he is uneasy, perhaps meeting strangers, or is, say, being careful, perhaps being involved in trading. In his villages he is outspoken, good-humored and animate. He likes wagers, practical jokes and telling stories. He is probably one of the world's greatest visitors and, too, one of the world's greatest hosts, one of his great pleasures in life being the giving of gifts and the feasting of friends.

I drank deeply from the water bag, and then closed it, and replaced it by the lodge wall. The lodge has a diameter of some fifteen feet. This is actually quite spacious. A circular enclosure, of course, geometrically, contains more space, for a given perimeter, than any other figure. Such lodges are conveniently and comfortably inhabited by families of from five to eight red savages. To be sure, much time, most of the year, is spent outdoors. Also, what might seem crowded to one with a particular acculturation may simply seem appropriate and right, even intimate and cozy, to one with a differing acculturation. Family and communal closeness, for better or for worse, are characteristics of the life of the red savage. I do not think he would want it any other way. To be sure, it is not unknown for a man to occasionally seek the lodge of his warrior society, where his children and woman cannot follow him. In his club, so to speak, he might be able to find a bit of peace and quiet which seems to have eluded him at home. Too, of course, meditation and the seeking of visions and dreams are solitary activities. A man may indicate that he is meditating by as little as putting his blanket over his head, even in a crowded camp. He will then be left alone. Dreams and visions, on the other hand, are usually sought in the wilderness.

"Howo, Tatankasa!" said Cuwignaka, thrusting his head into the lodge. "Come on. Come along, Red Bull!"

"I am coming," I said. I went outside. It was still quite dark. I could see shapes moving about, however. Cuwignaka had the two travois already hitched up.

There was much movement and excitement in the camp. I wandered off, behind the lodges.

"Where have you been?" asked Cuwignaka, when I returned.

"Where do you think?" I asked. "I was relieving myself."

I saw two red savages riding by. They were Sleen Soldiers. One was Hci.

"We will be leaving any moment," said Cuwignaka.

"I doubt it," I said.

Hci turned back his kaiila and brought it to a stop before us. He wore breechclout and moccasins. About his neck was a necklace of sleen claws. His long hair was braided. He carried his bow, not yet strung, and a quiver of arrows, at his left hip. On his belt, that holding the breechclout, there was a knife, in a beaded sheath. Hci's kaiila wore a jaw rope, looped over the back of its neck. This rope, however, is not used, or much used, in either the hunt or war. The rider guides the animal primarily by his knees. His hands, thus, are freed for the use of the bow, or other implements. There was, however, a rope looped about the neck of the kaiila. This rope is thrown to the side and behind the kaiila. If the rider, then, is dismounted in the tumult of the hunt, he may, hopefully, by seizing this rope, sometimes a strap, retain control over his mount and, hastily, safely, regain his seat. Hci's animal, incidentally, was a prize kaiila. This was indicated by its notched ears. The Kaiila notch both ears of such a kaiila. Certain other tribes, such as the Fleer, notch only one ear, usually the left.

"Remember, pretty Siptopto," said Hci, sneeringly, to Cuwignaka, "you are not to hunt. You are to remain back from the hunt. It is yours only to cut meat, with the other females." 'Siptopto' was an insulting pet name by which Hci occasionally addressed Cuwignaka. It was the sort of name, though not necessarily, that might be given to a female slave. It means "Beads."

"I am not a woman," said Cuwignaka.

"You will stay back from the hunt," said Hci. "You will cut meat with the other women."

"I will stay back from the hunt," said Cuwignaka. "I will cut meat with the women."

"You, and the slave," said Hci.

"We will stay back from the hunt," said Cuwignaka. "We will cut meat with the women."

Hci then turned his kaiila about, and went, following his fellow rider.

"Make ready your arrows!" I heard again. "Make ready your arrows! Sharpen your knives! Sharpen your knives! We are going to make meat! We are going to make meat!" Slowly, through the camp, in the darkness, now crowded with men and women, rode Agleskala, the crier of the Sleen Soldiers.

Behind him, in a line, coming from the vicinity of the lodge of the Sleen Soldiers, the society lodge, came several members of the Sleen-Soldiers Society. They were garbed and accoutered much as had been Hci. Two, however, carried long, heavy, stout hunting lances, rather than bows and arrows.

Following them, being careful not to precede them, were some of the first of the hunters.

"Hou, Witantanka!" called a girl to one of the warriors. "Greetings, One-Who-Is-Proud!"

"Hou, Akamda," said he to the girl, halting his kaiila. 'Akamda' is a word usually designating fringe, such as might occur on leggings or shirts.

"Is a warrior of the Isanna going hunting?" she asked.

"Maybe," he said. "Is a maiden of the Isbu coming out to cut meat?"

"It is possible," she said. "How many arrows do you have?"

"Twenty," he said.

"Then maybe you will be able to get one beast," she said. Hunters pride themselves on making single-arrow kills.

"Twenty Pte will let out their water and roll behind me, dying, in the dust," he said.

"Cinto!" she laughed. "Oh, yes! Surely!"

"Once my kaiila slipped," he said. "But it was long ago."

"If you use more than one arrow in any beast," she said, "I will tell everyone."

"Would you?" he asked.

"Yes," she said. "And no more riding after the animal, to pull out the first arrow. You are an idiot. You could have been killed."

"I would not do that," he said.

"Miniwozan saw you," she said. 'Miniwozan' does not translate well. It signifies a mist, or a slowly falling rain.

"Miniwozan, then," he said, "was too close to the herd."

"Perhaps," granted Akamda.

"It was probably another," he said.

"It was you," she said.

"Maybe I did it," he said.

"If you are gong to do that sort of thing," she said, "you should wait until the animal is dead, and the herd is passed by."

"Do you think I could do such a thing?" he asked.

"I think maybe you could do it," she said.

"Maybe," he said.

"Do not use more than one arrow," she said.

"I never use more than one arrow," he said, "almost never."

"Good hunting," she said.

"If I use more than one arrow, you will not tell anyone, will you?" he asked.

"I will tell you," she said, "you may be assured of that."

"But you will not tell others, will you?" he asked.

"No," she said, "except maybe Miniwozan."

"Do not bother," he said. "I will have it announced by the village crier."

"Be careful, Witantanka," said the girl.

"In the time of the dancings and the feasts, after the hunting is finished," he said, "I may be looking for a girl to ride with me about the camp."

"Behind you, on your kaiila?" she asked.

"Yes," he said. "Would you like to ride with me, behind me, on my kaiila, about the camp?" he asked.

"Maybe," she said. "I will think about it." This was tantamount to an offer of marriage.

"I think I will go hunting now," he said. "I must take my place."

"Oglu waste, Witantanka," she said. "Good luck, Witantanka."

Some more hunters drifted past us.

A few yards ahead of where we waited by the lodge there was a group of mounted kaiila riders. There was an older fellow there, a member of the Sleen Soldiers. He was addressing a cluster of some five or six young men, almost boys. It was the first hunt, I gathered, in which they would fully participate, not riding merely at the fringes, observing the older men, but entering among the beasts themselves. I walked up, to where I might hear what was going on. "Remember," the older fellow was telling them, "you do not hunt for yourself today. You hunt for others. Doubtless there will be hunters who will not be successful today. You will hunt for them. And there are those in the camps who are weak and frail. You will hunt for them. And there are those who are sick, and those who are hurt. For all of these, and others, those less fortunate than yourselves, you hunt today. But always, remember, you hunt not only for yourself. You never hunt only for yourself. You hunt for the Kaiila."

"Howe, howe," acknowledged the boys.

"Good hunting," said he to them. "Oglu waste! Good luck!"

They then turned their kaiila about, to take their places.

In a boy's first hunt he gives his kill, or kills, to others. Only the first beast's tongue, its most prized meat, will he have, it being awarded to him for his efficiency and valor. The purpose of this custom seems to be to encourage the young man, from the very beginning, to think of himself in terms of the gallantry and generosity of the warrior.

I walked back to where Cuwignaka was waiting.

"We will soon be going out," said Cuwignaka.

"I think you are right," I said.

The lodges, incidentally, in a hunt of this sort, are not struck. The Pte, in a herd of this size, moving as slowly as it must, and in virtue of the kaiila and travois, would be within reach for three or four days. The entire encampment of red savages, of course, may be swiftly moved. In less than twenty Ehn an entire camp can be struck, packed and gone. This is a function, of course, of the lodges involved. One woman, working alone, can put one up in fifteen Ehn and strike it in three.

"Canka," said Cuwignaka, as Canka stopped his kaiila near us.

"Greetings, my brother," said Canka.

"Greetings, my brother," said Cuwignaka happily. "What are you going to do this morning?"

"I think I will go out to look at the Pte," said Canka, smiling.

"Where is Winyela?" asked Cuwignaka. "Is she going out? Do you want her to come with us? We will look after her."

"She is going out," said Canka. "But I am sending her out with Wasnapohdi, the slave of Wopeton, the trader. She has been with the hunt before. She will not get too close. She will show her how to cut meat."

"Winyela is white," said Cuwignaka. "She will throw up the first time she has to cut meat. She will do it poorly."

"If she wastes meat, I will beat her," said Canka.

"You have never beaten her in your life," said Cuwignaka.

"If she wastes meat, I will beat her," said Canka.

"Good," said Cuwignaka, approvingly.

"I see, little brother," said Canka, "that you, too, are going out."

"Of course," said Cuwignaka.

"Do not get too close to the herd," said Canka.

"I won't," said Cuwignaka.

This warning on the part of Canka made me somewhat uneasy. I had thought that the dangers in this sort of business were borne primarily, if not exclusively, by the hunters. Yet, of course, it was clear that if the herd, or portions of it, were to veer or circle their movements might bring them into the vicinity of the travois and women. In such a case, of course, one must slash the travois straps, mount up, and make away as best one can. To be sure the greatest dangers were clearly borne by the hunters who must ride among the running beasts themselves, and attempt their kills from a distance just outside the hooking range of the trident, from a distance so close that they might almost reach out and touch the animal.

"You and Tatankasa will be out there alone," said Canka. "I will not be near you."

"I do not understand," said Cuwignaka.

"Beware of Hci," said Canka.

"We will," said Cuwignaka. The hair on the back of my neck rose up.

"Have you seen an arrow of mine?" asked Canka. "I am missing one of my arrows."

"No," said Cuwignaka.

"I must have misplaced it," said Canka.

"Yes," said Cuwignaka.

"I must take my place," said Canka.

"Good hunting. Be careful," said Cuwignaka. "Oglu waste!"

"Oglu waste," said Canka, and then turned his kaiila away, to take his place.

Agleskala now made his third and last circuit of the camp. "Make ready your arrows," he cried. "Make ready your knives. We are going to make meat! We are going to make meat!"

"We are going to make meat!" cried out several of those about us.

"We are going to make meat!" said Cuwignaka, happily.

The Sleen Soldiers, riding abreast, in a long line, which no hunter, no matter how eager, must cross, in the first streaks of dawn, left the camp. Behind them came the hunters, of the Isbu, of the Casmu, of the Isanna, of the Wismahi, and of the Napoktan, riding five abreast. Dust lifted about the paws of their kaiila. Then came the women, with the kaiila and travois, the poles leaving lines in the dust, and with them, joining them, came Cuwignaka and myself.

5

CUWIGNAKA AND I WILL GO TO THE DRAW

"Help me," said Wasnapohdi, "please."

We helped her put the huge bull on his belly in the grass, pulling the legs out. Cows, which are lighter, are usually skinned on their sides, and then turned, sometimes by ropes tied to their legs, drawn by the kaiila.

Wasnapohdi thrust her knife in behind the neck, to make the first slash, from which the skin would begin to be folded back, to expose the forequarters on each side. Subsequently the hide, in the normal fashion, can be cut down the middle.

The liver had already been removed from the animal, by the hunters. It is a great delicacy, and is commonly eaten raw.

"How is Winyela doing?" I asked. I saw the girl to the side on the grass, kneeling, her head down.

"She is sick," said Wasnapohdi.

I walked over to the girl. It did not smell too nicely near her.

"How are you feeling?" I asked.

"I am all right," she said. "In a little while I will try to cut the meat again."

"You are a female, Winyela," said Wasnapohdi, sweating, working. "You must learn this."

"I will try again, in a little bit," said Winyela.

"There is a cow over there," said Wasnapohdi, kneeling on the back of the animal, pointing with the bloody knife, "felled by one of Canka's arrows. I will have her work on her. That way, if she does poorly, since it is his own kill, and not that of another, he can be more lenient with her."

"Do you think he will be lenient?" I asked.

"No," said Wasnapohdi, returning to her task.

"I am not afraid," said Winyela.

"Oh?" I asked.

"No," she said. "No matter what I do, I know that Canka will never punish me."

"Why is that?" I asked.

"He likes me," she said.

"And do you like him?" I asked.

"I love him," she said, "dearly, more than anything."

"Bold slave," I said.

"A slave may be bold," she said.

"That is true," I said.

"Nonetheless," said Wasnapohdi, grunting, at her work, "do not be surprised if you find yourself well quirted."

"Canka would never do that to me," she said.

"Have you never brought him the quirt?" I asked.

"Once," she said, "the first evening in his lodge, he made me bring him the quirt, on my hands and knees, in my teeth."

"What do you suppose the meaning of that was?" I asked.

"That I was a slave, that I was subject to discipline," she said.

"And do you think he will have forgotten that?" I asked.

"I suppose not," she said. "But he did not use it on me, not then, nor has he used it on me later."

"I see," I said.

"Canka," she said, "will never punish me."

I smiled. I did not think the girl understood, fully, that she was a slave. Did she not know that, as a slave, she was subject to discipline, and that any master, regardless of his feelings, would impose it on her? The domination of slaves is not a haphazard or tentative thing. They are owned. They will serve, perfectly. If they do not, they will be punished, severely, or, if the master wishes, slain.

"Perhaps I am too pretty to whip," said Winyela.

"I would not count on it," said Wasnapohdi, irritatedly.

"At any rate," said Winyela, "Canka, I think, likes me. He will never beat me."

"Say that again," said Wasnapohdi, pausing in her work, breathing heavily, "when you find yourself on your knees, stripped, your wrists bound before you, to the whipping stake, every inch of your body bared to the stroke of his quirt."

"You are so silly!" laughed Winyela.

"Help me put the meat I am cutting on the travois," said Wasnapohdi.

"Must I touch it?" asked Winyela.

"Yes," said Wasnapohdi.

"I do not really wish to do so," said Winyela.

"Maybe Canka will not beat you," said Wasnapohdi, "but I assure you that I would have no compunction in doing so. Hurry now! Get busy, or I will take a bone and lash the hide off your pretty rump."

"Sometimes," said Winyela to me, getting to her feet, "Wasnapohdi is vulgar."

"Do you obey?" inquired Wasnapohdi.

"I obey," said Winyela, loftily, tossing her head.

"Put your head down, and say that, humbly," said Wasnapohdi.

"I obey," said Winyela, her head down.

"More humbly," said Wasnapohdi.

"I obey," said Winyela, more humbly, half sobbing, putting her head down further.

"Good," said Wasnapohdi. "Now, come here."

Wasnapohdi thrust eight or ten pounds of bloody meat into the unwilling hands of Winyela.

"Later," said Wasnapohdi, "you will cut up that cow over there. I will show you how."

"That will not be necessary," said Winyela. "I have seen how it is done."

Winyela then turned about and carried the meat to the travois. I took some from Wasnapohdi and carried it, too, to their travois.

"Do not be a little fool," I said to her, at the travois. "Let Wasnapohdi help you. She is your friend."

"I can do it myself," said Winyela. "And if I do not do it well, it does not matter."

"Do not be too sure of that," I said.

"Canka would never strike me," she said. "Too, he will do whatever I want."

"Do not forget," I said, "who is the master, and who is the slave."

"In the lodge of Canka," she said, "I can do whatever I please."

"Perhaps he will find it necessary to remind you that you are a slave," I said, "that you must obey, and be pleasing, perfectly, in all respects."

"Perhaps," she laughed.

"Perhaps you wish to be reminded that you are a slave," I said.

"That is absurd," she said.

"Do you know that you are a slave?" I asked.

"I know it," she said, "of course."

"But do you know it in the heart, and in the heat and humility of you?" I asked.

She looked at me, puzzled.

"Do you know it in the deepest love of you?" I asked.

"I do not understand," she said.

"That is where you want to know it," I told her.

"I do not understand," she said, angrily.

"Beware," I said, "lest your secret dream come true."

"Canka will never beat me," she said. Then she drew the hide cover over the meat, to protect it from the flies.

I looked about. From where we stood I could see at least a dozen fallen animals, their bulk, like dark mounds, dotting the plains. Too, here and there, we could see women, with their kaiila and travois, working, or moving about.

"Cuwignaka and I must get back to work," I said.

"I wish you well, Slave," said she.

"I wish you well, too, Slave," I said. I then went to join Cuwignaka.

"Canka will never beat me," she called after me.

"Perhaps not," I said.

"Come, Winyela," called Wasnapohdi. "There is meat to put on the travois."

"I am coming," responded Winyela.

"My, there is a pretty girl," said Bloketu, the daughter of Watonka, the chief of the Isanna Kaiila. "But why is she wearing the dress of a white woman?"

"Perhaps she is a white female slave," said Iwoso.

"Greetings, Bloketu. Greetings, Iwoso," said Cuwignaka, grinning.

"You have cut a great deal of meat," said Bloketu, honestly observing this.

"We have already made four trips back to the village," said Cuwignaka.

I noted that both Bloketu and Iwoso were suitably impressed with this.

"How many trips have you made?" asked Cuwignaka.

"One," said Bloketu.

I was not surprised. We had seen more than one hunter, later in the afternoon, drift back to visit with her. Bloketu was a beauty, and the daughter of a chieftain.

"Iwoso is slow," said Bloketu.

"I am not slow," protested Iwoso.

"It is you who are lazy and slow, Bloketu," said Cuwignaka. "It is well known. You would rather primp, and pose and smile for the hunters than do your work."

"Oh!" cried Bloketu. Iwoso, her head down, smiled.

"It is not enough to be merely beautiful," said Cuwignaka.

"At least you think I am beautiful," said Bloketu, somewhat mollified.

"That is not enough," said Cuwignaka. "If you were my woman, you would be worked well. If you did not work well I would beat you."

"I suppose," she said, "you think you could work me well."

"Yes," said Cuwignaka. "I would work you well, both outside the lodge and, even better, within it."

"Oh!" said Bloketu, angrily.

"Yes," said Cuwignaka.

"I am the daughter of a chieftain," she said.

"You are only a female," he said.

"Come, Iwoso, my dear maiden," said Bloketu, "let us go. We do not need to stay here, to listen to the prattle of this silly girl in the dress of a white woman."

"You might make an excellent slave, Bloketu," said Cuwignaka. "It might be pleasant to put you in a collar."

Iwoso looked up, suddenly, her eyes blazing. Then she put her head down. I did not understand this reaction on her part.

"Oh, oh!" said Bloketu, speechless with rage.

"Hold," I said to Cuwignaka. "It is Hci."

Riding up, now, coming through the tall grass, was the young Sleen Soldier, the son of Mahpiyasapa, the chieftain of the Isbu. "You are too close to the herd," said Hci. I doubted that this was true, from the tremors in the earth, the dust and the direction of the tracks.

"I have been insulted, Hci," said Bloketu, complaining to the young man. She pointed to Cuwignaka. "Punish him!"

"Her?" asked Hci.

"Her!" said Bloketu, returning to the tribally prescribed feminine gender for Cuwignaka.

"What did she say?" asked Hci.

"She said that I was lazy and slow!" said Bloketu.

"Oh?" asked Hci.

"And that he could work me in his lodge, and well!" she said.

"Yes?" asked Hci.

"Too, he said that I might make an excellent slave, and that it might be pleasant to put me in a collar!"

Hci looked Bloketu over, slowly. She shrank back, abashed. Cuwignaka's assessment, it seemed clear, was one for which he thought there was much to be said.

"Please, Hci," she said.

He then turned his attention to the lovely Iwoso. "She should not be wearing leggings," he said to Bloketu. "Too, her dress is too long. It should come high on her thighs."

"She is only my maiden," said Bloketu.

"Where is her collar?" asked Hci.

"I do not put her in one," said Bloketu.

"She is no longer a child," said Hci. "She is a grown woman now. She is old enough, now, for the garb and collar of a slave. She is old enough, now, for a warrior."

Iwoso looked down, angrily.

"Yellow-Knife woman," said Hci, bitterly.

She looked up at him, angrily.

"A Yellow Knife did this to me," said Hci, pointing to the long, jagged scar at his chin, on the left side.

"He struck you well!" said Iwoso, angrily.

"I slew him," said Hci.

Hci then again turned his attention to Bloketu.

"Punish him," said Bloketu, pointing to Cuwignaka.

"Her?" said Hci.

"Her!" said Bloketu.

"I am a warrior," said Hci. "I do not mix in the squabbles of females."

"Oh," cried Bloketu, angrily.

I smiled to myself. It seemed to me that Hci had handled this business well. Surely it would have been beneath his dignity to meddle in such a business. Too, as a Sleen Soldier, on the day of a hunt, during their tenure of power, he had matters much more important to attend to than the assuagement of a female's offended vanity.

"The herd is too close," said Hci. "You are all to withdraw from this place."

We prepared to turn about.

"Separately," said Hci.

The hair rose again on the back of my neck.

"There," said Hci, pointing to the southwest, "is a fallen bull, a Cracked-Horns, of thirty winters."

"That is not good meat, or good hide," said Bloketu, puzzled.

"Attend to it, Bloketu," said Hci.

"Yes, Hci," she said. The two women, then, Bloketu and Iwoso, the travois poles marking the grass behind their kaiila, took their way away. I watched the grass springing up behind them. In a few minutes it would be difficult for anyone but a skilled tracker, looking for broken stems, to determine that they had gone that way.

"Over there," said Hci, to us, pointing east by southeast, "there is a draw. In the draw there is a fallen bull, a Smooth Horns, no more than some six winters in age. Attend to it."

"Yes, Hci," said Cuwignaka, obediently. A Smooth Horns is a young, prime bull. Its horns are not yet cracked from fighting and age. The smoothness of the horns, incidentally, is not a purely natural phenomenon. The bulls polish them, themselves, rubbing them against sloping banks and trees. Sometimes they will even paw down earth from the upper sides of washouts and then use the harder, exposed material beneath, dust scattering about, as a polishing surface. This polishing apparently has the function of both cleaning and sharpening the horns, two processes useful in intraspecific aggression, the latter process improving their capacity as fighting instruments, in slashing and goring, and the former process tending to reduce the amount of infection in a herd resulting from such combats. Polishing behavior in males thus appears to be selected for. It has consequences, at any rate, which seem to be in the best interests of the kailiauk as a species.

"There," said Hci, "your kaiila will be tired. Unharness them from the travois. Let them graze. Picket them close to where you are working."

"Yes," said Cuwignaka, angrily.

"Go now," said Hci, pointing.

"Yes, Hci," said Cuwignaka.

I was sweating, as the young Sleen Soldier rode away. "What was that all about?" I asked.

"This meat on our travois," said Cuwignaka, "is to be destroyed."

"I do not understand," I said.

"We will go to the draw," said Cuwignaka.

"Very well," I said.

6

WHAT OCCURRED IN THE DRAW

It was nearly dusk.

"This will be our fifth load of meat," I said.

"Oh, yes," said Cuwignaka, bitterly.

"Wait," I said.

Cuwignaka, too, lifted his head. We were in a long, narrow, generally shallow draw. Yet, where we worked, where the Smooth Horns had been felled, the sides were relatively steep, some twenty feet or so on our left, some thirty feet on our right.

I could feel tremors in the earth now beneath our feet.

"They are coming," said Cuwignaka. He bent swiftly to the twisted leather hobbles, almost like slave hobbles, on the forelegs, almost at the paws, of our kaiila. He thrust the paws free of the twisted, encircling leather. We had already, as Hci had commanded, freed the kaiila of the two travois.

"How many are there?" I asked.

"Two, maybe three hundred," said Cuwignaka, climbing lightly to the silken back of his kaiila.

I could now hear the sound, clearly. It carried through the draw, the deep thudding, magnified by, intensified by, that narrow corridor, open to the sky, of dirt and rock.

"Mount up," said Cuwignaka. "Hurry."

I looked to the meat.

Almost at the same time, suddenly, about a bend in the draw, turning, lurching, its shoulder striking the side of the draw, its feet almost slipping out from under it, in its turn, in the soft footing, covered with dust, its eyes wild and red, foam at its nostrils and mouth, some twenty-five hundred pounds or better in weight, snorting, kicking dust behind it, hurtled a kailiauk bull.

I leaped to the side and it rushed past me. I could almost have touched it. My kaiila squealed and, as I headed it off, it tried to climb the side of the draw, scrambling at it, then slipping back, falling, rolling, to the side.

Another bull, then, bellowing, hurtled past.

I seized the reins of the kaiila. The draw was now filled with dust. The ground shook under our feet. The thudding now became thunderous, striking about the walls, seeming all about us. The kaiila of Cuwignaka squealed and reared. He held it in his place, mercilessly. As my beast scrambled up, regaining its feet, I mounted it, and turned it away, down the draw. Cuwignaka and I, then, not more than a few yards ahead of the animals, which, in a body, buffeting and storming, tridents down, their heads low, as the kailiauk runs, came streaming, flooding, bellowing, torrentlike, about that bend in the draw, raced to safety.

We stood in the grass, about a hundred yards from the draw. I kept my hand on my kaiila's neck. It was still trembling. The mass of the animals which, stampeded, had come running through the draw, was now better than a pasang away. Here and there single animals roamed. Some even stopped, lowering their heads, to graze.

"Let us return to the draw," said Cuwignaka, mounting up.

I joined him and, slowly, our kaiila at a walk, we returned to the narrow draw. Its floor was torn with the passage of the animals. Many of the hoofprints were six and seven inches deep.

"The animals were probably isolated in the other end of the draw," said Cuwignaka. "Then a bull was cut out and run down the draw, to be felled where we found him."

"Is that likely?" I asked.

"I think so," said Cuwignaka. "Sometimes animals take shelter in a draw, or, running into one, begin to mill, and, for a time, will stay there, sometimes until morning."

"It was a trap," I said.

"Not really," said Cuwignaka. "We were told to unharness the kaiila. We were told to picket them, in effect, at hand."

I nodded.

"No harm was intended to come to us," said Cuwignaka.

We then, on our kaiila, entered the draw, straightening

ourselves on our kaiila as they descended the sloping entrance between the dirt sides.

"The meat is gone," said Cuwignaka, in a moment. "It is torn apart, destroyed, trampled, scattered."

Here and there I could see pieces of meat, trodden into the dust.

"We could save some of it," I said, "gather it and wash it later, at the camp."

"Leave it for the flies," said Cuwignaka.

"The travois, too, are destroyed," I said.

"Yes," said Cuwignaka.

The poles were broken and splintered; the crosspieces were shattered; the hides were rent. Bindings and harness were scattered about.

I surveyed the gouged floor of the draw, the trampled, half-buried meat, the remains of the travois. Many of the bones, even, of the animal on which we had been working were crushed and flung about. The carcass itself, most of it, had been moved several feet and flattened, and lay half sunk in the dust of the draw. The force of even a single kailiauk, with its speed and weight, can be a fearful thing. In numbers, it is awesome to contemplate their power.

Cuwignaka dismounted and began to gather in the rawhide bindings and pieces of harness from the shattered travois. They might be used again.

"I will help you," I said. I dismounted, and joined him. Our kaiila, not moving much, stayed close to us.

"The head is there," said Cuwignaka, indicating the head of the beast we had skinned, and had been fleshing.

"Yes," I said.

"When we are finished," said Cuwignaka, "we will take it out of the draw. We will take it up to the surface."

"All right," I said.

"Someone is coming," I said.

We looked down to the bend in the draw. About it, slowly, his kaiila walking, came a single rider.

"It is Hci," said Cuwignaka.

Hci halted his kaiila a few yards from us. He was naked save for the breechclout and moccasins. About his neck was the necklace of sleen claws. Across his thighs was his bow. At his left hip was his quiver. His arrows, extracted from their targets, the meat identified, at this time of day, would have been wiped clean of blood, even the lightning grooves inscribed in the long shafts. Stains would remain, of course, at the base of some of the feathers.

"Hou, Cuwignaka," said Hci.

"Hou, Hci," said Cuwignaka.

Hci looked about the draw. "You have lost the meat," he said.

"Yes," said Cuwignaka.

"That is not good," said Hci.

"No," said Cuwignaka.

"Your travois, too, have been destroyed," said Hci.

"Yes," said Cuwignaka.

"I told you the herd was too close," said Hci. "I told you to withdraw from this place."

Cuwignaka was furious, but did not speak. We knew that these words of Hci, to that extent, could be sworn to by Bloketu and Iwoso.

"But you did not listen," said Hci. "You chose, rather, to deliberately disobey a warden of the hunt."

"Why did you do this?" asked Cuwignaka.

"Now you have lost meat," said Hci.

"It is you who have destroyed the meat!" said Cuwignaka. "You have destroyed meat!"

Hci sat quietly on the kaiila. "I could kill you now, both of you," he said, "but I do not choose to do so."

I did not doubt but what Hci spoke the truth. We had only one knife with us, a cutting knife. Hci was mounted, and had his bow.

Hci then, quietly, rode towards us. When he reached our vicinity he stopped his kaiila. He indicated the head of the kailiauk. "That is to be taken out of the draw," he said. "Take it up to the surface."

"I will do so," said Cuwignaka.

Hci then, not hurrying, rode past us and made his way up the draw, some pebbles slipping back, on its slope, from the movement of his kaiila's paws.

We finished our work, coiling the rent harness and bindings from the travois. We slung them about our shoulders.

"I must leave the Isbu," said Cuwignaka.

"Why?" I asked.

"I am a shame to my brother," said Cuwignaka.

"This head will be heavy," I said. "If we are going to get it out of the draw, let us do so now."

"Yes," said Cuwignaka. We then, between us, carried the

head up, out of the draw, and, some fifty yards or so from the draw, placed it on the level.

"Why are we doing this?" I asked.

"The kailiauk is a noble animal," said Cuwignaka. "Let the sun shine upon it."

"This is interesting to me," I said.

"What?" asked Cuwignaka.

"This business," I said.

"What business?" he asked.

"This business about the head," I said. "This was important, apparently, to both you and Hci, that it should be brought up from the draw, that it should be placed on the level, that it should be put, I gather, in the sun."

"Of course," said Cuwignaka.

"In this, do you not see," I asked, "you are both Kaiila, you no less than he. In the end, you are both of the Isbu."

"But I am a shame to the Isbu," said Cuwignaka.

"How is that?" I asked.

"I have lost meat," he said.

"You did not lose meat," I said. "Hci is the one who lost the meat."

"I guess you are right," said Cuwignaka. "No one, though, will believe it."

"Hci is well known in the camp," I said. "You may be surprised who might believe you, and not him."

"Maybe you are right," smiled Cuwignaka.

"You should not be distressed," I said. "You should be proud."

"Why is that?" asked Cuwignaka.

"You have brought four loads of meat back to the village. I doubt that anyone has done as well."

"That is pretty good, isn't it?" said Cuwignaka.

"It is marvelous," I said.

"But men are stronger than women," said Cuwignaka. "They can cut meat better."

"But the men are needed for the hunt," I said.

"Yes," said Cuwignaka.

"And you are a man," I said.

"Yes," said Cuwignaka. "I am a man."

"Let us get the kaiila now," I said. "It is time to go back to the village."

"Four loads," said Cuwignaka. "That is pretty good, you know."

"It is marvelous," I assured him.

"I am ready to go back to the camp now," said Cuwignaka.

"Good," I said.

7

BLOKETU AND IWOSO COME VISITING

"He beat me," wailed Winyela, running up to me. "He beat me!"

"You are in the presence of a free man," I said, indicating Cuwignaka.

Swiftly she fell to her knees, and put her red hair to the dust. Her hair, sometimes braided, was now, as usual, unbraided. She, like most other slave girls, whether of the red savages or not, wore it long and loose. Among the red savages, of course, free women commonly braid their hair. The lack of braiding, thus, usually, draws an additional distinction between the slaves and free women of the red savages. The most common distinction, of course, is skin color, the slaves almost always being white and the free persons almost invariably being red. "Forgive me, Master," she said to Cuwignaka.

"All right," he said.

She straightened her body, but remained on her knees, before us. "He beat me!" she said. She was naked, except for Canka's collar. Her small wrists were bound before her body, with several tight loops of a rawhide thong.

"Stand," I said, "and turn, slowly."

She did.

"Kneel," I said.

She knelt.

"Yes," I said. "There is little doubt about it. You have been beaten."

"It is not funny," she said.

"Apparently with a kaiila quirt," I said.

"Yes," she said. Some of the braiding marks were still visible in her flesh.

"I thought he liked me," she said.

"You are still alive," I pointed out.

"He took away my clothes, and tied me at a whipping stake, on my knees!" she said.

"That is not uncommon in camps of the red savages, for

white female slaves," I said. "Besides you would not want your clothes bloodied."

She looked at me, angrily.

"Your hair was thrown forward," I said.

"Yes," she said.

"That is so it will not cushion the blows which might fall on your back," I said.

"Doubtless," she said.

"Too," I said, "you would not want to get blood on your hair."

"Of course not," she said.

"Do you think that you are the first girl who has ever been whipped?" I asked.

"No," she said.

"Apparently you did not spend all of your time on your knees, your hair thrown forward, your head and belly down."

"No," she said. "I was struck from my knees by almost the first stroke. I twisted and cried out. I must have supplied much amusement to the women of the red savages who were watching."

"They hate white slave girls," I said. "They enjoy seeing them beaten."

"Then I could cry out no more," she said. "I must simply lie there—"

"And take your punishment—?"

"Yes, and take my punishment—"

"As a slave—?"

"Yes," she said, "—as a slave."

I smiled. This was apparently the first full beating to which the former Miss Millicent Aubrey-Welles, the former debutante from Pennsylvania, had ever been subjected. It had not only physically punished her, and well, but, too, obviously, she had felt it as keenly humiliating. It had not only hurt her, but had horrified and scandalized her.

"You seem outraged," I said.

"I am," she said.

"Why?" I asked.

"I was beaten," she said.

"Do you find yourself eager for a repetition of the experience?" I asked.

"No," she said. "No!"

"The experience, then, was instructive?" I said.

"Yes," she said.

"Why were you beaten?" I asked.

"I cut meat poorly, out on the prairie," she said.

"Wasnapohdi warned you," I said. "You would not let her help. You would not listen."

Winyela squirmed angrily, on her knees in the dust, her small wrists bound tightly before her.

"You were displeasing," I said. "Be pleased that your punishment was not more severe than it was."

Winyela looked up at me, tears in her eyes.

"You might have been fed to sleen," I said.

She shuddered.

"Do you not realize, pretty Winyela," I said, "that you are only a slave?"

"He did not even give me back my clothes," she said.

"These are holiday times," I said. "Surely you have seen more than one white female slave naked in the camp."

"He even left me bound," she said, lifting her secured wrists.

"That is perhaps a bit of extra discipline," I said.

"I am ashamed," she said. "I want to hide. Please let me go into your lodge."

I considered this.

"Beaten slave," said a white female, in a scandalously short shirtdress, and collar, a brunet slave of the Wismahi, sneeringly, to Winyela.

"You may enter the lodge," I said to Winyela.

"Thank you," she whispered, and crept within. Cuwignaka remained outside. He had pegged down three hides and, one after the other, alternating his efforts, was scraping them. All about the camp hides such as these, pegged down, and meat racks, heavy with sheets of kailiauk meat, were in evidence. These are common sights in summer camps. The meat is left two or three days in the sun, this being sufficient for its preservation. It is taken in at night to protect it from the night air.

Inside the lodge Winyela lay on her stomach, on the robes, and, her head lying on her bound hands, wept.

"Do you wish to be beaten again?" I asked.

"No," she said.

"Then, doubtless, you are resolving to be a better slave," I said.

She looked at me, tears streaming down her cheeks, her eyes red.

"Do not be so upset," I said. "You are only a slave."

"Canka struck me," she said. "He beat me."

"And well," I said.

"Yes!" she said.

"Did you expect to be displeasing with impunity?" I asked.

She regarded me, red-eyed.

"I see you did," I said. "Well, now you have learned better."

"I was beaten!" she said.

"Your sense of outrage is inappropriate," I said. "I suggest you rid yourself of it, immediately, lest it become the occasion of further discipline."

"Discipline?" she asked.

"Slave discipline," I said.

She swallowed, hard.

"Replace it with a suitable attitude of trepidation," I said. "You are only a slave."

I observed her naked flanks, on the robes.

She shuddered.

"You should not feel outrage," I told her. "You are only a slave. That is an emotion which would be more appropriate in a free woman, one, say, stripped, and unjustifiably beaten, as though she might be a mere slave. Beatings, on the other hand, are the due of slaves, particularly ones which are in the least respect displeasing, as they might be of any other owned animal."

"I might as well belong to anyone," she said, bitterly.

"That is true," I said. "But you belong to Canka."

"Yes," she said, bitterly. "I belong to Canka." She put her head down, weeping. "I'm so ashamed," she said. "I was so humiliated."

"I understand," I said. The females of the red savages, with their laughter and catcalls, in particular, would not have made the lovely slave's ordeal any easier. Too, that a given girl has been beaten, and has thus, presumably, failed to be fully pleasing in some way, makes her an object of contempt and ridicule among other girls. Little love is lost, commonly, between competitive slave girls. Girls commonly like seeing other girls being beaten, whom they think are too proud, or whom they don't like. It is almost a holiday in the slave quarters when a high slave is to be whipped, particularly if she is then to be reduced to the status of a common girl.

"Am I permitted to feel shame, humiliation?" she asked, angrily.

"Of course," I said. "Those are emotions which are permitted to slaves."

"How generous are the masters," she said.

"Too, shame and humiliation, like chains and whips, can be useful disciplinary devices."

"Of course," she said.

"A shamed, humiliated slave, tied and beaten, is usually swift thereafter to learn her lessons," I said.

"I do not doubt it," she said.

"Tell me truthfully now," I said. "During the beating itself, before you were alone, writhing with the pain, what did you find most shameful, most humiliating?"

"Must I answer?" she asked.

"Yes," I said.

"That I knew, in my heart," she said, "that I deserved the beating, that I richly deserved it."

"Oh?" I asked.

"I did not listen to Wasnapohdi," she said. "I was proud and vain. I was clumsy. I was stupid. I cut meat poorly. I displeased my master."

"I see," I said.

"Then I found myself stripped and tied on my knees at the whipping stake. I was to be publicly punished. Then the quirt fell upon me."

"Many times, in private beatings," I said, "such things as shame or humiliation will enter very little into the situation."

She regarded me.

"Often," I said, "the girl merely fears the leather, or is wary of it, and, hoping to give it a wide berth, behaves herself accordingly. For most practical purposes she knows that if she behaves in certain ways she will not feel it, and if she behaves in other ways, she will feel it. It is almost like a law of nature. It is always there, of course, in the background, and she knows that she is subject to it. Similarly, of course, even in her deepest love, she knows that, ultimately, her very life is dependent on the whim of her master. She can be thrown to sleen, at a word from him, if he wishes."

"We are so owned," she whispered.

"Sometimes," I said, "girls, some girls, who are not sure of their slavery, and its limits, will test their masters."

"Oh?" she said.

"Like you," I said.

"I?" she asked, startled.

"And the masters are not found wanting," I said. "The beauty is quickly reassured as to the existence of boundaries."

"I?" she asked.

"Yes," I said.

"Do you think I want to be limited and controlled?" she asked.

"Yes," I said.

"That is absurd," she said. She rolled over on her back, on the dark robes, and threw her bound wrists over her head.

"You were not sure that you were really Canka's slave," I said. "You wished reassurance."

The beauty moved angrily. She did not answer.

"Have no fear, Winyela," I said. "The collar, as you have no doubt by now discovered, is truly knotted on your neck."

I looked at her small feet, at those trim ankles, at the sweet calves of her, her thighs, her belly, her breasts, the neck and shoulders, her throat, in Canka's collar, her profile, the lovely red hair, behind her on the robes.

"You're looking at me, aren't you?" she said.

"Yes," I said.

"I hate men," she said. She quickly half sat, half knelt, on the robes, her bound hands on the robes.

"No, you don't," I said. "You hate yourself, or something ugly in yourself, probably left over from Earth, that sick world from which you have come."

She threw herself on her side, facing me, her legs pulled up, her bound hands before her. "I am miserable," she said.

"You were confused," I said. "You only wanted to be put in your place."

"My place?" she said.

"Yes," I said, "your place, your place in the order of nature, that of a female at the feet of her master."

She did not respond.

"But it is a dangerous game," I said. "I would beware of playing it with Goreans. Suppose Canka had given you to boys, as a target for their arrows, or had rubbed you with blood, your own, and had set sleen on you."

"I am going to run away," she said, sullenly. She rose, angrily, to her feet. I noted how her small feet pressed in the robes.

"I would not advise it," I said.

"Oh?" she asked.

"There is nowhere to run," I said.

She walked angrily to the other side of the lodge, and then turned to face me, her bound wrists held then at her waist. She was beautiful. "It is true," she said, angrily. "There is nowhere to run." She looked down, at her left thigh. "I am even branded," she said, "like an animal."

"Like the animal you are," I said.

"Yes," she said, bitterly, "—like the animal I am."

"Kneel," I said, indicating a place before me, before where I sat, cross-legged, on the robes.

She knelt.

"Back on your heels," I said, "with your knees widely spread."

She complied.

"Put your shoulders back," I said. "Thrust your breasts out. Hold your wrists at your waist."

She complied.

I examined her. She was not only beautiful. She was very beautiful.

"This is my reality, isn't it," she said, "that of a slave, at the bidding of men."

"Yes," I said. "It is."

"May I lower my wrists?" she asked. "May I close my knees?"

"Yes," I said. Swiftly, she did so.

"I did not think that Canka would beat me," she said.

"Why not?" I asked.

"I thought he liked me," she said. Her wrists looked well, bound, atop her closed thighs.

"I suspect he does," I said.

"He beat me," she said, poutingly.

"You are a slave," I explained.

"I thought he liked me," she said.

"I would suppose that he does," I said. "Hitherto, at any rate, he has treated you with great lenience. That, in my opinion, was a mistake on his part. That lenience, if I am not mistaken, you will discover to have vanished. You will now discover, if I am not mistaken, that your life in his lodge will now be rather different."

"Different?" she asked.

"The discipline to which you will now find yourself subjected, I suspect," I said, "will leave you in little doubt as to your bondage. It will be unswerving, precise and exact. If you depart from the narrow line of slave perfection by so much as a hort you may expect a cuffing, or the lash."

She looked at me, with horror.

"In short," I said, "you will be subjected to exactly the sort of discipline which women such as you want, and need."

She put her head down, angrily. She moved her wrists in the unyielding bonds.

"How do you feel about Canka?" I asked.

She lifted her head, angrily. "I hate him!" she said. "He beat me!"

"Yes, he did," I said, "and well."

"I hate him!" she said.

"You wanted him to beat you," I said.

"But I did not think he would!" she said.

"You were mistaken," I said.

"Yes," she said, "I was mistaken."

"An interesting, if painful experiment, on your part, Winyela," I observed.

"I did not really think of it as an experiment," she said, "at least not consciously, or fully consciously."

"But it seems, rather clearly, to have been one," I said.

"Perhaps," she said.

"I do not think it will be necessary to repeat it," I said.

"No," she said, shuddering, "no."

"What have you learned from your little experiment?" I asked.

"That I am truly a slave," she said.

"And what else?" I asked.

"That my master is strong," she said.

"I do not think you will be permitted, from now on, to get away with any nonsense," I said.

"No," she said. "I do not think so."

"It must be a very frightening thing, to belong to a strong master," I said.

"Yes," she said.

"But then a true slave would not wish it any other way," I said.

"No," she said. "That is true."

"You are satisfied, now," I asked, "that the uncompromising and categorical domination for which you yearn will be applied to you?"

"Yes," she said.

"That you are truly Canka's slave?"

"Yes," she said. "But I am afraid now that he may not like me any longer, that I may have irritated or offended him."

"As you hate him," I said, "what does it matter?"

"Hate him?" she asked. "I love him. I love him, more than anything!"

"But he beat you," I said.

"I was an errant slave," she said. "Of course I would be punished!"

"I see," I said.

"But I am afraid he does not like me any longer," she wept.

"Why?" I asked.

"He was cold to me," she said.

"He was probably angry," I said.

"Do you think he will give me away?" she asked.

"I do not know," I said.

She put down her head, sobbing. She was only an article of property. She could change hands as easily as a pair of moccasins or a kaiila. "I displeased him," she said. "How absurd and stupid I was."

"Does Canka know that you are here?" I asked.

"Yes," she said.

"Were you ordered to report here?" I asked.

"I had to talk to someone," she said. "I would have come anyway."

"Were you ordered to report here?" I asked.

"Yes," she said. I had thought that that might be the case.

"Why?" I asked.

"He has set me an additional punishment," she said, straightening her body, putting back her shoulders, thrusting out her breasts, sucking in her gut, kneeling back on her heels, spreading her knees widely, and lifting her crossed, thonged wrists to her waist, "—Master."

I let her retain this posture, that she might fully understand it.

"I note that your wrists are bound," I said.

"Yes," she said.

"I had thought that that might be only a bit of extra discipline," I said. "I had not known, earlier, from your behavior, that you had been sent to report to this lodge."

She put her head down.

"You wished to talk," I said.

"Yes," she whispered.

"That is permissible," I said.

"Thank you," she said, "—Master."

"To wish to talk is permissible," I said. "Actually to talk, of course, whether you are given permission to speak, or not, is up to the master."

"Yes, Master," she said.

I regarded her. She was quite lovely.

"Master," she said.

"Yes," I said.

"I was not ordered merely to report to this lodge," she said. "I was ordered to report to you."

"Not to Cuwignaka?" I asked.

"No," she said.

"To me, personally," I said.

"Yes, Master," she said.

"Do you know what it means," I asked, "when a woman is sent to report to a man, and she is naked, and in bonds?"

"I am not familiar with Gorean ways," she said.

"Is the symbolism not obvious?" I asked.

"That she is placed at his disposal," she said, "in bondage."

"Of course," I said.

"Then regard me before you," she said, "placed at your disposal, in bondage."

"Interesting," I said.

"Interesting?" she said.

"Yes," I said.

"Why?" she asked.

"You are a beautiful slave," I said, "and the slave of a high warrior, one who has, even, served as Blotanhunka, a war-party leader, of the All Comrades."

She tossed her head.

"You are supposedly worth even five hides of the yellow kailiauk," I said. "That is what Grunt was supposed to receive for you, for your delivery to Mahpiyasapa."

She looked away.

"So, why, then," I asked, "have you been sent here, to be put at the disposal of one who is, like yourself, only a slave?"

"I am being punished," she said. "I have my orders." She looked at me. "Punish me," she said.

"What were your orders?" I asked.

She looked down.

"Speak them," I said.

"I am to report to you," she said. "I am to present myself before you, and as a female slave. I am to beg you to act as my master, for the afternoon. I am to serve you, and be pleasing, fully, in any and every way that you might desire, and I am to yield to you, withholding nothing, with the perfection of a female slave to her master."

"And I, only a slave," I marveled.

"Yes!" she said, tears in her eyes.

"It is a superb punishment," I admitted.

"Yes," she said, miserably, "it is superb!"

"You will be, in effect," I said, "the slave of a slave."

"Yes," she said, angrily.

"This thought seems to disturb you," I observed.

"I am a slave girl," she said. "I am the rightful property of free men, not slaves."

"Proud slave," I said.

"Canka well knows how to reduce me," she said. Then she looked at me. "Begin my punishment," she said.

"Report," I said.

She looked at me, in fury.

"Keep your back straight," I said.

"I am Winyela," she said, "the slave of Canka, of the Isbu Kaiila. On the orders of my master I herewith report myself to you. I present myself before you, a female slave. I beg you to be my acting master, for the afternoon."

"Very well," I said.

"I am now yours, for the afternoon," she said. "Do with me as you will."

"I doubt that Canka truly wants me to have you," I said. "Besides, I think you have been punished enough."

She looked at me, startled.

"Give me your wrists," I said.

She extended her wrists, and I unbound them, refastening the thongs, like a bracelet, on her left wrist.

"Lie down here," I said, "on the hides. Rest. After a time, I will take you back to the lodge of Canka."

"Do you not want me?" she asked.

"To see you is to want you," I said.

"You may have me," she said.

"You love Canka," I said, "and you are his."

I then covered her with a smaller hide.

"It is not cold," she said, smiling.

"I am only human," I said. "Do not weaken my resolves."

"Forgive me, Master," she smiled. Then, worn from her ordeals of the day, she was asleep.

I looked at her slender, luscious figure, under the hide. I clenched my fists. Then I left the lodge.

Outside the lodge, I saw Cuwignaka, on his knees, scraping at a pegged-down hide.

"Where is Winyela?" he asked.

"Inside, asleep," I said.

"I think she has had a hard day," he said.

"I am sure of it," I laughed.

"How was she?" he asked.

"I do not know," I said. "I let her sleep."

"But she was sent here to report to you, was she not?" asked Cuwignaka, pausing in his work.

"Yes," I said.

"Surely you did not neglect to note that she was naked and bound."

"No," I said. "Such details did not escape my attention."

"Do you know what it means," asked Cuwignaka, "when a woman is ordered to report to a man, and she is naked and bound?"

"I have some idea," I admitted.

"And you let her sleep?"

"Yes," I said.

"Why do you think Canka sent her to you?" he asked.

"I am not truly sure," I said.

"She had just been beaten," said Cuwignaka.

"Yes," I said.

"Is it not obvious, then, that this was intended as an addition to her punishment, that she, a slave, would then have to serve one who was also only a slave, and as her master?"

"Perhaps," I said.

"A splendidly humbling experience for a female slave," said Cuwignaka, "and one that teaches her her worthlessness and lowness superbly."

"Perhaps," I said.

"And you did not use her."

"No," I said.

"In this you have doubtless not fulfilled the will of Canka," said Cuwignaka.

"Do you truly think he wanted me to have her?" I asked.

"Certainly," said Cuwignaka.

"But she loves him," I said.

"What difference could that possibly make?" asked Cuwignaka.

"And does he not love her?" I asked.

"Yes," said Cuwignaka. "But he will want her sent back to his lodge as a better slave."

"I think she has been punished enough," I said.

"A bold decision for one to make who is only a slave," smiled Cuwignaka.

I grinned. "Perhaps," I said.

"Besides," said Cuwignaka, "Canka likes you."

"I, too, like him," I said.

"He knows that you are a strong man, and that you need a woman."

I shrugged.

"You wear a collar," said Cuwignaka. "It is frustrating for you in the camp. You cannot even touch a nude, white female slave without permission, taking her from her work in dressing skins or sewing."

"There is Wasnapohdi," I said.

"But she is often elsewhere," said Cuwignaka, "and Grunt, for purposes of business, often consigns her to others, sometimes for more than a day or two."

"That is true," I said.

"So why should you object," asked Cuwignaka, "if Canka, in his friendship for you, in a suitable context, for an afternoon, makes you a present of Winyela?"

"I do not object," I laughed. "It is only that I think, today, at least, she has been punished enough."

"That seems to be Canka's decision, not yours," said Cuwignaka.

"Doubtless you are right," I said. "He is her master."

"And you let her sleep!" scoffed Cuwignaka.

"Yes," I said.

"How tender-hearted you are!" he laughed.

"Perhaps," I said. It had been a long time since anyone had accused me of that.

Cuwignaka bent again to his work, with the bone scraper. "What are you thinking about?" he asked.

"I wonder what Wasnapohdi is doing," I said.

Cuwignaka laughed. "She is probably doing what I am doing, scraping skins."

"Do you want any help?" I asked.

"No," said Cuwignaka. "This is woman's work."

I laughed. This response, a joke on Cuwignaka's part, is a commonplace among the red savages. The offer of a man to help with a woman's tasks is almost always refused. The man has his work, the woman hers. The gender of a task commonly has a plausible rationale. It seems to be the men, for example, who are best suited to be the warriors and the women who are best suited to be the lovely, desirable prizes of such warriors. Similarly it seems men, with their strength, aggressiveness and size, would be better suited for the hunt, pursuing the swift, trident-horned, belligerent kailiauk at full speed than the slighter, softer women, and that the women, with their patience, their sense of color, with their small, nimble fingers, would be better suited to exacting, fine tasks such as beadwork and sewing. Similarly, it is natural to expect that the general, sex-linked orientations and predispositions, statistically obvious, both male and female, of human beings, presumably functions of genetic and hormonal differences, would tend to be reflected, broadly, in the sorts of tasks which each sex tends to perform most efficiently and finds most congenial.

Some tasks, of course, from the biological point of view, may be sex-neutral, so to speak. Whether sex-neutral tasks exist or not is an interesting question. Such a task would seem to be one in which the sexual nature of a human being, with all its attendant physiological and psychological consequences, was irrelevant.

It seems likely that sex-neutral tasks, at least of an interesting nature, do not exist. We shall suppose, however, for the purposes of argument, that there do exist such tasks. Let us suppose, for example, that the cutting of leather for moccasins is such a task. Now among the red savages this task, supposedly sex-neutral, for the purposes of argument, is always, or almost always, performed by females. This calls attention to an interesting anthropological datum. The performance of even tasks which may be "sex-neutral," tasks that do not seem to have an obvious biological rationale with respect to gender, tends to be divided, in culture after culture, on a sexual basis. Similarly, interestingly, whether for historical reasons or not, these cultures tend to be in substantial agreement on the divisions. For example, in almost all cultures, though not all, loom weaving is a female task. This tends to suggest that it is important in these cultures that sexual differences, in one way or another, be clearly marked.

The blurring of sexual differences, with its attendant deleterious consequences on sexual relations and identity, the reduction of male vitality and the frustration of female fulfillment, is not, for better or worse, encouraged. The denial and frustration of nature, the betrayal and subversion of sexuality, it is possible, may not be in the long-term best interest of the human species. Sexism, thus, in a sense, may not be a vice, but the hope of a race. Unisex, not taken for granted as an aspect of a pathological culture, but understood, in depth, could be of interest, it seems, only to somewhat short-sighted or unusual organisms.

I saw a white, female slave walking by. She was in someone's collar. She was stripped.

I had not been given a quirt, a permission quirt, beaded, such as might give a male slave power over such women. I looked at her. She was luscious. I could not so much as touch her.

"What are you going to do?" asked Cuwignaka.

"I think maybe I will go look for Wasnapohdi," I said.

"I thought you might," said Cuwignaka.

I looked about.

"Have you seen Grunt?" I asked. Wasnapohdi would presumably be somewhere in his whereabouts.

"I saw him this morning," said Cuwignaka. "He seemed troubled."

"Why?" I asked.

"I do not know," said Cuwignaka.

"Bloketu and Iwoso are in the vicinity," I said. I had seen them, when I had looked about. "It seems they are visiting."

"Of course," said Cuwignaka, working the hide.

"How is it that Bloketu hates you so?" I asked.

"I do not know," said Cuwignaka. "Once we were friends."

"They are coming this way," I said.

Cuwignaka bent even more closely over the hide. There seemed now a subtle anger in his movements.

It is common, of course, for women to mock one such as Cuwignaka. Bloketu, on the other hand, seemed to take a malicious and peculiar delight in doing so.

"I had a dream last night about Bloketu," said Cuwignaka.

"Oh?" I said.

"That I collared her and owned her," he said.

"And when she was stripped did you put the quirt to her well?" I asked.

"Yes," he said, "and then I much pleased myself with her."

"A good dream," I said.

"Yes," said Cuwignaka.

"Oh, Iwoso," called out Bloketu, coming up, "here is that pretty girl we met on the prairie, you know, the one in the white-woman's dress."

"I remember," said Iwoso.

"She had cut so much meat! The poles of the travois even bent!"

"Yes," said Iwoso. Iwoso looked behind her, as if she expected to see someone.

"But she was such a naughty girl," said Bloketu. "She disobeyed the Sleen Soldier and she lost all that meat."

Iwoso laughed.

"What is her name? It is Cuwignaka, isn't it?" laughed Bloketu.

"Yes," said Iwoso.

"Ah, Cuwignaka," said Bloketu, "you are fortunate that you are not the woman of a Kaiila warrior. If you were he might have taken that white dress off your pretty little body and lashed you well. Thus you might learn your lesson, not to lose meat again that way."

"It is he again," whispered Iwoso to Bloketu, looking behind her.

"Oh?" said Bloketu. She turned about, angrily.

On his kaiila, in his breechclout, his hair braided, without feathers, sat Hci. He looked down on the two girls, afoot.

"Are you following us about?" asked Bloketu.

"It is rumored that there may be peace with the Yellow Knives," said Hci.

"I have heard that rumor," said Bloketu.

"They are our enemies," said Hci. He looked at Iwoso.

"If you wish to court Iwoso," said Bloketu, "you may come to the lodge tonight and sit outside, cross-legged, playing the love flute. I will then decide whether or not I will permit my maiden to leave the lodge."

"You have not yet taken away her leggings, nor put her in a short dress and collar," said Hci.

"It is not necessary to follow Iwoso about like a panting sleen," said Bloketu.

"It is not for such purposes that I follow her," said Hci. "If I want her, I will come to your lodge. I will offer a kaiila for her and bring a rope."

"That you are a Sleen Soldier does not permit you to speak so!" said Bloketu.

"This morning," said Hci, "Watonka, and you two, left the camp of the Isanna."

"He was spying on us," said Iwoso.

"You met other riders," said Hci. "I found the tracks. What did you do?"

"Nothing," said Bloketu.

"Who were the other riders?" asked Hci.

"You are an expert tracker," said Bloketu. "You tell me. Surely you examined the dust for the print of moccasins?" Different tribes have, usually, slightly different moccasin patterns, resulting in subtly different prints. To be sure, it usually takes a sharp print to make these discriminations. There is no difficulty, of course, in distinguishing between boots of the sort common with white riders and moccasins, the almost universal footwear of the red savages. They are worn even in the winter. In the winter they are often lined, for insulation and warmth, with hair or dried grass.

"None dismounted," said Hci.

"They were Isanna hunters," said Bloketu.

"No hunting parties of the Isanna left camp this morning," said Hci.

"Oh," said Bloketu.

"Watonka himself had so ordered it," said Hci.

"They were Wismahi," said Bloketu.

"They were Yellow Knives," said Hci. "Three of them."

"You cannot know that," said Bloketu, angrily.

"It would be for such a reason that you would take the Yellow-Knife slave with you," said Hci, looking at Iwoso, "to converse with them."

"Slave!" cried Iwoso, angrily.

"Yes, slave," said Hci.

Bloketu looked about. "Do not speak too loudly," she said. "You are right, Hci. They were Yellow Knives. And Iwoso has been very helpful. She can speak with them, other than in sign, which we cannot. They contacted Watonka. They wish to make peace with the Kaiila."

"That is wonderful," said Cuwignaka.

"Attend to your work, Girl," said Hci to Cuwignaka, "or I will put you to sewing."

Cuwignaka, angrily, sat back on his heels. In sewing, commonly, among the red savages, a roll of rawhide string is held balled in the mouth, and played out, bit by bit. The warmth and saliva in the mouth keeps the string moist and pliable. The thrusting end is twisted and wet. It is then thrust through holes punched in the leather with a metal or bone awl. The moist thread, of course, as well as being easier to work with, tends to shrink in drying and make tighter stitches. With the ball of hide string in the mouth, of course, it is difficult to speak. When a woman, then, finds herself being advised by her man to attend to her sewing, she understands, well enough, that it is now time for her to be silent. She has been, in effect, ordered to put a gag in her own mouth.

"You may not know of this, Hci," said Bloketu, "but Mahpiyasapa and the other chieftains know of it. There will be a council on the matter."

"The Yellow Knives are our enemies," said Hci. "There will never be peace with them."

"Was it really the Yellow Knives who first contacted Watonka?" asked Hci.

"Yes," she said.

"I find that hard to believe," said Hci.

"Why?" asked Bloketu.

"I know Yellow Knives," said Hci, his hand straying to the long scar at the left side of his chin. "I have met them, lance to lance, club to club, knife to knife."

"There is more to life than collecting coups," said Bloketu.

"That is probably true," said Hci, regarding Iwoso. Quickly she put her head down. She was very pretty. She had been captured from Yellow Knives at the age of twelve. I thought I agreed with Hci. She was now old enough to be a man's true slave.

"Do not be afraid, Hci," laughed Bloketu. "There were only three of them, and this is the time of the great dances."

During the summer festivals, and the time of the great dances, warfare and raiding is commonly suspended on the prairie. This is a time of truce and peace. The celebrating tribe, during its own festival period, naturally refrains from belligerent activities. Similarly, interestingly, enemy tribes, during this period, perhaps in virtue of an implicit bargain, that their own festival times be respected, do not attack them, or raid them. For the red savages the festival times in the summer, whenever they are celebrated by the various tribes, are the one time in the year when they are territorially and politically secure. These are very happy times, on the whole, for the tribes. It is nice to know that one is, at such times, safe. More than one war party, it is recorded, penetrating deeply into enemy territory, and seeing the high brush walls of a dance lodge, and discovering that it was the enemy's festival time, has politely withdrawn. This sort of thing is not historically unprecedented. For example, in ancient Greece the times of certain games, such as the Olympic games, constituted a truce period during which it was customary to suspend the internecine wars of competitive cities. Teams and fans from the combatant *poleis* then could journey to and from the stadiums in safety. Two additional reasons militating against bellicosity and martial aggression during the summer festivals might be mentioned. First, the size of these gatherings, the enemy being massed, so to speak, tends to reduce the practicality of attacks. Bands of men are not well advised to launch themselves upon nations. Secondly, it is supposedly bad medicine to attack during the times of festivals.

"I do not trust Yellow Knives," said Hci.

"It is all right, Hci," said Bloketu. "Ask your father, Mahpiyasapa, if you like."

Hci shrugged, angrily.

"There is to be a council on the matter," said Bloketu.

It did seem to me plausible, if the Yellow Knives wished to sue for peace, and if they had contacted Watonka, or if he had contacted them, that it would have been done at this time, at the time of the gathering, of the dances and feasts. This would seem to be the ideal time for such probings, such contacts, and any pertinent attendant negotiations.

Iwoso looked up. Hci was still regarding her. Such obvious scrutiny would not have been appropriate, of course, if she had not been a slave. Iwoso, again, put down her head.

"Oh," laughed Bloketu, light-heartedly, as if desiring to shift the locus of discourse, "I see you were not really spying on us, at all, Hci. You were only pretending to do so! You are a sly young fellow! You wanted an excuse to follow Iwoso!"

"No," said Hci. This was a form of teasing which Hci did not enjoy.

"I know you find Iwoso attractive," said Bloketu, laughing. "I have seen you look at her."

"She is only a Yellow-Knife slave," said Hci.

"She has been with the Kaiila since the age of twelve," said Bloketu. "She is as much Kaiila as Yellow Knife."

"No," said Hci. "She is a Yellow Knife. It is in her blood."

"Perhaps, Iwoso," said Bloketu, "I will let Hci court you."

"No, please, no!" said Iwoso. I saw that she, genuinely, feared Hci, and deeply. I did not fully understand this at the time. I would later.

"Then I shall decide," said Bloketu to Iwoso, "whether or not you shall accept him."

"No, please," said Iwoso.

"Do you dispute me, my maiden?" asked Bloketu.

"No," said Iwoso, miserably.

"She should say that on her knees, with her head down," said Hci.

"You men would like us all to be your helpless slaves," said Bloketu, angrily.

I saw Cuwignaka looking at Bloketu. I thought he was, perhaps, in his mind, undressing her. He was speculating, perhaps, on what she might look like, divested of her high station, divested of the jewelry and finery of a chieftain's daughter, put to a man's feet, collared, waiting to be commanded.

"Do you want Iwoso?" asked Bloketu, angrily, of Hci.

Hci shrugged. "She is a Yellow Knife," he said. "She might do as a slave. I do not know."

"Do you want her?" asked Bloketu.

"She might look well naked," said Hci.

"You are speaking of my maiden," said Bloketu, scandalized.

"—On a rope, under a whip," added Hci.

"Bloketu!" protested Iwoso.

"If you want her," said Bloketu, angrily, "you must court her properly."

"I do not court Yellow-Knife women," said Hci. "I kill them, or collar them." He then pulled his kaiila about and, kicking his heels back into the flanks of the beast, took his leave.

"What an arrogant young man," said Bloketu.

"Do not let him court me," begged Iwoso.

"I might let him court you," said Bloketu.

"Please, no," said Iwoso.

"Then," said Bloketu, smiling, "I might let you spurn him. That would be an excellent lesson for the fellow. Let his suit be rejected, his wooing publicly scorned. It would be a good joke."

"I would rather," said Iwoso, "that you did not permit him to court me at all."

"Why?" asked Bloketu.

"Suppose I spurn his suit," she said, "and he is angry. Suppose he seizes me, and binds me, and carries me away."

"He would not dare," said Bloketu.

"I am only a slave," said Iwoso.

"Have no fear," said Bloketu. "You are my maiden."

"Please do not let him court me," begged Iwoso.

"I will do what I want," said Bloketu.

"Yes, Bloketu," said Iwoso.

"You are afraid of him, aren't you?" asked Bloketu.

"Yes," said Iwoso. "I would be terrified to have to go to his lodge."

"Interesting," said Bloketu.

"You are free, and the daughter of a chief," said Iwoso.

"That is why you cannot understand my fear. But I am only, really, a slave."

"Slaves are so fearful," said Bloketu.

"If you were a slave, you, too, would know fear," said Iwoso.

"Perhaps," said Bloketu.

"We are owned," said Iwoso.

I thought I saw the chieftain's daughter shudder, momentarily, a tiny shudder, one which seemed to be of fear and, if I am not mistaken, of deep excitement and pleasure, perhaps at the wickedly horrifying thought of herself being a slave, of herself being owned. At any rate, I did not think that the lovely Bloketu, if she were to find herself truly enslaved, would experience any difficulty in learning fear. She, like any other slave, I was certain, would acquire it quite easily. It is a property which attaches naturally to the condition. The slave girl is totally at the mercy of the master, in any and every way. It is not surprising, therefore, that she is no stranger to fear.

"If you permit Hci to court me," begged Iwoso, "please do not have me accept his suit."

"I will do what I want," said Bloketu.

"Please do not have me accept his suit!" begged Iwoso.

"We will see what mood I am in at the time," said Bloketu, loftily.

"Please!" said Iwoso.

"We will see how I feel at the time," said Bloketu, "whether Hci is nice or not, whether or not I am pleased with you. What I do then will depend on such things."

"Please," begged Iwoso.

"Do not anger me, maiden," said Bloketu, "or I may send you to him for the night, without your clothes and tied, maybe with a quirt tied around your neck, like you were a white female slave!"

Iwoso was immediately silent.

"That is better, my maiden," smiled Bloketu. "Remember you are not yet important."

Iwoso did not respond. I did not understand Bloketu's remark about Iwoso not yet being important. I gathered that something might possibly happen, following which Iwoso might become important. If that was the case, then, I gathered, she would not have to worry about Hci, or, I suppose, other warriors of the Kaiila.

"Are you obedient, my maiden?" asked Bloketu of Iwoso, sweetly.

"Yes, Mistress," said Iwoso, her head down. This was the first time I had ever heard Iwoso use this word to Bloketu. It is not unusual for a girl to discover that within her velvet bonds there are chains of steel.

"Why should Iwoso become important?" asked Cuwignaka, kneeling near the hide on which he was working. It seemed to me a fair question. Iwoso was, in the final analysis, in spite of being the maiden of a chieftain's daughter, only a slave.

"It does not matter," said Bloketu.

"I would like to know," said Cuwignaka. "I am curious."

"Such matters are not the proper concern of one who is only a pretty young girl like yourself," laughed Bloketu.

"I am not a female slave," said Cuwignaka, "expected to serve in ignorance, unquestioningly, supposedly concerned, truly, only with the pleasures of her master."

"Then you admit that you are a mere female," said Bloketu.

"No," said Cuwignaka.

"Listen to the pretty young thing!" laughed Bloketu.

"I am two years older than you, at least," said Cuwignaka.

"You lost meat!" laughed Bloketu.

"Tell me," said Cuwignaka.

"I think I will call a man, pretty Cuwignaka," she said, "to put you about your sewing."

"It has to do with the Yellow Knives, doesn't it?" asked Cuwignaka.

"Maybe," smiled Bloketu. I saw that she was very vain. Cuwignaka, too, must have understood this.

"If Iwoso is to become important," said Cuwignaka, "then doubtless you would be even more important."

"Perhaps," said Bloketu.

"And if you are important," said Cuwignaka, puzzled, "then surely Watonka, your father, would be even more important."

"Perhaps," said Bloketu.

"But how could one be more important than being a chief of the Isanna?" asked Cuwignaka, genuinely puzzled.

"May I speak, Mistress?" asked Iwoso.

"Yes," said Bloketu.

"If one can bring about peace between our peoples, the Kaiila and the Yellow Knives," she said, "one would surely, in the prestige of this, be very important."

"That is true," said Cuwignaka.

"In doing this," said Iwoso, "it would be like counting a hundred coups, almost like being a high chief of the Kaiila."

"That is very true," said Cuwignaka, kneeling back on the dirt, near the pegged-down hide.

Bloketu seemed relieved. Iwoso, I gathered, subtly, not quite sure of it, was a very clever young woman.

"It is my hope," Iwoso said, "to be of some small help in this business, the bringing about of peace between our peoples."

"You are a noble girl," said Cuwignaka. "I hope that you will be successful."

"Thank you," said Iwoso.

Something about this conversation disturbed me. I was not sure, however, what it was.

Cuwignaka picked up his bone scraper and, once again, began to give his attention to the hide on which he was working.

"Let us return now, Mistress," said Iwoso, "to the lodges of the Isanna." Iwoso, I noted, seemed in a hurry to take her departure.

"But did we not come here to visit with this pretty girl?" asked Bloketu. "Then we were interrupted by Hci."

Iwoso was silent.

"We will tarry a moment," said Bloketu. I saw that she had not fulfilled, to her satisfaction, her desire to have sport with Cuwignaka. I did not know why she hated him so.

"Do not wait on my account," said Cuwignaka, not looking up from his work.

"She seems very diligent," said Bloketu.

"Yes, Mistress," said Iwoso.

"What are you doing, pretty girl?" asked Bloketu.

"Scraping a hide," said Cuwignaka. "Probably what you should be doing."

"Saucy girl," chided Bloketu.

"I do not care to be mocked," said Cuwignaka.

"You are very famous," said Bloketu. "All the Kaiila know of you. The Dust Legs, too, with whom we trade, know of you."

Cuwignaka grunted, irritably. It was only too likely that, through trade chains, his story had widely circulated in the Barrens. The Dust Legs, for example, who do a great deal of trading, have dealings with several tribes which, in their turn, have dealings with others. For example, although the Dust

Legs and the Fleer are enemies, as are the Kaiila and the Fleer, the Dust Legs have dealings with the Sleen, and the Sleen, in turn, trade with tribes such as the Yellow Knives and the Fleer. Thus, indirectly, even tribes hostile to the Kaiila, or normally so, such as the Fleer and the Yellow Knives might, quite possibly, have heard of Cuwignaka.

"But what they probably do not know," said Bloketu, "is how pretty you are, and what a marvelous worker you are." Cuwignaka, to be sure, was a very hard worker. I did not doubt but what he was one of the hardest workers in the camp.

"It is too bad you lost all that meat," said Bloketu. "But such things can happen."

Cuwignaka did not respond to her.

"Doubtless you will not let it happen again," she said.

Cuwignaka did not respond.

"You are doing a nice job with that hide," she said.

Cuwignaka did not respond.

"All in all, I think you would be a very valuable girl to have in a lodge, Cuwignaka," said Bloketu. "If you are not careful, the young men will come courting you."

Cuwignaka worked steadily, angrily. He did not speak. I was afraid he would cut the skin.

"Can you cook, and sew?" asked Bloketu.

"I can cook," said Cuwignaka. "I am not much good at sewing."

"The young men will not mind," said Bloketu. "You are so pretty."

"Maybe not," said Cuwignaka. "You manage very well, it seems."

"Let us go, Mistress," said Iwoso.

"Be quiet," snapped Bloketu to Iwoso.

"Yes, Mistress," said Iwoso.

"What do you mean by that?" asked Bloketu, angrily, of Cuwignaka.

"It is well known among the Kaiila," said Cuwignaka, kneeling back on his heels, putting aside the bone scraper and looking up at Bloketu, "that you are not good for much."

"Oh?" said Bloketu. She was taken aback, a bit, I think, by finding herself, ultimately only a woman, suddenly, unexpectedly, the object of so challenging and frank a gaze.

"Yes," said Cuwignaka.

"The young men do not seem to mind," said Bloketu, collecting herself, loftily.

"That is because you are the daughter of a chief," said Cuwignaka.

"No," said Bloketu, angrily. "It is because I am beautiful."

"Who has told you that?" asked Cuwignaka.

"Many men," she said.

"It was dark outside," said Cuwignaka.

"No!" said Bloketu.

"They tell you that because you are the daughter of a chief," said Cuwignaka.

"No!" said Bloketu.

"They want a kaiila from Watonka," said Cuwignaka.

"No!" said Bloketu.

Cuwignaka shrugged. I smiled. Swiftly had the tables been turned on the beauty, putting her on the defensive. I saw, too, in so simple an exchange, that Cuwignaka was intellectually dominant over Bloketu.

"Everyone tells me I am beautiful," said Bloketu, angrily.

"Have I ever told you that?" asked Cuwignaka.

"In a way," said Bloketu, warily. "Out on the prairie you told me that it was not enough to be merely beautiful."

"Oh?" asked Cuwignaka.

"Yes!" she said.

"Well," said Cuwignaka, "that may be true. It is possible. It may be that it is not enough, at least among the Kaiila, where there is much work to be done, to be merely beautiful."

"Thus," she said, triumphantly, "you think that I am beautiful!"

"Did I say I was talking about you?" asked Cuwignaka.

"No," she said.

"Well, maybe I was not talking about you," he said.

"Oh!" she cried, angrily.

"That is something to think about," he said.

"Do you think I am beautiful?" she asked.

Cuwignaka looked up at her.

"Do you think I am beautiful?" she asked.

"Maybe," he said.

"Maybe?" she asked.

Cuwignaka then rose to his feet. He went to stand before Bloketu. He looked down upon her. He was a head taller than she. She stepped back a bit. "Yes, Bloketu," he said. "You are beautiful."

"Now you speak the truth!" she said.

"And I shall speak further truths," he said. "You are beautiful as a free woman, and you would be even more beautiful as a slave, stripped and kneeling before me, in my collar, in my lodge, waiting to be commanded."

"I am the daughter of a chief!" she said.

"You would look well, crawling to me," he said, "with a quirt in your teeth."

"Beware!" she said.

"It is well that you are of the Kaiila," he said. "Else I might take the warpath, to take you, to bring you back to my lodge as a naked slave."

"Oh!" she cried.

"I desire you, Bloketu," said Cuwignaka. "I desire you with the greatest ferocity with which a man can desire a woman, that he would have her at his feet, as his owned slave."

The girl then turned and fled away. She was terrified. Never, hitherto, had she dreamed she could be the object of such passion.

She was swiftly followed by Iwoso, her maiden.

Cuwignaka, standing up, looked after the two girls. "They are pretty, aren't they?" he asked.

"Yes," I said.

"Do you think they would make good slaves?" he asked.

"Yes," I said.

"Who do you think is the most beautiful, Iwoso or Bloketu?" he asked.

"Bloketu," I said.

"I do, too," said Cuwignaka.

"I was somewhat disturbed by portions of the conversation between you, and Bloketu and Iwoso," I said, "in particular, the business about the enlargement of Watonka's importance."

Cuwignaka grinned. "I am afraid," he said, "that Bloketu and Iwoso were not entirely candid with us about that matter."

"How is that?" I asked.

"It seems they would have us believe that Watonka's enhancement would be largely one of prestige."

"Would it not be so?" I asked.

"There would be much prestige, to be sure," smiled Cuwignaka, "but, too, doubtless, in the giving of gifts, many kaiila would change hands."

"I see," I said.

"Already Watonka is the richest of all the Kaiila," said Cuwignaka. "Should he be successful in bringing about this peace, as we shall hope he shall be, he will doubtless be the recipient of many kaiila, perhaps even a thousand, gifts from both the Yellow Knives and the Kaiila themselves."

"I see," I said.

"Over his herds the sky will be dark with fleer," said Cuwignaka.

I smiled. The location of large herds of kaiila is sometimes marked by the presence of circling, swarming fleer. They come to feed on the insects stirred up in the grass, activated by the movements of the beasts' paws.

"Thus," said Cuwignaka, "Bloketu would be important, being the daughter of such a man, and even Iwoso, only a slave, would become celebrated among several tribes, serving as a maiden in so rich a household."

I laughed. "It is easy to see why Bloketu and Iwoso might have been hesitant to speak of this aspect of the matter," I said, "seeing what profits might accrue to them."

"Particularly," smiled Cuwignaka, "since matters, at this time, are, I gather, so uncertain and tentative."

"Do you think that there will be peace between the Yellow Knives and the Kaiila?" I asked.

"I do not know," said Cuwignaka. "I hope so."

"There is a pretty slave," I said.

"Yes," said Cuwignaka.

The blond-haired girl, stripped, collared, regarded me with contempt, tossed her head, and passed on. She was the property of a red master.

"I remember her," I said.

"She came in with the Isanna," said Cuwignaka. "We saw her then."

"Yes," I said. She had been part of the loot display of the Isanna, a trinket in the procession of their splendor. She had been at someone's stirrup, naked, her hands bound behind her back, a quirt hung about her neck.

"She is arrogant," said Cuwignaka.

"Yes," I said. I remembered that she had, then, too, looked upon me with contempt. She was owned by a red master. I was only a white slave.

"She is probably kept in one of the Isanna's girl herds," said Cuwignaka.

I nodded. These herds, usually consisting of from forty to fifty white females, stripped, are usually kept a pasang or so from camp, with the kaiila herds. The Isanna women, on the whole, object to such women being kept in the private lodges.

Before the winter such herds are usually sold off. Those girls who are not sold off must be clothed and brought indoors. They are usually kept in the lodges of warrior societies or in private lodges. Some are kept in girl lodges, in the charge of a warrior who, for the tenure of his governance over them, acts as their master. Some, to their horror, are put in the keeping of a red female. Usually, after a day or two of this, they beg to kneel again, head down, at the feet of the men. In the summer most such girls, and others, too, being added to them, are put out again, with the kaiila. The Isanna is only the third largest band of the Kaiila. It is, however, indisputably, the richest. Its wealth, for example, in both kaiila and white females is well known on the plains. Boys, with ropes and whips, watch over the women. They may, of course, cut any woman they wish out of the herd and use her.

"I myself," said Cuwignaka, "would prefer to keep slaves in my own lodge."

"There would be too many of them for the Isanna to do that," I said.

"They are pretentious, and vain," said Cuwignaka. "They do not need that many women."

"They sell off the herds in the winter," I said.

"But only to increase them again, in the spring," he said.

"That white females are herded by the Isanna, more so than with other bands, or tribes," I said, "has, I gather, something to do with the Isanna women."

"Yes," said Cuwignaka. "They do not want them in the lodges."

"That is understandable," I said.

"But, in such things, the men should be the masters, fully," said Cuwignaka.

"That is true," I said.

"It is well known that the Isanna women are insufficiently disciplined," said Cuwignaka.

"Bloketu is insufficiently disciplined, for example?" I asked.

"Yes," said Cuwignaka, "Bloketu is insufficiently disciplined. Bloketu needs discipline, severe discipline."

"It might be pleasant to administer it to her," I said.

"Yes," said Cuwignaka, grimly.

I smiled. Fortunately for the lovely Bloketu she stood high among the Kaiila. If she were a foreign woman who had fallen into Cuwignaka's hands, I did not doubt but what she would learn discipline, well and swiftly.

I watched the rear of the blond girl moving away, between the lodges. It moved well.

"You are hot," smiled Cuwignaka.

I did not respond. I was in misery.

"Winyela sleeps within the lodge," said Cuwignaka. "Why do you not whip her awake, and use her? She is only a slave. Too, she was sent to you to be disciplined."

"No," I said.

"One should not be too soft with female slaves," said Cuwignaka.

"I know," I said.

"It is Canka's will that you use her, and well," he said.

"Do you think so?" I asked.

"Of course," said Cuwignaka. "He is a red savage. Do not be culturally confused."

I shrugged.

"He will wish for her to be returned to his lodge a better slave than she left it," said Cuwignaka.

"Perhaps," I said.

"Lash her awake," said Cuwignaka. "Set her, without mercy, about her duties. Let her be in no doubt that it is men who are her masters."

"I think I shall let her sleep," I smiled.

"As you wish," said Cuwignaka.

"She has suffered enough for one day, I think," I said.

"As you wish," said Cuwignaka.

"But," I said, "I think I shall go to see Grunt."

"And look for Wasnapohdi," laughed Cuwignaka.

"Maybe," I said.

"Poor Wasnapohdi!" laughed Cuwignaka.

8

I TAKE MY LEAVE FROM GRUNT'S LODGE

"I am sorry," said Grunt. "Wasnapohdi is not here. She is out picking berries. I do not know when she will be back. After that she is supposed to help some of the other women."

"Oh," I said.

"If I had known you might want her," said Grunt, "I could

have kept her here for you, naked, tied hand and foot, at the side of the lodge."

"That is all right," I said. "It is nothing."

"You made a mistake with Winyela," he said.

"Oh?" I said.

"She was sent to you to be punished," he said. "You should have done so."

"Do you think so?" I asked.

"I know red savages," he said. "Yes."

"I did not do so," I said. Indeed, I had even let her rest, and then sleep.

"That was a mistake," said Grunt.

"Perhaps," I said.

We spoke within Grunt's lodge, one put at his disposal by his friend, Mahpiyasapa, civil chief of the Isbu Kaiila.

"I spoke to Cuwignaka earlier today," I said. "He told me that you seemed troubled."

"Oh?" he asked.

"Yes," I said. Grunt wore the broad-brimmed hat, that one with which I was so familiar. It was interesting to me that he wore it even within the lodge. I had never seen him without it.

"Is anything wrong?" I asked.

"I don't think so," he said.

"What is it?" I asked.

"Have you heard the rumors?" he asked. "About the Yellow Knives? That they are going to send a delegation even into the camp?"

"I have heard rumors, even today," I said, "about the possibility of a peace being arranged with the Yellow Knives. I had not realized, however, that things had proceeded so far, that a delegation was to be welcomed into the camp."

"Yes," said Grunt.

"Negotiations are much more advanced than I realized, then," I said. "It seems, now, that there may be a real possibility for peace."

"I do not like it," said Grunt.

"Why?" I asked. "Surely you welcome the prospect of peace."

"I do not trust the Yellow Knives," he said.

"Why?" I asked.

"I have never had good relations with the Yellow Knives," he said.

I smiled. Grunt divided the tribes of red savages into those with whom he had had good relations and those with whom he had not had good relations. He had had good relations, for example, with the Dust Legs, the Kaiila and the Fleer. He had not, on the other hand, had good relations with the Yellow Knives. Grunt pulled down his hat farther on his head, an interesting gesture, one about which he was apparently not really thinking.

"Are they any worse, really," I asked, "than the Kaiila, or the Kailiauk or the Fleer?"

"I suppose not," admitted Grunt.

"If peace comes about," I said, "this might even open up new possibilities for trade."

"Let others, then, exploit them," said Grunt, irritably.

"You do not seem overly fond of Yellow Knives," I observed.

"No," said Grunt.

"Do they hate you?" I asked.

"I would not suppose so," he said.

"You seem to dislike them," I said.

"Do I?" asked Grunt.

"Yes," I said.

"Perhaps," he said.

"Why?" I asked.

"Never mind," said Grunt. "It is not important."

I rose to my feet. "It is getting late in the afternoon," I said. "It is time for me to awaken Winyela and return her to the lodge of Canka."

"I wish you well," said Grunt.

"I wish you well, too," I said.

I then took my leave from Grunt's lodge.

9

THIS OCCURRED IN THE LODGE OF CUWIGNAKA

Gently I put my hand on the girl's small, soft shoulder, it under the hide blanket. I shook her twice, gently.

"No," she said, "no. Surely it is not time already to go to the office."

"Awaken," I said.

She opened her eyes, registering her surroundings. She laughed softly, lying under the hide blanket. "I awaken naked, in a man's collar, on a distant world," she said. "No, it is not time for me to go to the office."

"No," I said.

She then rolled to her stomach and, under the hide blanket, stretched. Her body moved deliciously under the hide.

"That concealed slavery is behind you now," I said. "Your slavery is now of a more open nature."

"Yes," she said.

I then lifted the hide blanket back, and down to her calves. Such may be done with a slave. Her curves were marvelous.

I listened for a moment to the sounds of the camp outside. Somewhere I heard a girl crying out, being beaten. It was probably a white slave girl.

I looked at Winyela, on her stomach, on the dark robes.

I then, sweating, my fists clenched on the hide blanket, drew it back up, over her, to the middle of her back.

"I may be revealed," she said. "I am a slave."

I said nothing. I fought for my self-control.

She turned then, to her side, supporting herself on her elbow. This action caused the hide blanket to slip to her waist. "Thank you for letting me sleep," she said. "You were very kind."

"It was nothing," I said.

"I should like to thank you," she said. She reached her lips toward mine but I, by her upper arms, held her from me. "What is wrong?" she asked.

"The kiss of a slave can be but the prologue to her rape," I said.

"Oh," she said, smiling. She then drew back, and then, on her side, lay down. She pulled the hide blanket up about her neck.

"You must get up soon," I said. "In a while it will be time to return you to the lodge of Canka."

"If I dally," she asked, "will you quirt me?"

"If I think you dally overmuch," I said, "of course."

"Could you do that?" she asked.

"Yes," I said.

"Of course," she said, "for I am only a slave."

"Of course," I said.

"Sometimes it seems strange to me," she said, "thinking of myself as subject to the whip."

"There is nothing strange in it," I said. "You are a slave."

"That is true," she said.

"Master," she said.

"Yes," I said. It had surprised me, for a moment, that she had called me 'Master', but then I recalled that she had been given to me, for the afternoon. Indeed, for the afternoon, or, I supposed, until, within reason, I chose to return her to the lodge of Canka, she was, for all practical purposes, my own slave.

"You have treated me with great tenderness and kindness," she said.

I shrugged.

"May I surmise from this," she asked, "as I know little of slavery, and am new to the condition, that there can be tenderness and kindness for a slave?"

"There can be tenderness and kindness for a slave," I said, "of course. It is not permitted, however, to compromise in the least the iron discipline under which she is kept."

"I see," she said.

I regarded her.

"I want to be kept under an iron discipline," she said.

"I know," I said.

It was hard for me to forget that she was naked under the hide blanket.

"Do masters ever love their slaves?" she asked.

"Often," I said. Indeed, a female slave is the easiest of all women to love; too, of course, she is the most natural of all women to love; these things have to do with the equations of nature, in particular with those of dominance and submission. To a man a female slave is a dream come true. A free woman, understandably, cannot even begin to compete with a female slave for a man's love. That is perhaps another reason why free women so hate their vulnerable, imbonded sisters. If a free woman would assure herself of her man's love she could not do better than, in effect, become his slave. She can beg of him, if she senses in herself the true bondage of love, an enslavement ceremony, in which she proclaims herself, and becomes, his slave. In their most secret and intimate relations thereafter she lives and loves as his slave. If a woman fears to do this she may, on an experimental basis, resort to limited self-contracting, in which her documents will contain stated termination dates. Thus, by her own free will, she becomes a slave for a specific period, ranging usually from an evening to a year. The woman enters into this arrangement freely; she cannot, of course, withdraw from it in the same way. The reason for this is clear. As soon as the words are spoken, or her signature is placed on the pertinent document, or documents, she is no longer a free person. She is then only a slave, an animal, no longer with any legal powers whatsoever. She is, then, until the completion of the contractual period, until the expiration date of the arrangement, totally subject to the will of her master.

"And still keep them as slaves?" asked the girl.

"Of course," I said.

"Then I could be loved," she said, "and still kept as a slave, totally."

"Of course," I said.

"Even to being beaten?" she asked.

"Yes," I said.

"Of course," she said, "for I would still be only a slave."

"Of course," I said. "How is your back?" I asked.

"Sore," she said.

"You have felt the quirt," I said. "You will be a better slave for it."

"How strange it is to think of myself in such terms, she mused.

"What terms?" I asked.

"That I am a slave," she said, "that I am owned, that I belong to a man."

"Perhaps it seems strange to you, sometimes, lingeringly," I said, "because you are from Earth. It is not strange on Gor, of course. Bondage for a beautiful woman, such as yourself, is a common reality on Gor."

"I gather that it is so," she said.

"It is," I said. "On Gor thousands of beautiful women, branded, and in collars, serve, and must serve, their masters with the fullness of their female perfections."

She nodded. She had seen female slaves. She herself had been sold in the town of Kailiauk, near the Ihanke.

"And you, in the Barrens," I said, "are such a woman."

"I know," she said. She had seen slaves, too, in the Barrens, of course, generally white women, the helpless, obedient, collared slaves of red savages.

"It is your reality," I said.

"I know," she said.

"I think it is time we went to the lodge of Canka," I said.

"Yes, Master," she said. She then sat up on the robes. She held the hide blanket about her neck.

I almost wanted to cry out, to tear it from her, to fling her beneath me.

"I love Canka," she said. "I love him, more than anything."

I nodded.

"And I want him to love me," she said, "even though I am only a slave, if just a little."

"I understand," I said. It was natural for a slave helplessly in love with her master to hope that he might see fit to cast her at least a particle or crumb of his affection. That much he might bestow even upon a pet sleen.

She looked at me. "Canka wanted me punished," she said.

I shrugged.

"But you did not do so," she said.

"No," I said.

"Punish me," she said.

"No," I said.

"Very well," she said.

She, moving slightly, but mostly sitting as she was, let the hide blanket slip to her thighs. It seemed an accident.

"Let us hurry to the lodge of Canka," I said. I did not know if I could retain my control.

"Please," she said, "let me adjust my collar." She then, carefully, with her small hands, aligned the beaded collar on her throat. At certain points she ran a finger around and under it, adjusting it for comfort. She then, again, aligned it, setting the central knot under her chin. "There," she said. "That is better, and more comfortable. How does it look?"

"Fine," I said.

"Good," she said. "It is important to us that our collars both look well and be comfortable."

I was driven half wild, seeing her small hands so careful and attentive upon that encircling badge of servitude, calling attention to it, adjusting it. It was, of course, a slave collar.

"Let us go," I said.

"My hair," she said, "please—Master."

I watched her putting back her head and, carefully, apparently paying me no attention, arrange her long, lovely red hair. This action, of course, raised the line of her lovely breasts.

"One of the things most startling to an Earth girl, brought to Gor," she said, "is that she finds herself the object of such ardent desire."

"Perhaps," I said. To be sure she would have encountered little on Earth to prepare her for the sexuality of Gorean men.

"Another thing which they find startling, and almost unbelievably so," she said, fussing with her hair, "is how irreservedly and passionately, and sometimes mercilessly, they are used."

I nodded. Such women, to be sure, would seldom be given much choice in the matter.

"And how ruthlessly they are owned and dominated, and made to obey," she said.

I did not speak.

"But then," she said, softly, putting her head down, her hands still at her hair, her breasts still lifted, in what was almost a delicate token of submission, "that is fitting and proper, for they are only slaves."

"Yes," I said. My fists were clenched.

"How does my hair look?" she asked, bringing her hands down and lifting her head.

"Fine," I said.

She then turned and, putting her right leg under her and lifting her left knee, she threw aside the hide blanket. She smiled at me. She had done this shamelessly, as a slave. The body of a slave, of course, is public, in a way that it would be unthinkable that the body of a free woman could be public.

"I think you find me attractive," she said.

"Yes," I said.

She then knelt back on her heels, facing me, but her hands were on the robes.

"Alas," she said, in mock sorrow, "how weak and vulnerable are slaves."

"Yes," I said.

"How helpless and powerless we are," she said.

"Yes!" I said, angrily. I saw that she had allure, and power.

"But perhaps we are not completely powerless," she said. She put her hands behind her head and straightened her back. She thrust out her breasts and stretched.

"Perhaps not," I said.

She then lowered her hands and looked at me. She was kneeling, facing me, then, her hands on her thighs. Her thighs were closed.

"I am more powerful," she said, "than was that little snip and chit, Millicent Aubrey-Welles, from Earth." This was who she had once been. Then she had been enslaved.

"How is that?" I asked. At the merest word from one such as the former Miss Millicent Aubrey-Welles, from Pennsylvania, a free woman, a Gorean slave girl, such as Winyela, would have to grovel, lick her feet and serve her in any way that she might desire.

"I am much more powerful than she," she said.

"How is that?" I asked.

"I am a slave girl," she said.

"You speak in riddles," I said.

"More powerful, of course," she said, "only in certain ways."

I smiled. I saw that she did now wish to be quirted for insolence. A slave, of course, can be quirted for any reason, or for no reason.

"In what way," I asked, "could a slave girl possibly have more power than a free woman?"

She smiled. She lowered her head, demurely. "Some men," she said, "find us attractive."

"That is true," I said. How unpretentiously, and delicately, she had put this point. I could not help, in spite of myself, but agree with her. How could the capacity of a free woman to stimulate male desire even begin to compare with that of the female slave? The female slave, in her helplessness, her vulnerability and beauty, is the most exciting and desirable of all females. Even to look upon one can drive a man mad with passion.

"Even a magnet," she said, "which may be moved about, and put where one wishes, has a little power."

"Yes," I said. How exciting, I marveled, are such women. How natural it is that they should find themselves, perhaps to their horror, perhaps to their deep excitement and pleasure, so stimulatory to male desire. Who can begin to quantify, or measure, the attractiveness of the female slave? Does she not seem to be the object designed by nature to be at the feet of men? Wars are fought to obtain them. Tributes, in part, are levied in terms of them, along with gold and Sa-Tarna grain.

"I can see," I said, "that the female slave, in her beauty, may possess, upon occasion, at least, some meager particle of power which does not appertain to the free woman."

"I think so," she said.

My response, I thought, appropriately dismissed from serious consideration the fantastic desirability and attractiveness of the female slave. Let them not grow arrogant. Let them continue to fear the whip.

"But how," I asked, "in what other way, other than in possible attractiveness and desirability, could a slave have more power than a free woman?"

"If one can do things another cannot, and if one is permitted to do things which another, in effect, could not, then, I suppose, one has, in a sense, powers which the other does not."

"I see," I said. "Powers in the sense of capacities and permissions."

"Yes," she said. "Slave girls, for example, can, and must, do things and perform acts, superbly, lovingly and unquestioningly, which would be forbidden to free women, or unthinkable for them. Indeed, some of the performances expected of slave girls, and some of the services rendered by them to their masters, are doubtless beyond even the ken of our ignorant free sisters. They probably do not even suspect their nature."

"They may suspect," I smiled. The liberties, in certain senses, permitted to slave girls doubtless constituted an additional reason why free women so hated and envied them. The free woman, in a sense, is paradoxical. She professes to despise the slave girl; she professes to loathe her and hold her in contempt; but, too, obviously, she is almost insanely jealous of her. Can it be that she, too, in her secret heart, wishes to kneel before a man, naked and in his collar, totally subject to his will?

"But some of the things they probably do not even know of," she said.

"That is probably true," I said. It was true that free women tended to be somewhat naive and ignorant. Some of them, at any rate, when enslaved, seemed quite startled to discover the nature of some of the even routine performances and services that would now be expected of them.

"Too," said the girl, "we are better at certain things than free women, such as serving and pleasing men."

"That is true," I said. The docility, deference and perfection of a slave girl's service are legendary. They had better be. She is owned. Too, the intimate and fantastic pleasures they can give men are well known, at least among free men.

"Too," she said, "we are permitted to act in certain ways in which I think it would be unlikely that a free woman could, or would, act."

"Oh?" I said.

"Yes," she said. She then slid to her stomach on the robes, and rolled upon them, and then lay on her back. She lifted a leg, and put her hands to it, and then lowered it, its heel, the knee bent, on the robes. She looked at me. "I could now," she said, "pose nude before you, as I might please. I might writhe here, in a girl's mute petition for attention. I could, on my back and belly, in effect, dance for you, my head never rising above the knee of a standing man. I could crawl to your feet, begging, licking and kissing."

"I am only human," I said, angrily. "Let us go now to the lodge of Canka."

She rose to her hands and knees. Her breasts depended beautifully. "Have I disturbed Master?" she asked.

"No," I said, angrily. "Of course not."

"That is good," she said. She then crawled to me, and knelt before me.

"That is the position of a tower slave," I said.

"Oh," she said. The position of the tower slave, in most cities, is very similar to that of the pleasure slave. The major difference is that the tower slave, whose duties are commonly, primarily, domestic, kneels with her knees in a closed position, whereas the pleasure slave, in a symbolic recognition of the fuller nature of her bondage, and its most significant aspects, kneels with them in an open position. The tower slave, of course, like any other slave, is fully at the disposal of the master, in any and every way. The distinction between the tower slave and the pleasure slave, though honored in some markets, some specializing in girls sold primarily for housekeeping purposes and others in girls sold primarily for the pleasures of men, is not really a hard-and-fast distinction; it is not absolute; indeed, it can even be transitory. A girl who is ordered to open her knees, or who finds them kicked apart, for example, realizes that she has now become a pleasure slave. Similarly a girl in one context may function as one kind of slave and in another context, as another sort. Serving a supper to a young man and his mother, for example, the girl may appear merely efficient and deferential. She kneels nearby, her knees closed. After the mother departs, however, she may kneel differently before the young man, with her knees open, his.

Winyela opened her knees, spreading them widely, kneeling back on her heels.

"You may retain the position of the tower slave," I said, sweating.

"Please, Master," she said. "I am a Pleasure Slave. It will be better for my discipline to be forced to remain kneeling in this, the more revealing and degrading position. Too, this position, so open and exposed, can be of service in reminding me, lest I be tempted to become arrogant or proud, of my lowliness, my purposes and condition."

"You would choose," I asked, "to kneel in the position of the pleasure slave, that position of female degradation and debasement, imposed on certain females by men, of utter female vulnerability, helplessness and beauty?"

"Yes, Master," she said. "Considering the nature of my bondage it is suitable for me. It is, considering the sort of slave I am, fitting and proper for me."

"You like it," I said.

"I am comfortable in it," she said, evasively.

"You like it," I said.

"Yes, Master," she said. "I find it deeply exciting and thrilling. I love kneeling in it."

"You are proud to kneel in it," I said, startled.

"Yes," she said.

"Brazen hussy," I said.

"Yes, Master," she said.

I looked at her. She straightened her body even more. "It seems to suit you well," I said.

"It suites me perfectly," she said.

"Why?" I asked.

"I am a pleasure slave," she said.

I rose to my feet. I prepared to snap my fingers.

"I love being owned by men," she said. "I do not find it degrading or debasing. I find it exalting and fulfilling. Do not despise me for what I am."

"And what are you?" I asked.

"A woman," she said.

"And a slave," I said.

"Yes," she said, "a woman, and a slave."

I extended my hand. I would snap my fingers. When I snapped my fingers she would rise to her feet and follow me, heeling me, like the sleek domestic beast she was, to her master's lodge. One of the first things a girl is taught to do is to heel.

"Have I not convinced you, Master," she asked, "that a slave has certain powers?"

"Perhaps some piteously limited powers," I said, "such as might characterize any owned beast."

"Of course," she laughed.

"You are truly a pleasure slave, aren't you?" I asked.

"Yes," she said.

"You seem much different now from Miss Millicent Aubrey-Welles, the upper-class girl, the debutante, from Pennsylvania," I said.

"That little chit," she laughed. "She, too, was a pleasure slave, and in her heart she knew it. The best thing that ever happened to her was to be brought to Gor and put in chains."

"Perhaps," I said.

"There is no doubt about it," she said.

"Do you remember her?" I asked.

"Of course," she said. "But I am no longer she. I am now Winyela, only a slave."

"That is true," I said. Only a slave, I thought to myself, ruefully, only a slave! She was exciting and beautiful, and owned. It was all I could do not to seize her and put her mercilessly to my purposes. How natural it seemed that the men of Gor should keep such women in cages and chains, and force them, under whips, to please them.

"To be sure," I said, "I see that you have powers which mere Millicent did not."

"Yes," she said. "I now have the powers of a slave." That was true. It could not be gainsaid.

"We must go to the lodge of Canka," I said.

"But you have not punished me," she said.

"No," I said.

"Canka wanted me punished, you know," she said.

"I do not know if he really wanted you punished or not," I said.

"Of course he did," she said. "He is a red master."

"I suppose you are right," I said. I recalled that Cuwignaka and Grunt had also, both, been of this opinion.

"But you did not do so," she said.

"No," I said.

"I am unpunished," she said.

"Yes," I said.

"Punish me," she said.

"No," I said.

"My master wanted me to be punished," she said. "I am ready to be punished. I want to be punished."

"It is all right," I said.

"Punish me," she said.

"No," I said.

"You have no intention, then, of punishing me?" she asked.

"No," I said.

"Canka wanted you to have me," she said. "Do you not find me attractive? Do I not have at least the negligible charms of a slave?"

"You are attractive, and beautiful," I said. "And, if you do not mind my saying so, you have been somewhat blatant about your charms."

"In a collar, a girl may flaunt herself," she said.

I nodded. It was true. The collar has an interesting effect on female sexuality. It liberates the girl to be herself.

"Will you not give me but one kiss?" she asked.

"No," I said. "It is well known to what the kiss of a slave girl must lead."

"What?" she asked, innocently.

"Her ownership, domination and rape," I said.

"Oh," she said.

I snapped my fingers.

The girl, immediately, stood.

"You see, pretty Winyela," I said, "you are ultimately powerless. I snap my fingers and you must stand, prepared then to follow me, unquestioning, your will nothing, to your master's lodge. Your clever tricks now avail you naught."

She put down her head.

I laughed with triumph, seeing her standing there, her head down. "You see," I said, "you are ultimately powerless."

She lifted her head, and smiled. "I am not completely powerless," she said.

"What do you mean?" I asked, puzzled.

"I will show you," she said, "how a slave can seduce a man."

Suddenly she reached out and, putting her lovely, bared arms about my neck, pressed her lips to mine. "Ai!" I cried, in anger, in fury. But I could not, then, for a moment, release her. She was a female slave. It is not easy to surrender a female slave from one's arms. Then, angrily, I pulled away from her. Her kiss, that of a female slave, burned on my lips. I shook with emotion. I was furious. The kiss, too brief, delicious, startling, warm, soft, raged in my body. It was like a chemical agent, a catalyst, introduced unexpectedly into my system. Reactions and transformations, eruptive, excruciating and compelling, irresistible and violent, seemed to explode in every compound and tissue in my body. Then she lifted her lips again to me. "Taste again of the lips of a slave, Master," she said. Then she was in my arms, crushed to me, and it seemed that there was only she, and the thunder and light in my blood. Then she was lifted in my arms. "See my collar!" she laughed. "I see it," I said, angrily. "I am a slave!" she said. "Yes," I said. "Do you like the taste of a slave, Master?" she asked. Then she reached out again to me, her arms about my neck, and, again, our lips met. I was then furious. I hurled her to my feet.

"Slut! Animal! Slave!" I cried.

"Yes, Master," she said, laughing.

She rose to her hands and knees and looked up at me, delighted. "I do not think you will resist me now," she laughed.

"Slave!" I cried, angrily.

"Yes, Master," she laughed.

I then, to her horror, strode to the side of the lodge and picked up the kaiila quirt which lay there.

"Please, no!" she said, frightened. "Do not whip me!"

But I laid the quirt to her well, five times, first striking her from her hands and knees to the robes, and then, as she twisted and rolled, helpless to avoid the blows, lashed her upon them.

"You wanted to be punished," I said.

"I did not want the punishment of the whip!" she wept.

"You will take what punishment your master decides to give you," I said.

"Yes, Master," she wept, her body marked, at my feet.

"On your back," I snapped. "Make slave lips. Throw apart your legs!"

Swiftly the girl complied, tears in her eyes. She then lay there, her lips pursed to kiss, her ankles widely spread.

I looked down at her. She looked up at me, tears in her eyes.

A girl who is commanded to make slave lips, or who receives the command, "Slave lips," must form her mouth for kissing. She then, commonly, is not permitted to break this lip position until either she kisses or is kissed. Needless to say, a girl cannot speak when her lips are in the unbroken, fully-pursed slave-lips position. The command which commonly follows the "Slave-lips" command is, "Please me."

I threw the quirt down beside the girl. She looked at it, there, gratefully. No longer was it in my hand. To be sure, it was where I might easily seize it up.

I then crouched beside her and lifted her to a half-sitting position. She closed her legs somewhat. I then kissed her, and this permitted her to break the slave-lips position.

"I do not think you will now hesitate to have me," she said.

"I do not think so," I said.

"It will be a great indignity for me, a great punishment, to be had by you," she said, "for you, too, are only a slave."

"Doubtless," I said.

"Following the instructions of my master, Canka," she said, "I am to yield to you, fully, irreservedly, as a slave girl to her master."

"Yes," I said.

"I am to hold nothing back."

"No," I said.

"But even were I not under such commands," she said, "I know I could not help but yield to you. I have felt your hands before. I know that you can, if it pleases you, make me cry myself your slave."

"Perhaps," I said. I had handled this slave before. We both knew what I could do to her.

"I am ready," she said. "Please begin my punishment."

"Very well," I said.

She lay back, softly, in my arms. "That was a splendid punishment," she said, "Master."

I said nothing. To be sure, I had enjoyed administering it to her. It is pleasant to take a woman and reduce her to a cringing, cuffed, orgasmic slave.

"I am yours for the afternoon," she said.

"That is true," I said.

"It is still early," she said.

I doubted that it was that early. Still the cooking fires had not yet been lit for the evening meal.

"Master," she said.

"Yes," I said.

"Punish me again," she wheedled, putting a finger on my shoulder, and then kissing me, "—please."

"Do you beg it?" I asked.

"Yes," she said. "I beg to be punished again."

"Very well," I said. I took her and threw her again beneath me. She cried out with delight.

"I love my master, Canka," she said.

"I know," I said.

"I want to be fully pleasing to him."

"You had better be," I said.

"That is true," she laughed. "It is strange," she said.

"What?" I asked.

"I am Canka's slave," she said. "Yet, I love him so much that even if I were not his slave, I would want to be his slave."

"Interesting," I said.

"I am only his enamored slave," she said.

"I know," I said.

"Do you want to know something?" she said.

"Surely," I said.

"Love," she said, "puts any woman in bondage, and the more deeply she is in love, the more deeply she is plunged into bondage."

"Perhaps," I said.

"I think it is true," she said.

"Perhaps you are right," I said. "I do not know."

"But if this is true," she said, "it would seem to follow that no woman could be truly in love who is not a female slave."

"What follows, I think," I said, "is that any woman deeply and truly in love is, in effect, a female slave."

"Imagine, then," she breathed, "the love that might be felt by an actual female slave, a woman actually owned, for her master. How helplessly she would be his!"

"Bondage," I said, "with its ownership and domination of the woman, is a soil in which it is natural for love to blossom."

"I know that that is true," she said.

"And the bondage of chains is then, not unoften, succeeded by the bondage of love."

"And think how deep is the bondage of the female slave," said the girl, "whose bondage is the bondage of both chains and love."

"Yes," I said. Her bondage was indeed the deepest bondage in which a human female could conceive of herself being placed, being only, strictly, the property of her beloved master.

"Do you know something else?" she asked.

"What?" I asked.

"You are my friend," she said.

"Beware that you are not quirted, a hundred strokes," I said.

"You are my friend," she said. "I know that it is true."

I did not bother responding to her. How preposterous was the girl's conjecture. Did she not know she was naught but a female slave?

"Can masters and slaves be friends?" she asked.

"Yes," I said. "But the girl, of course, is always to be kept in the perfection of her slavery."

"Of course," she said. "Master," she said.

"Yes," I said.

"I love Canka," she said. "But I displeased him. What if he

doesn't want me any longer? What if he sells me or gives me away?"

"I do not think he will do that," I said.

"How am I to act when I return to his lodge?" she asked. "What am I to do?"

"You are a slave," I said. "Be loving, obedient and pleasing, fully."

"I shall try," she said.

I then explained to her what she might do upon her return to the lodge of Canka.

"Oh, yes," she whispered. "Yes!"

It would be important for her to convince him that she had learned something from her travails of the day.

"I smell cooking fires," she said, happily. She made as though to rise, but I thrust her, roughly, back down on the robes. "Master?" she asked.

"You are eager to return to the lodge of your master," I observed.

"Yes, Master," she said.

"But until I choose, within reason, to relinquish you," I said, "you are still to me as my slave, are you not?"

"Yes, Master," she said.

"Well," I said, "I do not choose, at this moment, to relinquish you."

"Please, Master," she wept.

"You are nude, and attractive," I said. "I am going to have you again now, and at my leisure."

"Please, Master!" she protested.

"Do you object?" I asked.

"No, Master," she said, frightened.

"And how will you yield to me?" I asked.

"With perfection," she said, "as my master ordered." She looked at me, and laughed. "You brute," she said. "You know you will make me yield wih perfection, whether I wished to or not!"

"Perhaps," I said.

"Modest tarsk!" she laughed. "Oh!" she cried. "Oh! Oh!"

"It seems to be true," I said.

"Yes," she said, "yes!"

"You will, further," I said, "utter low-volume sounds, indicative of arousal."

"Yes," she said. "Yes."

This device, forcing the slave to furnish an audible analogue or correlate for her sensations, has three principal utilities. It helps to intensify the slave's responses, she responding in part to, and being in part aroused by, her own sounds of arousal. Secondly, the sounds, her helpless moans and cries, her whimpers, her sighs, her gasps, please, and can be stimulatory to, the master. Thirdly, the sounds aid him in his management and control of her. By means of them he can, in effect, map her beauty, guiding himself in his ownership of her, detecting the zones of her greatest sexual helplessness and, by varying the nature of his rhythms and touches, how they can be most efficiently and brilliantly exploited, the end in view, of course, being to produce the most yielding and orgasmically helpless slave possible.

"Ohhh," she said, softly.

"And when I am finished with you," I said, "I shall rise to my feet and snap my fingers. You will then, without further ado, rise to your feet and follow me, silently, humbly and unquestioningly, heeling me, as the mere beast you are, to the lodge of your master."

"Yes, Master," she said. "Ohhh. Ohhh!"

I smiled to myself. The little beast had tricked me. I thought my vengeance on her was suitable.

"Ohh!" she cried. "Ohh! Ohhhh!"

Yes, I thought, quite suitable.

10

AN IMPROVED SLAVE IS RETURNED TO HER MASTER

We stood before the lodge of Canka.

He emerged from the lodge.

Immediately Winyela, a penitent slave, lowered herself to her knees, and then to her belly before him.

"You may kiss his feet," I said.

She began to kiss the moccasined feet of her master.

"I was displeased with her," said Canka to me.

"She knows," I said.

Canka reached down and pulled her up to her knees and then, by the hair, he bent her back, and then twisted her about.

"She does not appear to be much disciplined," he said.

"I think the discipline to which she was subjected will prove to be adequate," I said. "If it does not, it may, of course, be doubled, or trebled."

"That is true," said Canka. Winyela, then, released, was again at his feet. Imploringly, beseechingly, again on her belly, as she had been before, she continued to press her lips to his moccasins.

"Do you think she is improved?" asked Canka.

"I think so," I said.

I looked down at the girl. I had little doubt she had learned her lessons. The highly intelligent woman, incidentally, as would be expected, learns her slave lessons, and that she is a slave, much more quickly than the stupid woman. It takes some stupid women as much as two days before they learn that they are truly in a collar. If a slave continues to prove recalcitrant, of course, she gains nothing by this. She will merely be disposed of.

"It is my hope," said Canka, "that she will not repeat her earlier mistakes."

"I do not think she will," I said, "and, of course, if she is not pleasing in some way she may be swiftly brought into line."

"She is responsive to the quirt?" asked Canka.

"Yes," I said.

"And to the touch of the master?" he asked.

"Yes," I said, "and, as befits a slave, helplessly and superbly so."

"Good," he said. He then stepped back from the contrite girl, bellying to him, kissing his feet, suing for his forgiveness and mercy.

"Have you firmly resolved to improve your qualities of pleasingness to your master?" I asked.

"Yes, Master," said the girl, on her stomach.

"With your permission," I said to Canka.

"Of course," he said.

"You may now indicate your new attitude toward your master," I told her.

"Yes, Master," she said. She then rose to her hands and knees and head down, crawling, entered Canka's lodge.

He looked at me, puzzled.

In a moment she re-emerged from the lodge as she had entered it, crawling, with her head down. Grasped between her small, fine white teeth was the center of a heavy, braided, beaded-handled kaiila quirt. Canka watched, as she, unbidden, brought him the quirt. She lay it at his feet, from her teeth, and then knelt before him, her head down. Her hands were on her thighs. Her knees were widely separated. This knee position indicated that she knew herself to be a woman held in the deepest and most intimate form of slavery.

"Thus," I said, "does she display her new understanding of her condition. Thus does she indicate her new attitude towards her master."

I saw that Canka approved of what he saw, and well.

"Behold her," I said, "a humbled, submitted slave. Her name is Winyela. She is the property of the warrior, Canka, of the Isbu Kaiila."

"Look up," said Canka to the girl.

There were tears in her eyes.

"She desires to speak," I said.

"You may speak," said Canka.

"I am yours, and I love you, my master," said the girl. Then she lowered her head.

Canka reached down and picked up the kaiila quirt. Then he indicated, with the quirt, that the girl should enter the interior of the lodge. She crawled to the lodge, head down.

"I see," said Canka, "that you have returned me a better slave than the one I sent you."

I said nothing.

"I am very pleased," he said.

"That pleases me," I said.

"I did not wish to have to kill her," he said.

"I do not think that will be necessary," I said. "I think you will now find that she is a good slave, and that all is in order."

Canka grinned.

"She is within," I said. "She awaits her master."

"Thank you," said Canka, "—my friend."

"It is nothing," I said, "my friend."

Canka then entered his lodge. A moment later I heard Winyela crying out, rapturously, doubtless locked in his arms. I had suggested the business of the kaiila quirt to her before we had left Cuwignaka's lodge. I had thought it might please Canka, and give Winyela a way to demonstrate, graphically and meaningfully, unmistakably, that she was now, knew herself to be, and desired not to be other than, the total slave of her master.

I then walked away. As I left, I heard her crying out in ecstasy and heard, too, the uncompromising, triumphant roars, unrestrained, bestial and victorious, of his ownership of her, a slave, a girl named Winyela, whom I had prepared for his lodge.

11

IT IS IN THE TIME OF FESTIVALS

"Canka is extremely pleased," said Cuwignaka, coming up to me. It was the day following Winyela's disciplining and my delivery of her, suitably informed and improved, to the lodge of Canka.

"I am pleased to hear it," I said. I was fond of Canka and, too, I supposed, I should be pleased, as I was, in strict fact, his slave, and had had what amounted, as I now understood clearly, to what was a charge, or at least an invitation in the matter.

"He is permitting her a dress of soft tabuk skin," said Cuwignaka, "creamy white and soft-tanned, though, to be sure, of slave length. Too, he has given her beads and moccasins. He has braided her hair. He has painted her face, for the time of the feasts."

"Marvelous," I said. It is not unusual for a master to care for a slave's hair. Too, they will, upon occasion, groom kaiila and tie streamers and ribbons in their long manes. That he had painted her face was also impressive. Usually, among the Kaiila, it is free women who are permitted face paint, and then, commonly only at times of great festivals. This paint is commonly applied by the woman's mate.

"I have never seen Canka so happy," said Cuwignaka.

"I am pleased," I said.

"You should see Winyela," he said. "She is joyful, alluring and superb."

"Excellent," I said. I was pleased to think that I may have had a hand in her transformation. To be sure, I had done little other than to put them together as true master and true slave.

"I, myself," said Cuwignaka, "feel the need of a slave."

"Grunt would be pleased," I said, "at your least indication of interest, to strip Wasnapohdi and put her to your feet."

"That is true," said Cuwignaka.

"She is hot and beautiful," I said.

"I was thinking more of my own slave," said Cuwignaka.

"You could probably buy one cheaply from the Isanna," I said. "They have many sleek-flanked slaves in their girl herds."

"I was thinking more in terms of a red slave," said Cuwignaka.

"Doubtless you have considered the warpath," I said, "the capture of a girl, the bringing of her back, naked and bound, a tether on her neck, running her at the flank of your kaiila."

"Twice I did not take the warpath," said Cuwignaka, "because I had no quarrel with the Fleer. It would now seem somewhat hypocritical on my part, would it not, to take the warpath not to deal vengeance and destruction to the enemy, but merely for my own selfish purposes, to procure a female."

"Perhaps you are right," I said. "How do you feel about kaiila raids?"

"I see little wrong with them," said Cuwignaka. "That is not so much war as it is a sport. We raid the Fleer. They raid us. And so it goes."

"What, then," I asked, "about a girl hunt, or a girl raid?"

"Perhaps," said Cuwignaka. "That, too, is more in the nature of a sport than anything else."

I knew that red savages occasionally went on girl raids. To be sure, the kaiila raid was much more common. The exploit marking, painted on the forequarters of a kaiila for a captured kaiila, resembles an inverted 'U'. This convention has a heritage, clearly, it seems to me, which traces back to an animal other than the kaiila, an animal, indeed, indigenous not to Gor, but to a distant world, one from which came the ancestors of the red savages. It seems clearly to be related not to a pawed, but to a hoofed animal. The usual exploit marking for a captured female is also a conventional representation. It resembles a pair of parentheses enclosing a vertical line. It seems to be a stylized representation, rather brazen, I think, of delicate female intimacies. There is, incidentally, no common, often-used sign for a captured male, comparable to that for the captured female. Males of the enemy are seldom captured. They are usually killed. In the coup codes, opaque red circles on feathers usually stand for enemies slain.

"But," said Cuwignaka, "I was thinking not so much in terms of any red slave, as of some red slave."

"I see," I said. "Well, my friend, put the dream of Bloketu from your mind. She cannot be captured. She is Kaiila, and she is the daughter of a chief."

"I know," smiled Cuwignaka. Such a woman, even though

she might be haughty and insolent, stood outside of Kaiila capture permissions. She was safe from the Kaiila.

"What is that you have there?" I asked. When Cuwignaka had come up to me he had been carrying an oblong object, wrapped in rawhide.

"I have not forgotten it," he laughed. "I bring it from the lodge of Canka."

"What is it?" I asked.

"You may keep it," said Cuwignaka, "until the end of the festivals."

"What is it?" I asked.

"Look," he said, unwrapping the object.

"Ah!" I said.

"Canka was very pleased with your work with Winyela," said Cuwignaka.

"Apparently," I said.

"He desires that you keep this until the festivals' end."

I looked at the object. It was a heavy, supple, beaded kaiila quirt. It was a symbol, of course, more than anything else. It gave its bearer warrior rights to open slaves, those not housed in private lodges, for the duration of the festivals. It was good for all of the girl herds of the Kaiila.

"This is very generous on the part of Canka," I said.

"He likes you," said Cuwignaka. "Also, as you know, he never wished to make you his slave. It was only that he had to do that, or have you attacked on the prairie, for having freed me from the stakes. Indeed, he is only waiting, I think, for an appropriate and safe time to free you. He must, of course, as having been a Blotanhunka, be judicious and politic in how he handles this matter."

"He is very generous," I said.

"I think he will free you during the feasts and giveaways," said Cuwignaka, smiling. "It would seem natural to do it then. Too, I think you will now be fairly safe among the Kaiila, even without a collar. They are used to you now, and they know that you are my friend."

"This is welcome news, indeed," I said. For too long had I been inactive in my true mission in the Barrens, that of attempting to contact the Kur war general, Zarendargar, Half-Ear, and warn him of the death squad, determined remnants of which still survived, that was hunting him, that commanded by Kog and Sardak, the latter of Blood, a high officer, of the Kurii. My only clue to his whereabouts was a story hide, now in the keeping of Grunt. On this hide, among other things, was the representation of a shield bearing Zarendargar's image. If I could find the owner of this shield I might then, hopefully, be able to locate Zarendargar.

"Too," said Cuwignaka, "I think Canka may buy a woman for you, as a gift, after the festivals, one to do your unpleasant work and warm you, helplessly, in the furs."

"He must indeed be pleased with Winyela," I smiled.

"He is," said Cuwignaka. "And, too, I might mention, though I do not know if it is appropriate to do so or not, that they are much in love with each other."

"She must, nonetheless, be kept as a complete slave," I said.

"Have no fear," said Cuwignaka. "She will be."

I was pleased to hear this. The Earth redhead, under an iron discipline, would blossom most beautifully in her love.

"Should Canka get me a woman," I said, "I will put her, too, of course, completely at your disposal. I will see that she provides you, too, unquestioningly, with any intimacy that you might desire."

"How well things are going for us all!" said Cuwignaka. "A Yellow-Knife delegation is due in camp today. This is the time of the dances and feasts. Canka is happy. You may soon be free and I, Cuwignaka, Women's Dress, will enter tomorrow the great lodge of the dance."

In the center of the camp a great circular brush lodge had been erected. Its high walls, some forty feet in height, built on poles, from platforms, and ceilinged with poles and branches, enclosed a dancing space, cleared, circular and packed down, of about fifty feet in diameter. In the center of this space was the pole which had been formed, some days ago, from the tree which Winyela had felled. Fixed in the earth, buried to a depth of about seven or eight feet, and supported, too, with a circle of heavy stakes, to which it was bound, it was about twenty-two feet in height. Two forks had been left on the pole, one about ten feet from the ground and one about fifteen feet from the ground. In the lower fork, rolled in a bundle, were the jewelry and clothes Winyela had worn when she had cut down the tree. From the higher fork dangled two leather representations, one of a Kailiauk and the other of a male, with an exaggerated phallus. These representations were doubtless intended to be significant in the symbolism and medicine of the dance. This dance, to the red savage, is holy. It is sacred to him. It is a mystery medicine. I shall not, therefore, attempt to reduce it to simple terms or translate it into simplistic concepts. It does have to do, however, at least, obviously, with such things as luck, hunting and manhood.

"I am happy for you, Cuwignaka," I said.

"I have waited for years to enter the dance lodge," he said. "It will be one of the great things in my life."

"I am happy for you," I said.

12

I UTILIZE THE ENTITLEMENTS OF THE BEADED QUIRT

"What do you want?" cried the boy, reining in his kaiila but feet before me. His words had a sibilant, explosive quality. This is a general characteristic of many of the languages of the red savages. It is even more pronounced, of course, when the speaker is excited or in an emotional state.

"Greetings, young man," I said, calmly. "You are Isanna, are you not?"

"I am Isanna," said the youth. "Who are you?" Another two lads, on kaiila, now approached me, remaining, however, some yards away.

"I am Tatankasa, a slave of Canka, of the Isbu," I said.

"He is a great warrior," said the youth, impressed.

"That is my understanding," I said.

"What are you doing here?" asked the youth.

"A man hunger is on me," I said.

"You should have a beaded quirt," said the youth.

"He is the slave of Canka," said another. "Let us not require the quirt."

"Behold," I smiled. I unwrapped the object which I carried.

"A beaded quirt," said the first youth, pleased.

"Yes," I said. About my left shoulder, in five or six narrow coils, there was a rope of braided rawhide. It was a light rope but it was more than sufficient for the sort of animal in which I was interested.

"You should have said you had the quirt," said the youth. Then he said to the two others, "Round them up!"

They raced away, through the grass.

"Follow me," said the first youth, and he then turned his kaiila, and led the way from the place. These youth were naked save for the breechclout and moccasins. They carried ropes and whips.

In a few moments we had surmounted a small rise, and I was looking down into a wide, shallow, saucerlike valley, some half of a pasang in width. "Hei! Hei!" cried the boys, in the distance, bringing together the members of the herd. Their ropes swung. Their whips cracked. Then the herd was together, well grouped by its young drovers. It now occupied, its members bunched and crowded closely together, a small, tight circle. It was now, in effect, a small, relatively fixed, directionless, milling mass. In such a grouping it may be easily controlled and managed. In such a grouping it has no purpose of its own. In such a grouping it must wait to see what is to be done with it. It must wait to see in what direction it will be driven.

"Hei! Hei!" called the young drovers, kicking their heels back into the flanks of their kaiila, waving their ropes, cracking their whips.

The herd now, the young drovers on either side of it, and slightly behind it, began to move in my direction.

"Hei! Hei!" cried the young drovers, ropes swinging, whips cracking. The herd then began to run towards me. I could see the dust it raised. Lagging beasts were incited to new speeds, treated to the admonishments of hissing leather, falling across their backs, flanks and rumps. Then one of the lads sped his kaiila about the herd, heading it off and turning it. He had done this expertly. Not more than a few yards away, below me, below where I stood on the small rise, the herd was again in a small tight circle, turned in on itself, purposeless, milling, stationary.

"You boys drive them well," I said.

"Thank you," said the young man on the kaiila, with whom I had been waiting. "We practice it, of course. If danger should threaten we wish to be able to move them quickly into the vicinity of the camp."

"It is the same with kaiila," said another lad.

I nodded. These lads, and lads like them, were set to watch the herds, not to defend them. At the first sign of danger, such as the appearance of an enemy party, they were to bring the herds back to the village, sending one lad ahead to sound the alarm. Under no circumstances were they to engage the enemy. Red savages do not set boys to fight men. Too, the lads were in little danger. It would be very difficult for a mounted warrior, even if he wished to do so, to overtake a boy, lighter in weight than he, on a rested kaiila, by the time the lad could reach the lodges, usually no more than two or three pasangs away.

"It is a fine herd," I said. It was the third such herd I had looked at this morning.

"We think so," said the first lad, proudly. "There is one with nice flanks," he said, indicating a brunet with his whip.

"Yes," I said.

The girl, frightened, seeing our eyes upon her, tried to slip back, unobtrusively, among her fellow lovely beasts.

"I have used her myself," said the first lad. "Do you wish to have us cut her out of the herd for you?"

"No," I said.

"There is a pretty one," said another lad, "the one with brown hair and the little turned-up nose."

"She is pretty," I said. "What is her name?"

The lads laughed. "These are herd girls," said one of them. "They have no names."

"How many are here?" I asked. I had not bothered to count.

"Seventy-three," said the first lad. "This is the largest of the Isanna girl herds."

"And the best," added another lad.

"They seem quiet," I said.

"In the herds they are not permitted human speech," said one of the boys.

"No more than she-kaiila," laughed another.

"They may, however," said the first, "indicate their needs by such things as moans and whimpers."

"This helps in their control," said another lad, "and helps them to keep in mind that they are only beasts."

"Do you drive them sometimes to water?" I asked.

"Of course," said one of the lads.

"We feed them on their knees," said another lad.

"They supplement their diets by picking berries and digging wild turnips," said the first lad.

"We make them chew carefully and watch closely to see that they swallow, bit by bit, in small swallows, sip roots, as well," said another.

"We then examine their mouths, forcing them widely open, to determine that they have finished their entire allotment of the root," said another.

I nodded. Sip roots are extremely bitter. Slave wine, incidentally, is made from sip roots. The slaves of the red savages, like slaves generally on Gor, would be crossed and bred only as, and precisely as, their masters might choose.

"Do you often have strays?" I asked.

"No," laughed a lad, slapping his whip meaningfully into his palm.

"At night," said another lad, "to make it harder to steal them, we put them in twist hobbles and tie them together by the neck, in strings, their hands tied behind their backs. These strings are then picketed near the village."

"Do any ever try to escape?" I asked.

"No," said one lad.

"Not more than once," laughed another.

"That is true," said the first lad. "No such beast ever tries to escape from the Isanna more than once."

"Some who try to escape are killed by sleen on the prairie," said one of the lads. "The others are trailed and brought back to the camp where they are tied down by our women and, over three days, taught that escape is not permitted."

"What is the penalty for a second attempt at escape?" I asked.

"Hamstringing," said one of the lads, "and then being left behind when the camp moves."

"I see," I said. "May I speak to one of them?"

"Surely," said the first lad.

I approached the women.

"You," I said, indicating a dark-haired woman, "step forward."

She came forward immediately, and knelt before me.

"You may speak briefly to me," I said. "After that, you are returned, once more, to the linguistic condition of the herd, that condition in which, without the permission of a master or masters, or one acting in such a capacity, you may not use human speech. Do you understand?"

"Yes, Master," she said.

"Is there any escape for you?" I asked.

"No, Master," she said, frightened, and then put down her head, trembling. I saw, too, several of the other women shrink back.

"Are you certain?" I asked.

"Yes, Master," she said, frightened.

"What of these other women," I asked, "do they, too, know that?"

"Yes, Master," said the woman. "We all know it! We all know that escape is impossible for us!"

"You may withdraw," I said.

Quickly the woman scrambled back, into the herd.

Several of the other women in the herd, I had noticed, had been following these conversations, my conversation with the boys and then, later, my conversation with the woman. In their eyes I had seen terror. Well did they understand, I saw, the hopelessness of even the thought of escape. Even if they should elude their red pursuers, which seemed almost unthinkable, there would be waiting for them only the prairie, and the sleen. These women, like most white women in the Barrens, and they well knew it, to their terror, lived at the mercy of, and on the sufferance of, red masters.

"In a moon or two it will be time to thin the herds," said one of the lads.

"We will trade some off and sell some others," said another lad.

"It seems that any of these would be worth keeping," I said, admiringly.

"It is a sleek herd," said one of the boys. "Doubtless several will be clothed and taken into private lodges for the winter moons."

"They are useful for digging under the snow for kailiauk chips," said a lad. Kailiauk chips were a common fuel on the plains.

"They are good, too," said the first lad, "for squirming in the robes."

"Yes," said another.

"If you like," said the first lad, "we will cut a girl out of the herd for you."

"He is the slave of Canka," said another lad. "Give him a good one."

"Would you like the dark-haired one you spoke to?" asked a lad. "It will take only a moment to put a rope on her neck."

"No," I said. "Thank you." To be sure the dark-haired woman was a lovely specimen, a fine example of the lovely two-legged beasts in the herd. She was sweetly breasted, narrow-waisted and widely hipped. She had a delicious love cradle. I had little doubt but what she might be worth two hides.

"There is a good one," said one of the boys, pointing out an auburn-haired beauty. "One lash of the quirt and she juices superbly."

"Actually," I said, "I am looking for a particular beast. May I examine the herd, to see if it is here."

"Of course," said the first lad.

I had thought that I had seen the particular animal I sought, shapely and blond, trying to hide itself in the herd.

It would take but a moment to make the necessary determination. I thrust the quirt I carried and the hide in which it had been wrapped, in my belt.

I entered among the women. "Give way," I said. "Kneel." The herd knelt.

I threaded my way among the kneeling slave beasts of the Isanna. Then I stopped beside one. She knelt low, her head down to the grass. I stood beside her and she began to tremble. I then took her by the hair and, crouching beside her, threw her, twisting her, to her side in the grass. My hand in her hair I then turned her face forcibly towards me, and held it thusly, so that I might see her features, fully. Yes, it was she whom I sought. I then put her again to her knees, pushing her head down to the grass.

"Place your wrists behind you, crossed," I said. She did so and, in a moment, with one end of the light, narrow rope I carried, removed from my shoulder, I bound them together. I then took the rope up from her wrists and, pushing up her collar, looped it five times about her throat, and then took the free end of the rope under the rope leading up from her bound wrists, and then brought it forward. In this fashion a convenient, unknotted tether is formed. This type of tether is suitable for short leadings. The free end of the tether is slipped under the bond leading up from the wrists to prevent the girl from slipping it by the simple expedient of lowering and dipping her head a few times. She would still, of course, even in such a case, remain bound by the wrists.

The usual tether, it might be mentioned, is tied snugly but not tightly. There should be room to place two fingers between the throat and the inside of the tether. Any pressure felt by the prisoner must be felt on the back of the neck. A good Gorean tether constitutes no impediment whatsoever to a girl's breathing. An exception is the choke collar which does interfere with a girl's breathing, but only if she is in the least bit recalcitrant. In the cities it is more common to use collars and leashes than tethers, or knotted tethers. The common leash has a snap clip, sometimes a locking one. This snap clip has a variety of uses. It can snap about a link or ring in its own leash, the leash then functioning as a self-contained collar-and-leash device, or about such things, say, as a collar, collar ring or neck bond, perhaps of rope or chain.

"On your feet," I said. The girl stood. I then led her forth from the herd, a sleek, curvaceous animal on her tether, my choice. She hurried behind me, that the slack in the tether not be taken up, as it was a wound, and unknotted tether, that it not tighten on her throat.

"She is pretty, but she is not the best choice," said the first lad.

"Oh?" I said.

"She is a block of ice," he said.

"I saw her twice, in the village," I said, "once in the entry of your band into the camp, and then, again, a day or so later. She seemed of interest."

"We send them into the villages, upon occasion, some of them," said the first lad, "to work, if there is a call for them, or to deliver roots and berries which they have gathered to the women. Too, of course, they are useful in twisting grass for tinder and gathering wood and kailiauk chips for fuel. These things, then, too, they must deliver to the villages."

"Surely some are sent in occasionally for wench sport," I said.

"Sometimes we deliver a string of five or six into the camp for that purpose," said the first lad.

"Does this wench," I asked, indicating the girl on my tether, "often occupy a place in such a string?"

"No," laughed one of the lads.

"She is a block of ice," said the first lad.

"Choose another," invited one of the lads.

"How long may I keep her?" I asked.

"Until sundown," said the first lad. "She must then be put with the others."

I glanced at the slender ankles of my charge. I thought they would look well in close-fitting leather hobbles, twist hobbles, knotted on the outside of the left ankle, which she, her hands bound behind her back, would be unable to remove. Such hobbles are also used, of course, for the two front legs of kaiila.

"My thanks, lads!" I said. "You have been very helpful!"

I then led the girl from the vicinity of the herd, to a place I had picked out, in the shelter of some trees, near a small stream.

I had glanced back once. The lads and I exchanged waves. Several of the women in the herd, I had noted, had seemed quite pleased to see the blonde being led away on my tether. I gathered that she was an arrogant, proud girl, and not popular with her fellows. From what I knew of her, I did not find this surprising.

"Here we are," I said, entering among the trees.

In a moment I had tied her tether about a branch. I looked about myself.

A parfleche, containing some food, hung in one of the branches. I had placed it there earlier. With it, too, I had placed a large hide, rolled. That hide I now unrolled and spread, carefully, on the grass. The small hide, that in which the quirt had been wrapped, I dropped to one side. "That hide," I said, indicating the smaller hide, "is about the size of a Tahari submission mat."

I looked at the girl.

"You may kneel," I said.

She knelt, her tether looping gracefully up to the branch about which I had fastened it.

"I see that you speak Gorean," I said. That pleased me for it was much easier for me than the complexities of Kaiila. She did not respond.

"Spread your knees, widely," I said.

She did so.

I regarded her. In this place, until sundown, she was mine.

"In the herd," I said, "you attempted to conceal yourself from me."

She looked away, angrily.

"You seem very quiet," I said. "Perhaps your tongue has been removed, or slit, for insolence." I went to her and held her head back, my hand in her hair. "Open your mouth," I said. She did so. "No," I said. "That is not the case."

She made an angry noise.

"At least you are capable of sound," I said.

She tossed her head.

I then walked about her. "Your curves," I said, "suggest that you do not need to be a block of ice. They suggest that you are capable of responding as a hormonally normal woman. I see that you are not branded."

I then crouched before her and touched the side of her neck. She pulled away, angrily.

This gesture displeased me. The slave must welcome the touch of a man. Indeed, she must even beg for it.

Angrily I drew the quirt from my belt. She eyed it, fearfully. She shook her head. She uttered tiny, protesting, begging noises. She lifted her head, turning her head so that the side of her neck faced me, that I might touch it, if it pleased me.

"Ah," I said, "of course. You are a herd girl. You may not use human speech without permission." I had taken it for granted, mistakenly, as it had turned out, that the prohibition against human speech imposed on the herd girl would cease to obtain when, say, as in the present context, she had clearly been removed from the vicinity of the herd. I understood now that this was not the case. This made sense, of course. One would not expect human speech from a she-kaiila, for example, even if she were not in her herd. Too, I now had a much clearer notion of the effectiveness of the discipline under which the red masters kept their white beauties.

She nodded her head, vigorously.

"I wonder if I should give you permission to use human speech," I mused. "Perhaps, rather, I should feed, train and use you as a mere curvaceous brute, not bothering to complicate our relationship by according you human speech."

She made piteous, begging noises.

"It has been a long time since you were permitted to speak, hasn't it?" I said.

She nodded.

"Do you wish to be permitted to speak?" I asked.

She nodded, anxiously.

"Do you beg it?" I asked.

She nodded, desperately.

"Very well," I said. "You may speak." I usually permitted my slaves to speak. Sometimes, however, when it pleased me, I had them serve me mutely, as only delicious beasts. Only one or two slaves had I never permitted to speak in my presence, and those I had, later, sold off.

"That is good," she said, "to be able to speak!"

"You may thank me," I informed her.

"I do not wish to do so," she said.

"The permission accorded," I said, "may as readily be withdrawn."

"Thank you," she said. It pleased me to obtain this small amount of courtesy, this conciliatory token, from this woman.

"Thank you—what?" I asked.

"You are a slave!" she said. "You wear a collar!"

"Thank you—what?" I asked.

She was silent.

"Are you familiar with the quirt?" I asked.

"Thank you, Master," she said, quickly. "Yes, Master!"

"I see you have felt it," I said.

"Yes, Master," she said.

"Do you know what you are doing here?" I asked.

"You are going to use me," she said, "one or more times. Then you will return me to the herd. I am ready. Let us get on with it."

I regarded her.

"I do not wish to be quirted," she said.

"Why, a moment ago, did you withdraw from my touch?" I asked.

"I found it irritating," she said. I saw her body, as she said this, tighten, and draw back. It was very different from the normal body of a slave, which seems so warm and soft, so vital and alive, so eager to be touched, caressed and held. I saw that she was a rigid, unhappy woman.

"You are not branded," I said.

"No," she said.

"Are you from a Waniyanpi compound?" I asked. The Waniyanpi, slaves of red savages, lived in tiny, isolated agricultural communities. They supplied their masters with corn and vegetables. They subscribed to a unisex *ethos*.

"No," she said.

"How did you come to the Isanna?" I asked.

"You do not need to know anything about me, to have me," she said.

"Speak, Slave," I said. I touched the quirt to the palm of my left hand.

"Yes, Master," she said quickly. "I was once a woman of Ar."

Her accent, soft and liquid, had suggested this to me.

"I was of the merchants. I formed a company to trade along the Ihanke. I hired five men. I regarded the red savages as ignorant barbarians. I sent my men to nearby trading points, opened by the Dust Legs to any white traders. I furnished them with inferior trade goods, which they were to misrepresent to the savages. I would become rich in hides and horn. Imagine my surprise when, standing on the front porch of my small trading post, I saw my five men, afoot, bound and gagged, each dragging a travois, returning from the Ihanke. At the same time I felt myself seized from behind by red savages, Dust Legs. I was stripped and bound. I was shown the materials on the travois. They were the inferior trade goods I had sent to the trading points, being returned. One item, however, on one of the travois was not mine. It was a fine kailiauk robe. One of the Dust Legs showed it to me, and then pointed to it, and then to me, and then threw it on the porch of the trading post. It was their payment for me. I was then carried into the Barrens. I have been a slave of red savages ever since."

"At least you were properly paid for," I said.

"Yes," she said, angrily.

"How did you come to the Isanna?" I asked.

"The Dust Legs traded me to the Sleen," she said, "and the Sleen traded me to the Yellow Knives."

"It seems that no one was eager to keep you," I said.

"Perhaps not," she said.

"What did you bring?" I asked.

"The Sleen got me for two knives," she said, "and the Yellow Knives had me for a mirror."

"The Dust Legs," I said, "apparently originally conjectured that you would be worth a hide. You then went for two knives, and then for a mirror."

"Yes," she said, bitterly.

"You have not failed to note, I suppose," I said, "that you have seemed to undergo a certain decrease in value."

"No," she said, angrily, "I have not failed to note that."

"How did you finally come to the Isanna?" I asked.

"I was taken in a girl raid by the Isanna, with two-dozen others," she said. "We were herded into the Isanna country."

I nodded. This was around Council Rock, north of the northern fork of the Kaiila River and west of the Snake River.

"But you are not kept in a private lodge," I said. "You are kept in a girl herd."

"I was tried out, and then put in the herd," she said.

"You are apparently not regarded as much of a slave," I said.

"I am beautiful," she said, squirming in her bonds, the tether, attached to the branch, above her head, on her neck. "You saw that I was marched at the stirrup of an Isanna warrior in the Isanna procession into the camp of the Isbu!"

"That is true," I said. "You were seen fit to be displayed as Isanna loot."

"Yes," she said.

"Then you were sent back to the herd," I said.

"Yes," she said, sullenly.

"Why," I asked, "did you, in our two previous meetings, regard me with such contempt?"

She tossed her head.

"I advise you to speak, Slave," I said. I tapped the quirt in my palm.

"You are only a male slave," she spat out, suddenly. "I despise male slaves. I hold them in contempt. I am too high for them. I am too lofty for them. I am above them! Girls such as I belong to and are for free men!"

"I see," I said.

"Too," she said, "I am the property of a red master."

I nodded. I saw that she had come to know and respect red savages. From a woman who had once regarded them as dupes and ignorant barbarians she had now come, as their slave, to understand them as the redoubtable hunters and warriors they were. Astride their kaiila, lance in hand, they were the rulers of the prairies, the Ubars of the plains. In the Barrens, obviously, it is something of a distinction for a woman, particularly a lowly white woman, to belong to one.

"But you are apparently not much of a property for your master," I said.

"Oh?" she said, angrily.

"You are kept in a herd," I reminded her.

She looked away, angrily.

I freed her tether from the branch and, slipping it back under the bond coming up from her wrists, I unlooped it from her neck. I then freed her hands. I dropped the rope to the side.

"Perhaps you had better keep me bound, or put me in a leg stretcher," she said.

"That will not be necessary," I said.

She rubbed her wrists. I had perhaps bound her too tightly. But then it is important that a girl knows herself bound.

"What are you going to do to me?" she asked.

"Many things," I said, "but among them I am going to improve your master's property."

She looked at me.

"Get on your hands and knees," I said.

She complied.

"See the quirt?" I asked.

"Yes, Master," she said.

"I will give you a moment or two to crawl to the robe which I have spread on the grass," I said. "After that, if you are anywhere else for the next Ahn, the quirt will be used on you, and liberally. And, indeed, it may, if I choose, be used on you, even on the robe."

"I understand, Master," she said.

"Go," I said.

She crawled to the robe. Crouching on it, she looked at it, and its edges. It was an island of safety for her, or possible safety. Off it, in the next Ahn, she knew she would be whipped. On it, she did not know. This was, of course, a familiar master's tactic, usually used only with new slaves, young, inexperienced girls, fearful of the sexual aspects of their slavery. They find themselves in a large room, usually empty, or rather empty, save for an imposing couch. They are then informed that they will be whipped anywhere in the room except on the couch and may, perhaps, be whipped upon it. Needless to say, the girl scurries to the couch, regards it, in effect, as a place of possible refuge, in spite of the fact that her sexual exploitation and domination will clearly take place upon it, and, for the time limits set, whatever they may be, fears to leave it. Some masters, if not pleased, will force the girl from the couch, and, keeping themselves between the girl and the couch, whip her, then letting her, after a few strokes, flee back to the couch. There, in that place of possible safety she will try again, desperately, to be more pleasing. This may be the last time in months, incidentally, that the girl will be on the surface of the couch. Until her slave skills improve her place will be on furs, or a mat, or on the bare stones or tiles, at the foot of the couch. Indeed, some masters will sleep even a superb slave at the foot of the couch. Perhaps it is too obvious to mention but a point served by this original use of the couch is to break down the new slave's fear of the couch and encourage her to see it in a favorable light, indeed, as a place of relative safety, comfort and favor. In a possibly hostile environment she desires its protection and significance. She wishes to be upon it. Later, of course, for nobler reasons, she will presumably come to view it with even greater eagerness and affection. On it she will be permitted to serve her master and on it, in turn, she will come to know his touch, as a loving, yielding slave.

"Get on your left hip," I said, "your right leg extended, the palms of your hands on the robe."

"You can't kill me," she said. "I do not belong to you!"

"That is an interesting question," I said. "As I hold the beaded quirt I think I do, in this context, have such rights over you. At any rate, even if I do not, a complaint to the boys, relayed by them to your master, would surely be in order. He may then decide whether or not your least difficulty or disobedience is to be punished by death. And since you are a herd girl, I doubt that he will think twice about the matter. That is better." She had assumed the position which I had prescribed.

"Do not complain to the boys," she said. "They are cruel!"

"They are not cruel," I said. "They are only good herders."

"If I do not please you," she said, "just quirt me."

"Have no fear," I said. "If I am not pleased you will be well quirted. Then I will decide whether or not to complain to the boys."

She moaned.

"You have good slave curves," I said, regarding her. "You may thank me."

"Thank you, Master," she said.

"One wonders why, then, you are so valueless. You went for a hide, and then two knives, and then only a mirror. Now you are in a herd. Why are you worth so little?"

"I do not know, Master," she said.

"The boys tell me that you are a block of ice," I said.

"I cannot help it if I am unresponsive," she said. "It is my nature."

"I also gather," I said, "that you are arrogant and surly. You are thus, in various respects, a poor slave."

She tossed her head, irritably.

I struck her once, on the right thigh, with the quirt. She cried out with pain, and looked down at the welt.

"I would think twice, if I were you," I said, "before I made angry little noises or impatient gestures."

"Yes, Master," she said.

"Do you find men attractive?" I asked.

"Since I may be raped at their pleasure," she said, "what difference does it make?"

"Do you find them attractive?" I asked.

"Sometimes," she said, "they make me feel uneasy."

"What were your relations with men, prior to your enslavement?" I asked.

"Cannot you simply take me and be done with it?" she asked.

"Speak," I said.

"At one time," she said, "in spite of being a proud free woman of Ar, I felt the desire for the companionship of men."

"I understand," I said.

"I decided that I would permit them, certain ones of my careful choosing, of proper means and stations, to become acquainted with me, and that I might then, from among these, favor certain ones with the dignity and honor of my friendship. Then, perhaps, in time, if I felt so inclined, I might, if he were thoroughly pleasing and wholly suitable, consider acceding to the pleas of one to enter into companionship with me."

"And how did matters proceed?" I asked.

"I called together a number of young men," she said. "I informed them of my willingness to form acquaintances, and specified to them the strict conditions to which these relationships, absolute equality, and such, would be subject."

"And what happened?" I asked.

"All withdrew politely," she said, "and I never saw them again, with one exception, a little urt of a man who told me he shared my views, fully."

"You entered into companionship with him?" I asked.

"I discovered he was interested only in my wealth," she said. "I dismissed him."

"You were then angry and hurt," I said, "and began to devote yourself wholly to the pursuits of business."

"Yes," she said.

"Too," I said, "I gather, from other aspects of your story, that you became mercenary and greedy."

"Perhaps," she said.

"And then you were captured, and brought into the Barrens, and made a slave," I said.

"Yes," she said. "May I break this position?"

"No," I said.

"Do you like what you see?" she asked.

"You had better hope that I like what I see," I said.

She swallowed, hard.

"Yes," I said. "I like what I see."

"I suppose I should be grateful," she said.

"I think that I would be grateful if I were you," I said, "since you are a female slave."

"Of course," she said. "I do not wish to be quirted, or slain."

"Yes," I said.

"Do you enjoy posing naked women for your pleasure?" she asked.

"Yes," I said.

"Oh," she said.

"I think you feared your womanhood," I said. "That seems clear, even from your behavior in Ar. This is not unusual, incidentally, in a free woman, because deep womanhood, they sense, involves love, and love, for a woman, seems always to involve a bondage, if not of ropes and chains, of one sort or another."

She looked at me, tears in her eyes.

"Then, when you were, in effect, rejected as a woman, you were hurt and angry. You determined never to endure another such humiliating rejection. Too, understandably, you became hostile towards men. You would hate them. You would outdo them. You would have your vengeance on them. You came to fear certain sorts of feelings. You drew back even further from your womanhood."

"No, no, no," she wept, "I am a poor slave only because I am unresponsive! That is my nature! I cannot help it!"

"That is not your nature," I told her. "And you are going to help it."

"Master?" she asked.

"Crawl to the grass, there," I said. "Hurry!"

She crawled to the point, trembling, where I had indicated.

"Kneel to the whip," I ordered her.

She knelt there, trembling, her head down to the grass, her wrists crossed beneath her, as though bound.

I struck her thrice.

"Are you a whipped slave?" I asked.

"Yes," she wept, "I am a whipped slave."

"You belong to men," I told her. I gave her another stroke.

"Yes, Master!" she said.

"Are you going to be pleasing?" I asked. Another stroke.

"I will try to be pleasing!" she wept.

"I am sure you will, my dear," I said. "But the interesting question is whether or not you will succeed." I then gave her two more strokes.

"Oh," she wept. "Ohh."

"Do you beg now," I asked, "to return to the robe?"

"Yes, Master!" she said.

"Return, then, to the robe, Slave," I said.

Swiftly she crawled back to the robe. She lay on her stomach on its surface, grateful to be again within the perimeters of its relative safety. She was half choking and crying.

"On your back, Slave," I said, "hands at your sides, palms up, right knee lifted."

Wincing, she complied.

"What is the place of women!" I demanded.

"At the feet of men!" she wept.

"And where are you?" I asked.

"At your feet!" she wept.

"What are you?" I asked.

"A slave, a slave!" she said.

"Men have been patient long enough with you, Slave," I said. "That patience is now at an end."

"Yes, Master!" she wept.

"No longer are you a free woman," I said. "That is all behind you now. You are now only an imbonded female, only a slave, at the mercy of men."

"Yes, Master," she gasped, frightened.

"Accordingly," I said, "you are no longer to think of yourself as, or permit yourself to act like, a free woman. You are now, henceforth, to think and act like a slave. You are to feel as a slave, and live and love as a slave!"

"Yes, Master," she wept.

"Slave," I said.

"Yes, Master," she said.

"No impediment exists now," I said, "between you and your womanhood."

"No, Master," she said, frightened.

I dropped the quirt down near the robe. I then crouched down beside her. "When I touch you," I said, "you will feel, deeply and fully, richly and beautifully, gratefully, joyfully and submissively, and later, when you yield, you will yield totally and completely, irreservedly, helplessly, holding nothing back."

"But then I should be naught but a slave," she said, "helpless in the arms of her master."

"Yes," I said.

She looked at me, frightened.

I knelt beside her. "Sit up," I said. "Put your arms about my neck."

She obeyed.

"Slave lips," I commanded.

She pursed her lips and then I, gently, kissed them. "That was not so fearful now, was it?" I asked, drawing back.

"What do men, truly, want of slaves?" she whispered.

"Everything," I said.

"And what must a slave give them?" she asked.

"Everything," I said, "and more."

"I had feared, and hoped, it would be so," she said.

I smiled.

"You see," she said, "I am a slave."

"I know," I said. She was a woman.

"Have you read the *Prition* of Clearchus of Cos?" she said.

"What is a former free woman of Ar doing reading that?" I asked. It was a treatise on bondage.

" 'The slave,' " she quoted, " 'makes no bargains; she does not desire small demands to be placed upon her; she does not ask for ease; she asks nothing; she gives all; she seeks to love and selflessly serve.' "

"You quote it well," I said.

"You have read it?" she asked.

"Yes," I said. I remembered the passage clearly. The girl had perhaps, at one time, memorized it.

"I have always been fascinated with bondage," she said, "but I never expected, then, to find myself a slave."

"Kiss me, Slave," I said.

"Yes, Master," she said.

"Do you fear now," I asked, "as a slave, that you will be rejected?"

"I see now," she said, "as a slave, that it does not matter. It is not mine to fear such things, but rather to see to it that I am completely pleasing. If I am rejected, it matters not, for I am only a slave. As a slave I am nothing. I am meaningless and worthless. Thus what does it matter if I should be despised and spurned? I must then, only, try again, seeking anew, helplessly, to serve and love."

I did not respond to her. I did not think it necessary to tell her, and she would, in any case, soon learn it, that the least of the slave's fears is rejection. Rather she must fear quite the opposite. She must fear that the very sight of her will drive a man half mad with passion, and that he may not wish to rest until he gets his chains on her.

"In the *Prition,*" I said, "Clearchus, of course, is primarily concerned with only one form of bondage, that of the love slave."

"That is true," she said.

"There are many slaveries," I said, "and some are doubtless quite fearful and unpleasant."

"Yes," she shuddered. She had heard, I gathered, of certain agricultural slaveries, and of slaveries such as those in the public kitchens and laundries. Too, she was doubtless familiar with contempt slaveries and vengeance slaveries. One form of vengeance slavery is the proxy slavery, in which one woman, totally innocent, is enslaved and made to stand proxy for a hated, at-least-temporarily-inaccessible woman, even being given her name. The proxy, of course, being enslaved, is truly enslaved. Even if the hated woman is later captured the proxy is not freed. She is generally, merely, given away or sold.

"The common denominator," I said, "appears to be that the woman must be totally pleasing and, in all ways, is totally subject to the will of the Master."

"Yes, Master," she said.

"You may now kiss me again, Slave," I said.

"Yes, Master," she said.

I then lowered her to the robe. Her arms were still about my neck.

"Are you going to teach me to be pleasing?" she asked.

"Yes," I said.

"You will then," she smiled, "be improving, as you suggested, my master's property."

"Yes," I said. "But I am going to do more than teach you how to be pleasing."

"Oh?" she asked.

"Yes," I said. "When I am finished with you, my naked, collared beauty, you will be quite different than you are now."

She looked at me.

"I am going to make you into a man's dream of pleasure," I said.

"Do so," she said.

"Please, please," she wept. "Do not leave me! I beg you! Touch me more, please! I beg you to stay with me! I did not know it could be anything like this! Please, I beg you, touch me again!" She clutched me. Her tears were on my arm and chest.

"Do you beg it, as a slave?" I asked.

"Yes, Master," she said. "I beg it as a slave!"

"Very well," I said.

"What a fool I was as a free woman!" she whispered.

"You were only ignorant," I said.

"I did not know what it was like to be a slave, the helplessness, the sensations."

I did not respond.

"I did not know such feelings could exist," she said. "I never felt anything like them. They are so overwhelming."

"They have to do with dominance and submission," I said.

"I was afraid, in my yielding," she said, "that I might die."

"It was only a small slave orgasm," I said.

She looked at me, wonderingly.

"Beyond what you have experienced," I said, "lie indefinite horizons of ecstasy. No woman yet, I speculate, has numbered them."

"It is so much more than mere physical feeling," she said.

"It is such feeling in a cognitive matrix," I said. "It is psychophysical. It is an indissolubly emotional, physical and intellectual whole."

"I shall now need, often, the touch of a man," she said.

"Yes," I said.

"You have done this to me," she chided.

"It should have been done long ago," I said.

"But now," she said, "what if a man does not choose to satisfy me?"

"Try to be such that he will show you kindness," I said.

She shuddered. She was now much more at the mercy of men than she had ever suspected she could be. The slave fires in her belly, as it is said, had now been lit. She was now susceptible to the torments of the deprived slave. Free women, whose sexuality is usually, for most practical purposes, sluggish and inert, often have difficulty in understanding the desperation and intensity of these needs on the part of a female slave. They think that she is different from, and inferior to, themselves. If they themselves should be enslaved, of course, they are likely to soon revise these opinions. They, too, then may well find themselves moaning and scratching in their kennels, begging rude keepers for their touch, and being despised, in turn, by free women.

"You have ruined me for freedom," she said.

"Do you object?" I asked.

"No," she said. "I want to be a slave. I love being a slave."

"That is fortunate," I said, "for that is what you are."

"I have been a slave for months," she said. "I regret only that I have wasted all this time. I have waited until today to discover what it can be, truly, to be a slave."

"What do you feel about men?" I asked.

"They are interesting and beautiful," she said.

"Beautiful?" I asked.

"To my eyes," she smiled.

"And what else?" I asked.

"I know that they are my masters, that I need their touch and that I wish to serve them."

"Can you conceive of yourself kneeling before a man, head down, begging him for his caress?" I asked.

"Clearly," she said, "now that my sexuality has been awakened."

"Will he accede to your plea?" I asked.

"It would be my hope that he would," she said.

"Sometimes he may, sometimes he may not," I said. "There may come times when you will be grateful for so little as a cuffing or a kick."

"I must accept what I am given," she said. "I am a slave."

I then took her again in my arms. "Yes!" she breathed.

I lay on my side and the girl put a tiny piece of pemmican in my mouth.

I enjoyed having her feed me. She had, earlier, brought me water in her mouth, but, in its transfer, at the touch of her lips, it had only led to a new ravishment of her. I had then gone to the stream to satisfy my thirst.

"It is nearly sundown," I said.

"Then I must be returned to the herd," she moaned. "I must then be taken near the village with the others. I must then be hobbled and, a rope on my neck, be picketed with my string. How can I bear, now, to return to the herd?"

"I doubt that you will now be long kept in the herd," I said.

"I now need a man," she said. "I will do anything to be taken into a lodge, to serve."

"You are helpless now, aren't you?" I said.

"Yes, Master," she said. "May I leave the robe?"

"Yes," I said.

She went to the small hide in which the quirt had been wrapped. She picked it up and brought it to the edge of the robe. She spread it out there. "You told me," she said, smiling, "that this hide was about the size of a Tahari submission mat."

"Yes," I said.

"Behold," she said, smiling, her head down. "I kneel upon the mat."

I regarded her. A thousand memories rushed to my mind, of the vast, tawny Tahari, of its bleakness, and its dunes, of its caravans, of its oases and palaces. In the Tahari culture the submission mat has its place.

"In the Tahari," she asked, "might not girls, such as I, kneel on such mats?"

"Yes," I said. Many times I had seen such slaves, blond and beautiful, kneeling on such mats before dark masters.

"Oh!" she cried, seized and taken.

The girl knelt before me on the robe. Her head was down. "I beg your caress, Master," she said.

I smiled. Well did she remember our earlier conversation.

I looked at the sun through the trees. I thought there was time.

"Earn it," I said.

"Yes, Master," she said, happily.

Later I held her, again, in my arms. "We must start back now," I said.

"I know," she whispered.

I got up, and gathered my things together. "Roll the robe," I said. She did so. Then she knelt on the grass.

"Bind my hands and arms," she said, "so tightly that I cannot move them. Then march me back to the herd, a rope on my neck."

"No," I said. "You will walk back, quietly, before me."

"Yes, Master," she smiled.

I tied my things together with the rope. Then, the girl preceding me, we left the small grove. I looked back on it once. I had had a good time there.

13

I LEARN OF THE PRESENCE OF WANIYANPI

"Bring her forth, the red-haired slave," said Mahpiyasapa, chieftain of the Isbu Kaiila, standing before the lodge of Canka.

Canka stood, unafraid, his arms folded. "Winyela," he called.

The girl, frightened, emerged from the lodge and knelt down, near its threshold.

"It is she," said one of the men with Mahpiyasapa.

"It is she, who danced at the pole," said another.

"A pretty slave," said another.

"I want the woman," said Mahpiyasapa to Canka, indicating Winyela.

"You may not have her," said Canka.

"Speak, Wopeton," said Mahpiyasapa to Grunt, whom he had brought with him.

"My friend, Canka," said Grunt, "the woman was brought into the Barrens for Mahpiyasapa. He had ordered such a woman last year. It was for him that I purchased her in Kailiauk, near the Ihanke, and for him that I marched her eastward on my chain. The bargain was an old one, sealed last year. He is your chief. Give him the woman."

"No," said Canka.

"I was to receive five hides of the yellow kailiauk for her," said Grunt. "I do not wish, however, to have bad blood between two great warriors of the Isbu. Give her to Mahpiyasapa. I will forgo the hides."

"No," said Mahpiyasapa. "It will never be said that Mahpiyasapa did not speak with a straight tongue. When I receive the woman I will give you the hides."

"He may not have the woman," said Canka. "By capture rights she is mine. Mahpiyasapa, my chieftain, knows this. Mahpiyasapa, my chieftain, is Kaiila. He will not violate the customs of the Kaiila."

"There is truly to be peace between the Kaiila and the Yellow Knives," said Mahpiyasapa. "Watonka has arranged it. Even now civil chieftains of the Yellow Knives reside in his lodge."

"What is this to me?" asked Canka

"You have not behaved well," said Mahpiyasapa. "The woman should be mine. As chief I could take her to my lodge. But as chief I will not do this. I do not want to make you angry."

"Let me buy you two women, and give them to you for her," said Canka.

"That is the one I want," said Mahpiyasapa, indicating Winyela.

"That one," said Canka, "is mine."

"I want her," said Mahpiyasapa.

"She is mine, by capture right," said Canka.

Mahpiyasapa fell silent. He was angry.

"I am sorry, my chief," said Canka, "if I do not behave well. I am sorry if I have not acted in a way that is becoming to me. Had it been another woman I do not think I would have hesitated to bring her, her neck in a rope, to your lodge. This woman, however, as soon as I saw her, I knew that I wanted her. I know I could not rest until her neck was in my collar, until she was mine."

"I do not want her for myself," said Mahpiyasapa. "I want her for Yellow Knives. I and my fellows are going about the

"Good," said one of the lads.

"Back to the herd, girl," said another lad, urging his kaiila towards her.

She scrambled back to the herd, quickly inserting herself among her fellow, lovely beasts. Some of the other animals regarded her with envy, and wonder. She was much different now, clearly, than she had been earlier in the day. The acceptance of her womanhood, and her submission to men, and surrender to them, in her heart, is a pivotal thing in the psychic life of a female. A similar moment of great psychic import occurs, of course, in the life of a man when he accepts manhood. Thenceforth, he repudiates lies and spurious images. Thenceforth he will be a man.

"It is sundown," said one of the lads. "We must get these she-kaiila to the village, where we shall hobble and picket them for the night."

Some of the beasts, I saw, regarded the blond girl, now, with loathing. Others, however, came up to her and kissed her, gently, welcoming her to the sisterhood of the collar. How wretched and peevish are those, themselves so resentful and constricted, who begrudge others the vitalities and pleasures of their honesty.

"Hei!" called two or three of the lads, lifting their coiled ropes.

"My thanks, lads!" I yelled.

They waved, acknowledging my words. I stepped back, watching, then, the herd being slowly moved toward the village.

The blond girl turned once, and waved to me, and then blew me a kiss in the Gorean fashion, kissing and brushing it to me with her fingers. I returned the kiss, and waved, too. Then I made my own way back to the village. I was to meet Cuwignaka at the lodge of Canka. We were to have boiled meat for supper.

"That was good," I said.

"Thank you, Master," said Winyela.

"Do not spoil the slave," warned Canka.

"Sorry," I said.

"It was splendid!" said Cuwignaka.

"Thank you, Master," said Winyela, smiling. The repast had been far more than boiled meat. It had been, in effect, a rich stew, crowded with vegetables and seasonings. Some, I knew, Winyela had begged from Grunt.

"Do you not think so?" asked Cuwignaka of Canka.

"Maybe," said Canka.

"Did my master enjoy his meal?" asked Winyela.

"Maybe," said Canka.

"A miserable slave hopes that her pathetic efforts to be pleasing to her master have been successful," she said.

"It was not bad, maybe," said Canka.

"Do not spoil the slave," warned Cuwignaka.

"I love serving you, Master," said Winyela.

"Even if you did not like serving me," said Canka, "you would do it, and perfectly."

"Yes, Master," she said.

"For you are a slave," he said.

"Yes, Master," she said. "And your slave."

He regarded her.

"If I do not please you, beat me," she said.

"Have no fear," said Canka. "If you are not pleasing, it will be done."

"Do you think she will be often beaten?" asked Cuwignaka.

"I do not think it likely," I said.

"Master," whispered Winyela to Canka. Her eyes were moist. I saw his eyes, glinting upon her fiercely.

"There were many vegetables in the stew," I said to Cuwignaka, pretending not to notice the intensity between Canka and Winyela. Indeed, we had had to eat much of the stew from small bowls, filled by Winyela with a kailiauk-bone ladle. Some larger pieces of vegetable and meat, we had, however, in the informal fastion of the Barrens, taken from the pot on our knives. Canka, perhaps because company was present, or because he wished to further impress her slavery upon her, had fed Winyela. This is occasionally done with a slave. It helps to remind them that they are domestic animals, and that they are dependent for their very food upon their master. I had noticed, during the meal, how she had taken food from his fingers, biting and sucking, and kissing, furtively at them. During the course of the meal she had been becoming more and more excited. Too, I had thought that Canka had given her smaller bits and pieces, and had held on to them more tightly, than was necessary to merely feed her. "That is unusual, isn't it?" I asked.

"Yes," said Cuwignaka. "That is produce, for the most part, from the fields of the Waniyanpi."

"I had thought it might be," I said. The Waniyanpi were, substantially, agricultural slaves. They farmed and gardened, and did other work for their red masters. "Were men sent forth to the compounds to fetch the produce?" I asked.

"The Waniyanpi have delivered it," said Cuwignaka. "It is done that way when it is the great camp which is in question."

"I see," I said. During the feasting times, those generally correlated with the coming of the kailiauk, the locations of the great camps of the various tribes were well known. This made feasible the delivery of produce, something which would be correspondingly impractical most of the year, when the tribes had separated into scattered bands, and sometimes even smaller units, with temporary, shifting camps. "Are there Waniyanpi now in camp?" I asked.

"Yes," said Cuwignaka, "but they will be leaving soon."

"How soon?" I asked.

"I do not know," said Cuwignaka.

"I met some Waniyanpi," I said. "They were from a place they referred to as 'Garden Eleven.' I wonder if those in camp would be from there."

"They might be," said Cuwignaka. "Why?"

"I thought it might be interesting to renew my acquaintances among them," I said. "Too, I would be interested to learn of the whereabouts and condition of one who was once the Lady Mira, of Venna, who, enslaved, was sentenced by her red masters to reside with the Waniyanpi."

"I remember her," said Cuwignaka, bitterly. "Long days I spent, chained to her cart."

"Surely you are sorry for her," I said, "given, in particular, the almost unspeakable cruelty, for a woman, of her sentence, of her punishment?"

"She was a proud and arrogant woman," said Cuwignaka. "I do not pity her."

"But she has known other forms of life," I said. "It is not like she was born and raised in such a compound."

"I do not pity her," said Cuwignaka.

"Surely she, now, honored and denied, celebrated and deprived, would be ready to beg for her own stripping, for the stroke of a man's lash, for the feel of her ankles being tied apart, widely and securely, in a leg stretcher."

"I do not pity her," said Cuwignaka. "She was harsh and cruel. Let her languish, an unfulfilled slave, in the compounds of the Waniyanpi."

"You are cruel," I said.

"I am Kaiila," shrugged Cuwignaka.

"Perhaps if she prostrated herself, naked, before you, begging for mercy, you might be disposed to show her some lenience," I speculated.

"Perhaps, if I thought she was now ready to be a woman, and had learned her lessons," said Cuwignaka.

"Ah," I said, "I see that you might be swayed to generosity."

"Of course," grinned Cuwignaka. "I am Kaiila." He then gestured to Canka and Winyela. She was now in his arms, her head back. She was sobbing with pleasure. She was oblivious of our presence. "Too," he said, "there is something to be said for female slaves."

"That is true," I said. How beautiful was Winyela, lost in her helplessness, her pleasure and love. How marvelous and beautiful are women! How glorious it is to own them, to be able to do what one wishes with them and to love them! But then I thought soberly of she who had once been the Lady Mira, of Venna, who had once, as the agent of Kurii, been my enemy. No such fulfillments and joys, it seemed, were for her. She had been condemned instead to the compounds of the Waniyanpi. She had been sentenced to honor and dignity, and equality with the pathetic males of the compound. She would not know, it seemed, the joys of being run, naked, a rope on her neck, a slave, at the flanks of a master's kaiila, the pleasures of, tremblingly, loving and serving, knowing that he whom one loves and serves owns one, fully, the fulfillments of finding oneself, uncompromisingly and irrevocably, in one's place in the order of nature, lovingly, at one's master's feet.

"We shall come back later," said Cuwignaka to Canka, getting up. But, Canka, too, I fear, lost in the sweetnesses and beauties, in the love and pleasure, of his woman, did not hear us.

Cuwignaka and I, smiling, left the lodge.

"Where are the Waniyanpi?" I asked.

"In the lower end of the camp, at the edge of the camp," said Cuwignaka, "where the drainage is worst."

"I should have known," I said.

"We put them there," said Cuwignaka.

"Of course," I said.

"Are you going to see them?" asked Cuwignaka.

"Yes," I said.

"I do not think I will come," said Cuwignaka. "I do not much care for the company of Waniyanpi."

"Very well," I said.

"Meet me back at the lodge of Canka, later," said Cuwignaka.

"Why?" I asked. I thought perhaps Canka and Winyela might prefer to be left alone.

"I heard from Akihoka, who is friends with one of the Sleen Soldiers, that Hci is going to be up to something tonight," grinned Cuwignaka.

"What?" I asked.

"I am not sure," said Cuwignaka, "but I think I know. And I think I know how we can foil him."

"What is this all about?" I asked.

"It has to do with the giveaways," said Cuwignaka.

"I do not understand," I said.

"Meet me back here, later," said Cuwignaka.

"Very well," I said.

"I am so much yours," we heard Winyela say, from within the lodge. "I am so much yours, my master!"

Cuwignaka and I smiled, and then we took our separate ways.

14

WANIYANPI

"Pumpkin!" I said, pleased.

"Peace, and light, and tranquillity, and contentment and goodness be unto you," he said.

"I had heard that there were Waniyanpi in camp," I said. "I had hoped that it might be you, and others from your group."

"We have delivered vegetables to our masters," said Pumpkin. "You remember Carrot and Cabbage?"

"Yes," I said. "Greetings, Fellows."

"Sweetness be unto you," said Carrot.

"Sweetness be unto you," said Cabbage.

"Who is this?" asked a dark-haired woman, belligerently. She, too, wore the garb of the Waniyanpi. That is a long, gray dress, which falls between the knees and ankles. Her feet, too, were wrapped in rags. This garb is unattractive on women, doubtless intendedly so. On men, similarly, it appears ungainly and foolish.

"I do not think you met Radish," said Pumpkin.

"No," I said.

"Who are you?" asked Radish.

"Radish is the leader of our small expedition to the camp," said Pumpkin, "and is, for most practical purposes, first in the compound, in our home, Garden Eleven, although we all are, of course, the same."

"Of course," I said.

"Who are you?" asked Radish.

I looked at her. She was surly, and, obviously, badly in need of a whipping.

"I am Tatankasa, Red Bull," I said, "the slave of Canka, Fire-Steel, of the Isbu Kaiila, of the Little-Stones band of the Kaiila," in a mixture of both Kaiila and Gorean.

I continued to look at her. I did not think that she was, objectively, a bad-looking woman. Beneath the ugly garment she wore there were the suggestions of an attractive figure. I wondered what she would look like naked and bound, kneeling at a man's feet, under his quirt.

"You are a slave," she said.

"So are you," I said.

"We wear no collars," she said.

"You do not need collars to be recognized as slaves," I said.

She glared at me, angrily. I considered stripping her, and putting her to my feet.

"Many who are slaves do not wear collars," I said. "Many who are slaves do not even know that they are slaves."

"That is true," said Pumpkin, agreeably.

"Do not speak further to this person," said Radish, turning away.

"How long are you going to be in camp?" I asked.

"I am sorry," said Pumpkin. "I should not speak further to you now. It is the wish of Radish."

"You are a slave. She is a slave. You are all supposed to be the same. What does it matter?" I asked.

"I suppose it does not matter," said Pumpkin. "But I would not wish to displease Radish."

"Why not?" I asked.

"Waniyanpi are supposed to be loving, accommodating and pleasing," said Pumpkin. 'Waniyanpi' is a Kaiila expression. It means "tame cattle."

"And is Radish loving, accommodating and pleasing?" I asked.

"Not really," said Pumpkin. "That is an interesting thought." He looked at me. "We are leaving in the morning," he said.

"I told you not to talk to him," said Radish, from a few feet away.

"Please be quiet, Radish," said Pumpkin. She turned away, angrily.

"Sweetness be unto you," said Pumpkin.

"How far away is your compound?" I asked.

"Some one hundred pasangs from here," said Pumpkin.

"I did not know you had kaiila," I said.

"We do not," said Pumpkin. "We came afoot, dragging travois, laden with our produce, in the charge of a boy."

"I thought Radish was the leader of the expedition," I said.

"She is the Waniyanpi leader," he said. "We all, of course, must take our orders from our red masters."

"How is she who was the Lady Mira, of Venna?" I asked. The Lady Mira, of Venna, had been an agent of Kurii. She had been in political command, under Kog and Sardak, of a force of approximately a thousand mercenaries, the human contingent accompanying Kog and Sardak, and their death squad, into the Barrens. The military command of these mercenaries, also under Kog and Sardak, who would have retained supreme command, had been in the hands of Alfred, a mercenary captain from Port Olni. The chain of command, then, for most practical purposes, except tactical stiuations, would have been Kurii, then the Lady Mira, and then Alfred, the captain from Port Olni. After the joint attack and massacre of a few weeks ago, the Lady Mira had been captured and, presumably because she had been found with soldiers, sent to a Waniyanpi compound. Alfred had managed to escape with a mounted force of perhaps some four hundred riders. He, presumably, had, by now, made his way back to the Ihanke, to civilization and safety. Small bands of warriors, the sorts which make up common war parties, would not be likely to attack a force of that size.

"The Lady Mira, of Venna?" asked Pumpkin.

"The blond woman, given to you by the red savages after the battle," I said. "I think you were going to call her 'Turnip.' "

"Turnip, of course," said Pumpkin.

"How is she doing?" I asked.

"She is fitting in very nicely," he said. "She has embraced the teaching zealously. She is now a happy and confirmed Same."

"And what if she were not?" I asked.

"Then," said Pumpkin, "regrettably, we would have to put

her out of the compound, into the Barrens, without food and water."

"You would kill her?" I said.

"No, no!" said Pumpkin. "Waniyanpi are not permitted to kill. We would only have to put her out."

"You would, then, let the Barrens do your killing for you," I said.

"She might survive," he said.

"Possibly," I said.

"It always makes us sad to have to put someone out," he said.

"I can imagine," I said.

"Surely you cannot expect us to permit the existence of false ideas in the compound?" he asked.

"Why not?" I asked.

"I do not know," he said.

"Perhaps you fear your beliefs, if presented with plausible alternatives, might fare badly?"

"No, no," he said. "Truth does not need to be afraid of falsity. Truth is not fearful and weak."

"I am glad to hear it," I said. "So what is wrong with having a few false ideas around?"

"It is against the teaching," said Pumpkin.

"Why?" I asked.

"I do not know," said Pumpkin.

"Perhaps it is feared someone might believe one," I said.

"How could anyone do that?" he scoffed.

"Perhaps some depraved or benighted individual," I suggested.

"Perhaps," he said.

"Thus," I said, "ignorance is the bulwark of truth."

"Perhaps," granted Pumpkin.

"But here is an interesting thought," I said. "What if your beliefs are not true, but false. How would you ever find out about it?"

"I suppose we might not," said Pumpkin. "Thus, it is fortunate for us that our beliefs are true."

"How do you know?" I asked.

"It is one of our beliefs," he said.

"Sameness is a lie," I said. "And it is not even a subtle or plausible lie. It is obviously and patently a lie."

"It is not to be questioned," said Pumpkin. "Even if it is a lie it is a lie which lies at the very foundation of our society. It is the premise of our world. All worlds have their myths. The alternative to the myth is chaos."

"The alternative of falsehood," I said, "is not chaos, but truth."

"One must believe something," said Pumpkin.

"Try truth," I said.

"Would you like to see Turnip?" he asked.

"Is she here?" I asked.

"Yes," he said. "We did not wish to bring her, but the boy who was in charge of us picked her out to come along, thus giving us, appropriately, an exactly equal number of males and females."

"Why 'appropriately'?" I asked. "If you are all the same, what difference should it make? Why not all males or all females, or any ratio?"

"I suppose you are right," said Pumpkin. "We ourselves do not distinguish between males and females."

"That, at least, if peculiar, is consistent," I said. "But you have noticed, surely, that there seem to be some differences between males and females."

"We try not to notice that," said Pumpkin.

"Have you noticed," I asked, "that males are better at dragging heavy weights across the prairie than women?"

"We notice, of course," said Pumpkin, "that not all Sames are of equal size or strength."

"And have you noticed, further," I asked, "that there seems to be a correlation between the stronger Sames and those the red savages regard as males, and between the slighter, weaker Sames and those the red savages regard as females?"

"I try not to notice such things," said Pumpkin.

"Were you harnessed to a travois?" I asked.

"Yes," said Pumpkin.

"How many pulled it with you?" I asked.

"I, alone, drew it," he said.

"And what of some of the other travois," I asked, "those drawn by the smaller, slighter Sames. How were they harnessed?"

"Five to a travois," shrugged Pumpkin. "But the trek is long, and the weight is heavy."

"I see," I said. "Where is Turnip?"

"I will show you," said Pumpkin. "She is with one of the groups. You will be pleased to see how she turned out."

I followed Pumpkin through, and behind, several lodges. Then, in a few moments, we came to a place where a low, sloping shelter, of travois poles, sticks and canvas, had been erected. I could see some similar shelters in the nearby vicinity.

"Have these women been brought to the camp to be bred with other Waniyanpi?" I asked. "It seems they have been prepared for what you folk refer to as 'the Ugly Act.' Is the day of Waniyanpi Breeding at hand?"

"No," said Pumpkin, laughing. "It is done for other reasons."

The five women sitting near the shelter, in their drab garments, all had sacks tied over their heads, knotted under their chins. For the day of Waniyanpi Breeding, male Waniyanpi from one compound are marched, hooded, to the vicinity of some other compound. Near it they are led to hooded, stripped Waniyanpi women, selected for breeding, from the other compound, lying bound in a maize field. There, then, between hooded couples, under the whips of red masters, are fulfilled the offices of the day of Waniyanpi Breeding. This is supposedly the only physical contact, incidentally, which takes place between Waniyanpi men and women.

As would be expected, their tiny, pathological culture, implicitly or explicitly, to one degree or another, is opposed to sexuality. For example, sexual inertness and frigidity are praised as virtues. Similarly, an attempt is made, through such things as verbal abuse and ridicule, to make individuals with truly powerful sexual drives succumb to irrational guilts and shames. "True persons," which is a euphemism for conformists to the social norms, are supposed to be "above sex," or, at least, to recognize its "relative unimportance," or to understand that it may be acceptable, in some "place," or other, which is never clarified. That a given individual of strong passions could scream with the need for sexual release is something that they cannot understand or which, somehow, terrifies them. They are flowers and, it seems, lack the senses which would enable them to understand such things as hungers and storms. Buttercups and lions will perhaps always be mutually unintelligible to one another. Most simply, perhaps, sexuality is regarded by the Waniyanpi as being inimical to Sameness, as being subversive of the Identity thesis so essential to its madness. Too, in an interesting concession to putative sexual difference, sexuality, by the Waniyanpi, is regarded as being demeaning to women.

It is not clear, historically, whether the values of slaves were imposed on the Waniyanpi by their masters, or whether the

Waniyanpi invented their *ethos* to dignify and enoble their own weakness. It may be mentioned that, interestingly, since the Waniyanpi repudiate nature, and natural relationships, that there is, in the compounds, an unusual incidence of homosexuality, both of the male and female varieties. This is perhaps a natural enough development considering the conditioned obstacles placed in the way of more usual relationships. It also fits in better with the values of Sameness. To be sure, officially the Waniyanpi disparage all sex, despite the relative countenance tacitly afforded by their *ethos* to the homosexual relationship. Where natural sexuality is prohibited there is little alternative, obviously, but to choose among competitive perversions. The prescribed choice for the Waniyanpi, of course, is lofty abstinence, pretending no problems exist. The reason that Waniyanpi breeding takes place in a maize field, incidentally, seems to be that, in the medicine beliefs of the red savages, the example of their breeding is supposed to encourage the maize to flourish.

"What are the other reasons?" I asked.

"There are two," said Pumpkin, regarding the hooded women. "The first is that we thus hide their faces from the red savages, and thus reduce the probability of their being taken away from us."

"Their clothing," I said, "to a large extent, hides their figures."

"Yes," said Pumpkin, embarrassed.

"Frankly," I said, "I do not think they are in much danger. The red savages have their pick of many women, lovely, vital women, many of them nude and collared, and trained, like she-kaiila, to service their pleasures. I do not think they would be likely to be much interested in Waniyanpi females." Such females, I adjudged, from seeing Radish, and the men, would be unpleasant and rigid, or, more likely, dismal, miserable, drab, lackluster and uninteresting. It would be difficult, in a slave market, even to give away such women. It was interesting to speculate whether under a proper regimen of whipping, bonds and training something might be done with them. "What is the second reason?" I asked.

"We do not want them to see red-savage males," he said.

"Why?" I asked.

"It makes it harder for them, sometimes, then," he said, "to be content, again, in the compounds. It makes it more difficult for them, sometimes, to continue to accept and practice the teaching, for them to adhere to the truths of Sameness."

"I understand," I said. That true men existed was something which, for most purposes, was to be kept from the Waniyanpi women. It was better for them, perhaps, not to know of their existence. Let them continue to think of men along the lines of the despicable, pathetic males of the Waniyanpi compounds. That would surely make their life easier. How miserable and frustrated they might be, to see a real man, and, their womanhood awakening, to know that they, Waniyanpi females, must continue, as though nothing had happened, to devote themselves to gardening and hypocrisy. It made sense that they should be hooded in the vicinity of the camp, particularly a summer camp. Surely it would be embarrassing, too, to Waniyanpi men, such as Pumpkin, if one of their females should tear off her clothes and throw herself naked to the feet of a red warrior, begging for the tightness of his ropes and the slash of his quirt.

"That one is Turnip, is it not?" I asked, indicating one of the seated women.

"Yes," said Pumpkin.

"Why is Radish not hooded?" I asked.

"She is so strong that she does not need the hood," said Pumpkin. "Too, for most practical purposes, she is first in the compound. It was on her orders that we hooded the other women."

"She did not trust them," I said.

"Of course she trusts them," said Pumpkin. "They are all wonderful Sames."

"Then why are they hooded?" I asked.

"Even a Same," said Pumpkin, "might occasionally have a moment of weakness."

"I see," I said. "It has been nice speaking to you, Pumpkin. You may now go."

"Of course," said Pumpkin. "I trust her. She is a wonderful Same." He then withdrew. I watched him leave. I rather, for no reason that was clear to me, liked Pumpkin. This time, in speaking to him, he had seemed somewhat less dogmatic than he had the first time, a few weeks ago, in the vicinity of the battlefield. He had a strong native intelligence, I suspected, which, for too long, had been somnolent. He had kept himself from thinking for years. Now, I suspected, he might be wondering whether or not he might think, and, if so, what might come of it. This can be an exciting time in the life of any human being. Somewhere beneath the gray garb of Pumpkin, I suspected, might lurk the heart of a heretic.

I walked over to the vicinity of the hooded Waniyanpi women, those near the closest shelter of sticks, poles and canvas. There were five of them. They were seated, mostly cross-legged, on the ground. Gray sacks had been tied over their heads, knotted with cords under their chins. I went and stood before she whom I took to be Turnip, the former beautiful agent of Kurii.

In moccasins my approach was undetected.

I cleared my throat, that they might know of my presence.

She whom I took to be Turnip, and the others, as well, lifted their heads in the sacks.

"Pumpkin?" asked the woman whom I took to be Turnip.

I did not respond. The women had remained seated, as they had been. Assuming that I must be a Waniyanpi male they did not, of course, show me respect, let alone submission.

"Carrot? Cabbage?" asked the woman.

I had cleared my throat, to announce my presence to the women. This sound, polite, almost apologetic, had been performed deliberately. It would be a way, I conjectured, in which a Waniyanpi male, courteously, might announce his presence to his lovely, hooded colleagues. I wished to see their reactions. They had been as I had expected, in effect, nothing.

"Squash? Beans?" she asked, her voice now slightly faltering.

I did not, again, respond.

"Surely you are of the Waniyanpi?" she said. It did not occur to her that one who was not of the Waniyanpi would approach them, drab Waniyanpi women.

"No," I said.

Hurriedly, then, the five women knelt. They knelt with their knees pressed closely together and their heads inclined. Deference, thus, slaves, did they display, knowing themselves in the presence of one who was not of the Waniyanpi. Only their own men it was whom they needed not, and did not, show respect. How different, I mused, would have been their responses, from the beginning, had they not been females of the Waniyanpi, but Gorean pleasure slaves. To be sure I had not announced my presence to them, and by design, as might have a typical Gorean male. Such a male, entering among hooded slaves, in particular, pleasure slaves, might have signified his presence by smiting his thigh once, or by twice clapping his hands, sharply, perhaps, at the same time, calling, "Position." Such women, then, had they been hooded Gorean pleasure slaves, and not Waniyanpi females, would have scrambled to kneel, and beautifully and vitally. Too, they would have knelt with their knees widely spread, exposing the soft interiors of their opened thighs, indicating thereby, and sensitively and beautifully, their vulnerability to male might and their submission to male power.

Gorean pleasure slaves, incidentally, are occasionally used hooded. The hood, of course, can increase the female's sense of vulnerability and sexual helplessness. She does not know, for example, where she will be next struck or caressed. Similarly the hood is sometimes used when the master lends or consigns the slave to others, she being hooded, perhaps, before the guests arrive, or, perhaps, after she has served them their supper and liqueurs. She may then, perhaps with other slaves, hooded, too, be turned about, and then knelt at the feet of one or another of the guests. She, and the other slaves, too, of course, must then serve the guest, or guests, to whom they have been assigned with perfection. Too, their use may be gambled for, or lots drawn for it.

I crouched before the woman whom I took to be Turnip. I held her by the upper arms. She raised her head, in the sack.

"No," she said, "you are not Waniyanpi. I can tell by your touch."

"Oh?" I said.

"That you touch me, as they would not," she said, "but, too, how you touch me, how you hold me."

"How is that?" I asked.

"With authority," she said, "as a man holds a woman."

"I see," I said.

With my hands, and thumbs, then, gently, I pressed back the sack, closely, about her face, that the outlines of her features might emerge through the cloth.

"You are she," I asked, "who was once the Lady Mira, of Venna?"

"Yes," she said, "yes."

"Formerly of the merchants?" I asked.

"Yes," she said. I saw her lips move under the cloth.

"Formerly a mercenary," I said, "formerly an agent in the service of Kurii?"

"Who are you?" she asked, frightened.

"You may respond to my question," I informed her. My thumbs, then, were at her throat. She felt their pressure.

"Yes," she whispered. "I was formerly a mercenary. I was formerly in the service of Kurii."

"What are you now?" I asked.

"Only a Waniyanpi slave," she said.

"It is true," I told her. I removed my thumbs from her throat.

"Who are you?" she asked.

"We met," I said, "a few weeks ago, in the vicinity of the field of battle. You had been stripped and yoked by your red masters. You were tethered to a wagon axle. It was before you were taken to a Waniyanpi compound."

"It was you," she said, "who struck me with a quirt and forced me to give you an account of the battle."

"Yes," I said.

"You were merciless," she said. "You made me speak as though I might have been a slave."

"It was appropriate," I said. "You were a slave."

"Even then?" she asked.

"Yes," I said.

She reached out her hand, timidly. She touched, and felt, the collar at my throat.

"You, too, now, are a slave," she said. "We are both the slaves of red masters."

"Yes," I said. "We are both perhaps fortunate to have been spared. It is their country."

"Perhaps there could be a little tenderness between slaves," she said.

"I understand that you are now called 'Turnip,'" I said.

"Yes," she said. "I am Turnip."

"I am Tatankasa, Red Bull," I said. "I am the slave of Canka, Fire-Steel, of the Isbu Kaiila."

"You have at least a single master," she said. "We belong to the band, to the Isbu Kaiila."

"How are you faring?" I asked.

"What a silly question!" she laughed, rather pronouncedly. "I am faring very well, of course!"

"I am glad to hear it," I said.

"Becoming of the Waniyanpi has changed my life," she assured me, speaking clearly and a bit loudly. "I cannot tell you how fulfilled and happy I am. It has wrought a most wondrous transformation in my existence."

"I see," I said.

"We are joyful dung," she said. "We are sparkles on the water, making the streams pretty. We are flowers growing in the fields. We are nice. We are good."

"I understand," I said.

"I am now a convinced and happy Same," she said. "I am

now not a not-the-Same. That must be clearly understood. I am not a not-the-Same. I am a Same."

"I understand," I said.

"I have fully and happily embraced the teaching," she said. "It will not be necessary, as first it might have appeared, to put me out into the Barrens, without food and water. All is one, and one is all, and the same is the same. The teaching is the truth, and the truth is the teaching."

I glanced about, at the other Waniyanpi women kneeling near her. They were, I take it, her harness mates, responsible with her, I supposed, for drawing one of the travois.

"Are you happy?" I asked her.

"Yes," she said. "I am wonderfully and gloriously happy. That must be clearly understood."

"I understand," I said.

"Oh," she said, lifted in my arms. I then carried her several yards away, among the lodges. I then lowered her to her knees in a quiet spot.

"Are we alone?" she begged.

"Yes," I said.

She began to sob inside her hood.

She reached out, desperately, and held me about the legs, I standing before her. She pressed her cheek against my thigh. I could feel the hood, hot and damp, soaked with tears, between her cheek and my leg.

"Save me from them," she wept. "They are lunatics. They foreswear the most obvious truths of human nature. Among them the males cannot be men and the females cannot be women. It is a sick, perverted world! They struggle against passion. They are afraid to feel. They are terrorized by desire. They pervert their reason. They deny their senses. They are mad, all of them!"

I crouched down and took the sobbing woman in my arms.

"They will make me ashamed of my body," she wept. "They may drive me insane, I do not want their dismal peace, their pathological tranquillity, their vacuous serenity. I am not a turtle. I am not a vegetable. I am a woman. I want to be what I am, truly. I do not want to be ashamed of my needs or my sex. I want to live, and feel!"

She was Gorean woman. This had made the transition to a Waniyanpi community additionally difficult for her. The transition, presumably, because of their conditioning and upbringing, having acclimated them to what, in effect, were

Waniyanpi values, would doubtless have been much easier for a woman from Earth.

"It is not wrong to want to be alive, is it?" she asked.

"No," I said, "it is not wrong to want that."

"They pretend to be happy," she said, "but they are not happy. They are miserable, and filled with hate."

"Let us rejoice," I said, "that their madness is confined to a handful of isolated compounds in the wilderness." How frightful it would be, I thought, if such an arid lunacy should infect a wider domain.

"Save me from them," she begged.

"It is not practical," I said.

She sobbed anew, and I held her more closely.

"You were found with the soldiers," I said. "That is doubtless why you were sent to a Waniyanpi community. It is your punishment."

"A most just and suitable punishment," she said, bitterly.

"Yes," I said. It was a particularly terrible punishment, of course, for a woman such as she, one who had some idea of the possibilities of life and feeling.

"Better to be the lowest slave, naked and chained, of the cruelest master on Gor," she said.

"Yes," I said.

"Look," she said, drawing back, sobbing, putting her hands to the hood. "They are afraid even to let us see true men."

"It is perhaps more merciful that way," I said. "That way, perhaps, you will experience less distress and torment when you return to the Waniyanpi compound."

"But I have known true men," she said.

"That makes it much harder for you, of course," I admitted.

"I hunger for the touch of a true man," she said. "Waniyanpi males are weak, pathetic and meaningless."

"It may not be their fault," I said. "They may be only trying to fulfill the stereotypes of their culture."

"We were made to chew sip roots on the way to the camp," she said, "to protect us, if our red masters should choose to seize and rape us."

"The precaution, however," I said, "proved unnecessary, did it not?"

"Yes," she said. "We are only Waniyanpi females. No man wants us."

I did not speak.

"They do not fear our men, do they?" she asked.

"No," I laughed. "Even a boy would think nothing of using you in the presence of an entire work crew of Waniyanpi males, if he felt like it. They would not interfere."

"Why are we not desired?" she asked.

"You are taught, explicitly or implicitly," I said, "to behave and dress unattractively, even, so to speak, to think unattractively. Most males, thusly, assuming them to be vital and healthy, would not be likely to find a Waniyanpi woman of much interest. They might tend to think of them as being, in some odd way, repulsively unnatural, or, perhaps, worse, as being mentally ill. Too, of course, in the camps of our red masters you must realize that there are alternatives available."

"We are not really like that," she said.

"I do not suppose you are," I said.

"We have needs and hungers, too," she said.

"I suppose you do," I said. It did seem to me that the usual male assessment of the Waniyanpi female was likely to be somewhat hasty and negative. Men are often too abrupt, it seems to me, in their judgments. They might profit from some instruction in patience. Such women, unfulfilled as females, starved for male domination, I supposed, taken sternly in hand, stripped and put to a man's feet, might prove to be grateful and rewarding slaves. In a matter of days, I suspected, it might be difficult to tell one, licking and kissing at one's feet, warmly, lovingly and gratefully, from a more normal slave.

"I suppose, if a man were sufficiently desperate," she said, "he might find us of interest."

"Probably," I said. Studies and case histories suggested that this sort of thing was true.

"The least desirable," she said, bitterly, "are the last desired."

"Perhaps," I said.

"It is so ironic!" she said.

"What?" I asked.

"When I was free, in Venna, and elsewhere," she said, "I was desired and could not be obtained. Now that I am a slave and can be obtained, I am not desired."

"I see," I said.

"It is a new experience for me, and one not to my liking, not to be desired."

"Oh?" I said.

"I had thought, when free," she said, "that if ever I fell slave, men would put me frequently to their pleasure."

"That is common with slaves," I said. "It was a fair assumption."

"And that I must needs fear only that I might not sufficiently please them."

"To be sure," I said, "a natural fear with slaves."

"But not once," she said, "have I been put to the service of my masters."

"Surely you have frightened fleer from the maize, gardened and picked produce," I said.

"But not once," she said, angrily, "have they put me to their intimate service, forcing me to perform with the skills and talents of the female slave."

"It is perhaps just as well," I said. "You were a free woman, and you have not had much training. If you did not do well, you might be whipped severely, or perhaps slain."

"Oh," she said.

"Being a slave girl is very different from being a free woman," I said. "From a free woman a man expects little, or nothing. From a slave girl, on the other hand, he expects, as it is said, everything, and more."

"I understand," she said.

"A free woman may be valueless and, if she wishes, account this a virtue. A slave, on the other hand, must be superbly pleasing. She must see to it, with all her intelligence and beauty, that she is her master's attentive, sensitive, skillful treasure."

"I would like to be such a treasure to a man," she said.

I did not speak.

"May I call you 'Master'? " she asked.

"Yes," I said.

"Master," she said.

"Yes," I said.

"When I was free, I was regarded as being very beautiful. Indeed, it was said by some that I was as beautiful, even, as a slave."

"A high compliment," I acknowledged. I recalled the first time I had ever seen her, on her curule chair, on her high cart, in the column of the Kurii and mercenaries. She had worn the robes of concealment, but only a wisp of diaphanous silk, presumably by intent, had feigned to hide her features. I recalled, even then, wondering what she might look like in the shimmering dancing silks of an enslaved female or, say, stripped and collared, crawling to a man's feet.

"Master," she said.

"Yes," I said.

How different, then, was that absurd pretense of a veil, that sweet diaphanous sheen of material, compared to the rude, coarse sack which had now been tied over her head. How disgusting were the Waniyanpi.

"Surely I am no less beautiful now than I was then," she said.

"Perhaps," I granted her.

"And now I am a slave," she said.

"That is true," I said.

"Have me," she begged, suddenly. "Touch me. Caress me. Hold me. Take me!"

"But you are a Waniyanpi female," I said, "above sex. That has been decided by your masters."

"I am a slave," she said. "I need the touch of a man."

"But you have been rescued from sex," I said. "You have been accorded honor and dignity. You have been made identical to a certain form of male. This is supposed to be what you want. You are now, your nature betrayed and nullified, supposed to be happy and fulfilled."

"I am miserable," she wept.

"Interesting," I said.

"I am a woman," she said. "I need attention as a woman. Comfort me. Hold me. Be kind to me."

I did not speak.

"Whip me, beat me, if you wish," she said, "but pay attention to me as a woman. I am a woman. Let me, I beg you, be a woman."

"That is not permitted, as I understand it," I said, "to the Waniyanpi female."

"I have been put with the Waniyanpi," she said. "It was my punishment. But I am not one of them. Take pity on me. Have mercy on me. I am not truly a Waniyanpi female. I am a woman. I have the feelings of a woman. I want the sensations of a woman. I need the sensations of a woman. Have mercy on me, Master!"

"You do not now seem to be a proud agent of Kurii," I said.

"I am no longer an agent of Kurii," she said. "I am now only a female slave."

"And a pleading slave, it seems," I said.

"Yes," she said, "I am now only a pleading female slave."

I did not speak.

"I know, now," she said, "that I am not garbed attractively

and that a sack has been put over my head but underneath these things I am a woman, with a woman's needs and desires. That cannot be concealed by all the lies and the coarse, cruel cloth in the world. No shameful or pernicious raiment, no imposed masking of the features, no falsity of the tongue or mind can change what I am, a woman."

I did not speak.

"I strive to interest you," she said.

"It would not be good for me to accede to your request," I said. She must, after all, return to the compound of the Waniyanpi.

"You saw me stripped and in a yoke," she said, "tied to the axle of a wagon."

"Yes," I said.

"Am I not attractive?" she asked.

"You are," I said.

"And do you not find me attractive?" she asked.

"Yes," I said.

"Have me," she said.

"It would not be wise," I said. I did not think it would be good for her.

"I beg to be put to your service, Master," she said.

"And if you were," I asked, "what would you fear?"

"Only that I might not please you sufficiently," she said.

"The answer is suitable," I said.

"Touch me, have me," she begged.

I did not respond to her.

"You are still there, are you not?" she asked, frightened, kneeling, reaching out. "You have not left me?"

"No," I said. "I am here."

"I have chewed sip root," she said, plaintively. "We women from the compound, dragging the travois, were all made to do that, to protect us should we be taken and raped by our masters."

"I understand," I said.

"You have nothing to fear," she said.

"I understand," I said. It would be difficult to explain to her, I conjectured, that my concern in this matter was not for myself, but for her. The memory of a man's touch, of any man's touch, I thought, would be a cruel souvenir for her to carry back to the compound. I did not think that memory would make the bleakness and loneliness of the compound easier to bear. It is better, perhaps, for one who must live on porridge never to know the taste of meat and wine. If one must live with the Waniyanpi, perhaps it is best to be of the Waniyanpi. It is, at any rate, safer. Sanity can be perilous in a country of lunatics.

"Please," she begged. "Touch me, hold me, let me know that men still truly exist."

"You surely, as a former free woman," I said, "have known the touch of men, their arms."

"But only on my own terms," she said, "never as what I am now, a slave."

"I see," I said. To be sure, perhaps it is only the female slave, the woman at the total mercy of a master, who can know, truly, what it is to be in the arms of a man, what it is, truly, helplessly, to feel their touch.

"Please," she said.

"You must be returned to the Waniyanpi," I said.

"Have me," she begged. "I will serve you even as a slave."

"What did you say?" I demanded.

"I will serve you even as a slave," she whispered, timidly.

I seized her, cruelly, by the upper arms. I shook her once, viciously. "Oh!" she cried, in misery.

"You are a slave," I told her. I then shook her again, and flung her, viciously, to the dirt.

"Yes, Master!" she said, in the hood. "Yes, Master!"

"You are no longer a proud free woman," I told her. "You are now a slave, and only a slave! If you are used, of course, you will be used as the mere beast, and slave, you are!"

"Yes, Master!" she whimpered.

I looked down at her, angrily. Arrogance, even inadvertent arrogance, in a slave is not accepted. She lay on her side, in the dirt, her head in the hood. The gray dress had come up now, high on her right thigh. Her leg was beautiful. I clenched my fists, that I might not subject the frightened, lovely imbonded beast to the treatment suitable to her condition.

"Let me be a woman," she begged. "Let me be a woman!"

I considered the Waniyanpi. "It is against the law," I said.

I then lifted her up and threw her, she helpless and hooded, over my shoulder.

"I hate you, I hate you," she wept. "I hate you!"

I then carried her back to the shelter and put her, again, with her sisters, her harness mates, other females of the Waniyanpi.

15

HCI'S TRICK

"Behold!" said Hci. "In good faith do I greet you! In the time of the festivals, now, let us make good feelings between us."

"Greetings," said Canka, standing before his lodge.

Behind Hci were two of his fellows, of the Sleen Soldiers. One held a string of twenty kaiila.

"Demonstrating the warmth that is in my heart for you," said Hci, "I give you twenty kaiila!" He motioned for the fellow with the kaiila to come forward.

"Do not!" said Canka.

"They are yours!" cried Hci, with an expansive wave of his hand.

"I do not have twenty kaiila," said Canka. "I am not the son of a chief."

"You need not return me kaiila," said Hci, concernedly. "You will not lose honor, as you know, if you return to me, in magnanimous reciprocity, something of comparable value."

"But what might I have of comparable value?" protested Canka, angrily. It seemed clear that he was to be outdone in the giving of gifts, in the display of generosity. Technically, of course, Hci should not have offered gifts to Canka of a value which Canka could not repay. Such might shame or embarrass the recipient.

"Her," said Hci, pointing to Winyela, standing near the lodge entrance. "I will take her!"

Winyela turned white.

"No!" cried Canka. "I will not give her up! She is mine!"

"I have given you a gift of great value," said Hci, as though puzzled. "You will give me nothing in return?"

"You may not have her!" said Canka.

"Very well, my friend," said Hci. He looked about at his fellows, and the others, too, of which there were now several, about. He smiled broadly. "The kaiila, however, having been given, are yours. I do not regret my generosity. I regret only that you have taken so surly an attitude in this matter."

One of the Sleen Soldiers with Hci slapped his thigh with amusement. There was laughter, too, from others gathered about. More red savages, as if from nowhere, the word of Hci's visit to the lodge of Canka apparently having rapidly spread, appeared. There was now a crowd in front of the lodge.

"I have given Canka twenty kaiila," said Hci to the crowd. "In return he does not give me even one she-kaiila." He pointed to Winyela.

There was laughter from the crowd.

"Take back your kaiila!" said Canka, angrily.

"How can that be done?" asked Hci. "They have already been given."

"I give them back to you!" said Canka, in fury.

"Very well," said Hci, smiling. His fellow of the Sleen Soldiers tightened his grip on the lead rope.

"Hci is very clever," said Cuwignaka to me. "He knows Canka does not wish to surrender Winyela. His caring for her is now well known in the camp. Even so, he did not put his plan into effect until after Canka had refused to give her to his father, Mahpiyasapa, for the Yellow Knives. If Canka would not surrender her to Mahpiyasapa he would not, of course, surrender her to Hci in an exchange of gifts."

"Hci, then," I said, "did not expect to obtain Winyela."

"Of course not," said Cuwignaka. "I do not even think he wants her. She is pretty but there are many pretty girls in camp. The Isanna have more than two hundred. Too, he may be the son of a chief, but he is still only a young man. He would not want to pay twenty kaiila for such a woman. For a young man that would be a crazy price to pay. She is only a white slave. A young man would not want to pay more than four or five kaiila for such a woman. Most white slaves go for a hide or less. Besides, after the cutting of his face, Hci has, for the most part, avoided the company of women, even slaves. Hci, I think, would rather kill Fleer and Yellow Knives than master slaves."

"He is, then, risking nothing," I said.

"And, in shaming Canka, gaining a great deal," said Cuwignaka. "He is a clever fellow. I like him."

"I am sorry, my friend, Canka," said Hci, grinning, "that you have lost honor in this matter. I hope that you will forgive me. In a way it is surely my fault. It did not occur to me that, in making peace between us, I should not offer you splendid gifts. I never conceived of it being possible that you lacked the nobility and generosity of the Kaiila warrior. It is well that you are only of the All Comrades. Such as you would never be accepted in the Sleen Soldiers."

I tensed, for I feared that Canka would draw his knife and rush upon Hci. Hci, too, I think, was prepared for such an eventuality, and, I suspect, would have welcomed it. His knees were slightly flexed. His hand was near his knife sheath. Only too ready, I suspected, was Hci to submit the differences between himself and Canka to the arbitration of steel.

"Ho, ho!" suddenly laughed Cuwignaka, slapping at his leg. "Hci does not see the joke!"

Both young men looked at Cuwignaka as though he might have taken leave of his senses.

"It is a good joke, Canka," said Cuwignaka. "You have fooled him well. For a moment even I was fooled!"

"What are you talking about?" said Canka.

"Did you truly think, Hci," laughed Cuwignaka, "that my brother, Canka, who has served as a Blotanhunka, and who is of the All Comrades, not merely of the Sleen Soldiers, would not take your twenty kaiila for a mere slave?"

"I will never surrender her," said Canka.

"May I speak to my brother?" asked Cuwignaka, laughing.

"Certainly," said Hci. He then turned to the crowd. "It is lovely Siptopto, Canka's sister. Why should a sister not be permitted to speak to her brother? Is it not a sister's privilege to speak to her brother?"

"Cinto!" said several in the crowd. "Surely! Certainly!"

"Thank you," said Cuwignaka.

"Do not stand between us," said Canka.

Cuwignaka placed himself directly between the two young savages, facing Canka, his back to Hci. He placed his hands fraternally upon Canka's shoulders, an action which also, of course, had the consequence of assuring himself that Canka remained where he was. He spoke softly to Canka for a moment, and then stepped back. "The joke has really gone far enough, my brother, I feel," said Cuwignaka, rather loudly.

"You are right, Cuwignaka," said Canka. "Forgive me, Hci," he said. "I did not really mean to make sport of you."

Hci regarded him, puzzled.

"She is yours," said Canka, indicating Winyela. Winyela looked agonized. I thought for a moment she might fall.

"She is mine?" asked Hci.

"Of course," said Canka. "Put a rope on her neck. Lead her away." He then, firmly, took the lead rope of the kaiila string from the Sleen Soldier who held it.

"Mine?" asked Hci.

"Yes," said Canka. "You said that you would take her. Take her."

"It is twenty kaiila!" said Hci.

"The terms of the exchange were yours," said Canka. "I find them peculiar. But I certainly accept them. Take her."

"Please, Master," wept Winyela, piteously throwing herself to her knees at the feet of Canka, "do not let me go! Do not give me to him! I love you! I love you!"

"Silence, mere slave," said Canka, sternly.

Winyela put her head down. Her body was shaken with wild sobs.

"Do you think you are more than a mere object," he asked, "to be done with as I please?"

"No, Master," she wept. "No, Master."

Hci was standing there, stunned.

"What are you going to do with her?" asked Canka, pleasantly.

Hci, I saw, had not planned on getting the girl, as Cuwignaka had speculated. He had not really thought about doing anything with her.

"My father wanted her," said Hci. "I will give her to him, for the Yellow Knives."

"That is a good idea," said Canka, warmly.

"Hci," laughed a man, "has given twenty kaiila for a white slave!"

"I do not think I will let him do my trading for me," said another man.

"It is two jokes," laughed another. "Hci was fooled into thinking Canka would not trade, and then Canka outwitted him, making a trade much to his profit!"

"If only I could do as well in the exchanging of gifts!" said another fellow.

There was general laughter.

"Come, Girl," said Hci, angrily, to Winyela. He wished, clearly, to swiftly depart from this place where, suddenly, the tables being turned, he found himself, he, Hci, the son of a chief, not only outdone but made to look foolish. This would muchly sting his vanity.

"Go with him," said Canka to Winyela.

She rose unsteadily to her feet.

Hci turned away. But he had not taken more than a stride or two before Canka called after him, "Hold, Hci, my friend!"

Hci, angrily, his hand at his knife hilt, turned.

"This is the time of making peace," said Canka. "This is the time of feasting and dancing. This is the time of the giving of gifts."

Hci glared angrily at him.

"I give you twenty kaiila!" said Canka, lifting the lead rope of the kaiila. "They are yours!"

"I have nothing to give you worth twenty kaiila!" shouted Hci, in fury.

"I will take her," said Canka, pointing to Winyela.

"No," said Hci, suddenly. "I know now you want her. I will keep her!"

"Do so," laughed Canka. "But then," he said, turning to the crowd, "let it be told about all the fires how Hci lost his honor, how he did not participate in the giving of gifts, how he proved in this that he was only a small and petty man, that he lacked the nobility and generosity of the Kaiila warrior!"

"I am a Kaiila warrior!" shouted Hci, in fury. "I am not small and petty! Hci is generous! Hci is noble! Hci is a generous and noble warrior! Hci is a warrior of the Kaiila! Hci does not lose his honor!"

"Oh?" asked Canka.

"She is yours!" said Hci.

"And the kaiila are yours," smiled Canka, handing the lead rope of the kaiila string to one of the Sleen Soldiers with Hci.

Winyela fell at the feet of Canka. I feared she might lose consciousness.

Hci regarded Canka with fury. His hand opened and closed at his knife sheath.

"I think Canka wants the woman," said a man.

"I think so, too," said another.

"Interesting," said another.

"There are three jokes," said one of the men. "Canka pretended not to want to trade, and then he traded, outwitting Hci, and then, wanting the woman, he again outwitted Hci, forcing him, against his honor, to trade her back."

I smiled. I myself thought the honors in this lively exchange would be more fittingly accorded to Cuwignaka than to Canka. His cleverness, it seemed to me, it was which had won the day and prevented probable bloodshed. Canka, I was sure, was under no delusion on this score.

"It is a good story," said a man. "Through the years it will bear much retelling."

"And it is not an owned story," said a man. "We all may tell it."

"Yes," said another. Many stories among the red savages are owned stories, stories which only one man has a right to tell. If one would wish to hear the story one must ask its owner to tell it. It is a privilege to own a story. It can make one an important person, too, to own a story, to be he to whom one must come if one wishes to hear it. Sometimes they are told on special days, story-telling days, and many people will come to listen. Some men own little but their story, but owning a good story, in the opinion of the red savages, makes a man rich. Such stories, like other forms of personal property, can be given away or sold. They are, however, seldom sold, for the red savages do not like to think that a story can have a price. They like to think of them as being too precious to sell. Thus, like all things precious, or priceless, they are either to be kept or given away, kept as treasures, or awarded, freely, as by a man whose heart sings, as gifts. Sometimes a man bequeaths his story to his heirs; some stories, for example, have been in families for generations; sometimes, on the other hand, he will give it to someone who loves it, and whom he thinks, in turn, will tell it well.

"Tomorrow," cried Hci, angrily, pointing his finger at Canka, "my father will take the woman! Tomorrow, by noon, he will take her from you, for the Yellow Knives!" He then, in fury, turned about and strode between the lodges. He was followed by his fellows of the Sleen Soldiers, the lead rope of the kaiila string in the hands of one of them.

"Do you think he will do that?" I asked Canka.

"No," said Canka. "Mahpiyasapa is angry with me, but he is a good chief. He knows the ways of the Kaiila. He would never take the woman from me against my will."

Canka then crouched down, next to Winyela. He lifted her to a kneeling position and held her against him, closely.

"Do not be afraid," said Canka, soothingly.

"You gave me away," she whispered.

"Only for a moment," he said, "and only within our ways. I was in no danger of losing you."

"You gave me away," she said, numbly.

"It is over now," said Canka. "I will not do it again."

"Do you not like me?" she asked.

"Yes," said Canka, "I like you."

"Do not let me go, ever," she begged.

"I will never let you go," he said. "I love you."

She looked at him, startled, and then, trembling and sobbing, pressed herself into his arms. "I love you, too, my Master," she wept.

Canka let her cry for a time, holding her in his arms. Then he lifted her in his arms and carried her gently into the recesses of his lodge.

"Canka handled Hci quite well, I think," said Cuwignaka.

"I think Cuwignaka handled Hci quite well," I said. "Certainly Canka knows that and, I suspect, unfortunately, Hci knows it as well."

"Hci is a clever fellow," said Cuwignaka. "I think it is time he was given a taste of his own medicine."

"Those who dispense such medicine," I said, "seldom enjoy receiving it in turn."

"I think now I have a little satisfaction for Hci's trick in the draw, and the losing of the meat," chuckled Cuwignaka.

"Do you think trouble will come of this?" I asked.

"No," said Cuwignaka. "Hci is angry, but he can do nothing. Within our ways he is helpless."

"But what if he goes outside of your ways?" I asked.

"He will not do that," said Cuwignaka. "Hci, when all is said and done, is Kaiila. He is honorable."

"He threatened Canka that Mahpiyasapa would take Winyela tomorrow," I said. "He certainly could not know that that is true, and it is, I gather, in all probability, false. Similarly, outrightly, it seems, he lied in the matter of the meat."

"That is true," said Cuwignaka, thoughtfully. "He really should not have done that."

"No," I said.

"It is not a becoming thing for a person to do," said Cuwignaka.

"Too," I said, "such things as civilization, and friendship and interchanges depend muchly upon trust."

"Also," said Cuwignaka, "it could be dangerous."

"How is that?" I asked.

"One's shield might betray one," said Cuwignaka.

I regarded Cuwignaka.

"Yes," said Cuwignaka. "It is a well-known fact. One's shield may choose not to defend one, if one is a liar."

"Shields do not behave like that outside of the Barrens," I told Cuwignaka, smiling.

"You are skeptical, I see," said Cuwignaka. "Well, be assured, my friend, I am speaking of the shields of the peoples of the Barrens and within the Barrens. These are not your ordinary shields. These are made with the aid of spells. The medicines of war are important in their construction and designs. They are not merely equipment, not merely contraptions of metal or leather. They are holy. They are precious. They are friends and allies. Surely you have seen them suspended from tripods behind the lodges, being sunned?"

"Yes," I admitted.

"That is to soak up power from the sun."

"I see," I said.

"You would not do that with an ordinary shield, would you?" asked Cuwignaka.

"Not generally," I admitted.

"Thus," said Cuwignaka, "they are not ordinary shields."

"In battle," I said, "surely some warriors are more successful than others."

"Of course," said Cuwignaka. "Their war medicine is probably stronger."

"I see," I said.

"Let us return to our lodge," said Cuwignaka.

"You speak Gorean," I said. "You have lived with white men."

"Yes?" asked Cuwignaka.

"Do you really believe this business?" I asked.

"What business?" he asked.

"About the shields," I said.

"Of course," said Cuwignaka.

"Be serious," I said.

"I do not know," smiled Cuwignaka. "Maybe. Maybe not."

"Do all of your people believe such things?" I asked.

"Most, I would suppose," said Cuwignaka.

"What of warriors, like Canka and Hci," I said, "would they believe such things?"

"Of course," said Cuwignaka.

"Let us go to our lodge," I said.

"Yes," said Cuwignaka. "I must rest. Tomorrow I must dance. Tomorrow will be a glorious day!"

16

OIPUTAKE

"Master! Master!" cried the blond-haired girl, delightedly, seizing me by the hand.

She drew me happily behind a lodge. She was naked, save for her beaded collar. It was the morning of the day of the great dance. Behind the lodge she knelt down before me. I was a man. "I am so happy, Master," she said. "I am so happy!"

"Why are you not in the herd?" I asked, fearful for her. "You have not run away, have you?" I asked. The penalties for a girl straying from her herd, or running away, were not light. The first offense involved being turned over to the women of the red savages for days of torment and torture. The second offense was to be punished by hamstringing and abandonment.

"No," she laughed, on her knees before me. "I have been taken out of the herd! I am no longer in it!"

"Your collar is different," I observed. This was an attractive collar, with red and yellow beading.

"I have a new master," she said, proudly, happily.

"What happened?" I asked.

"Last night," she said, "I, with others, was exchanged in the giveaways. My former master, I think, thought he was ridding himself of a poor girl, but I, as soon as I found myself within the skins of my new master's lodge, began to serve him, deliciously, and as a subdued slave. He was elated. I think he was much pleased with me. He said I was a marvelous gift. He even gave my old master an additional kaiila. My old master was furious then, at having let me go. But he cannot do anything about it now. I now belong to my new master."

"Wonderful," I said.

"I now have a name!" she said.

"What is it?" I asked.

"Oiputake," she said.

"That is the word for a kiss," I said.

"Yes," she smiled. "And sometimes," she laughed, "I do not know when my master is merely calling me or ordering me to please him!"

"As you are a slave," I said, "I do not think I would take chances in the matter."

"I cannot," she laughed. "If I am in the least doubt, I kiss him."

I smiled.

"And he, the marvelous monster, in my control, takes liberal advantage of that ambiguity!"

"Oiputake," I said.

"Yes, Master," she said, leaning forward, kissing me on the thigh.

"I see there are some advantages," I said, "in giving a girl such a name."

"You men are all alike, in owning us, in mastering us," she laughed.

"Perhaps," I said.

"My Master informs me," she said, "that if I continue to please him he might even permit me clothing."

"Splendid," I said.

"And he might braid my hair," she said.

"He must beware," I said, "lest he become weak."

"I think there is little danger of that," she laughed. "He is a red savage."

"Would you like him to become weak," I asked, "so that you might wind him about your little finger?"

"No," she said. "I want only, in all things, to be his perfect slave."

"He is a red savage," I said. "I think there is little danger that you would be permitted to be anything else."

"No, Master," she laughed.

"You seem happy," I said.

"I am," she said, "unspeakably happy. And I owe it all to you."

"To me," I shrugged, "or to some other man."

"It was you," she said. "And I shall never forget it." Her eyes clouded. "There is only one thing," she said.

"What is that?" I asked.

"I am so helpless now," she said. "My needs—"

"Yes," I said.

"My appetites have been ignited," she said. "My needs have been so aroused. It puts me so much, now, at the mercy of men." She squirmed, on her knees. She rubbed her thighs together.

"That is common in a female slave," I said.

"I can hardly look at an attractive man now," she said,

"without feeling warm, and receptive, let alone being in a collar, and naked on my knees before one."

"I understand," I said.

"At one time," she said, "I would never have dreamed that I might one day beg a man for his touch, but last night, in the arms of my master, I did so."

"I understand," I said.

"Tearfully," she said, "I, once a proud free woman of Ar, now only a slave, pleaded for his caress."

"And was he kind?" I asked.

"Yes," she said. "I love him!"

"You might have been whipped instead," I said.

"I know," she said, "for I am only a slave. I love him! I love him!"

"I am happy for you," I said.

"Thank you, Master," she said.

"Did you yield well to him?" I asked.

"Yes," she said. "I yielded to him from the bottom of my belly."

"Superb," I said.

She squirmed on her knees, before me.

"Are you in distress?" I asked.

"But these feelings," she said, "which you first induced in me—"

"Yes?" I said.

"They make me helpless before almost any man," she said.

"What feelings?" I asked.

"Sometimes I cannot help myself," she said.

"What feelings?" I asked.

"Sometimes my heart palpitates and my breath quickens," she said. "Sometimes my entire skin seems suddenly suffused with warmth. It seems my breasts and thighs want to be touched. I want to be held. I want to be caressed. My belly grows hot and receptive. I feel desire. I am open, and wet. The smell of my needs is upon me."

"Kiss my feet," I told her.

She bent down and kissed my feet. She then lifted her head, and looked at me, tears in her eyes.

"Do such feelings disturb you?" I asked.

"Sometimes," she said, "I am so ashamed of these changes in my body."

"They are nothing to be ashamed of," I said. "Be pleased, rather, that your body, at last, freed of inhibitions, constructions and rigidities, is in perfect working order."

"Perfect working order?" she asked.

"Of course," I said. "The feelings you describe, and many others, like them, are the natural and spontaneous reactions of the healthy and passionate woman in the presence of an attractive male. Rather than feel shame at experiencing them you should feel concern if you did not. The failure to feel such feelings, in situations in which it would be natural to feel them, would presumably be a clue as to the presence of some unfortunate barrier or blockage, either physical or, more likely, psychological."

"But do good women have such feelings?" she asked.

"I do not know," I said. "But sick women do not."

She looked at me.

"What is a 'good woman,'" I asked, "one who is natural, spontaneous, feminine and loving, or one who conforms to certain cultural stereotypes, the results, usually, of attempts on the part of aggressive mental cases to impose their maladies, from which they seem unable to escape, on others?"

She did not speak.

"Some virtues," I said, "require a cure."

"But such feelings," she said, "could make a woman a slave."

"Yes," I said.

"I see why some women fear them," she said.

"So do I," I said. "But you are a slave, so you need not be concerned about such matters. Enslaved, you are free, interestingly and paradoxically, to be free."

"You make me feel free," she said.

"Beware you are not whipped," I said.

She contritely kissed my feet.

"Master," she said.

"Yes," I said.

"I do feel distress," she said.

"I know," I said.

"Real distress," she said.

"You are a female of strong, though once rigidly suppressed, drives, who has been enslaved," I said.

"Master?" she said.

"Too," I said, "the feelings of the normal woman, under the condition of forthright and explicit slavery, are often multiplied a hundred fold, and, in some women, it seems, a thousand fold."

"I cannot stand it, Master," she said.

"Grovel," I told her.

"Surely you would not make me do that?" she said.

I pointed to the ground at my feet, uncompromisingly. She slipped to her belly before me. I felt her lips and tongue on my feet.

"The important thing," I said, "is to be what you are. If you are a slave, be a slave."

"Yes, Master," she said.

"What are you?" I asked.

"A slave," she whimpered, kissing at my feet.

"Then be a slave," I said.

"Yes, Master," she said.

The collar looked well on her neck, under her hair.

"You treat me," she said, "like I was—like I was—"

"A slave," I said.

"Yes," she said.

"You are a slave," I said.

"Yes, Master," she said.

"So expect to be treated as one," I said.

"Yes, Master," she said.

I let her please me for a time in this fashion, bellying before me, kissing, and licking and sucking at my feet.

"You grovel well, Slave," I said.

"Thank you, Master," she said.

"You would not begrudge a fellow the enjoyment of his sovereignty, would you?" I asked.

"No, Master," she said.

"You look well at a man's feet," I said.

She moaned in humiliation, and in severe sexual distress.

"You may thank me," I said.

"Thank you, Master," she said.

"You're welcome," I said.

"You enjoy my debasement," she said. "You enjoy it!"

"Yes," I said. "So do you."

Her small shoulders shook. I saw that what I had said was true.

"You may kneel before me," I said.

She rose to a kneeling position before me. "You have not touched me," she said, "and yet you have much aroused me."

I did not respond to her. Human females are such rich and wonderful creatures. Their sexual life, and feelings, are subtle, complex and deep. How naive is the man who believes that having sex with a woman is so little or brief a thing as to fall within the parameters of a horizontal plane, the simple stimulations of a skin, the results attendant upon a simplistic manual dexterity. How woefully ignorant are the engineers of sexuality. How much to learn have even her artists and poets! Women are so inordinately precious. They are so sensitive, so beautiful, so intelligent and needful. No man has yet counted the dimensions of a woman's love. Who can measure the horizons of her heart? Few things, I suspect, are more real than those which seem most intangible.

"Without even touching me," she said, "you have much aroused me. And now I kneel helplessly before you."

Her distress was obvious. She was a slave, and needed desperately to be taken. And yet I had done little but treat her as a woman, and impress, categorically, male domination upon her. I did not think she was now in doubt as to her sex.

"When I led you behind the lodge," she said, "I was grateful and happy. It was my intention to make you a gift, of my own free will, of my pleasures. But now you have made me needful. Now you have put me at your mercy!"

"It is suitable, Slave," I said.

"Will you not be kind?" she asked.

I did not speak to her.

"You see me helpless and needful," she said, "begging."

"It befits you," I said, "Slave."

"Men do this to us," she said. "They make us this way, and then they decide whether or not they will even touch us!"

"Sometimes, too, as I understand it," I said, "a girl is made to perform."

"Perform?" she asked.

"Yes," I said, "she is made, so to speak, to earn her havings."

"Yes, Master," she said. "That is not uncommon."

"Are you prepared to work for your havings," I asked, "to earn them?"

"Yes, Master," she said. "I will do anything."

"But you must do anything anyway," I said, "for you are a slave."

"Yes, Master," she moaned. "Yes, Master."

I looked down upon her.

She squirmed, and clenched her small fists. There were tears in her eyes.

"I am in need," she said.

I crouched next to her, and felt her, gently. She pressed her small, hot, wet, rounded belly into my hand, her eyes closed.

"I see that you do not lie," I said.

"No, Master," she said.

"The collar looks well on your neck," I said.

"Yes, Master," she said.

"And your hair is beautiful," I said.

"Thank you, Master," she said.

"Do you beg to be had?" I asked.

"Yes, Master," she said.

"Are you prepared to earn your having?" I asked.

"I will do anything," she said.

"Kiss me," I said.

"For so little," she asked, "I can earn my having?"

"But it must be the kiss of a slave," I informed her.

"Yes, Master," she said.

Our lips then met, sweetly and tenderly, fully, lingeringly. Her lips, opened, soft, those of a submitting slave, at first met mine timidly, and then, as she understood that she was not to be spurned, or struck, more fully, more boldly, until her kiss was deep, helpless and warm, and she seemed one with the kiss, and lost within it, and then, again, timidly, she drew back, having proffered herself to me as a slave, to observe what might be my reaction, to see in my eyes if she had been found pleasing, and what would be her fate.

She looked at me.

I was pleased with her. She had not even been taught the kisses of a slave.

I lowered her gently to her back.

I looked down upon her.

"Touch me," she pleaded. "Please, touch me. I beg you to touch me, Master."

"I do not think that much touching will be necessary," I said.

Then no sooner than I had entered her, she, as I had expected, given her condition of arousal, clutching me, and gasping, exploded into orgasm.

"Yes, Master," she said. "Yes, Master! Thank you, Master! Yes, Master!"

I thought I had done a good job with her. I thought her master would be pleased with her. She had once been a frigid free woman. She was now a promising slave.

Some red savages passed us from time to time, going about their business, but they paid us little attention. We were only slaves.

"Thank you, Master, for touching me," she whispered, "for consenting to put me to your uses."

"You served well, Slave," I said.

"I am pleased," she said, "if I have served you well, and in the way of a woman."

"And of a slave," I said.

"Yes, Master," she smiled, kissing me.

She drew back, then, and lay on her side, with her legs drawn up. The marvelous, turned breadth of her thigh was beautiful. How delicious are such creatures. How natural it is that men should choose to institutionalize their ownership.

"Things are going well for the Kaiila," I said. "Your master has acquired a beautiful white slave. My Master, and friend, Canka, of the Isbu, has retained his own slave and love, a girl named Winyela, also a luscious white slave, and my friend, Cuwignaka, after years of waiting is, at last, going to enter the lodge of the great dance." I smiled to myself. How naturally I had thought of the former Miss Millicent Aubrey-Welles, of high family, and once a debutante in Pennsylvania, as only another luscious white slave in the Barrens. This was appropriate, of course, for that was now all she was, that and her master's love.

"I am happy for him," she said.

"There is plenty of meat in the camp," I said, "and this is a time of festivals and dances, of feasts, visitings and giveaways."

"I myself was exchanged in a giveaway," she smiled.

"Much to the chagrin, as it turned out, of your former master, I understand," I said.

"Yes," she smiled.

"And perhaps most splendidly," I said, "it seems that there is soon to be peace between the Kaiila and the Yellow Knives. Even now civil chiefs of the Yellow Knives are in the camp."

"They are not civil chiefs," she said.

"What?" I asked.

"I have seen the Yellow-Knife chieftains in the camp," she said. "I saw them coming to the camp days ago, when I was in the herd. I saw them last night at a late feast, when I was being brought to my master's lodge. I saw them this morning, near the lodge of Watonka, in the Isanna camp. They are not civil chieftains."

"You are mistaken," I said.

"I was a slave of Yellow Knives for a time," she said. "I know."

"They are not civil chieftains?" I asked.

"I saw the civil chieftains of the Yellow Knives at a

council," she said. "It was only some weeks ago. Shortly thereafter I was taken by Isanna warriors in a raid."

"It seems too early for there to have been a council," I said.

"There was a council," she said.

"Had the Pte arrived?" I asked. I would have expected such a council to be correlated with the coming of the Pte and the gathering of Yellow-Knife bands for the great hunts. The Pte would be expected to arrive in the territories of the Kaiila before arriving in those of the Yellow Knives.

"No," she said.

"Interesting," I said. "Do you know the topic or topics of the council?"

"No," she said.

"Some weeks ago," I said, "there was a raid on a large wagon train and a mercenary column of soldiers. Do you know of this?"

"Yes," she said. "Captives were brought to the Yellow-Knife camp."

"Was the council before or after the raid?" I asked.

"Several days after it," she said.

"That, too, is interesting," I said. "You are certain that you do not know what the council was about?"

"No, Master," she said. "I was not taught to speak Yellow Knife. I know almost nothing of it. Among them I performed, on the whole, only the most menial of labors, commonly guided in my work only by cuffings and the blows of whips. To them I was only a kind of she-kaiila, a two-legged beast of burden."

"Such labors," I said, "seem fittingly assigned to sexually inert slaves."

"Yes, Master," she said, "but they are imposed, too, sometimes, even on the most passionate of their women."

"Of course," I said.

"In this council," she said, "I saw the civil chieftains of the Yellow Knives. They are not the same men who are now in the camp."

"You are mistaken," I said.

"No, Master," she said.

"Have you seen these men in camp before," I asked, "the Yellow Knives?"

"Yes, Master," she said.

"They are civil chieftains," I said.

"No, Master," she said.

"Do you know what they are?" I asked.
"Yes, Master," she said.
"What are they?" I asked.
"War chiefs," she said.

17

AN ASSESSMENT OF THE INFORMATION OF OIPUTAKE

"Canka!" I cried. "Where is Canka!"

The young warrior was not in his lodge. Near it, sitting cross-legged, a robe well over his head, half concealing his face, rocking back and forth, was a figure.

"Akihoka," I cried, "where is Canka."

"He has gone hunting," said Akihoka.

"When will he be back?" I asked.

"He should not come back," moaned Akihoka. He rocked back and forth. "He was my friend," he moaned. "He was my friend."

"I do not understand," I said. "What has happened?"

"You are the second to seek him today," said Akihoka, bent over, muchly hidden in the robe.

"I do not understand," I said. "I have information. I must see him. It may mean nothing. It may mean much!"

"Sleen Soldiers came for him," moaned Akihoka. "But he was not here. He was hunting."

"Why should Sleen Soldiers come for Canka?" I asked, alarmed.

"He tried to kill Mahpiyasapa," moaned Akihoka, rocking in misery.

"That is preposterous," I said.

"They have the arrow which was shot at Mahpiyasapa," said Akihoka, rocking back and forth. "It is the arrow of Canka. Too, Hci saw Canka fleeing from the place."

"Canka would not shoot at Mahpiyasapa," I said. "Mahpiyasapa is his chief."

"It is said that he feared Mahpiyasapa would take the red-haired woman away from him."

"Mahpiyasapa would not do that against his will," I said, "and Canka knows that."

"Hci said that he would last night," said Akihoka.

"Hci," I said, "spoke in anger."

"Hci saw him fleeing from the place," said Akihoka, grief-stricken.

"I thought you said Canka had gone hunting," I said.

"It is said he shot at Mahpiyasapa, and then went hunting," said Akihoka.

"That is absurd," I said. "No one shoots an arrow at his chief, and then just rides off hunting."

"The arrow is the arrow of Canka," said Akihoka, almost chanting in grief. "Hci saw him running from the place."

"Who else saw him?" I asked.

"No one," said Akihoka.

"Does this seem likely to you," I asked, angrily, "in a crowded camp?"

"It was the arrow of Canka," said Akihoka. "They have the arrow. It is the arrow of Canka. Hci saw him running from the place."

"Hci is a liar," I said.

"No," said Akihoka.

"Why not?" I asked.

"He has sworn by his shield," said Akihoka.

"Clearly it must have been Hci himself who fired the arrow," I said.

"Mahpiyasapa is the father of Hci," said Akihoka. "Hci would not try to kill him"

"I do not think he would try to kill him either," I said. "I think it was Hci's intention merely to make it seem that an attempt had been made on his life."

"Hci would not do that," said Akihoka.

"Why not?" I asked.

"Hci is Kaiila," said Akihoka. "Shame, shame," he moaned, rocking in the robe. "It is shame for Canka. It is shame for the All Comrades. I have sorrow for Canka. He was my friend. He was my friend."

"Hci," I said, firmly, "did not see Canka running from the place." I recalled that Canka had, on the first morning of the great hunt, inquired of Cuwignaka the location of one of his arrows. As long ago, then, as that time, it seemed to me that Hci had been fomenting his plan. In the openness of the living of the red savages, where things are not hidden and locked up, and where theft is not expected, and is generally regarded as almost unthinkable, it would not be a difficult matter, provided one was a bit careful, to take an arrow.

"Hci swears it," said Akihoka.

"Hci swears falsely," I said.

"Hci swears by his shield," said Akihoka.

"Then Hci swears falsely by his shield," I said.

Akihoka stopped rocking. He pulled the robe down from his head, about his shoulders. "You are white," he said. "You are only a slave. You know nothing of these things."

"In your heart you know as well as I," I said, "that Canka would not try to kill Mahpiyasapa. I am sure even Mahpiyasapa, in his heart, knows that, too."

"But Hci has sworn by his shield," he said.

"He has sworn falsely," I said.

"How can that be?" asked Akihoka, puzzled.

"It has to do, doubtless, with the vanity of Hci, and his hatred for Canka," I said.

Akihoka looked down at the dirt. It was not easy for him, a Kaiila warrior, to comprehend that such a thing, even though it seemed so plausible, might have taken place. It was as though his trust in deep things had been shaken.

"By the love you bear Canka," I said, "ride after him. Go out to meet him. Find him. Tell him what has occurred. I assure you he knows nothing of it. This was done now, indeed, I do not doubt, because he had left the camp."

Akihoka looked up at me.

"Find him before the Sleen Soldiers do," I said. "It might mean his life. Tell him what has occurred. Then he must decide what to do."

"He will come back," said Akihoka.

"Then let him come back knowing what has occurred," I said. "Go after him."

"I know where he will be hunting," said Akihoka.

"Hurry," I said.

Akihoka threw off the robe. "I will go," he said.

"Where is Winyela?" I asked.

"I do not know," he said.

"Did Sleen Soldiers come for her," I asked, "to take her to the lodge of Mahpiyasapa?"

"No," said Akihoka.

"You see?" I said. "Mahpiyasapa, even under these conditions, does not have her brought to him. Even under these conditions he still regards her as Canka's woman. He must know that Hci is lying."

Akihoka turned about and raced away, between the lodges.

He would jerk loose the picket rope of his kaiila and mount it in a bound. In moments he would be outside the camp.

I looked after Akihoka. Already he had vanished from sight.

I felt a cool breeze. I felt sorrow for Mahpiyasapa. It must be a terrible thing for a father to realize that his beloved son has betrayed his codes.

Then I recalled the information I had received but moments before from the lovely blond slave, Oiputake. I was in a quandary. I had hoped, of course, to convey this information to Canka. This seemed appropriate not only because he was, strictly, my master, but also because he was highly placed in the All Comrades. He might then have made a judgment on it, assessing its significance, if any. I would have gone first to Cuwignaka, as I knew him best and had the highest regard for his perceptiveness and common sense, but that action I had rejected, of course, because at this time he would be, with other young men, dancing in the great lodge. I did not know what to do. I could, of course, kneel to random individuals, met here and there, and tell them what I had learned, but I feared I might be dismissed as a raving slave. Who would believe the words of a slave, and I had this cognizance, too, only from another slave. What, too, if she were mistaken?

Grunt, I thought, Grunt! He will know what to do! Too, he is a close friend of Mahpiyasapa. Mahpiyasapa will listen to him. I must seek out Grunt!

18

I CONTINUE TO SEEK AN ASSESSMENT OF OIPUTAKE

"Where is Grunt!" I cried.

Wasnapohdi, startled, looked up. She was kneeling within the lodge which Mahpiyasapa had set aside for the use of Grunt, his friend.

"He is not here!" she said.

"Where is he?" I asked.

"I do not know!" she said. She seemed frightened. "Have you heard about Canka?" she said.

"Yes," I said. "But I do not believe it."

"Nor do I," she said. "It cannot be."

"Why are you alone in the lodge?" I asked. "Why are you not working?"

"I am hiding," she said.

"You need not be afraid," I said. "The business with Canka has nothing to do with you."

"I am not hiding because of that," she said.

"Do you have any idea where Grunt is?" I asked.

"He may be with Mahpiyasapa," she said. "He left after he found out about Canka."

"That is a splendid thought," I said. "I shall go to the lodge of Mahpiyasapa!" I turned to leave but then, suddenly, turned back. "Why are you hiding?" I asked.

"I have seen him!" she whispered.

"Canka?" I asked, startled.

"No," she said, "Waiyeyeca, One-Who-Finds-Much, he who once owned me!"

"Several have owned you," I said.

"I spoke to you of him," she said, "when first we met, shortly after Grunt, my master, had acquired me at the trading point."

"The boy?" I said.

"Yes," she said.

"I remember," I said. Long ago, at a Dust-Leg trading point, Grunt had obtained Wasnapohdi for three fine hatchets. In talking to me, afterwards, she had told me something of herself. She had been born in a Waniyanpi compound, one owned by the Kailiauk, a tribe federated with the Kaiila and speaking a closely related dialect. He who obtained her from this compound was a Kaiila warrior. At that time she was only eight years old. He had taken her home with him and given her, as a slave, to his ten-year-old son. She had thus learned to serve and placate men early. Yet as children they had been more as companions and playmates than as master and slave.

Then once, when they were alone, when she was but fifteen and he seventeen, far from their camp, gathering berries together, he had been unable any longer not to see her as a woman. She had looked up to see him, almost angrily, cutting and carving at a branch, notching it at the ends for thongholds. She was frightened and began to cry. She had seen such devices before, and knew their use. She was ordered to remove her clothing, and to lie down, with her legs widely apart. Then she felt her ankles tied in this position, the branch behind them, widely apart, by means of the notches and thongs. She had no doubt as to what would be her fate. She was to be used for the first time, and as the slave she was. By dusk, freed of the branch, she had lain on her belly before him, kissing his feet. That night, when they had returned to the village, she did not ride behind him in his kaiila, as she had that morning. She accompanied him, rather, on foot, marched at his stirrup, her hands bound behind her back, a thong on her neck, run to the pommel of his saddle. That morning two children had left the village; what returned to it that night were a young master and his claimed slave.

Wasnapohdi put down her head, trembling.

I think that the young master and his slave had been much in love. His affection for the girl, for she was only a slave, had brought much ridicule on him from his peers. To this sort of thing he, a red savage, had been extremely sensitive. In the end, perhaps to refute or mitigate charges of affection for the girl, or perhaps because he suspected they might be true, and interpreted his feelings in such a matter as unseemly weaknesses in a young warrior, he had sold her. After that she had had several masters. Grunt, as I have mentioned, had finally acquired her from Dust Legs.

"His name is Waiyeyeca?" I asked.

"Yes," she said.

"What is his band?" I asked.

"Napoktan," she said.

"The Bracelets band," I said.

"Yes," she said. Their territory lies roughly northwest of the Kaiila River, north of the northern fork of the Kaiila River, and east of the Snake River. Napoktan warriors commonly wear two copper bracelets on the left wrist.

"Did he see you?" I asked.

"No," she said.

"Do you still love him?" I asked.

"I do not know," she said. "It has been a long time, years. He sold me!"

"You are a slave," I said. "Surely you do not object to being sold."

"I thought he loved me!" she said.

"Perhaps he did," I said.

"He sold me!" she said.

"Perhaps he did not regard you as sufficiently beautiful," I said.

"Perhaps!" she said, angrily.

"If he could see you now," I said, "if he could see how beautiful you have become, doubtless he would regret his earlier decision, keenly."

"Perhaps!" she said, in fury.

"Have you no work to do?" I asked.

"I am hiding," she said.

"Why?" I asked.

"I am afraid for him to see me," she said, tears in her eyes. "He sold me! I loved him! I do not want to open these old wounds! I do not want to go through all that heartache again! I have suffered enough!"

"Nonsense," I said. "You are merely looking for an excuse to get out of work. I know the tricks of a lazy girl when I see them."

"No," she said, agonized, "really!"

"What are you supposed to be doing?" I asked.

"Polishing trade goods," she said.

"Inside the lodge or outside?" I asked. I knew what the answer must be.

"Outside, I suppose," she said, "so that I may better see what I am doing."

"Then get outside and polish trade goods," I said.

"Please, no," she said. "He might see me!"

"The Napoktan camp is not close," I said. "That is highly unlikely."

"He might see me!" she protested.

"What if he does?" I asked.

"What if he sees me, and wants me?" she asked. "What if he carries me away, or buys me?"

"He will not simply carry you away," I said. "Grunt is a guest of the Kaiila."

"But what if he wishes to buy me?" she asked, in misery.

"Then that is simply a matter of prices," I said.

"No, no," she wept. "You do not understand!"

"I understand very well," I said. "You are a slave. You are a piece of property. A man sees you and decides whether or not he is interested in you. If he is, he makes Grunt an offer. It is accepted or rejected. Perhaps bargaining ensues. If they do not come to terms, then you remain Grunt's. If they do come to terms, then you simply have a new master, whom you must then serve completely and with total perfection."

She collapsed on a robe in the lodge, clutching at it with her small fingers, weeping bitterly.

"I believe you were given a command," I said. "I trust that

you do not desire for me to repeat it, as your discharge of the task might well, then, be preceded by a severe whipping."

"No, Master," she wept. "I do not desire for you to repeat your command."

"If your obedience is insufficiently prompt," I said, "I may add to my command the stipulation that you will polish the trade goods outside the lodge naked."

"My obedience is prompt, Master," she wept, getting up. She began to gather together several pots and pans from Grunt's store of trade goods.

"I am well aware of the tricks of lazy girls to escape from their work," I told her.

"Yes, Master," she wept. "Yes, Master."

I then hurried from the lodge. I wished to find Grunt, to query him as to the possible significance, if any, of the information I had earlier received from Oiputake, as to the identity of the Yellow Knives in the camp.

"Tatankasa!" called a little boy. "Throw the hoop for me! Throw the hoop for me!"

"Have you seen Wopeton, the Trader?" I asked.

"No," he said. "Throw the hoop!"

"Forgive, me, Small Master," I said. "I am on business."

"Very well," he said.

I sped on, toward the lodge of Mahpiyasapa.

"Hold!" called a lad.

I stopped, and fell to my knees before him. It was the lad who had been first among the herders, when I had carried the beaded quirt to the girl herd.

"Greetings," said he.

"Greetings, Master," I said.

"The blond slave whom you took for wench sport," he said, "is no longer in the herd. She was exchanged in a giveaway and her new master, reportedly, is quite pleased with her. It seems she is now to serve in his low lodge, away from the herd, convenient to him, as a prize slave."

"That is good news, Master," I said.

"The credit for this goes to you, I think," said the lad. "You melted the ice in her belly. You made her become a woman, and need men."

"Thank you, Master," I said.

"She has been named Oiputake," he said.

"Yes, Master," I said. "Master!" I said, suddenly.

"Yes," he said.

"Why are you in the village now," I asked, "at this time of day?"

"The herds have been brought in," he said, "to the edges of the village."

"What of the guards and pickets?" I asked.

"They, too, have been brought in," he said.

"Why?" I asked.

"It is upon the orders of Watonka," said the lad.

"The western edge of the camp, then, is unguarded," I said. The security for this perimeter was the responsibility of the Isanna.

"It is all right," said the lad. "It is the time of the feasts, of the festivals."

"Have you seen Wopeton, the Trader?" I asked.

"No," he said.

"May I leave?" I asked.

"Surely," said the lad, puzzled.

I leaped up and again hurried toward the lodge of Mahpiyasapa. I passed within a hundred yards of the great dance lodge, formed of towering walls of brush. Within would be the pole, the ropes and the skewers, and, painted and bedecked, dancing, the young men.

"Mahpiyasapa is not here," said the woman, kneeling near his lodge, one of his wives. Her gnarled fingers held a bone scraper. She was sharpening the scraper on a stone in front of her. On the scraper there were six dots. It has been used for six years. Two of her fingers had been cut off at the first joint. She had lost two sons.

"Do you know where he is?" I asked.

"No," she said.

"Thank you, Mistress," I said. I rose to my feet, and stepped back. I did not know what to do now, or where to go.

"Why should he not be in the council?" she asked, not looking up.

"Of course," I said. "My thanks, Mistress!"

"It will do you no good," she said. "You cannot see him there, if he is there. It is not permitted."

"I really seek Wopeton," I said. "Might he be in the council?"

"It is possible," she shrugged. She did not look up from her work.

"My thanks, Mistress," I said. "You have been very kind."

"If he is in the council," she said, "you will not be able to see him either."

"My thanks, Mistress!" I said. I turned about and hurried from the place. She had been very helpful. I did not think that I would have managed as well had I been a white female slave. Had I been such she might have put me to labors or kept me on my belly, in the dirt, my mouth filled with dirt, before her, for hours. Women of the red savages bear little affection towards the lovely white properties of their men. White slave girls will often flee at the mere approach of a red female and will almost never meet the eyes of one. In my intense awareness of this being the day of the great dance, probably a function of Cuwignaka's almost overwhelming concern about it, and in my concern over the fate of Canka, and my concern with the information obtained from Oiputake, I had forgotten that this day, too, was the day of a peace council, a day in which was to be seen, supposedly, at least the first stages of the ratification of a peace agreement between the Yellow Knives and the Kaiila. I made my way rapidly towards the council lodge. I did not know if I could draw Mahpiyasapa out of the council, or if it would be wise to do so, but I was confident that I could, somehow, if he were there, make contact with Grunt.

I was thrown rudely back by the two young warriors. "Kneel, Slave!" snarled one of them.

I knelt swiftly. Knives were drawn upon me.

"Forgive me, Masters," I said. "It is needful that I speak with Wopeton."

"He is not within," said one of the warriors.

"Convey then, I beg you," I said, "my need to speak with Mahpiyasapa."

"Neither is Mahpiyasapa within," said the warrior.

"Neither is within?" I asked.

"No," he said.

"Forgive me, Masters," I said.

"They may come later," said one of the warriors. "The council has not yet begun."

"Yes, Masters," I said. "Thank you, Masters." I crawled back a pace or two, on my knees, keeping my eyes on their knives. Then I rose to my feet and, facing them, backed away. They sheathed their knives and resumed their stance, arms folded, before the threshold of the great lodge. Its poles were fifty feet in height and it was covered with more than a hundred skins.

I looked about. Again I did not know what to do. I must wait, I suppose, to see if Grunt, or Mahpiyasapa, appeared. By now, however, I would have supposed they would have been within the council lodge. Surely the council was due to soon begin.

"Slave," said a fellow, sitting cross-legged, some yards off, beckoning to me.

I went to him and he indicated a place near him where I might kneel. I did so. He was grooving a stone for a hammer-head. This is done with a dampened rawhide string, dipped in sand, and drawn again and again, patiently, across the stone. I watched him work. "Today," he said, "the council will not hear the voice of Mahpiyasapa."

"Why, today, will the council not hear his voice?" I asked.

"Today," said the man, drawing the rawhide string across the stone, "Mahpiyasapa is in sorrow. He has gone from the village, to purify himself."

"Why should he be in sorrow?" I asked. This was unwelcome news, indeed, that he might not be in the camp.

"I think it is because Canka tried to kill him," said the man, watching the movement of the string.

"Oh," I said. I did not know this man, and I did not see much point in conveying to him my suspicions as to what had actually occurred in this disturbing incident.

"You are Canka's slave, aren't you?" asked the man.

"Yes," I said.

"And you have not been taken, or slain," he said.

"No," I said.

"Interesting," he said, dipping the string again in water, and then in sand.

Mahpiyasapa's sorrow, I had little doubt, was occasioned by the perjury of Hci, and not by some putative treachery on the part of Canka. This, too, I had little doubt, was in the mind of the man who had chosen to speak to me. He was not a fool. In his shame and sorrow Mahpiyasapa had not gone to the council. Perhaps he felt he could not, there, face his peers. In the small confines of a sweat lodge, fasting, and with steam and hot stones, he would try to come to grips with these things which had happened. He might then go to some lonely place, to seek a dream or vision, that he might know what to do.

"Master," said I.

"Yes," said the man.

"Is it your understanding that Wopeton accompanied Mahpiyasapa?"

"That is what I think," said the man, drawing the wet string, sand adhering to it, firmly and slowly, carefully, across the stone. He had probably been working for more than two days on the stone. I could see the beginnings of the groove in its surface.

"Thank you, Master," I said.

"And that, too, is interesting," said the man, looking at the stone.

"Yes, Master," I said. The stones for use in the sweat lodge are heated in a fire outside the lodge and, held on sticks, taken within, where water is poured upon them, creating the needed heat and steam. When a stone cools it is then reheated. This part of the work, heating the stones, bringing the water, reheating the stones, and so on, ideally, is not done by the individual or individuals within the sweat lodge. Ideally, it is done by an assistant or helper. I had little doubt that Grunt was acting in this capacity for his friend, Mahpiyasapa. Mahpiyasapa, in this time, in his shame and misery, could not bring himself to face his own people.

I backed off a bit, on my knees, and then rose to my feet, and then withdrew from the presence of the fellow who was patiently working on the stone. I turned about and looked again at the huge council lodge. The two guards were still at the threshold. Between them, various men were entering. Expected to attend such a council, of course, on the part of the Kaiila, were not only the civil chieftains of the various bands of the Kaiila but their high men, as well, the councils of the various bands, and trusted warriors, and men of probity and wisdom. Such councils tend to be open to the noble, the proven and worthy. In that lodge, this afternoon, would be gathered, for most practical purposes, the leadership and aristocracy of the Kaiila nation. How absurd, then, to me, appeared my suspicions and fears. Where men so numerous, and noble and wise, were gathered, surely naught could be amiss. Who was I, an ignorant slave in their midst, to concern myself with their affairs? Too, Oiputake must have been mistaken. The Yellow Knives in camp could not be war chiefs. That would make no sense.

I took my way from the vicinity of the council lodge.

"Where is Watonka?" I heard a man ask.

"He has not yet arrived," said another man.

"Is he making medicine?" asked a man.

"I do not know," said another.

"He is waiting for the shadow to shrink," said another. "He will then come to the council."

I then, for no reason I clearly understood, turned my steps toward the lodges of the Isanna.

The three men, arms folded, standing in the vicinity of Watonka, who stood on a bit of high ground, near the Isanna lodges, I did not doubt were Yellow Knives. It was not that there was anything in particular about them that seemed to differentiate them from the Kaiila, but rather that there seemed something as a whole about them which was different, doubtless the cumulative effect of many tiny details, perhaps in the beading of their clothing, the manner in which certain ornaments were carved, the notching of their sleeves, the manner of fringing leggings, the tufting at the base of the feathers in their hair, the cut and style of their moccasins. They were not Kaiila. They were something else. They seemed stolid and expressionless. Watonka was looking to the sky, to the southeast. At the feet of Watonka there was a slim, upright stick. In the dirt, about the stick, were drawn two circles, a larger and a smaller. In the morning, when the sun was high enough to cast a shadow, the shadow, I surmised, would have come to a point on the outer circle. At noon the sun, it seemed, in this latitude, casting its shortest shadow, would bring the shadow to or within the smaller of the two circles. When the shadow, again, began to lengthen, the sun would be past meridian. I looked up at the sun, and down to the stick and its shadow. It was, I conjectured, less than half of an Ahn before noon.

Watonka, in marked contrast to the three warriors, whom I took to be Yellow Knives, seemed clearly ill at ease. He looked to the warriors, and then, again, looked to the sky, to the southeast. The day was bright and clear. Near the men, a bit to one side, were Bloketu and Iwoso. Bloketu, too, seemed ill at ease. Iwoso, on the other hand, like the other three, who were presumably Yellow Knives, seemed quite calm. These six, and two others, nearby Isanna warriors, with lances, wore yellow scarves diagonally about their bodies, running from the left shoulder to the right hip. The purpose of these scarves, I supposed, was to identify them as, and protect them as, members of the peace-making party. Too, of course, they might have been intended to fulfill some medicine purpose, perhaps suggested in a dream to one of them.

I did not know if Bloketu would be permitted into the council or not. Normally women are not permitted in such places. The red savages, though often listening with great attention to their free women, and according them great honor and respect, do not choose to relinquish the least bit of their sovereignty to them. They will make the decisions. They are the men. The women will obey. Iwoso, on the other hand, I supposed, would be required in the council lodge. She was probably the only person in the camp who spoke both Yellow Knife and Kaiila fluently. Iwoso, interestingly, had a coil of slender, supple rope at her belt. Judging by the sun, and the shadow by the stick, I would have supposed that Watonka and his party should have been making their way to the council lodge. The council, as I understood it, was to begin at noon. The manner in which the men wore their yellow scarves, I noted, gave maximum free play, if they were right handed, to their weapon hands.

"Bloketu," I said, going to her.

"Mistress!" she corrected me.

"Mistress," I said.

"Why are you not kneeling?" she asked.

I fell to my knees. "I would speak with you, if I might," I said.

"It was your master, Canka," she said, angrily, "who tried to kill Mahpiyasapa this morning."

"May I speak with you?" I asked.

"Yes," she said.

"Alone," I asked.

Iwoso looked suddenly, sharply, at me.

"You may speak before my maiden," said Bloketu. "What does it matter? Why should a slave not speak before a slave?"

"Forgive me, Mistress," I said. "I may be ignorant, and a fool."

"That is not unlikely," she said.

"But I have reason to believe that the three men with your father, the Yellow Knives, are not as they seem."

"What do you mean?" she asked.

"I think they are not civil chieftains of the Yellow Knives," I said. "I think it is possible they are war chiefs."

"Lying slave!" cried Iwoso angrily, lunging at me and striking me. I tasted blood at my mouth.

"What is going on?" asked Watonka, looking towards us.

"This slave is an amusing fool," laughed Bloketu. "He thinks our guests are not civil chieftains of the Yellow Knives, soon to be our friends, but war chiefs."

This was translated by Iwoso speedily to the three Yellow Knives. Their expressions did not change.

"That is absurd," said Watonka, looking rapidly about. "I vouch for these men myself."

"You could not know such a thing," said Bloketu.

"There is a slave in camp," I said, "a blond female who was owned by Yellow Knives for a time. It was she who recognized them. It was she from whom I learned this."

"She is obviously mistaken," said Bloketu. These things, and what follows, were being translated, quickly, by Iwoso for the Yellow Knives.

"The tongues of lying slaves may well be slit," said Watonka, angrily. He drew his knife.

At this point one of the Yellow Knives put his hand on Watonka's arm. He spoke, and his words, for all of us, were translated by Iwoso.

"Do not harm the slave," he said. "This is a time of happiness and peace."

I looked up, startled. The man must indeed by a civil chieftain.

"Dismiss him," suggested the Yellow Knife.

"You are dismissed," said Watonka, angrily.

"Yes, Master," I said, getting up.

"Beat him," said Watonka to the two Isanna warriors.

Suddenly I was prodded with the butts of the two lances, and then struck viciously about the head, the shoulders and body. I fell to my knees, my head covered, my body shuddering under the lashing and jabbing of the wood.

"Let him go," suggested the Yellow Knife.

"Go," said Watonka.

I struggled to my feet and, my face bloody, my body aching, stumbled backward, and then turned, and limped away. I heard laughter behind me. I had been well beaten. No bones, it seemed, were broken. I had little doubt that my body was black and blue. I spit up, into the dirt. I almost fainted. Then I staggered away, laughter ringing about me, a humiliated and punished slave. I had done, however, what I could. I had brought Oiputake's information to the attention of one even so great as to be a civil chieftain of the Kaiila, to Watonka, the civil chieftain of the Isanna. It seemed to me I could not have done better unless I had managed to speak, perhaps, to one such as Mahpiyasapa. Suddenly I felt anger, irrationally, towards Mahpiyasapa and Grunt, and toward Canka, and even towards my friend, Cuwignaka. I had not been able to speak to them. In my sickness and misery it seemed almost as though it was they who, thus, had been responsible for my beating. Then I shook the foolishness of this from my mind, and made my way back towards the lodge I shared with Cuwignaka.

It was at this time, I think, about a quarter of an Ahn until noon.

19

I SPEAK WITH CUWIGNAKA

"Cuwignaka!" I cried, startled, entering the interior of our lodge.

He was sitting, cross-legged, within the lodge. His head was down. His head was in his hands. He lifted his head. "They would not let me dance," he said. "Cancega, himself, medicine chief of all the Kaiila, at the behest of Hci, refused me entrance into the dance lodge."

"You must have heard," I asked, "of the alleged attack by Canka on Mahpiyasapa?"

"Yes," he said, bitterly. "Hci has won," he said. "Hci has won all."

"I am sorry, my friend," I said, "about the dance. I am sorry." I sat down, cross-legged, near him.

"If I am not permitted to dance," asked Cuwignaka, "how can I prove to them I am a man?"

"I am sorry, my friend," I said. In these moments, in my sorrow for Cuwignaka, I forgot my own bruises and pain. I knew that Cuwignaka, for years, had dreamed of entering the lodge of the great dance, there to test and prove the manhood from which his people seemed determined to preclude him. It was there, too, perhaps, in the loneliness and pain of the dance, that he wished himself to learn the truth in this secret and momentous matter.

"Tatankasa," said Cuwignaka, suddenly, "what is wrong?"

"Nothing," I said.

"You are hurt," he said, concerned.

"It is nothing," I said.

Cuwignaka crawled over to where I sat. He put his hand at the side of my head. "Your head has been gashed," he said.

I winced. "I was beaten," I said.

He went then to the side of the lodge and brought back a cloth. He wiped blood away from the side of my head.

"Who did this?" he asked.

"Two men, warriors of the Isanna, on the command of Watonka," I said.

"What did you do?" asked Cuwignaka.

"It was foolishness," I said. "I meddled in matters in which I knew nothing. I should have known better."

"But what did you do?" he asked.

"It is nothing," I said. I did not want him, in his great disappointment, to concern himself with my foolishness.

"Tell me," he said. I took the cloth from him and folded it, and held it against the wound, to stanch the flow of blood.

"I am sorry about the dance," I said. "I know how keenly you desired to enter the lodge."

"Why were you beaten, my friend?" he asked.

"This morning," I said, "converse did I hold with a blond slave, after amusing myself with her. I had used her before. She was formerly a herd girl. A woman once of the high city of Ar, she had been captured by Dust Legs and suitably enslaved. She was later traded to Sleen who, in turn, traded her to Yellow Knives. She came to the Isanna among the fruits of a girl raid. On the basis of her experience with the Yellow Knives she had told me that the three Yellow Knives in the camp are not civil chieftains, as is claimed, but war chiefs."

"She is obviously mistaken," said Cuwignaka.

"Obviously," I said. I moved my body. It hurt to move it.

"You told this to Watonka?" asked Cuwignaka.

"I would rather," I said, ruefully, "have told it to someone else, and, actually, it was to Bloketu that I told it. It was only that Watonka was there."

"It is too bad to be beaten over such a thing." said Cuwignaka.

"I agree," I smiled. I pulled the cloth from my head. It stuck with the blood, and then pulled free. But the wound did not begin again to bleed. "I do not think Watonka would have paid us attention," I said, "except that Iwoso leaped at me, striking me, crying out that I was a lying slave."

"That reaction seems excessive on her part," said Cuwignaka. "After all, what business is it of hers?"

"Watonka, too, was very angry," I said. "I feared he might

attack me with his knife. One of the Yellow Knives, one of the civil chieftains, intervened. I was only beaten."

"That seems thoughtful for a Yellow Knife," said Cuwignaka.

"He said it was a time of happiness and peace," I said.

"He is obviously a civil chieftain," said Cuwignaka.

"Yes," I said.

"Or pretending to be," said Cuwignaka, carefully.

"I am sore," I said.

"He did not wish to have blood spilled," said Cuwignaka.

"That seems so," I admitted.

"Why?" asked Cuwignaka.

"There might be many reasons," I speculated.

"Perhaps he thought the spilling of blood might not be suspicious shortly before the opening of a council on peace," said Cuwignaka.

"Perhaps," I said.

"But, too," said Cuwignaka, "such an act might have called much attention to itself. People might inquire, for example, why it was done, what it was all about."

I shrugged. "Perhaps," I said.

"Why should Watonka and Iwoso have been so angry?" he asked.

"I do not know," I said.

"What was Bloketu's reaction?" he asked.

"I do not think she wished to see harm come to me," I said.

"This incident occurred just outside the council lodge," said Cuwignaka.

"No," I said. "It occurred among the lodges of the Isanna."

"But this happened recently, did it not?" asked Cuwignaka.

"Yes," I said, "just a bit ago."

"Watonka and the others were on their way to the council lodge?" asked Cuwignaka.

"No," I said. "They seemed to be waiting, among the lodges."

"This is very interesting," said Cuwignaka, cautiously. "One would think that they would have been on their way to the council, if not within the council lodge, by then."

"Perhaps," I said. It was not clear to me what Cuwignaka was driving at.

"The great men of the Kaiila should all be within the council lodge," said Cuwignaka. "Why not Watonka?"

"Mahpiyasapa is not there either," I said. "He has gone off somewhere."

"That is a different matter, I think," said Cuwignaka.

"I think so," I said.

"At the time for the council to begin," mused Cuwignaka, "Watonka seems in no hurry to be within the lodge."

"That seems so," I said.

"The lodge contains the great men of the Kaiila," said Cuwignaka, "but Watonka, and the Yellow Knives, are not there."

"No," I said.

"Tell me, my friend, Tatankasa," said Cuwignaka. "Does there seem anything unusual to you, today, about the camp? Is there anything noticeably different?"

"The herds have been brought in, close to the camp," I said. "I saw one of the lads that commonly watches one of them, one of the girl herds. From him I learned, too, that the pickets and guards of the Isanna have been brought in."

"On whose orders?" inquired Cuwignaka.

"Watonka's," I said.

"Why?" asked Cuwignaka.

"I do not know," I said. "I suppose because it is a time of peace. It is the time of dances, of feasts and festivals. There is no danger. Tribes do not attack one another at such times."

"True," said Cuwignaka, slowly. "It has been so for a hundred winters."

"I was alarmed when I first learned this," I said, "but, I gather, you agree there is nothing to worry about."

"The camp is exposed on the west," said Cuwignaka.

"Yes," I said.

"Why would Watonka do this?" he asked.

"It is a time of peace," I ventured.

"Also," said Cuwignaka, "presumably even a large war party would hesitate to attack a camp of this size."

"Yes," I said.

"When you saw Watonka, and the Yellow Knives," said Cuwignaka, "what were they doing? Think carefully."

"Nothing," I said.

"Think carefully," said Cuwignaka.

"The Yellow Knives were standing in the vicinity of a small, raised place, prominent among the Isanna lodges. On this small, raised place stood Watonka. On this small, raised place, too, was a stick, surrounded by two circles, a larger and a smaller. I take it that the measurement of time was being accomplished by this stick and the circles. The inner circle, I think, would have had the edge of the shadow reach it or fall within it about noon."

"Interesting," said Cuwignaka.

"Yes," I said. "Why would they not simply judge noon by the position of the sun?"

"The stick is more accurate," said Cuwignaka. "Too, the shadow may be watched intently, as the sun may not be."

"The council is to begin at noon," I said. "Doubtless they were interested in a more precise judgment of time than might be afforded by simple visual sightings."

"Why?" asked Cuwignaka.

"I do not know," I said. To be sure, this question seemed a sensible one. Red savages are not ordinarily concerned with such precise measurements of time.

"Was there anything else that might have seemed unusual which you noted?" asked Cuwignaka.

"One thing or another," I said.

"What?" asked Cuwignaka.

"Watonka seemed interested in watching the sky," I said.

"The sky?" asked Cuwignaka.

"Yes," I said.

"Did he watch the entire sky?" asked Cuwignaka.

"No," I said. "He seemed interested in only one direction."

"What direction?" asked Cuwignaka, alarmed.

"The southeast," I said.

"I am afraid, Tatankasa," said Cuwignaka. "I am very afraid."

"Why?" I asked.

"It is from the southeast that the Pte came," said Cuwignaka.

"Yes?" I said.

"They were early this year," said Cuwignaka. "The Pte were very early. They should not have come as early as they did."

"That is true," I said. We had speculated on this matter before. To be sure, it had not seemed to be of much concern to Cuwignaka until now.

"You seem alarmed," I said. Cuwignaka's anxiety made me uneasy.

"It cannot be," said Cuwignaka, firmly.

"What?" I asked.

"Was there anything else unusual about Watonka, and the Yellow Knives?" pressed Cuwignaka.

"He, and his entire party, including Iwoso and Bloketu, wore yellow scarves, or sashes, about their bodies," I said.

"Why?" asked Cuwignaka, frightened.

"To identify them, I suppose," I said.

"To whom?" asked Cuwignaka. "They are well known in the camp."

I suddenly felt chilly. "I do not know," I said.

"Do you recall, Tatankasa," asked Cuwignaka, "some days ago, when we spoke with Bloketu and Iwoso outside our lodge. I was scraping a hide."

"Yes," I said.

"Iwoso was to become important, it seemed," he said. "From this we conjectured that Watonka, and Bloketu, too, would then be even more important."

"Yes," I said.

"How could one be more important among my people than to be the civil chieftain of a rich band?" asked Cuwignaka.

"To become, I suppose, a high chief of all the bands," I said, "a chief of the tribe, as a whole."

"But there are no first chiefs, no high chiefs, among the Kaiila, except maybe, sometime, a war chief," said Cuwignaka. "It is not our way."

"Perhaps there could be prestige, and riches, garnered in gift giving, as the result of arranging the peace," I said. I recalled we had thought about this matter along these lines before. It had, at that time, seemed a sensible way of viewing matters.

"Watonka is already rich in women and kaiila," said Cuwignaka. "There is only one thing he cannot be rich in, among our peoples."

"What is that?" I asked.

"Power," said Cuwignaka.

"What are you saying?" I asked, alarmed. "I am becoming afraid."

"What time is it?" asked Cuwignaka.

"It must be noon, by now," I said.

"There is no time to lose," said Cuwignaka, leaping to his feet.

"What is wrong?" I asked.

"The camp is going to be attacked," said Cuwignaka. "The pickets, the guards, have been withdrawn from the west. The Pte were early! Watonka looks to the sky, to the southeast!"

"I do not understand," I said.

"Why were the Pte early?" asked Cuwignaka.

"I do not know," I said.

"They were being hunted, being driven, by a new people," said Cuwignaka. "Something is behind them. A new force has come into our country."

"But Watonka was looking to the sky," I said.

"That is what makes me most afraid," he said. "It is like the old stories, told long ago by travelers, warriors who had ridden farther than others."

"What can we do?" I asked.

"We must alert the camp," said Cuwignaka.

"Even if you are right," I said, "even if the camp should be in danger, even if attack was imminent, no one will believe us. You wear the dress of a woman. I am a slave. We will be only mocked, only laughed at."

"One will not laugh at us or mock us," said Cuwignaka. "There is one who will listen."

"Who is that?" I asked.

"Hci," said Cuwignaka, angrily.

He then rushed from the lodge and I, rising to my feet, hurried after him. Outside he looked wildly to the sky, to the southeast, and then began to run between the lodges. I, too, looked at the sky. It was clear.

20

KINYANPI

"Behold," laughed Hci, sitting with cronies, cross-legged, outside the lodge of the Sleen Soldiers, "it is the pretty sister of Canka, and Canka's slave, Tatankasa."

"Listen to me, Hci," said Cuwignaka, "please!"

"Kneel," said Hci to us.

We knelt.

"She tried to enter the lodge of the dance," laughed Hci, pointing at Cuwignaka. "She is not permitted to do so!"

There was laughter from the young man sitting in the circle.

"I must speak to you," said Cuwignaka.

"I am busy," said Hci. There was laughter.

"I must speak to you!" said Cuwignaka.

"Do not come to plead lenience for your foolish brother,

who tried to kill my father, Mahpiyasapa, this morning?" inquired Hci.

"The camp is in danger," said Cuwignaka.

"What?" asked Hci.

"The Yellow Knives with Watonka are not civil chiefs," said Cuwignaka. "They have been recognized by a blond slave, once the property of Yellow Knives. They are war chiefs."

"That is absurd," said Hci.

"The pickets and guards have been drawn in from the west," said Cuwignaka. "Watonka has not gone to the council, nor have the Yellow Knives. The Pte were early! Watonka looked to the sky, to the southeast!"

"To the sky?" said one of the men with Hci.

"It is as in the old stories," said one of the men.

"These are lies," said Hci. "This is a trick. You are trying to make me look foolish."

"The guards have been drawn in from the west," said one man. "I know that."

"The Pte were early," said another. "We all know that."

"Who says Watonka is not in the council lodge?" asked Hci.

"Shortly before noon," I said, "I saw him still in the camp of the Isanna, with the Yellow Knives. I do not think it is his intention to go to the council lodge. I saw him watching the sky, to the southeast."

"Others were in the council lodge?" asked Hci.

"Most others, yes," I said. "I think so."

"The greatest men of our people, most of them, are in that lodge, Hci," said Cuwignaka, "gathered in that one place. Surely you understand what that could mean?"

"This is all a trick on your part," said Hci.

"No," said Cuwignaka.

"If what you say is correct," said Hci, "Watonka would be a traitor. He would be betraying the Kaiila."

"I am convinced that that is the case," said Cuwignaka.

"It cannot be," said Hci.

"To achieve his personal ends," said Cuwignaka, grimly, "even a good man can sometimes do great wrong. Can you believe that, Hci?"

Hci looked down, angrily.

"Can you believe it, Hci?" asked Cuwignaka.

Hci looked up, angrily. "Yes," he said.

"Act," said Cuwignaka. "The Sleen Soldiers have police powers in the camp. Act!"

"It is a trick," said Hci, angrily.

"It is past noon," said Cuwignaka. "There is little time."

"It is a trick," said Hci.

"I swear that it is not," said Cuwignaka. "Had I a shield I would swear by it."

Hci looked at him, startled.

"That is a most holy and sacred oath," said one of the Sleen Soldiers, frightened.

"Would you truly swear by a shield?" asked Hci.

"Yes," said Cuwignaka. "And when one so swears, then one is to be believed, is one not?"

"Yes," said Hci. "One is then to be believed."

"No one would betray the shield oath," said a man.

Hci trembled.

"Are you so fond of Yellow Knives?" asked Cuwignaka. "Have you not fought them?"

Hci looked at Cuwignaka. His hand, inadvertently, went to the whitish, jagged serration at his face, the residue of the canhpi's slash years ago.

"You probably know Yellow Knives as well as any man in the camp," said Cuwignaka. "Do you truly believe they desire peace?"

"No," said Hci.

"Act," said Cuwignaka.

"Would you truly swear by your shield?" asked Hci.

"Yes," said Cuwignaka.

Hci rose to his feet. "Agleskala," he said, "go to the council lodge. If Watonka is not within, use the powers of the Sleen Soldiers. Empty the lodge."

"What are you going to do?" asked Cuwignaka.

"I am going to blow the whistle of war," he said. "I am going to fetch the battle staff."

There was a scream from somewhere among the lodges to our left.

The sun seemed suddenly dark in the cloudless sky. The sky itself seemed blotted out with swift torrents of terrible forms. It was as though a storm had suddenly materialized and come alive. Over our head there was the snapping and cracking of a thousand thunders.

"It is too late!" I cried.

"It is the Kinyanpi!" I heard. "It is the Flighted Ones! The Kinyanpi!"

21

YELLOW KNIVES

One of the Sleen Soldiers, rising to his feet, spun awkwardly, kicking dust, the arrow having entered through the chest, its point protruding above his left hip.

Hci looked upward, wildly.

The tarn alighted, its talons seizing Agleskala. In its strike I think his back was broken. Hci and I stumbled backward, swept to the side by the strokes of the wing, the blows of the air. We could scarcely see for dust. The rider, clad only in a breechclout, his body bright in purple and yellow paint, thrust towards us with the long tarn lance. In the movement of the tarn, again taking flight, the thrust was short. Hci and I, from the dirt, looked upward. A hundred feet in the air the body of Agleskala was released.

"Weapons! Get weapons!" cried Hci.

An arrow struck near us, sinking almost to the feathers in the dirt.

I smelled smoke. I heard screaming.

"Kaiila!" called out Hci. "Get kaiila!"

"Run!" cried a man. "There is no time to make war medicine!"

"Arm yourselves!" cried Hci. "Get kaiila! Rally by the council lodge! Fight!"

"Run!" cried another man.

"Run!" cried another.

"Look out!" I cried.

Another tarnsman, low on the back of the mount, it swooping toward us, only a few feet from the ground, lowered his lance. I seized Hci and dragged him down. I saw the feathered lance, like a long blur, sweep over us. Then the bird was climbing again.

"Tarnsmen cannot take the camp," I said. Lodges were burning. Women were screaming.

The men who were with us had scattered.

"Do not touch me!" cried Hci, in fury.

I removed my hands from him.

"The people will run to the west!" said Cuwignaka.

"They must not!" I said.

We saw a rider on a kaiila racing towards us. Then, suddenly, he reeled from the back of the beast. He struck the ground, rolling, scattering dust. We ran to him. I lifted him in my arms. His back was covered with blood, filthy, now, too, with dirt. "They are in the camp!" he gasped.

"Who?" demanded Hci.

"Yellow Knives!" said the man. "Hundreds. They are among the lodges!"

"They have come from the west," said Cuwignaka, grimly.

"Watonka must die," said Hci.

I put the body of the man down. He was dead. A woman fled past us, a child held in her arms.

Hci rose from our side and went into the lodge of the Sleen Soldiers. I looked upward. This section of the camp was no longer under direct attack. The primary interest of the tarnsmen, I had little doubt, would have been the council lodge and the area about it. The lodge itself, because of its size, would be conspicuous. Too, they had doubtless been furnished with a description of it by Watonka or those associated with him. It was no wonder he was not eager, this day, to enter the lodge.

"I am going to Grunt's," I said. "My weapons are there. He has kept them for me. Too, Wasnapohdi is there. She may need help."

"There is a lance in my lodge," said Cuwignaka.

"We will get it on the way," I said. This was the same lance which had been fixed, butt down, in the turf beside Cuwignaka near the scene of battle several weeks ago. He had been staked down naked, to die. About the lance, wrapped about it, had been a white dress. It was that which he now wore. I had freed him.

We saw two men running past.

"Let us hurry," I said.

22

CUWIGNAKA REQUESTS INSTRUCTION

"Use the lance!" I cried.

We had turned, startled, not more than a few yards from our lodge, from the interior of which Cuwignaka had recovered the lance.

The rider on the kaiila, bent low, his lance in the attack position, charged, dust scattering back from the pounding paws of the kaiila.

Cuwignaka ducked to the side, lifting and raising his arms, the long lance clutched in his fists. There was a shiver of wood as the two lances, Cuwignaka's on the inside, struck twisting against one another. The point of the other's lance passed between Cuwignaka's arms and his neck. The man was taken from the back of the kaiila by Cuwignaka's lance. The kaiila sped away.

"He is dead," said Cuwignaka, looking down.

"Free your lance," I said.

Cuwignaka, his foot on the man's chest, drew loose the lance.

"It is safer in such an exchange," I said, "to strike from the outside, fending his lance away, trying to make your strike above and across it."

"He is dead," said Cuwignaka.

"If he had dropped his lance more to the right you would have moved into it," I said.

"I killed him," said Cuwignaka.

"It is unfortunate that we did not obtain the kailla," I said.

"He is dead," said Cuwignaka.

"Attend to my lessons," I said.

"Yes, Tatankasa," said Cuwignaka.

"Hurry," I said. "We are near Grunt's lodge."

"Are you all right?" I asked Wasnapohdi, entering Grunt's lodge.

"Yes," she said, kneeling fearfully in its recesses. "What is going on?" she asked.

"Watonka has betrayed the camp," I said. "It is under attack by both tarnsmen and Yellow Knives. Has Grunt come back?"

"No," she said. "Cuwignaka, are you hurt?"

"No," he said, trembling. "The blood is not mine."

"Where are my weapons?" I asked Wasnapohdi.

"I killed a man," said Cuwignaka.

"Here," said Wasnapohdi, going to a bundle at the side of the lodge, unwrapping it. Within it was my belt, with the scabbard and knife sheath, and the small bow I had purchased long ago in Kailiauk, with its sheaf of twenty arrows.

"Tatankasa," said Cuwignaka.

"Yes?" I said. I took the belt in my hands. I had not worn it since I had accepted the collar of Canka.

"Do not arm yourself," said Cuwignaka. "You might be spared, as a slave."

I buckled the belt about myself, I lifted the short sword in the scabbard and dropped it back in place. I tested the draw of the knife. The sheath hold was firm but the draw was smooth. I bent the bow, stringing it. I slung the quiver over my shoulder. I would use the over-the-back draw. I took two arrows in my hand, with the bow, and set another to the string.

I looked at Cuwignaka.

"The camp is large, and populous," I said. "It cannot be easily taken, even by surprise. There will be resistance."

Cuwignaka shook his head, numbly. "I cannot fight," he said. "I never could."

"Come, Wasnapohdi," I said to the girl. "We will try to find others. I will try to get you back to Grunt."

She stood, to follow me.

"If necessary, Wasnapohdi," I said to her, "fall on your knees before Yellow Knives, and tear open your clothing, revealing your breasts to them. If they find you attractive they may not slay you. They may only put their ropes on you."

"Yes, Master," she said.

"But I do not need to tell you that, do I," I asked, "for you are a woman."

"No, Master," she whispered. Men are the warriors and women, she knew in her heart, were among the fitting spoils of their victories.

At the interior threshold of the lodge I turned again to face Cuwignaka.

"I killed a man," he said, shuddering. "I could never do that again. It is too terrible a thing."

"The first is the hardest," I said.

"I cannot fight," he said.

"If you remain here," I said, "you must prepare to lie down and die with the innocent."

"Do you respect me, Tatankasa?" he asked.

"Yes," I said, "but death will not. It respects no one. It respects nothing."

"Am I a coward?" he asked.

"No," I said.

"Am I wrong?" he asked.

"Yes," I said.

"I do not know what to do," he said. "I am troubled."

"I wish you well, mitakola, my friend," I said. "Come, Wasnapohdi."

I briefly reconnoitered, and then left the lodge, Wasnapohdi following me. We threaded our way among the lodges, some of which were burned. Meat racks, with the sheets of dried meat, had been overturned. Pegged-down hides had been half torn up and trampled. I turned once, suddenly. It was Cuwignaka. He was still visibly shaken. He clutched the lance in his hands. "I am coming with you," he said. We then continued on our way.

"Back!" I said. "Down!"

We stepped back and crouched down behind a lodge. Eleven riders passed.

"Yellow Knives," I said.

In the belts of several of them were thrust bloody scalps, the blood run down their thighs and the sides of their legs, across their paint.

"If you do not fight," I asked Cuwignaka, "who will protect the weak, the innocent?"

"I cannot fight," he said. "I cannot help it. I cannot."

"Where are we going, Master?" asked Wasnapohdi.

"Toward the place of the council lodge," I said.

"That was doubtless the center of the attack," said Cuwignaka.

"We do not have kaiila to flee with," I said. "If there is resistance it seems natural to expect it at that point, particularly if it is organized. That is the center of camp. Men can reach it most easily, and strike out from it most easily."

"That is true," said Cuwignaka.

"Come along," I said.

"Step carefully," I said. "Several have died here."

We picked our way through twisted bodies.

Wasnapohdi threw up.

"These are your people," I told Cuwignaka.

"I cannot fight," he said.

The girl, lying on her back, nude, looked up at us, wildly. Her knees were drawn up. Her ankles were crossed and bound. Her wrists, behind her, were fastened at the small of her back and, by a double thong, looped twice, tightly, about her body, held in place there. I ran my finger under the belly thongs. She winced. In her body there were deep marks from them. I then let the thongs return to their place. The fellow who had tied her had done a good job. The thongs were merciless. A woman, of course, too, because of the glorious nature of her beauty, the sweet flaring of her hips, the lovely swelling of her upper body and breasts, cannot even begin to slip such a bond. A strand of leather, too, short and taut, pulling up her legs, connected her wrists and ankles. It is an efficient tie. In it a woman is utterly helpless. Nearby, in the dirt, its tying string cut away, lay a leather, beaded collar. The girl squirmed. On her left breast, in black paint, probably traced there with a finger, there was a rude mark, to identify her. So easily may a girl change masters.

The girl, squirming, looked wildly up at me.

"Come along," I said to Cuwignaka and Wasnaphohdi.

We left the girl behind us, whimpering. She would stay where she was. Later her new master, if he remembered, would return for her, to claim her. If he did not she was, in any case, clearly marked. When the loot was sorted out it would be at his feet that she would be placed.

"Be quiet," I whispered. "There are others here. This is obviously a collection point."

"How horrifyingly they treat us," gasped Wasnapohdi. "How horrifyingly they tie us, and put us about, as though we might be cord wood."

Even as she spoke a white slave girl, naked, her hands bound behind her, running before a kaiila, stumbling, prodded by the butt of a lance, was herded into that crowded place between the lodges. She fell among the other women. Some cried out as the kaiila stepped among them. The girl's captor dismounted and put his lance down. He then turned the girl to her back and, among the other bound women, threw her legs apart. She cried out, his will imposed upon her. He then threw her to her stomach and, with a short leather strap, bound her ankles together. He then turned her about, and jerked her to her knees, facing him. She was shuddering, and could scarcely utter articulate sounds. He then took a small leather sack from his belt and spit into it. He dipped his finger into the sack and, pressing it firmly down in the sack, swirled it about. He then put the sack down. On his finger was black paint. The pigment is fixed in kailiauk grease. He held her steady with his left hand behind her shoulder and, with his finger, traced a mark on her left breast. He looked at it, and then wiped his finger on his thigh and replaced the sack at his belt. She looked down at the mark. It was the mark of her master. She was then, by the hair, thrown down among the other women. The man retrieved his lance and then, swiftly, remounted his kaiila. In a moment he had left the place. The woman lay on her back, with the others, left behind. On her left breast, in black paint, was an identificatory mark. Most of the others there, too, wore such marks, but, in their cases, the marks were different.

"Some of these women," I said to Cuwignaka, "are red, doubtless former free women of the Kaiila."

"Women are born to serve men," said Cuwignaka.

Some of the women, though only a few, were marked not with paint, but with tags, devices of wire with an attached leather disk. The wire is thrust through an ear lobe or the septum and twisted shut, thus fastening the tag on the female.

"Do you think that is true, Wasnapohdi?" I asked.

"Yes, Master," she said, lowering her head. "I think so."

"Why?" I asked.

"Our deepest fulfillments," she said, "are found in obedience, service and love."

"But are these not the primary duties required of the female slave?" I asked.

"Yes, Master," she said.

"It thus seems," I said, "that there is some sort of interesting relationship between the achievement of female fulfillment and the harsh institution of uncompromising female slavery."

"Yes, Master," she said.

I smiled.

"But we would like to choose our masters," she said.

"Unfortunately," I said, "that is not possible."

"I am a female slave," she said. "I am well aware of that, Master."

"Sometimes, perhaps," I said, "a woman must find herself at the feet of the very man whom she would have chosen, had she the choice, as her master."

"Perhaps, Master," she said. "But even if she is not so fortunate as to be owned by such a man, there is a gratification for her in being made to kneel and obey, and, will-lessly, serve, a gratification connected with the fulfillment of her nature as lover and slave, and connected, too, with the knowledge that she is now at last in her place in nature, and will be kept there."

"I see," I said.

"Too," she said, "it is hard not to fall in love, eventually, with one who is one's master."

"That makes it easier, of course, to control the girl," I said.

"Doubtless, Master," she said, I thought with a trace of bitterness.

Bondage, I thought, must, doubtless, sometimes, be a hard lot for a female. Even whether a girl is clothed or not is up to the master.

"Do you think these women," I asked, surveying the trussed women at the collection point, "will make good slaves?"

"Any woman," she said, "with the proper master, will make a superb slave."

"Look upon them," I said. "You see them nude, helpless and bound, thrown together as the mere properties they are."

"Yes, Master," she said.

"Doubtless you feel keen pity for them," I said.

"Yes, Master," she said. "Master!"

I held her so that she could not move. My hand was upon her.

"But you are aroused, Wasnapohdi," I told her.

"Yes, Master," she whispered.

"Why is it," I asked, "that the sight of one female in bondage makes another desire to be placed in the same condition!"

"I do not know, Master," she said.

"Do you desire to be nude, and bound among them?" I asked.

"No, Master," she said. "I am already with masters."

"I am not a master," said Cuwignaka.

"Is he a master?" I asked Wasnapohdi. She was a female. She might be able to tell such things.

"There is that in him which could be a master," said Wasnapohdi. "I sense it."

"I wear the dress of a woman," said Cuwignaka. "I will not even fight."

"There is in you that which could be a master," said Wasnapohdi. "I can sense it."

"That is absurd," said Cuwignaka.

"It is you who must decide," she said.

"Look at these women," I said to Cuwignaka. "Many of them are former free women of the Kaiila. Many men, as they are of their own people, regardless of what would be in the best interest of the women, would fight to free them. In such matters they would not consider what would make the women most happy but rather would take their enslavement, irrationally, as being somehow demeaning or insulting to them personally. Thus, for their own vanity, really, in the final analysis, they would fight to free them. Too, sometimes men who desire to own slaves but are themselves too weak to do so, or, because of rigidities or cripplings, are psychologically incapable of doing so, will, out of envy, jealousy and spite, fight to free them, in order to deny others the pleasures which they, because of their handicaps and inhibitions, cannot grant to themselves. If I, for one reason or another, cannot have these extraordinary pleasures, then neither, too, shall anyone else, so to speak. What I want and cannot have I will deny to others, so to speak. Moral fervor is often the outcome of inadequacy. Happy men do not make good zealots. Once again, of course, the best interests of the women, and whatever might be their true nature, are not considered. They, as usual, though putatively the objects of these wars, are the forgotten ones. All women know that truly strong-drive men desire to own them; a male with strong drives will never be truly content with anything else. Truth is not terrible; it is merely real."

Cuwignaka looked at me, not speaking.

"But will you not fight for these women, even for reasons of vanity?" I asked.

"No," he said. He shook his head. "I do not want to fight. I cannot fight. I am sorry, my friend, Tatankasa. I cannot fight."

"I cannot make you couch a lance," I said. "I cannot put a knife into your hand."

"I am sorry, Tatankasa," he said.

"Let us go," I said. "We must try to make the center of camp."

"It is the dance lodge," I said.

To our right was the great, circular brush lodge. It was some forty feet in height. It enclosed a packed-down dancing space of some fifty feet in diameter. It was ceilinged with poles and branches. In the center of the lodge, visible now through a hole torn in the brush, was the tall, slim, peeled, twice-forked pole which, days ago, Winyela had felled. The paraphernalia of the dance, with the exception of some long, narrow, braided ropes, had been removed from the pole. The pole itself had apparently been attacked with hatchets and knives. It was marked and gashed. From the sides of the dance lodge huge gouts of brush had been torn away. It was through these gaps that Yellow Knives had perhaps entered the lodge. Inside, in several places, the dust was bloodstained. In places, marked by successions of linear stains, and marks in the dust, bodies had apparently been dragged from the lodge. This, presumably, would have been done later by Kaiila.

"This place, as I understand it," I said, "is holy to your people. It has been desecrated."

Cuwignaka shook his head. "I cannot fight," he said.

"Do not look down," I warned Cuwignaka. "It will disturb you."

"Tatankasa!" he said.

"I have seen it," I said. "Come along."

But Cuwignaka knelt down among the dead. He lifted the small body in his arms.

"Let us go," I said.

"It is only a child," he said.

Wasnapohdi averted her eyes. She looked sick. It was not pretty.

"We knew him," said Cuwignaka.

"There is the mother," I said.

"We knew him!" said Cuwignaka.

"Yes," I said. He had been a lad from among the Kaiila. He was well known to both Cuwignaka and myself. We had thrown the hoop for him many times, he then firing his small arrows through it. In the camp he had been known by the names of Hala and Owopte. 'Hala' is Kaiila for the Gorean hinti, which are small, active insects. They resemble fleas but are not parasitic. The boy had been small for his age, and energetic. There is no simple translation for 'Owopte' but, literally, it means the place from which a turnip is dug. He had used to go out with his mother to dig turnips when he had been a little boy. That was a pet name which she had given him. He had been fond of the vegetable. He had not lived long enough to choose a suitable adult name for himself.

"He is dead," said Cuwignaka.

"Yes," I said.

"Why have they done this to him?" asked Cuwignaka, rocking the body in his arms.

"I do not know," I said. I could understand, to some extent, the stripping, the cutting and slashing, the mutilation, the cutting and uprooting of bloody trophies, where male adults, warriors, were concerned. In a sense it was a celebration of relief, of life, of victory, of jubilation and triumph. It did not make much sense to me where women or children were concerned. Confirming my suspicions in this matter, it might be noted that many warriors will usually reserve such grisly attentions, with the exception of scalping, for adult, enemy males. Too, such things are more common with younger warriors than mature warriors. There are many putative explanations for these practices, having to do with such things as insulting the enemy, terrorizing others and even delaying or interfering with the deceased's entrance into, or activities within, the medicine world, but I suspect that the deepest, least rationalized explanations lie in the vicinity of the ventilation and expression of emotions such as hatred, relief and elation, of joy, gladness and triumph. Such practices among most peoples are not as institutionalized as among the red savages but I think that those who know war, on whatever remote fields, will not find themselves unfamiliar with the counterparts of such practices. They are not restricted to the grasslands east of the Thentis mountains. They are not unknown outside of the Barrens.

"He is only a child," said Cuwignaka, rocking the body, pressing his cheek against the affronted head, the exposed bone, the lacerated, bloody skin. "Why have they done this?"

"I do not know," I said.

"Yellow Knives have done this," he said.

"Maybe those called the Kinyanpi," I said. "I do not know."

"Enemies have done this," said Cuwignaka.

"Yes," I said.

Cuwignaka put the body down, carefully. He then looked at me. "Teach me to kill," he said.

23

CUWIGNAKA AND THE SLAVE

"Down," I whispered.

We lay behind the lodge. Five Yellow Knives, in single file, astride kaiila, moved quickly past. As the last one passed I stepped out behind them. The strike must be below the left shoulder blade. It must be made swiftly enough for the carrying force of the small bow not to be dissipated; it must be made from a distance sufficient, given the spacing of the riders and the sound of the Kaiila's paws, to cover the sound of the string. I then fitted another arrow to the string.

"They will not know for a time that they are now only four," I said.

"Leave it," I said. But Cuwignaka was at the body. "I do not want it," I said. Cuwignaka thrust it in his own belt, dark and bloody against the white cloth of the dress he wore.

"We need kaiila," I said.

"We will get them," said Cuwignaka.

"Oh!" cried the woman, one of two, nude and bound, sitting on the ground, their legs widely apart.

The Yellow Knife with them whirled about but only to meet Cuwignaka's lance.

The woman screamed. Cuwignaka jerked his lance free. She began to sob, frightened, hysterical. "Be silent, Slave," snarled Cuwignaka. She looked up at him, frightened, sobbing. He struck her alongside the head with the shaft of his lance. Such things slaves understand. Her outburst might have alerted other Yellow Knives. Her blubbering, too, might convey to them that something unusual had occurred. She lay on her side in the dirt. She looked up once at Cuwignaka and then, quickly, averted her eyes from his. He was looking down at her, angrily. She trembled. Whereas a free woman may often make a man angry with impunity, she being lofty and free, this latitude is seldom extended to the slave. When a slave makes a man angry she knows that there may very well be consequences to her action, that she, vulnerable and owned, subject to discipline and punishment, may very well be held to account, and, indeed, is quite likely to be held to account, and strictly, for any dissatisfaction which she may have engendered.

"There are no kaiila here," I said. I was not clear why Cuwignaka had stopped here.

"This either has been, or is intended to be, a collection point," said Cuwignaka. He gestured to the two women, one sitting on the ground, her legs widely apart, the other lying on her side, her arms, too, in their particular tie, largely between her legs.

"You think, then," I said, "that girls are either to be brought to this place, or are to be taken from this place?"

"Yes," said Cuwignaka, "and judging from the tie, which does not suggest that they are soon to be marched away, I would think they are being brought to this place."

"I see," I said. Thusly, presumably men would come with kaiila, either to bring more women, or to herd these away. We, then, would be waiting for them. "We should not be waiting too closely to this spot," I said, "for those coming in may be looking for the guard."

"We will look for tracks," said Cuwignaka. "I do not think it will be difficult."

"It is interesting that there was a guard here," I said. There had not been one at the other point.

"That indicates, I think," said Cuwignaka, "that we may, at last, be closer to the center of Kaiila resistance."

"It is some five Ahn until dark," I said.

"By that time it is my hope to have kaiila and join with the resistance," said Cuwignaka.

I nodded. If a flight from the camp, with refugees, was to be made, presumably it would be most effectively conducted after dark.

"You should be sitting up," said Cuwignaka to the girl lying on her side. The side of her face bore a long welt from where she had been struck with the lance shaft. "It will look more natural."

"Yes, Master," she whispered.

Cuwignaka looked at me, puzzled, and then smiled. How naturally the female had used the expression 'Master' to him.

"I think you are right about the tie," I said.

"Yes," he said. We looked at the two women, now both sitting, with their legs apart. It is an efficient tie. It is known to the slavers of the cities, and to the men of the cities, of course, as well as to the savages of the Barrens. The girl is made to sit down, with her legs apart. She is then made to put her arms inside her legs. The left wrist is then taken under the left leg and placed against the outside of the left ankle, where, on the outside of the ankle, it is tied tightly in place. The right wrist is then treated similarly, passing under the right leg and being tied tightly on the outside of the right ankle. This makes the girl quite helpless. It also makes it impossible for her to close her legs.

Neither of the girls dared to meet our eyes. They looked down, frightened.

The conjecture of Cuwignaka with respect to their tie and its significance was as follows: Normally, when a woman is brought to a collection point or holding area she is either herded there or led there on a tether. In either case her legs are free. Since her wrists will usually have been bound behind her back at the time of her capture, particularly if she is a new capture, all that remains to be done in the holding area, thus, is to throw her to the ground and put her in a quick ankle-tie. This ankle tie, then, if she is to be moved in the near future, may swiftly be removed and she, already hand-bound, is promptly ready again for the tether or the blows of her herder. The more elaborate ties of the two girls at this point suggested, then, that women were being brought to this point, rather than being taken from it. For example, to take a woman from this point would require two separate operations rather than one. She would have to be freed of her present bonds and then have her hands retied. The ties of the women at this point suggested, too, that they were being readied not for an imminent transfer to another location but for the pleasure of warriors. Their ties, thus, were an indication of the confidence and arrogance of the enemy.

Cuwignaka knelt beside the body of the fallen Yellow Knife. He drew forth his knife. The bound women shuddered. Then they, as Wasnapohdi, looked away.

"I think you had best dispose of our friend there," I said, indicating the Yellow Knife.

Cuwignaka nodded. I did not much care to look at it, particularly after Cuwignaka had finished with it. Too, if other Yellow Knives should approach the area it scarcely seemed appropriate to have it lying about.

In a moment Cuwignaka had returned.

I saw no sign of approaching Yellow Knives.

He looked down at the woman who had screamed, and cried, she whom he had silenced with the command of a master and a blow to the side of the face.

He put the point of his lance under her chin and lifted her head. She was terrified. I could see that he was still angry. The point of his lance dipped, aligned then with the beauty of her soft, bared breasts. Then the point was raised again, lodging itself again under her chin, holding her head up again, cruelly, that she must look at him.

"Forgive me, Master," she whispered. There was a drop of blood at her chin.

I myself did not blame her for crying out. She had been frightened. She had been startled. Too, her weeping had been uncontrollable. She had been only a blubbering slave. I wondered if he would kill her.

"Forgive me, Master," she begged.

He looked down at her, angrily. Then he withdrew the lance point from her chin.

Relieved of its pressure she put herself to her back in the dirt before him. She looked up at him, frightened. "Please, forgive me Master," she begged.

"You are well tied for the pleasures of Yellow Knives," said Cuwignaka scornfully, looking down upon the supine, exotically bound suppliant.

"Forgive me, Master," she begged. "Please." She opened her legs to Cuwignaka, spreading them even more widely than the nature of her tie required.

"Why should Yellow Knives be first?" I asked.

Cuwignaka looked at me.

"Please, Master," begged the girl.

"Have you ever had a woman?" I asked.

"No," he said.

"Take her," I said. "I will keep the watch."

The girl gasped, lifted and held.

"Master!" she breathed.

"Aiii," cried Cuwignaka, softly.

"Master, Master," she said. Cuwignaka seemed loathe to let her go. Then he thrust her from him, to her side in the dirt. He stood up.

"I did not know such pleasures could exist," he said, "such feelings! Such triumph! Such glory!"

"There is no substitute for a slave female," I said. This had been known to men throughout history.

Cuwignaka gently, by the hair, pulled the girl to a sitting position. She turned her head and kissed and licked at his leg.

"Do you think she received pleasure?" he asked.

"Yes," I said.

"Might not a slave dissemble in such a matter?" he asked.

"Certain things their bodies cannot dissemble," I said. I took the girl by the hair and, gently but firmly, pulled back her head. "Do you see these discolorations," I asked, indicating irregular reddish splotches on her fair skin, "the results of capillary distention?"

"Yes," he said.

"They are correlated with her pleasure."

"Interesting," said Cuwignaka.

I then turned the girl in profile to him. "Consider her nipples," I said. "They are hard and high, distended, sweet and swollen with blood."

"Yes," said Cuwignaka.

"This sign, too," I said, "invariably indicates the presence of sexual pleasure in the human female."

"Are such things generally known to masters?" asked Cuwignaka.

"I would suppose so," I said. I then released the girl's hair and she put her head forward, and down, humbly.

"It would not be in a girl's best interest, then, to dissemble in such a matter," said Cuwignaka.

"No," I said. "And after a beating or two she will strive with all her might to experience authentic sexual pleasures, and as deeply and fully as possible."

"Excellent," said Cuwignaka.

"And thus, in a sense," I said, "she sets herself the task of making herself all the more helplessly her master's slave."

"Superb," said Cuwignaka.

The girl turned her head again and, softly, timidly, kissed him on the leg.

"But whether she experiences pleasure or not is unimportant," I said, "for she is only a slave."

"Of course," said Cuwignaka.

The girl put down her head.

"We must get kaiila," I said.

"We will look for tracks," he said.

At the perimeter of the holding area we looked back at the two women sitting, bound, in the dirt. The one who had been so frightened of Cuwignaka, and who had placated him with her bound beauty, was looking after us.

"I had not known such pleasures could exist," said Cuwignaka.

"They can be as long or as brief, as superficial or as profound, as you wish," I said.

He then gave his attention to the ground, looking for tracks.

I looked back for a time at the two nude, bound women, women who were owned by men, who could be bought and sold, who were slaves.

"Perhaps you should not have had a slave," I said.

"Why not?" he asked.

"They may spoil you for other women," I said.

24

WE OBTAIN KAIILA

The three girls screamed, their tethers dropped, their hands tied behind their back.

The Yellow Knife behind them, the arrow in his chest, slipped back, awkwardly, turned, and fell heavily into the dust.

The other Yellow Knife dropped his lance into the attack position, cried out rage and kicked his heels back into the flanks of the kaiila. The animal leapt toward Cuwignaka.

"Stay to the outside of his lance!" I cried. Cuwignaka had no shield. He must fend the stroke with his own lance. Had he a shield he might have sought an inside attacking position, fending to the left, striking then toward the opened center. I fitted another arrow to the string. I took it from my hand, where I had held it in readiness, oriented linearly with the bow itself. In the warfare of the red savages the first feed is usually from the bow hand or from the mouth to the string; the second feed is from the quiver to the hand or the mouth. Needless to say the arrow may be moved much more swiftly from the bow hand or the mouth to the string than from the quiver to the string.

Cuwignaka struck the lance away to his right with his own lance. The passage was so swift he could not bring his own lance over that of his foe. The kaiila stopped almost short, in a scattering of dust, jerked back on its haunches and wheeled about. I lifted and lowered the bow. I could not get a clear shot. In the second passage Cuwignaka darted to his right. His opponent cried out in fury, unable to clear the neck of his kaiila with the lance. Cuwignaka's upward thrust, however, was easily turned by the Yellow Knife's stout war shield, of rawhide thickened and hardened by shrinking over heated stones, from the neck, between the shoulders, or the humped back, behind the head, bearing the trident of the bull kailiauk.

Again I lowered the bow, cursing, furious, changing my position.

The kaiila again spun about, scratching, snorting, with an explosion of dust.

The rider brought the lance over the beast's neck, inside of the shield on his left arm. In this position, the enemy to the left, the rider affords himself the protection of the shield. This is commonly regarded as more than adequate compensation for the somewhat reduced fanlike ambit of play, that between the shield and the neck of the kaiila, then open to the lance. The kaiila was a trained beast. Its left ear was notched. It would doubtless maneuver in such a way as to keep Cuwignaka on its left in its charge, even changing its attack trajectory, if necessary, to do so.

I tried to get to the rider's right. Already he had charged. I heard the two shafts crack together, Cuwignaka fending the driving point away, and then, to my dismay, I heard a swift, striking sound, and saw Cuwignaka struck from the side of the kaiila, and reeling and staggering backwards, then sprawling, his legs loose under him, to the dust, struck by the passing shield, the weight of the kaiila and rider behind it, his own lance spun from his grip. With a trained kaiila, the animal aligning itself in such a way as to optimize the play of the rider's lance, there is little defense against this sort of thing. Being close enough to sturdily fend the blow brings one, if one is afoot, and shieldless, normally, close enough to risk the strike of the shield. The blow was such that I feared, for a moment, his head struck to the side, that his neck might be broken. The rider spun the kaiila about, to his right, keeping his shield between himself and my arrow. Cuwignaka was on one knee, half risen, shaking his head. His weapon was a dozen feet away. The rider dropped his point for the kill.

"Down!" I cried.

Cuwignaka hurled himself headlong under the paws of the kaiila and the lance thrust down, driving into the dust. The kaiila almost atop Cuwignaka then turned again and, again, the lance thrust down. Cuwignaka desperately seized it and it, braced under the Yellow Knife's arm, lifted, pulling him to his feet, skidding and half dragged in the dust. The rider cried out in anger. Cuwignaka clung to the lance. There was blood at the side of his head and run into his left eye. I was now only a few feet from the rider. The rider was bent down, struggling to retain control of the lance. Cuwignaka was between him and my weapon. The rider, not unaware of my presence, jerked the kaiila about, bringing his shield once more between us. The rider jerked at the lance and it tore against the palms of Cuwignaka's hands, blood at the wood. Then he swung the lance down and against the side of the kaiila and Cuwignaka lost his balance and the lance, rolling under the paws of the beast. The Yellow Knife, with a whoop of triumph, brandishing the lance, sped his kaiila forward, to turn it for another passage. I lowered my bow. Cuwignaka was on his feet, sprinting after the rider. I smiled. He would, if the Yellow Knife did not vary his pattern, have time to make his desperate connection. The Yellow Knife jerked his kaiila to a halt, it rearing up, fighting the jaw rope, clawing at the air, and Cuwignaka, almost at the same time, leaped to its back, behind the Yellow Knife. They plunged to the dust. In a moment, Cuwignaka rose to his feet, his knife bloody.

"I will get the kaiila," I said.

25

WE SPEAK WITH A KAIILA WARRIOR

"Look," said Cuwignaka, pointing.

A rider was approaching, the feathers on his lance streaming behind it, the lance upright.

We had mounted the two kaiila taken from the Yellow Knives. It felt good to have such beasts beneath us. I had put my bow in the bow case of the Yellow Knife I had slain and added his arrows to my quiver. I had taken, too, his lance and shield. Cuwignaka had recovered his own lance and had added to his armament, too, the shield of the Yellow Knife he had slain. Wasnapohdi, afoot, was at the left flank of my kaiila.

"He is Kaiila," I said.

"It is Hci," said Cuwignaka.

The son of Mahpiyasapa pulled his mount up short near us. "Two Yellow Knives came this way," he said.

"They went no further," said Cuwignaka.

Hci looked down at the two bodies, separated by several feet. "Who did this?" he asked.

"You are alone," said Cuwignaka. "Was it your intention to attack the two Yellow Knives by yourself?"

"Yes," said Hci.

"You are a brave man," said Cuwignaka.

"How is it that you have kaiila?" asked Hci. "Their markings indicate that they are Yellow Knife."

"These Yellow Knives had no further need of them," said Cuwignaka.

"How is it that a slave is armed?" asked Hci, regarding me.

"He has my permission," said Cuwignaka.

"Who slew these Yellow Knives?" asked Hci.

"Are you disappointed that it was not you?" asked Cuwignaka.

"No," said Hci. "It does not matter. I have taken many coups today."

I noted that Hci's shield, almost as though it were alive, seemed to move. It seemed he had to hold it steady, close to him. I had never seen anything precisely like this before.

"Who slew them?" asked Hci.

"Two who lay in wait for them," said Cuwignaka. He, too, obviously, noted the shield of Hci. It seemed that Hci, almost with the strength of his arm, must restrain it. Then the shield was again calm, again seemingly no more than a device of leather, one painted with designs and ornamented with feathers.

"Isbu?" asked Hci.

"One was Isbu and one was not," said Cuwignaka.

"Do you know their names?" asked Hci.

"Yes," said Cuwignaka.

"What are they?" asked Hci.

" 'Cuwignaka' " and 'Tatankasa'," said Cuwignaka.

"This is a dark and bloody day for the Kaiila," said Hci. "Do not make sport with your cleverness."

"Forgive me," said Cuwignaka.

"You have presumed, even, to put bloody trophies at your belt," observed Hci. "Whence did you obtain them?"

"I took them from some fellows I found lying about," said Cuwignaka, dryly.

"Do not forget that you are only a woman and a slave," said Hci, regarding us.

"I am not a woman," said Cuwignaka, quietly.

"You have kaiila now," said Hci. "That is good. You now have an opportunity to flee."

"Is the camp lost?" asked Cuwignaka.

"No," said Hci. "We are holding it."

"We shall not fly then," said Cuwignaka.

"Those who slew the Yellow Knives," said Hci, "have they fled?"

"No more than we," said Cuwignaka.

"Should you come again into contact with them," said Hci, "inform them that our forces may be joined near the council lodge."

I had thought that the resistance would organize itself in that area. It was at the center of the camp. Too, it was on high ground.

"I understand," said Cuwignaka.

"Will you deliver the message?" asked Hci.

"You may consider it delivered," said Cuwignaka.

"Good," said Hci. He then turned his kaiila, but, again, pulled it up short. He turned back to face us. "Mahpiyasapa has returned," he said. "He and Kahintokapa, of the Yellow-Kaiila Riders, are commanding the defense. We fear only the return of the Kinyanpi, the Flighted Ones."

"May I speak?" I asked.

"Yes," said Hci.

"Such may be met," I said. "Watonka and his party wore yellow scarves or sashes that they might be recognized by the Kinyanpi. Your warriors, too, might adopt that device. In this way the Kinyanpi may be confused as to who to fire upon, particularly in the minglings of combat. Too, consider the deployment of archers in the corridors of aerial attack, to protect your riders. Sharpened stakes can discourage talon attacks. Ropes stretched between lodges can interfere with low-flight attacks and impede attempted landings. Cloths and covers, even separated and strung above the ground, can provide protective concealments, some serving to hide what is actually beneath them, particularly from high altitudes, others serving as patterns distractive to archers, patterns which make it difficult to target the objects they shelter, both with respect to their movements and locations."

"Have you seen such things done effectively?" asked Hci.

"Yes," I said.

"I will speak to Mahpiyasapa," said Hci.

"Grunt is my friend," I said. "Did he return to the camp with Mahpiyasapa?"

"Yes," said Hci. "He is with us."

"Good," I said.

"Hci," said Cuwignaka.

"Yes?" said Hci.

"What of Watonka?" asked Cuwignaka. "Does he fight with the Yellow Knives?"

"It had been my intention to kill him," said Hci. "I rode to the camp of the Isanna. I found him there. He was already dead. So, too, were some others. I think they were killed by the Yellow Knives who had been with them. It had been done not with arrows, but knives. Too, the Yellow Knives were gone. It was probably done when the attack of the Kinyanpi began. They did not need him any more then."

"What of Bloketu?" asked Cuwignaka.

"The traitress?" asked Hci.

"Yes, Bloketu, the traitress," said Cuwignaka.

"I do not know," said Hci.

"You did not find her among the dead," said Cuwignaka.

"No," said Hci.

"The Yellow Knives must have taken her," said Cuwignaka.

"Perhaps," said Hci.

"I myself had little doubt as to the fate of the lovely, betrayed traitress. I recalled the coils of supple rope which Iwoso, her maiden, had worn at her belt. Too, I had little doubt that Iwoso, long before the attack, working in secret, in anticipation, had prepared a beaded collar for her mistress. Iwoso, for her part in the attack, would now be an important woman among the Yellow Knives. A woman of such importance, of course, should have her own maiden.

"As you are only a woman and a slave," said Hci, "it would be my advice, since you have kaiila, that you flee."

"Thank you for your consideration," said Cuwignaka. Indeed, in my opinion, Hci was, at least in his own mind, trying to be courteous and helpful. He did think of Cuwignaka, for the most part, as though he were a woman, and he would think of me, naturally enough, in terms of my collar. His remark was intended to be, and I think Cuwignaka understood it in this way, in our best interest. It seemed a new Hci with whom we spoke, one far less vain and arrogant than the one we had known.

"If you wish, on the other hand, to come to the area of the council lodge, to huddle there with the women and children, you may do so," he said. "The way to the council lodge, at this point, is clear."

"Thank you," said Cuwignaka.

"But there will be fighting there," said Hci.

"We understand," said Cuwignaka.

Hci then turned his kaiila about and rode from us.

"Did you see the movement of his shield before?" asked Cuwignaka.

"Yes," I said. "I have never seen anything like that. It is eerie."

"I am afraid," said Cuwignaka.

I felt suddenly chilly. Then I shook the chill from me. The sky was bright. In it were billowy white clouds. It was a good day for war.

"Shall we go to the council lodge or flee?" I asked.

"We shall decide the matter in a way becoming to my people," said Cuwignaka. "Do you see that lonely fleer in the sky?"

"Yes," I said.

"If it should fly to the north or west," he said, "we shall go to the council lodge."

"And if it should fly to the south or to the east?" I asked.

"Then," said Cuwignaka, "we shall go to the council lodge."

"It is going north," I observed.

"Then the matter is clear," said Cuwignaka. "We will go to the council lodge."

"I was hoping that that would be the outcome," I said.

"So, too, was I," said Cuwignaka.

"It was very clever fleer," I said.

"I was sure it would be," said Cuwignaka.

We adjusted our weapons.

"Let us go," I said.

"What of these?" asked Cuwignaka, gesturing with his lance to the three white slaves who had been in the charge of the Yellow Knives. They stood to one side, frightened. Their long tethers dangled from their necks to the dust. They were stripped. Their hands were bound behind their backs.

"You are in the presence of a free man," I said to them, indicating Cuwignaka.

Quickly they fell to their knees, putting their heads to the dust.

"We will leave them," I told Cuwignaka. "They are only female slaves."

"I, too, am only a female slave, Master," said Wasnapohdi, looking up at me.

"You may accompany us," I said.

"Thank you, Master," she said.

The other slaves lifted their heads, remaining on their knees, bound, in the dust.

We left them behind, then, making our way toward the council lodge. They, like other loot strewn about, robes and saddles, must wait to see who it was who would pick them up, who it was to whom they would then belong, whom they must then serve, absolutely and unquestioningly, with every perfection and particle of their intelligence and beauty.

26

ONCE MORE TO TREAD DISPUTED, BLOODY DUST

"Well done!" I called to Cuwignaka.

His kaiila in the clash of shield and lances had lost its footing, spinning and falling back to its haunches. Cuwignaka had retained his position on the animal. As it scrambled up he had caught a passing Yellow Knife under the shield. The momentum of the Yellow Knife had wrenched Cuwignaka to the side but, again, he had kept his position. The same momentum, in its force, blood leaping from his side, carried the Yellow Knife from the point of the lance. In a few yards he had been unable to cling to the animal and had slipped from its back, under the paws of other beasts.

I looked about myself.

Hci and Cuwignaka, to my right, were almost side by side.

I buffeted aside the attack of a Yellow-Knife lance, it furrowing the hide of the shield I bore. There were men afoot amongst us, too, both Yellow Knives and Kaiila. The Yellow Knife whirled his kaiila about, as I did mine. Lances struck on shields. We were then apart from one another. Ear-splitting shrieks and cries filled the air. Red savages are not wont to conduct their altercations in dignified silence. There is a purpose to such things, of course. They serve to heighten aggression and ventilate emotion. They may also have a role to play in the intimidation, and consequent inhibition, of the enemy, perhaps in virtue of making one seem a more fearsome or terrible foe. Most interestingly, such cries, particularly if unexpected, may freeze, or startle, the enemy, thus, for a brief, valuable moment, providing the aggressor with a relatively inactive, stationary target for a particular stab or thrust. This sort of thing occurs in the animal world, incidentally, as when the cry of the male larl freezes game for the coordinated attack of his mate, the she-larl. Too, those who have been trained in the use of the bayonet will not find such things unfamiliar.

"Beware!" I cried.

A Kaiila turned, catching the canhpi of a Yellow Knife on his shield.

I yanked back my leg, bloody. I struck down to my right with the butt of my lance. A Yellow Knife, afoot, reeled back. He was struck by the forequarters of another Yellow Knife's kaiila and fell to the ground. There a Kaiila warrior leapt upon him, knife rising and falling.

Suddenly my lance was pinned between my mount and that of another warrior, one of the Kaiila. For an instant I could not free it of the press of the animals and then I wrenched it free.

I saw Cuwignaka fend away an attack against Hci, thrusting his kaiila, his shield lifted, literally between that of Hci and his assailant. Hci himself was thrusting away an attacker on his right.

In feeling I was not really much aware of the cut on my leg but I inspected it, visually, to ascertain its depth and nature. It is important to be objective about such matters. In particular, if the flow of blood is considerable or steady, it must be stanched. Some men have bled to death from wounds of which they, in the heat of battle, in the excitement and press of combat, were scarcely aware. The blood from the wound, however, was shallow and run from the cut itself. Already its flow was slowing. It was not dangerous. There were neither veins nor arteries in the area.

I kicked back my heels into the flanks of my kaiila and it lunged ahead. My lance dug into the chest of a Yellow Knife afoot. I jerked loose the lance. The thrust is made with the blade parallel to the ribs. This facilitates its removal.

Men clashed on either side of me.

I saw a white female slave, nude, terrified, running, buffeted, among the men and animals.

It made no sense to me that she should be loose on the field.

She was beautiful.

I saw a young Kaiila warrior, his lance transferred to his left hand, reach down to seize her by the hair, to appropriate her for himself.

"No!" I cried. "No!"

The young warrior looked up, startled.

Bearing down on him, lance leveled, was a painted Yellow Knife.

I brought my kaiila about and, desperately, thrust the lance into the charging Yellow Knife, to my right. It went half through him, his force driving his body along the wood. His gut struck my hand and the lance, in his scream and the twisting of the kaiila, was lost. Behind him, as I had feared, came his flankers, those working with him, to protect him in his charge, those who would give him time to free his lance. The short sword of Port Kar leapt forth from my sheath. I met the lance of the man on my left with the shield, turning its stroke. The other fellow, who had been to the left of the lead warrior, pulled his kaiila toward me. I turned, taking his lance thrust, too, on the shield. As he thrust at me again I struck off the end of the lance. Such blades are, for the most part, unknown in the Barrens. They can part silk dropped upon them. Startled, crying out, he pulled his kaiila back, and turned, and fled. I struck out at the fellow on my left and a segment, cleaved, flew from his shield. Wide-eyed, he, too, withdrew.

Such blades, of course, are infantry weapons. Their weight and length is designed to achieve a desiderated optimum. They are heavy enough to have considerable striking force in saberlike trajectories and light enough to have something of the swiftness and play of the foil. They are long enough to outreach a dagger-armed opponent and short enough, and maneuverable enough, to work their way, beating and thrusting, behind the guard of longer, heavier weapons. They are not, however, a good weapon for use from either the back of a kaiila or a tarn. That sabers are not used more widely on Gor is, I think, a function of the tendency of many mounted warriors to rely too exclusively, in my opinion, on their skills with the lance. The scimitar of the Tahari, a useful weapon from kaiilaback, is an interesting exception to this general tendency.

Here and there, some leaning awry, thrust in the dirt, were lances.

I rode to one and, sheathing my sword, took it in hand. It was also a Yellow-Knife lance.

I turned about on the kaiila and saw the girl who had been running through the men and beasts. She was standing still, bewildered, shuddering, a few yards away. I rode the kaiila to where she stood.

"Do you understand Gorean?" I asked.

"Yes, Master," she said.

"Are you the slave of Yellow Knives?" I asked.

"Yes, Master," she said.

"You are mistaken," I said. "You are the slave of Kaiila."

"Yes, Master," she said, shuddering.

"Open your mouth," I said, "widely."

I laid the point of the lance in her mouth, well in her mouth, depressing her tongue. She looked at me, frightened. The slightest thrust would drive it through the back of her neck.

The young man whom I had protected rode up beside us. She regarded him in terror, her eyes wide, unable to move, her mouth about the lance.

"I think you know this woman," I said to the young man.

"Yes," he said. "We met recently."

"She is now a Kaiila slave," I said.

"Yes," he said.

"You understand how she was used, do you not?" I asked.

"Yes," he said, bitterly.

"It will now be decided, my dear," I told the girl, "whether you will live or die."

She whimpered piteously, her eyes wide, unable to speak, the lance point depressing her tongue.

"Do you find her of interest?" I asked the young man.

"Yes," he said.

"What is your name?" I asked.

"Cotanka," said he, "of the Wismahi." As is often the case with the names of the red savages they do not translate simply and directly into a different language. The expression 'cotanka' usually designates a fife or flute, but it may also be used more broadly to refer to any wind instrument whatsoever. Given the cultural milieu involved and the narrower understanding of that expression within that milieu perhaps the best translation, supplying connotations familiar to the red savages, might be 'Love Flute'.

"It seems," I told the girl, "that you may be permitted to live, at least for a time."

She looked at me, wildly, piteously, gratefully, her tongue still unable to move, because of the lance point.

"The young man finds you, at least at present, of some *interest*," I said.

She whimpered, the sharpened metal in her mouth.

"Do you understand what it means," I asked, "when a man finds a woman of *interest*?"

She nodded, a tiny motion, but desperate, fervent.

"I think it would be in your best interest," I said, "to strive to be pleasing, fully."

She nodded again, tears in her eyes, desperately, fervently.

"When I give you the word," I said, "you will turn about and run to the lines of the Kaiila. There you will find a white man, who wears a broad-brimmed hat. His name is Grunt. You will throw yourself to your belly before him and tell him that you are the slave of Cotanka, of the Wismahi."

She nodded, her eyes wide.

I removed the point of the lance from her mouth. It was wet and muddy, from her saliva and from the dust, in which it had been thrust, point down, to the binding, from which I had retrieved it. She coughed and spit. She ran her tongue out, at the side of her mouth, leaving a stain of mud at the corner of her mouth.

She stepped back, terrified, shuddering. She wiped her forearm across her mouth.

"What is your name?" I asked.

"I have no name," she said. "Cotanka, my master, of the Wismahi, has not yet given me one."

"It is a suitable answer," I said. "Who are you?"

"The slave of Cotanka, of the Wismahi," she said.

"What are you to do?" I asked.

"I am to seek out one called Grunt," she said, "and tell him who I am, that I am the slave of Cotanka, of the Wismahi."

"And how are you to do this?" I asked.

"Lying on my belly before him," she said.

"As befits a slave," I said.

"Yes, Master," she said.

"Go, Slave," I said.

"Yes, Master!" she cried. She then turned about and ran, stumbling, back toward the Kaiila lines.

"I think she will make you a suitable slave," I said to the young man.

"I think so," he said.

"Let us return to the fray," I suggested.

"Let us do so," he agreed.

We then wheeled our kaiila about, once more to tread disputed, bloody dust.

27

FIGHTING

"They are coming! They are coming!" we heard. "The Kinyanpi! They are coming!"

Several times in the afternoon had the battle whistles, formed from the wing bones of taloned Herlits, blasted in the air, and the feathered battle staffs raised and lowered, communicating their signals to the combatants, not only to the Kaiila but to the Yellow Knives, as well. I did not know the codes, nor, for the most part, did Cuwignaka, as he had not been trained in the whirling, shifting tactics of his people, but Hci, and others, knew them well, much as Gorean soldiers know the meaning of the movements of standards, the blasts of battle trumpets and the beating of tarn drums. We followed their lead. Not once had Mahpiyasapa, communicating his will by the whistles and battle staffs, permitted his brave, ragged lines to pursue retreating Yellow Knives. I think this was wise for, as far as we could conjecture, we were muchly outnumbered. Surely fresh Yellow Knives had, from time to time, swept into the combat. Others, too, had been seen on nearby hills. The feigned retreat, drawing pursuers, strung out and disaligned into ambush, is a favorite tactic of red savages. Too, we wished to hold the camp. In it were women and children. In it was the meat which must nourish the Kaiila in the impending winter.

"They are coming," we heard. "The Kinyanpi!"

"Maybe it is smaller birds, a flock, much closer," said a man.

We heard blasts on the whistles of war.

"It is the Kinyanpi," said a man.

"Let us mount up," said Cuwignaka, swallowing down a piece of pemmican.

I continued to wipe down the flanks of the kaiila.

Warriors about me were mounting. Many of the animals were covered with dust to the belly. The hair about the lower jaws of many of them was stiff with dried blood, from the control of the jaw ropes. Blood, too, was on the braided leather.

I heard men about me. Some recounted their coups aloud to themselves. Some called upon their medicine helpers for assistance, usually birds and animals. Others sang their medicines of war. Still others spoke to their shields and weapons, telling them what would be expected of them. Many sang their death songs. "Though I die it is true the sun will blaze in the sky. Though I die it is true the grass will grow. Though I die it is true the kailiauk will come when the grass is high."

I made the jaw rope snug again on the lower jaw of my kaiila. Then, shield and lance in hand, I mounted.

"Do you think we can stand against the Kinyanpi?" asked Cuwignaka.

"I think so," I said. "Kahintokapa has prepared well." Archers concealed under robes and hidden among lodges lay between the Kinyanpi and our main forces, at the western edge of the camp. If the Kinyanpi attacked as they had before they would encounter, unexpectedly, sheets of arrows fired from close range. They would then, too, if they maintained their early attack pattern, strike into the ropes strung between lodges. These were intended to serve the same purposes as the swaying, almost invisible tarn wire sometimes strung in the high cities, wires which can cut the wings from a bird or tear off the head or arm of a rider. Sharpened stakes, too, fashioned from lodge poles, supported by shorter, crossed poles, archers at their base, could be oriented to the trajectory of the attack. This would tend to prevent, we hoped, not only swooping, talon attacks but also the close-quarters work of which the red savage, with his small bow, is fond.

We expected the Kinyanpi to be much less effective at a greater distance. Too, if the Kinyanpi were at heights of even fifty or a hundred feet, it would be difficult for them to fire accurately through the overhead network of ropes and cloths which we had suspended between several of the lodges. This form of reticulation is calculated to have a confusing and distractive effect on swiftly moving, airborne archers. By the time a target can be identified there is usually not enough time to fire. The ground-based archer, on the other hand, the defender, has the solid earth beneath him, and he, because of his nearness to the openings in the network, or loosely linked canopy, can both track the approaching enemy and fire through it with ease and efficiency. In this respect it functions something like a window. It is difficult to hit a particular window, particularly at late notice, while one is moving at high speed, but it is not difficult to see what is approaching through one and to fire through it. The defender, meanwhile, between passes, may change his position or, if you like, window.

"Do you think the Yellow Knives will coordinate their attack with that of the Kinyanpi?" asked a man.

"I think they should," I said.

"I think they have had their stomach filled at the moment with fighting," said Cuwignaka. "I think they will wait to let the Kinyanpi do their work for them."

"Perhaps," I said.

"If we can stand against the Kinyanpi," said the man, "I think we can hold the camp."

"I think so," I said.

"I can see them," said Cuwignaka, turned on his kaiila. "I can see the riders clearly. They are coming in, as before."

"I think it will be the last time the Kinyanpi will attack a Kaiila camp so incautiously," I said.

We then turned to face the Yellow Knives, some three hundred yards away. We were in long lines, our ranks two and three deep. We kept a distance of a lance length between riders. This was to minimize hits by the Kinyanpi. Our kaiila shifted under us. We waited, under the network of ropes and cloths. I heard songs of war.

There was a sudden, horrified scream of a tarn, impaled.

"Shields overhead!" I cried.

A tarn, its wings like thunder, smote the air below us, some twenty feet over our heads, and then another.

Other tarns, I could see, had suddenly swerved or begun to climb.

The kaiila under us turned, startled, scratching at the dust.

"Watch the Yellow Knives!" I called to Cuwignaka.

"They are not moving," said Cuwignaka. "They are holding in place."

A tarn then was caught under the ropes. Screaming, it tore its way free, pulling leather and cloth with it. Its rider was held on its back, lifeless, his knees under the girth rope, his body riddled with arrows. Two other birds hung in the netting, one with its neck broken and the other with a wing half torn away. The riders were pulled from their backs and hacked to pieces. The tarn with the useless wing snapped with its great back at its foes and then was killed with lance thrusts. One rider fell from the back of a struck tarn and caught in the netting, hanging head down. His hands were held and his throat was cut. Another perished similarly, lances thrust upward through the ropes and cloth, until he could be pulled down, falling to the ground, there to die under knives. I saw, looking wildly about, tarns flying erratically, hit with arrows. I saw two fall. One rider I saw fall from the back of a tarn, some few hundred yards to the west and north of the camp. I looked wildly back to the west. The Yellow Knives had not moved.

"How many were there?" I asked Cuwignaka.

"Forty, fifty?" speculated Cuwignaka. "I do not know. Not so many as before."

I did not know, either, how many were in the original attack. Surely those numbers would still be in the vicinity. I would have guessed some two hundred riders would have struck in the first attack, that which had taken the camp by surprise. Cuwignaka's speculations as to the numbers involved in the recent skirmish was congruent with my own estimations. The majority of the Kinyanpi, for some reason, it seemed, had been held back. This puzzled me. The attack, of course, I told myself, might have been primarily an excursionary probe, a venture to determine the nature and strength of our defenses. If that were the case, I thought grimly to myself, its riders would have ample information to report to their superiors.

"Why do you think so few attacked?" I asked Cuwignaka.

"I do not know," he said. "Where a smaller number attacks a larger number there is more glory."

I smiled to myself. Perhaps Cuwignaka was right. While I had busied myself with the prosaic categories of military arithmetic and motivation, I had perhaps neglected the mentality of the enemy, which, in some cases, as in that of red savages, might be eccentric and unusual, at least when viewed from an inadequate or alien perspective. If glory is more important to the enemy than normal military objectives, calculated in costs and units, then one, accordingly, is advised to make certain adjustments in one's thinking about him.

"But," said Cuwignaka, "that is not really our way. Surviving is more important than glory."

"Then why did so few attack?" I asked.

"I do not know," said Cuwignaka.

I was irritated. Now, my edifice of explanation had tumbled. Now, no more than Cuwignaka, did I understand the nature of the recent attack.

"Look," said a man.

"I see," I said.

A single tarnsman, high in the sky, was flying toward the Yellow Knives. Then he alit, among them.

"Surely now they will coordinate their forces," said Cuwignaka.

"I think so," I said.

28

FIGHTING CONTINUES

"See?" asked Cuwignaka.

"Yes," I said. Before the lines of the Yellow Knives, some three hundred yards away, to the west, riders rode back and forth, with feathered lances.

It was now late in the afternoon.

"They are preparing for an attack," said Cuwignaka. "They are exorting their warriors to be brave."

"Yes," I said. I had now, again, taken my place in the Kaiila lines. I had ridden to the perimeter of our rearward lines, there, for the second time, to inspect the deployment of archers, the placement of the stakes, the rigging of the overhead nets. I found all in order. Had I not done so I would have conveyed my suggestions to Cuwignaka who, in turn, would have relayed them to Hci. He, then, would have brought them to the attention of Mahpiyasapa or of Kahintokapa, One-Who-Walks-Before, who was in charge of this sector of our position. Kahintokapa, of the Casmu band, was a member of the prestigious Yellow-Kaiila Riders. This rather roundabout procedure, providing we had the time in which it might function, seemed advisable to both Cuwignaka and myself. We doubted that either Mahpiyasapa or Kahintokapa would much relish receiving direct advice from two fellows as lowly in the camp as ourselves. On the other hand, Hci had been scrupulously honest, somewhat to our surprise, in making it clear to his father and to Kahintokapa the source of his earlier recommendations for defense against the attacks of the Kinyanpi. That he had even considered my counsel, let alone heeded it and conveyed it, and as mine, to Mahpiyasapa and Kahintokapa, had surprised both Cuwignaka and myself. Neither of us had expected this, not of Hci, from whom we looked for little but arrogance and vanity. Too, to our surprise, when we had come to join the warriors they had opened their ranks to permit us to take our place among them. We had not fled. We had not gone to wait with the women and children. We had come with shields and lances. They opened their ranks. We then, one who wore the dress of a woman, and one who was only a slave, took our place among them.

"I think they will be coming soon," said Cuwignaka.

"Yes," I said.

At our rearward lines I had seen Kahintokapa. He had raised his hand to me, palm open, in greeting. I had returned the gesture. It was almost as though I were not a slave. He had his shield again in its cover, as he had had earlier. He would withdraw it from the cover for combat, of course.

"They are probably waiting for the Kinyanpi," said Cuwignaka.

"I think so," I said.

In my return to our lines I had stopped to see Grunt. He was near the area where the women and children were gathered. He, with some of the women, was nursing the wounded. Wasnapohdi was with him. That we had turned the attack of the Kinyanpi had inspirited him. "The camp can be held, I am sure of it!" he had said.

"I think so," I had said.

"The Yellow Knives have been quite successful," he had said. "They have obtained numerous kaiila, much loot and many women. Surprise is now no longer with them. I know such men. They will soon withdraw. Obtaining further loot would be too costly to them."

"They have not yet withdrawn," I had said.

"I do not understand that," he had said.

"Nor do I," I had admitted. It had seemed strange to me that the Yellow Knives, after the difficulties of taking the camp had been made clear to them, had not withdrawn. One would have expected that of red savages.

"They remain in the field?" he had asked.

"Yes," I had said.

"Interesting," he had said.

When I had left Grunt I had ridden a hundred yards or so away, to look at the remains of the council lodge. Little now remained but its poles. It had been the central target of the initial attack of the Kinyanpi, the Flighted Ones. Hundreds of arrows, I had heard, had penetrated its lodge skins. In it, and about it, had been the scene of a massacre. It was little wonder that Watonka had not been eager to attend the council. It was fortunate that Mahpiyasapa, with Grunt, had been outside the camp at the time of this attack. Most of the accumulated leadership, wisdom and experience of the Kaiila people, in all the bands, had perished in a matter of Ehn. One of the few survivors had been Kahintokapa, who had cut his way through the skins and fled. A task force of Yellow Knives had penetrated the camp, too, to that point, and it was they who had killed and mutilated the wounded, and burned the lodge. A similar task force had attacked the dance lodge. These task forces had then withdrawn. Shortly thereafter the resistance had formed, led by Mahpiyasapa and Kahintokapa. I looked into the darkened circle outlined by the long poles. Within it, still, were bodies, and the upright shafts of countless arrows. It had indeed been a dark and bloody day for the Kaiila. Many things, incidentally, puzzled me about this attack, generally. One was the alliance and cooperation of the Yellow Knives and Kinyanpi. These were not traditional allies. It seemed to me unusual that they had acted in this carefully coordinated fashion. Alliances between tribes unfamiliar to one another commonly took place only in resistance to white intrusion into the Barrens. Another peculiarity of the attack lay in the nature of its engineering. It did not follow the normal, rather restrained, small-scale, almost ritualized patterns of conflict common among the red savages. For example, the meretricious proposal of a spurious peace, to lure the leadership of a people into a small area, there to be devastatingly attacked, while not beyond the intelligence or cunning of red savages, did not seem at all typical of their approach to military matters. Certainly it was a surprising kind of generalship to find in the Barrens. It seemed to have little to do with traditions of honor and the meticulous counting of coup. Lastly, it seemed almost incomprehensible, given the nature of the beliefs of the red savages, that the attack had been mounted on a people at the time of the festivals. This, in the Barrens, is something in the nature of blasphemy or sacrilege. It was hard for me to believe that the Yellow Knives, red savages themselves, could have even conceived of such a thing. This, again, I had to observe, suggested, at least, the advent of a new form of generalship, the adoption of novel tactics, in the Barrens. To be sure, I had to admit that this sort of thing, particularly with the collusion of Watonka, apparently slain later by those whose interests he had served, had been quite effective. That was undeniable.

I looked again at the bodies, and arrows, within the remains of the council lodge.

I was not pleased with what I saw. I then turned my kaiila away.

I had then ridden back toward my place in our forward lines. In this short journey I had passed several kaiila, picketed under the ropes and cloths. There were not enough for all those who would have to ride. I also passed large stocks of meat, gathered from the drying racks by the women and put on robes under the netting. This meat would be important for the Kaiila. It could make the difference between surviving the winter and losing many lives in the cold and snows. I also passed some lines and circles of female slaves. Most were kneeling and stripped, and secured with hair ties. Long hair is enforced on most Gorean slaves by their masters. It is aesthetically beautiful and much, from the point of view of diverse coiffures, revealing new dimensions of the slave's loveliness, may be done with it. Too, as is well known among masters and slaves, its application, in the expression and pursuance of a slave's submission and service, can do much to enhance and deepen a master's pleasures; it is erotically useful. Too, in the absence of more customary restraints, such as, say, binding fiber or graceful, steel shackles, it may serve as a bond.

The commercial value of long hair might also be mentioned. Aside from the obvious fact that it might improve the price of a girl in her sale or resale, it can also be sheared and sold. Free women sometimes buy hair for wigs or falls, and, although the hair they purchase is always certified as coming only from free women, there is little doubt that it is often taken from female slaves.

Too, interestingly, female hair is prized for catapult ropes. It is not only stronger and more resilient than hemp but it possesses better properties of weather resistance, being less affected by moisture and temperature changes. When a city is under siege, particularly if the siege is prolonged, even free women will often have their hair shorn, contributing it then to the supplies for municipal defense. Considering the usual vanity of Goreans, both male and female, over their appearance, this is a patriotic sacrifice of no little magnitude. It is particularly significant when one understands that the women know very well that if they fall into the hands of the enemy, with their hair shorn, they may expect to be sold into low slaveries, such as agricultural servitudes or those of the mills. Sometimes, as time passes, the foremen in such places come to realize that they have an incredible beauty in their power. They often hide such women from their superiors, keeping them for themselves. An additional advantage of long hair in a female slave, incidentally, is that it gives the master additional power over her, for, as he is the master, it is his decision whether or not she shall be able to keep it. One of the commands a Gorean woman most fears to hear, whether she is a captive or a slave, is "Shear her."

The kneeling position is, of course, a suitable one for slaves. A slave will normally assume such a position on entering the presence of her master or a free person. She will probably remain in it until permitted to rise. It is a common position, too, for her to assume when she is in attendance of a master, for example, awaiting his notice or commands. Too, she will usually speak to her master from this position, unless, of course, she is lying down, as in making her reports to him, inquiring as to his will, answering questions, and so on. Some masters approve it, too, for purposes of general conversation. Most masters, incidentally, enjoy talking with their slaves, immensely; after all, the slave is not a mere contractual partner, in effect, a business associate; she is a prized possession; she is a treasure, and she is all one's own.

Some Goreans think of the Free Companionship as being a form of contract slavery; this is not, of course, precisely correct; on the other hand, if more women took that definition seriously, I have little doubt but what free companionships would be far more rewarding than they now are, for many couples. They might then, under that interpretation, and held contractually enforceable on the woman, be that next best thing to her actual slavery. There is no full and adequate substitute, of course, given the dominance/submission ratios and the order of nature, for the uncompromised, and full and total bondage of the female. Once this is institutionalized and legalized, as it is on Gor, we have, then, the union of nature and civilization, a union in which civilization no longer functions as a counterbiological antithesis to nature but rather, perhaps, as an extension and flowering of nature herself, a union in which natural relationships are fulfilled and furthered.

That most of the kneeling women were stripped did not mean that most of them were from the outlying herds. For the most part those herds had probably, by now, fallen to Yellow Knives. Rather the stripping of these women, most of whom would presumably be slaves from the inner parts of the camp, was, in large measure, a security precaution, the camp being under attack. It is difficult for a naked woman to conceal weapons. That most of the women wore bonds was also a security precaution. It is common for Goreans, in times of crisis or danger, to secure their slaves. At such times slaves, like other animals, must be strictly controlled. It would not do, for example, to have them running about, adding to the confusion. Similarly, slaves are to be absolutely unable, even if they wish, to interfere with the defense or abet the attackers, in any way; similarly, they are to be precluded from attempting to take advantage of the confusion, perhaps in order, foolishly, to attempt to escape. They are the prizes of the action, not participants in it. Helpless, they must abide its outcome. It will be time enough later for them to learn their fate.

They were fastened, for the most part, in two different forms of hair ties. In one, the wrists of one woman were bound before her body, lifted and raised, in the hair of the woman before her. Another woman's wrists, then, would be bound in her hair, and so on. Some of these women were coffled in lines, and others in circles, the last woman's hair serving to bind the wrists of the first woman. The other form of hair tie had the hands of a woman tied behind her back to the hair of the woman who, her head lowered, knelt behind her.

Once again, some were secured in lines, and others in circles, the hands of the last woman being tied in the hair of the first. This second form of hair tie, done in lines, incidentally, resembles a common coffle arrangement, achieved with a set of relatively short thongs, each about five feet in length. The first woman's hands are bound behind her back with one end of such a thong and then the other end is taken up and knotted about the neck of the woman behind her; this woman's hands are then bound behind her with another thong, its free end then being taken up and bound about the neck of the woman behind her, and so on. An advantage of this coffle arrangement is that women may be easily taken from it, and added to it.

A similar arrangement, of course, may be achieved with chains, each length of chain terminating at one end with a pair of slave bracelets and, at the other end, with a closable, lockable neck ring. The last woman on the coffle, of course, has the neck ring attached to her own bracelets and chain locked about her own neck. An advantage of the chains over the thongs, of course, is that the chain cannot be chewed through. Some of the other girls under the ropes and cloths were tied in more conventional fashions. Some were not even tied at all. An example was Oiputake, or Kiss, whom I well knew. It was she whom I had taken from a herd earlier, and improved. Too, it was she who had alerted us to the fact, thinking little of it at the time, that the Yellow-Knife chieftains in camp were not civil chieftains but war chiefs.

"Master!" she had cried out to me, extending her hand to me.

"Be silent, Slave," I had told her.

"Yes, Master," she had said. I had then ridden on. I did not wish to converse with her at the time. She could not follow me. She stood within a small dirt circle, probably drawn with the heel of a moccasin about her. It was a confinement circle. She could not leave it without the permission of a free person. I did stop my kaiila briefly beside a blond girl, lying on her belly in the dirt. She trembled, knowing I had stopped near her.

"Who are you?" I asked.

"I am a nameless slave of Cotanka, of the Wismahi," she said.

She was the slave who, earlier, had been used by Yellow-Knives as, in effect, a lure girl, one used to distract or, say, entrap a warrior. Cotanka had been fortunate. He had not been killed. He now owned her. I did not think her lot would be an easy one. She wore the "bonds of the master's will." Grunt had put her in them. She lay on her stomach. Her wrists were crossed behind her. Her ankles, too, were crossed. She was "bound." She could not rise to her feet. Yet there was not a rope or a strap on her body. She was "bound by the master's will." She could not move from this position unless, at the word of a free person, she was freed from it. To break the position otherwise is to be instantly slain.

No longer now were some of the Yellow Knives riding about, back and forth before their lines, moving their lances about, preparing their parties for combat, exorting them, doubtless, to boldness and bravery.

The kaiila of the enemy were now aligned towards us.

"Make ready your lances, make ready your knives," chanted Mahpiyasapa, riding before our lines. "May your eyes be keen. May your movements be swift and sure. May your medicine be strong!"

"They will be coming soon," said Cuwignaka.

"Yes," I said.

"What are they waiting for?" asked a man.

"The Kinyanpi," said another.

I glanced over to Hci. I saw his shield move, as though by itself. Then he steadied it. I felt the hair rise on the back of my neck. I felt goose flesh.

This movement of the shield had not been unnoticed by Mahpiyasapa. He rode to Hci.

"What is wrong with your shield?" he asked.

"Nothing," said Hci.

"Fall back," said Mahpiyasapa. "Do not fight." Then he rode from him.

Hci, however, did not leave his place in our lines.

"Perhaps the Kinyanpi will not come," said a man.

"The Kinyanpi!" cried voices to our rear, the shout being relayed from man to man.

I looked back.

"It is the Kinyanpi," said Cuwignaka, looking back, too.

"Yes," I said. They were coming in two flights, two darknesses, one from the east, one from the southeast.

We then gave our attention to Mahpiyasapa, awaiting his signal.

Mahpiyasapa, before our lines, lifted and lowered his lance.

We had little doubt as to what the tactics of the Kinyanpi would be this time. They would not repeat their earlier mistake of a direct, low-level attack against our defenses. They would either keep their height and rain arrows down upon us or act in support of the Yellow Knives. As we could protect ourselves reasonably well with shields from simple, distance archery it seemed obvious, then, that our two enemies would act in conjunction. If we warded blows of Yellow Knives we could not, at the same time, protect ourselves from aerial fire. Similarly, if we attempted to protect ourselves from aerial fire, by lifting our shields, we would be exposing ourselves to the Yellow Knives' plane of attack. Presumably we would await the attack of the Yellow Knives under the ropes and netting. This would make overhead archery more difficult for the Kinyanpi but would also give the Yellow Knives the momentum of attack.

As soon as Mahpiyasapa had lowered his lance we placed about our bodies yellow scarves and other strips of yellow cloth. It was in this way that Watonka, the Yellow-Knife war chiefs, Bloketu, Iwoso and others had been identified as personages not to be fired upon by the Kinyanpi.

Again Mahpiyasapa raised and lowered his lance, and then he pointed it toward the enemy.

As one man, kaiila squealing, warriors howling, feathers flying, lances lowering, our lines leapt toward the enemy.

We struck them, they milling, startled, wheeling about, kaiila rearing, a full Ihn before the turf was dark with the wild, swiftly moving shadows of the Kinyanpi overhead.

The engagement was brief, perhaps only four or five Ehn, and the Yellow Knives, howling and whooping, in full flight, speeding away, forsook the field. I lifted my bloody lance in salute to Cuwignaka. The Kinyanpi, too, had withdrawn. Scarcely a dozen arrows had fallen amongst us. Of these, of those that had found targets, they reposed in the bodies of Yellow Knives. In what consternation must the Kinyanpi have viewed the plethora of yellow signals beneath them. Surely they would have understood that most of such might be worn by Kaiila, but, in flight, moving swiftly, uncertain of their desiderated targets they had, for the most part, restrained their fire.

"They will not be back!" laughed a man.

"See the signal of Mahpiyasapa," said another. "Let us return to our lodges."

We turned our kaiila about and, slowly, not hurrying, well pleased with ourselves, tired, but quietly jubilant in our victory, made our way back toward our camp.

"Look!" said a man, pointing back, when we had reached again our former lines.

"I do not believe it," said another.

We looked back, those three or four hundred yards, across the field. At the crest of a rise, once again, suddenly emerging, silhouetted against the sky, were lines of Yellow Knives.

"They have regrouped," I said. This was evident. Yet I had not expected it. This manifested a type of discipline that I would not have expected of routed red savages, and certainly, in any case, not this soon.

"I thought they had gone," said a man.

"I, too," said another.

"Surely they have enough women and kaiila," said a man. "It seems like they should have left long ago."

"There seems little enough for them to gain in further fighting," said a man.

"They would have to pay dearly for anything further," said another.

"Yet they are there," said another.

"Yes," said another.

"It is not like Yellow Knives," said a man.

"I do not understand it," said another fellow.

"Nor I," said another.

I, too, wondered at the reappearance of the Yellow-Knife lines.

It was dusk. This, too, was puzzling. Red savages, on the whole, prefer to avoid fighting in darkness. In the darkness it is difficult to be skillful and, in the absence of uniforms, friends may be too easily mistaken for foes. Some savages, too, prefer to avoid night combat for medicine reasons. There are many theories connected with such things. I shall mention two. One is that if an individual is slain at night, he may, quite literally, have difficulty in the darkness in finding his way to the medicine world. Another is that the individual who is slain at night may find the portals of the medicine world closed against him. These beliefs, and others like them, it seems clear, serve to discourage night combat.

One may, as in many such cases, then, wonder whether night combat is discouraged because of such beliefs, or whether such beliefs may not have been instituted to discourage night fighting, with all of its confusions, alarms and terrors. On the other hand, there is no doubt whatsoever that many red savages take such beliefs with great seriousness. The life world, and consciousness, of the red savage, it must be clearly understood, is quite different from that of, say, a secular rationalist or a scientifically oriented objectivist. One of the most common, and serious, mistakes that can be made in crosscultural encounters is to assume that everyone one meets is, in effect, very much like oneself. Their personal world, the world of their experience, their experiential world, may be quite different from yours. If it is not understood in its own terms, as he understands it, it is likely to seem irrational, eccentric or foolish. Properly understood, on the other hand, his world is plausible, in its terms, as is yours. This is not to say that there is nothing to choose between life worlds; it is only to say that we do not all share the same life world.

"Why are they not going away?" asked a man.

"It will soon be dark," said another.

"They must have very strong medicine," said another.

"Perhaps," said another, uneasily.

I saw Hci struggle for a moment to again control his shield. Then, again, he had steadied it.

"What are they waiting for?" asked a man.

"Their ranks are opening," said a man.

"Something is coming through them," said another man.

"It is a sleen," said one man.

"No," said another.

"It is on all fours," said another man.

"Surely it is a sleen," said another.

"It is too large to be a sleen," said another.

"Aiii!" cried a man. "It is rising to its feet. It is walking on two feet!"

"It is a thing from the medicine world!" cried a man.

"It is a medicine helper of the Yellow Knives!" cried another.

Almost at the same time, from behind us, there were cries of consternation. "Riders!" we heard. "Riders!"

We wheeled our kaiila about. At the back of the camp, there were screaming and the sounds of numerous kaiila, squealing and snorting, their clawed feet tearing at the grass. At full speed, pennons flying, lances lowered, bucklers set, in sweeping, measured, staggered attack lines, waves of riders struck the camp.

"They are white men!" cried a man near me.

I saw a woman, running, caught in the back with a lance, between the shoulder blades, flung to the dust, the lance then withdrawn. It had been professionally done.

"White men!" cried another man near me.

I saw another man toward the rear, an archer, discharge an arrow, and leap to the side, to avoid a rider. He was hit by the next rider, one of those in the succeeding wave, its riders staggered with those of the first. In this type of formation, given the speed of the charging kaiila, the distance between successive waves is about forty to fifty feet. This is supposed to provide the next rider with a suitable response interval. If the first rider misses the target the second, thus, has time to adjust for its change of position. From the point of view of the target, of course, which may even be off balance, it is difficult, in the interval involved, to set itself for a second evasive action. Its problems are further complicated, also, of course, by the imminent arrival of even further attack waves. The primary purpose of the staggering of the attack-wave riders is to bring a target which may have escaped from the attack lane of one rider almost immediately into the attack lane of another.

Certain psychological factors, also, in this type of situation, tend to favor the attacker. As a target's attention tends to be absorbed in avoiding one attack it is less prepared to react efficiently to another. Also, the elation and relief which tends to accompany escape from one danger tends to result, often, in a reduction, however brief, in the target's capacity to cope with another. This is a moment within which the target may find itself within the lance range of the next rider. This type of formation is generally not useful against an enemy which is protected by breastworks, pits or stakes, or a settled infantry, its long pikes set, fixed butt down in the turf, the weapons oriented diagonally, the points trained on the breasts of the approaching mounts. It is also generally ineffective against another cavalry for it permits a shattering and penetration of its own lines. It tends to be effective, however, against an untrained infantry or almost any enemy afoot. The archer, struck by the rider, spun to the side, the lance blade passing through his neck.

"White men!" I heard.

"Turn about!" cried Mahpiyasapa. "Fight! Defend the camp!"

The lines spun about and the men of Mahpiyasapa, whooping and crying out, dust scattering, sped back under the ropes and between the lodges to engage this new enemy. I held my position.

The white men were undoubtedly the mercenary soldiers of Alfred, the mercenary captain of Port Olni. With something like a thousand men he had entered the Barrens, with seventeen Kurii, an execution squad from the steel worlds, searching for Half-Ear, Zarendargar, the Kur war general who had been in command of the supply complex, and staging area, in the Gorean arctic, that which was being readied to support the projected Kur invasion of Gor. This complex had been destroyed. Evidence had suggested that Zarendargar had escaped, and was to be found in the Barrens. Once Zarendargar and I, in the north, as soldiers, had shared paga. I had come to the Barrens to warn him of his danger. Then I had fallen slave to the Kaiila. A wagon train of settlers, with which Alfred had joined forces, had been attacked. A massacre had taken place. Alfred, however, with some three to four hundred mounted men, leaving most of his command to perish, had escaped to the southeast. From the southeast, I remembered, the kailiauk had come early. From the southeast, too, had come the Kinyanpi.

Earlier I had conjectured that Alfred and his men had returned to civilization. I now realized that was false. Somehow they had come into league with the Kinyanpi and, perhaps through them, and in virtue of some special considerations, the nature of which I suspected I knew, been able to make contact with, and enlist the aid of, Yellow Knives. A fearful pattern had suddenly emerged. The discipline of the Yellow Knives now became more meaningful. So, too, did their apparent willingness to fight in the half darkness of dusk. Suddenly, too, starkly plausible, became such untypical anomalies of the Barrens as the meretricious proposal of a false peace, the spurious pretext of a council in order to gather together and decimate the high men of the Kaiila, and even the unprecedented sacrilege of attacking a people at the time of its great dances and festivals. These things spoke not of the generalship of the Barrens but of a generalship alien to the Barrens, a generalship of a very different sort of mind. Even so small a detail as the earlier, small-scale attack of the Kinyanpi now became clear. It must have been indeed, as I had earlier conjectured, an excursionary probe to determine the test defenses, before the main force, held in reserve, was committed. The generalship again suggested that of the cities, not of the Barrens, that of white soldiers, not red savages.

I looked wildly back toward the Yellow Knives. As I had expected they were now advancing. Their feathered lances were dropping into the attack position. Their kaiila were moving forward, and gradually increasing their speed. By the time they reached the camp the kaiila, not spent, would be at full charge. The Yellow-Knife lines were now sweeping past the creature which had emerged earlier from their ranks. It stood in the grass, the warriors sweeping about it. It was some eight feet tall. It lifted its shaggy arms. It was a Kur. We would be taken on two fronts.

Behind me there was fighting. I turned about. I saw soldiers cutting down portions of the ropes and cloths.

"Kinyanpi!" I heard. "They are coming again!"

"It is the end," I thought. "The Kurii have won." The Kurii, now, allied with the Yellow Knives, and supported by the Flighted Ones, the Kinyanpi, could systematically search the Barrens, unimpeded in their search for Zarendargar, and if an entire people, the nation of the Kaiila, should stand in their way, then what was it to them, if this nation should be destroyed?

I heard the whooping of the Yellow Knives growing closer.

I then turned my kaiila and rode toward the back of the camp.

29

HOW IT CAME ABOUT THAT GRUNT SURVIVED

A slave girl screamed, buffeted to the side by the forequarters of my kaiila. She turned, struck, from the animal, her hands tied behind her back, lost her footing and fell. I saw the frightened eyes of another girl, her wrists lifted, bound together with hair, thrown before her face. The hair that bound them hung free before the wrists, dangling from them, in jagged strands, marking where it had been hastily cut free from the hair of the girl before her in a holding coffle. Her own hair, similarly, had been cut short, closely, at the back of her neck, where the girl behind her, with swift strokes of a blade, had been freed.

"Run," a free woman was screaming. "Run! Seek your safety!"

I saw another free woman cutting at the hair of other kneeling beauties, freeing them from the cruel hair coffles, that they might flee as best they might.

Another woman was cutting the bonds at the ankles of another lovely slave. That slave's ankles had been bound more conventionally, with tight thongs of rawhide. When the thongs sprang apart, leaping from the knife, I saw deep red circles in the girl's ankles I doubted that she would even be able to rise to her feet for a few Ehn.

I pressed my kaiila forward, through the crowd.

I saw Oiputake to one side.

"Where is Cotanka?" a girl was crying out. "I am the slave

of Cotanka! Where is Cotanka!" It was she who earlier, in effect, had functioned as a lure girl. I had captured her. As Cotanka had accepted her as a slave, she had been spared, at least for a time.

I heard a girl beneath me scream as the paws of my kaiila passed over her. I could see another girl, too, ahead of me, to my right, lying on the ground, trembling. There was the mark of a kaiila paw on her back. Other riders, earlier, had passed this way.

To my left and forward, a great section of the overhead netting had been cut down. Some slaves were there, standing or kneeling in the fallen mesh. It was not a capture net, of course, but a mesh designed, in effect, to provide a camouflage against, or a distraction for, overhead archers. The slaves, thus, were not entrapped. I thought it might be a reasonably safe place for them to be. The Kinyanpi, presumably, would not be likely to fire on a nude white slave any more than on an unmounted kaiila. Both would fit not into the category of enemy but rather into the category of booty. It would be a greater danger, presumably, for a girl to hide in a lodge where, perhaps being mistaken for a free person, she might be struck by arrows, the skins of the lodge cover perhaps being riddled from above by the swift, flighted riders. I thrust with my lance upward, through the netting, driving it through the body of a soldier, cutting at it. He fell across the netting, then tumbled through it. Then I was beyond the area of the slaves.

The battle, I saw, at an instant's glance, was hopeless.

I heard the heavy vibration of a cable of a crossbow. A Kaiila warrior pitched backwards off his kaiila.

I heard the screaming of a free woman.

"Run!" cried a man, riding past. "Run!"

I looked back. The Yellow Knives would have to make it through the confusion of slaves.

"Yellow Knives are coming!" I cried out, pointing back. "Yellow Knives, to the west!"

Mahpiyasapa looked about, wildly. Then he fended himself from a lance attack.

A dark shadow hurtled past. My shield lifted, I deflected an arrow from above.

A child ran past.

"Form lines," cried Mahpiyasapa. "To the east! To the west! Women and children between the lines!"

I saw Hci, with an expert thrust, past the buckler of a soldier, drop the fellow from his saddle.

The whooping of Yellow Knives was then upon us. We were cut into small groups, our lines shattered. The battle became a tangled, bloody melee.

I saw Cuwignaka rolling in the dust, his kaiila gone. I turned my kaiila against the forequarters of a riderless mount, pressing it toward Cuwignaka. Cuwignaka was on his feet, blood about his head. A Yellow Knife, afoot, rushed upon him, knife raised. They grappled. Then the Yellow Knife fell backward, blood at his throat. Cuwignaka, a knife run with blood in his hand, blood on his hand and wrist, too, stood in the dust. I lost sight of him as two warriors passed between us. Then I had my hand on the jaw rope of the riderless kaiila and dragged it, snorting and squealing, to Cuwignaka. He yanked free a lance from the body of a fallen Yellow Knife. He was then, in an instant, on the back of the animal I had brought him, and in command of it.

I saw Mahpiyasapa fell a Yellow Knife with his lance. "Shields overhead!" I cried. A hail of arrows fell amongst us. Then great wings smote the air above us, the air tearing at our clothes, raising dust in affrighted clouds on the field.

"I am here!" called Cuwignaka.

"I am going to find Grunt!" I cried, through the dust. To my left I saw a child run through with a soldier's lance. I saw two women running wildly through the dust.

I struck aside a lance and urged my kaiila toward where Grunt had been tending the wounded.

The area here was like a charnel house. The grounds were covered with the twisted bodies of the slain and mutilated. I wondered if any had escaped. Lodges, even, though not all of them, had been thrown down and burned.

"Aiii!" I heard. I lifted my shield but the Yellow Knife, his eyes wild with fright, rode past, his braids flying behind him.

"Something over there," said Cuwignaka, half a kaiila length behind me, pointing.

We urged our mounts up a small rise, and then down, partly, over it. Here, too, we found the bodies of men who had been wounded. Too, here, among them, were even bodies of one or two of the women who had been, with Grunt, tending to them.

"Grunt is alive!" I said.

Grunt, bodies about his feet, stood on a small rise.

"Away!" Grunt was crying, waving his arm aversively, at two Yellow Knives, mounted, looking at him. "Away!"

In the slaughter it seemed that only Grunt, and Wasnapohdi, too, protected by him, crouching behind him, her head down, the jaw rope of a kaiila clutched in her two hands, had not been killed.

The two Yellow Knives, suddenly, turned about and sped from Grunt.

I choked back a wave of repulsion.

I recalled that long ago, even before I had come to Kailiauk, near the Ihanke, or Perimeter, I had questioned a young man, a tharlarion teamster, as to how it was that Grunt, of all white men, at that time, was permitted to travel so far and with such impunity in the Barrens. "Perhaps the savages feel they have nothing further to gain from Grunt," the young man had laughed. "I do not understand," I had said. "You will," he had said. But I had never understood that remark, until now.

"You see why he is still alive," said Cuwignaka. "It has to do with beliefs about the medicine world."

"I think so," I said.

I moved the kaiila down the rest of the shallow slope, toward the small rise on which Grunt, Wasnapohdi behind him, stood. When Grunt had come into the Barrens he had had with him, among his other trade goods, a coffle of slaves. Although these women had been lovely he had not made use, as far as I knew, of any one of them. He had, on the other hand, invited me to content and relieve myself with them as I would, expecting little of me in return other than that I would handle them as what they were, slaves, and prepare them, to some extent, for they were new slaves, for their future tasks, those of providing a master with exquisite, uncompromised pleasures and services. He had had me teach even the virgins their first submissions. One such had been the former Miss Millicent Aubrey-Welles, the debutante from Pennsylvania, who was now Winyela, the slave of Canka, of the Isbu Kaiila. At the time I had never dreamed we would one day be owned by the same man. It was now clearer to me, as it had not been before, why Grunt had not performed these tasks himself.

"Greetings," said Grunt.

"Greetings," I said.

"Now you see me as I am," said Grunt. "Do not attempt to conceal your repulsion."

I shrugged.

"It has already been done to him," said Cuwignaka. "It is like one cannot be killed or who, killed, has come back from the dead. It is like something from the medicine world."

"Yes," I said.

"Occasionally it proves useful," said Grunt.

It was the first time that I had ever seen Grunt without the familiar, broad-brimmed hat.

"It was done to me five years ago," he said, "by Yellow Knives. I had been struck unconscious. They thought me dead. I awakened later. I lived."

"I have heard of such cases," I said.

"It is hideous," he said.

"Some of the skin has been restored," I said. In other places I could see little but scar tissue. In places, too, the bone was exposed.

"More, too, was done," said Grunt, bitterly.

"It is fortunate that you did not bleed to death," I said.

"Is it?" asked Grunt.

"Yes," I said.

"Perhaps," he said.

"Do many know?" I asked.

"You did not know," said Grunt. "But it is generally not unknown."

"I see," I said.

"Wasnapohdi did not know," he said. "When she first saw she threw up in the grass."

"She is only a slave," I said. Wasnapohdi kept her head down.

"Do you wonder," he asked, "why Grunt seeks the Barrens, why he spends so little time with his own people?"

"The camp is going to fall, imminently," I said. "It is my suggestion that you ride for your lives."

"I prefer the Barrens," said Grunt, angrily. "They have strong stomachs in the Barrens!"

"Riders!" said Cuwignaka. "And kaiila!"

We spun about on our kaiila.

"They are Kaiila!" said Cuwignaka.

Some five warriors, of the Napoktan Kaiila, each drawing a string of kaiila, pulled up near us.

"The women and children," said Cuwignaka, pointing, "are in that direction."

"Wasnapohdi," cried one of the warriors, "is it you?"

Wasnapohdi, from her crouching position, fell immediately, seemingly unable to help herself, to her knees in the grass. She looked up, her lower lip trembling, tears suddenly brimming in her eyes. "Yes, Master!" she said.

"Hurry!" cried the leader of the warriors, and, suddenly, they sped away, in the direction Cuwignaka had indicated.

I had heard the way in which Wasnapohdi had said the word 'Master' to the young man. It had not been used in the mere fashion in which any slave girl might use the expression 'Master' to any free man, expressing her understood lowliness and deference before him, but rather as though he might be her own master.

Grunt, I noted, had drawn on his broad-brimmed hat. He had not wished to be seen as he was before the young warriors.

"That is Waiyeyeca," I said to her.

"Yes, Master," she said, tears in her eyes. I understood now why she had hidden from him in the camp. She feared her feelings. There was no doubt now in my mind, nor, I think, in hers, that she indeed did love him. In her eyes, and in her voice, and in the way in which she had said 'Master' to him, I saw that she still, in her heart, regarded herself as his slave.

Grunt, too, a shrewd man, had noticed this.

Wasnapohdi rose to her feet, looking after the riders. She put out her hand. Tears were in her eyes.

"Let me follow him, Master," she said to Grunt. "Please!"

"Have you received permission to rise, Slave?" asked Grunt.

She looked at him, startled. Then Grunt, with a savage blow of the back of his hand, struck her to the grass at his feet. She looked up at him, disbelievingly. There was blood at the side of her mouth. Her hands were then taken before her body and her wrists, crossed, were, at one end of a long tether, tightly tied. She was then jerked to her feet. "You do not belong to him," said Grunt. "You belong to me."

"Yes, Master," she said, tears in her eyes.

Grunt mounted. He looped the free end of her tether three times about the pommel of his saddle. "If we survive," said Grunt, "you will discover that your breach of discipline has earned you a superb lashing."

"Yes, Master," she wept.

With all her heart she wished to run after Waiyeyeca, but

she would go with Grunt. Her will was nothing. She was a slave.

"I was too much absorbed with myself," said Grunt. "Sometimes I let things bother me too much. I thank you both, my friends, for bringing me to my senses."

"Ride," said Cuwignaka. "It is nearly dark. Hopefully many will be able to escape from the camp, riding or afoot."

"Surely you will come with us?" said Grunt.

"No," said Cuwignaka.

"The fighting is the business of warriors," said Grunt.

"We are warriors," said Cuwignaka.

"I wish you well," said Grunt.

"We wish you well," I said.

"*Oglu waste!*" said Cuwignaka.

"*Oglu waste!*" said Grunt. "Good luck!"

He then moved his kaiila away, through the gloom. We saw Wasnapohdi cast an anguished glance over her shoulder, in the direction in which Waiyeyeca had ridden. Then, by the wrists, weeping, stumbling, the tether taut, she was pulled along, by the side of Grunt's kaiila.

"He is the only man I know who has survived that," said Cuwignaka.

"In itself," I said, "it is not likely to be lethal. It is only that it is commonly done only to the dying or dead."

"You are right, of course," said Cuwignaka.

"Grunt seems rather sensitive about it," I said.

"It saved his life today," said Cuwignaka. "He should be pleased."

"I suppose one could get used to it," I said.

"It is hideous," said Cuwignaka.

"To be sure," I granted him, "it is not likely to start a fashion."

"I do not think so," laughed Cuwignaka.

"He is a good man," I said.

"Yes," said Cuwignaka, "and a kindly one."

"Yes," I said.

"I wonder if Wasnapohdi will ever realize how Grunt was concerned to save her life."

"She will doubtless understand sometime," I said. "She is an intelligent woman."

"Mahpiyasapa knows the camp is lost," said Cuwignaka.

"Yes," I said. "The young warriors were bringing in kaiila, to help evacuate the women and children."

"Do you think there will be enough kaiila?" asked Cuwignaka.

"I do not know," I said.

"There will not be," said Cuwignaka.

30

SARDAK

Thrusting and stabbing we cut through soldiers.

"Kaiila! Friends!" I cried, lance uplifted.

"Tatankasa! Cuwignaka!" cried a man.

The thin, ragged, linear oval of warriors, some hundred yards in length, opened, admitting us. Within it, crowded, were women and children, and kaiila.

Mahpiyasapa and his lieutenants, with their cries, the movements of battle staffs, the blasts of war whistles, had succeeded in forming fresh lines, constructing a defensive perimeter.

We wheeled our kaiila about, taking our place in the lines.

Arrows from soaring Kinyanpi fell amongst us.

Here and there, at points on our perimeter, Yellow Knives and soldiers, in fierce, brief exchanges, tested our strength.

"No man is to flee until Mahpiyasapa gives the signal," said a man.

"We must hold out until darkness," said another.

"We must then, sheltering the women and the young, try to break through their lines."

"I understand," I said.

"The night is overcast," said another. "It will be difficult for the Kinyanpi to follow us."

"It will soon be dark," said a man.

"Wait for the signal of Mahpiyasapa," cautioned another.

Hci drew his kaiila back from the lines, and turning it about, brought it alongside of Cuwignaka's beast.

"I did not think you would come back," he said.

"I am Kaiila," said Cuwignaka.

Hci then returned to his place in the lines.

"I think we can hold these lines until dark," I said to Cuwignaka.

"I think so," said Cuwignaka. "Otherwise it will be a slaughter."

Suddenly we heard the shaking of rattles, the beating of small hand drums. The Yellow Knives opened their lines. The soldiers, too, drew back. In the corridor then formed, in the gloom, their bodies painted, brush tied about their wrists and ankles, chanting, stomping, turning about and shuffling, came dancers. They wore masks.

"Yellow Knives," said a man, frightened.

"They are making medicine," whispered another.

The masks they wore were large, almost as broad as their shoulders. I could see their faces, painted with yellow stripes, through the mouth holes of the masks. The masks themselves were painted. They were made of wood and leather.

"They are calling on medicine helpers!" said a man, terrified.

Such masks, to the red savage, are not simply masks. They are themselves objects fearful with power. The visions recorded on such masks might, in the lore of the red savages, derive from the medicine world itself.

Men shifted uneasily on their kaiila. One or two of the beasts backed from the line.

"Hold your places!" said Mahpiyasapa. "We do not fear wood and leather!"

I smiled to myself. The remark of Mahpiyasapa, it seemed to me, smacked of heresy. On the other hand, it was certainly not in the best interests of his position to promote the plausibility of Yellow-Knife medicine.

"It is false medicine!" called Mahpiyasapa. "Do not fear it! It is only wood and leather!"

I smiled again to myself. Mahpiyasapa had made a suitable adjustment, implicitly drawing a distinction between true and false medicines, the medicine of the Kaiila presumably being true medicine, and that of the Yellow Knives false. A more typical distinction would have been not between true and false medicines, but between weaker and stronger medicines. The red savage is usually quite willing to grant that the enemy has medicine; it is his hope, however, of course, that his medicine will prove stronger. On the other hand, if the medicine of the Yellow Knives was false medicine altogether, then what had he to fear?

The test for the stronger medicine, incidentally, implicitly, appears to be victory or success. The matter is perhaps rather similar to the claim that the will always acts on the stronger motive, the stronger motive being implicitly defined as that motive on which the will acts. In a creature priding itself on its rationality this penchant for irrefutable fables is, at least at first glance, somewhat remarkable; scrutinized more closely, however, it appears that such fables, in many cases, play psychologically significant roles; this perhaps explains their prevalance in all, or most, cultures, and their appearance in all, or most, human beings; allegiance to such fables, for example, it is clear, can be conducive to tribality; tribality, in turn, is often conducive to group survival. It is thus possible, interestingly, that a readiness to subscribe to ideologies, with no particular regard for their nature, has been selected for. Clearly, however, these belief systems must be at least of certain general sorts; for example, a belief that individuals could drink sand would not be likely to achieve an impressive longevity; it might last approximately seventy-two hours.

The most successful belief systems normally have two significant properties in common; first, they have nothing to do with the real world and, secondly, they claim to have a great deal to do with it. The second property seems to be important in encouraging people to take it seriously and the first in assuring that it need never collapse in the face of facts, regardless of what the facts turn out to be. The real role of such belief systems, thus, is not to tell people about the world, for they are actually irrelevant to the world, but to supply them with psychological and social benefits. To simply see such belief systems as false or meaningless is perhaps to fail to understand what one is dealing with. They are not libraries but fortresses. It is an interesting question whether or not such competitive belief systems can be replaced with truth; truth, like the belief systems, is irrefutable, but its irrefutability is not a function of emptiness, of cognitive vacuity, but of its rectitude.

Truth, you see, has reality on its side. Truth's problems do not derive primarily from the complexity of nature but from the simplicity of people. It is always more convenient to adopt a slogan than conduct an inquiry. Too, the often cold and flinty nature of truth may, to many people, understandably, constitute a poor substitute for the comforts of self-deception. Harmless lies, perhaps, improve the quality of human life. They do not, of course, improve its nobility or grandeur. I suppose a choice, as in many matters, must be made. Some will sleep late. Others will seek the stars.

"Fear nothing," cried Mahpiyasapa. "The medicine of the Yellow Knives is false medicine!"

"What manner of medicine beasts are they, those portrayed on the masks?" asked a man.

"I do not know," said another, uneasily.

"I have never seen such things," said a man.

"Surely such things could exist only in the medicine world," said a man.

"Such things would surely be fearful and invincible medicine helpers," said a man, shuddering.

"The medicine of the Yellow Knives is false medicine," said a man. "Mahpiyasapa is right."

"Suppose it is not," said another man.

"Such things do not exist," said another man. "They do not exist even in the medicine world."

"Whence, then, came the visions for such masks?" asked another, uneasily.

"If they did exist in the medicine world," said the first man, "they would not favor the Yellow Knives."

"True," said another man.

"What if they did?" asked another.

"Then," said the first man, "we would be doomed."

I leaned forward on the kaiila. I could now see, reasonably well, the visages portrayed on the masks. The hair on the back of my neck rose. The visages, clearly, were those of Kurii.

"Hold your lines," I begged the men about me. "Hold your lines, no matter what happens!"

"Your medicine is false," cried Mahpiyasapa to the Yellow Knives, though doubtless they could not understand him. "We do not fear it. It is only wood and leather!"

A horrifying sound came then from the ranks of the Yellow Knives and soldiers. It was a long, howling cry. It must have struck terror, too, into the hearts of the Yellow Knives and soldiers. The sound was unmistakable. I had heard it on the rocky slopes of Torvaldsland, on the sands of the Tahari, in the jungles of the Ua.

Emerging then from the ranks of the enemy came a gigantic Kur, some nine feet in height, some nine hundred pounds in weight. It carried a huge shield and lance, the accouterments of a man. Behind it, on each side, similarly armed, came others.

"Aiii!" cried a man, turning his kaiila.

"Hold your lines!" cried Mahpiyasapa.

But the lines, men screaming, kaiila wheeling about, were shattered. Fear became flight, and flight rout, and rout slaughter. Yellow Knives and soldiers pressed in. Women and children screamed.

"Run!" cried Mahpiyasapa. "Run!"

Men fled. Women and children sought the free kaiila which had been brought for them.

I lowered my lance. I trained it on the heart of the gigantic Kur. It was Sardak, the leader of the death squad from the steel worlds. Then soldiers came between us and I could not reach him. A woman on a kaiila, a child before her, clutching her, bounded past.

"Cuwignaka!" I called.

"I am here!" he cried.

I saw him, afoot. He had discarded his lance. He thrust a second child, behind the first, to the back of his kaiila. "Run, little brothers!" he cried, slapping the kaiila sharply. Squealing, it bounded away.

"Come!" I cried to him. "Come! Ride behind me!"

He shook his head. "There are not enough kaiila!" he said.

I dismounted, next to him. Two kaiila, bearing Yellow Knives, charged past. All was confusion. Men fought here and there about us.

"Get on your kaiila, you fool!" cried Cuwignaka. "Ride! Run!"

"Look!" I said.

Hci sat on his kaiila, almost as though stunned. He seemed paralyzed, frightened, immovable.

"Look out!" I cried. I saw a Yellow Knife wheel his kaiila about and drop his lance into the attack position.

"Look out!" I cried.

Hci turned, seeing the man. The Yellow Knife, the advantage of surprise lost, pulled back on the jaw rope of his kaiila. The animal almost backed to its haunches. Then it was on its feet again. The man, the point of his lance moving slightly, studied Hci. Hci regarded him.

"Beware!" I cried.

It was almost as though Hci did not see the man, almost as though he was looking through him, almost as though the very real man, and the physical point of the lance, of sharp bronze, were little more than tokens or emblems of something he feared far more.

Hci did not bring his kaiila about. He did not set himself to repel the charge.

The Yellow Knife hesitated, frightened, puzzled. This inactivity, so unexpected, so unnatural, so eerie, unsettled him.

Did he see a man before him or something else, perhaps a guest from the medicine world, something through which he might charge, touching nothing, something that might disappear like smoke behind him?

Then Hci cried out in anguish. His shield began to rise. It seemed, for a moment, that he tried to struggle with it, but, inexorably, as though with a will of its own, it rose.

The Yellow Knife aligned his lance.

Hci, resigned, no longer fighting, calmly, not moving, sat astride his kaiila, his arms lifted to the moons of Gor.

"Look out!" I cried.

The Yellow Knife's lance took him low in the left side, hurling him from the kaiila, and then the Yellow Knife, with a whoop of victory, whirled away.

"His shield would not defend him," said Cuwignaka, in horror. "His shield betrayed him! I have heard of such things. I never saw it until now!"

A soldier, on a kaiila, bolted past. His lance was black in the dusk.

I seized a woman running past. I caught her wrist before she could drive her knife into me. With a cry of pain she dropped it. I slapped her. I threw her to the back of my kaiila. Cuwignaka took the child who had been with her and threw him to the back of the beast, behind her.

"You will not go?" asked Cuwignaka of me.

"I will not leave without you," I said.

"Go!" said Cuwignaka, slapping the kaiila sharply. "Go!" It bounded away in the darkness, darting through the confusion.

A tarn's wings smote the air above us, not twenty feet over our heads. Dust swirled up from the ground. I was buffeted from my feet by the forequarters of a running kaiila. I climbed to my feet. I wiped dust from my eyes.

"I am here, said Cuwignaka, seizing me by the arm. "Come with me."

"Kinyanpi," I said, "they will be patrolling the outskirts of the camp. They will be searching the fields for fugitives."

"That is why we must stay in the camp," said Cuwignaka.

We made our way then, through the shadows, sometimes running, sometimes crouching down, sometimes crawling, from the scene of the slaughter. In a few moments we had hidden ourselves in one of the lodges. A short time later we heard the thunder of kaiila paws leaving the camp.

"They are mounting a pursuit," I said.

"They are tenacious," said Cuwignaka.

"It is the discipline of the soldiers and the beasts," I said.

"Probably," said Cuwignaka.

"Where are you going?" I asked.

"He may not be dead," said Cuwignaka.

"Hci?" I asked.

"Of course," said Cuwignaka.

"You are going back?" I asked.

"Yes," he said.

"I will come with you," I said.

"You need not do that," said Cuwignaka.

"I will come with you," I said.

"It will be dangerous," he said.

"It will be less dangerous for two than for one," I said.

"Mitakola," said Cuwignaka.

"Mitakola," I said. This, in the language of the Kaiila, means 'my friend'."

I did not find it necessary to tell Cuwignaka that I myself had intended to return for Hci. Before we had left the center of the camp I had seen him move.

We left the lodge stealthily. Our business must be done soon, before the return of the Yellow Knives and the soldiers. After their return the discipline would be at an end. Then would be the time of the falling upon the slain, the time of the knives, the time of the trophies.

31

IN GRUNT'S LODGE

"I lied," said Hci.

He lay in the darkness, in Grunt's lodge. I had wished to return to this lodge. There were objects in it which remained of interest to me. In it, too, were stocks of dried meat and wakapapi, pemmican.

"It was I who took the arrow of Canka," he said. "It was I who feigned an attack on Mahpiyasapa. It was I who accused Canka of attempting to kill him."

"That is known to us," said Cuwignaka. "I think, too, it is understood by Mahpiyasapa, and many others."

"I swore upon my shield," said Hci.

Cuwignaka did not respond.

"It knew," said Hci. "It fought me. Dishonored, it would not defend me."

"Rest now," said Cuwignaka.

We could hear the sounds of revels in the distance, where, together, Yellow Knives, soldiers and Kurii celebrated their victory.

"You came back for me," said Hci.

"Yes," said Cuwignaka.

"Why?" asked Hci.

"I am Kaiila," said Cuwignaka.

"I did not think you were Kaiila," said Hci.

"You were wrong," said Cuwignaka.

"Yes," said Hci. "I was wrong."

"Is he dead?" I asked.

"No," said Cuwignaka. "He is sleeping."

32

WHAT CUWIGNAKA DECIDED TO DO

"They enjoy their revels," said Cuwignaka.

We lay on our stomachs, on the small rise, overlooking the campfires of the victors.

I had a determination to make. Cuwignaka, too, who had insisted on accompanying me, also had a determination to make, something in which he was interested.

"There," I said, "in the great circle, in places of honor, the beasts, you see?"

"Yes," said Cuwignaka.

"They are Kurii," I said. "They were with the mercenaries of Alfred, the captain from Port Olni. They were housed in the small wagons near the end of his column."

"When I was with the column, as a slave," said Cuwignaka, "I never saw them."

"Their presence was kept secret, too, from the soldiers," I said.

"You are sure they are not from the medicine world?" asked Cuwignaka.

"You do not believe in the medicine world," I said.

"I believe in what I see," said Cuwignaka.

"They are as real as you or I," I said. "They have their histories and their purposes, like men."

"They terrify my people," said Cuwignaka.

"Do you see the largest one?" I asked.

"Yes," said Cuwignaka. It was squatting in a place of great honor, at the height of the large circle, its weight resting on its feet and the knuckles of its hands. On one side of it sat Alfred, captain of the mercenaries, with certain of his lieutenants. On the other side of it sat the three war chiefs of the Yellow Knives, those who had been earlier in the camp. Doubtless they had used their time with Watonka to well scout the camp. With them were certain of their high warriors.

"That is the leader of the Kurii," I said. "It's name, in Gorean, is Sardak. Behind it is another high Kur, one called, in Gorean, Kog."

"Such things have names?" asked Cuwignaka.

"Yes," I said. "How many do you count? Be careful. It is important."

"Seven," said Cuwignaka.

"I, too, count seven," I said. There had been seventeen of the small wagons, of the sort which I had conjectured contained Kurii, with the mercenary column. Given the irritability and territoriality of the Kur, it had seemed likely that there would have been but one Kur to a wagon. This gave me a figure of seventeen Kurii in the original death squad, including its leaders, Sardak and Kog. When Grunt and I had come to the field of the massacre we had learned from Pumpkin, the Waniyanpi slave, Waniyanpi being used to clear the field, that the bodies of nine such beasts had been found. I had been unable to determine, at that time, whether or not Kog and Sardak had been among the slain. The bodies of the beasts had been dragged away, into the fields, by red savages. It seemed they did not know much what else to do with them. I had learned later from the former Lady Mira of Venna, whom her red masters had decided to make a Waniyanpi slave, that a small group of Kurii had apparently made its way, at least largely unopposed, from the field. The savages, it seemed, were reluctant to attack them. She had speculated that there had been some seven or eight beasts in this group. I also knew of the survival of one Kur whom I had encountered, personally, on the field, preventing it from attacking a party of Waniyanpi. It had had wounds, and a great deal of dried blood matted in its fur. I speculated that it might have fallen in the fighting, and lost consciousness, from the loss of blood, and then, later, awakened. It seemed unlikely that it had been one of the party which had escaped, and had then been sent back, perhaps to look for food. It was probably separate from the group which had escaped. It had then withdrawn from the field. I had not pursued it. As nearly as I could determine now, it had not made contact with the others. It had, perhaps, perished on the prairie.

"One would be enough," said Cuwignaka.

"What do you mean?" I asked. I did not think that any one Kur, singly, would be likely to look forward to meeting Zarendargar, Half-Ear, in a battle to the death.

"One would be enough to hearten the Yellow Knives," he said, "one would be enough to frighten and dispirit the Kaiila."

"Of course," I said. In my own concerns, in my own purposes in the Barrens, to locate and warn Zarendargar of his danger, I had given too little thought to the obvious role of the fierce Kurii in the military politics of the vast grasslands east of the Thentis mountains. Cuwignaka, as a matter of fact, did not even know of my true mission in the Barrens. He thought me one who merely dealt in trading, much like Grunt.

"The Kaiila are broken," said Cuwignaka, bitterly.

"Many must have escaped," I said.

"They are disunited and scattered," said Cuwignaka. "The meat for the winter is lost."

"Doubtless some will survive," I said.

"Perhaps like Dust Legs," said Cuwignaka, "traders, diplomats, interpreters, serving the needs of others, not as Ubars of the plains, as masters of the grasslands in their own right."

I felt ashamed. How stupid I had been. How absorbed we can be sometimes in our own concerns, and sometimes, then, so little alert to the affairs of others. I was concerned with the life of a friend. Cuwignaka was concerned with the survival of a people.

"Perhaps the Kaiila will rise again," I said.

"No," said Cuwignaka. "Nothing, now, can save them."

"You do not know that," I said.

"What can save them?" asked Cuwignaka.

"Nothing, perhaps," I said. "I do not know."

Cuwignaka looked down from the small rise, onto the broad, firelit spaces of the revels and feasts.

"There are the victors," he said.

The area, a large one, was crowded. There was a great circle, in which dignitaries had their places, and many smaller circles. In the center of each there was a fire. In the center of the great circle the huge fire blazed from a kindling of broken lodge poles. Slave girls, stark naked, kneeling and sweating, tended hundreds of cooking pots. Other slave girls, similarly stark naked, hurried about, serving the men, bringing them food and water, and, when desired, themselves. The ankles of the cooks wore six-inch tethers, keeping them close to their pots. The ankles of the serving slaves wore longer tethers, permitting them to walk with ease, but not to run. When one of the soldiers or Yellow Knives wished one of these girls he simply unfastened the tether from one of her ankles and, when finished, put it again in place. Sometimes the girls were pulled into the shadows, and sometimes not. I saw two soldiers fighting over one. The collars of most of these girls had been cut from their throats, for they had been Kaiila collars. Most of the girls, on their left breast, fixed there in black paint, wore a mark. It identified them, making it clear to whom they belonged.

"Yes," I said.

We saw a Kur leap up and seize a slave girl. He lifted her well above his head, by an arm and thigh. She was screaming, her body helpless, bent in a lovely bow. The Kur then lowered her and put his great jaws half about her waist. Her eyes were wild. He let her feel the print of his fangs. Then he flung her from him, into the dirt. He then bounded up and down, turning, in a small circle. The girl, terrified, crawled away. The Kur, its lips drawn back from its white fangs, returned to its place.

"It is Kur humor," I said.

"You are sure they are just like us?" asked Cuwignaka.

"There are some differences," I admitted.

"There are lance dancers," said Cuwignaka.

"I see them," I said.

From between lodges there was emerging a long line, of perhaps forty to fifty men, bearing lances. The line, snakelike, weaved its way toward the fires, and then began, its dancers shuffling, bending down, rising up, chanting, to wind its way among them.

"It is a dance of the Snake Society, a warrior society of the Yellow Knives," said Cuwignaka. "We have a similar dance among the Kaiila, but any warrior who has counted coup may dance it."

"At least she is still alive," I said.

"Yes," said Cuwignaka.

"I gather that that is the determination which you wished to make in this small reconnaissance," I said.

"Yes," said Cuwignaka.

"She is now fetching for Iwoso," I said.

"Yes," said Cuwignaka.

"Do you think she will make her a good maiden?" I asked.

"Of course," said Cuwignaka.

"Does it outrage you to see her as a female slave?" I asked.

"She betrayed the Kaiila. No," said Cuwignaka.

"She now returns and kneels before Iwoso, head down, handing her food."

"That must be very pleasant for Iwoso," said Cuwignaka.

"She does it well," I said.

"Good," said Cuwignaka.

"She appears to have been much beaten," I said.

"Good," said Cuwignaka. "That will accustom her the more quickly to her new condition."

"Do you think she will make Iwoso a good slave?" I asked.

"I think she will make anyone a good slave," said Cuwignaka.

"She seems to be the only red slave at the feast," I said.

"We know there are other red slaves," said Cuwignaka. "We saw several."

"Do you think the fact that she is the only red slave at the feast, the only one among all the white slaves, is deliberate?" I asked.

"Of course," said Cuwignaka. "That is done to humiliate her. It is a stroke worthy of Iwoso's high intelligence."

"You have noted, also, I suppose," I said, "that she is one of the few slaves who wears a collar and that she is the only slave, or one of the few, whose ankles are not thonged."

"That her ankles are not thonged is intended as a further humiliation," said Cuwignaka. "That suggests that she, though red, is of even less value than a white female. In any case, of course, escape is impossible."

"Yes," I said.

"The collar is doubtless Iwoso's," said Cuwignaka.

"Doubtless," I said.

"Iwoso must have received much pleasure in secretly preparing it for her," said Cuwignaka, "and again when she first put it on her."

"Iwoso's triumph seems complete," I said.

"Yes," agreed Cuwignaka.

"Look," I said.

"I see," said Cuwignaka.

A warrior had seized the red slave by the hair and pulled her, twisting her, to her feet. He then held her before him, bent backwards, examining the sweet bow of her beauty.

Iwoso leaped to her feet. She shouted something, angrily, at the man. He, laughed, hurled the red slave away from him, a dozen feet away, into the dust.

"The lance dancers are approaching," I observed.

"Iwoso does not want the slave to learn the pleasures of men," said Cuwignaka. "Doubtless she fears it will spoil her as a serving slave for a woman."

"She is right," I said.

The lance dancers, then, were swirling about the fallen red slave, weaving and spinning, in spiraling, swiftly moving circles about her. Some of them merely laid the cold metal points of the lances, or the sides of the lance blades, on her flesh. Others jabbed her, dancing, with the points. She lay in the dust, her hands over her head, her knees drawn tightly up, small, shuddering and trembling, helpless under the points.

Iwoso leapt among the dancers, scolding and shouting, thrusting them away. There was much laughter from the Yellow Knives and the dancers.

Iwoso then crouched down and, taking a braided, rawhide rope from her waist, presumably the same one I had seen her with earlier, even before the first attack on the camp, tied it about the neck of the helpless, terrified slave. She then drew her, on her hands and knees, back to her place. She made her lie down there, on her side, with her knees drawn up. She struck her twice with a switch. The slave cried out, squirming under the blows, but kept her position. The mistress then resumed her place, sitting down, cross-legged, with the men, in the great circle. She retained the slave's leash in her hand, looping it, shortening it, so that it was only about a yard in length. The lance dancers, in their serpentine pattern, swirled away.

"I did not know that Bloketu was so beautiful," I said. It is difficult for a woman to conceal her beauty when she is permitted to wear only a collar, or a collar and leash.

"I wonder if Iwoso is even more beautiful," said Cuwignaka.

"Perhaps someday masters will know," I said.

Cuwignaka looked at me, and smiled. "Perhaps," he said.

"It is dangerous to remain here," I said. "I suggest that we withdraw."

Cuwignaka's attention was again on the great circle.

"It is dangerous here," I said. "Perhaps you can manage to take your eyes off Bloketu."

"She is beautiful, isn't she?" said Cuwignaka.

"Yes," I said. "It is my speculation that the perimeter of the camp and the areas about the camp may still be under surveillance, the perimeter being guarded to prevent the return of Kaiila to the camp for such things as food, the fields to detect the movements of possible fugitives. Similarly I think it would be difficult to obtain kaiila and escape without abandoning Hci and the kaiila, in any event, as we have determined, are well guarded."

"She is so beautiful," said Cuwignaka.

"Accordingly, it is my recommendation that we remain in the camp tonight. I think this is in the best interests not only of Hci but of ourselves. We must then attempt to depart in the morning, after the watches have been recalled or relaxed, or the camp, as a whole, has been left."

"Quite beautiful," said Cuwignaka, admiringly.

"So, what do you think?" I asked.

"About what?" asked Cuwignaka.

"About remaining in the camp tonight," I said.

"Of course," said Cuwignaka. "I could not, in any case, leave the camp before morning."

"Why not?" I asked, puzzled.

"Surely you know what day this is," he said.

I looked at him.

"This is the very height of the time of our feasts and festivals," he said.

"Yes?" I said.

"So what day is it?" he asked.

"I do not know," I said.

"Have you forgotten?" he asked.

"It seems so," I said.

"This is the first day of the great dance," he said.

"What of it?" I asked.

"I am going to dance," said Cuwignaka.

"You are insane," I said.

"The portals of the dance lodge will be unguarded now," he said. "There will be none to deny me entrance."

"There will be none to dance with you," I said, "none to share the loneliness, the pain."

"I will dance alone," said Cuwignaka.

"Today," I said, "the Kaiila do not dance."

"One will," said Cuwignaka.

"The lodge of the dance has been rent," I said. "The pole itself had been defaced and profaned, its trappings stripped away. Your body would not be properly painted. You would not have brush at your wrists and ankles. You could not dare to blow upon the Herlit-bone whistle."

"Do you really think such things are necessary?" asked Cuwignaka, smiling.

"I do not know," I said.

"Little is actually needed for the truth of the dance," said Cuwignaka. "I will have the pole, myself and my manhood. It will be enough."

"It takes some men two or three days to free themselves from the pole," I said.

"I do not have that much time," said Cuwignaka. "I will free myself by morning."

"You will kill yourself," I said.

"I do not think that is likely," said Cuwignaka.

"Do not dance," I said.

"At one time or another in his life," said Cuwignaka, "every man, in one way or another, must dance. Otherwise he is not a man."

"There are many ways to dance," I said.

"I will dance in the way of my people, the Kaiila," said Cuwignaka.

"You do not even believe in the medicine world," I said.

"I believe in the dance," he said.

I was silent.

"I may need some help," said Cuwignaka, "in attaching the ropes, in placing the skewers in my flesh. Will you help me?"

"Yes," I said.

"Then, when I am finished with the dance," said Cuwignaka, "and have rested a little, we will be on our way. We will rig a travois for Hci. We will leave the camp before dawn. I know a small arroyo nearby. We will hide there and then, perhaps tomorrow evening, take our leave."

"Where will we go?" I asked.

"Hci needs care," said Cuwignaka.

"I understand," I said. "Look," I said, gesturing to the broad, firelit spaces below us.

"The Yellow Knives prepare to dance," said Cuwignaka.

We saw Yellow-Knife warriors setting up small poles, some five to six feet in height, attaching grisly trophies to the tops of the poles.

"They will celebrate their victory," said Cuwignaka. "Those are trophy poles. They will dance trophy dances."

"I do not care to watch," I said.

"Let them dance," said Cuwignaka. "Another, in another place, will also dance."

"You are determined?" I asked.

"Yes," said Cuwignaka.

"You will dance?" I asked.

"Yes," said Cuwignaka. "I will dance."

33

MIRA

We heard the rattling and beating, the clanging, from a distance.

Fleer circled in the sky.

We then, the grass to our waist, dragging the travois on which Hci lay, and other articles, surmounted a rise, surveying the maize fields below us, the buildings and palisade of the compound beyond them.

The fact that we did not have kaiila had, it seemed, worked to our advantage. Several times in the past few days we had seen solitary Kinyanpi scouts in the sky. Each time we had hidden in the deep grass.

We then, grateful for the slope, drew the travois downward, toward the valley below.

At one edge of the field a crude wooden platform had been erected, some seven or eight feet high, its surface reached by a ladder. Above the platform, on poles, a cloth canopy had been stretched. It was being moved by the wind. Beneath the canopy, one with a string of pans and cups tied together, the other with a wooden spoon and a flat, metal pan, were two Waniyanpi women. One was shouting and gesticulating, shaking the pans and cups; the other was shouting and pounding on the flat, metal pan with the wooden spoon.

The fleer, then, the members of a common flock, as the fleer usually flies, departed. They would probably return at a later time.

One of the women on the platform seized the arm of the other and pointed in our direction. She who had first seen us then put down her string of pans and cups and, hastily, descended from the platform. She began to run toward the palisade in the distance. The other woman, shading her eyes, watched us approach. As we came closer she seemed suddenly to react. She put down her pan and spoon and, like the other, hastily descended from the platform. She, however, unlike the other, began to run towards us.

"Go away," she cried to us, coming towards us, through the grass. "There is danger here!"

I scanned the skies. "Let us get out of the open," I said. "Let us go to the maize, near the platform."

"There is danger here," she said, hurrying then along beside us.

"There is danger here, what?" I said.

"There is danger here—Masters," she said.

In a few moments we had reached the edge of the maize field, near the platform.

"You may kneel," I told her.

"I may kneel?" she asked.

"Yes," I said.

"Yes, Master," she said, gratefully, and knelt before us.

"What is the danger here?" asked Cuwignaka. "Are there Kinyanpi about, Yellow Knives, soldiers?"

"There are no soldiers nor Yellow Knives," she said. "Kinyanpi occasionally fly past, but fewer now than before. I think they are bringing their searches to a close."

"What, then, is the danger?" asked Cuwignaka.

"You will not be welcome here," she said. "They are turning everyone away."

"This man is wounded, grievously," I said, indicating Hci.

"They are turning everyone away," she said, "even the wounded. They have turned away even women and children."

"This man needs help," I said.

"It does not matter," she said. "I am sorry."

"He may die," I said.

"I am sorry," she said.

"Is this not Garden Eleven, a Waniyanpi compound owned by the Kaiila," demanded Cuwignaka.

"Now we are owned by Yellow Knives," she said. "Soldiers have told us."

"You are still owned by the Kaiila," said Cuwignaka, angrily. "You will provide us with food and shelter."

"We are afraid," she said. "We do not know who owns us."

"Someone is coming," I said.

Approaching, along the side of the maize field, coming from the direction of the palisade and buildings in the distance was a group of Waniyanpi. In their lead was the woman I had met, briefly, at the Kaiila camp, Radish. Near her was the woman who had run to fetch them, she who had earlier had the pans and cups on the platform. Behind Radish came Pumpkin, large and ungainly, as usual, in the drab, rude dress that was the uniform of the Waniyanpi. There were about fifteen persons in the group, both men and women. I recognized Carrot and Cabbage.

"Turnip," cried Radish, angrily, "what are you doing, kneeling before a man? Get on your feet!"

"You do not yet have permission to rise, " I said.

"Yes, Master," she said, happily.

"Get up!" said Radish.

"Apparently you did not hear," I said. "The slave has not yet received permission to rise."

I folded my arms and regarded the insolent Radish.

Turnip, whose beauty could be conjectured, even beneath the gray, rude garb of the Waniyanpi, lowered her head, humbly, her long, blond tresses hanging forward. She had once been the Lady Mira, of Venna, an agent of Kurii. Then she had fallen into the hands of red savages. She was now only a slave.

"Go away," said Radish, angrily. "There is no room here for you."

"I would speak with a man," I said. "What man is in charge here?"

Radish reacted as though struck. "I speak for all of us," she said.

"Pumpkin," I asked, "is it you? Are you leader here?"

"No, no," said Pumpkin, quickly, looking down. "There is no leader here. We are all Sames. We are all the same. There are no leaders. We are all the same. Peace, and light, and tranquillity, and contentment and goodness, be unto you."

"Sweetness be unto you," said Carrot.

"Sweetness be unto you," said Cabbage.

"You seem to me the natural leader here, Pumpkin," I said.

"No," he said, "no, no."

"You have surrendered your sovereignty?" I asked. "This woman, then, is your leader?"

"There is no leader," mumbled Pumpkin, not meeting my eyes. "We are all Sames. We are all the same."

"You, then," I asked, viewing Radish, "are the leader."

"Perhaps," she smiled.

"Radish is strong and forceful," said Carrot.

"She is not the leader," Cabbage assured me. "It is only that we do whatever she says."

"Is this true, Pumpkin?" I asked.

"We do whatever Radish tells us," he said, again not meeting my eyes.

"We have a man here," I said. indicating Hci, "who is grievously, sorely, wounded. We need food and shelter."

"Find it elsewhere," said Radish.

"Pumpkin?" I asked.

He did not respond, but put down his head. This hurt me, for I had hoped that in Pumpkin, somewhere, perhaps deeply buried, was a man.

"Carrot?" I asked. "Cabbage?"

"I am sorry," said Carrot.

"It is not just you," said Cabbage. "Yesterday Radish even put two young people out of the compound, a young man and woman. She found them touching one another."

"Terrible!" said one of the Waniyanpi women, though I do not think she believed it.

"Go away!" said Radish, pointing out over the prairie. "Go!"

"No, Tatankasa, Mitakola," said Cuwignaka, "do not kill them!"

Radish drew back. My hand, in anger, had gone to the hilt of my sword.

"They banish even their own people," said Cuwignaka.

"I am a woman," said Radish, uncertainly.

"I thought you were a Same," I said.

"Their blood is not worthy of your sword," said Cuwignaka.

"Kill us if you wish," said Pumpkin.

"We will not resist," said Carrot.

"Resistance is violence, and violence is wrong," said Cabbage.

"Aggression must be met with love," said Carrot.

"Conquerors have often found that a useful philosophy to encourage in subject peoples," I said. I took my hand from the hilt of my sword.

"We need your aid," I said to Radish.

"You may not have it," she said, emboldened. "Go away."

I looked at the men. "You are vile hypocrites," I said.

"No," said Pumpkin, "not really. It is only that we are Waniyanpi."

"We do whatever Radish tells us," said Carrot.

"Yes," said Cabbage.

"You have surrendered your manhood," I said. "You are spineless weaklings."

The men hung their heads.

"Let us go, Tatankasa," said Cuwignaka, "Mitakola."

I looked at Pumpkin. He, of all of them, I had had hopes for.

"Pumpkin," I said.

He lifted his head but then, again, put it down, not meeting my eyes.

"Come along, Mitakola," said Cuwignaka.

"Get up, Turnip," said Radish, angrily. "You shame the Waniyanpi!"

"I have not yet been given permission to rise," said Turnip.

"You are kneeling before a man!" screamed Radish. "Get up!" I wondered what it was in Turnip's deferential attitude, in her posture of submission, which so inflamed Radish.

"Yes," said Turnip, "I am kneeling before a man!"

"Get up!" screamed Radish.

Turnip turned to me, facing me. "I kneel before you, Master," she said. "I incline my head to you, as a woman, and a slave."

"Get up!" screamed Radish, beside herself with rage.

"I kiss and lick your feet, Master," said Turnip.

There coursed through the women present, other than Radish, a thrill of horror and pleasure. I heard several of them gasp.

Turnip knelt before me, the palms of her hands on the grass, her head down. I felt her lips and tongue, sweetly and softly, delicately, kissing and caressing my feet.

"You are cast out!" screamed Radish. "You are out of the compound!"

Turnip paid Radish no attention. She lifted her head to me, and smiled.

"Take off the garb of the Waniyanpi!" screamed Radish. "You are not worthy of it!"

"You may rise," I told Turnip.

Turnip rose to her feet and, over her head, drew off the dismal, gray dress he had worn.

Underneath the dress she was stark naked. She then stood before us, very straight and very beautiful. The women, with the exception of Radish, looked upon her admiringly, thrilled that she was so beautiful. The men averted their eyes, frightened and shamed.

"Exercising the prerogative of any Kaiila warrior, over any slave in a compound of the Kaiila," said Cuwignaka, clearly and loudly, "I now claim this woman as my personal slave." He then regarded her. "You are now my slave," he said.

"Yes, Master," she said. She knelt down swiftly and inclined her head to him. I was pleased to see that she did this quickly. She now understood that she was no longer a Waniyanpi slave but was under a man's discipline.

"And your use," said Cuwignaka, pointing to me, "is his."

"Yes, Master," she said, happily. As a slave myself, of course, I could own nothing, not even the collar I wore. On the other hand I could certainly have the use of a slave, who would then be to me as my own slave, in all things.

"It will be up to him, of course," said Cuwignaka, "as to whether or not he chooses to accept your use."

"Accept my use, Master," she begged. "Please."

"What if I do not accept her use?" I asked Cuwignaka.

"Then we will leave her behind, cast out of the Waniyanpi compound, to die," said Cuwignaka.

"Please accept my use, Master," she begged.

I looked down upon her.

"I learned long ago, at the paws of a master's kaiila, that I was a slave," she said. "I learned it, too, in receiving the blow of a quirt, of a strong man." This was a blow I had administered to her sometime ago, preparatory to questioning her in the matter of the attacked wagon train and column. "I learned it, too," she said, "naked, in a yoke which had been fastened on me by red savages, when I was marched to the compound. Mostly I have learned it here, in the long hours I have had to think, in the fields and in the compound. No longer am I in doubt as to what I am. I am a slave."

A thrill passed through the Waniyanpi women present, with the exception of Radish.

"Long ago," she said, "when you were free, and I had just been sentenced to a Waniyanpi compound, you refused to carry me off, making me your own slave. Perhaps, then, regarding me as a mere encumbrance, I having been so recently free, you did not take me with you. Perhaps, on the other hand, it amused you, as it seemed to, that I, someone you seemed to regard, somehow, as a foe of some sort, or lovely enemy, was to be sent to a Waniyanpi compound. Now, however, our realities have changed. If it had been your desire to see me suffer in a Waniyanpi compound, you have now had your wish. I will never forget the horrors of my experiences there. You may now, if it pleases you, take me from it, as I beg you. Too, now you, too, have fallen slave. You, now, are no more than I. Perhaps a slave, then, may see fit to accede to the pleas of another slave, rather than dismiss her petition as casually, as thoughtlessly, as cruelly, as might a free man. Also, you being a slave, too, perhaps you have been denied the use of women or deprived of their caresses, or perhaps, not being free, you have not been permitted to use them with the same liberal audacity as a free man, or as frequently as you might desire. If that is so, I might be of somewhat greater interest to you now than I was before. Lastly I would no longer be an encumbrance to you for I am, obviously, no longer a free woman. No longer am I an inconvenience and a bother, something to be concerned about and watched out for. Now I am only a property that begs to love and serve you."

"You seem a different woman than before," I said.

"I now realize that I am a slave, Master," she said.

"If I accept your use," I said, "you must understand that I do so—unconditionally."

"No strong man accepts a woman on any other terms," she said. "I would not have it any other way."

"Do you understand what it is to be a man's total slave?" I asked.

"Yes," she said.

"Speak," I said.

"The slave is totally subject to the master in all ways, and in all things. She is his to do with as he pleases. She depends on him for her food and the merest scrap of her clothing, if any. She is subject, completely, to his discipline, to his abuse and his whip. She is owned, like a sandal or saddle. She may be slain even on a whim, if her master wishes."

"Are these, and other such conditions, acceptable to you?" I asked.

"Yes, Master," she said.

"I accept your use," I said.

"Thank you, Master!" she cried. She seized me about the legs and kissed me. I felt her tears through my tunic.

"Stand," I said.

Joyfully she stood.

"Do you think your lot with me will be easy, Slave?" I asked.

"No, Master," she said, happily.

I went to the travois on which Hci lay. On it, too, were various articles and supplies. I cut a length from a narrow, braided rawhide rope.

"He is going to put her in a collar!" said one of the Waniyanpi women, excitedly, awe in her voice.

"Yes," said another, breathlessly.

"Come away!" said Radish to the women and men. But the women would not be budged. The men too, their eyes cast down, save for furtive glances, seemed loath to leave.

I took the narrow rope, then, and looped it about her neck, three times. I then knotted it and ran my finger about, under the loops, making sure that they were unslippable and snug, but not in the least uncomfortable. The point of the collar is to mark the woman as a slave and, in many cases, by means of devices such as a particular kind of knot, a tag, an engraving on metal, or a plate attached to it, to identify the master, not to cause her discomfort. Most of the time she will not even be aware she is wearing it. She may always, of course, be reminded. And if she is in doubt, she may always touch it. It is on her. I let the two loose ends of the braided, rawhide rope, some seven or eight inches in length, dangle between her breasts. They would also make a convenient, short leash, to pull her about with, if I wished.

I looked at the woman, collared. The three loops were about her neck. The ends dangled down, between her breasts. This collaring arrangement, though not unfamiliar on Gor generally, particularly after the fall of a city, when metal collars may not be available in abundance, or in rural areas, is unusual in the Barrens, where leather, thong-tied beaded collars are almost universal. I did not think, accordingly, that there would be much doubt as to who it was, to whom her use belonged.

I thought she would make a lovely slave.

"She is collared!" said one of the women, breathlessly.

"Yes!" said another.

"Come away!" said Radish.

I noted that even the men, furtively, with but one exception, observed the collaring of the beautiful female. I saw that they, too, wished they had a female to collar. I wondered if the sight of her collaring might arouse their manhood. The one exception was Pumpkin. He kept his eyes cast down, determinedly. He was sweating. His fists were clenched. I saw that he, in the approved fashion of the Waniyanpi, would turn his manhood against himself, using it to frustrate himself, using it to cause himself suffering, denying it its fulfillment, its sovereignty and dominance.

"Take the place of my friend, in the traces of the travois, Slave," I said.

"Yes, Master," she said.

Cuwignaka slipped from the broad, over-the-shoulder strap he had used to exert leverage on the travois and then helped the girl to adjust it on her body. She then stood before the travois, very straight and beautiful, the strap on her body. The men and women, with the exception of Pumpkin and Radish, looked on, thrilled, and in awe and envy. The woman was obviously a slave. She would serve in any way her masters chose. She could serve even, obviously, as a draft beast.

"Come away!" said Radish.

The men and women did not move.

"Pumpkin," said Radish. "Pumpkin!"

I saw how she appealed to him, as to a natural leader.

"Yes, Radish," he said.

"Come away," she said. "Come away, Pumpkin!"

"Yes, Radish," he said, and turned meekly about. He took his way from the place. The others, and then Radish, casting a look of hatred behind her, followed.

I walked over to the girl.

She lifted her head proudly, the strap about her body.

"We have little food," I said. "There will be great danger."

"I am a slave," she said. "Whip me, if I do not please you."

"It is a fitting answer," I said. I regarded her. She was very beautiful.

"It seems to me you took a great risk," I said. "You were very bold, very brave."

"Not really, Master," she said.

"How did you know I would accept your use?" I asked.

"I knew it," she said. "I sensed it."

"When?" I asked.

"As soon as you had me kneel before you," she said.

"Interesting," I said.

"I am a woman," she said. "We can tell such things."

"Interesting," I said. How subtle and deep was the intelligence of women, I thought. How much they know. How much they can sense. How simple and crude, how naive, sometimes seems the intelligence of men compared to the intelligence of women. What deep and wonderful creatures they are. Who can truly understand the emotional depths and needs, eons old, of these flowers of nature and evolution? How natural, then, it is, that the truly loving man will concern himself not with her distortions and perversions, ultimately barren, but with her emotional and sensuous truths, ancient and deep within her, with what might be called her biological and natural fulfillment. Then I shook such thoughts from my mind, for she was simply a slave, and was to be treated as such.

"Oh!" she said.

I cinched the strap closely on her body.

"Master is rough," she said.

"Be silent, Slave," I said.

"Yes, Master," she said, smiling.

"What, now, is our destination?" I asked Cuwignaka.

"We will go north," he said. "We will build a raft for the travois and cross the Northern Kaiila. We will then proceed north and west of Council Rock, into the land of the Casmu Kaiila. There is a place there I know. It is a camping site favored by Kahintokapa."

"I wonder if he survived," I said.

"Let us hope so," said Cuwignaka.

"What sort of place is this?" I asked.

"It is secluded," said Cuwignaka. "There is wood and water. Game is generally available in the vicinity."

"Do Kaiila, generally, know of this place?" I asked.

"Yes," he said. "We are generally familiar with one another's camp sites. This is important if we wish to gather the bands. It can also be important in the winter. Sometimes there is food in one place and not in another."

"Various survivors, then," I said, "might possibly have gone to this place."

"That is not unlikely," said Cuwignaka.

"Let us then be on our way," I said. I picked up the other strap, the rigged harness, the trace, and slipped it over my shoulder, about my body.

"It is we who will pull the travois, is it not?" asked the girl.

"Yes," I said. "We are slaves." Actually I wished Cuwignaka to rest. He was still weak from the dance. Four times in the last five days the wounds on his chest had begun to bleed.

"I am pleased to be harnessed with you, to pull with you, Master," she said.

"Do not slack," I said, "or you will be severely beaten."

"I shall not," she said. She looked behind herself, uneasily, at Cuwignaka. "Master," she said, "I am bare."

"I am well aware of that, my lovely harness mate," I said.

"Will he whip us?" she asked, in a whisper.

"He will if he wishes," I told her.

She swallowed hard.

"When I give the signal," I said, "lean forward and step out with your left foot. Lengthen your stride somewhat, and I shall shorten mine. I shall set the pace. If you cannot keep it, beg for its reduction."

"Yes, Master," she said.

"Now," I said, "step forward."

"Yes, Master," she said.

"I love working beside you, pulling with you, Master," she said.

"I, myself," I said, "would prefer for this work to be done by four or five slave girls, naked, and under whips."

"Yes, Master," she said, looking down.

We continued on our way, northward, drawing the travois through the tall grass.

She was doing very well. Either she did not wish to slacken her efforts or feared, mightily, to do so. Such a slackening, of course, would have been instantly detectable to me, her harness mate. She would then, of course, have been whipped, and made to draw more than her share of the weight.

"Master," she said, after a time.

"Yes," I said.

"Am I to be permitted clothing?" she asked.

"Not for a time," I said. "Perhaps, later. We will see. Perhaps by your performances, if they are sufficiently superb, you may, in time, be adjudged worthy of a scrap of cloth."

"Yes, Master," she said, happily. "Master," she said, a little later.

"Yes," I said.

"I do not have a name," she said.

"That is true," I said.

We continued to draw the travois through the tall grass.

"Am I to be named?" she asked.

"Perhaps," I said.

"I would like to have a name," she said.

"It is probably a good idea for animals like you to be given names," I said.

"Yes, Master," she said.

"Perhaps we should call you 'Ahtudan'," I said.

"What does that mean?" she asked.

" 'Something to be spit upon,' " I said. "It is a fitting name for a slave, it is not?"

"Yes, Master," she said, her head down.

"Perhaps we could call you 'Cesli' or 'Cespu'," I said.

"What do those names mean?" she asked.

" 'Cesli'," I said, "means dung."

"Oh," she said.

"Either of men or animals," I said.

"I see," she said.

" 'Cespu' means 'wart' or 'scab,' " I said.

"I see," she said.

"Let us save those names," said Cuwignaka.

"Oh?" I said.

"Yes," he said.

"Very well," I said. I smiled. In Cuwignaka there was a warrior.

"Is it all right with you," I asked the girl, "if we save those names?"

"Yes, Master," she laughed.

"What about 'Turnip'?" I asked.

"Oh, please, Master, no," she laughed. "That reminds me so of the Waniyanpi."

"Your life has changed considerably, as you will soon learn," I said. "That name, thus, would no longer be appropriate for you."

"I am pleased to hear it," she said.

"Perhaps I should call you 'Wowiyutanye'," I said.

"What does that mean?" she asked.

"Temptation," I said.

"Master flatters me," she said, head down, smiling.

"I have a name for you," I said.

"What, Master?" she asked, eagerly, apprehensively.

"It is not a sophisticated name," I said.

"No, Master," she said, "for I am only a slave."

"It seems to me a simple, suitable name for a slave," I said.

"Yes, Master," she said. Whatever name it was she would wear it. Animals must wear whatever names are given to them.

"I name you—" I said.

"Yes, Master?" she said.

"I name you 'Mira'," I said.

"Thank you, Master," she said. "Master well knows how to humble a slave! Once that name was worn by a slave who did not know she was a slave. It was then a slave's name but not a slave name. Then the slave was legally imbonded. She learned then, and soon, that she was truly a slave. Her nature was revealed. Her truth was manifested. The name then again was put on her, this time as a slave name. Now the name is not only a slave's name, as it always was, but is a slave name as well, and recognized and acknowledged publicly, by the slave and others, as such. How cleverly, then, this reminds the slave that she was never anything, even before the technicality of her legal imbondment, but a slave!"

"Do you think you will prove to be a satisfactory slave?" I asked.

"I will try with all my heart, Master," she said.

"Do you want to be a slave?" I asked.

"Yes, Master," she said, "with all my heart."

"See that you serve well," I said.

"Yes, Master," she said.

"Pull, Slave," I said.

"Yes, Master," she said.

34

SQUASH AND STRAWBERRY

"Tie me and use me as a slave," she begged.

I thonged her hands casually, efficiently, behind her back. I then threw her to the grass at my feet.

She reared up on her elbows. "I beg slave rape," she gasped.

I dropped to the grass beside her and put my left hand in her hair, pulling her head back to the grass. I pulled it back, and held it, in such a way that she must look back, and up, at the sky. I broke off a long stalk of grass.

It had been four days since we had crossed the Northern Kaiila. In our passage we had seen, to our right, Council Rock, rearing high, almost anomalously, out of the plains, prominent amidst a group of smaller, associated bluffs.

"Master?" she asked.

I began to tease her with the stalk of grass.

"Are they near?" I asked Cuwignaka.

"Yes," he said.

He was sitting nearby, cross-legged, mending one of the traces on the travois.

"Oh, oh!" said the girl.

"Are they armed?" I asked.

"No," he said.

"Did you put out a little pemmican?" I asked.

"Yes," he said.

"Oh!" said the girl. "Oh!"

We spoke in Kaiila. The girl did not know this language. She did not even know what we were talking about. In her presence we had discussed the matter only in Kaiila.

"Oh, please, Master, stop!" begged the girl. She began to squirm and whimper. She could not free herself, of course, for my left hand held her hair and my right leg was across her legs. She, helpless, was well held in place.

"I did not want you to do this, Sweet Master," she said. "Please, I beg you, stop!"

She squirmed, recoiling and shuddering, as it pleased me to make her do.

"Oh, please!" she said in misery. "Please, my Master!"

She did not even know of the proximity of the others. They had been with us since even before we had crossed the Northern Kaiila. They, like the girl, as we had ascertained to our satisfaction, did not understand Kaiila, or did not much understand it. We had made remarks in their hearing to which they, if they had understood Kaiila adequately, presumably would have responded, probably by swift flight. It seemed quite clear that they did not know that we were aware of their presence. Sometimes Cuwignaka had left a little pemmican behind at our camp sites, as though inadvertently. It was time, now, we had decided, to make their acquaintance.

"Oh, please, stop, Master!" she begged. "I will do anything! I will do anything!"

"But you must do anything, anyway," I said. "You are a slave."

"Yes, Master!" she cried.

I desisted in touching her body lightly, unexpectedly, here and there, with the stalk of grass.

"Do you think you can yield well?" I asked.

"Yes, Master! Yes, Master!" she gasped.

I put the stalk of grass to the side.

"Kiss," I said.

She reared up on her elbows, struggling, reaching forward, and put her mouth to mine.

Then she lay back, looking at me.

Sometimes, in the cities, one puts a woman in slave chains, making her helpless, her limbs fastened apart, and then addresses her beauty, lightly, with a feather. In a few moments she is usually begging to serve you in any way you might wish. There are many ways to teach a woman that she is in your power, and truly yours. This is only one.

"Are you subdued?" I asked.

"Yes," she said, "totally."

"And how will you yield?" I asked.

"With perfection," she said.

I then began to caress her, with my hands, and with my mouth, my tongue, lips and teeth. She began to moan and whimper.

"They are coming closer," said Cuwignaka, casually. "They seem to be interested in your handling of the slave."

I continued to attend to the lovely, bound woman whose use I owned.

She was almost beside herself with orgasmic sensation.

"Please," she begged. "Yes!" she said.

Then she writhed beneath me, mine.

"Yes," she wept. "Yes!"

"They are quite close now, a few feet away," said Cuwignaka, casually, "a few feet to your right, in the grass, one a bit behind the other."

"Please!" begged the girl.

"Very well," I said.

"I yield me," she cried. "I yield me yours!" She was so marvelous. How glorious are women.

"They seem fascinated," said Cuwignaka.

"Let me know if there is any change in their location," I said.

"I wish that I could hold you," she said.

"You cannot," I said. "You are bound as a slave."

"Yes, Master," she said.

I held her, closely. She pressed herself against me, helplessly. Whether she was held or not was my decision. She could be, if I chose, spurned in a moment, thrust aside in the grass.

I kissed her, softly. She was very beautiful.

"They are changing their position," said Cuwignaka, working on the trace from the travois. "One is falling back. The other is going for the pemmican."

"All right," I said.

The girl looked up at me, lovingly. Again I kissed her.

"Oh!" she said.

I had leapt from her side. I lunged through the grass. With one hand, before he could leap up, I had seized the young fellow by the collar of his garb and hauled him to his feet.

"Greetings," I said to him, in Gorean.

"Greetings," he stammered. He still clutched the tiny pemmican cake.

I pulled him toward the center of our camp where Cuwignaka, now on his feet, waited. There, too, risen now to her elbows, her hands still tied behind her, startled, was the slave girl, Mira, once the Lady Mira, of Venna, with whom I had been pleasuring myself. On the travois, sleeping, was Hci.

In the grass now, standing, some yards away, frightened, the grass to her waist, was a young girl, some sixteen or seventeen years of age, blond. She, like the young man, wore the garb of the Waniyanpi.

I transferred my hold on the lad's garment to my left hand

and, with my right, beckoned the girl to approach. "Come here," I said.

Timidly, she approached. Then she stood, too, with us.

I released my grip on the lad's garment. "Who are you?" I asked.

"I am Squash," he said.

"I am Strawberry," said the girl.

"We have been following you," said the lad.

"We know," I said.

"We took pemmican," said the lad. "Are you going to kill us for stealing?"

"It was left for you," I said.

He extended his hand to me. In it was the small cake of pemmican which he had just seized up from the grass. "I took this, just now," he said.

"You are the male," I said. "It is yours."

He looked at me, puzzled. "I am not a male," he said. "And she is not a female. We are Waniyanpi."

"That is over now," I said.

The girl was looking at Mira, fascinated. "Turnip," she asked, "is it you?"

"She was once Turnip," I said. "She is now Mira, a slave girl. She cannot respond to you. I have not given her permission to speak."

The girl looked at me, in awe.

"Turn on your side, Slave," I said. "Show them that your hands are thonged."

Immediately Mira obeyed. The young man and woman saw that her wrists were tightly bound with thongs.

"Be now as you were before," I said, "up on your elbows."

Immediately Mira obeyed.

"What is that on her neck?" she asked, referring to the narrow, dark, braided rawhide rope, looped three times about the slave's neck and knotted before her throat, the two loose ends dangling between her breasts.

"It serves as a slave collar," I said.

"I see," said the girl, stepping back a bit. She put down her head. She drew a quick breath. She blushed.

"You may lie down," I told the slave.

She lay back in the grass, naked and bound, near our feet.

"You two are far from your compound, are you not?" I asked.

"Yes," said the young man, putting down his head.

"We were recently at a Waniyanpi compound," I said. "It was Compound Eleven, I believe."

The young man did not respond.

"That was your compound, was it not?" I asked.

"Yes," he said.

"We heard there of two young people who were put out of the compound, a young man and a young woman," I said. "Doubtless you are those two."

"Yes," admitted the young man, not raising his head.

"You followed us here, from its vicinity," I said.

"Yes," he said.

"Why?" I asked.

"We hoped you would lead us to food," he said. "We did not know what else to do."

"Your crime, as I recall, was to found touching one another."

"No," said the young man. "No!"

"Kneel down," I told the young woman, "before this young man, and strip off that foolish garb."

The young man looked at me, startled. "Do not avert your eyes from her," I told him.

The girl pulled up the long, clumsy dress, to her knees, and then knelt before the young man. She then drew the dress over her head and put it to the side. In this way she was on her knees before him, as she bared her beauty to him.

"Do not avert your eyes," I warned the young man.

"Ohhh," he said, softly. "She is so beautiful."

"Does it now seem to you so shameful, or horrifying, to touch her?" I asked.

"No," he said. "No!"

"No longer are you Waniyanpi," I said. "She may now be touched freely, however and as often as you wish."

"I cannot believe such freedom," he said. "It is so different! It is glorious!"

"It is your freedom, not hers," I said.

"What?" he asked.

"Do not forget that she is a female," I said.

He regarded me, puzzled.

"She seems hungry," I said. I had noted that she was eyeing the cake of pemmican in his hand.

"Forgive me, Strawberry!" he said. "I am so thoughtless!" He quickly broke the cake of pemmican in two.

I put my hand on his arm. "You are the male," I said. "It is yours, not hers."

"I will share it with her, of course," he said.

"She has not yet begged," I said.

He looked at me, startled. Then he, in confusion, looked again upon the girl.

"I beg for something to eat," she said, smiling.

He quickly gave her half of the tiny cake of pemmican and she, on her knees, naked, swiftly, ravenously, ate it.

He then, musingly, regarding her, finished the remaining part of the cake of pemmican.

"Hold still," I told him. With a knife I cut away much of the long, gray skirt of the Waniyanpi garb he wore. I cut the sleeves away, too. Then, with a part of the material, I made a belt. I belted the garment then, tunicwise, about his waist.

"How strong your legs look," said the girl, softly, admiringly, looking up at him, "and your arms!"

"You are permitting her to speak?" I asked.

"Yes," he said.

"Very well," I said.

The girl put down her head, smiling. Whether or not she would be permitted to speak had been discussed.

"The camp is quite close," said Cuwignaka. "Let us be on our way."

"You are welcome to accompany us," I told the young man, "and you may, if you wish, bring the female."

"I want to bring her," he said.

"Very well," I said.

Again the girl smiled. It had been explicitly discussed, whether or not she would be brought with us.

"I will conceal, as I can, the signs of our encampment," said Cuwignaka.

"I will load the travois," I said.

"Are you truly a slave—Mira," asked the girl.

Mira cast a glance at me.

"You may respond," I told her.

"Yes, I am a slave," said Mira, "totally."

"What was he doing to you, before?" asked the girl.

"You watched?" asked Mira.

"Yes," said the girl.

"He was enjoying me and using me as what I am, a slave," she said.

"Are you embarrassed?" asked the girl.

"No," said Mira. "A slave is not permitted modesty."

"You seemed ecstatic with pleasure, overcome with gratitude and joy," said the girl.

"It was my yielding," she said.

"Need you have yielded like that?" asked the girl.

"Yes," said Mira. "The slave is given no alternative other than to yield to the master fully."

"But you would want to yield like that, wouldn't you?" asked the girl.

"Yes," said Mira.

"Then the slave is forced to do what she, in her most secret heart, most deeply desires to do," said the girl.

"Yes," said Mira. "But you must understand that a slave's lot is not an easy one. We are often worked long and hard."

"But is there not a pleasure in such a service?" asked the girl.

"At one time I would not have thought so," said Mira, "but I know now, now that I am an owned slave, that there is."

"How must a slave act?" asked the girl. "What must a slave do?"

"We are to be absolutely docile, totally obedient and fully pleasing," said Mira.

"Horrifying!" said the girl.

"Perhaps," laughed Mira.

"And what if you are not?" asked the girl.

"But we are," laughed Mira. "The masters see to it."

"But what if you rebel?" asked the girl.

"Only stupid girls rebel," said Mira, "and they are soon taught its uselessness."

"But can you not even protest?" asked the girl.

"We may protest, of course, if the masters see fit to permit it," said Mira, "but then, when we are finished, our discipline is reimposed upon us, perhaps even more severely."

"Discipline?" breathed the girl.

"Yes," said Mira, "the slave girl is subject to discipline and punishment. She is owned, like a sleen or tarsk is owned. She is owned, literally owned. You must understand that in its full sense. Accordingly, anything may be done with her that the master wishes. She may even be slain, if the master wishes."

"Then the slave girl is totally helpless," said the girl. "She is totally at the mercy of the master."

"Yes," said Mira.

"I would like that," said the girl.

"Oh?" asked Mira.

"Are you happy?" asked the girl.

"Yes," said Mira, "incredibly so."

"Do you not desire freedom?" asked the girl.

"The only freedom I would now desire," said Mira, "would be the freedom to be totally a slave."

"I have so much love in me," said the girl, "I, too, would be a slave."

"But you have no master," said Mira, smiling.

"Stand," I said to Mira.

She struggled to her feet.

I unbound her hands and put the thongs in my belt. She then knelt before me and kissed my feet.

"What are you doing?" asked the girl.

"I am kissing the feet of he who is to me as my master," said Mira.

The young girl then rose to her feet and went and knelt before the young man.

"What are you doing!" he cried, startled.

"I am kissing your feet," she said.

"That is a slave's act!" he cried.

She lifted her head, proudly, defiantly. "Yes!" she said.

He shrank back, frightened. "We are Sames," he said.

"No," she said, "we are not. You are a man and I am a woman."

"No," he cried. "No!"

"I would be a slave," she said.

"No, no," he cried. "No!"

"Do I displease you?" she asked. "Am I not attractive? Am I not desirable? Am I not beautiful? Do you, truly, not wish to own me?"

"Of course I want to own you!" he said. "Just to look at you is to want to own you! For years I have wanted to own you!"

"Own me," she said.

He cried out in misery and bent over, clenching his fists.

"What is wrong?" she asked.

"It is the thought of owning you," he said. "It is so overwhelming. It would mean such power, such joy!"

"Own me," she said.

He looked down at her, trembling.

"There is something to be said for the idea," I said, "particularly if you are not going to leave her behind."

He looked at me, puzzled.

"She is a white female," I said. "Few white females, if any, in the Barrens are free. We are going to an encampment of red savages. She is attractive. If you do not want to enslave her, I have little doubt but what someone else will do so."

He looked down at her.

I went to the travois and freed the coil of narrow, braided rawhide rope I had used for Mira's collar. I cut off a suitable piece. I then replaced the balance of the rope on the travois, securing it in place.

"Stand," he said to the girl. She stood.

I handed him the length of rope. He stood there, looking at her, the rope in his hands.

"You understand, do you not," I asked the girl, "the meaning of this?"

"Yes," she said.

"You may freely enter into the state of bondage," I told her, "but you may not freely leave it. This thing, once it is done to you, is, on your part, irreversible. It is not then within your power to break, alter or amend it in any way. You will then, you see, no longer be a free person, but only a slave."

"I understand," she said. She then turned to the young man. "I am ready," she said. "Make me a slave."

He then looped the dark, narrow, braided rawhide rope three times about her neck. He adjusted it so that it was snug and not too tight, and the ends were even. He then tied the two loose ends together, closing the collar. He jerked the two loose ends, sharply, snapping them in contrary directions, making the knot tight. A narrow, inverted triangle of flesh showed between the first two coils of the collar, wrapped closely about her neck, and the knot. He released the two loose ends of the collar, below the knot, and they fell lightly, dangling, as was the case with Mira's collar, between her breasts. The subtle touch of the leather on the breasts of a slave can be useful to a slave, particularly when she is naked, reminding her that she is a slave. Also, as I have suggested, they provide a convenient, short leash wherewith one might drag her about and control her, as one pleases. The collar, as was the case with Mira's, would serve not only to mark the girl as a slave but, in its way, would distinguish her from the common properties of the red savages, whose collars are usually of beaded leather. It was natural that the young man, whose experiences in such matters were limited, should follow the general collar design I had used with Mira. I had no objection. Indeed, it seemed appropriate that both girls, both former Waniyanpi girls, should be similarly collared. I would later explain to him the identificatory aspects of the collar, and he might then, if he wished, change it, or personalize it in some way, perhaps with a special knot, tag or ornament. On the other hand, too, if he wished to leave it as it was, I had no objection. Both we and the girls, and soon so, too, would others, well understood the bondage relations in which they stood.

"She is a pretty slave," I said.

Then they were in one another's arms. "I have always wanted to own you!" he cried, his voice rich, husky and wild.

"Any man may now own me," she said, "for I am a slave, but it is you who do own me! It is you who do own me!"

"I love you," he cried, crushing her to him.

"And I love you, my Master," she cried. "I love you, my Master!"

"I must have her," cried the young man to us. "I cannot wait. Go on without us!"

"We can wait," I said.

He then lowered the naked, collared slave, so beautiful, so vulnerable, so helpless, so tremulous, so eager, so ready, so loving, to the grass. "I am so happy!" she said. "I am so happy!"

"The camp," said Cuwignaka, "is just over this rise."

Cuwignaka and I trudged upward, through the grass. It was late afternoon.

Behind us, some fifty yards, came the travois. The young lad who had been once of the Waniyanpi had insisted on helping to draw it. We had rigged a center trace. He now drew it, flanked on either side, also in harness, by a female slave, Mira on his right and the blond girl, who also had been once of the Waniyanpi, on his left. A man's slave usually heels him, following behind him, or behind him on his left. He had made a tunic for his slave. He had fashioned it for her from her former Waniyanpi garb. It was incredibly short. It was sleeveless. It had a deep, plunging neckline. It, too, was belted tightly, with a belt of rolled cloth, which device served well to accentuate the delicate lineaments of her lovely figure. Such tiny, skimpy garments, so straightforwardly and brazenly revelatory of a woman's beauty, are usually regarded by free women as scandals and outrages. Nonetheless they are the sorts of garments in which a girl, if she is a slave, will come to expect herself to be placed, if she is permitted clothing at all. Indeed, slave girls tend to enjoy such garments. They appreciate the freedom of movement which they permit and relish, too, the insolent exposure and display of their desirability and beauty to the bold appraisal of men. The young man's slave seemed quite pleased with her garment. It was, of course, all she wore. Mira I was keeping naked. I would decide later whether or not to permit her a garment. I smiled to myself. She had once been an agent of Kurii. She would, accordingly, drink deeply of slavery under my tutelage. She would learn it well.

"There," said Cuwignaka, standing on the crest of the small hill, in the deep grass, "below, is the camp, nestled in the trees, by the small stream. You can see some lodges."

I stood, stock-still, on the crest of the small hill, beside Cuwignaka. I scarcely glanced into the shallow valley, at the trees along the stream, the lodges hidden among the trees.

It was something else which drew my attention. It was on a rise behind the camp.

"What is wrong?" asked Cuwignaka.

I could not speak. My blood began to race, my heart to pound. I began to breathe swiftly. I trembled.

"What is wrong, Mitakola?" asked Cuwignaka.

"There," I said. I pointed to the rise overlooking the camp.

"What?" he asked.

"There!" I said. "There!"

On that rise there were two trees, white-barked trees, some fifty feet tall, with shimmering green leaves. They stood within some thirty to forty feet of one another and both were outlined dramatically against the sky.

"What?" asked Cuwignaka.

I stared, tremblingly, at the lonely pair of trees. "The trees," I said. "The trees." They were Hogarthe trees, named for Hogarthe, one of the early explorers in the area of the Barrens. They are not uncommon in the vicinity of water in the Barrens, usually growing along the banks of small streams or muddy, sluggish rivers. Their shape is very reminiscent of poplar trees on Earth, to which, perhaps, in virtue of seeds brought to the Counter-Earth, they may be related.

"It is from those trees," said Cuwignaka, "that this place has its name."

"What is the name of this place?" I asked.

"Two Feathers," said Cuwignaka.

"I thought that was a name," I said.

"It is a name," said Cuwignaka, "the name of this place."

"Who is high man here?" I asked.

"It would be Kahintokapa, One-Who-Walks-Before, of the Yellow-Kaiila Riders," said Cuwignaka, "if he survived."

"He must have survived!" I cried.

I began to run wildly down the slope toward the camp.

"Wait!" cried Cuwignaka. "Someone is coming!"

"Tatankasa!" cried Canka, rushing towards us from the camp. But I ran past him. I ran as though mad. He, and perhaps Akihoka, who had gone to fetch him back from hunting, must have made contact with fugitives from the festival camp and then, with them, come to this camp.

"Master!" cried Winyela.

But I ran past her, too.

"Wait!" I heard Cuwignaka calling out behind me.

But I could not wait. It was late afternoon. This would be the time for the sunning of shields, hanging on the shield tripods behind the lodges, the entrance of the lodge facing east, the back of the lodge facing west.

Women looked up, startled, as I hurried through the camp. "Tatankasa!" cried more than one.

"Tatankasa!" called out Mahpiyasapa.

I, a slave, fell to my knees before him. He was chief of the Isbu Kaiila.

"You live!" he cried. "My heart sings!"

"Master," I cried. "Where is the lodge of Kahintokapa!"

"There," said Mahpiyasapa, puzzled, pointing.

"My thanks, Master!" I cried.

I clenched my fists.

"You may rise," said Mahpiyasapa, discerning my urgency.

I leaped to my feet.

"Tatankasa!" cried Mahpiyasapa.

"Yes?" I said.

"Know you aught of Hci?"

"Let your heart soar and sing, Master," I said. "Your son lives!" I pointed behind me, to the slope, down which the young, former Waniyanpi lad, and Mira and the former Waniyanpi girl, now a master's slave, drew the travois. Mahpiyasapa, his face radiant with joy, hurried from my side. I saw Canka and Cuwignaka embracing. Winyela, overjoyed, stood by. Others, too, from the camp, were running out to meet them.

I quickly turned my steps toward the lodge of Kahintokapa. I came to it, and then I stopped. Then, slowly, I walked about the lodge. I felt the warm sun on my back. Never before had I seen the shield of Kahintokapa outside of its shield cover, even when I had first seen him, long ago, with Canka and the members of the All Comrades, near the site of the battle of the wagon train, near, too, where the mercenaries had fought, and Alfred had escaped with a contingent of some three to four hundred men.

It is not uncommon for a warrior to keep his shield in its case or cover when not fighting. It is removed from the case, or cover, also, of course, when it is sunned, set forth to draw in power and medicine from the yellow, life-giving, blazing star of two worlds, Sol or Tor-tu-Gor, Light Upon the Home Stone.

I stood for a long time on that late-summer day, looking at the shield, hanging on the shield tripod. It turned, slightly, in the breeze, back and forth. I took care, in deference to the feelings of the red savages, not to let my shadow fall across it, while it was being sunned. Similarly, one does not pass between a guest and the fire in a lodge without begging his pardon.

I heard Cuwignaka and Canka coming up behind me. They, too, regarded the shield.

"You see it?" I asked.

"Of course," said Cuwignaka.

"The hunter, long ago, in the snows," I said, "was Kahintokapa."

"I do not understand," said Cuwignaka.

" 'Two Feathers'," I said, "was not a man's name, but the name of this place."

"Of what is he speaking?" asked Canka.

"I do not know," said Cuwignaka.

"Look upon the shield," I said.

We all regarded the shield. It bore, painted on it, with meticulous detail, outlined in black, colored in with pigments, the visage of a Kur. It was a broad, savage head. One could see the protruding canines. The eyes, I thought, had been particularly well done. They seemed to look upon us. The left ear had been half torn away.

"It is Zarendargar, Half-Ear," I said.

"Who is Zarendargar?" asked Cuwignaka.

"One with whom I once, long ago, and in a far place, shared paga," I said.

"That is the medicine helper of Kahintokapa," said Canka.

"I would like to make its acquaintance," I said.

"These things are personal," said Canka. "These things are private. They are seen in dreams, in visions. How can one man see the medicine helper of another man?"

"I must speak to Kahintokapa," I said.

"Kahintokapa is grievously wounded," said Canka.

"Will you make known my desires to him?" I asked.

"We both will," said Cuwignaka.

I looked at the visage on the shield. The likeness had been well captured. Even now, among certain articles on the travois, brought from the lodge of Grunt at the festival camp, was the story hide, acquired long ago in the delta of the Vosk, some four pasangs from Port Kar. On this hide was portrayed the story of a hunt and of the finding of a medicine helper. This hide had been the clue which had brought not only Kog and Sardak, and their allies, to the Barrens, but myself as well. At the narrative's termination on the hide the artist had drawn a likeness of the medicine helper, portrayed as though on a shield. The image had been that, clearly, of Zarendargar. Now, deep within the Barrens, north of the Northern Kaiila River, in the country of the Casmu Kaiila, I looked upon the shield itself.

I turned about.

Several people were gathered about.

I looked past the people, away from the camp, out over the grasses.

Then I turned again to Cuwignaka and Canka.

"I would speak to Kahintokapa," I said.

"You would seek this medicine helper?" asked Canka.

"Yes," I said.

"If you do," said Canka, "you must do so in accordance with our ways."

"I will, of course," I said, "abide by your wishes."

"Cuwignaka and I will speak to Kahintokapa," said Canka. "We will speak on your behalf."

"I am grateful," I said.

35

IN THE VISION PLACE

"The body was never recovered," I said.

"It would make a difference to a Tuchuk," said Kamchak, of the Tuchuks.

A cold wind swept across the flat summit of Ar's Cylinder of Justice.

The stones were cold some twenty pasangs west of the Casmu-Kaiila camp at Two Feathers.

Again I held grass and earth with Kamchak, of the Tuchuks. I could feel it, cool in my hands, between my fingers.

It began to rain. The rain washed the dirt and grass from my hands. The bridges of Tharna had been gray and cool in the soft, long, slow rains.

In this distance I heard the roars of the crowds in Ar's Stadium of Tarns.

I emerged from the baths of Ar. They seemed suddenly cold.

The silver mask seemed unnaturally large. The woman's voice, from behind it, seemingly far away, was wild with rage. "We shall meet again!" I heard.

The tarn smote its way from the roof of the palace. Air tore past us.

The Dorna was a ship, a tarn ship, a ram ship, shallow-drafted, straight-keeled, single-banked, lateen-rigged, carvel-built, painted green, difficult to detect in the rolling waters of Thassa, out of Port Kar.

Lara, who had been Tatrix of Tharna, kneeling before me on a scarlet rug, in the camp of Targo, the Slaver, lifted, supplicatingly, holding them in her hands, two yellow cords to me.

Misk, at night, stood in the grasses near the Sardar, lofty, slender, grand against the moons, on a small hill, the wind moving his antennae.

I should have returned that night, perhaps, to the tavern of Sarpedon in Lydius, to see Vella dance. I had had business.

How splendid women look in the collars of men!

The sky was white with lightning. There was a great crash of thunder.

"It is a hurricane of stones!" cried Hassan, the wind tearing back his burnoose.

"Maybe it will be cold tonight," speculated Imnak, bending over the slate point of his harpoon, methodically sharpening it with a stone, in the light of the small sleen-oil lamp.

"Yes," I agreed.

The northern waters are cold. Torrents descended, lashing the sea. The serpent of Ivar Forkbeard, its mast and spar lashed down, pitched in the waves near the Skerry of Einar. I heard Ivar Forkbeard's great laugh.

Lighting crashed above the red crags of the Voltai.

"Let him be whipped," said Marlenus of Ar.

Blows fell.

My cheek lay on the cold wet stones. One does not leave the vision place. Rain fell. I put out my hand and clutched ice. It rattled and struck about me, leaping up from the stones. My back was cut. The white clay on my body was streaked. I covered my head and lay on the stones. One does not leave the vision place.

It was hot.

I could hear the birds in the jungle of the Ua.

"Let us continue on," said Kisu, and, again, the river before us, broad between the moist, tangled green thickets of the banks, backed on each side by the enclosing jungle, we dipped our paddles into the muddy, sluggish water.

I felt lightheaded. Perhaps it was the sun. The Ur force is being disrupted, I heard. It seemed the ground was far beneath me. My feet could hardly touch it.

I lay on my back. The high, hot sun of the Tahari burned in the sky.

"Drink," said Hassan, bending over me. "Alas," he said, "the water bag is empty."

"At least," said Samos, "it is cooler now. That is a relief."

"Yes," I said.

"I am sorry you are so hungry," said Imnak. "I would like to give you something to eat, but there is no food in the camp. I think maybe one should go hunting."

"Yes," I said. "Let us go hunting."

"Are you not coming?" asked Imnak.

"I am weak," I said. "I am tired. I think I will lie here for a little while."

"You have drunk very little, and you have not eaten in three days," said Imnak.

"Yes," I said.

"That is probably why you are so hungry," speculated Imnak.

"That is probably it," I agreed.

"There is a storm coming, Captain," said Thurnock. "Sensible ships, in such a season, are safe in port."

"Even warriors long sometimes for the sight of their own flags, atop friendly walls, for the courtyards of their keeps, for the hearths of their halls. Thus admit the Codes."

I struck the sword from the hand of Marlenus of Ar.

"One must seek medicine helpers in certain ways," said Canka. "If you would do this thing, you must do so in the correct manner."

"I will abide by your wishes," I said.

"There is no assurance the medicine helper will come," said Kahintokapa.

"I understand," I said.

"In seeking medicine helpers, sometimes men die," said Kahintokapa.

"I understand," I said.

"This thing is not easy," said Cuwignaka.

"I understand," I said.

The shield of Hci rose like a moon, inexorably, exposing him to the lance of the Yellow Knife. The moon raced through the clouds. There are many ways to understand what one sees.

"A storm is coming, Captain," said Thurnock.

A small package, oblong, heavy, brought from among the articles in Grunt's lodge, in the festival camp, lay near me on the stones.

I struggled to sit up, cross-legged, on the stones. I put my hands on my knees.

I felt rain.

Lightning burst in the sky and thunder rolled and crashed about me, like waves between the banks of the horizons.

Torrents of cold rain descended in diagonal sheets, pounding at the rocks, tearing at the leaves of nearby trees.

"Who is that woman?" I asked.

"It is said she was once the daughter of Marlenus of Ar," I was told. "Then, for dishonoring him, she was disowned." Her figure, veiled, clad in the robes of concealment, had vanished, gone from the corridor.

"You are a weakling!" she cried, in the hall of Samos. "I hate you!"

"You would let me go," she asked, "rather than throw me to your feet and whip me, and master me?"

"Give her passage to Ar," I said.

"Here is the slave, Captain," said Thurnock. He threw her to the tiles before my curule chair. "On your knees before your master, Slave," he said.

She looked up at me.

I fondled the whip, thoughtfully, idly, that lay across my knees.

"I love you," cried Vella, suddenly beside me, kneeling at the side of my curule chair, her hands on my arm. "I love you! I will please you more. I will please you a thousand times more!"

Lightning lit the sky. Thunder cracked. Rain tore its way downward.

"It is a severe storm," said Ivar Forkbeard, near me, on the deck of his serpent.

Then lightning again illuminated the stormy sky and the driving torrents of rain, and then the lightning and rain were gone, and then there were great ringing blows, and the great hammer of Kron, of the Metal Workers, lifting and falling, smote on a mighty anvil, showering sparks in the night, which fell into the calm sea and glowed there like diamonds, and I rolled to my back and looked upwards to see that the diamonds were in the sky, and were stars.

It begins in the sweat lodge. This is a small lodge, rather oval and rounded. A man may not stand upright within it. One constructs a framework of branches. This framework is then covered with hides. In the center there is a hole, in which the hot stones, passed in from the outside on a forked stick, are placed. Cups of water are poured on the stones. When the stones cool they are removed from the lodge and reheated. There are many rituals and significances connected with the sweat lodge, having to do with such things as the stones, the fire, the orientation of the lodge, the path between the lodge and the fire, the amounts and ways in which the water is poured, and the number of times the lodge is opened. I shall not enter into these matters in depth. Suffice it to say that the ceremony of the sweat lodge is a detailed, complex, sophisticated and highly symbolic ritual. The purification of the bather is its principal objective, the readying of the bather for the awesome task of seeking the dream or vision. My helpers, tending the fire and aiding with the stones, were Canka and Cuwignaka.

I did not follow the order of the ritual in all respects nor keep the ceremony in the exactitude of all its details. I would not do this because of reservations on my part, having primarily to do with skepticism concerning the existence of a medicine world, and because I was not Kaiila. Not being Kaiila I would have felt it improper or irreverent, if not dishonest, profane, sacrilegious or blasphemous, to do so. My feelings and decisions in these matters were understood and respected by Canka as well as Cuwignaka. Nonetheless, as one sits alone in the darkened interior of the sweat lodge, with one's head down between one's knees, to keep from fainting and to help stand the heat, one has a great deal of time to think. I do not think that it is a bad idea for a man to be alone sometimes, and to have some time to think. This is a good way, for example, to get to know oneself. Many men, it seems, have never made their own acquaintance. It would not hurt most of us, I suspect, once in a while, to go to a sweat lodge.

After one emerges from the sweat lodge one goes to a stream and washes in the cold water. One cleans, with a knife or sharpened stick, even under one's fingernails. A small fire, of sweet-brush and needles, from needle trees, is then built. One rubs the smoke from this fire into one's body. Then one rubs white clay on one's body. These things hide the smell of men. It is thought that most medicine helpers do not like the smell of men and if they smell this smell they will be loath to approach. Everything possible is done, of course, to encourage the approach or appearance of the medicine helper.

One then goes to the vision place.

It is a high place, and rocky. There are some trees about. One can look down and see the grass below, moving in the wind.

There one fasts. There one waits.

One may drink a little water. It takes a long time to starve to death, weeks. It does not take long, however, to die of thirst. How long it takes to die of thirst varies with many things, with the man, with his bodily activity, with the sunlight or shade, with the winds and the temperatures. But it does not take long. It is a matter of days, usually three or four. It is good, thus, to drink some water.

One waits. One does not know if the medicine helper will come or not.

It is lonely in the vision place.

I lay on my back, looking up at the stars.

They are very beautiful in the Barrens.

The rocks on which I lay were cold and wet. It had rained earlier in the evening.

It is very quiet in the vision place.

I was very hungry, and thirsty, and cold.

Sometimes, I knew, the medicine helper does not come. Sometimes men wait in vain. Sometimes they must go back to the camp without a vision. Sometimes they try again, another time. Sometimes they stay longer at the vision place. Sometimes they die there.

Perhaps the medicine helper will not come, I said to myself. Then I laughed, but with little mirth, for I was Tarl Cabot. I was not of the Kaiila. How absurd that I lay here, on these stones, daubed with white clay, in a vision place, alone with the trees and stars. I was not of the Kaiila.

I was terribly weak.

I wondered if the smoke of sweet-brush and needles, if the rubbing with white clay, might not have its effect not so much in encouraging the approach of medicine helpers but in lessening the probability of the approach of sleen. Similarly, the lack of activity on the part of the vision seeker may not be stimulatory to the sleen's attack response, Akihoka tells a story about his own vision seeking. A sleen came and lay down quite near to him, and watched him, until morning, and then rose up and went away. Some vision seekers, on the other hand, are torn to pieces by sleen. Akihoka's medicine helper is the urt. He received his vision on the second night.

I fell asleep.

It was gray and cold, a bit after dawn, when I awakened. It was still muchly dark.

How is it that these people can have visions, I asked myself.

Perhaps, in time, the tortured body has had enough. Perhaps it then petitions the brain for a relieving vision.

It helps, of course, to believe in such visions, and to take them as indications of the medicine world.

Unnatural states of consciousness occur, surely, in the vision place. It is something about the hunger and thirst, the loneliness, I suppose. It is difficult, sometimes, to distinguish between dreams and visions, and realities.

One does not really need a vision. A dream will do.

But some men are not good at having visions, and some men cannot remember what they might have learned in dreams. They cannot remember what they did in the dream country, only that they were there.

But, in such cases, the red savages are merciful. They know that not all men are alike. It is enough to try to dream, to seek the vision. After all, if the medicine helpers will not come, that is their prerogative. A man who fails to attain a vision, or who cannot obtain a suitable dream, may purchase one from another, who is more fortunate, one who will share his vision or dream with him, or sell him one he does not need. Similarly, one may make a gift of a dream or vision to someone who needs it, or would like to have it. Such gifts, to the red savages, are very precious.

No more can be expected of a man than that he go to the vision place. That is his part. What more can he do?

The medicine helper is not coming, I said to myself. The medicine helper will not come.

I have come to the vision place. I have done my part. I am finished with it.

I then heard a noise.

I feared it might be a sleen.

I struggled to sit up, cross-legged. I could not stand. I heard small stones slipping and falling backward, down the slope. I put my hand on the hilt of my knife. It was the only weapon I had in the vision place. But my fingers could scarcely close on the beaded hilt. I could not grasp it tightly. I was too weak.

I saw the head first, then the body of the creature. It crouched down, a few feet from me.

It was very large, larger than a sleen. I put my hands on my knees.

It lifted the object, wrapped in hide, which I had placed before me. Then, with its teeth, it tore off the leather.

In the half darkness, it was not easy to see its lineaments or features.

It approached me, and took me in its arms. It pressed its great jaws against my face and, from its storage stomach, brought up water into its oral cavity, from which, holding it there, and rationing it out, bit by bit, it gave me of drink. It gave me then, similarly, a soft curd of meat, brought up, too, from the storage stomach. I fought to swallow it, and did.

"Are you the medicine helper of Kahintokapa?" I asked, in Kaiila. "Are you the medicine helper of One-Who-Walks-Before?" I asked, in Gorean.

"I am Zarendargar," came from the translator, in Gorean, "war general of the Kurii."

36

THE PIT

I scanned the skies.

"Hurry!" I ordered the girl.

"Yes, Master!" she said, cutting at the grass with a turf knife.

One covers the framework of branches and poles, over the pit, with plates of sod, with living grass. In this way, the grass does not discolor in a matter of hours. Sometimes one must wait for two or three days in the pit.

The pit is some ten feet in length, some five feet in width and some four feet in height. It must be long enough to accommodate the hobbling log, the hunter and, at times, the bait.

We heard a cry, as of a fleer. Cuwignaka had seen it first.

"Down!" I said, seizing the girl, pulling her down into the high grass.

I cursed, looking upward. A solitary rider, one of the Kinyanpi, was taking his way northwestward.

This was an area in which they, too, did this sort of hunting.

"Get back to work," I told the girl.

"Yes, Master," she said.

The hobbling log had been dragged to this place, by two kaiila, in the night. The dirt from the pit is hidden under brush or scattered in the grass.

"It is finished," said the girl, putting the last plate of sod in place.

"Put the turf knife in the pit," I said.

"Ye, Master," she said.

She placed the turf knife in the pit, through the hole which we had left as its entrance. The turf knife is a wooden-bladed, saw-edged, paddlelike tool. It is used to cut and saw sod and, when the handle is held in the right hand and the blade is supported with the left, it may be used, also, rather like a shovel, to move dirt.

I then tied one end of a rawhide rope about her right ankle. The rope was about fifteen feet in length.

"Get into the pit," I said.

"Yes, Master," she said.

I then followed her into the pit and, within it, we sat down, facing one another. The hobbling log was on my left and on her right. I looped the rope on her right ankle twice about the hobbling log. A much stouter rope was already tied about it, with its loose end, several feet in length, coiled atop it. Other ropes lay near us in the pit.

I looked up, through the opening in the pit. It was about eighteen inches square. A similar opening, somewhat smaller, was at the other end of the pit. It had its purpose. I could see the sky through the opening, and the clouds.

"We now wait," I said.

"Yes, Master," she said.

37

WHAT OCCURRED IN THE PIT

"You are a pretty she-property," I said.

"Thank you, Master," she said.

"Perhaps I will feed you," I said.

"Thank you, Master," she said.

"You may approach," I said, "on all fours."

"Thank you, Master," she said. She crawled toward me, on all fours, in the narrow pit. I put small pieces of pemmican in my hand. She fed from my hand. I put more pemmican in my hand. I then lowered my hand. I felt her kissing, nibbling and licking at my hand, taking the pemmican from it. I put more pemmican in my hand and then lowered it still further. I felt her hair on my body. She nibbled and kissed at my hand, delicately removing pemmican from it, her head following my hand, as I lowered it yet further, and then, with extreme delicacy, with tenderness and gentleness, she nibbled and kissed at my body. "Master desires his slave," she whispered.

"No," I said, restraining myself. I thrust her back. "Go to your place, Slave," I said.

"Yes, Master," she said, and returned to her place.

"I must remain alert," I said. "I must keep my senses sharp."

"Yes, Master," she smiled.

I noted that she knelt now in her place, rather than sat there. I did not effect anything critical. I had merely ordered her to return to her place. I had not specified that she was to sit there.

I threw her the water bag. She kissed the spike, softly, tenderly, watching me. Then, unexpectedly, mischievously, she quickly swirled her tongue about the spike, and kissed it again. She then took it deeply into her mouth and lifted the bag, holding it with both hands.

"It is not necessary to drink like that," I said.

She put her head back yet further, and drank more.

Holding the water bag as she did, high, with her head back, arched her back and lifted the line of her breasts, beautifully. She had turned subtly, displaying herself to me in profile.

I observed how she drank.

"You are a lascivious slave, Mira," I informed her.

She turned her belly to me, still drinking. The water bag now prevented her from seeing me.

Unable to see me, with her hands high, and occupied, she could be easily approached and, unexpectedly, embraced, or attacked.

I wondered if I should have permitted her clothing. Perhaps if I had given her some clothing she would have been less distracting. Yet as a slave is clothed her clothing is often less of a concealment than it is a device to make her seem more vulnerable, more helplessly, whether she wishes it or not, tantalizingly attractive. The clothing of a slave is usually little more than an invitation to its removal, and her rape. The collar, too, of course, and she was already in a collar, a leather-rope collar, makes her exquisitely attractive, indicating her status, that she is only a lovely, owned she-animal, to be done with as one pleases.

"It is enough," I said, angrily.

She brought the water bag down. "I did not mean to drink too much water," she said, innocently. She replaced the leather cap on the spike of the water bag.

I took the water bag back from her, and put it beside me. "Sit," I told her.

"Yes, Master," she said, and sat down, with her back against the other side of the pit.

She began to play with the narrow, dangling, braided-rawhide rope ends of her leather-rope collar, that which I had put on her in the vicinity of the compound of the Waniyanpi. She fiddled with them, and sometimes jerked on them, showing me, thusly, as though inadvertently, that the collar was well fastened on her.

"Master," she said.

"Yes," I said.

She looked at me, and, as though not knowing what she was doing, drew on the rope ends, holding them out a bit from her body. This demonstrated, as though thoughtlessly, the possible leash function of the rope ends.

"Yes?" I said, irritably.

"I am sorry if I drank too much water," she said.

"You are doubtless tired," I said, "and should rest. Lie down, on your side."

"Yes, Master," she said, and lay down, on her side, her head away from me, one of her feet drawn up more than the other. She lay looking at the side of the dirt pit, her head in the crook of her left arm.

"You are a pretty slave," I said.

"Thank you, Master," she said.

"The rawhide rope on your ankle looks well," I told her. This was the rope which I had tied on her ankle earlier, before I had ordered her into the pit. Its other end was looped twice about the hobbling log.

"My master put it on me," she said. "Thank you, Master." Women look well in bonds. The purpose of this bond, however, was her own protection. I wondered if she understood that. Perhaps she thought it was merely to hold her in the pit with me. But my will alone could have done that. She was a slave.

She stretched a bit. How maddeningly desirable are slaves!

If, outside the pit, she should panic, and try to run, she might, by the rope on her ankle, be kept from doing so; that might save her life; similarly, if she should be paralyzed with fear and find herself unable to move, it might be used to drag her back into the pit. Also, of course, if, unfortunately, she should be seized, it might give us some time to encourage her captor, with blows, and lances and cries, to release her, before it could break and she could be carried off.

"Must you lie like that?" I asked.

"It is the shape of my body, Master," she said. "It is my hope that you do not find me displeasing."

Light filtered into the pit.

Similar pits, though much smaller, are used for the capture of the taloned Herlit. In the case of the Herlit it is dragged bodily into the pit. There it may be dealt with in various ways. It may be strangled; it may be crushed beneath the knees, with the hunter's weight; or it may be put on its belly, its back to be broken by a swift blow of the foot. In the latter two fashions, the wings are put to the side. This avoids damage to the feathers. It is not easy to kill such a bird with the bare hands, but that is the prescribed methodology. It is regarded as bad form, if not bad medicine, to use a weapon for such a purpose. An adult Herlit is often four feet in height and has a wingspan of some seven to eight feet. The hunter must beware of being blinded or having an artery slashed in the struggle. The fifteen tail feathers are perhaps most highly prized. They are some fourteen to fifteen inches in height, and yellow with black tips. They are particularly significant in the marking of coups. The wing, or pinion, feathers, are used for various ceremonial and religious purposes. The breath feathers, light and delicate, from the base of the bird's tail, are used, with the tail feathers, in the fashioning of bonnets or complex headdresses. They, like the wing feathers, may also be used for a variety of ceremonial or religious purposes. The slightest breeze causes them to move, causing the headdress to seem almost alive. It is probably from this feature that they are called "breath feathers." Each feather, of course, and its arrangement, in such a headdress, can have its individual meaning. Feathers from the right wing or right side of the tail, for example, are used on the right side of the headdress, and feathers from the left wing or left side of the tail are used on the left side of the headdress. In the regalia of the red savages there is little that is meaningless or arbitrary. To make a headdress often requires several birds. To give you an idea of the value of Herlits, in some places two may be exchanged for a kaiila; in other places, it takes three to five to purchase a kaiila. We were not today, however, hunting Herlits.

"Master is looking at me," she said.

I looked away from her, angrily. Then I looked back at her, again.

She lay naked in the pit, before me, on her left side, her head in the crook of her left arm, her right leg, the braided-rawhide rope on its ankles, drawn up a bit more than her left. She was exquisitely curvaceous. Doubtless she knew well how she lay before me. I wondered if she should be beaten or caressed, whipped or raped.

Sometimes slaves are skillful in immeshing masters in the toils of their beauty. How often do they conquer us with their softness! How often are we the victims of their delicious, insidious charms and wiles! What drums and alarms are found, upon occasion, in their glances and smiles. What battalions can march in a tearful eye and a trembling lip. What potent strategies can lurk in the line of a breast or the turn of a hip. How a bent knee and a bowed head can wrench a man's guts. Helplessness and vulnerability seem strange shields; how implausible is gentleness as an instrument of diplomacy; what an unlikely weapon is her tenderness. Who is most powerful, I wondered, the master or the slave? Then I realized that it is the master who is most powerful for he may, if he wishes, put her on the block and sell her or dispose of her in any way he pleases. In the end, in the final analysis, it is he, and not she, who holds the whip. It is she who, in the end, must kneel at the feet of a master, completely at his mercy, her will, in the final analysis, nothing. It is she who, in the end, in the final analysis, is owned, and must please, absolutely.

"Master is still looking a me," she said.

"Be quiet!" I said. I had heard a noise.

Cautiously I crawled to the larger of the two openings in the ceiling of the pit.

"It is an urt," I said, "curious. It has now gone away."

I returned to my place.

It can be nerve-racking, waiting in the pit. In our hours in the pit we had had several occasions for concern. Twice we had heard the single note of the fleer from Cuwignaka, signaling the passage, overhead, of flighted ones, the Kinyanpi. Once a tabuk, a prairie tabuk, tawny in the Barrens, single-horned, gazellelike, had grazed nearby. It had browsed within feet of us. In a sense this had pleased me, suggesting that our quarry might be in the vicinity; in a sense it had displeased me, suggesting that abundant, alternative game might also be in the vicinity, the tabuk tending to travel in herds. Some varieties of prairie tabuk, interestingly, when sensing danger, tend to lie down. This is counterinstinctual for most varieties of tabuk, which, when sensing danger, tend to freeze, in a tense, standing position and then, if alarmed further, tend to scurry away, depending on their agility and speed to escape predators. The standing position, of course, as is the case with bipedalian creatures, tends to increase their scanning range. The response disposition of lying down, apparently selected for in some varieties of tabuk, tends to be useful in an environment in which high grass is plentiful and one of the most common predators depends primarily on vision to detect and locate its prey. This predator, as would be expected, normally attacks from a direction in which its shadow does not precede it. Any tabuk, of course, if it is sufficiently alarmed, will bound away. It can attain short-term speeds of from eighty to ninety pasangs an Ahn. Its evasive leaps, in the Gorean gravity, can cover from thirty to forty feet in length, and attain heights of ten to fifteen feet. Once we had heard two notes of the fleer, but, that time, as it had turned out, the source of the signal had not been Cuwignaka but, to our frustration, an actual fleer.

I sat back, against the rear of the pit.

I looked at the hobbling log, to my left, and the rope attached to it, coiled atop it. I looked to the walls of the pit, to the ceiling, with the poles and sod, and at the light, filtering downward into the pit, and then again I looked at my naked slave.

How shamelessly she lay before me!

Surely she knew how she lay before me. She lay before me as a curvaceous slave before her master.

I forced myself to look away from her. I counted several Ehn. Idly, in the dirt, beside me, I traced designs. Then I discovered they were cursive Kefs, the common Kajira sign, sometimes called the staff and fronds, that sign which marks the thigh of so many enslaved Gorean beauties.

I looked back at the girl.

"Do I distract you?" she asked.

"No," I said, angrily.

"Oh," she said.

She squirmed a little, apparently merely to change her position.

I made an angry noise.

"Master?" she asked.

"It is nothing," I said.

"Oh," she said.

I observed how her toes were pointed, this curving her calves deliciously. Her belly, too, was sucked in a bit, accentuating the loveliness of her breasts and the flare of her hips. How lasciviously, how desirably, she lay before me, and yet with what seeming indifference, with what a seeming innocence, with what a seeming lack of awareness! She sighed, and smiled, and looked away. How inadvertently she had seemed to do that. The she-sleen! I clenched my fists. She knew well what she was doing. She lay before me with the lascivious, apparent nonchalence of a slave who, supposedly unaware, knows well that her master's eyes are upon her.

"Master?" she asked.

"Rest," I said.

"Yes, Master," she said, and smiled. "If master should desire aught, let his slave be summoned. She will respond with instant and perfect obedience."

"It is well," I said.

"Yes, Master," she said.

She then closed her eyes, pretending to sleep.

I regarded her. I could not take my eyes from her. I owned her. Well was I pleased that she had fallen to my leather.

She opened her eyes, and smiled.

"Rest," I said.

"Yes, Master," she said, and again pretended to sleep. There was a tiny smile about the corner of her lips. How shamelessly she lay before me, and yet with what an apparent lack of awareness!

The she-sleen was cunning, and delicious. Well did she know what she was doing to me. I looked away from her and began to sweat. Again I clenched my fists. I must not permit myself to be diverted from the business of the day.

I looked back upon the slave.

She again closed her eyes, pretending again to sleep. She squirmed a little, and made a tiny noise, as though in weariness. I saw that she expected to conquer.

"Slave," I said.

"Yes, Master," she said.

"You do not seem to be sleepy," I observed.

"No, Master," she said.

"But it does not matter, whether you are or not," I said.

"No, Master," she said.

"For you are a slave," I said.

"Yes, Master," she said.

"Slave," I said.

"Yes, Master," she said.

"Crawl to me on your belly," I said.

"Yes, Master," she said, smiling.

"Now kneel before me," I said, "with your knees wide, with your wrists crossed behind you, touching, as though bound."

"Yes, Master," she said. She was then before me, in a posture of my dictation, and, as it is said, bound by my will.

I withdrew an object from my pouch.

"Master?" she said.

I held the object before her. She regarded it with dismay. "I have already chewed sip root within the moon," she said.

"Open your mouth," I said.

"Yes, Master," she said.

I then thrust the object into her mouth.

"Chew it well," I said, "and swallow it, bit by bit."

She grimaced, at the barest taste of the object.

"Begin," I told her.

She began.

"Not so quickly," I told her. "More slowly. Very slowly. Very, very slowly. Savor it well."

She whimpered in obedience.

She did not need the sip root, of course, for, as she had pointed out, she had had some within the moon, and, indeed, the effect of sip root, in the raw state, in most women, is three or four moons. In the concentrated state, as in slave wine, developed by the caste of physicians, the effect is almost indefinite, usually requiring a releaser for its remission, usually administered, to a slave, in what is called the breeding wine, or the "second wine." When this is administered she usually knows that she has been selected for crossing with a handsome male slave.

Such breedings commonly take place with the slaves hooded, and under the supervision of the master, or masters. In this way the occurrence of the breeding act can be confirmed and authenticated. Sometimes a member of the caste of scribes is also present, to provide certification on behalf of the city. Usually, however, in cities which encourage this sort of registration it is sufficient to bring the papers for stamping to the proper office within forty Ahn. Such rigor, however, is usually involved only in the breeding of expensive, pedigreed slaves. Most slave breeding is at the discretion of the private master or masters involved. Slaves from the same household, incidentally, are seldom mated. This practice is intended to reduce the likelihood of intimate emotional relationships among slaves. Furthermore, male and female slaves are usually kept separate, female slaves commonly performing light labors in households and male slaves working in the fields or on the grounds. Sometimes, to reward male slaves, or keep them content, or even to keep them from going insane, a female slave is thrown to them. This is sometimes a girl of delicate sensibilities from the house who has not been perfectly pleasing; she then finds herself thrown naked to work slaves. In slave matings, since most crossings do not take place within the same household, a stud fee is usually paid to the master of the male slave. The active ingredient in the breeding wine, or the "second wine," is a derivative of teslik. In the matter of bitterness of taste there is little to choose from between raw sip root and slave wine, the emulsive qualities of the slave wine being offset to some extent by the strength of the concentrations involved.

"I have finished it," gasped the girl, shuddering.

"Open your mouth," I said, "widely."

I forced her mouth open, even more widely, with my thumbs and forefingers. I examined her mouth, closely. The sip root was gone.

She still held her wrists crossed, touching, behind her. She was still bound, as it is said, by the master's will.

"You are unbound," I told her. She removed her hands from behind her back.

She looked at me, knowing that I was her master.

"Lick and wipe your mouth," I told her. She ran her tongue over her lips, and wiped them with the back of her right forearm.

If I should choose to kiss her I did not desire to taste the residue of sip root.

"Hands on thighs," I said, "head down."

She complied. It is pleasant to command women.

"Do you think that you will conquer?" I asked.

"No, Master," she whispered.

"Would you like more sip root?" I inquired.

She shook her head, rigorously. "No, Master," she said. She had not needed the sip root, of course.

It is occasionally useful to have the slave perform arbitrary and unpleasant acts. It helps to remind them that they are only slaves, and are subject to the master's will.

"Lift your head," I said.

She did so.

"Please me," I said.

"After what you have done?" she asked. "After what you made me do!"

"Please me," I said, "—perfectly."

"Yes, Master!" she said, frightened. She then began, anxiously and fearfully, desperately afraid, to kiss and caress me.

I then looked down at her, in my arms, snuggled against me, lifting her lips to mine.

"Who will conquer?" I asked her.

"You," she said, "you, Master!"

"You will see to it, won't you?" I asked.

"Yes, Master," she said, desperately.

It is occasionally useful to enlist the woman's aid in her own conquest. If she is not conquered, authentically, and in her own understanding, and to the master's satisfaction, she is subjected to severe punishment, and may even be slain. Accordingly, with all of her will and feeling, she bends every effort toward her own defeat. She does not rest until she knows herself, and her masters know her, to be naught but a submitted, vanquished slave.

I kissed her, and her lips, open, hot, seemed to melt beneath mine. How well her slave's body, hot and naked, yielding, felt in my arms!

"Be cruel to me," she begged. "I am yours. I am owned. I am a slave!"

Some women can resist, for a time, some masters, but what woman can long resist both herself, turned against herself, by the master's will, and the master, as well? What a splendid ally the woman makes, in her own conquest! Should she not be used more often? Too, when a woman has aided in her own conquest, her defeat, brought about in part by her own will, has a special memorableness for her, a special, self-revelatory significance for her. She has, in her defeat, of her own will, acknowledged herself a slave. This understanding, and acknowledgment, openly made, is often the difference in a woman between joy and fulfillment, and egotism, hostility and frustration.

"Who has conquered?" I asked the woman.

"You have conquered, completely, Master," she said. "I am a slave. I am yours alone."

"Strictly," I said, "you belong to Cuwignaka. It is your use which is mine."

"Yes, Master," she sobbed.

"You are his alone, as of now," I said. "But if he should

give you away, or sell you, then you would belong to another."

"To you," she wept. "To you!"

"To anyone," I said.

"Yes, Master," she sobbed.

"Why?" I asked.

"Because I am a slave, only a slave," she wept.

"Yes," I said.

"Yes, my Master," she sobbed.

"Hold!" I said. "Listen!"

She clutched me, her eyes closed.

I heard the two notes, as of a fleer.

"Do you not hear it?" I asked.

"It is a fleer," she said. "It is only a fleer."

She moaned as I thrust her from me. I licked my lips. I could still taste a little of the sip root, kissed from her mouth. It was bitter.

She extended her hand to me. "Master!" she said.

I crouched in the pit. I lifted my head, peering through the larger of the two apertures in the ceiling of the pit.

Again we heard the two notes, as of a fleer, more insistently.

I stood then in the pit, my head and shoulders outside of the opening.

"Master," she said.

"It is not a fleer," I said.

I crouched down again, then, in the pit. I yanked at the rawhide rope, twice looped, tied, on her right ankle. It was tight. Its other end was looped twice about the hobbling log. I then seized the woman, my left hand in her hair, my right hand in her collar, and pulled her up, beside me.

"Master!" she cried, in misery.

I thrust her up, through the opening.

"Do you see it?" I demanded.

"Yes," she said, after a moment. "It is very high."

"Is it circling?" I asked.

"It is hard to tell," she said. "I think maybe it is."

"Good," I said. "Then it is probably hunting." The leisurely, high-altitude hunting circles of our prey sometimes manifested a diameter of pasangs.

"Does it see you?" I asked.

"I do not think so," she said.

"Move a little, walk about," I said. I saw the rawhide tether shift.

The distance vision of our prey would be truly remarkable. It is particularly good at the detection of movement. It is said it can see an urt move across open ground at a distance of two pasangs. It is said it can detect an irregular movement of grass, not correlated with wind direction and velocity, from a distance of one pasang. I was confident we could rely on its vision.

"It is circling," she said.

"Does it see you?" I asked.

"Now," she said, frightened. "Now I think it does."

"Do not lose track of it," I said. "Do not appear to notice it, but do not lose track of it. Your life could depend on this. Note exactly, as well, the location of the opening."

"I know well where it is, Master," she said. "Do not fear."

"The matter must be close," I said. "You understand that?"

"Yes, Master," she said, "yes!"

Our quarry must not be allowed a great deal of time for investigation.

"It sees me!" she moaned.

"Good!" I said. "Do not appear to much notice it."

"It is coming!" she said. "It is coming, very swiftly!"

"Do not appear to much notice it," I said.

"I am frightened!" she said.

"Breathe deeply," I said. "Keep your body ready, a little tense, but not tight."

"It is coming very swiftly," she said.

"Do not lose track of it," I said. "Keep in mind clearly, as well, the location of the entrance of the pit."

"I am frightened!" she cried.

Suddenly the tether seemed to jerk from the pit and then, in a moment, it had jerked tight. I heard her cry out with misery. I thrust my head and shoulders from the pit and saw her, on her belly, in the grass, her right leg stretched out, almost straight, behind her, the tether tight on it. She had tried to run.

I hoisted myself out of the pit, screaming and cursing, waving my arms. The quarry, startled at my unexpected appearance, veered away, passing within feet of me, the great shadow suddenly between me and the sun, and then the sun again blazed on the late-summer grass, tumultuous and whipped, twisted, by the passage of the quarry. The sweat on my face felt cold, from the wind which had rushed past.

"On your feet," I said.

Tremblingly, she rose to her feet.

I looked after the receding figure in the afternoon sky.

"I could have been killed," she said.

"You lost us the quarry," I said.

"I could have been killed," she said, trembling.

"You are only a worthless slave," I told her. "You have lost us the quarry."

"Forgive me, Master," she said, her head down.

"Into the pit, Slave, and be quick about it," I said.

"Yes, Master," she said.

I followed her into the pit. She knelt at one end, near the larger opening, her head down.

"Forgive me, Master," she whispered.

"Another such performance and you shall be well punished," I informed her.

"Yes, Master," she said.

"It may return," I said.

She shuddered.

In a few Ehn, as I had hoped, we heard again the two notes, as of the fleer.

"It is perhaps hungry," I speculated.

She lifted her head, her eyes wide with terror.

"I did not think he would forget you, my luscious, nude bait," I said. I regarded her. Most women, for some reason, stand in mortal terror of such things. This is particularly true of women who have some familiarity with them, who know something of their swiftness, their savagery and their ferocity, who have some knowledge of what they can accomplish.

"Do not make me go out of the pit again," she begged.

"Out," I told her.

Fearfully, scarcely able to move, she crawled out of the pit.

"It is there," she said, "in the sky. It is circling. I sense myself the center of that circle."

"Splendid!" I said.

"Let me hide," she begged. "Let me hide!"

"No," I said.

She suddenly screamed and the tether, length by length, leaped from the pit and then, again, jerked taut.

"Idiot slave!" I cried.

"I'm tied! I'm tied!" she wept.

I stood up, lifting my head and shoulders above the entrance to the pit. She was sitting in the grass, at the end of the tether, weeping hysterically. "I'm tied," she cried, fighting to thrust the tether from her ankle.

The quarry was still in the sky.

By the tether I pulled her to within a few feet of the entrance.

"Get on your feet," I cried, "Slave!"

Unsteadily, trembling, her head lifted, she rose to her feet, her hands out to help her maintain her balance.

"I'm frightened," she wept.

"Where is it?" I asked.

"I don't know," she wept. "It's gone! It's gone!"

"No," I said. "It will not be gone."

The girl's head was lifted, scanning the sky. It seemed empty, save for the high, billowing clouds.

"Be alert," I said. "It will not be gone."

"I can't see it," she cried, joyfully. "I can't see it!"

"It is not gone," I said. "It is somewhere. Be alert!" Suddenly the hair stood up on the back of my neck. The quarry had seen the fear responses of the girl. Twice she had tried to run. Now it seemed to have disappeared.

"It is gone," she said.

"It has alighted," I said.

"What am I to do?" she asked.

"Scan in a low circle, about you," I said.

The quarry knew the girl's location. The girl did not know its location.

There is, within normal limits, and assuming the dimension is under surveillance, a direct correlation between height and detectability. It is for such reasons that an upright carriage increases the capacity to detect the approach of a predator or the position of game. It is for such a reason that the larl commonly crouches when stalking prey.

"I see nothing," she said.

"Be alert," I said.

I wondered how long it would take, say, a startled tabuk or ground animal, of a burrowing sort, to regain its composure, to return to its normal activities.

"It is gone," she said.

"Do not relax your vigilance," I cautioned her. "It will presumably be moving with great speed and will be some ten to fifteen feet in the air. You will not see it, probably, given your height, and the grass, until it is within a few hundred yards of you. Even so, however, this will permit you ample reaction time. You have a great advantage, you see, in that you are expecting it."

"I think it is gone," she said.

"Perhaps," I said.

"It would have come by now, surely," she said.

"Perhaps," I said. "Perhaps, not."

The sky seemed placid, the clouds slowly changing their shapes in the air currents. I watched them for awhile. I supposed that a tabuk, by now, might have returned to grazing.

"It is coming!" she cried, suddenly.

"Into the pit!" I cried. "Hurry!" There had been no mistaking the urgency in her voice.

"I cannot move!" she cried. "I cannot move!"

I threw myself half out of the pit and with my right hand seized her right ankle, and then, with my left, seized her left ankle. She screamed, throwing her hands before her face. Bodily I dragged her down beside me. Almost at the same instant, flashing over the opening, I saw immense, extended talons closing, and the rushing passage of a huge, dark shape, the grass leaping up and seeming to be almost torn up, almost uprooted, following it.

She clutched me, shuddering.

"You have not been pleasing," I told her. I then thrust her from me.

"Is it gone?" she begged, sobbing.

"It will be back," I said. "Stay near the opening."

I unlooped the tether on her leg from the hobbling log. She watched me, frightened. The other end was still tied tightly on her right ankle. I then went to the other end of the pit, where the smaller opening was, and uncoiled the line which lay there, formerly atop the hobbling log.

"What do we do now?" she asked.

"Wait," I said.

She lay down in the pit, making herself as low, and small, as possible.

We did not wait long.

We heard a sudden, striking, thudding sound. It was almost as though half of a kaiila had been suddenly dropped to the earth. It was a sound which, when one has once heard it, one is not likely to mistake it for another. The vibrations were felt through the walls of the pit.

"It is here," I said.

The girl, looking up, suddenly screamed with fear. A large, bright, round eye peered through the opening in the ceiling of the pit.

A beak, yellowish, some two feet in length, scimitarlike, poked into the pit.

It withdrew.

We then heard a taloned foot cutting at the sod and poles over our head.

"We are safe here!" cried the girl.

"No," I said.

The beak again entered the pit and pushed downward. It poked against the girl's body. She screamed. It snapped at her and she shrank back, to the opposite end of the pit, covering her head, screaming. This excited the predator. Half of its head thrust into the pit, after her. Then it screamed, too, a shrill scream, and, withdrawing its head, it began to cut and tear at the roof of the pit. I saw a talon emerge through the sod roof. I saw poles lifting and splintering.

In this moment, its attention fastened on the girl, on tearing away the obstacle which lay between him and her, I thrust through the smaller opening and, with a swirl of rope and two hitches, fastened the hobbling log on its right leg. I then screamed and thrust at it, and it spun about. I fended its beak away with my forearm.

"Well done!" cried Cuwignaka, springing up from the grass. He interposed himself, and a lance, between me and the predator. The beak snapped the lance off short. Hci, swinging ropes, crying out, emerged, too, from the nearby grass. Cuwignaka and I backed off. The bird, smiting its wings, darted towards us but, screaming, fell short on its belly in the grass, feathers flying about. It only then realized it was impeded. It turned about, wildly, the leg, and rope, turning under him. Cuwignaka struck it on the beak with the shaft of the lance, distracting it. Hci, running up, struck it with the coils of rope in his hand. The bird, then, rising up, wings beating, took to flight, jerking the hobbling log from the pit, tearing it up through the sod roof and poles.

"Strong! Strong! Marvelous!" cried Cuwignaka.

He had not understood the strength of such a creature.

Struggling, wings beating, screaming, the bird, lunging and falling, and climbing again, fought the weight. It struggled to perhaps a hundred feet in the air and then, bit by bit, the log swinging, fighting, it began to lose altitude. Cuwignaka and Hci ran beneath it, in the grass. I wiped sweat from my forehead. I was elated.

I returned to the pit, its roof now half torn away. In one end of it the girl crouched. I leaped down into the pit beside her. "On your belly," I told her. I then pulled her right ankle, to which the tether was still tightly attached, high, up behind her. With some of the tether, close to the knot on her right ankle, I tied her hands together behind her back. I then looked down upon her, she now on her side, with her wrists tied behind her, fastened to her right ankle, pulled up, closely behind her. She was well secured. I then, with extra ropes taken from the pit, went to aid Cuwignaka and Hci.

38

A SLAVE IS PUNISHED

"It is a splendid catch," I said.

Ropes bound the beak of the bird tightly shut. It lay on its side. Its feet, too, were bound together. Ropes, as well, encircled its wings, binding them to its body. Already we had put a girth rope about it, of the sort beneath which the Kinyanpi, in flight, inserted their knees.

It was now late afternoon.

We had transported the bird to this grove of trees on a travois, drawn by two kaiila. It was only a pasang or so from the pit, which we had rebuilt.

The bird struggled, and then lay still.

"A splendid catch," I said.

"We must try again, tomorrow," said Cuwignaka.

"Yes," I said.

We then turned about, and walked to another part of the grove. It was in this part of the grove that we had our kaiila tethered, and had made our camp.

There, near our things, stood my slave, who had once been the lofty Lady Mira, of Venna, an agent of Kurii.

I looked at her. She lowered her eyes.

"Fetch me a coiled rope," I told her. "And then get on all fours."

She did so.

"You ran twice," I told her.

"Forgive me, Master," she said.

"Then once, frozen with fear, you needed to be dragged, perforce, into the pit."

"Forgive me, Master," she begged.

"I am not pleased," I said.

"Forgive me, Master!" she begged.

Cuwignaka and Hci stood by while the slave was beaten. Then I cast aside the coiled ropes, to a place among my other things. She lay now at my feet, on her belly, shuddering and sobbing, clutching at the grass.

"Now," I said, "get up and put out our food."

"Yes, Master," she said, struggling to her feet.

"And tonight," I said, "after we have eaten, and when we are sitting about, you will serve each of us in turn, and for as many rounds as we wish."

"Yes, Master," she said.

"And furthermore," I said, "you will do so with absolute obedience and in complete silence."

"Yes, Master," she said.

"It will be a pleasant evening," said Cuwignaka.

"Yes," said Hci, "but there is another whom I would rather have in my thongs."

"I think I know who she is," laughed Cuwignaka.

"And is there not one," asked Hci, "whom you, my friend, Cuwignaka, would rather have licking your feet in terror?"

"Perhaps," smiled Cuwignaka.

"The pit is slow work, Tatankasa, Mitakola," said Hci. "Even with good fortune we cannot snare enough tarns by winter to combat the Kinyanpi."

"Using the pit, I hope to catch only two or three," I said.

"That will not be enough," said Hci.

"Not in themselves," I admitted.

"Ah!" said Hci. "But that will be very difficult and dangerous."

"I do not see another way," I said. "Do you?"

"No," said Hci.

"Are you with us?" I asked.

"Of course," he said.

We then went and sat down where Mira, on leaves, had set forth our food.

We chewed the cold pemmican. We would not make a fire in this place.

From time to time, chewing, we cast a glance at Mira. She knelt to one side, her head down.

She was very beautiful. It was difficult not to anticipate the pleasures we would later receive from her.

I threw her a piece of pemmican.

The three moons, visible through the branches, had risen.

I looked again at Mira.

She lifted her head, chewing, and our eyes met. Then she looked down, again, shyly, smiling.

She was a common slave, who, tonight, would serve as a slave in common.

39

THE FEATHER

"It is exhausted, but it is still dangerous!" I cried. I held one end of the rope about the flopping bird's neck, keeping it taut, and Hci, on the other side, held the other. "Be careful," I called to Cuwignaka.

Speaking soothingly, he approached the bird.

We were in the vicinity of the tarn pit. This was the second tarn we had caught. The first one we had caught yesterday.

Cuwignaka suddenly leaped forward and locked his arms about the bird's beak. He was almost thrown loose as the bird shook his head. Holding the beak with one arm, then, he whipped rope about it and, in moments, had tied it closed. In a few moments we had secured its wings and then, working together, Hci and I, bound its legs together.

I took the hobbling rope from its right ankle, that which had fastened it to the hobbling log. It shuddered, lying on its side. "It is ready for the travois," I said.

I then turned about and went back to the tarn pit. Its roof was gone, torn away and scattered when the concealed hobbling log had been jerked upward through it.

I looked down into the pit. The girl lay on her stomach, her hands over her head, shuddering and sobbing below me.

"Are you all right?" I asked. I had not bothered, this time, to bind her.

"Did I not please you last night?" she sobbed.

"Yes," I said, puzzled.

"But you put me out on the tether," she said.

"Of course," I said.

Her body trembled, uncontrollably.

"It is over now," I told her. "We have it."

She sobbed, hysterically. I did not think she could control the movements of her body. "You did not do badly," I assured her.

She whimpered, shuddering.

"Why are you so upset?" I asked.

She sobbed, hysterically, shuddering. To be sure, it had been a close thing.

I slipped into the pit beside her and took her in my arms. "It is over now," I reassured her. "It is all right now."

She looked at me, her eyes wide, frightened. "What you can make us do," she gasped. I stroked her head, gently. I had once seen a similar hysteria in an urt hunter's girl, in Port Kar. She had barely missed being taken by a giant urt in the canals. But the spear thrust of the hunter had been unerring and turned the urt at the last instant and the second thrust had finished it off. Girls in Port Kar will do almost anything to keep the rope off their neck and keep out of the canals. To be sure it is normally only low girls or girls who may have displeased a master in some respect who are used for such work.

"Last night," she said, "did I not please you well?"

"Yes," I said, "you did, and tonight you will please us again, and in the same way."

She moaned.

"You did not do badly today," I reassured her, "truly. For example, tonight it will not be necessary to beat you again, with coiled ropes. That should please you."

"Yes, Master," she said.

"Indeed," I said, "you did not do badly, at all. Perhaps I will have one, or both, of your ears notched, as our friends, the red savages do, with prize kaiila, trained for the hunt or war, that you may be recognized as a valuable, trained tarn-bait girl."

She pressed herself against me, sobbing.

"It is a joke," I said.

"Yes, Master," she said.

I saw that she was not in a mood to appreciate such humor. I myself, however, for what it is worth, had not thought that it was bad at all.

"Do you, and the others, not care for me?" she asked.

"You are only a slave," I reminded her.

"Of course, Master!" she said. "How foolish of me, to think that one might care, in the least, for one who is only a slave!"

"You are only a property," I told her, "and worthless, except that you might have some small monetary value."

"Yes, Master," she said.

I did not see any reason to tell her that slaves are the most treasured, despised and loved of all women. Being Gorean she knew this.

"But cannot a master," she asked, "sometimes feel some small affection for a property, even, say, for a pet sleen?"

"Perhaps," I said, "but that would not mean, then, that the sleen was other than a sleen."

"No, Master," she said.

"Or the slave other than a slave," I said.

"No, Master," she said.

I kissed her, gently.

"You do feel some tenderness for me," she said. "I am a woman. I can tell!"

"Perhaps it will be necessary, after all, tonight, to whip you," I said.

"No, Master," she said. "Please, no!"

"Do not expect affection," I said. "Expect, rather, Slave, only to serve your master with total perfection."

"Yes, Master," she said.

"And even if a master, some master, sometime, should be moved to feel some tenderness, or a bit of affection, doubtlessly foolishly, toward you, remember that it changes nothing, that you remain only what you are, a slave."

"Yes, Master," she said.

"Even the most loved slave," I said, "should a master be so foolish as to love a slave, remains, in the end, and do not forget it, radically, and only, a slave."

"Yes, Master," she said.

I kissed her again, softly.

"You can do anything with us, can't you?" she asked. "It depends only on your will."

"Yes," I said.

"Do not put me out of the tether again, Master," she begged. "Keep me for only silken work. I will endeavor with all my heart to be a most perfect and pleasing slave."

"Is this she who was once the lofty Lady Mira who speaks," I asked, "she who was once the proud free woman of Venna?"

"Yes, Master," she said.

"And is now naught but an abject slave?"

"Yes, Master," she said.

"Your will is nothing," I said. "It will be done with you, totally, as masters please."

"Yes, Master," she said.

"Perhaps you understand now," I said, "a little better than before, what it is to be a slave."

"Yes, my master," she said. She laughed, ruefully.

"What is wrong?" I asked.

"I was thinking of when I was a free woman," she said. "How contemptuous I was of the slave girls in the cities, how I scorned them, and despised them, so helpless in their lowly, silken slaveries, and yet, now, how I envy them their slaveries!"

I smiled.

"What lucky, soft little things they are," she said, "being sold naked off sales blocks to the whips and chains of strong masters, with little more to worry about than the heat of the kitchens, the steaming water of the laundering tubs, the dangers, from young, prowling ruffians, of shopping in the evening! How warm and safe they are locked in their kennels at night or cuddling, in furs, chained at the foot of their masters' couches! What need have they to fear sleen and tarns! They need fear only their masters!"

"The lot of a slave girl in the cities is not always easy," I said. "Most are owned by one master, alone, and must share his compartments with him, in complete privacy. There, as slave girls elsewhere, they are at the master's mercy, completely."

"It is not so different in the Barrens," she said, "when one is alone with the master, when the lodge flaps are tied shut, from the inside."

"Perhaps not," I smiled.

"And in the cities," she said, "it is so beautiful, the towers, the bridges and sunsets, the people, the flower stalls, the market places, the smells of cooking."

"Yes," I said, "the cities are beautiful." Some of the most beautiful cities I had seen were on Gor.

"I lived in Ar for a year," she said. "Not far from my apartments there was a pastry shop. Marvelous smells used to come from the shop. In the evening, when the shop was closing, slave girls, in their brief tunics and collars, would come and kneel down, near the hinged opening to the open-air counter. The baker, who was a kind-hearted man, would sometimes come out and, from a flat sheet, throw them unsold pastries."

I said nothing.

"How amusing I found that at the time," she said. "But, too, I sometimes wondered if the pastries I bought at that shop tasted so good to me as those the girls had begged did to them. They seemed so delighted to receive one. It was so precious to them."

I said nothing.

"If I were a slave in Ar," she said, "and I were permitted to do so, I think I should go to that pastry shop and, in my tunic and collar, kneel there with the other girls, hoping that I, too, might receive such a pastry."

I smiled. How beautiful she was, and how helpless, a slave.

"In street shopping," she said, "I was always heavily veiled. The baker would not recognize me."

"Perhaps some of the other girls were former customers as well," I said.

"Perhaps," she smiled. "That is an interesting thought."

"The transition between a free woman and a slave girl can occur suddenly on Gor," I said.

"I am well aware of that, Master," she smiled. Sometimes a girl is captured in her own bed, raped and hooded, and carried to a market, all in the same night.

"But, on the whole," she said, "how I scorned slaves, how I hated them!"

"Oh?" I asked.

"Do you know the slaves I hated the most, those I most despised?" she asked.

"No," I said.

"The pleasure slaves!" she said. "How I hated them! They were so beautiful and desirable! Sometimes I would take a whip into the streets and deliberately jostle one, and then make her lie down and whip her across the legs!"

"The same thing, now, could be done to you," I said.

"I know," she said.

"Why did you hate them so?"I asked.

"They were lucky enough to be in a collar, and not me!" she said.

"It seems, then," I said, "that you hated them because you were jealous of them, that, in reality, you envied them."

"Yes," she said, "I was jealous of their beauty and desirability. I envied them their happiness."

"Did you know this as a free woman?" I asked.

"Yes," she said, "but I do not think that I would have freely admitted it."

"Deceit is a freedom of free women," I said.

"But it is not a freedom permitted to slave girls, is it, Master?" she asked.

"No," I said.

"Every woman, in her heart," she said, "longs to kneel before a strong man, to be subject to his whip, to be owned, to be mastered, to know that she has no choice but to give him total love and service."

"The master will not permit the girl to give him less than everything."

"And the slave desires to give the master everything," she said, "and more."

"Are you happy," I asked, "being a slave?"

"Yes, Master," she said. "I have never been so happy before in my life."

"You are now in your place in nature," I said.

"Yes, my Master," she said. She kissed me.

"No longer, now," I said, "do you need to envy slave girls."

"No longer do I envy them their slavery," she said, "for now I, too, am a slave. In my bondage I am as rich and favored as they."

"But surely," I said, "you are aware of the miseries and terrors which may occasionally characterize the lot of female slaves."

"Of course," she said, "for we are at the mercy of our Masters, in all things."

"Yet you are not displeased to be a slave?" I asked.

"No," she said.

"Why?" I asked.

"That we may, at our master's whim, be subjected to miseries or terrors, even to torture and death, if he wishes, makes clear to us that we are truly slaves, that we are truly owned, that the domination to which we are subject is truly total and absolute."

"I see," I said.

"We would not have it any other way," she said.

"I see," I said.

"But we know," she said, "that though we are in one sense fully without power, that in another sense we may do much to control the happiness and quality of our lives. We need, generally, only be absolutely obedient and fully pleasing."

"That is generally true," I admitted.

"Too," she said, "in bondage we find that we live our truth. How else could we be happy and fulfilled?"

"I do not know," I said.

"And I think it is obviously true," she said, "that men

desire us, treasure us, and love us, as well as command us, in ways that a free woman can never understand or know."

"That is a secret between masters and slaves," I smiled.

"Perhaps," she laughed. "But I doubt that it is a well-kept secret or free women would not hate us so!"

"Perhaps," I smiled.

"There are risks in all conditions," she said. "Free persons, men, at least, for example, if need be, are expected to accept great hazards on behalf of their cities. That is not expected of slaves."

"That is true," I said. Slaves, like kaiila and furniture, being properties, were not expected to participate in municipal defense. To be sure, they might be ordered to strengthen walls and reinforce gates, and such.

She put her arms about my neck, and kissed me. "Suppose you were a conqueror and found me in a burning city," she whispered. "You would not be likely to slay me, would you?"

"No," I said.

"You would make me yours," she said. "You would tie me to the stirrup of your kaiila. You would make me march in your plunder column."

"You might be harnessed to a wagon, to help draw loot," I said.

"Yes, Master," she whispered. "But I would be alive."

"Slavery is sometimes accorded to free prisoners," I said. "This is particularly the case with free women who, when stripped, are found desirable enough for the collar." This may be done in various ways. Normally, a free woman, unceremoniously, is simply enslaved. She deserves no consideration, whatsoever. She is a female of an enemy city. Accordingly, she belongs at the feet of the conqueror, with other spoils. A warrior may secure such women with devices so simple as thumb-cuffs, like tiny, joined rings, and snap-lock, or pronged, tension-closed, nose-rings, with strands of wire, to fasten them together.

The material for securing ten women, in such cases, fits into a corner of the warrior's pack and weighs no more than a few ounces. If the cities are long-time, hereditary enemies snap-lock, or pronged, tension-closed, earrings might be used instead of nose-rings, as a gesture of contempt, a pierced ear, or ears, on Gor, culturally, commonly, being regarded as the mark of the lowest, the most sensuous and the most despicable of slaves. To be perfectly honest, however, ear piercing for Gorean slaves is now much more common than it was a few years ago. Perhaps the time will come when the slave will be a rarity who has not felt the two thrusts of the leather-worker's needle. The growing prevelance of ear piercing probably has to do, at least significantly, with its tendency to stimulate the sexual aggression of the Gorean male. Accordingly, girls with pierced ears, "pierced-ear girls," tend to bring higher prices in the markets. Slavers, thus, prior to putting their properties on the block, are more and more inclined to have this done to them.

Some girls, knowing how desirable this can make them, beg their master to have their ears pierced. The piercing of the ears is not only symbolic and aesthetic to the master and the slave but it can be tactually arousing, as well, playing with the earring, the girl feeling it brush the side of her cheek or neck, and so one. Sometimes, however, the free woman in a captured city is not, say, simply stripped, thrown down and tied, later to be turned over to an iron master for the searing kiss of his white-hot metal. Sometimes, rather, she, stripped, and presented before officers, is offered the choice between swift, honorable decapitation and slavery. If she chooses slavery, she may be expected to step onto a submission mat, and kneel there, head down, enter a slave pen of her own accord, or, say, fully acknowledging herself a slave, belly to an officer, kissing his feet.

The question is sometimes put to her in somewhat the following fashion. "If you are a free woman, speak your freedom and advance, now, to the headsman's block, or, if you are truly a slave, and have only been masquerading until now as a free woman, step now, if you wish, upon the mat of submission and kneel there, in this act becoming at last, explicitly, a legal slave." She is then expected, sometimes, kneeling, to lick the feet of a soldier, who then rapes her on the mat. It is commonly regarded as an acceptable introduction for a woman to her explicit and legal slavery.

"But what does such a woman know?" laughed Mira. "They are ignorant."

"Perhaps one such as yourself might be set to their training," I said.

"I would make them learn quickly," she laughed.

"Your mood now," I said, "seems lighter."

"Yes," she said. "Thank you, Master."

I kissed her.

"It is so ironical," she laughed.

"What?" I asked.

"How I at one time so hated slaves and now have never been so happy as when I am a slave myself!"

"No longer do you hate them," I said.

"No," she said, "for now I am, too, a slave."

"And no longer do you envy them either," I said.

"It is not necessary for me to envy them any longer that they are slaves," she said, "for that is a condition which I, too, now, helplessly share."

"Then you no longer envy them?" I asked.

"But I do," she laughed, "and since I so despised them and held them in such contempt before, this seems now doubly amusing!"

"I do not understand," I said.

"How laughable and delicious would the little collared chits find it that I, who so scorned them, am not only now, too, a slave, but a low slave, one with only a leather collar, one not even permitted clothing, a cheap, inexpensive slave, thousands of pasangs from civilization, a meaningless slave in the wild grasslands east of the Thentis mountains, one of so little worth that she may even serve as naked bait for tarns!"

"In silk, and a golden collar, and taught the lascivious movements of pleasure slaves, you might bring a good price, even in the cities," I said.

"Thank you, Master," she said.

"It is the girls in the cities, I take it," I said, "those of the sorts with whom you were familiar as a free woman, that you envy."

"Yes," she said.

"Those girls whom you so scorned before?" I asked.

"Yes," she said. "Now, laughably, I must look up to them, for they are higher than I."

"It is amusing, I suppose," I said.

"As a free woman," she said, "never did I suspect that one day I might actually aspire, from a far lower slavery, to wear such a tunic and collar and, like them, so helpless and subservient, serve in a city."

"These things are relative," I said.

"Now such a thing is beyond my reach," she said, "unless a master should grant it to me."

"Yes," I said, "for you are a slave."

"You see now," she smiled, "why it is that I envy such slaves."

"Yes," I said. "You wish now that only such a slavery was yours."

"Yes," she said.

"But it is not," I said. "You are a slave in the Barrens."

"Yes, Master," she said.

"Tatankasa!" cried Cuwignaka. "Come quickly!"

I leaped out of the pit.

"There!" cried Cuwignaka, pointing upward. "One of the Kinyanpi!"

I shaded my eyes.

"It is not a wild tarn," said Cuwignaka. "There is something on its back."

"Yes," I said.

"It must be a man, bent over," said Cuwignaka.

"But, why?" I asked.

"He is perhaps trying to conceal that the tarn is not wild," said Cuwignaka.

"Perhaps he is wounded," said Hci, fitting an arrow to a bow.

"You are sure you have been seen?" I asked.

"The captured tarn was seen," said Cuwignaka. "I am sure of it. The bird changed its direction. Too, by now, doubtless we have been seen."

"It is circling," said Hci.

"We cannot hide the captured tarn," said Cuwignaka.

"Our plans are foiled. Our hopes are dashed," said Hci.

"One of the Kinyanpi, having made this determination, having detected our presence in the tarn country," I said, "would presumably return to his camp, later to return with others."

"Why is he still circling?" asked Cuwignaka.

"I do not know," I said.

"What is it, Master?" asked Mira. She had emerged, frightened, from the pit. She stood a little behind me, and to my left. I did not strike her. I had not ordered her to remain in the pit.

"We are not sure," I said.

"I think the bird intends to land," said Cuwignaka.

"That is incredible," I said. "Surely one warrior of the Kinyanpi would not wish to challenge three armed men."

"It is going to land," said Cuwignaka. "I am sure of it."

"You are right," I said.

"Why does the warrior not show himself?" asked Hci.

"I can see legs," said Mira.

"I will go a bit behind the path of the bird's approach," said Hci, exercising the tension in the small bow he had armed. "Then when the warrior dismounts he may, if we wish, be easily slain."

I nodded. A man's shield can protect him in only one plane of attack.

"Why would he land?" asked Cuwignaka.

"I do not know," I said.

The bird soared towards us and then, several yards away, turned its wings, braking, and hovered for a moment in the air, its claws dropping, and then landed.

We closed our eyes, briefly, against the storm of wind and dust which temporarily assaulted us.

Mira threw her hand before her mouth and screamed. "Withdraw," I told her.

I went forward and seized the guide-ropes of the tarn, near the beak. It shook its head. The guide-ropes, or reins, of the tarn, as the Kinyanpi fashion them, seem clearly to be based on the jaw ropes used generally in the Barrens by the red savages to control kaiila. This suggests that the Kinyanpi had probably domesticated kaiila before tarns and that their domestication of the tarn was achieved independently of white practice, as exemplified, say, by the tarnsmen of such cities as Thentis. The common guidance apparatus for tarns in most cities is an arrangement involving two major rings and six straps. The one-strap is drawn for ascent, and the four-strap for descent, for example.

"What could have done this?" asked Cuwignaka, in awe.

I heard Mira, a few yards behind us, throwing up in the grass.

"I am not sure," I said.

Hci came up to join us, from where he had been crouching down in the grass.

"Aiii," he muttered.

"What do you think?" asked Cuwignaka.

"Never have I seen anything like this," said Hci. To be sure it was awesome to contemplate the forces and pressures that could have done it.

The tarn, besides its rude bridle, wore a girth strap.

I glanced back at Mira. She was on her hands and knees in the grass, sick.

She was correct that she had seen legs. The knees were thrust under the girth strap. There were also thighs and a lower abdomen. There was no upper body.

"I do not understand this," said Cuwignaka, in a whisper.

"Only something from the medicine world could have done this," said Hci.

I looked up, scanning the sky. Whatever had done this must still be about, somewhere.

"Why has the bird landed?" asked Cuwignaka.

"It is a domestic tarn," I said. "Probably it wishes to be freed of the remains of the rider. It saw men."

"I am uneasy," said Cuwignaka.

"I, too," said Hci.

"This is a great boon for us," I said. "Remove the legs from the girth strap."

"How is that?" asked Cuwignaka. He and Hci removed the legs from the girth strap and discarded them in the grass. Sleen could find them later.

I patted the tarn on the neck. "This is a domestic tarn," I said. "It is trained. Not only will it be unnecessary to break it but it will be of great use, in a brace harness, in training the two tarns we have already caught." This is a common method of training new tarns.

"Mira!" I called, sharply.

She ran to me and knelt before me, putting her head to my feet.

"You may be pleased to learn," I told her, "that for our purposes we now have tarns enough. It will no longer be necessary, at least at this time, to put you out again on the tether."

"Thank you, Master!" she cried and, almost uncontrollably, half sobbing, kissed my feet in gratitude.

"Destroy the tarn pit," I said, "and address yourself to the task of concealing all signs of our activities here."

"Yes, Master," she said, leaping to her feet.

"And take that tether from your ankle," I said.

"Yes, Master," she said, and knelt down on one knee, her hands at the knot.

"We will fetch the kaiila and attach them to the travois," I said. "We will take this tarn to our temporary camp."

"Yes, Tatankasa," said Cuwignaka.

"We do not wish to remain in the open longer than necessary," I said.

"No, Tatankasa," said Hci.

I glanced down at Mira. She was now sitting in the grass, her fingers fighting the knot.

"If you have not finished with your work here before we

leave," I told her, "follow the travois tracks in the grass back to our temporary camp."

"Yes, Master," she sobbed.

"Tonight," I said, "after food and woman, losing no time, we shall proceed toward Two Feathers."

"Good," said Cuwignaka.

"Our plans proceed," I said to Hci, "expeditiously and apace."

"Splendid," said he.

"Master!" sobbed the girl.

"What?" I asked.

"I cannot undo the knot," she said, tears in her eyes. "You have tied it too tightly!"

I handed the reins of the tarn to Cuwignaka. I crouched down beside the girl.

"I have tried," she said. "I have tried! Please, don't whip me!"

I unfastened the knot.

"Thank you, Master!" she said.

"Quickly now, to your work," I said.

"Yes, Master!" she said. "Oh!" she cried, in surprise and pain. I had sped her on her way with a proprietary slap.

I turned, grinning, to face Cuwignaka and Hci. Cuwignaka, not unwillingly, returned the reins of the tarn to me.

"Can you ride such a beast as this, truly, Tatankasa?" asked Hci.

"Yes," I said.

"It amazes me that such a thing can be done," he said.

"It can be done," I assured him.

"Perhaps the Kinyanpi have some special medicine, some special powers," he said.

"No," I said. "They are men, such as you and me."

"The back of the bird, the feathers, are drenched with blood," he said.

"It is dried now," I said.

"It is not yet that dry," he said, pinching some between his fingers. There was a reddish smudge there, not a brownish-red powder.

"You are right," I granted him.

"This was done, then, not so long ago," he said.

"That is true," I said. I had not seen any reason, earlier, to point this out.

"The rider," he said, "surely only something from the medicine world could have done that to him. It is like finding only a foot in a moccasin."

"Are you afraid?" I asked.

"Yes," said Hci.

"I find that hard to believe," I said.

"You know what it is that I fear, do you not, Cuwignaka, Mitakola?" asked Hci.

"Yes," said Cuwignaka.

"What?" I asked Cuwignaka.

"It is nothing," said Cuwignaka. "It is only a matter of myth."

"What?" I asked.

"He fears that it could only have been the work of Wakanglisapa," said Cuwignaka.

"Wakanglisapa?" I asked.

"Yes, Wakanglisapa, 'Black Lightning,' the Medicine Tarn," said Cuwignaka.

"That is foolish, Hci, my friend," I said.

"I do not think so," he said. "While I crouched in the grass, awaiting the landing of the tarn, I found something. I would like to show it to you."

Neither Cuwignaka nor myself spoke. We watched Hci return to the place in the grass where he had waited, bow ready, for the landing of the tarn. In a moment or two he had returned to where we stood.

In his hands he carried a large feather.

"It is black," said Cuwignaka.

"There are many black tarns," I said.

"Consider its size, Tatankasa, Mitakola," said Cuwignaka, in awe.

"It is large," I granted him. It was some five feet in length. It could only have come from a very large tarn.

"It is the feather of Wakanglisapa, the Medicine Tarn," said Hci.

"There is no such beast," I said.

"This is his feather," said Hci.

I said nothing.

Hci examined the skies. "Even now," he said, "Wakanglisapa may be watching us."

I, too, scanned the skies. "The skies seem clear," I said.

"The beasts of the medicine world," said Hci, "may appear, or not, as they please."

"Do not be foolish, my friend," I said.

Hci thrust the feather down, like a lance, in the dirt. I looked at it. Its barbs moved in the wind.

"Let us draw the travois ourselves," said Hci. "It will save time."

"Cuwignaka and I will draw it, after we have tied the reins of this tarn to one of the poles," I said. "You go ahead, to fetch the kaiila, and then meet us."

"I think it will be better if we all remain together," said Hci.

"You feel there is danger?" I asked.

"Great danger," said Hci.

"We shall wait then, too, for the slave," I said.

"It is well, unless we wish to risk losing her," said Hci.

"Let us not risk losing her," I said. "She may be worth as much as a kaiila."

"Yes," said Hci. It seemed not improbable that the former Lady Mira of Venna might bring that much in a bartering.

In a few moments the slave had joined us. She had worked swiftly. She had not needed to be hastened with blows.

"It is not necessary to tie me by the neck to a travois pole, Master," she said.

I slapped her, snapping her head to the side.

"Forgive me, Master," she said.

"It seems you still have much to learn about being a slave," I said.

"I am eager to learn," she said, her head down.

"I will help," said Hci.

"No," I said. "Your wound might open."

"I will keep watch on the skies, then," said Hci.

"Good," I said.

"What are you doing?" asked Hci.

I had uprooted the feather and placed it on the travois, with the bound tarn.

"I am taking the feather," I said. "It may prove useful."

"I do not know if that is wise, Tatankasa," said Hci. He shuddered.

"It is all right," I said. "I have an idea." If Hci were convinced that such a feather was that of the fabled medicine tarn, Wakanglisapa, perhaps others, too, might so regard it.

I checked that the reins of the unbound tarn were bound securely to the right travois pole, looking forward. I then checked the slave's rope, that it was securely bound on the left travois pole, looking forward, and that a similar, uncompromising security was manifested in the neck-knot, at the other end of the rope, under the girl's chin.

"The knots are tight. I am well tethered, Master," she said. When my hands were at the knot she suddenly, desperately, licked and kissed at my wrists. Her eyes looked at me, beseechingly. She lifted her lips to mine. I took her nude, tethered body in my arms. It is glorious to kiss a slave, a woman one owns.

"Let us be on our way, Tatankasa," said Cuwignaka.

"Yes," I said. I disengaged myself from the slave, and slipped into the harness beside Cuwignaka. We would draw the travois together. We did not enter the girl into the harness. We did not wish to be slowed by her shorter steps and lesser strength. I did not doubt, however, that the girl, not having to pull, would be able to keep up with us. If nothing else the neck tether and blows from Hci would see to it.

"Do you see anything, Hci?" asked Cuwignaka.

"No," said Hci.

"You do not believe in Wakanglisapa, do you?" I asked Cuwignaka.

"Sometimes," said Cuwignaka, uneasily, "I do not know what I believe."

"I see," I said.

"There is the feather," said Cuwignaka.

"It is only the feather of a large tarn," I said.

"Something did what it did to the rider, to he of the Kinyanpi," said Cuwignaka.

"That is true," I granted him.

"And it is still out there," said Cuwignaka.

"Somewhere, doubtless," I said.

"It was Wakanglisapa," said Hci.

"Do you see anything?" I asked.

"No," said Hci.

"Then do not worry," I said.

"Tatankasa," said Hci.

"Yes?" I said.

"Leave the feather," said Hci.

"No," I said. I then, followed by Cuwignaka, threw my weight against the harness. The travois moved forward easily. The tarn, even an adult one, is a bird and is light for its bulk.

"One thing puzzles me in this," I said, after a time, to Cuwignaka. "Why would a tarn, if it was a tarn, have attacked a rider in flight. That is extremely unusual."

"It is explained in the legend of Wakanglisapa," said Cuwignaka.

"Tell me," I said.

"It is said that Wakanglisapa prizes his feathers and is jealous of them, for they contain powerful medicine."

"So?" I said.

"Perhaps the rider had found the feather and was carrying it, when Wakanglisapa came to reclaim it."

"I see," I said.

"We did find the feather in the vicinity," said Cuwignaka. "Perhaps it had been dropped by the rider."

"That is possible," I said.

"That is why Hci wanted the feather left behind," said Cuwignaka.

"I see," I said.

"He is afraid that Wakanglisapa may come searching for his feather."

I shivered. "Do you see anything, Hci?" I asked.

"No," he said.

40

IN THE COMPOUND OF THE WANIYANPI

"There is a fire in here," said Pumpkin, from outside of the threshold. "Let me go in first."

Hci, Cuwignaka and I sat behind a fire, in the center of the large, half-sunken, earthen-and-wood lodge of the Waniyanpi. We faced the threshold.

"There may be danger," I heard Radish say, from outside the threshold.

"Do you wish to enter first?" asked Pumpkin.

"No," she said. "No! You enter first."

"I shall," said Pumpkin.

We sat behind the fire, in what, in a lodge of red savages, would be the place of honor.

Mira knelt behind us, in the position of the pleasure slave. I had permitted her clothing, but clothing only of a certain sort.

The lodge in which we waited was not untypical of the communal lodges of the Waniyanpi. It was some fifty feet in diameter, with an earthen bench or projection about the interior edges. Its roof is rounded and slopes upward towards the center. This roof ranges from five to eight feet in height, from the surface level, as opposed to the interior floor level; it is formed of poles covered with sod; it is supported at the edges of the log walls, against which, on the outside, dirt is banked, and by log stanchions arranged in a circle on the floor. At the apex of the lodge is a smoke hole and beneath the smoke hole, at the center of the lodge, is the fire hole. It was in this fire hole that we had built our fire. The smoke hole, incidentally, because of its size, and the size and structure of the lodge, tends to be somewhat inefficient. It is quite different from the smoke holes of the conelike hide lodges common with the red savages which, because of flaps, responsive to the movements of poles, function like efficient, adjustable flues.

There are no windows in the lodges of the Waniyanpi. Even with the fire lit, they are half dark.

"He is coming in," said Cuwignaka.

"Yes," I said.

The lodges of the Waniyanpi, as I have suggested, are communal lodges. The entire community lives within them. One advantage of such lodges, and of communal living, generally, is that it makes it easier to impose social controls on the members of the community. It is natural, accordingly, for certain sorts of authoritarianisms to favor such arrangements. Where there is no place for difference it is natural that difference will have no place. The strongest chains are those a man does not know he wears.

"It is a large man," said Cuwignaka.

"It is Pumpkin," I said.

I despaired, then, for a moment, of my plan. But then, I reminded myself, how insuppressible is man, how tenacious is truth.

"Is it you?" asked Pumpkin, coming forward, blinking against the light of the fire.

"Greetings," I said. "We have made ourselves your guests."

"You are welcome," said Pumpkin, ungainly in his Waniyanpi garb.

"Is it safe?" called Radish, from outside the threshold.

"Yes," said Pumpkin. "Come in."

Pumpkin then saw Mira.

She wore a brief halter of Waniyanpi cloth which, by design, did little to conceal the beauty of her breasts; about her waist a string was tied; two pieces of Waniyanpi cloth, about a foot wide and two feet long, were thrust over and behind the string, one in front and one in back; these two pieces of cloth could be casually jerked loose, if one wished; similarly, the knot, at the left hip, was made so that a mere tug could free it, causing the garment to fall; in this fashion the lower garment may be removed from her a bit at a time or, as a whole, if the master wishes; a similar knot, joining the halter's neck and back strings, could be similarly freed. The slave, accordingly, can be stripped a bit at a time, or almost instantly, as one wishes. Such garments are not unusual for slaves.

Pumpkin stared at Mira, unbelievingly.

"Master?" she asked.

"Is it you—Turnip?" he asked.

"I am Mira," she said, "the slave of Red Bull."

"Are you not Turnip?" he asked.

"I was once Turnip," she said. "I am now no longer Turnip. I am now Mira, the slave of Red Bull."

I had had two major purposes in mind in dressing her as I had. I wished, first, for the Waniyanpi males, and females, too, to see her as she was, as what she was, a slave, an owned woman, one who belonged to men and must please them. Secondly, I wished for them all to see, and see clearly, how beautiful and desirable she was, the lovely slave.

I saw that the Waniyanpi men, and women, too, looked upon her. Some of the Waniyanpi males tried to avert their eyes but, in a moment, gazed eagerly again upon her. She was simply too beautiful and exciting to look away from.

I smiled. The Waniyanpi could not take their eyes from her. She lowered her head, timidly, blushing, startled at suddenly finding herself the object of this attention. The Lady Mira of Venna, the free woman, I speculated, had never found herself looked upon in this fashion, with such awe, with such desire and admiration, with such rapture and pleasure. But then she was not a slave.

"Get her out of here!" screamed Radish. "Can't you see? She is a slave!"

Radish ran about the fire and struck Mira, striking her to her side on the dirt floor. Mira, on her side, cowered at her feet.

"Get out of here!" screamed Radish. "Get out of here! There is no place for such as you here! Get out! You are an animal! Go graze with the verr! Go swill with the tarsk! Get out! Get out!"

Mira, frightened, trying to cover her head, looked to me.

"She does not have my permission to leave," I informed Radish.

"Get out! All of you!" screamed Radish.

"I have bidden them welcome," said Pumpkin.

"I am the leader here!" cried Radish.

"I thought we were all Sames," said Pumpkin.

"Send them away!" cried Radish.

"I have bidden them welcome," said Pumpkin. His voice was not pleasant. Radish, suddenly, frightened, backed away. I think she suddenly realized, perhaps for the first time, explicitly, in her life, what a man such as Pumpkin, with his power, and his will, might do.

"You are welcome," said Pumpkin, turning to us.

"Thank you," I said.

"Tonight," said Pumpkin, "share our kettle."

"That is a Gorean invitation," I said. "Where did you hear it?"

"Many years ago, from a man," said Pumpkin, "one who had not always been of the Waniyanpi."

"What became of him?" I asked.

"He was killed," said Pumpkin, "by Yellow Knives."

"Now," said Carrot, "Yellow Knives are our masters."

"No," said Cuwignaka. "The Kaiila are your masters."

"The Kaiila are gone," said Cabbage. "They are vanquished and scattered."

"They will return," said Cuwignaka, his voice like iron.

We spoke in Gorean. I was just as pleased. This meant that Hci could not follow what was said. It would not have done my plans any good if he had leapt across the fire and thrust his knife into Cabbage's throat.

"Alas," said Pumpkin. "We have only porridge."

"To share the kettle of a friend," I said, "is to dine with a Ubar."

"That, too, is a Gorean saying, isn't it?" asked Pumpkin.

"Yes," I said.

"Let us all sit," said Pumpkin, "saving those whose turn it is to prepare the porridge."

The Waniyanpi, most of them, then gathered about the fire and sat down. They seemed pleased, most of them, that there were guests. An iron rack was brought, from which a kettle was suspended. The fire was built up.

"I will stir for you, Carrot," said a dark-haired girl.

"I will stir for you, Cabbage," said a blond girl.

"It is my turn," said Cabbage.

"Please," said the girl, glancing at Mira.

"Very well," said Cabbage.

"Carrot and Cabbage must then, later, stir twice," said Radish.

"No," said the dark-haired girl.

"No," said the blond-haired girl.

"Do you recall Squash and Strawberry, the two young people who were recently put out of the compound?" I asked Pumpkin.

"Yes," he said, sadly.

"They are safe now," I said, "in a Kaiila camp."

"I am so pleased to hear it!" exclaimed Pumpkin.

"Wonderful!" said several of the Waniyanpi. I saw that they had not truly wanted the young couple, who had been caught touching one another, to die. I had suspected that that would be the case.

"It was Radish who wanted them put out," said Carrot.

"They were caught touching," said Radish, angrily.

"Squash has now taken a Kaiila name," I said, " 'Wayuhahaka', which means 'One-Who-Possesses-Much.' "

"But he possesses little or nothing," said Radish.

"He has found his manhood," I said, "and nothing, ever again, will take it from him."

"That is not a fitting name for a Same," said Radish.

"He is no longer a Same," I said.

"Disgusting," she said.

"He is also learning the bow and the lance," I said to Pumpkin.

"Interesting," he said.

"Strawberry remains Strawberry," I said. "That name, at least at this time, is being kept upon her. He has not yet seen fit to change it."

" 'Being kept upon her'?" asked Radish. " 'He has not yet seen fit to change it'?"

"He found her pleasing," I said. "He has made her his slave."

"His slave!" breathed the dark-haired girl stirring the porridge.

"Yes," I said.

She stopped stirring the porridge.

"Then he can take off her clothes, if he wishes," said the blond girl, pausing in her stirring as well.

"Whether she is clothed or not now," I said, "is completely up to his will."

"He can touch her whenever he wishes?" asked another Waniyanpi woman.

"Of course," I said. "Whenever, however, and for as long as he pleases. And, as she is a slave, she may now wheedle for his caress, and beg for his touch."

"If she is a slave, she must obey him, mustn't she?" asked the dark-haired girl.

"She must obey him perfectly, and in all things," I said.

"Stir the porridge," said Radish.

The two girls again commenced their stirring.

"She is a slave, isn't she?" asked the Waniyanpi woman who had spoken before, she who was not engaged in the stirring, pointing at Mira.

"Yes," I said. Mira lowered her head, modestly.

"Do not look upon her," snapped Radish, "particularly those of you whose garments are of larger sizes!"

"Anyone may look upon her who pleases to do so," said Pumpkin.

Mira blushed. She kept her head down. Pumpkin was right, of course. Slaves, being properties, may be looked upon by anyone who pleases to do so.

"I do not want her here," said Radish, angrily.

"Why not?" I asked.

"She is a slave," said Radish.

"I thought all the Waniyanpi were slaves," I said.

Radish looked at me, angrily.

"To be sure," I said, "the universalization of slavery is its best concealment."

"The porridge is ready," said the dark-haired girl with the spoon.

It was popping and bubbling.

"Let us eat," said Pumpkin.

"What is she doing?" asked Radish, irritably.

"She is serving," I said.

Mira knelt near me, head down, her arms extended, proffering me a bowl of the Waniyanpi porridge.

The porridge had been removed by a hook from the rack and placed on another rack, to the side. The blond girl had brought out wooden bowls and spoons.

"Each here serves themselves, in turn," said Radish.

"Your porridge, Master," said Mira.

"Thank you," I said, taking the porridge.

She then returned to the line, to fetch porridge for Cuwignaka and Hci.

"She is pretty, isn't she?" said the dark-haired girl, she who had shared in the stirring of the porridge, to Carrot. He was watching Mira.

"Yes," he said.

"Am I pretty?" she asked.

"You are not pretty, and you are not ugly," he said. "You are a Same. Sames are not pretty and they are not ugly. They are all the same."

"Oh," she said.

Mira then returned from the porridge kettle and knelt near Cuwignaka. Head down, her arms extended, she proffered him porridge as she had me.

"Thank you," said Cuwignaka.

She then rose up and returned, again, to the line near the kettle.

"She serves well," said Pumpkin.

"Women learn quickly," I told him.

The dark-haired girl and the blond girl, who had shared in the stirring, who were sitting, cross-legged, near Carrot and Cabbage, rose to their feet, going again to the porridge line.

"I have thought about the things we discussed," said Pumpkin. "I have thought about them, many times."

"I had thought you might," I said. Indeed, that was why I had come to the lodge of the Waniyanpi.

Mira returned to our vicinity now and knelt near Hci, proffering him a bowl of porridge as she had to Cuwignaka and me. He took it with one hand. He spoke to her in Kaiila and snapped his fingers. She put her head down to the dirt before him. He spoke again. She kissed the dust before him, humbly. He spoke again and she straightened up and then again lowered her head to the dust before him. He spoke again and she withdrew to her former position where she knelt as before. Again he spoke, and she lowered her head, humbly.

"She obeys with perfection," said Pumpkin.

"How thrilling it would be to be so under the command of a man and to obey him with such perfection," said a Waniyanpi woman, softly, almost to herself.

"Thank you, Hci," said I, in Kaiila.

"Thank you, Hci," said Cuwignaka.

"It is nothing," said Hci.

Hci's lesson had not been lost upon us. Cuwignaka and I, perhaps inadvertently, had been too soft with Mira. The slave who is treated too leniently may begin to forget that she is a slave. It may be necessary, then, to remind her. Beatings can be useful for this purpose.

The two girls who had gone to the porridge line, the dark-haired girl and the blond girl, had returned a bit before, each with their bowl refilled with porridge. They had been in time, standing, watching, to see Mira put through her paces by Hci. They were almost trembling.

The dark-haired girl knelt down near Carrot. "I have brought you some more porridge," she said.

He looked at her, startled.

"Would you like some more?" she asked, timidly.

"Yes," he said, taking her bowl.

"Here," said the blond girl, kneeling down near Cabbage, pressing her bowl of porridge towards him.

"Thank you," he said, startled.

"Each here," snapped Radish, "fetches his own porridge."

"No," said the dark-haired girl.

"No," said the blond girl.

"I think maybe, even though you are a Same, that maybe you are pretty," said Carrot to the dark-haired girl.

"Could you command me," she asked, "as that other girl is commanded?"

"No," he said, "of course not! You are a Same!"

"Oh," she said.

"Do you not have pressing business elsewhere?" Radish asked me.

"No," I said.

"I think it is time that you left our domicile," she said.

"I have not yet finished my porridge," I said.

"Do not be rude, Radish," said Pumpkin. "These are our guests."

Radish tossed her head, which seemed an uncharacteristic, almost feminine gesture for her, and looked away.

I handed the residue of my porridge, in its wooden bowl, back to Mira. I left the spoon beside me. She would not be so stupid as to ask for it. Slaves commonly eat without utensils. The porridge, by now, of course, had cooled.

"If necessary," said Radish, "you can be put out by force."

"I do not think so," I said.

"What do you want here?" she asked. "Why have you come here?"

"Surely the pleasure of sharing a kettle with friends is reason enough," I said.

She glared at me in fury.

Mira had fallen upon the porridge with gusto. She now, with her fingers and tongue, was wiping the bowl clean. She did not eat now as might a rich, free woman, from a golden service with Turian prongs, sumptuously, in some fine house. She ate now as a slave, and was grateful for her feeding.

"I think it is time, now, for you to leave," said Radish, acidly.

I then rose from beside the fire and walked about it, taking a position among several of the Waniyanpi. They drew back, rather in a circle about me.

"To me, Mira," I snapped.

Swiftly she leapt to her feet and hurried about the fire, to stand before me.

She was very beautiful, in her strings and rags.

"Remove your clothing," I told her.

She reached behind her neck, to undo the halter, this action lifting the line of her breasts, beautifully.

A gasp of awe escaped the Waniyanpi.

She reached to the knot at her left hip. A cry of pleasure escaped the Waniyanpi.

The former Lady Mira of Venna now stood before me, a naked slave.

"To my lips, Slave," I said.

She melted into my arms, embracing and kissing me, as a slave into the arms of her master.

"Aiii!" cried several of the men, softly.

"Ohhh," breathed several of the women.

Deeply then did I kiss the slave.

She seemed lost in my touch. She whimpered. She abandoned herself in my arms, surrendering fully, as a slave must, or be beaten, to the master.

"Put them out!" I heard, a screaming as though from faraway. "Put them out!"

I became vaguely aware of the pounding of small fists on my back. Then whoever was doing this was pulled away.

I looked about. Pumpkin, forcibly, was restraining Radish.

"Put them out!" Radish was screaming hysterically. "Put them out!"

The dark-haired girl, then, she who had helped with the stirring of the porridge, slipped suddenly, defiantly, from her garment. The blond girl did so, too. These two, then, were as bared as Mira.

"No!" screamed Radish, looking at them. "No!"

"Yes!" cried the dark-haired girl.

"Yes!" cried the blond girl.

"Put them out!" cried Radish, pointing to the two girls, and to Carrot and Cabbage. "Put them all out!"

"Yellow Knives!" cried a man, near the door.

There was an instant silence in the Waniyanpi lodge. Radish turned pale.

"There are two of them," said the man. "They are at the entrance to the compound."

"What is going on?" Hci asked Cuwignaka.

Cuwignaka spoke briefly to him, and he nodded. Cuwignaka and Hci then stood up. I stepped away from Mira. Cuwignaka, Hci and I exchanged glances. We loosened our weapons. We had not counted on the appearance of Yellow Knives.

"I will see what they want," said Pumpkin. He turned about and left us.

"They will not go away," said Radish. "I know it!"

"What do you think they want?" I asked her.

"I do not know," she said. "Food? Shelter? They make demands on us as they please."

"They take what they want," said a man.

"Am I pretty?" asked the dark-haired girl of Carrot.

"Yes," he said, "oh, yes! You are pretty! You are beautiful!"

"Am I pretty?" asked the blond girl of Cabbage.

"Yes," he said. "You, too, are beautiful!"

"Take me in your arms and put your lips to mine," said the dark-haired girl to Carrot.

"But that would be to touch you!" he said.

"I am naked," she said. "Kiss me, I beg you."

"That is touching!" he whispered.

"I cannot be a woman if you will not be a man," she said.

He took her in his arms and they kissed. The blond girl, too, then, was in the arms of Cabbage.

"You are fools!" said Radish.

Carrot and Cabbage, then, Carrot with his arm about the dark-haired girl and Cabbage with his arm about the blond girl, turned, with the rest of us, to regard the threshold.

It was quiet in the lodge of the Waniyanpi.

I heard the fire crackle in the fire hole.

I glanced at the two girls, one with Carrot, the other with Cabbage.

They had stripped themselves. They were clearly slaves. It was now only a question of who would be their masters. Normally red savages are not interested in Waniyanpi women but I had little doubt that in the case of these two wenches the Yellow Knives would be prepared to make an exception. They were desirable and beautiful; this was not because of their mere nudity but rather, I think, because of something else, something which had taken place within them, something psychological; this might perhaps best be characterized as a surrender to their womanhood; in any event they were now no longer mere Waniyanpi females but prizes and treasures; they were now eminently worthy of having their wrists bound before their bodies and being led behind a master's kaiila. I did not think that the Yellow Knives would see fit to neglect them; only too obviously were they now ready to be put beneath the will of a man. I observed them, and Carrot and Cabbage. I wondered if Carrot and Cabbage would object, if the Yellow Knives entered and, finding the girls of interest, and deciding to take them, tied them and led them away. I supposed not, for they were Waniyanpi males. Then I looked at their eyes. Their eyes were stern. I smiled to myself. Perhaps, after all, they were men.

"They will enter," said Radish. "I know it!"

"You must hide," said a man.

"No," I said.

"If they find you here, they will kill you," said a man.

"No," I said. "If they find us here, it is they who will die."

"You must leave!" said Radish.

"No," I said.

"It is not just you who are in danger," said Radish. "Do you not understand? They will think that we have welcomed you!"

"You have," I said. "The meal was superb. Thank you."

"They may not just want to kill you," she said. "They may wish to kill us all!"

"Perhaps," I said.

"You must leave," she said. "Your presence here jeopardizes us all!"

"I do not think so," I said.

"Leave!" said Radish.

"You cannot expect them to just walk out," said a man. "What about the Yellow Knives?"

"Perhaps they could escape out the back," said a man. "Digging out, under the logs."

"I do not think there is time for that," said another.

"Too," said another, "it might be difficult to conceal the signs of such an escape, so quickly."

"True," agreed another.

"You are right!" cried Radish. "If they are caught leaving, or if signs of their escape are found, it will be clear to the Yellow Knives, in either case, that they were here."

"That seems true," said a man.

"There is a chance!" said Radish.

The Waniyanpi regarded her, with interest.

"There is only one thing to do!" she said. "I see it now, clearly!"

"What is that?" asked a man.

"Seize them," she cried, wildly, pointing at us. "Seize them!"

No one moved.

"Seize them!" she cried. "Do you want to die? Do you want to be killed? Seize them!"

"Why?" asked a man.

"I do not want to die!" she cried. "I do not want to be killed by Yellow Knives!"

The Waniyanpi looked at one another.

"Seize them, bind them!" she cried.

"Why?" asked a man.

"That they may be turned over to Yellow Knives, you fool!" she cried. "We can pretend that we have captured them. We were only waiting for Yellow Knives to come to the compound, that we might deliver them to them!"

"The Yellow Knives would kill them," said a man.

"Yes," said Radish, "but we would be spared! We would be alive! Do you not see? It is our only chance!"

"We will not do this," said a man.

"Carrot," said Radish, "seize them."

"No," said Carrot.

"Cabbage," said Radish, "seize them!"

"No," said Cabbage.

"I command it!" cried Radish.

"No," said Carrot.

"No," said Cabbage.

"Someone is coming!" said a man near the threshold.

Hci went to one side of the threshold. Cuwignaka went to the other. I remained where I was. They drew their knives.

"Do not strike!" I said to them.

Pumpkin stood in the threshold. He carried a feathered lance. I recognized it. It was one of two which the Waniyanpi had retrieved in the area of the battle, some weeks ago, between the soldiers and the savages. Apparently this lance, at least, had been saved. I was startled to see it again. I had not realized that the Waniyanpi would have kept it.

The point of the lance was bloody.

"Where are the Yellow Knives?" asked Radish.

"I slew them," said Pumpkin.

"You slew them!" she cried, in horror.

"Yes," he said.

"You are insane!" she cried.

"Where is the other lance?" Pumpkin asked Carrot.

"Hidden, near the edge of the maize field," said Carrot.

"I thought so," said Pumpkin. "In the morning, fetch it."

"I will," said Carrot. The dark-haired girl, stripped, trembling, held Carrot's arm, tightly.

"You did not truly slay the Yellow Knives, did you?" asked Radish.

"Yes," said Pumpkin. "I did."

"You are insane!" she cried. "You are insane!"

He regarded her, evenly, not speaking.

"We are doomed," she said. "We are all doomed!"

"Take off your clothes," he said.

She looked at him, speechless.

"Completely," he said.

"Never!" she cried.

"Now," he said.

I noted that the other Waniyanpi women, other than the two who had already stripped themselves, removed their clothing. Radish looked wildly about. Then she looked to the bloody point of the feathered lance. Then she looked into the eyes of Pumpkin. She shuddered. She saw that he would not brook disobedience.

"Good," said Pumpkin.

I saw that Radish, as I had once conjectured, was, all things considered, not a bad-looking woman. Indeed, all things considered, she was rather attractive.

"I am the leader!" she said.

"Turn about, slowly, and then again face me," he said. "Good," he said. I saw that Radish, indeed, was an attractive woman.

I saw then that the Waniyanpi males were examining the

other women as well. Some they had turn before them; some were, by the arms, forcibly turned about, for inspection; in the case of others the males themselves walked about the women, and the women knew themselevs being boldly beheld and appraised. This gave great joy to the men. I think that many of them, never before, had realized how soft and beautiful, how desirable, are women.

"Pumpkin!" protested Radish, tears in her eyes.

"I am not a vegetable," he said. "I am no longer Pumpkin."

"I do not understand," said Radish.

"I am taking a new name," he said. "I am taking the name 'Seibar'. I am now Seibar." 'Seibar', incidentally, is a common Gorean name. It was the surname, for example, of a slaver in Kailiauk. Too, I had known two people in Ar by that name.

"Pumpkin!" she said.

"I am Seibar," he said.

"That is not a Waniyanpi name," she said.

"True," he said.

"This is insolence," she said. "This is insubordination! Let me put on my clothing, quickly!"

"Whether or not you wear clothing," he said, "is my decision, and I will decide the matter if, when and how I please."

"I am the leader!" she cried.

"Kneel," he said.

One by one the Waniyanpi women knelt. Radish watched them in misery.

"Now," said Seibar.

Radish knelt. She looked well at his feet.

"I am the leader!" she cried.

"No," he said. "You are only a woman."

"We are all Sames!" she cried.

"No," he said. "You are a woman. I am a man. We are not the same."

"The Teaching!" she cried. "Remember the Teaching!"

"The Teaching is false," he said. "Surely you have known that. Surely you have used it long enough, for whatever reasons, to subvert, deny and hide your sex."

"No," she said. "No!"

"But now, no longer will you betray and conceal your sex. You will now, henceforth, objectively and openly, be what you are, a woman."

"No!" she cried.

"Your lies, your subterfuges, your pretenses, are at an end."

"No," she wept.

"You will, henceforth, acknowledge your sex and be true to it. You will, henceforth, without deception, without qualification, in your thoughts, and in your most secret thoughts, and in your deportment, behavior and appearance, dare to express, and express, your full femaleness, totally and honestly."

"No, no," she wept.

"Henceforward," he said, "you will be precisely what you are, a woman."

"Please, no," she said.

"I have said it," said Seibar.

"Please," she wept. "Please, please."

"It has been said," he said.

She put down her head, shuddering.

"Naturally, there are sanctions attached to this command," he said.

"I understand," she said.

"And I do not think disobedience will be difficult to detect," he said.

She nodded. An expression, a gesture, even a tone of voice or a tiny movement, might reveal reservation or disobedience. Safety, in such a situation, inasmuch as it lay anywhere, surely lay in abject and total compliance, beginning with interior submission, and issuing then in appropriate behaviors. Radish would no longer be permitted to suppress her womanhood. She must now reveal it, and in an uncompromising and authentic fashion. It had been decided by Seibar.

"What are you?" asked Seibar.

"I am a woman," said Radish. There were tears in her eyes. She half choked on the words.

"Ohhh," said one or two of the Waniyanpi women, softly, thrilled, hearing Radish's admission.

Seibar handed the lance he held to Carrot, who placed it against the wall. He then, with a strap, crouched down, before Radish.

"What are you doing?" she asked.

He tied the strap about her right ankle and then, leaving her about six inches of slack, tied it also about her left ankle. He then took the strap up, and forward, between her legs, where, crossing her wrists, he proceeded to bind them together, tightly, before her body. He jerked shut the last knot, decisively. "Binding you," he said.

She tested the tight, flat leather circles confining her wrists, a small movement, one not intended to be observed. She turned white. She knew herself helpless.

"On your feet, woman," said Seibar, hauling her by an arm to her feet.

She could not stand straight, as he had left her only some eighteen inches of strap between her left ankle and her bound wrists.

"Go to the men in this room and tell them what you are," said Seibar.

Radish, bent over, with short steps, those of a length permitted her by her leather shackles, made her way to Carrot. She looked up at him, tears in her eyes. "I am a woman," she said.

"Yes," said Carrot.

"I am a woman," said Radish to Cabbage.

"Yes," said Cabbage.

At last Radish stood before me. "I am a woman," she wept.

"That is easy to see," I said.

Seibar then, by the arm, led her to an open place in the lodge.

Suddenly she broke loose from him and turned about, almost falling. She pulled futilely at the straps. "I am not a woman!" she screamed. "I am not a woman!"

Seibar, slowly, began to wrap leather straps about his right hand, that he might have them firmly in his grip. The ends of these straps, of which there were five, dangled then from his fist, some two feet or so in length. He approached Radish. She regarded him in terror. He swung the straps slowly before her eyes. She regarded them, almost as though mesmerized.

"I lied," she said. "I am a woman. I am truly a woman!"

"Kneel," he said.

Radish lost no time in falling to her knees.

"You have been arrogant and pretentious," he said.

"She has had people put out of the compound," said a man.

"She wanted us to bind our guests and turn them over to Yellow Knives," said another man.

"She has pretended to be a man!" said another man.

"She has betrayed her sex," said another man.

"No," said Radish. "No!"

"And you have tried to weaken, to reduce and destroy true manhood," said Seibar.

"No," she cried. "No!"

"Men are now no longer tolerant of this," said Seibar. "They have had enough."

"I meant no harm!" cried Radish.

"We are rising," said a man.

"Yes!" said another. "Yes!" said another. "Yes!" said another.

Radish looked wildly about. Then, again, she looked at Seibar.

"We are choosing, you see, my dear Radish," said Seibar, "to reassert our natural sovereignty. The experiment in perversion, falsehood and disease is done. Now, again, we will be men."

"Seibar!" she wept.

"Yes!" cried the men.

"Surely you have feared that this might one day happen," he said.

She looked at him, wildly.

"Put your head to the dust," he said.

She did so. She trembled. "I am a woman!" she cried. "I am a woman!"

"And one who has not been pleasing," said Seibar.

Then he lashed her, and well.

Then, in a few moments, she lay on her side at his feet, bound, sobbing, marked, disciplined.

At a sign from Seibar Carrot and Cabbage lifted her to her feet. They held her in place. She looked out at Seibar, through her hair and the tears in her eyes. She could not stand.

"Put her out," said Seibar, "as she did others."

"No," she wept. "No!"

"Do not fear," said Seibar. "I will have them remove your bonds once you are hurled beyond the gate. You will then have the same opportunities for survival which you have accorded others."

"Seibar, please, no!" she wept.

"Only then will the gate be closed against you," he said.

"Please, no!" she wept. She struggled, hysterically. "Let me kneel!" she begged Carrot and Cabbage.

At a sign from Seibar they permitted her to fall to her knees.

"I beg to be shown mercy," she said.

"The same mercy which you have shown others?" asked Seibar.

"No," she wept, "true mercy!"

"Why should it be shown to you," he asked, "as it was not to them?"

She put down her head, sobbing. For this she had no answer.

"We shall open the gate," said a man.

"Beloved Mira," cried Radish, looking at Mira, wildly, "what shall I do?"

Mira shrank back, startled. "I am only a slave," she said. "You are a free woman."

"What shall I do?" she begged, tearfully.

"You have but one slim chance," said Mira.

"Speak," begged Radish.

"The only avenue of escape which lies open before you," said Mira, "is too debasing and degrading. I dare not even mention it to you."

"Speak, speak!" begged Radish.

"Sue to be his slave," said Mira. "As a wholly submitted woman, one he owns, he may be disposed to show you mercy."

"I do not know what to do," wept Radish.

"If you are a free woman," said Mira, "go nobly forth into the Barrens, there to perish of hunger or thirst, or of animals or exposure. If you are a slave, sue to be his slave."

"I do not know what to do!" she wept.

"Do what is in your heart," said Mira.

"Beg mercy for me, plead for me, intercede for me!" begged Radish.

Mira came and knelt before Seibar, her head down. "Have mercy upon us, Master," she said. "We are only women, one bond and one free. We know your strength. We know what you can do. We do not dispute your sovereignty. We beg for mercy, if only for a time. We beg for kindness, if only for a moment."

"Your slave speaks eloquently," said Seibar.

"She has experienced the might of men, and knows what they can do," I said.

The woman in the leather shackles, then, with her wrists bound before her body, suddenly sobbed, and shook with ungovernable, overwhelming emotion. The movement, like a shudder, had been unrestrained, uncontrollable. Something deep and profound had obviously occurred within her. "Yes," she whispered to herself. "Yes!"

She put her head down and, unbidden, tenderly, submissively, softly, began to kiss the feet of Seibar.

"Look up," said Seibar.

She lifted her head. Her eyes were moist. They were incredibly soft and tender. I think that never before had she seen Seibar like that.

"And doubtless you, too, subscribe to the discourse of this slave," said Seibar, indicating Mira.

"With but one exception, yes," said the leather-bound woman.

"Oh?" asked Seibar.

"She is mistaken in one detail," she said.

"What is that?" asked Seibar.

"She said that there were two women who knelt before you, one bond and one free. In this she was in error. There were two women who knelt before you, but one was not bond and one free. Both were bond."

Mira, tears in her eyes, suddenly seized the woman bound beside her, and kissed her.

I took Mira by the hair and threw her to the side.

"Yes," said the leather-bound woman looking up at Seibar. "I am bond."

"Beware of the words you speak," said Seibar. This was true. Such words, in themselves, in the appropriate context, effected enslavement. Intention, and such, is immaterial, for one might always maintain that one had not meant them, or such. The words themselves, in the appropriate context, are sufficient. Whether one means them or not one becomes, in their utterance, instantly, categorically and without recourse, fully and legally a slave, something with which masters are then entitled to do with as they please. Such words are not to be spoken lightly. They are as meaningful as the collar, as significant as the brand.

"The words I speak, I speak knowingly," she said.

"Speak clearly," he said.

"I herewith proclaim myself a slave," she said. "I am a slave."

"You are now a slave," I said to her, "even in the cities. You are a property. You could be returned to a master as such in a court of law. This is something which is recognized even outside of the Barrens. This is much stronger, in that sense, than being the slave of Kaiila or Yellow Knives."

"I know," she said.

Seibar looked down upon her.

"I am now a legal slave," she said.

He nodded. It was true.

"A few moments ago," she said, "I for the first time confessed myself to myself a slave, a confession which I now acknowledge and make public. For years I had known that I was a slave, but I had denied this, and fought it. Then, suddenly, I no longer wanted to fight this. When we fight ourselves it is only ourselves which must lose. In that moment I surrendered to my secret truth. What I have done now is little more than to proclaim and make public that secret truth. Beyond that admission there lies little more than the effectuation of a technicality."

"But the technicality has now been effectuated," said Seibar.

"Yes," she said, putting her head down, "it has now been effectuated."

"Whose slave are you?" he asked.

"You have stripped me, and bound me, as a slave," she said. "I have felt your lash. I am yours."

"Have I collared you?" he asked.

"No," she said, keeping her head down, "but it is my hope that you will do so."

"Have I indicated any interest in having you as a slave?" he asked. "Have I given you any reason to believe that I might accept you as a slave?"

"No," she said, keeping her head down, "you haven't."

"Whose slave would you be?" he asked.

"Yours," she said.

"Speak," he said.

She raised her head, but did not meet his eyes. "I am Seibar's slave," she said.

"Now, perhaps I will give you to another," he said.

She still did not meet his eyes. "It may be done with me as you please," she said.

"Do you think I do not understand," he said, angrily, "that you have made yourself my slave in the hope that you might thereby escape the fate of being out into the Barrens?"

"Whatever might have been my motivation," she said, "the fact remains, in any case, that I am now fully your slave, and may be done with wholly as you wish."

"You had your chance to go nobly into the Barrens, with

the dignity of the free woman. Now perhaps I shall have you put out in shame, in the dishonor of a slave!"

"You may do with me as you please," she said, softly.

"Would that not be amusing?" he asked angrily.

"Yes," she said, "very amusing." She looked at him, with tears in her eyes. "If I am to be put out," she said, "may I beg one boon."

"What is that?" he asked.

"Your collar," she said. "Put it on my neck. Tie some knot in it which is yours, so that if men find me they may say, 'Here, see this knot. It is Seibar's. This woman was his slave.' "

"You ask for my collar?" he said.

"I beg it," she said.

He took one of the straps he had used in her whipping. He looped it twice about her neck and tied it.

"You have it," he said.

"Thank you," she whispered.

She then lifted her head to his, where he crouched down before her, and tried to touch her lips to his. Her small hands moved futilely in their bonds, at her knees.

He did not permit her lips to touch his. "That would be touching, would it not?" he asked, ironically.

"Yes," she whispered.

"How clever you are!" he said, angrily. "What a sly, scheming, shameless she-sleen you are!"

"How you must hate me," she said.

"Do you think I cannot see through your games, your trickery?" he cried.

"Do you think it is only because I do not want to die?" she wept. "Do you think it is only because I do not want to be put out into the Barrens?"

"Yes!" he said.

"No," she said. "No!"

"No?" he asked.

"No!" she wept.

"Speak," he said, angrily. "I grow weary."

"But I am a slave," she said, frightened. She looked at me, pleadingly, for understanding.

"Accordingly, miserable, imbonded slut," I said, "you must speak the truth."

She put down her head. She squirmed in her bonds.

"Much a command be repeated?" asked Seibar.

She lifted her head, tears in her eyes. "I am a slave," she

said, "and I must tell the truth. Forgive me, I beg you. Forgive me. Beat me if you wish."

"Yes?" said Seibar.

"I want your touch," she said. "I beg it!"

"Shameless slave," he chided.

"As a slave may be, and should be," she said.

He regarded her, not speaking.

"For two years," she said, "I have wanted to be your slave, to be subject to your will, to be owned by you, to be yours, fully. I have dreamed of your touch, and, if it should please you, your lash."

"Lying slave," he snarled.

"I want to obey you," she said.

"Lying slave!" he said.

"I love you," she said.

"Liar!" he cried.

"Alas," she said, "how can I convince you?"

"You cannot!" he cried.

"Of course not," she said, "if you will not permit it."

"Put your hands on her body," I said.

Siebar put his hands on her body.

"I love you," she said.

I touched her. "She speaks the truth," I said.

"I love you," she said. "Kiss me. Then put me out, if you wish. I will then go gladly, if it be your will."

He kissed her. I smiled. Then, with a cry of rage, of frustration, he struck her across the mouth. She then lay on her side on the dirt floor.

"Do you think she speaks the truth?" he asked.

"Yes," I said. "If I were you, I would give her a trial. See if she works out. If she does not prove satisfactory, she may always, then, be put out."

Seibar kicked the girl, with the side of his foot. "What is your name?" he asked.

"I have no name," she said.

"It is a fitting response," I said.

"A slave's response?" asked Seibar.

"Yes," I said.

"Do you think she is truly a slave?" asked Seibar.

"Yes," I said, "that is obvious. It is now only a question of whether or not you have any interest in her."

Seibar looked down at her.

"What is a fitting name for a slave?" he asked.

" 'Tuka'," I said. "That is not a bad name." 'Tuka' is a

common slave name on Gor. It is simple, sensuous and luscious. Most masters have probably known one or more girls with that name.

"You are Tuka," said Seibar, naming her.

"I am Tuka," she whispered, happily, named.

"Kneel," said Seibar. The girl struggled to her knees. She looked up at him. There was love in her eyes. He looked down at her, an incredible tenderness in his countenance. I saw that he must guard against weakness. But I felt sure that he would do so. Only too well would he be aware of the penalties and consequences attached to weakness, consequences ultimately tragic for the welfare of both sexes.

"Shall I open the gate?" asked a man.

"No," said Seibar. "The slave, at least for a time, will be kept."

The men and women in the lodge let out a cheer. Mira rushed to Tuka and kissed her.

"Well done," I said to Seibar.

"I am a slave. I am your slave," said the dark-haired girl kneeling before Carrot.

"I am a slave. I am your slave," said the blonde, kneeling before Cabbage.

One by one the Waniyanpi women, timidly, beautifully, knelt before various men, imbonding themselves to these new masters.

I hoped they knew well what they were doing, for they were then slaves.

Men and women, crying out with pleasure, with tears, in floods of emotion, kissed, and touched one another, and loved.

"We can take the bodies of the Yellow Knives away," said Cuwignaka to Seibar. "We will cut them up and leave them on the prairie. No one, thusly, will know that they met their end here."

"That will be helpful," said Seibar.

"Thusly, too," I said, "you may then return to being Waniyanpi, if you wish."

Seibar looked about. "We will fortify the compound," he said. "We will never again be Waniyanpi."

"There is always time to be a coward," I said.

"We have tasted manhood," said Seibar. "We will never go back. We will now die, or be men."

"It might be well, for a time," I said, "to express your

manhod only within the secrecy of your own lodge. It might be well, for a time, to pretend to be still Waniyanpi."

Seibar smiled.

"I have a plan," I said.

"I did not think that your visit here was one of a purely social nature," he said.

"Free your slave of her bonds," I suggested. "You will, anyway, later tonight, not want her ankles so closely tied. She may then serve us, while we talk."

"You would speak before slaves?" he asked.

"Of course," I said. "They are only slaves."

"Masters?" asked Tuka, kneeling, holding the tray. We took the fried maize cakes from the tray. Then the tray was empty, save for one object, a segment of a dried root, about two to three inches long and a half inch wide.

"Open your mouth," said Seibar to Tuka.

She did so immediately, unquestioningly.

"This is for you," he said.

She nodded.

He broke the root in two and thrust it in her mouth. "Chew it well," he said, "and swallow it, every particle."

She nodded.

"Open your mouth," he said.

She did so. The sip root, every bit of it, was gone.

"You may now take the tray away, and then return," he said.

"Yes, Master," she said, happily.

Mira had shown her how to kneel, lower her head and proffer the tray, properly. Tuka, I saw, would be an apt pupil in bondage. Slaves learn quickly. They are beaten if they do not.

"And those," I said, "are the details of my plan."

"It is bold and simple," he said.

"You see the significance of your role?" I asked.

"Yes," he said.

"You understand, of course," asked Cuwignaka, "that there is great danger in this?"

"But for all of us," said Seibar.

"Yes," said Cuwignaka.

"You honor us with such responsibility," said Seibar.

"Rewards, I assure you," said Cuwignaka, "will be commensurate with risk."

"We have received our manhood," said Seibar. "That is reward enough."

The slave then returned to our area and knelt down, closely, behind Seibar.

"You are then with us?" I asked.

"I am," he said. We then clasped hands.

"Let us rehearse these details again," I said. "There must be no mistake."

"Very well," he said.

As we spoke the slave, apparently unable to control herself, and not struck back or disciplined, began, at first timidly, then more boldly, to kiss and fondle Seibar. Soon she began to gasp and pant, pressing herself against him. At last he took her in his arms and put her on her back, across his legs. Her body was then like a bow, her head down on one side, in the dust, and her heels on the other side. "Keep your hands back, over your head," he said. "Yes, Master," she whimpered. He then, as we talked, caressed her. Soon her hands were clenching and unclenching and she was whimpering, writhing helplessly. Then, mercifully, he lifted her up by the shoulders and she put her head against his chest, her arms about his neck. Her eyes were wide. She squirmed, almost in shock, astounded, unable to believe the sensations she felt in her body.

"I think the plans are clear," I said.

"Yes," said Seibar.

"We must be on our way," I said.

We stood up. "You may kiss the feet of our guests, Tuka," said Seibar.

"Yes, Master," she said.

"Do not be weak with her," I said.

"I will not," he said. I smiled. I saw that it was true.

"Tuka," said Seibar, "fetch what was once your blanket and put it with mine, on the shelf, by the wall, where I sleep."

"Yes, Master!" she said. I smiled. I saw that Tuka, at least, would not be tied by the neck, out in the yard for the night.

Seibar and I again clasped hands, sealing our bargain.

"I have done as you wished," said Tuka, returning, dropping to her knees before her master.

"I am weary," said Seibar. "I think I will tie your ankles together."

"Please do not tie them together, Master," she said.

"Very well," he said. He then indicated that she should rise and she did so. He then lifted her in his arms. She kissed at him eagerly.

"I wish you well," I said.

"I wish you all well," he said.

We then, Hci, Cuwignaka, Mira and myself, took our leave. I did look back once, to see Seibar placing Tuka gently on the blankets in his sleeping place, on the dirt shelf, near the log-and-dirt wall.

They seemed oblivious of their surroundings. They were absorbed in one another. They were master and slave.

41

HCI WILL COME WITH US

"I tell you it exists!" exclaimed Hci.

"Did you see it?" I asked.

"No," he said. "Mira saw it."

"She is only a slave," I said.

The girl, near the lodge at Two Feathers, amidst trees, knelt, trembling.

"You were gone," she said, shuddering, "with Cuwignaka and Canka, training tarns. It came like a great, black thing, screaming. Leaves were torn from the trees in its passage!"

"It is gone now," I said.

"It is real, Tatankasa," said Hci. "Make no mistake about it. It exists!"

"It is only a tarn," I said.

"It is Wakanglisapa," said Hci, "the medicine tarn."

"I do not believe in the medicine world," I said. "I do not think it exists."

"It is following us," said Hci. "It is looking for its feather."

"That is absurd," I said.

"Get rid of the feather," said Hci. "Return it to the Barrens. Throw it away. Burn it. It is dangerous!"

"We may have need of it," I said.

"Get rid of it!" said Hci.

"It is only a feather," I said.

"Than the feather of Wakanglisapa there is no medicine more dangerous or powerful," said Hci. "That is why he has come looking for it."

"The medicine tarn does not exist," I said.

"She saw it," said Hci, pointing to Mira. Mira was half white with fear.

"It was only a tarn," I said.

"It was Wakanglisapa, the medicine tarn," said Hci. "He is angry." He looked at the sky, apprehensively. The moons were now out. White clouds scudded across the sky.

"I see no signs of a tarn now," I said.

"He has followed us," said Hci.

"It is probably a different tarn," I said.

"It is Wakanglisapa, the medicine tarn," said Hci.

"You are one of the bravest men I have ever known, Hci," I said. "How can you think in this way? How can you act like this?"

"You know more of tarns than I, Tatankasa," he said. "Do tarns behave in this fashion?"

"No," I admitted, "not normally."

"Then it is no ordinary tarn," said Hci.

"I do not know," I said. "Perhaps not."

"Do you not remember the warrior of the Kinyanpi?" he asked.

"Yes," I said. I shuddered.

"That could only have been the work of Wakanglisapa," said Hci.

"Wakanglisapa does not exist," I said.

"I am not afraid of men," said Hci. "I am not afraid of what I can see. I am not afraid of what I can fight."

"I understand," I said.

"Do these things seem normal to you?" asked Hci.

"No," I said.

"Do they not seem strange?" asked Hci.

"Yes," I admitted.

"Do you understand them?" asked Hci.

"No," I said, "not really, certainly not fully."

"Get rid of the feather," said Hci.

"No," I said.

"Get rid of it," he said.

"I do not believe in the medicine world," I said. "I do not think it exists."

"I know the medicine world exists," said Hci.

"How do you know that?" I asked.

"Once," said he, "I grievously lied. Later, in battle, my shield betrayed me. It would not obey me. I could not control it. It refused to protect me. Of its own will it rose, exposing me to the lance of my enemy."

"We know what happened," I said. "What we do not know, really, is why it happened. Such things are not absolutely unknown, even to the physicians in the cities. There are technical names for them. They are still not well understood. Often their causes are deep and mysterious."

"The shield rose," said Hci.

"The shield cannot rise by itself," I said. "It was your arm that rose."

"I did not lift my arm," said Hci.

"Such movements, over which we have no control," I said, "are sometimes connected with such things as guilt, and a conviction of the fittingness of certain behaviors. They result from undetected occurrences in the brain. It is like one part of you at war with another part. They seem to occur by themselves. They can be frightening."

"The shield rose, like a moon," said Hci.

"Doubtless it seemed so," I said.

"It rose," said Hci, "as firmly and inexorably as a moon."

"We understand things in various contexts of belief," I said. "When something happens it might be interpreted one way in one context of belief and in another way in another context of belief."

"This is hard to understand," said Hci.

"That is because you are thoroughly familiar with only one context of belief," I said, "your own. Thus, you are not accustomed to draw a distinction between what is to be interpreted, so to speak, and its interpretation. These two things tend, then, in your understanding to merge into only one, in this case that your shield betrayed you."

"It did," said Hci.

"Look up," I said. "See the moons?"

"Yes," he said.

"Do you not see how they fly through the sky?"

"It is the clouds moving in the wind," said Hci, "going the other way. That is why it makes the moons look like they are moving."

"Look again," I said.

Hci again regarded the sky.

"Can you see the moons flying?" I asked.

"Yes," he said, after a time. "I can see it that way."

"You see," I said, "there are many ways to understand what we see."

"I understand," said Hci. "Are all explanations of equal merit?"

"No," I said. "Most are presumably false."

"How do we know when we have the one true explanation?" asked Hci.

"I suppose we can never be absolutely certain," I said, "that of all the theoretically possible explanations, all explanations which would respond effectively to all conceivable tests, all explanations which would agree in explaining phenomena and in yielding predictions, that we have the one true explanation."

"That is interesting," said Hci.

"That we cannot prove that an explanation is absolutely correct does not, of course, entail that it is not correct."

"I understand that," said Hci.

"We can sometimes be rationally certain of the correctness of an explanation," I said, "so certain that it would be foolish not to accept it."

"I understand," said Hci.

"Good," I said.

"Do you know the medicine world does not exist?" asked Hci.

"I do not think it exists," I said.

"Do you know it does not exist?" asked Hci.

"No," I said. "I do not know that it does not exist."

"Perhaps it exists," said Hci.

"Perhaps," I said. "I do not know."

"You do not believe it exists," said Hci.

"No," I said.

"I do believe it exists," he said.

"I understand," I said.

"Perhaps, then," he said, "it is your explanation which is false, not mine."

"Perhaps," I said.

"This is the Barrens," he said.

"That is true," I said.

"Perhaps things are not the same here as in your country," he said.

"Perhaps," I said. I supposed it was an act of faith that nature was uniform, surely an act of rational faith, but an act of faith, nonetheless. The universe was surely vast and mysterious. It was perhaps under no obligation to conform to our preferences. If it did seem congenial to our limitations perhaps this was because we could experience it only within these same limitations. We might unknowingly live in the midst of dimensions and wonders, things beyond the touch of our tools, things beyond the reach of our imaginations and intellects, things too different to know. Yet what bold, gallant mice we are. How noble is man.

"You are determined to keep the feather?" asked Hci.

"Yes," I said. "Are you coming with us tonight?"

"Wakanglisapa can bring ruin to all our plans," he said.

"Nonsense," I said. "Are you coming with us?" I asked.

"Yes," he said.

"We must start soon," I said.

"I must do something first," he said.

"What is that?" I asked.

"Sing my death song," he said.

42

THE SKY SEEMS CLEAR BEHIND ME

"Hurry!" I cried, on tarnback. "Hurry!"

"It is no use!" cried Hci, a few yards away, on tarnback, some two hundred yards above the rolling grasslands beneath us. On my right, urging his tarn ahead, was Cuwignaka.

"They are gaining!" cried Hci. "They will catch us!" It was now half of an Ahn past dawn.

I looked back, over my shoulder. Five riders, men of the Kinyanpi, pursued us, relentlessly. We heard their whooping behind us.

We were slowed by the lines we held. Behind each of us, strung together by neck ropes, swept five tarns. The Kinyanpi hobble lines had not been well guarded. In the vicinity of a Yellow-Knife camp, their allies, amongst tribes unfamiliar with tarns, they had feared nothing. We did not expect that such laxity would be repeated in the future.

A white female slave, one whipped from a Yellow-Knife lodge, had seen us. She had given the alarm. Ironically, in the moonlight, I had recognized her. She was a short-legged, luscious blonde, a former American. Her name, when Grunt had owned her, when she had been a member of his coffle, had been Lois. She, with three others, Inez, Corinne and Priscilla, had been taken from Grunt by Yellow Knives in the vicinity of the field where the battle had taken place between a coalition of red savages and the soldiers of Alfred, the mercenary captain from Port Olni. Sleen, at the same time, had taken two others of Grunt's girls, Ginger and Evelyn, and his two male prisoners, Max and Kyle Hobart, the latter presumably to serve as boys, given such duties as watching over kaiila. Another girl, too, at the same time, had been taken from Grunt, the former debutante from Pennsylvania, once Miss Millicent Aubrey-Welles, a girl he had planned to sell to Mahpiyasapa, civil chieftain of the Isbu Kaiila, for five hides of the yellow kailiauk. This girl, however, had not been taken by Yellow Knives or Sleen; she had been taken by a Kaiila warrior, Canka; she was now Winyela, his slave. When the luscious, short-legged blonde had seen us, she who had been Lois when wearing a collar of iron in Grunt's coffle, she had turned about and fled back among the lodges, screaming, spreading the alarm. I did not think that she recognized us but, even if she had, she would still have done what she did. Slave girls on Gor obey their masters with perfection.

"We have as many tarns as we can well handle now," I had said to Cuwignaka and Hci, slipping the noose over the head of the last tarn. "Let us go!"

We would have preferred to walk the tarns a bit from the camp, before taking to flight, but we had not time, the camp being roused, to do so. Accordingly we swiftly took to flight, the screaming of the birds, the smiting of their wings, serving further to alert the camp, both Yellow Knives and Kinyanpi. Too, doubtless we were well seen in flight, against the moons.

It seemed we had hardly seen the camp fall away beneath us but what red tarnsmen were aflight, plying their pursuit in our hurried wake. Five came first and behind these, I did not doubt, would swarm others.

"We cannot outdistance them!" cried Hci.

I again looked over my shoulder. They were even closer now.

"Come closer!" I cried to Hci. I then, as he did so, hurled the line I carried to him, it falling across the back of his tarn where he seized it, wrapping it about his fist.

"I am turning back!" I cried. "Go on without me!"

"We will release the tarns!" cried Cuwignaka.

"No!" I said.

"We will turn with you to fight them!" called Hci.

"No!" I said. "Conduct the tarns to camp! We must have them!"

"No!" cried Cuwignaka.

"You will not risk all!" I said. "You will continue on your way!"

"Tatankasa!" cried Cuwignaka.

"The Kaiila must live!" I said.

"Tatankasa!" cried Hci.

"I have a plan!" I said. "Go! Go!" Then, remonstrating no further with them, I swung the tarn about. I jerked back on the reins, then held them back. Beating its mighty wings the bird hung almost motionless in the air, its back a steep line. From beneath the girth rope I drew forth an object which I had placed there, which had been pressed between the girth rope and the body of the tarn. It was the large black feather which I had obtained in the vicinity of the tarn pit, days ago, that feather the possession of which had so distressed my friend, Hci. I brandished it over my head, grasping it in the middle, like a spear or banner.

That feather, I had hoped, would be even more meaningful, more terrifying, to the Kinyanpi than to Hci.

It was a feather of a sort with which I thought they, the Kinyanpi, might be even too familiar.

Belief in the medicine world, I hoped, would hold as potent a sway over the minds of the Kinyanpi as it seemed to over the minds of so many of the red savages, friends and foes alike.

The leader of the Kinyanpi, when some fifty yards from my tarn, suddenly drew back on the reins of his tarn, and held it in a hovering position. His fellows joined him. He pointed at me. They shouted among themselves, over the beating of the birds' wings.

I held the feather up, prominently, almost brandishing it. I wanted them to make no mistake about it.

I did not reach for weapons. What need had he of weapons who controlled the medicine of Wakanglisapa? And what medicine or weapons might hope to prevail against it?

Unfortunately, when the leader had drawn back his tarn he had seemed to do so more in surprise than fear. It was more as though he had been taken unawares than frightened. I had hoped they would all retreat in terror. Unfortunately, they were not doing so.

The birds, wings snapping and striking, their backs almost vertical, the men leaning forward on them, were an impressive sight.

I rejoiced in one thing. Each moment was precious. Cuwignaka and Hci, each moment, were speeding farther and farther away.

I then, to my dismay, saw the five riders freeing their weapons. It was clearly their intention to attack.

They were brave men.

Too, I had perhaps miscalculated. If the feather was not that of Wakanglisapa they would assume they had nothing to fear. If it was the feather of Wakanglisapa, then why should they not attempt to capture it, to secure its mighty medicine for themselves?

The five riders then broke their formation by swerving to the side and began to circle, to build up momentum, and then, soon, they had brought their birds onto an attack course.

I thrust the feather back under the girth rope, angrily, cursing. Much good had it done me! I strung the small bow at my side. I drew forth three arrows from the tabukhide quiver behind my left hip. I put one arrow to the string. I held two with the bow.

They were coming swiftly.

Their formation resembled the perimeters of a geometrical solid. Their point rider would pass within lance range. The other four riders were somewhat behind him, on the left and right, top and bottom. Whatever adjustment is made to meet the point rider will presumably provide at least one of the following, flanking riders with an exploitable advantage.

I would try to pass swiftly through the formation, compounding the velocities and, in the passage, turn back to fire over my left shoulder.

I must wait for the exact moment to speed the tarn forward. They must expect me to hold my ground.

The lead rider was now in the neighborhood of a hundred yards away. I saw the lance lower, the Herlit feathers on it torn backward in the wind against the shaft. It reminded me for a moment of the ears of a sleen, laid back in its attack.

Another few yards and I must snap the reins of the tarn, kicking back at it, screaming, starting it forward.

I kicked back but then, suddenly, drew back on the reins. The tarn, arrested in its lunge, screamed, rearing back, startled, wild, in the air. I was flung back. I held my seat.

The lead rider, when only a few yards away, had jerked back wildly on the reins of his tarn. I saw him swerving up, and to my right, and then back. He was not even looking at me. He was looking at something, apparently, behind me. His face seemed contorted with terror. He swung his tarn about and began to flee. Almost at the same time the flanking riders had, in seeming terror, in disarray, their formation lost, burst like a star about me and then, frantically, on all sides of me, as though I might no longer be of interest to them, wheeled their tarns about and, like their leader, sped away.

I turned about on the back of the tarn. I saw nothing. Only the clouds, the sky.

I shuddered, seemingly suddenly chilled, and then turned the tarn about.

I set a course away from Two Feathers, in case I was followed. Then, later, I would make suitable adjustments.

The sky seemed clear. The early morning air was fresh and cool.

"And thus it happened," I told Cuwignaka and Hci. "They turned away, suddenly, at the last moment, and fled."

"They saw something behind you," said Hci.

"What was it?" asked Cuwignaka.

"I do not know," I said.

"It could have been only one thing," said Hci.

"What?" I asked.

"Wakanglisapa," said Hci.

"I saw nothing," I said.

"The beasts of the medicine world appear or not to men, as they please," said Hci.

"Wakanglisapa does not exist," I said.

"It is interesting," said Hci.

"What?" I asked.

"You held the feather. Yet you were not attacked. I do not understand that."

"Do not try to explain things in unlikely categories," I said.

"Perhaps you were protected by the medicine of the feather," said Hci.

"I am sure there is a rational explanation," I said.

"There may be," said Hci. "Wakanglisapa may not be your enemy."

"Wakanglisapa does not exist," I said.

"He may be your ally," said Hci.

"Wakanglisapa is a myth," I said. "He does not exist."

"What shall we do now?" asked Cuwignaka.

"We will proceed with our plans," I said. "We will send riders to the Dust Legs, the Fleer and the Sleen."

"The Fleer will not cooperate," said Hci. "They are blood enemies of the Kaiila."

"The Sleen are not likely to be of help either," said Cuwignaka.

"The riders will be sent out," I said.

"Very well," said Cuwignaka.

"We must now, in the next weeks, train tarnsmen," I said.

"They will need a Blotanhunka," said Cuwignaka.

"Canka," said Hci.

"Counting your tarn, Hci," I said, "and not counting my tarn or the tarn of Cuwignaka, we have sixteen tarns. We will form two groups, each with a leader and seven men. The Blotanhunka of one group will be Canka. The Blotanhunka of the other group will be Hci."

"Hci?" asked Hci.

"Yes," I said.

"Perhaps it should be Cuwignaka," said Hci.

"You are a far greater warrior than I, Hci," said Cuwignaka.

"You would trust me to be Blotanhunka?" asked Hci.

"Yes," I said, "and so, too, now, will the men."

"In you is the blood of Mahpiyasapa," said Cuwignaka. "You are a great warrior. You are a natural leader of men."

"I will do my best," said Hci.

"How much time do we have?" asked Cuwignaka.

"The Kaiila have little meat," I said. "Winter is coming."

"The riders must make their journeys," said Cuwignaka. "The men must be trained."

"I wish to be ready no later than the end of Canwapegiwi," I said, "the moon when the leaves become brown." It is in Canwapegiwi that the autumnal equinox occurs.

"That is soon," said Cuwignaka.

"The hunting must be done," I said. "The winter must be prepared for."

"That is soon," said Cuwignaka.

"I only hope," I said, "that it is not too late."

43

WHAT OCCURRED WHEN WE VISITED A YELLOW-KNIFE CAMP

"You must make swifter progress in learning Yellow Knife," said Iwoso to Bloketu, in Kaiila.

"It is hard for me," said Bloketu. The two girls knelt, Bloketu behind Iwoso. Bloketu was combing Iwoso's hair. They were in a lodge. We could observe them through the tiny aperture we had opened in the rear of the lodge, behind them, with the point of a knife. A small fire burned in the lodge. The two girls knelt behind the fire, between it and the rear of the lodge, opposite the entrance.

"I learned Kaiila swiftly," said Iwoso.

"You were captured as a child," said Bloketu. "It took you two years before you spoke Kaiila passably."

"Are you insolent, Maiden?" inquired Iwoso.

"No, Mistress," said Bloketu, quickly.

"Perhaps I should switch you again, tomorrow," said Iwoso.

"Please do not do so, Mistress," said Bloketu. I gathered that Iwoso's switchings, in their way, tended to be quite efficient. They were probably administered to the bare skin, with the girl tied in such a way as to maximize their effect.

"Beg properly," said Iwoso.

"Bloketu, the maiden, begs her mistress not to switch her," sobbed Bloketu.

"Perhaps," said Iwoso. "We shall see what my mood is tomorrow."

"Yes, Mistress," said Bloketu.

"Continue combing," said Iwoso.

"Yes, Mistress," said Bloketu.

There was a yellow, beaded collar about Bloketu's reddish-brown neck. Such collars tie in front. It was snug. It was doubtless Iwoso's.

"As you will recall," said Iwoso, "I learned Kaiila very quickly."

"Yes, Mistress," said Bloketu.

"You, on the other hand," said Iwoso, "are quite slow."

"Yes, Mistress. Forgive me, Mistress," said Bloketu.

"But you are not really that unusual," said Iwoso. "Kaiila women are generally stupid. They are almost as stupid as white female slaves."

"Yes, Mistress," said Bloketu.

Bloketu wore an unfringed, unornamented shirtdress. It was extremely simple and plain. It contrasted markedly with the exquisite, almost white, soft-tanned tabukhide dress, with its beads and finery, worn by her mistress. She, too, had not been given knee-length leggings, of the sort common with the women of the red savages, or moccasins. Her feet were wrapped in hide.

"It is pleasant owning you," said Iwoso.

"Yes, Mistress," said Bloketu.

"Even though you are worthless," added Iwoso.

"I was the daughter of a chief!" cried Bloketu.

"Even the daughters of Kaiila chieftains are worthy only to be the slaves and maidens of Yellow Knives," said Iwoso.

"Yes, Mistress," said Bloketu, sobbing.

"Do you like your clothes?" asked Iwoso.

"Yes, Mistress," said Bloketu.

"They are far better than you deserve, aren't they?" asked Iwoso.

"Yes, Mistress," said Bloketu.

"That is because I am kind," said Iwoso.

"Yes, Mistress," said Bloketu.

"Do you think that I am too kind?" asked Iwoso.

"I do not know," said Bloketu.

"Answer 'Yes' or 'No,' " said Iwoso.

"Please, Mistress," moaned Bloketu.

"Yes or no?" asked Iwoso.

"No, you are not too kind," said Bloketu.

"You dare to criticize me?" asked Iwoso, imperiously.

"No, Mistress," said Bloketu.

"You seem to suggest by your remark that I am perhaps insufficiently kind," said Iwoso.

"No, Mistress!" said Bloketu.

"Your answer, then, is 'Yes'?" inquired Iwoso.

"Yes, yes!" said Bloketu.

"Yes, what?" asked Iwoso.

"Yes, Mistress," said Bloketu.

"Yes, Mistress, what?" asked Iwoso.

"Yes, Mistress, you are too kind!" said Bloketu.

"You dare criticize me again!" said Iwoso.

"No, Mistress," wept Bloketu.

"But you are perhaps right," said Iwoso. "Atfer all, a slave must tell the truth."

Bloketu sobbed.

"I have been much too lenient with you," said Iwoso. "I now see that, upon reflection. Thank you, Bloketu. I shall attempt to mend my ways. I must try in the future to treat you more as you deserve, with much greater harshness."

"Please, no, Mistress," begged Bloketu.

"After all, you are only a slave."

"Yes, Mistress."

"Are you crying?" asked Iwoso.

"You tricked me!" said Bloketu.

"It is not difficult to trick a stupid slave," said Iwoso.

"No, Mistress," sobbed Bloketu.

"How offensive that I was once your maiden," said Iwoso. "How appropriate that you are now mine."

"Yes, Mistress," said Bloketu.

"Do you know one of the great pleasures of owning a slave?" asked Iwoso.

"What, Mistress?" asked Bloketu.

"Knowing," said Iwoso, "that one may do with her whatever one pleases, fully."

"Yes, Mistress," said Bloketu, frightened.

"Continue combing," said Iwoso.

"Yes, Mistress," said Bloketu.

"Do you know that some men have been known to find the bodies of female slaves of interest?" asked Iwoso.

"I have heard that," said Bloketu.

"Only low men, of course," said Iwoso.

"Of course, Mistress," said Bloketu.

"What do they see in such luscious, obedient sluts who must please or die?" asked Iwoso.

"I do not know, Mistress," said Bloketu.

"You are a female slave," said Iwoso.

"Yes, Mistress," said Bloketu.

"What do you think of men?" she asked.

"I fear them terribly," she said, "particularly since I became a slave."

"Interesting," said Iwoso.

Bloketu trembled.

"I have seen men looking at you," said Iwoso. "Do you know that sometimes they are looking at you?"

"Sometimes, Mistress," she said.

"Your body is nicely curved," said Iwoso. "Doubtless some of these men, doubtless low men, might find you of interest."

"Of interest, Mistress?" asked Bloketu, frightened.

"Yes," said Iwoso, "—sexually."

"Perhaps, Mistress," said Bloketu, frightened.

"Perhaps I shall have you thrown to them," she said.

"Please, no, Mistress," begged Bloketu.

"I own you," she said. "I will do with you whatever I want."

"Yes, Mistress," sobbed Bloketu.

"Your father was a traitor," said Iwoso. "And you, too, were a traitor. Sometimes I think the best thing to do with you would be to bind you and have you turned over to the remnants of your people, for their judgment. Doubtless they have ways of dealing with traitors."

"Do not give me for judgment to my people," begged Bloketu.

"Do you beg, rather, to remain my maiden?" asked Iwoso, amused.

"Yes! Yes!" said Bloketu.

"Beg properly," said Iwoso.

"Bloketu, your maiden, begs mercy of her Mistress," said Bloketu. "She begs to be permitted to remain the maiden of her mistress."

"Perhaps," said Iwoso. "We shall see."

"Yes, Mistress," said Bloketu.

"Continue combing," said Iwoso.

"Yes, Mistress," said Bloketu.

With one long, even, swift stroke of the knife I opened the back of the lodge. Cuwignaka and Hci, swiftly, before the girls could react, had pressed into the lodge and seized them, throwing them to their backs and holding their mouths shut.

I followed them into the lodge. I handed each a rolled ball of hide and fur. These were thrust, loosening and opening, into the mouths of the girls, expanding immediately to fill their oral cavities. I then handed Cuwignaka and Hci two, long, flat strips of leather. With these, looped about and then drawn back tightly between the teeth, and then looped about again, and again drawn back tightly between the teeth, and then tied behind the neck, the packing of hide and fur was inflexibly, unexpellably, fixed in place. The girls looked up at us, terrified, gagged.

We then, with thongs, Cuwignaka working with Bloketu and Hci with Iwoso, tied each girl's hands together before her body. Cuwignaka then removed the pieces of hide, tied on with strings, which had served Bloketu as a substitute for moccasins, from her feet. Hci removed Iwoso's moccasins. He then, too, drew from her legs the soft, almost white, tabukhide knee-length leggings which she had worn. Cuwignaka then, with another thong, tied together Bloketu's ankles and Hci, working swiftly, served Iwoso in the same fashion. Quickly then, with knives, their clothing was cut from them. Only the collar was left on Bloketu's neck, Iwoso's collar.

We looked down upon our handiwork. We were pleased.

I then produced two long, specially prepared leather sacks. Iwoso shook her head wildly.

We then slipped each girl, feet first, into a sack. These sacks, by design, are a relatively close fit for a girl. In them she can do little more than squirm. Each sack, further, has two sturdy leather handles which come up, high, quite high, one on either side of the occupant's head; if these handles are held together, or tied together, the closure between them will usually be twelve to eighteen inches over the girl's head. By means of these handles, of course, the sack may be provided with a variety of means of transport.

We then, by means of eyelets at the top of the sack, and thongs, and looping the thongs about the necks of the girls and tying them through the eyelets, fastened each girl in her sack. It was now impossible for them to inch or squirm their way free. Hci, with evident pleasure, tied the thongs under Iwoso's chin. There is also an interior edge, some twelve to eighteen inches in height, on each sack. This edge, however, we had left folded in. By means of this edge, and its own eyelets, which are aligned with the lower eyelets, to make lacing in the lower position convenient, the sack may be, if one wishes, brought out to its full length and closed completely over the head of the girl. This, too, of course, makes it impossible for the occupant, then totally inclosed, to free herself.

Iwoso made angry noises, almost inaudible, muffled in her gagging.

"Would you like to tell us that we will not be able to get away with this?" asked Hci.

Iwoso nodded vigorously, and Hci smiled. She then, in fury, in frustration, was silent, her words having been so easily anticipated.

"You look well tied in a slave sack," said Hci to Iwoso.

Iwoso's fury was but inadequately expressed because of her bonds, the sack and the gag.

"I am sorry, Lady Iwoso," I said, "but we did not have any sacks on hand which were appropriate for free women, sacks compatible with their dignity. We had to make do with what we had."

Iwoso regarded me with fury, and then looked away.

Bloketu made piteous, tiny noises, trying to attract the attention of Cuwignaka.

At last he looked at her.

She whimpered piteously.

"Be silent, slave and traitress," he said to her.

She put her head back, moaning. Tears ran from her eyes. She trembled. She had hoped to trade on the affection which she knew he had once held for her. Surely he would let her go! Surely he would show her mercy! But her pleas had gone unheeded. She shuddered, helpless in the confining leather. Her eyes were wild. Her worst fears, it seemed, might now be realized, that she be returned to the Kaiila nation, there to face the stern justice of her people.

"Go to your stations," I said to Cuwignaka and Hci. "Leave the kaiila hobbled outside. I will meet you at the prearranged rendezvous."

"The Kaiila will rise again," said Hci.

"Our plans proceed apace," said Cuwignaka.

"Yes," I said. "The council of all the bands of the Kaiila, of the Isbu, the Casmu, the Isanna, the Napoktan and the Wismahi, of all the remnants of the Kaiila people, will take place at Council Rock at the end of Canwapegiwi."

Cuwignaka, Hci and I clasped hands. Then Cuwignaka and Hci, as silent as shadows, moving through the cut I had made in the back, left the lodge.

I looked at the fair captives, helpless in their sacks, and then built up the fire a bit. I must wait for a time.

Iwoso uttered tiny, desperate, entreating noises. "Please be silent, Lady Iwoso," I said to her, putting my finger gently across my lips.

She was then silent.

The fire, then, after a time, suitably subsided.

It had served as a clock. Factors such as impatience can occasionally distort one's subjective estimations of the length of various temporal intervals. These confusions and distortions, of course, are eliminated, at least to a large extent, by having recourse to various stages in some presumably continuous, objective process. Is this not the sort of thing which is involved in the ringed candles, in the tiny stream of water in the clepsydra, in the falling sand in the Ahn glass, in the alternation of day and night, and in the calendar of the stars? I stirred up the fire again, so that I might better see what I was doing. By now Cuwignaka and Hci should be in place.

I stood up.

The girls looked at me in fear.

Their fears were not allayed in the least when I, having fetched a stout rawhide rope, crouched down next to them and tied one end of this rope about the handles of Bloketu's sack and the other end about the handles of Iwoso's sack.

Iwoso began to utter desperate noises, moving her head, the gag packed in her mouth.

"You would like to speak, would you not, Lady Iwoso?" I asked.

She moved her head affirmatively, desperately.

"If I removed your gag," I asked, "would you promise to be quiet?"

She nodded her head affirmatively, vigorously.

"Could I depend on your word in such a situation?" I inquired.

She nodded, vigorously.

"I could, of course, hold a knife point at your throat," I said, "and at the slightest sign of trickery or refractoriness plunge it into your throat."

She turned pale.

"Under such conditions would you still care to speak?" I asked.

She nodded.

My hands moved toward the gag. Then I stopped. "I dare not remove the gag," I said. "You are an extremely intelligent and clever woman. You would doubtless trick me somehow."

She shook her head negatively, reassuringly.

"Perhaps I should remove your gag," I mused.

She nodded.

"No," I said. "I must not do so. Indeed, I have been warned, even before we left our camp, against doing so. Masters fear I would be tricked. Thus you must, at least for a time, continue to wear it."

Iwoso looked at me for a moment in fury, and then put her head back in helpless frustration.

"I am sorry," I said.

Iwoso looked at me, puzzled.

"I can understand your feelings," I told her. "How offensive it is that you, a lofty free woman, are tied naked in a sack, as though you might be a mere slave, as though there might be no difference between you and the Kaiila slave girl who lies beside you."

Iwoso's mind, I had little doubt, that quick, clever mind, was working feverishly.

Then she looked at me with soft, mild reproach. She nodded her head, pathetically.

"I am sorry, Lady Iwoso," I said. Then I began to loop the rope carefully, from its center, that the ends of which were attached to the handles of the girls' sacks.

Iwoso, then, began to whimper timidly, piteously, trying to attract my attention.

I looked down at her.

Her eyes were soft, and pleading, and seemingly submissive and humble. She moved her head, lifting her mouth, with its heavy, sodden packing and its tight straps, toward me.

"Do you wish to speak to me?" I asked.

She shook her head negatively.

"That is good," I said.

She whimpered, piteously, again lifting her head toward me, the gag bound so tightly, so effectively, in her mouth.

"Do you want me to remove the gag?" I asked.

She shook her head again, small, piteous movements, negatively.

"What, then?" I asked.

She whimpered, lifting her head again to me.

"It is uncomfortable, isn't it?" I asked.

She nodded vigorously.

"Red savages," I said, "sometimes treat women too fiercely, do they not?"

Iwoso nodded her agreement.

"I suppose," I said, "that it would do no harm if I loosened it a little."

Iwoso whimpered, gratefully.

Bloketu then lifted her head, piteously, whimpering pleadingly. "Be silent, slave slut," I said to her. "You are not a free woman. You will continue to wear your gag in its full effectiveness, as a slave."

Bloketu lay back, tears running out of her eyes.

I then unknotted the gag behind the back of Iwoso's neck. I loosened the straps with my finger and then, putting my finger in her mouth, loosened the packing as well. Then, as though fearing I had been too lenient, I retightened the straps, closely, but not as tightly as they had been earlier. I then fastened the straps together behind her neck with a simple over-and-under knot. This would hold for a time because of the tightness of it and the strap friction. It would not hold, however, for very long, particularly if tested. I then pretended to secure that knot with a second knot, to prevent slippage. I did not, of course, actually do so. The stressing and jerking of the straps, which Iwoso could feel through the back of her neck, was the result, merely, of my looping part of one strap about the other and then jerking against it, the second strap end, of course, falling free as soon as I released it, leaving only the first knot in place, the simple over-and-under, or overhand knot. The security knot, as far as Iwoso could tell, was in place.

Bloketu lay on her back, sobbing.

"Is that better?" I asked Iwoso.

She whimpered, pleadingly.

"I dare not make it any looser," I said.

She whimpered, more pleadingly.

"I can always," I said, "make it tighter."

She shook her head, negatively.

"It is better, isn't it?" I asked.

She nodded her head.

"Perhaps I should make it tight again, as it was," I said.

She shook her head negatively, pleadingly.

"Are you grateful?" I asked.

She nodded her head.

I then looked away from her and returned my attention to the coiling of the rope. Inwardly I smiled. Did she really think that a woman such as she, luscious slave meat, would be truly accorded any consideration whatsoever?

I then, taking the rope with me, exited through the cut in the back of the lodge. I unhobbled the kaiila waiting there. It had a high-pommeled saddle on its back. It was to be ridden neither in the hunt nor to war. I looped the rope about the pommel of the saddle, dropping a few coils of it to either side, it then, on either side, descending to the ground and trailing back into the lodge. I threw a robe over my head and shoulders. I then mounted. Then, not hurrying, the robe muchly about me, I moved the kaiila away from the lodge, drawing from the lodge, through the cut in its back, by means of the rawhide ropes attached to their handles, the two sacks.

I heard Iwoso making tiny, desperate noises. I think, then, she was truly frightened. I think then she fully realized, perhaps for the first time, that it might actually be possible for us to take her, with all the consequences which might then accrue to her in virtue of this, from the Yellow-Knife camp.

But I was, as yet, in no hurry to leave.

Without haste, muchly concealed in the robe, I moved the kaiila out into the broad, empty lane between the Yellow-Knife lodges, almost a busy, triumphal way. In such a lane sometimes young swains, on kaiilaback, in their paint and finery, parade before damsels; in such a lane sometimes are kaiila races held; and in such a lane, sometimes, slave girls, for humiliation or punishment, or sport, are dragged back and forth in sacks.

I felt the tension in the ropes, on either side of the kaiila, as I entered into the long lane, some two hundred yards in length, the sacks, their weight negligible for the strength of the kaiila, being drawn lightly behind.

As I rode slowly along I looked back. The heads of the girls were off the ground, held off the ground, when we were in motion, by the construction of the sack with its handles, and the draw of the rope. Iwoso was uttering tiny, desperate noises. They were muffled and almost inaudible. They reminded me of the squeakings of an urt in terror. I did not think they could be heard more than a few feet away. Surely not in the lodges on each side of that broad thoroughfare. A domestic sleen did emerge from between the lodges, its ears pricked up, but when it saw what was ensuing, it turned away, paying us no more attention. Such sights and sounds were not unfamiliar to it.

I looked back again. Iwoso was squirming madly in the sack. Did the well-tied little thing really think she could free herself? Did she not know she had been tied by a warrior, Hci, of the Kaiila? But there is a simple way to stop such squirming. One increases the speed of the kaiila. I did so.

When I came to the end of the thoroughfare I turned the kaiila in a broad circle, not to foul the lines to the sacks, and began to retrace its length, even more quickly.

The sacks into which the girls had been inserted, naked and bound, were slave sacks. They are extremely stout, heavy sacks and heavily, and doubly, sewn. The intent of this is to make them sturdy leather prisons, containers from which a girl cannot escape and in which she is absolutely helpless. A consequence of the thickness of the material and the sturdiness of the construction, of course, is that the sack, almost inadvertently, affords the girl a great deal of protection. Neither Iwoso nor Bloketu would sustain skin or body damage as a result of what was being done to them. And certainly we would not have wanted them marked. Most men prefer soft, smooth slaves. Indeed, in the cities, some slaves are even shaved or depilated.

I turned the kaiila about, again, at the far end of the thoroughfare or promenade, that long, dusty avenue between the Yellow-Knife lodges, and began to make my way back, once more, along its length.

I looked back. Dust, from the paws of the kaiila, was billowing behind me. Let the girls fight for breath. I grinned. I wished that I were within the coup system. Surely some sort of high coup would be involved, dragging a high lady of the Yellow Knives, one of their own proud free women, in a sack, up and down, back and forth in their own promenade lane, like a common slave girl. Surely that would be worth at least a feather or some sort of marking on a feather.

I increased my speed.

I wondered if Iwoso had speculated on why their heads had been left uncovered, or why we had not inclosed one girl completely and left the head of the other free, why we had treated the slave and the free woman identically. Slave girls, when being transported in sacks, for example, on wagons or on the shoulders of men, are usually completely within the sack, it being tied shut over their head. This helps keep the girl in ignorance as to her whereabouts and what is going on about her. This is thought suitable for slaves. She is also, after having been in a sack for a time, likely to be extremely grateful to he who releases her and very fearful that he might, if displeased with her, return her to it. Also, of course, many sorts of commodities on Gor are transported in this fashion. In the cities, of course, when inserting girls within sack bonds, it is common to observe a difference, where it exists, between a slave and a free woman. Commonly a slave would be inclosed completely in the sack and a free woman, if no risk were involved in doing it, would be bound in the sack only from the neck down. This kind of difference in binding, or shackling, in which the free woman wears easier or more comfortable bonds than the slave, is in deference to the status of the free woman. When she, too, is enslaved, then, of course, she and the slave will be likely to wear identical bonds. To be sure, much depends on context.

For example, if the two sacks were to be dragged in the dust behind tharlarion then it might be the case that the free woman, for her greater comfort, would be inclosed completely in the leather confinement and the slave would be bound only from the neck down, this once again, and again to the detriment of the slave, observing the distinctions in bindings between them. Iwoso, of course, would presumably not be familiar with binding distinctions in the cities. Had she, thus, been bound more leniently than Bloketu, particularly since she was being bound by Hci, who seemed to bear her great hatred, she might have become suspicious. Thus we left the heads of both of the girls uncovered. This fitted in well, incidentally, with common practices among the red savages in dragging slaves about for, say, punishment or sport.

The heads of the slaves are usually left free. Similarly they are seldom gagged. In these ways they provide greater amusement for the spectators. Their expressions may be the more easily seen and their cries for mercy, or promises of better service, or assurances of reformed behavior, or even of perfect behavior, may be the more clearly heard. Sometimes the young men organize races in which slave girls are dragged behind the kaiila. When the young men set themselves to the development of such plans small slave girls in a camp, particularly white ones, tend to become afraid, for they know that they are not much weight for a kaiila to pull.

I turned the kaiila in a wide circle at the end of the promenade, the bags, like swift, twin plows, taut on their ropes, throwing up two trails of dust.

By now it seemed to me that Iwoso would have had time to expel her gag.

I hoped that I had loosened it sufficiently.

I looked back. The bags and ropes were covered with dust. I slowed my speed a little.

Suddenly there was a wild screaming from behind me, and a wild crying out, in what I assumed must be Yellow Knife.

I stopped the kaiila for a moment. It had certainly taken her long enough to get the gag out of her mouth.

Iwoso was sitting up in her sack, her head between its handles. She leaned forward, screaming. Such noise, I was confident, would soon rouse much of the camp.

I then, in order to be near the far end of the promenade, that nearest the open prairie, moved the kaiila appropriately down the long track between the lodges. By the tension on the rope attached to the handles of her sack Iwoso was then jerked backwards and again, almost horizontal, was being dragged behind me in the dust. This time, however, she was screaming wildly. I thought it well to hasten the kaiila, to convince her that I might be alarmed. I saw more than one Yellow-Knife warrior emerging from a lodge. They, I noted, like warriors of the Kaiila, and of the red savages generally, apparently slept naked. The slaves of such warriors, too, are often slept naked, particularly when they are within arm's reach of their masters.

At the end of the promenade, by the last few lodges, I again stopped the kaiila.

From this point I could easily escape into the night.

"Please be silent, Lady Iwoso!" I called to the Yellow-Knife maiden.

She saw fit, however, as I had conjectured, to ignore my suggestion, well-intended though it might have been.

I could now see more than one man running after us. I was more worried about those I could not see, who might be busy unhobbling kaiila behind their lodges.

Some men and women, too, stood near the nearby lodges, as though trying to grasp what might be taking place.

I permitted Iwoso, for a few moments more, to sit there behind me in the dust, tied in her sack, crying out. I was pleased to note that she was uttering a complexity of verbiage and, thus, was presumably not merely attempting to summon help. She seemed to be intent upon communicating something of consequence to the Yellow Knives. I did not speak Yellow Knife but I was reasonably confident as to what the main content of her message would be. This was a message, too, which I was confident she would wish to deliver for, in delivering it, she would be attempting to lay the groundwork for her eventual, if not immediate, rescue.

"That will be sufficient, Lady Iwoso," I told her, in Kaiila, and then, with perhaps an overly dramatic gesture, but one whose effect was not lost on the Yellow Knives, I threw aside the robe I had worn. It landed, happily, on a Yellow Knife who was charging from the side, causing him to lose his balance and fall. I kicked back into the flanks of the kaiila and the animal bolted forward. Iwoso was again jerked to the near-horizontal, that position approved for females being dragged in a slave sack, and was, in an instant, speeding cooperatively behind me. A Yellow-Knife warrior lunged wildly for the sack but fell short, sprawling in the dust. I had timed it rather well. A few yards out into the prairie I did stop again. I looked back. The camp was well astir. I heard shouts of rage. Men were running about. Then I again urged my kaiila into the night, drawing the two sacks behind me in the grass. I did not have time to dally. I had two women to deliver, one to Cuwignaka and one to Hci.

I must make it to a certain flat, barren rock. The mode of their delivery we had rehearsed several times, under similar conditions, with Mira. I could not hope, of course, in the ordinary run of things, to outdistance pursuing Yellow-Knife kaiila, certainly not with so short a start and drawing the weight of two such deliciously packed slave sacks. We did not want to cut the sacks free, of course. We wanted what was in them.

I heard cries behind me.

Pursuit was closer than I liked.

In a few Ehn I arrived at the rock, urging my kaiila up its sloping face. It scrambled, slipping, but then caught its footing, and attained its summit, some forty feet above the level of the plain.

The three moons were full, and beautiful.

I dismounted and pulled the two slave sacks across the stone to my feet. I removed the rope by means of which the two sacks had been drawn from the pommel of my saddle. I then removed the rope's ends from the large, closed, high handles of the sacks.

Across the prairie I could see riders approaching, some four or five in the lead, and others, drawn out, behind them.

I cut the rope apart in the center. I then threaded one length of the rope through the handles on Bloketu's sack and tied the two ends together, drawing it up from the handles in such a way as to make a long, double loop, the two high portions of the loop well above the handles and adjacent to one another; I then, with the other length of the rope, did the same thing with Iwoso's sack.

The lead riders, then, had stopped. They seemed confused about the trail. Perhaps it had crossed another trail. Certainly it did not seem likely that it would lead to this upjutting, flat-topped, weathered rock. Other riders, then, from the village, caught up with them.

I scanned the skies. There was no sign of Cuwignaka or Hci.

I looked down at Iwoso, laced securely, helplessly in her sack. "You seem to be missing your gag," I said.

She remained absolutely quiet. Had she not tricked me into

the loosening of her gag, in the lodge, giving her an opportunity to cry out and raise the alarm, an opportunity which she had well exploited? It was little wonder she was quiet. Doubtless now, so fully at my mercy, she must be wary of my wrath. I glanced at Bloketu. Her gag was still fixed as firmly, as perfectly, in her mouth, as the first moment it had been put there.

The riders were now again approaching.

Slave sacks, as you may have gathered, are known not only among the red savages but also among the men of the cities. Given their obvious utility, among men who own and master women, they may have arisen independently in both places. Their appearance in diverse loci, for example, need not imply borrowing. Such sacks, however, do have a utility among the men of the tower cities which they are not likely to have, or would seldom have, among the bold savages of the Barrens. To understand this utility it is well to understand that on Gor slaving, like marketing and farming, is a business. One of the problems which often arises in this business is that of getting the capture from, say, her own bedroom to your pens where she may be properly branded and collared, and taught to kiss and obey, later to be retailed naked from a suitable outlet, into her new life as a slave.

I heard cries below me. The riders below had seen the approach of the tarn almost as soon as I had.

Cuwignaka would be in the lead. The large wooden hook dangled from the girth rope of his tarn.

"There are the sounds of pursuers," said Iwoso. "They will soon be here. Free me. You cannot escape."

I lifted Bloketu to her feet, holding her with my left arm, the double loop in my right hand.

"What are you doing?" asked Iwoso.

I kept my eye on the approaching tarn.

"Free me," said Iwoso. "You cannot escape."

Cuwignaka's tarn seemed suddenly upon us. It was moving at great speed. The wooden hook was no more than four or five feet from the surface of the rock. Iwoso, startled, at my feet, screamed. I flung the double loop over the hook. Bloketu, at what must have been a breathtaking acceleration, was jerked upward and away.

"No, no!" screamed Iwoso.

I lifted her to her feet. She squirmed in the sack, her eyes wild with terror.

"Please, no!" whispered Iwoso. Then I had flung the double loop on her sack over the hook on Hci's tarn and she, her scream fading in the distance, was lofted away into the night.

The Yellow Knives, below, looked upward in consternation. I trusted that Canka, on one of the tarns we had purloined from the Kinyanpi, would soon make his appearance.

One of the Yellow Knives pointed to me. I was still on the rock. Two or three of them, suddenly, began to urge their kaiila toward me.

I turned about. Canka's tarn swept by. My own tarn, on a long tether, held by Canka, was only yards behind. I heard the scratching of kaiila claws on the rock face. I extended my hands and thrust my arms through the rope netting, it dangling from the girth rope of my tarn, and whipping and snapping, too, at the surface of the rock it skimmed. I seized then the netting with my hands and felt myself drawn up and away from the rock. After I had caught my breath I climbed by the netting and girth rope to the back of my tarn and took my place there. Canka, with a cry of congratulations, hurled me the tether and I coiled it and put it beneath the girth rope. The tarns of Cuwignaka and Hci, with their lovely cargos, were now far in the distance. I circled once, broadly, looking back. Several of the Yellow Knives, on their kaiila, were now on the large, flat surface of the rock.

I then turned my tarn to follow the tarns of my friends.

To be sure, we had given up one kaiila, but that, perhaps, was not too much considering that we had obtained Iwoso. It was the first time, I supposed, that the Yellow-Knife beauty had been, in effect, exchanged for a kaiila. I did not know whether or not it would be the last.

I looked up at the glorious sky, with its moons and clouds. I began to sing, a warrior song, one from Ko-ro-ba.

After a time, looking back, I became aware of another shape in the sky. It was two or three hundred yards behind me, above me and to my right. It was a great, black tarn. I turned my tarn to meet it. We circled one another. Then I took my tarn down to the prairie. The other tarn, too, then, alit near me, on the grass.

"Greetings, old friend," I said. "It has been a long time."

44

YELLOW KNIFES COME TO COUNCIL ROCK

"Oh!" said Iwoso, wincing, as I pulled tight the knots on her wrists, fastening them back and on each side of the stout post.

"How dare you treat me like this?" asked Iwoso.

"Rejoice," I told her, "that you are not being bound in whipping position."

"Whipping position?" she said. "But I am a free woman!"

"It is not only slaves who may be whipped when their captors please," I told her.

She shrank back, her back against the post. To be sure, she was not tied with her belly against the post and her hands over her head, out of the way of the lash, or kneeling, her hands tied in front of her, about the post, common whipping positions.

I then crouched down and roped her ankles, closely, to the post.

"I am a free woman," she said. "It is undignified for me to be tied to a post."

"Hci has decided it," I said.

"Hci!" she cried. "What right has he to decide such things?"

"He is your captor," I said.

"Oh," she said, frightened. I suspect that there were few things which the sly, clever Iwoso feared in this world, but, high among them, I had little doubt, were the scarred face and fierce heart of Hci, of the Isbu Kaiila.

I then stood up and unlooped some more rope.

There were two posts. They were wedged deeply in a fissure in the surface of Council Rock, near the brink of the escarpment. From the position of the posts one could see the prairie, hundreds of feet below, for pasangs about, particularly to the west. The posts, too, because of their position near the edge of the escarpment, commanded a fine view of the main, sloping trail leading up to the summit.

I then, looping rope about Iwoso's belly, twice, snugly,

pulled her back against the post, roping her closely to it. There was a deep notch in the back of the post, into which the rope fitted, to prevent slippage.

"You might have permitted us clothing," said Iwoso.

"No," I said. Bloketu, naked, was already bound to the first post.

Not only would the girls command an excellent view of the prairie, especially to the west, and of the main trail to the summit, but those who might approach from this direction or ascend the trail should, similarly, be able to entertain an excellent view of the girls.

They were prominently displayed.

"As a free woman," said Iwoso, "I am not used to being exhibited naked."

"It has already been decided," I said.

"By Hci, of course?" she said.

"Yes," I said.

"Of course," she said, bitterly.

I then unlooped some more rope.

"It is an excellent view," commented Iwoso, lightly.

"Yes," I said.

"To what do we owe this extraordinary privilege," she asked, "that we are permitted this view, this fresh air, that we have been relieved of our hoods and our bonds in the prison lodge?"

I looped the rope twice about her neck and then three times more under her chin and about the post, slipping it deeply into the notch in the back of the post which, like the lower notch, serves to prevent slippage.

"Today," I said, "you are to be judged."

"Judged!" she cried.

"Yes," I said. I then jerked tight the knot, the rope secure in its notch, behind the post. Iwoso's head, like Bloketu's, was then roped back helplessly against the post.

"But I am an animal," cried Bloketu. "I am only a slave!"

"You will be freed prior to your judgment," I told her. "You may then, in the full accountability, helplessness and vulnerability of the free woman, face justice."

Bloketu moaned in misery.

Iwoso began to squirm madly in the ropes. I regarded her. "Struggle, free woman," I said. "It will do you no good."

Iwoso, irrationally, frenziedly, fought the ropes. Then, regarding me in misery and terror, she ceased her struggles. She was held, of course, as helplessly as before.

"Bring me a kaiila," she whispered. "Help me to escape. I will make you rich among the Yellow Knives!"

"What of her?" I asked, indicating Bloketu.

"She is only a slave," said Iwoso. "Leave her. Let her face justice."

Bloketu regarded her, piteously.

"Do not even dare to speak, Slave," said Iwoso.

"Forgive me, Mistress," said Bloketu. On her neck, thrust up, over the ropes holding her neck to the post, she still wore Iwoso's collar. Cuwignaka had not seen fit to remove it from her.

I regarded Iwoso. She stood before me, roped to the post, absoutely helpless in her bonds.

"I am sorry," I said. "My sympathies are with the Kaiila." I then turned away.

"Warrior," called Iwoso, ingratiatingly.

I paused.

"Please come back," entreated Iwoso.

She had called me "Warrior" though I still wore Canka's collar, though I was still a slave. She meant, thus, to flatter me. Iwoso, I conjectured, did little without purpose.

I turned about. "Yes," I said.

"I am tied tightly," she said. "Can you not loosen my bonds, but a little?"

I looked at her.

"Please, please," she said.

"You are beautiful," I said.

"Roped and stripped as I am, handsome warrior," she said, "if I should indeed be beautiful I could never hope to conceal it from you."

"That is true," I said.

"Please," she wheedled.

"Perhaps," I said.

I crouched by her ankles. "Oh!" she said. I then stood up and attended to her wrists. "Oh, oh!" she said. I then attended to the rope at her belly and then to that on her neck. "Oh! Oh!" she said.

I then stood back.

"You have not loosened my bonds!" she said.

"No," I said. "I seem, rather, inadvertently doubtless, to have tightened them."

She looked at me, angrily. It was not easy for her to do so now, her head held back so closely against the post. "Beast! Sleen!" she said.

I turned away again.

"Oh, Warrior, Warrior!" she called, desperately, softly.

"Yes?" I said, returning to where she might see me, though, by intent, with some difficulty.

"How does the council go?" she asked.

"What council?" I asked.

"The great council of the Kaiila, of all the remnants of the Kaiila," she said, "of the Isbu, the Casmu, the Isanna, the Napoktan and Wismahi?"

"The council?" I asked.

"That being held now," she said.

"How did you know about the council?" I asked.

"You mentioned it," she said, "in the Yellow-Knife camp, in my lodge."

"Oh," I said.

"Too," she said, "do you not think I could see all the lodges when I was being brought to the post?"

"I suppose it does not make any difference that you know about it," I said, "as you are a prisoner. It would not do, of course, for the beasts to learn of it, or the white soldiers of your people, the Yellow Knives, or the Kinyanpi."

"No," she said, "for they might take you here, surprising you and surrounding you, you being isolated in this place, you being, for most practical purposes, trapped with little possibility of escape on Council Rock."

"It is doubtless well," I said, "that our gathering here, this council, is a closely guarded secret, that our enemies know nothing of it."

"Yes," she said, "else the work begun at the summer camp might for most practical purposes be concluded here. The Kaiila might, for most practical purposes, be wiped out."

"Fortunately," I said, "our enemies have no way of knowing where we are."

"We were days in our hoods," said Iwoso. "They were lifted only a bit, at irregular intervals, I think, to permit the placing of food in our mouths, the holding of a wooden bowl of water to our lips. It was difficult to keep track of time."

"I understand," I said. The hood often tends to produce spatial and temporal disorientation. This is regarded by many as one of its values. Some slavers use hoods to considerably reduce a girl's taming time. Hoods, of course, have many values. One of them is to teach a girl that she is helpless and dependent. Another is punishment.

"Could you tell a poor free woman, one bound as helplessly as a slave, handsome warrior," she asked, "what is the day?"

"I suppose it could do no harm," I said.

"Please, handsome warrior," she begged.

"It is the last day of Canwapegiwi," I said.

"Ah!" she cried, elated.

I smiled to myself. Had she not seen the dust as yet? It had been there, visibly, far off, in the west, for better than a quarter of an Ahn. The movements of the white soldiers and the Yellow Knives, even from the time they had crossed the Northern Kaiila, four days ago, had been under surveillance by our scouts.

"You seem pleased," I said.

"It is nothing," she said.

Did she truly think that it was a mere accident that she and Bloketu had been brought to the posts this mornnig, interestingly, on the last day of Canwapegiwi?

Without seeming to Iwoso then began to scan the terrain below, doubtless with some anxiety.

"Are you looking for something?" I asked.

"No," she said, quickly, "no!" She looked back at me.

"Oh," I said.

I then, turning away from the ledge, not facing the west, began to coil some rope which was lying about, one of several such lengths which seemed, purposelessly, to be scattered near the edge of the escarpment. When I was behind Iwoso I looked at her again. As I had thought, she had returned to her scrutiny of the surrounding plains. I wondered how long it would take her to detect the dust. I had seen it when I had first come to the edge of the escarpment but, to be sure, from the scouts, I had known where to look. It was obvious, but not dramatically so.

Then I suddenly saw her body move. She had then, I was sure, registered the dust.

"Are you sure you don't see something out there?" I asked her, coming up behind her.

"No," she said, suddenly, "no!"

"I thought you might have seen something," I said.

"No!" she said.

"I wonder," I said, musingly, and looked out over the prairie, to the west.

"Am I not beautiful, handsome warrior?" she asked.

I turned to face her. I scrutinized her frankly, as she

shrank back, as one may scrutinize a captive female or a slave.

"Yes," I said. I then made as though to turn back and again regard the prairie.

"Look upon me, handsome warrior," she suddenly begged.

I turned then to again regard her.

"I am only a captive woman," she said, poutingly, lowering her eyes, "one stripped and roped to a post, one whom you can uncompromisingly view, one who cannot protect herself, one who is absolutely helpless before you."

"Yes," I said.

"You can do anything with me you want," she pouted.

"Yes," I said.

"No!" she said. "Please continue to look upon me!"

"Why?" I asked.

"Can you not tell?" she asked, smiling, as though chiding me with a gentle, embarrassed reproach.

I shrugged.

"No!" she said. "Please continue to look upon me!"

"Why?" I asked.

"Look," she said. She thrust her body toward me, pressing it piteously, squirmingly, against the ropes that bound it to the post.

"What is wrong?" I asked.

"Do not make me speak!" she said.

"Speak," I said.

"I am a woman," she said, "and I wish to be touched and loved."

"Oh?" I said.

"Yes!" she said.

"Surely you can speak more clearly," I said.

"I am a woman," she said, "and my body hunger cries out in my belly! My desire in much with me! My wants are much upon me!"

"Speak more clearly," I said.

"I am a woman," she said, "and my feminine needs, irresistible, overwhelming, clamoring, pleading, making me helpless and yours, prostrate me before you!"

"You speak like a slave," I said.

"And perhaps now," she said, "for the first time, I begin to understand something of the nature of those feelings which can so afflict those unfortunate women, making them so helpless, begging their masters for their touch."

"Is it my understanding," I asked, "that you wish to serve at the post, as a slave might, licking and kissing?"

"Yes!" she said. She then closed her eyes and pursed her lips.

"I shall call Hci," I said.

"Hci!" she cried, opening her eyes and regarding me wildly.

"Yes," I said. "He is your captor."

"Never!" she cried.

"Oh," I said, and turned again to the prairie.

"Yes!" she cried. "Call Hci!"

"You wish to lick and kiss your captor, as a slave might?" I asked.

"Yes!" she said.

"Do you beg it?" I asked.

"Yes," she said. "Yes!"

"Very well," I said. "Hci!" I called.

Hci, interestingly, was not very far away and, in a moment or two, he was approaching Iwoso's post. I winked at Hci. "This woman," I said, "has begged to lick and kiss her captor, as a slave, at the post."

"Well?" asked Hci. He stood quite close to Iwoso. She turned her head to the side, that her lips might not brush his. She began to tremble. I think that, as a mature female, she had perhaps never been that close to a male, and certainly not in this fashion. Hci was stripped to the breechclout and Iwoso shrank even further back as the handle of his knife, thrust in its sheath, touched her above the belly on the right.

"Well?" said Hci.

Timidly Iwoso turned her head to him and their lips, gently, touched. She then kissed him twice, timidly, on the check. He did not move. Iwoso, then, frightened, but more boldly, began to kiss him softly about the mouth and face.

These kisses, now, clearly, I saw, went beyond the feigned obedience ingredient in her strategem; some of these kisses were like questions, after which she would wait to see how he might react; others were like tiny explorations or experiments, testings or tastings, to satisfy her female curiosity; others were like small, tender placatory submissions; others were like gentle, moist offerings, hoping that he might be pleased. Iwoso, I saw, doubtless contrary to her original intentions, was actually kissing Hci.

"Lick, as well as kiss," said Hci.

Iwoso, softly, then, complied.

I was reminded of the girls at the training stakes in the pens of slavers, in the cities. One of the first things a girl is taught to do is to lick and kiss under duress. One of the next things she is taught to do, in her training chains in a furred alcove, is to make love instantly, at so little as the snapping of fingers or the barking of a command.

"Here," said Hci, pointing to the hideous scarring at the left side of his mouth.

Iwoso regarded him.

"A Yellow Knife did that," said Hci. " I killed him."

Softly, then, Iwoso began to lick and kiss at the rugged, whitish tissue at the side of Hci's face.

Then Hci drew back his head. He looked deeply into Iwoso's eyes. He was disturbed, I think, at what he saw there. They were wide, and deep, and tender and moist.

"You pretend well," said Hci, sneering.

Tears sprang into Iwoso's eyes.

"Slave lips," said Hci, angrily.

Iwoso looked at him, puzzled.

"Purse your lips, as a white female slave," said Hci.

Iwoso did so.

"Now kiss," said Hci, angrily.

Iwoso did so, fully upon the lips, as a slave girl.

"I suggest that you do so more fervently," said Hci.

Iwoso complied, pressing her lips more desperately, more helplessly, more fervently, to those of Hci.

"Declare your love," said Hci, sneeringly.

"I love you," said Iwoso, frightened, not even seeming to understand the words she spoke.

"Again," said Hci.

"I love you," said Iwoso, numbly. "I love you."

"Speak the words with more meaning," commanded Hci.

"I love you," said Iwoso, desperately. Then she looked deeply into Hci's eyes. Then, frightened, she looked away. Then, half choking and shuddering, she burst into tears.

"Well?" said Hci.

She trembled at the post.

"Well?" asked Hci.

Iwoso looked again at Hci. Tears were running down her cheeks. It seemed she was terribly frightened. Then it seemed that something within her broke or gave way. "I love you!" she wept suddenly. "I love you!"

"Better," said Hci.

"No," she wept, plaintively, " I do love you!"

"Of course you do!" laughed Hci.

"I love you!" she said.

"Yellow-Knife slut!" cried Hci.

"I do love you!" she cried. "I do love you, truly!"

He then, with the flat of his hand, struck her a savage blow across the face, turning her head in the neck bonds, bringing blood to her lips and mouth.

"Lying slut!" he cried.

Iwoso, shuddering, turned her head away, weeping.

"Cuwignaka!" called Hci.

Cuwignaka came over to the post.

"Kiss him," ordered Hci, "fully upon the lips, as a slave, and declare your love for him."

Iwoso kissed Cuwignaka. "I love you," she said.

"Now kiss him," said Hci, indicating me, "similarly, and and declare your love for him."

"I am a free woman!" she cried. "He is a slave!"

"Do so!" said Hci.

Iwoso pressed her lips to mine. "I love you," she said.

"More fervently," said Hci, angrily, "with more meaning!"

"No!" said Iwoso.

Hci's knife whipped from its sheath. I feared he was going to disembowel her at the post. There was a spot of blood on her lower abdomen. Indeed, I think he might have done so had her compliance not been instantaneous and perfect.

"I obey!" she cried.

She pressed her lips deeply, desperately, frightened, to mine. "I love you!" she said, frightened. "I love you!"

"Behold the fickle slut," sneered Hci, "kissing and declaring her love upon command, like a slave!"

I regarded Iwoso. As she was a free woman it would not be necessary to whip her for having hesitated in obeying a command.

"I hate you!" said Iwoso, weeping, to Hci. "I hate you!"

Hci sheathed his knife. "Excellent," he said.

"Sleen! Beast!" she cried to him.

"Now we see Iwoso as she truly is," said Hci, "the sly, vicious Yellow-Knife slut."

"Sleen!" she cried, weeping.

"You look well, Yellow-Knife slut," said he, "roped naked to a Kaiila post."

"Sleen!" she screamed.

"Yellow Knives!" we heard men cry about us. "Yellow Knives!" Men were rushing about. Each knew his position and his business. Over the past few days we had rehearsed this many times.

We looked down to the prairie, to the west. Not a pasang away, across the prairie, all attempt at concealment discarded, waves of Yellow Knives, feathers flying, dust billowing behind them, charged toward Council Rock.

"You are surprised!" cried Iwoso, wildly. "Now you will all die! Now you are lost! There is no escape for you! You will all be trapped on Council Rock!"

"It goes as we have planned," said Hci to Cuwignaka.

"Yes," said Cuwignaka.

"You cannot escape!" cried Iwoso, elatedly. "Now you are done, Kaiila sleen!"

At this point I could see only Yellow Knives but I did not doubt but what Alfred, the mercenary captain from Port Olni, with the remnants of his command, probably some three hundred cavalrymen, or so, following the engagement at the summer camp, was not far behind. Certainly, according to our scouts, he had been with the Yellow Knives at the time of the crossing of the Northern Kaiila. He would wish the Yellow Knives to make the first strike, doubtless, absorbing and presumably subduing the brunt of the resistance, thus sparing his own men. Similarly, in this fashion, if such matters entered his mind, there would presumably be fewer, if any, prisoners to be concerned about. I did not think that the Yellow Knives would have disputed this plan. They would have been eager to be the first upon the Kaiila.

"They will soon be at the foot of the trail!" cried Iwoso. "Your escape is cut off!"

We saw Mahpiyasapa, civil chief of the Isbu, hurrying past. But a step behind him was the redoubtable Kahintokapa, of the Casmu, of the Yellow-Kaiila Riders.

"Do you not know how it is that they found you?" cried Iwoso, weeping. "It is my doing! I told them! In my lodge I overheard this foolish slave mention the place and time of the council! I tricked him into loosening my gag! I managed later, before being dragged from the Yellow-Knife camp, to rid myself of it! I then, in Yellow Knife, informed my people of your future whereabouts!"

"It was by intent and calculation that Tatankasa spoke of the council in your lodge," said Hci.

"Too," said Cuwignaka, "it was in accord with our plans that your gag be loosened."

"Do you truly think, woman," asked Hci, "that you would

have been permitted a gag the perfection of which you could in the least diminish had it not pleased your captors to have it so?"

"I cried out to my people," said Iwoso. "I told them about the council!"

"That, my pretty, naked, roped Yellow-Knife slut," said Hci, "was in accord with our plans."

"But even now I tricked you," she said, "by distracting you from seeing the approaching dust, by pretending to sexual need!"

"The dust," I said, "was visible long before you noticed it, before you initiated your clever, diversionary strategem."

"Knowing that," she said, "you let me behave as I did!"

"Yes," I said.

"It was pleasant seeing you pretend to sexual need, pretty Iwoso," said Hci.

She looked at him, aghast.

He took her chin and held her head. "You pretend well to sexual need, Iwoso," he said. I saw that she shuddered, Hci's hand controlling her. Then, angrily, he thrust her head, in its neck bonds, to the side.

"The Yellow Knives approach incautiously, anxiously," said Cuwignaka. "Doubtless they fear some might escape."

"Yes," I said.

"Things go well," said Cuwignaka.

"Yes," I said.

"They are at the foot of the trail!" sobbed Iwoso, looking down. "You cannot escape! You are lost!"

The Yellow Knives now, to be sure, swirled about the foot of the trail, that leading to the summit of Council Rock. This trail ranges generally from about five to ten feet in width. Some were even now urging their kaiila upward, doubtless desiring to be the first to count coup. Others, jostling and milling about, in dust and feathers, pressing and gesticulating, fought for a position on the narrow upgrade.

"It was I who brought them here!" cried Iwoso.

I did not think it wise that the Yellow Knives were urging their kaiila so speedily upward, and in such numbers, on so narrow a trail. To be sure, they were eager. Also, of course, it is sometimes difficult to separate the red savage from his kaiila. This sometimes renders his strategies somewhat inflexible. The tactical situation, in my opinion, called for an assault on foot. But the Yellow Knife would not be likely to think in such terms, at least not immediately. He, like most of the red savages, seemed to be a born cavalryman. They would learn, swiftly enough, of course, that the trail, here and there, abruptly narrowed. Indeed, in places, usually about blind turns, we had artificially narrowed it.

"You are finished now, Kaiila sleen!" cried Iwoso.

"Are you proud of yourself, and of your role in this?" asked Hci.

"Yes," she cried. "Yes!"

"Interesting," said Hci.

"Now you will all be killed!" cried Iwoso. "Now even your women and children will be killed!"

"There is not one woman or child in this camp," said Hci.

"What?" she asked.

"No," said Hci.

"All the lodges!" she cried.

"They are mostly empty," said Hci. "The women and children are elsewhere, and safe."

"I do not understand," said Iwoso.

"This is a camp of warriors," said Hci.

"But the council!" cried Iwoso.

"There was never a council," said Hci.

"But what are you doing here?" asked Iwoso.

"Waiting for Yellow Knives," said Hci.

"We have had them under surveillance for four days," said Cuwignaka.

"I do not understand!" said Iwoso.

"You have played your role well," said Hci.

"My role?" she asked.

"Yes," said Hci, "your part in our plans."

"I do not understand," she said.

"You have been manipulated," said Cuwignaka.

"You have served our purposes well," said Hci.

"You have been duped," said Cuwignaka. "You have been tricked."

"Without understanding it," said Hci, "you have been as obedient and compliant as a slave."

"No!" cried Iwoso, squirming in the ropes.

"Have you not brought the Yellow Knives here?" asked Hci.

"Yes," said Iwoso. "Yes!"

"You have lured them into a trap," said Hci.

"No!" she cried.

"Check her bonds," said Hci.

I did so. "She is well tied, and absolutely helpless," I said.

"I do not believe you!" she cried to Hci.

We heard the scream of a kaiila some two hundred feet below. Two kaiila, with their riders, slipping and scrambling, slid from the trail and then, unsupported, flailing, turning in the air, the riders and their mounts separating, they fell a hundred feet, struck some rocks, bounded out from the escarpment and fell the final two hundred feet to the lower, sloping face of Council Rock, and then, a moment later, struck the prairie below.

"I do not believe you!" cried Iwoso to Hci. "It cannot be!"

"Check the bonds of her slave," said Hci.

"You are a liar!" screamed Iwoso.

"Why else do you think that you and your miserable slave have been brought forth and roped so prominently to these posts at the edge of the escarpment? That you may, as it amuses us, see what you have brought about!"

"No!" cried Iwoso.

"But your presence here serves another purpose, as well," said Hci. "It is to be expected that the Yellow Knives, seeing you, a high lady of their tribe, tied naked, as a slave, with a slave, will be incensed, that they will be outraged at this insult, that they will fight even more desperately, frenziedly and irrationally to free you, and thus, concomitantly, will be more susceptible to errors in judgment and tactics. Too, later, when they come to realize how they must have been tricked, how you brought them into this trap, perhaps they will see fit to riddle your pretty body, and that of your slave, with arrows."

Iwoso regarded Hci with horror.

"Oh!" cried Bloketu.

"This one, too, is now well secured," I said.

We heard the scream of another kaiila and saw it, and its rider, plunging downward.

"Neither of you," said Hci, regarding the two women, "roped as you are, will make difficult targets."

"Please untie me," begged Iwoso.

"Please untie me, Cuwignaka!" begged Bloketu.

Cuwignaka, in fury, went to Bloketu and slapped her head, back and forth, in the neck bonds.

She regarded him, startled, blood at her mouth.

"How do you dare, without permission, to so put the name of a free man on your slave lips?" asked Cuwignaka.

Bloketu looked at Cuwignaka, startled, disbelievingly. He was now a man who had punished her.

"I am sorry," she whispered.

His eyes were fierce. I think she scarcely understood that it could be Cuwignaka.

"—Master," she added.

On the trail below, only some twenty feet or so below the ledge, charging upward, Yellow Knives, four or five abreast, mounted on painted kaiila, swept toward the top of the trail, some hundred feet or so to our right.

But a moment before the vanguard of this charging force could attain the summit the high, heavy structure of timbers and sharpened stakes was thrust into place. The stakes, anchored by the timbers, were tied together like fierce wooden stars. Kaiila, screaming, unable to check their forward momentum, plunged onto the stakes. Impaled and torn, pressed from behind, filling the air with hideous noises, they reared and twisted, throwing riders and biting and clawing at one another. More kaiila rushed forward, charging behind them, striking into the bloody, halted mass. Riders slipped down among the animals, screaming. More kaiila, from behind, pressed forward. Dozens of animals and many riders were forced from the trail, sliding and plummeting down the steep face of Council Rock.

I saw one of the war chiefs of the Yellow Knives, whom I remembered from the summer camp, in his kaiila slip over the ledge. Still more Yellow Knives, not clear on what was ahead, were trying to force their way upward on the narrow trail. Men fought to escape the edge, cutting at one another even with knives. But those at the edge, often, other Yellow Knives pressing forward, were thrust, even fought, from the trail.

The air was rent with screaming, that of beasts and men. Bodies, those of kaiila and Yellow Knives, slipped from the edge, plummeting downward. Lances snapped against the stone and the barricade. Men trying to crawl among the paws of the milling, frenzied beasts were trampled. Some riders near the barricade, halted in their charge, seeing the impossibility of advance under the current conditions, were trying to back their beasts from the barricade. This forced other beasts and men from the trail. Others, wildly, fought to turn their beasts. Some of these, successful, began to try to force their way back down the trail.

There was much shouting as well as screaming. I saw the movement of battle staffs. Their visibility, of course, was minimal, given the twistings of the irregular, tortuous trail. More efficient were the blasts of war whistles. The trail then, long and winding, visible in many of its lengths from the height of the escarpment, seemed choked with Yellow Knives. It was like an odd, upward-moving, arrested river of beasts and men, suddenly stopped, immobilized, in its flow. We could even see many Yellow Knives, puzzled, milling about, near the foot of the trail, hundreds of feet below. The trail, within its narrow boundaries, the rock on one side, the fall on the other, constituted a suitable trap, or slaughter channel, for our paralyzed, bewildered, confined enemies.

"No!" screamed Iwoso. "No!"

Lodges, with their poles, were thrown back and men emerged, dragging at the ropes of small travois, heavily laden with stones. Others, with their hands, and levers, began to roll larger stones, even boulders, toward the edge of the escarpment.

"No!" cried Iwoso.

"Shall we gag her?" asked Cuwignaka.

No," I said. "Let her cries, if they will, distract our attackers."

To this point we had struck not a blow. Yet I think that more than a hundred and fifty Yellow Knives might already have perished, victims of that steep, dreadful trail, crowded from it, driven from it, trampled upon it, and some even falling under the weapons of their own fellows, fighting for space on the rugged ascent. Then began the lethal hail of stones, hundreds flung from above, dozens rolled and toppled over the edge. These stones, striking down, could not fail to find marks. They plunged into the seething mass at different points on the trail. Some of the larger stones even did their work more than once, striking men or kaiila from the trail at one point and then, bounding downward, striking the face of the rock here and there, to shatter into yet more men at a lower point in the ascendant trail. Some finally plunged, rolling and bouncing downward, into the Yellow Knives far below on the grass.

Yellow Knives raised their shields but this did little good for the potency of the stones lay primarily not in their capacity to cut or penetrate but to transmit their considerable force, bluntly, crushingly, suddenly, to the target surface. Arms were broken in the shield straps. Men were struck from the backs of kaiila. Animals, maddened, screaming, hissing, snorting, squealing, reared and bolted. Dozens of men and animals, buffeted, losing their footing, crowded from the edge, slipped, scratching and screaming, down the rock's steep face.

Iwoso regarded the scene of carnage with horror.

Frenzied blasts on war whistles, relayed to the bottom of the trail, finally had their effect. Slowly, with difficulty on the narrow trail, some backing down, some turning, some falling, the Yellow Knives on the lower lengths of the trail, pressing back among their fellows at the foot of Council Rock, freed the lower ascents, enabling their trapped fellows on the upper reaches of the trail, those so exposed to our pleasure, to begin their own laborious, tortuous descent. Their retreat was harried by the further flinging of stones and rolling boulders.

The barricade at the summit of the trail, with its sharpened wooden stakes, with their bloodied points, was even temporarily removed, to permit the rolling down the trail of a great boulder. This the rear guard of the Yellow Knives, packed against their retreating fellows, the rock on one side, the drop on the other, their eyes wide with horror, must watch bounding inexorably toward them. Then it struck amongst them. It took perhaps a dozen men from the trail and then bounded down the rock face and, a few Ihn later, skipping and leaping almost like a pebble, possessing such terrible forces, yet seeming so small from this height, it caromed off the foot of the rock face and then landed, rolling and bounding, among scattering Yellow Knives on the grass below.

Iwoso looked at Hci. She was helpless in her ropes. He did not speak to her.

The stones had been gathered over a period of days and brought to the height of Council Rock. The girls, of course, would not have known this, for they had been in their bonds and hoods in the prison lodge.

"The trail is clearing," said Cuwignaka. "Do you think they will go away?"

"No," I said.

"Where are the soldiers?" asked Cuwignaka.

"They must be somewhere about," I said.

"Look," said Hci, pointing downward.

A single rider, a Yellow Knife, in breechclout and paint, and with a full bonnet of Herlit feathers, was urging his kaiila up the trail. In some places the upgrade on this trail was some forty-five degrees and the kaiila, scratching and scrambling, lunged and fought his way upward.

"That is a brave man," said Cuwignaka.

"He is probably looking for a coup," said Hci.

The rider, tall on the kaiila, singing medicine, disdaining to lift his shield, rode past, below us.

"I recognized him," said Cuwignaka. "He is one of the war chiefs who dealt with Watonka."

"You are right," I said. There were three such chiefs. One had perished in the first attack.

Mahpiyasapa did not give the order to fire on the man. It was not merely that he respected his bravery. It was also that he was permitting the man to scout the position. A certain form of assault, it might seem, would be effective.

The man halted his kaiila only yards from the barricade, with its terrible, bloody points.

Then he turned his kaiila about, not hurrying.

"He is truly brave," said Cuwignaka, admiringly.

"He is a war chief," said Hci.

The man stopped his kaiila beneath us. He ceased singing his medicine and looked upward. He saw the two stakes, some twenty to twenty-five feet above him, and the naked, roped beauties who graced them.

"Do not speak," said Hci to Iwoso, "or you will be slain."

Iwoso was absolutely silent. Warriors of the Kaiila do not make idle threats.

The warrior, looking upward, scarcely noticed Bloketu. He did, however, for a time, regard Iwoso. His face was absolutely expressionless. Then, slowly, he resumed his descent, once more singing his medicine song.

"He is furious," said Hci. "Superb!" Then he turned to Iwoso. "They will fight fiercely to rescue you," he said.

Iwoso looked at him, frightened.

"But they will not be successful," he said.

Iwoso fought the ropes, futilely.

"You may speak now," said Hci, watching the retreat of the Yellow Knife.

Iwoso's lovely, curved body squirmed inside the confining ropes.

"Perhaps you should speak now, while you have the opportunity," said Hci, "for later perhaps you would have to request permission to speak, and if men did not please to give it to you, then you might not speak."

Iwoso looked at Hci in anger. Her lips trembled. But she did not speak. She pressed her body once again, futilely, against the ropes. Then she stood disdainfully at the post, roped helplessly to it.

"They are coming again," said Cuwignaka, "this time single file. They will not crowd themselves on the trail."

"They are still on kaiilaback," I said. "They learn their lessons hard."

"Kahintokapa will count fifty," said Hci. "He will then give the signal."

My count and that of Kahintokapa, near the trail summit, near the barricade, tallied exactly. When the first fifty riders had passed the chosen point on the trail the second barricade, bristling, too, with stakes, on ropes, was lowered to the trail, shutting off the upper segment of the trail as effectively as a gate. The first fifty riders, not realizing they were cut off, continued upward. The later riders stormed against the barricade, the successive riders piling up behind them, forced the first riders forward, onto the stakes, and several riders, as the file behind them doubled and then bulged, were forced from the trail. The second barricade was defended by a fusilade of arrows sped from the small bows of Kaiila warriors suddenly appearing at the upper edge of the escarpment. Meanwhile, Kaiila bowmen, firing from behind the first barricade, and crawling over and through it, loosened war arrows into the enemy. Disadvantaged were the Yellow Knives to be on kaiilaback in such close quarters. And as they lowered their shields to defend themselves against the almost point-blank fire of the Kaiila other Kaiila archers, from above, over the edge of the escarpment, fired down upon them. Some of the men afoot, with their weight, throwing it against the beasts, even forced the beasts and their riders from the trail. Survivors, turning their kaiila about, fled back down the trail, there to encounter the second barricade. One man, with the downward momentum of the slope, managed to leap his kaiila over the lower barricade. Two others, on foot, crawling through the barricade, managed to escape. He who had leapt his kaiila over the lower barricade was the second war chief of the Yellow Knives, he who had ascended the trail only Ehn earlier. It was a fine, agile beast.

"I do not think they will come again on kaiilaback," said Cuwignaka.

"I would think not," I said.

Cuwignaka's speculation, as it turned out, was sound.

In about an Ahn, in the vicinity of noon, we saw some three or four hundred Yellow Knives ascending the trail, on foot, slowly, conserving their energy.

"You are finished now!" said Iwoso. "You are finished!"

In the way of defenders we had only some two hundred men, what we had been able to gather of the remnants of the Kaiila bands after the battle of the summer camp. Stones would not be likely to be too effective against men on foot. The barricades, too, to men on foot, though they would surely constitute impediments to their advance, would scarcely constitute insuperable obstacles. Further, the Yellow Knives, like other red savages honed to warlike perfection over generations of intertribal conflict, were fine warriors. I did not doubt but what, man for man, they might be the equivalent of the Kaiila. The delicate balances of tribal power would not have been sustained for generations, in my opinion, had radically disparate distributions of martial skills been involved.

"Already they are moving over and through your lower barricade!" cried Iwoso.

"Yes," said Hci. We had not chosen to defend it.

"In their numbers," cried Iwoso, elatedly, "they will storm your upper barricade, overwhelm the defenders and then be amongst you!"

"It is unlikely that one of them will reach the upper barricade," said Hci.

"What do you mean?" cried Iwoso. "What are you doing?" She struggled to see behind her but, because of the post and her neck bonds, could do so but very imperfectly.

From the lodges near the edge of the escarpment men again drew forth travois. On these were great bundles of arrows, hundreds of arrows in a bundle. Many of these arrows were not fine arrows. Many lacked even points and were little more than featherless, sharpened sticks. Yet, impelled with force from the small, fierce bows of the red savages at short range, they, too, would be dangerous. For days warriors, and women and children, had been making them.

"You must think not only in terms of numbers, Iwoso," I said, "but fire power, as well."

She looked, startled, at one of the huge sheafs of arrows being spilled near her.

"Sometimes," I said, "there is little to choose from, between ten men, each with one arrow, and one man with ten arrows."

Hci and Cuwignaka fitted arrows to the strings of their bows.

"This strategy was once used," I said, "by a people named the Parthians, against a general named Crassus."

Iwoso looked at me, puzzled.

"It was long ago," I said, "and it was not even in the Barrens."

"Fire!" called Mahpiyasapa.

Torrents of arrows sped from the height of the escarpment. In moments the shields of the Yellow Knives bristled with arrows. Return fire, in the face of such unrelenting sheets of flighted wood, was almost unthinkable. The small shields of the Yellow Knives, too, provided them with little protection. They were not the large, oval shields of Turia, or the large rounded shields common to Gorean infantry in the north, behind which a warrior might crouch, hoping for a swift surcease to the storm of missiles. It did not take long for the assaulted Yellow Knives to realize that they were exposed to no ordinary rain of arrows, a shower soon finished, but something unnatural to them, something unprecedented in their experience. By now, surely, ordinary quivers would have been emptied a dozen times. One broke and ran and, by intent, he, and the next two, were permitted to flee. Thus encouraged the Yellow-Knife lines suddenly broke and the trail seemed suddenly to erupt with men intent only on escape. They made easy targets.

"See the Yellow Knives?" Hci asked Iwoso. "They flee like urts."

She looked away from him.

He then began to look at her.

"What are you doing?" she asked.

"Looking at you, closely," he said.

"Please, don't," she said.

"You are rather pretty," he said, "for a Yellow Knife."

She tossed her head, angrily.

"I wonder if you would make a good slave," he mused.

"No!" she said.

"I wonder if I might find you of interest," he said.

"Never," she said, "I would never be your slave! I would rather die!"

"There are the soldiers," said Cuwignaka, pointing out toward the prairie.

"Yes," I said. "Doubtless they delayed their arrival, assuming that, by now, the Yellow Knives would have completed their business here."

Hci joined us at the edge of the escarpment.

"You are hideous!" Iwoso called to Hci. "No woman could love you! I hate you! I hate you!"

"What do you think the Yellow Knives will do?" asked Cuwignaka.

"I think they will make camp, investing our position," I said.

"I think so," said Hci.

"I would die before I would be your slave," called Iwoso, sobbing, to Hci. "I would die first!"

"There," I said, pointing, "is Alfred, and his officers. Doubtless they are receiving full reports."

"Do you see any sign of the beasts?" asked Cuwignaka.

"They are probably in the rear, with the column," I said. "Their effect on the Yellow Knives is likely to be the more significant the more unfamiliar they are to them."

"Their commander, too," said Hci, "may favor holding them in reserve."

"That is probably true," I said.

"Perhaps they are not with the column," said Cuwignaka.

"Perhaps," I said.

"I hate you!" cried Iwoso.

"Look," I said.

"I see," said Cuwignaka.

"I hate you!" cried Iwoso. "I hate you!"

"Be quiet, woman," said Hci. "We do not have time for you now."

"They are going to reconnoiter," I said. "It should have been done long ago."

Alfred, with his officers, and several Yellow Knives, began then, slowly, to ride south.

"They will scout us well," said Cuwignaka.

I nodded. In a few moments the riders bent eastward and began to circle our position. Alfred, a fine captain, would study it with great care.

"The Yellow Knives have sustained great losses," said Hci. "I fear they will withdraw."

"I do not think so," I said. "The soldiers are here now. Too, we must not discount their faith in the beasts."

"I have had reservations from the beginning," said Hci. "Of what value is a trap from which what is trapped may withdraw?"

"Without others," said Cuwignaka, "we cannot spring the trap."

"They may not come," said Hci.

"That is true," said Cuwignaka.

"What are you talking about?" asked Iwoso.

I turned to face her. "We are not the trap," I said. "We are the bait."

"I do not understand," she said.

Hci walked over to stand near Iwoso. His arms were folded. She shrank back against the post.

"You are a Yellow Knife," said Hci. "Do you think the Yellow Knives will withdraw?"

"I do not know," she said.

"If they withdraw," said Hci, "you must abandon all hope of rescue."

She shuddered.

"It would then have to be decided what is to be done with you," he said.

"And what would be done with me?" she asked.

"You are rather pretty," he said.

"No," she said, "not that!"

"Perhaps," he said.

"Do not look at me like that!" she said. "I am a free woman!"

His eyes assessed her, speculatively, appraisingly. She squirmed in the ropes, helpless, unable to keep herself from being candidly viewed.

"Please," she said.

"Your body seems not unsuitable for that of a slave," said Hci.

"I will never be a slave!" she said. "I will never be a man's slave!"

"Surely such a woman should be a slave," said Hci.

"Perhaps," said Cuwignaka.

"Never!" cried Iwoso.

"She squirms nicely in the ropes," said Hci.

"Like a slave," said Cuwignaka.

"Perhaps she might be found of interest by some low man," said Hci.

"Perhaps," said Cuwignaka.

Iwoso regarded them with fury. Obviously they had overheard her conversation with Bloketu in the lodge.

"Don't you think you would make a good slave?" asked Hci.

"No, no!" said Iwoso.

"Perhaps you are right," said Hci.

She looked at him, startled.

"You would probably make a poor slave," he said.

"Oh?" she said.

"Yes," he said.

"If I wanted to," she said, "I could be a superb slave."

"I doubt it," he said.

"Why?" she asked.

"Because you are frigid, like a free woman," he said.

"If I were made a slave," she said, "I would not be frigid. I could not be frigid. I would not be permitted to be frigid."

"I doubt that any man would find you of interest," said Hci.

"That is not true," she said. "Many men would find me of interest. They would be eager to buy me. I would bring many kaiila."

"Oh?" he asked.

"You yourself, but moments ago," she said, triumphantly, "were wondering if you might not find me of interest!"

"Was I?" he asked.

"Yes!" she said.

"I was only wondering," he said.

"Imagine me as your slave," challenged Iwoso. "Do you not find that of interest?"

"Perhaps," said Hci.

"At your feet, begging to serve and be touched."

"An interesting picture," admitted Hci.

"See!" she said.

"Would you like to be my slave?" asked Hci.

"You have tricked me," she said, suddenly, "making me speak like this!"

"Would you like to be my slave?" asked Hci.

"You are hideous," she said. "No woman could love you."

"Would you like to be my slave?" he asked.

"No!" she said.

"Truly?" he asked.

"Never," she said, "I would never be your slave! I would rather die!"

He reached his hand toward the side of her face.

"Don't touch me!" she hissed, drawing back.

"Before," said Hci, "I did not have time for you. Perhaps, now, I have time for you."

"Don't touch me!" she cried.

His hand paused, but an inch from her face.

She was drawn back, her head turned to the side, her eyes closed, tensed.

Then he lightly touched her cheek.

She shuddered, a movement that affected her entire body, moving suddenly within its ropes, from her head to her toes.

Outraged, she opened her eyes. She looked at Hci in fury. She then spat viciously into his face.

She then shrank back against the post, terrified, awed at the enormity of what she had done.

"Lick the spittle from my face, and swallow it," said Hci, quietly.

"Yes, my captor," she said, in a small voice.

She then, delicately and carefully, licked the spittle from Hci's face and, as she had been bidden, swallowed it.

"It is time to feed the women," said Hci.

Cuwignaka brought some pemmican and a small water bag from a nearby lodge.

"Do you beg food, Slave Girl?" he asked Bloketu.

She looked at him. If she did not beg, she would not be fed. "Yes, Master," she said.

He then thrust pieces of pemmican at once, her meal, into her mouth, to save time.

"Chew and swallow, Slave," he said.

Bloketu obeyed.

"Do you beg drink, Slave?" asked Cuwignaka.

"Yes, Master," she said.

He then gave her a draught from the water bag.

"Do you beg food, Free Woman," asked Hci.

"Yes, my captor," said Iwoso, humbly.

He then thrust pemmican into her mouth, as Cuwignaka had with Bloketu.

"Chew and swallow, Free Woman," he said.

Iwoso obeyed.

"Do you beg drink, Free Woman?" asked Hci.

"Yes, my captor," whispered Iwoso.

In a moment, when Iwoso had finished, Hci stoppered the water bag. "You may now thank us for your food and drink," he said.

"Thank you for my food and drink, Master," said Bloketu to Cuwignaka.

"Thank you for my food and drink, my captor," said Iwoso to Hci. If a girl's thanks, in such circumstances, are not deemed sufficiently sincere, or profuse, it is not clear if, or when, she will again be fed.

Cuwignaka, Hci and I then sat cross-legged at the edge of the escarpment.

We divided the balance of the pemmican and water between us.

"Do you think the Yellow Knives will attack again, today?" asked Cuwignaka.

"I do not think so," I said.

From time to time I glanced back at Iwoso. It seemed she could not take her eyes from Hci. I had seen how she had shuddered at his touch. Too, it was by him that she had found herself dominated, and so effectively and suitably, at the post. I saw that she was his slave. I wondered if she knew that yet.

"There is the white officer," said Cuwignaka. "He has apparently completed his circuit of our position."

Far below we saw Alfred, and his party, returning to the Yellow-Knife camp.

"Has he found weaknesses in our position?" asked Cuwignaka.

"He will think that he has," I said. I myself, at close range and with impunity, had scouted our position. I had also scouted it from a distance, from the presumed perspective of an enemy, from the grasslands below. From the surface of the prairie certain things, cleavages and fissures, certain irregularities in the rock face, appeared to be weaknesses. They were not.

"Let us hope that he is mistaken," said Cuwignaka.

"Aside from the main trail," I said, "there is no easy route, not even a narrow path, to the summit of Council Rock."

"It can be climbed," said Hci. "Men have done so."

"Yes," I said, "but I think our enemies will find it difficult, costly and dangerous to do so, particularly in the face of determined defense."

We watched the sun beginning to set over the western prairie. The smells of cooking fires drifted up from the Yellow-Knife camp.

"My captor," whispered Iwoso.

"Yes," said Hci.

"I am in pain," she said. "My body aches."

"Do you beg as a captive to be released from the post?" asked Hci.

"Yes, my captor," she said.

"Do you beg it as a humble captive?" he asked.

"Please do not make me so beg!" she said.

He looked out again over the prairie.

"Yes," she said, "I so beg it! I beg it as a humble captive!"

We stood up and turned about, regarding the girls.

Iwoso looked pleadingly at Hci.

"The proud Iwoso looks well clothed in humility," said Hci.

"It is all she is clothed in," said Cuwignaka.

Iwoso looked away, as nude as a slave.

"Bring their hoods," said Hci.

"Very well," I said.

In a few moments I returned with the hoods. The girls, in them, bound, would be returned to the prison lodge.

I freed the necks of Bloketu and Iwoso from the posts.

"You said that I was to be judged today," said Iwoso, "but you were wrong. I was not judged."

"That is thanks to the Yellow Knives," said Hci. "We had hoped that by now our business with them would have been concluded, but it has not been."

"When, then, am I to be judged?" she asked, lightly, as though scarcely interested.

"The business of battle is to be first concluded," he said. "Then, when you are totally within our power, when you are helplessly ours, when you are ours, fully, to do with as we please, then, and then only, will you be judged."

Her eyes widened in fear.

Then I drew the hood over her head and tied it under her chin. I then, similarly, hooded Bloketu. I then freed their hands from the post and, on either end of a common tether, I tied their hands together before their bodies. I then freed them from the posts and prepared to lead them to the prison lodge.

"Tie them well," said Hci.

"I shall," I said.

"In the morning," he said, "put them again, well roped, precisely as today, at the posts."

"I will," I said.

I then led them, hooded and stumbling, by the common tether on their wrists, to the prison lodge.

After a time, after I had secured the girls, hooded and tied, wrists to ankles, in the prison lodge, I returned to the edge of the escarpment.

"The next attack will doubtless occur at dawn," said Hci.

"No," I said.

"When, then?" asked Hci.

"Tonight," I said.
"The soldiers?" asked Cuwignaka.
"Yes," I said.

45

WHAT OCCURRED AT NIGHT AT COUNCIL ROCK

I felt the hand of Cuwignaka gently on my shoulder. I opened my eyes.

"The first," he said, "are nearly to the summit."

I sat up. "We will let a few attain the summit," I said, "that the others may be encouraged. Then we will greet them."

Hci was already awake. He stood nearby, his lance in his hand.

The night was cloudy and dark. I did not envy the soldiers. The back faces of Council Rock were extremely dangerous even in daylight.

We threaded our way through the lodges, across the top of our fortress.

Our lines were already in place, waiting.

"Sing no medicine," said Hci. "Be silent."

Hci, Cuwignaka and I, then, leaving our weapons at the lodges, dropped down to our hands and knees and then, in a few moments, to our bellies, crawling forward.

We were then about four or five feet from the edge.

We heard small scrapings.

We then withdrew.

"Climbing the rock face is extremely dangerous," I said. "Too, these men are cavalrymen. They are not used to such tasks. Surely some must have fallen."

"We heard no cries or screams," said Cuwignaka.

"Such would surely have alerted us, had we not already been anticipating their climb," said Hci.

"Their plan is surely a bold one," said Cuwignaka. "Surely, normally, we would not have expected an attack at night, and surely not from this quarter."

"It is interesting," I said, "that no cries have been heard."

"Perhaps they are all expert climbers," said Hci.

"That is unlikely," I said.

"Let us hide under kailiauk robes near the edge," said Hci. "We may then cut their throats, one by one, as they climb over the top."

"These men are professional soldiers," I said. "There will be command chains. If certain signals of clear passage are not conveyed there will be standing orders to withdraw. Such signals I want conveyed. Then we will attack."

"Thus," said Hci, "more men should be exposed, trapped, on the rock face."

"I would think so," I said.

"Good," said Hci.

"It is odd," I said, "that none seem to have fallen."

"Perhaps it is a diversion," said Cuwignaka. "Perhaps the true attack is to come elsewhere."

"I do not think so," I said. "In any event, Mahpiyasapa and Kahintokapa maintain their posts at the main trail, and we have stationed guards at intervals about the perimeter."

"One has attained the level," whispered Hci.

"I see," I said. There seemed a darkness in the darkness, which had moved. Then it lay very still.

"There is another," said Cuwignaka.

"Yes," I said. "Wait."

A certain subtle judgment must now be made. Enough men must be allowed to attain the surface to convince the enemy that their approach was undetected, that the orders for continuing the climb be transmitted, but not enough men that they might effectively hold a position behind which further climbers, in numbers, might be able to complete their ascent.

"Now?" asked Hci.

"No," I said.

In our lines we had fifty men. I would, accordingly, permit, as nearly as I could determine, something in the neighborhood of twenty-five soldiers to attain the level. This should be a number large enough for our purposes and yet small enough, I hoped, to be dealt with effectively and decisively.

"Now?" asked Cuwignaka.

"Wait," I said.

We watched the darkness grow at the edge of the rear escarpment.

"Now?" asked Hci.

"No," I said.

"Now?" asked Hci.

"Yes," I said, "now!"

Kaiila warriors, like unleashed sleen, rushed toward the ledge.

What was done there, stabbing down, cutting and hacking, took little time.

I remained a bit behind. I did not wish to be struck in the darkness. I was white.

Then, in a moment, I went and stood near the ledge. The rocky face was dark with darknesses. It was hard to tell what might be men and what shadows.

I spun and caught a lance being thrust toward me. "Tatankasa!" cried a man.

My clothes seemed suddenly soaked with cold sweat. I released the lance.

The soldiers seemed, for the most part, to have been swept from the ledge.

Bows and arrows were brought from the lodges. Men, with impunity, began firing into the shadows. More than once, below me, on the rock face, I saw a body pitch outward and then fall, silently, it seemed, into the darkness below.

"The torch!" I called. "Light the brush!"

An arm reached over the ledge, near me. I saw a face, wild. Hci thrust down with the point of his lance. The man plummeted backwards, down and away into the darkness.

The mystery of the silent climbers, however, had been solved. The man had been gagged. I could only conjecture how many might have fallen in the darkness, essaying that treacherous, terrible ascent.

A torch was brought. With it we set fire to the great bundles of brush, on ropes, which had been prepared earlier. These flaming bundles, on their ropes, were then hurled over the edge, to hang burning against the rocky face.

I again looked over the edge. The men, in great numbers, like insects, now illuminated, clung precariously to the rock. They could offer no defense. Barely could they hold their position. At their leisure the Kaiila bowmen picked their targets. Some men, in terror, lost their hold on the rock. Others, terrified, remained where they were, to die. Most began, in haste, to attempt the descent. Many of these fell. Some men released their hold altogether on the rock, hoping to risk less in the terrors of the slide downward than in facing the Kaiila arrows.

"How many died?" asked Cuwignaka.

I looked down. I could not see, in the darkness, to the foot of the mountain.

"I do not know," I said.

"Many?" asked Cuwignaka.

"Yes," I said. "Many."

46

THE SECOND DAY OF WAR

"I heard noises last night, cries," said Iwoso. "Oh!" she said.

I had tightened her neck bonds, pulling her head back against the post. She was then bound to the post as she had been the previous day, helplessly, identically, as Hci had wished.

It was near dawn. Bloketu was already bound to her post.

"There was an action," I said. "It need not concern you."

Iwoso struggled briefly in her ropes, futilely. I then tightened them.

"Must I be displayed like this?" she asked.

"Yes," I said. "Hci, your captor, finds it amusing."

She struggled, angrily, helplessly.

"Too, he thinks it might be of interest to you, to observe the issuance of these military affairs, particularly as you are not likely to be unaffected by their outcome."

She looked at me, frightened.

"Too, of course," I said, "your presence here, naked, in your ropes, tied like a slave, is calculated to be an incitement to the Yellow Knives."

"You use me in many ways, it seems," she said, bitterly, "to serve your purposes."

"You are a captive female," I said. "It is thus only natural that you be used to serve the purposes of your captors."

"You use me," she said, "as thoughtlessly and brazenly as a slave!"

I regarded her. "Yes," I said, "you might say that."

She looked away.

"I would like to make a recommendation," I said.

She did not look at me.

"Things were perhaps closer for you yesterday than you realize," I said.

She looked at me.

"It has to do with keeping you alive, my proud, pretty Iwoso," I said.

"Oh?" she said.

"Hci is your captor," I said, "and he is not a patient man. I think you should show him total respect and obey him with absolute perfection."

She looked at me, angrily.

"Do you understand?" I asked.

"Yes," she said.

I turned away, to look down at the Yellow-Knife camp.

"Almost as though I were a slave!" she said.

"Yes," I said, "almost as though you were a slave."

"Never!" she cried.

"As you will, Lady Iwoso," I said. I continued looking down at the Yellow-Knife camp. I could see, too, their kaiila, grazing behind the camp.

"Yesterday," she said, "I was weak! But I am not weak today!"

"The whip," I said, "is often useful in dispelling such illusions from the mind of a woman."

She was silent.

"Have you ever been whipped, Lady Iwoso?" I asked.

"No," she said.

"The Yellow Knives," said Cuwignaka, coming over to where I stood, "are beginning to mass at the foot of the trail."

"It would appear to be a major assault," said Hci, joining us.

"This time they will finish you!" called Iwoso.

"Iwoso seems to be in good spirits today," observed Cuwignaka.

"She is in fine fettle," I said.

"Tonight," said Iwoso, "I will be with my people, safe!"

"What are they carrying?" asked Hci.

"It looks like screens," I said, "probably of branches and hides." Such devices, I speculated, dismally, would arrest or turn most arrows from the bows of red savages. Their small bows, generally so ideal for their purposes, so advantaged in rapidity of fire, so useful from the back of a racing kaiila, lacked the driving power, naturally enough, of heavier weapons. In impact they were inferior not only to the peasant bow, Gor's fiercest missile weapon, but even the common, hand-drawn crossbow.

"Some soldiers are with them," I said.

"Yes," said Hci.

"Do you see any sign of the beasts?" I asked. I did not.

"No," said Hci.

"Free me," said Iwoso. "There are soldiers there. Free me, and sue for peace. Beg to be permitted to surrender. Some of you might be spared."

"There are not enough soldiers to control the Yellow Knives," said Cuwignaka.

"And I doubt," I said, "that either the soldiers or the beasts, having come this far, and sustained such losses, are much interested in the taking of prisoners." To be sure, beyond such considerations, there was little to do in the Barrens with prisoners, unless they were females, who might then be reduced as love prizes to suitable, helpless slaveries.

"Surrender!" said Iwoso. "Surrender!"

"What is wrong with Iwoso this morning?" inquired Hci.

"I do not think that she has taken leave of her senses," I said. "Rather I think that yesterday she was forced to look inside of herself, and there she discovered things which frightened her. She is now trying to fight them. She is now, in compensation, unwilling to accept these startling, alarming insights, trying to restore her former self-image, trying to be pronouncedly defiant."

"What are you saying?" asked Iwoso.

"She thinks that yesterday she was weak, but that today she is strong."

"Interesting," said Hci. He walked over to Iwoso. "Do you think that you are strong?" he asked.

"Yes!" she said.

"You are mistaken," he said.

"They are coming up the trail now," said Cuwignaka.

The Yellow Knives, probably some four or five hundred of them, with perhaps some fifty soldiers, were now climbing the trail. They moved slowly, to conserve their strength. Some of them held the screens they had constructed between themselves and our position. Others held them overhead, advancing beneath them. There was little doubt their main party would reach the barricade at the summit in much of its full strength. I looked at the ropes left lying at intervals along the edge of the escarpment. I had little doubt but what their utility was soon to be realized.

"In the distance, to the west," I said, "the prairies seem clear."

"Yes," said Cuwignaka.

"They are passing the first barricade," observed Hci. This, now, was the lower barricade, the first to be met in the ascent. We had lowered it into place yesterday, to make the retreat of kaiila difficult. Undefended, it posed no serious obstacle to men afoot.

Our approximately two hundred men were divided into five groups. Two of these groups, of some forty each, were stationed near the summit barrier. One of these groups, under Mahpiyasapa, was defensive. Given the narrowness of the trail, so few might, for a time, adequately maintain the barricade against much greater numbers, the effective application of these numbers being reduced by the nature of the terrain. The second group near the summit would appear to be being held in reserve, to reinforce as necessary the contingent at the barricade. It was, however, a strike force. There were three other groups, of some forty men each. They would have their diverse deployments.

In a few moments the Yellow Knives and the soldiers with them, shielded by their screens, were passing beneath our position, advancing toward the summit. A few moments later, screaming, crowding forward, they rushed toward the barricade.

"The men of Mahpiyasapa are holding," said Hci.

I nodded. They would certainly be able to do so, at least for a time.

"The enemy seems now to be suitably positioned for our purposes," I said. "Too, as we had anticipated, their attention is much concentrated on the barricade."

"Iwoso may cry out," said Cuwignaka.

"I do not think they would hear her," I said. "There is too much noise. They are too intent upon their business at the barricade."

"Nonetheless," said Hci, "it is a risk I do not choose to take."

"Are you going to cut her throat?" asked Cuwignaka.

Iwoso shrank back against the post.

"Should she be permitted to so easily escape the judgment of the Kaiila?" asked Hci.

"No," said Cuwignaka, his voice hard.

Iwoso, roped, trembled.

"A gag, if noted, might alert perceptive Yellow Knives," said Cuwignaka.

"Open your mouth, Iwoso," said Hci. "Widely."

He then bent down and picked up a small rock, about an inch in diameter, from the surface of our position.

He placed this in Iwoso's mouth. "Close your mouth," he said.

She complied.

"Do you wish to keep your tonque?" he asked.

She nodded, frightened.

"When we return," he said, "if this rock is not still in your mouth, your tongue will be cut out. Do you understand?"

She nodded, terrified.

Hci, Cuwignaka and I then hurried along the edge of the escarpment, about three hundred feet to our left, joining others, already waiting there.

Hci raised and lowered his hand. The forty men in his party, including myself and Cuwignaka, then, on the ropes left along the edge of the escarpment, held by the members of the fourth group, under the command of Kahintokapa, lowered ourselves to the trail below.

We moved swiftly.

Then we fell upon the Yellow Knives.

Eyes, wild, regarded us over their shoulders. Men attempting to escape us pressed forward, forcing their fellows toward the barricade, causing several to lose their footing on the trail. In the press, it was difficult for them to turn and fight. Arrow screens were broken and dropped.

Then Yellow Knives, in sufficient numbers, had managed to turn and face us.

"Back!" called Hci.

Swiftly we withdrew.

Elated, Yellow Knives rushed after us, down the trail. Men withdrew even from the barricade to join the pursuit.

At our withdrawal our fifth group, some fifty yards behind us, lowered itself from the escarpment. This was under the command of a Napoktan warrior. His name was Waiyeyeca. They carried lances strapped on their backs. As soon as we were among them they unslung these lances, bracing them like pikes on the trail. Pursuing Yellow Knives, thrust from behind, unable to stop, rushed onto the lances. The eighty of us, then, the lancers and Hci's group, held our ground. This was not difficult to do given the narrowness of the trail. War clubs, shields and knives met. Then over the barricade, now deserted by the enemy, passing between Mahpiyasapa's defenders, came our second group, that which, seemingly, had been held in reserve. It now struck the Yellow Knives on the trail itself. Most of the Yellow Knives, of course, hemmed in by their fellows, on the front and in the rear, and on the flanks by the drop and the wall, must remain inactive. Then, into this trapped mass, its arrow screens no longer in position, and many of them scattered and lost, sped hundreds of arrows. These were fired by the men of our fourth group, suddenly appearing at the top of the escarpment, that which had handled our descent ropes, that under the command of Kahintokapa, of the Yellow-Kaiila Riders. In that contingent, it might be mentioned, there served a blond youth, one who had taken the Kaiila name of Wayuhahaka, "One-Who-Possesses-Much," who had once been of the Waniyanpi.

Many of the Yellow Knives and soldiers, rather than face this withering fire, lowered themselves from the trail, slipping and sliding, then, abrasively, down the side of the rock face. Some may have survived. In moments then our groups, that of Hci and Waiyeyeca, and that from the barricade itself, met, Yellow Knives and soldiers slain or forced from the trail. Cuwignaka, in joy, embraced the leader of the group come down from the barricade. The name of the leader of that group was Canka.

I looked over the edge of the trail.

There were many bodies below. Some had caught on rocks. Others had fallen to lower segments of the trail. Some, even, had plunged bounding, and turning and striking, from plane to plane, to the grass.

"Yellow Knives on kaiila approaching the lower barricade!" called Kahintokapa, from above.

Ropes were thrown down to us. Our weapons and shields slung about us we then climbed these ropes to the height of the escarpment. By the time these Yellow Knives had dismounted and cast aside the lower barricade, it tumbling downward, breaking and shattering in its descent, and remounted, we were safe. Some of them rode about a bit on the trail but then, under sporadic arrow fire, they withdrew.

There were many Yellow Knives left on the trail below. I had recognized one of them. It was he who had been the second of the war chiefs from the summer camp. No longer did he sing medicine.

Kaiila warriors, laughing and joking, congratulated one another, exhibiting grisly trophies.

In the Barrens conflict is typically quarterless.

"Open your mouth," said Hci to Iwoso.

She did so, expelling the wet stone into the palm of his hand.

47

THE THIRD DAY OF WAR

"I think they will be coming in the neighborhood of noon," said Cuwignaka.

It was now the third day in the siege of Council Rock.

Yesterday afternoon we had seen Kinyanpi. Yesterday night we had lit a great brush beacon which we had prepared. This beacon, whether used for the emission of smoke in daylight hours, or for its flame at night, could be seen for pasangs across the prairie.

"The Yellow Knives, left to their own resources," said Hci, "would have withdrawn after the failure of the first day. It seems to me highly unlikely that the discipline of the soldiers and beasts can long be maintained over them."

"Doubtless they now have the backing of the Kinyanpi," I said. "Flighted scouts, at any rate, were observed yesterday."

"More than Kinyanpi will be required to bring them again to the barricade," said Hci.

"You expect, then," asked Cuwignaka, "only one more major assault."

"And it will be the most determined of all," said Hci, grimly.

"And who will be its leaders?" asked Cuwignaka.

"The beasts, of course," I said.

"Yes," said Hci.

"It is nearly noon," said Cuwignaka, looking upward.

"I hear drums," I said.

"Medicine drums," said Hci.

"Soldiers are leaving the camp," I said.

"Yes," said Hci.

"They are riding south," I said.

"Interesting," said Hci.

"There is a Kinyanpi rider," said Cuwignaka, pointing upward.

"Doubtless a scout," said Hci.

"There is movement now, in the Yellow-Knife camp," I said.

"They are coming," said Hci.

"Who is in their lead?" asked Cuwignaka.

"The beasts," I said.

"We do not know how long the day will last," said Hci. "Feed and water Bloketu."

She was roped to her post, just as she had been the first two days.

"Do you beg food and drink?" asked Cuwignaka.

"Yes, Master," she said.

He fed and watered her.

"Thank you for my food and drink, Master," she said.

"I beg food and drink," said Iwoso, suddenly.

"Shall I give her food and water?" asked Cuwignaka.

Iwoso looked at Hci. The decision would obviously be his. Yesterday she had not begged. Accordingly, as is customarily the case when begging is required, she had received neither food nor drink.

"Yes," said Hci.

Iwoso was then fed and watered. Her mouth, her head extended, clung greedily, desperately to the spout of the water bag. Then it was pulled from between her teeth. She tried to lick at the water at the side of her mouth.

"Do you think me weak, Iwoso," asked Hci, "that I have so soon permitted you food and drink?"

She looked at him, puzzled.

"Have you not asked yourself why I might do this, so soon?" he asked.

She looked at him, frightened.

"I am doing it to improve your appearance," he said, "much as one might water an animal before its sale, that you will look your best for the Yellow Knives."

"Again you use me for your purposes, tricking me!" she said.

"You may now thank me for your food and drink," he said.

"Thank you for my food and drink," she said, in fury.

"More humbly, more appropriately," said Hci.

"I thank you for my food and drink," she said. "I thank you for it—humbly," she said.

Hci looked at her.

"—My captor," she added.

Hci put his hand under her chin and held her head up. "Do you think her throat would look well in a collar?" he asked Cuwignaka.

"Yes," said Cuwignaka.

"I will never wear a collar!" said Iwoso, her head held up by Hci's hand.

"My collar?" asked Hci.

"Of course," said Cuwignaka.

"I will never wear your collar!" said Iwoso. "I would die first!"

"The beast in the lead," I said, "is called Sardak. That closest to him in Kog."

"They are fearsome things," said Cuwignaka.

"Surely," said Hci, joining us, "they are of the medicine world."

"Do not be afraid," I said to him.

"They expect all opposition to crumble before them, at their very appearance," said Cuwignaka, bitterly.

"They can bleed and die, like men," I told Hci.

"Things of the medicine world," said Hci, "may sometimes seem to bleed and die, but they do not truly do so."

"They are not of the medicine world," I said.

"I am uneasy," said Hci.

"The Kaiila must hold against them," I said.

"Soldiers," called a man, running along the escarpment, "roped together, are beginning to climb the back face of the mountain!"

"It is to be a coordinated attack," said Cuwignaka.

"Then," I said, looking upward, "I think we may soon expect the Kinyanpi."

"It is the end for you!" cried Iwoso. "You are finished!"

"Look!" cried Hci, suddenly, pointing upward.

We heard the drums on the trail, beaten by medicine men, dancing about the beasts. The Yellow Knives, in lines behind them, advanced.

"Look!" insisted Hci.

In the sky there was a tarn.

My heart leapt.

"We are doomed!" cried Hci.

Men about us screamed, and threw their arms before their faces.

We crouched down, dust and rocks flying past us, that we not be forced from the edge of the escarpment by the turbulent blasts of those mighty, beating wings. Then the monster had alit amongst us.

"It is Wakanglisapa!" cried Hci. "It is Wakanglisapa, the Medicine Tarn!"

I approached the beast slowly. Then I put out my hand and touched its beak. I then, as it lowered its head, took its head in my hands and wept. "Greetings, Ubar of the Skies," I said. "We are together again."

"There is a cloud in the east," said a man, "small, swiftly moving."

"It will be Kinyanpi," I said. "My friend has preceded them."

Men looked at one another.

"Bring a girth rope, and reins," I said. "And throw back the lodge covers and poles which conceal our tarns. We must greet our visitors."

Men hurried away.

Yesterday night the great beacon of brush had been lit on the summit of Council Rock. It had been the first in a line of ten such beacons. Each, in turn, as soon as the light of the preceding beacon had been visible, had been lit. Before morning, some singly, some in groups of two or three, under the cover of darkness, our tarns had been brought to Council Rock, there to be concealed within specially prepared lodges. There were eighteen of these beasts, that which had been a Kinyanpi mount which had come to us on the prairie, the two wild tarns we had captured by means of the tarn pits, and the fifteen tarns we had managed to secure in our subsequent raid. These tarns we had brought from Two Feathers to the Waniyanpi compound commanded by Seibar. There, concealed by day and trained by night, and housed within striking distance of Council Rock, they had waited for our signal.

I put the girth rope on the great black tarn. I fixed the reins upon it.

I heard the approach of the drums on the trail ascending to the summit.

"The soldiers on the back face near the top," said a man.

"Repel them as you can," I said.

Lodges were thrown back, with the poles and skins. Tarns were revealed.

I leaped to the back of Ubar of the Skies. My weapons were handed to me.

Canka, Hci and Cuwignaka hurried to mount their tarns.

Eagerly, awaiting no command or signal, his neck outstretched, Ubar of the Skies took to the air.

"Ko-ro-ba!" I cried, the name of the city to which I had first been brought on Gor, Ko-ro-ba, the Towers of the Morning.

The tarn screamed.

Blasts of air tore through my hair. The feathers on my tem-wood lance lashed backwards, like flags snapping in the wind.

I heard other tarns, too, screaming behind me, and heard the beatings of wings.

Council Rock fell away beneath me.

Like a dark streak, vengeful and fearful, the great black tarn clove the skies.

Suddenly bodies and tarns seemed to be exploding about me as we entered, penetrating, the startled formations of the Kinyanpi. No resistance in the air had they expected, nor none this soon. I saw eyes, wild, about me.

My lance took a rider from his mount, tearing him back out of the girth rope, and then he was spinning, wildly flailing, screaming and turning, growing smaller, journeying with terrible, accelerative force, seemingly eccentrically, to the turf below, it seeming to rock and shift with my movements, like liquid in a bowl.

Ubar of the Skies reared back, talons raking, screaming. I saw tangles of intestines torn from the body of a tarn. I turned the stroke of a lance with my small shield. I heard a man scream, his arm gone. The disemboweled tarn fell away from us, fluttering, spinning downward. With a shake of its mighty head my tarn flung the shield from its beak, a hundred feet away, the arm still inserted in the shield straps. Then the tarn was climbing, climbing. Tarns swirled about us, below us. Some struck one another. I gave the tarn his rein. Four tarns began to follow us. Still did my tarn climb. Through clouds, such bright, lofty fogs, did we ascend. Below us, like birds springing wonderously from the snow, tarns and their riders emerged from the clouds, following us.

"Will you seek the sun?" I laughed.

Could it be that, after all these years, the tactics of combat on tarnback remained so fresh, so vivid, in the eager, dark brain of my mighty mount? Could they be retained so perfectly, with such exactness, seemingly as terrible and sharp as in the days when they were first imprinted, high above grassy fields, the walls of Ko-ro-ba in the distance?

I fought for breath.

The mighty lungs of the tarn expanded. I could feel their motion between my knees. It drew the thin air deeply into those moist, widened cavities. Still we climbed.

Then we turned, the sun at our back.

The other tarns, strung out now, struggling, wings beating painfully, sporadically, against the thin air, hung below us. They were exhausted. They could climb no further. They began to turn back.

Out of the sun struck the great tarn. As I had been trained to do I drew as deep a breath as possible before the dive began. It is not impossible to breathe during such a descent, particularly after the first moments, even in the rushing wind, but it is generally recommended that one do not do so. It is thought that breathing may effect the concentration, perhaps altering or complicating the relationship with the target. The bird and the rider, in effect, are the projectile. The tarn itself, it might be noted, does not draw another breath until the impact or the vicinity of the impact, if the strike fails to find its mark. The descent velocities in a strike of this sort are incredible, and have never been precisely calculated. They are estimated, however, at something in the neighborhood of four hundred pasangs per Ahn.*

There were snappings, as of wood breaking, but it was not wood. The first tarn, that highest, was struck full in the back, the man broken between the two bodies. Its back was broken and perhaps the neck of the man in the same blow. As a hurricane can imbed a straw in a post so, too, are compounded the forces involved by the speed of the stroke.

Again the tarn aligned itself, smote downward, then lifted its wings, almost folded on either side of me, its talons, like great hooks, lowered.

It caught the second tarn about the neck, as it swerved madly, by the grasping talons of its left foot, and I was thrown about, upside down, the ground seeming to be over my head, and the two birds spun in the air and then my tarn disengaged itself, the neck of the other bird flopping to the side, blood caught in the wind, like red rain.

* No terrestrial conversion is supplied in the Cabot ms. for this figure. Equivalences supplied elsewhere in the Cabot mss. suggest a figure of a little over two hundred miles per hour. —J.N.

Its rider's scream alerted the third rider, but, in a moment, the talons had locked upon him, his bird exhausted, struggling in the air, and he was torn upward from the girth rope. He was released, falling through the clouds below us, disappearing. He would fall, I conjectured, through the Kinyanpi formation below, that formation being by now, I supposed, arrested by the other tarnsmen, those from Council Rock. Beneath those placid, fleecy clouds I had little doubt there was bloody war in the air.

The fourth rider made good his escape, descending through the clouds, disappearing.

I swung the tarn about, for a moment, over the clouds, and then entered them, several hundred feet from where the foe had disappeared.

An escape trajectory, if one is dealing with a wily foe, can prove to be a tunnel of ambush.

I took the tarn below the clouds and there again made visual contact with the foe. He was racing down to join his fellows.

This pleased me. I hoped that he would spread alarms among them.

I was less pleased by what else I saw and yet I knew I could have expected little that was different.

Our bold tarnsmen from Council Rock fought amidst circling Kinyanpi.

They were outnumbered easily by ten to one. The outcome of such an arrangement was surely a foregone conclusion unless some new ingredient might intervene, something unexpected or different, which might drastically alter the balances of battle.

That our men had lasted this long was a function of several factors, factors on which I had desperately relied. As nearly as I could determine, few tribes in the Barrens had mastered the tarn. That there were Kinyanpi had almost been taken as a matter of myth by the Kaiila until their dramatic appearance at the summer camp. This suggested that such groups were rare. The Kinyanpi, I conjectured, occupied a position rather analogous to that of Earth tribes who might have been among the first, in the sixteen and seventeen hundreds, to master the horse. Due to lack of competition their battle skills, originally developed in connection with the kaiila, would presumably have declined. Similarly, due also to a lack of competition, and the merciless selections of war, they had not yet become to the tarn as the normal warrior in the Barrens is to his kaiila, namely, a member of a matched fighting unit. On the other hand, the shield and lance skills of the Kaiila were fresh, and our men were tried warriors. Secondly, I had had the men and their tarns train as fighting units, not only the man and his mount, but the men and their mounts, in pairs and prides, as well. Signals were conveyed not by tarn drums, however, but, in one of the manners of the Barrens, by Herlit-bone whistles.

In one of my calculations I had been disappointed. I had hoped that the mere appearance of the great black tarn would inspire terror in the Kinyanpi and that they would withdraw.

Five riders had done so, when it had appeared suddenly, unexpectedly, behind me, in the vicinity of a Yellow-Knife camp in which they had been sojourning, where we had captured the fifteen tarns.

The riders below, however, perhaps because of their numbers, or perhaps their leadership, or their confidence in their medicine, had not done so.

Discomfited they might have been. Frightened they might have been. But they had not withdrawn.

"Down, Ubar of the Skies!" I cried.

Perhaps they had feared less than might have Yellow Knives, Fleer or Kaiila, because they were more familiar with tarns than such tribes. Perhaps they feared less because it was daylight. Perhaps they had feared less because the tarn bore reins, a girth rope, a rider, and had approached them from Council Rock.

Their apprehensions must be restored.

I had formed a plan.

Down we plummeted into the midst of the Kinyanpi. Screaming, men scattered on their tarns. We struck none. I had slung my weapons about me. My shield was at my hip.

The tarn hung, hovering, in the air, as the Kinyanpi regrouped.

I pointed to three of them, one after the other, and then, my arms folded, spoke a command to Ubar of the Skies. "One-strap." The bird began to ascend.

I had seen the surprise of the Kinyanpi when I had released the reins. Their eyes had widened when they had seen my arms were folded. Let it dawn on them that the tarn had obeyed my mere word. I did not look back, for fear of spoiling the effect. I hoped, of course, that the three men would be following me.

As soon as I had entered the clouds I whipped out my small bow and put an arrow to the string, and held two in the bow hand, and, reseizing the reins, brought the tarn about, and yet it seemed it needed no guidance. Dark and silent in the fog it veered about. One by one the Kinyanpi, consecutively, as I had hoped, entered the cloud. This was the tunnel of ambush, as it is called. A trained tarnsman is taught to avoid it. Three tarns, riderless, returned to the formation below.

I replaced the bow. Again, allowing a suitable interval, I plummeted the tarn downward, again into the midst of the Kinyanpi.

Interestingly, as nearly as I could determine, no fighting had taken place in my absence.

My tarn braked in the air, spreading and beating its wings. Again my arms were folded. I pointed dramatically at a fellow. He shook his head wildly and pulled his tarn away. I pointed at another fellow. He, too, declined my invitation. One of the Kinyanpi struck his painted chest, crying out. I pointed to him. Then I pointed to two others. They looked at one another, uneasily. Then, regally, I looked away. "One-strap," I said to Ubar of the Skies.

We ascended again to the clouds.

I listened carefully, every sense alert. The fellow who had struck himself on the chest was eager. I barely had time to enter the cloud, with apparent leisure, than I had turned and he was upon me. I had no time to draw the bow. The lance thrust at me and I clutched at it, and then caught it. Tarn to tarn we grappled for the lance. I let him think he was wrenching it away from me. This freed my right hand for the knife. He took it, to the hilt, in his left side, under the ribs. I cut the girth rope on his tarn and drew him across to the back of my own tarn. I killed him there. I then took the tarn to a place in the clouds which I judged to be above the Kinyanpi formation. There I released the body. It would fall through the formation.

"Hunt," I said to Ubar of the Skies. We moved quietly, a stroke at a time, through the sunlit vapor of the cloud.

Then, too, within the cloud, I saw the other riders below

me. They had kept together. They were wiser than the others. Then I could not see them in the cloud.

"Hunt," I whispered to Ubar of the Skies.

Ubar of the Skies, given his rein, began to circle, every sense in that great body tense and alert. I fitted an arrow to the string of my bow.

Sometimes it seemed almost as though we were motionless, floating, or arrested in time and space, and that it was the moist, nebulous substance of the cloud that flowed past us, almost as though we were immersed in a river of fog.

Then I saw shapes before us. Ubar of the Skies was approaching from behind and on the right. Most men are right-handed. It is more difficult, thusly, for them to turn and fire over their right shoulder. Ubar of the Skies was a trained tarn of war.

The arrow, fired from not more than fifteen feet away, entered the body of the rider on the right below the left shoulder blade and almost at the same instant Ubar of the Skies, screaming, with those hooklike, terrible talons tore the body of the rider on the left from the girth rope. I seized the reins of the tarn whose rider I had struck with the arrow. I lowered my head, avoiding the wing. Then the wing, for a moment, was arrested, caught against that of Ubar of the Skies. I jerked free, from the front, where it protruded, the arrow, drawing it through the body. I did not want visible evidence of how the rider had met his end. The tarn freed its wing and I was almost struck from the back of Ubar of the Skies. The other rider was screaming, locked in talons below me. I returned the bloody arrow to the quiver. As I could I drew the tarn whose reins I held beside us, leaning forward on the back of Ubar of the Skies. Such reins are not made for leading and the stroke of the wings, so close to my bird, was irregular, uneven and frantic. Then I cut the girth rope on the tarn, when we were over the Kinyanpi below, and let the body slide from its back. With little regret I released the tarn. It sped away.

The body would seem to have fallen from the sky, from the clouds, mysteriously, inexplicably, like a meteor amongst them, penetrating their formation, thence descending to its encounter with the grasslands below.

I hovered, high in the clouds, over where the Kinyanpi circled below.

I waited a suitable interval.

The man was screaming beneath me.

I recalled a child, slain and mutilated in a summer camp. "Teach me to kill," had said Cuwignaka.

"Release," I said to Ubar of the Skies.

The man, gesticulating, flailing, screaming, the sound rapidly fading, sank away from me, drawn by gravity, through the air.

I waited another suitable interval and then I, again, took Ubar of the Skies downward. Again I hovered among terrified Kinyanpi, my arms folded. Let them consider what medicine such a foe might possess.

I then, regally, imperiously, pointed to the chieftain of the Kinyanpi, he most prominent among them, he next to the bearer of the feathered staff, the battle staff.

He shook his head, wildly. I then, with a sweeping gesture, pointed to the east, that direction from which they had come. Wildly he turned his tarn and, crying out, followed by his men, fled.

"Quickly!" I cried to Cuwignaka, Canka, Hci and the others. "Back to Council Rock!"

Soldiers had established a hold on the eastern ledges of Council Rock, to which they had been climbing, those ledges opposite those above the trail, up which, slowly, medicine drums beating, medicine men dancing about the beasts, the procession of Yellow Knives, a few minutes ago, had begun its climb. Behind the soldiers who attained the ledge other soldiers, roped together, clambered upward. The eastern face of Council Rock seemed covered with men and ropes.

Then tarns, screaming, talons raking, wings beating, hurtled among the startled soldiers on the ledge, seizing and tearing at them, blasts of wind even from the wings forcing some back over the edge. The defenders leaped forward. We landed our tarns among a litter of bodies, red and white, on the ledge.

I looked down, at the ropes of men, not yet to the top. "Let those with tarns, who lost women and children at the summer camp, attend to these," I said.

In a moment tarns had swept again from the ledge and then, seizing ropes and men in talons, at the very rock face itself, dragged dangling, screaming men from the sheer surface; ropes and men, tangled, were pulled away from the surface; ropes and men, torn loose from hand and footholds, unsupported, sped twisting and turning to the rocks below.

I raced across the top of Council Rock, men behind me. The Yellow Knives, on the western side of Council Rock, prevented by the mountain from knowing what had occurred in the air to the east, and on the eastern faces of the rock, singing their medicine, their hearing throbbing with the beat of drums, had not desisted in their procession to the summit; they had continued to ascend the trail.

"You are done!" cried Iwoso. "You are finished!" Roped to the post as she was, she, too, was ignorant of the developments to the east.

Yellow Knives were not twenty-five feet below me, on the trail. In their lead surrounded by medicine men, beating on drums and dancing, were Sardak and Kog, and five others of the Kurii. I also saw, prominent among the Yellow Knives, Alfred, with soldiers, and a Yellow Knife I recognized as the third of the war chiefs who had been at the summer camp. He had not taken part, as far as I knew, in the earlier actions. It was his intention, however, I gathered, to participate in the anticipated resolution of the siege, in his forces' climactic victory.

Before resistance had crumbled at the appearance of the Kurii.

Even now the barricade at the summit was deserted.

Some fifty to seventy feet from the barricade the procession stopped.

The drums stopped. The medicine men stopped dancing. They drew back.

Kog and Sardak came forward, followed by the others.

The barricade was empty.

The trail was silent.

Then the barricade was no longer empty. Atop it, on the logs and stakes, the wind moving in its fur, stood a gigantic Kur.

Yellow Knives crowded back against one another, uneasily. They looked to Kog and Sardak, but these beasts, standing as though stunned, or electrified, on the stony trail, were oblivious of them.

The Kur on the barricade distended its nostrils, drinking scent.

Sardak stepped forward. He reared upright, increasing his scanning range. He moved his tentaclelike fingers on his chest, which gesture, I think, is a displacement activity. Some claim it has the function of cleaning the claws.

The ears of the beast on the barricade, one half torn away, flattened themselves against the side of the head.

Sardak's ears, too, lay back.

I saw that the claws of the rear appendages, or feet, of the monster on the barricade, had emerged. So, too, I noted, had those of Sardak.

The beasts did not speak to one another. Words were not necessary.

Swiftly, moving with incredible grace and lightness for its bulk, the beast on the barricade descended to the trail.

Sardak, the two rings of reddish alloy on his left wrist, advanced to meet it.

They stopped, some ten feet from one another, alone, facing one another on the trail, between the barricade and the other beasts and Yellow Knives.

They then began, keeping very low, on all fours, to circle one another.

Occasionally one would reach out, or snarl, or make a sudden movement, but not charging, to see the response of the other. Fangs were bared.

The hair on the back of my neck rose. Was it like this, I wondered, in the ancient days of the Kurii, long before the steel worlds, long before, even, the development of their technology. Is it like this, I wondered, even today, in the steel ships, in the "killings."

Then the two beasts, as though they had satisfied themselves, squatted down, their hind legs under them, facing one another. To a superficial observer, they might have seemed somnolent. But I could sense the ripple of muscle, the tingle of nerve, beneath the fur in those mighty bodies. They were somnolent as a gun is somnolent, one with a finger tensed, poised, upon its trigger.

Suddenly, as one, both beasts leapt at one another, and seemed, grappling, biting and tearing, claws raking, almost as if they were a single, blurred animal cutting and tearing at its own body. There was a scratching of claws on the stony trail. They rolled and tore at one another and blood, from drenched fur, marked the stone, leaving the pattern of the fur.

They then backed away from one another again, and again began to circle.

It had been no more than a passage at arms.

Again they sprang towards one another and again, sometimes, their movements were so rapid, turning and grappling, biting and tearing, that I could not even follow them. The energy and speed of such beasts is awesome.

Then they had again separated.

The medicine men of the Yellow Knives looked at one another, frightened. There was blood on the rock. Such things, then, could bleed.

Zarendargar, Half-Ear, my friend, had then, I suspected, made his determinations. I do not think Sardak understood this, at the time.

I fitted an arrow to the string of my bow.

Once more the beasts charged and met with fierce impact. Then Zarendargar was behind Sardak. Sardak flung his head back, to close the space between the skull and the vertebrae, his eyes like wild moons, but it was too late. The massive jaws of Zarendargar, inch by inch, Sardak held in his arms, forced the head forward. Then with a sound of tearing muscle and skin, and crushed bone, Zarendargar's jaws closed. Men watched, horrified, as Zarendargar, holding it by the neck, it half bitten through, in his jaws, shook the body, fiercely. He then flung it from him and leaped up and down, scratching at his chest. He flung his head up to the sun and howled his victory. For a moment or two the body on the rock still bled, the movements of the heart marked in the gouts of fluid that surged over the fur. The head lay askew, to one side, held by vessels and skin. Zarendargar screamed and leaped on the stone, and, scratching, climbed a bit up the rock face from the trail, and then fell back, and leaped again. The sun and sky were again saluted by the victory cry of the Kur. There was blood and fur at his mouth. I could see the double row of fangs, streaked with red, the long, dark tongue emergent like a serpent from the spittle and blood, the foam, of the kill. Kurii, I reminded myself, are not men.

Yellow Knives shrank back.

Zarendargar then lifted the body of Sardak in his hands and held it over his head. The arm of Sardak, with its two rings of reddish alloy, hung limp. The head hung a foot from the body. Then Zarendargar flung the body from the trail, down, down, onto the rocks below.

I loosened the arrow from my bow into the heart of Kog. He stiffened, the feathers almost lost in the fur, and then fell.

Kaiila warriors had now appeared on the ledges beside me, and were visible now, armed, at the barricade.

The Yellow Knives began to back downward. The war chief cried out to them, presumably ordering them to remain in place. A medicine man turned and fled. Kurii looked about, at one another. None seemed eager to advance on Zarendargar.

Zarendargar stood before the barricade, his arms lifted, snarling, his face and body bloody.

"Hold!" cried Alfred to those about him. "Hold! Do not fall back! Attack! Attack!" He cried out in Gorean. There were few there, I supposed, except for the handful of soldiers with him, who understood him. No one moved decisively. "Attack! Attack!" cried Alfred. He took a step forward but none, clearly, intended to follow him, "Attack!" he cried.

The Yellow Knives looked at one another. They were undecided. The Yellow-Knife war chief gestured toward the barricade. The Yellow Knives wavered. It seemed their medicine had failed them. They had lost their medicine.

At this moment Ubar of the Skies appeared behind me, outlined against the sky. He extended his mighty wings and smote them against the air. He uttered the challenge scream of the tarn.

The Yellow Knives then turned and fled.

Kaiila swarmed over and through the barricade, with clubs and lances, and shields and knives. There was confusion below.

Arrows were loosened from the height of the escarpment into the fleeing Yellow Knives. Fighting took place at a dozen places on the trail. Some of our men who were tarnsmen brought their tarns into the fray, raking down at the Yellow Knives. Yellow Knives, crowding, fleeing, forced many of their own number from the trail.

"Look!" I said. In the distance, coming from the west, were columns of dust.

"They are coming!" cried Cuwignaka, elatedly.

"Yes," I said.

These would be the Dust Legs, the Sleen and Fleer, tribes to whom we had sent riders.

We had been the bait, on Council Rock, to lure the Yellow Knives and soldiers into a trap, a trap which these other tribes, acting in coalition, were to spring shut. Clearly their best interests were involved in doing so. The Yellow Knives, in cooperating with white soldiers, had betrayed the Memory. In such a way, according to the Memory, an earlier tragedy, now almost lost in legends, had begun. The Barrens must be protected. Too, sacrilege had been performed, in the attack on a summer camp. Was this not to be avenged? Even more seriously Kinyanpi had come to the more western countries. Such alliances, those of Yellow Knives with forces such as those of the white soldiers and the Kinyanpi, threatened the delicate tribal balances in the Barrens. Such events might produce dislocations, interfering with the migrations of the Pte, the Kailiauk, and forcing tribes from ancestral hunting grounds. Our agents' arguments had been, it seemed, persuasive. Too late had the newcomers arrived to aid in the fray. Not too late, however, were they to close off a hundred avenues of retreat, to interfere with a thousand escapes, to wreak havoc among a withdrawing, demoralized, terrorized enemy.

I saw Alfred struck down from behind with the heavy, balled knob of a carved wooden canhpi.

Iwoso was white with terror, roped to her post, seeing the retreat of the Yellow Knives.

Threading his way among the fighting groups on the trail, slowly making his way upward, was he who had been the third of the three war chiefs at the summer camp.

I pointed him out to Hci.

"I have seen him," said Hci.

The man was carrying a bow and arrows. He moved with purpose. An arrow was fitted to the string.

His face, under the fearsome paint, was contorted with rage. He stopped below us, on the trail. Iwoso, helplessly roped to her post, moaned. She cried out something to him, pleadingly. She was in clear view, only a few feet above him. She was well displayed. Her ankles were roped back against the post; at the waist, too, she was fastened to it, the rawhide ropes deep in her belly, and deep, too, in the notch behind the post; her neck, too, was tied to the post; and her hands, as well, in tight, rawhide loops, rather at her sides and slightly behind her. She cried out again to him, pleadingly. She could do little more than squirm in her bonds, and scarcely that. I had seen to it. The arrow, from below, was aligned on her heart. It leapt from the string, speeding toward the naked, roped beauty. Hci interposed his shield, and the arrow, deflected, caromed off a hundred feet in the air. The Yellow Knife below, with a cry of rage, turned then, and fled down the trail.

"I have business," said Hci. Lightly, moving swiftly, discarding his shield, armed now only with his knife, he made his way from our position, to the trail summit, and to the barricade. I then saw him, in a moment, making his way down the trail.

Iwoso gasped, and tried to turn her head away, her neck in the ropes.

"Look," said Hci.

Iwoso looked, helplessly, commanded.

The scalp, freshly cut, bloody, dripping, hung before her face, held in Hci's fist.

"It is the scalp of he who would have slain you," said Hci, "he with whom you conspired."

She closed her eyes, shuddering.

"Look," said Hci.

She opened her eyes, looking again upon the bloody trophy.

"Do you understand?" asked Hci.

"Yes, my captor," she said, in a small voice.

Hci then put the scalp in his belt. Blood from it ran down his leg, down his naked thigh, as he wore the breechclout.

It was the scalp of he who had been the third of the war chiefs in the summer camp.

Iwoso then closed her eyes, in misery, turning her head away, her head held in place by the ropes under her chin.

I removed the girth rope from Ubar of the Skies. I took the reins from the sable monster.

"You are free, Sweet Friend," I said. I caressed that savage beak. It put it down, against my side. Ubar of the Skies was not a woman, something to be owned and dominated, something, even with the whip, if necessary, to be forced to love and serve, something which could not be fulfilled until it found itself helplessly, with no recourse whatsoever, will-lessly, at the feet of a master.

"The trail is clear," I said to Hci.

"Yes," he said.

The five Kurii, I saw, those who had been with Sardak and Kog, lay slaughtered on the trail. They had been riddled with arrows and hacked to pieces. Some, I think, may have been slain by Yellow Knives who, in wrath, sensing perhaps a betrayal or fraud in them, had fallen upon them.

It would be a long time, I thought, before Kaiila or Yellow Knives would be likely to again take such beasts for supernatural creatures, visitants from the medicine world.

"Do you see those dusts?" Hci asked Iwoso, pointing to various points in the west.

"Yes," she said.

"Those will be Sleen and Dust Legs, even Fleer," he said, "intercepting your people, doing massacre among them."

I could see riders, even, in the Yellow-Knife camp, below. Lodges were burning.

"There will be much loot, many kaiila," said Cuwignaka. "Doubtless they will find their journey worth their while."

"And they need not even have attacked a summer camp," said Hci, bitterly.

Iwoso sobbed.

"Need they?" asked Hci.

"No, my captor," said Iwoso.

"The Yellow Knives are defeated," said Hci to her. "They are scattered. They flee for their lives."

"Yes, my captor," she said.

"There is now no hope of rescue for you, my roped, Yellow-Knife slut," said Hci.

"No, my captor," she said.

"You are now totally alone," he said.

"Yes, my captor," she said.

"You now belong to the Kaiila," he said.

"Yes, my captor," she said.

48

TWO WOMEN

"Free this slave," said Hci to Iwoso, pointing to Bloketu.

"Yes, my captor," said Iwoso.

I looked down from the escarpment to the victory camp below, where, yesterday, the Yellow Knives had had their encampment. The site was now occupied by Dust Legs, Sleen and Fleer.

"I free you," said Iwoso to Bloketu. She fumbled with the knot on Bloketu's collar, removing it from her.

It was early in the morning.

We had brought the girls to the edge of the escarpment, near the posts. We had not roped them to them, however. They had spent the night, as the several nights previously, hooded and bound in the prison lodge. They were still stripped, as before. In another such lodge, hooded and bound, were Alfred, and four of his officers. He had not perished of the blow from the knob-headed canhpi. These were all who had survived of the soldiers.

"Kneel, Free Women," said Hci.

Both of the girls, naked, knelt on the stone at his feet.

"Put your heads down," said Hci.

They lowered their heads.

"I pronounce you both slaves of the Kaiila," said Hci.

They shuddered, slaves.

"Your former names, 'Bloketu' and 'Iwoso'," said Hci, "are now put on you as slave names."

They trembled, named.

"You may raise your heads," said Hci.

They did so, frightened, public slaves. Bloketu tried to read in the eyes of Cuwignaka, and Iwoso tried to read in the eyes of Hci, what was to be her fate. The status of being a public slave tends to be an ambiguous one. What is a girl to do, how is she to act, to whom is she to relate? In such a status she is an impersonal property, as of a state, clan or tribe. No particular master is likely to have any special concern for her, nor can she, as such a slave, ameliorate or improve her condition, or even secure, to some extent, her possibilities of survival, by becoming, in virtue of deep, sweet, delicate, intimate and exquisite relationships, so fulfilling to both the woman and the man, a prized possession of her owner, a treasure to her master.

Hci swung coiled ropes in his hand.

He then struck Iwoso.

"Have you ever been whipped?" he asked.

"Yours is the first blow that was ever put upon my body, Master," she said.

He then struck her again, savagely. "Oh!" she cried, putting her head down to the stone.

"Are you pretty?" asked Hci. "Answer 'Yes' or 'No'."

"No!" said Iwoso.

"Lying slave!" said Hci. He then struck her another blow.

"Are you pretty?" asked Hci.

"Yes," cried Iwoso. "I am pretty!"

"Pretentious, arrogant slave!" cried Hci. "Surely you know that that is a judgment more properly to be made by masters than imbonded sluts. It seems you must be whipped."

"Have mercy, Master!" cried Iwoso.

He then struck her, twice more. She sobbed, head down, at his feet.

"Do you persist in being disobedient?" he inquired.

"Master!" she wept, in protest.

"Answer 'Yes' or 'No'," he said.

"Master!" she cried.

"Yes, or no?" he asked.

"No," she wept. "No!"

"Thus," said he, "you admit to having been previously disobedient."

He then struck her, three times.

"Do you persist in being disobedient?" he then inquired, again.

"Yes!" she cried, miserable.

"Then, clearly," he said, "you are to be whipped, or slain." He then struck her five times.

"No," she wept. "No! No!"

"Then, again," said he, "you acknowledge a previous fault."

He then struck her once more.

She lay then, on her stomach, her soft body on the hard stone, her back striped, sobbing, at Hci's feet.

"Have you been tricked?" asked Hci.

"Yes, Master," she sobbed.

"As you see," said Hci, quoting Iwoso's remark to Bloketu in her lodge, overheard by us the night of their capture, "it is not difficult to trick a stupid slave."

"No, Master," she wept.

Bloketu, I thought, had been avenged.

"Have pity on me, Master," wept Iwoso.

"On your knees," said Hci. Both girls, then, were kneeling, stripped, at his feet.

"In virtue of the power vested in me as a commander in the Sleen Soldiers, and in accordance with the wishes of my father, Mahpiyasapa, civil chieftain of the Isbu Kaiila," said Hci, "I pronounce you both free."

They looked up at him, wildly.

"It is said," he said. "Bring the staff and thongs," he said to me.

I brought the long staff, about seven feet long. This was bound behind the necks of Bloketu and Iwoso. I then tied their hands together behind their backs.

"What is going on?" cried Iwoso.

"You have had a taste of slavery," said Hci. "Now you have been freed."

"But, why!" cried Iwoso.

"That you may, together, in the full accountability of the free person," said Hci, "face the justice of the Kaiila people."

Bloketu began to sob.

"No!" cried Iwoso. "No!"

49

JUDGMENT

"There is no doubt as to the guilt of these two," said Mahpiyasapa.

The men about him, and behind him, grunted their assent. "Cinto!" said several. "Surely! Certainly! Agreed!"

The two women, kneeling before the men, the staff bound behind their necks, their hands tied behind their backs, trembled.

"The testimonies have been taken," said Mahpiyasapa. "The evidence is clear. Concerning their complicity in the matter of the attack on the summer camp there is no doubt."

"Cinto!" said the men. "Agreed!"

"They have conspired against the Kaiila people," said Mahpiyasapa.

"Cinto!" said the men.

"They have betrayed the Kaiila," said Mahpiyasapa.

"Cinto!" said the men.

"Have you anything to say?" asked Mahpiyasapa.

The girls, their heads down, the heavy staff behind their necks, did not speak.

"You are found guilty," said Mahpiyasapa.

They trembled, sobbing.

"As one of you was once the daughter of a Kaiila chieftain, Watonka, who was once a great warrior amongst us, and was once my friend, and one of you was once her maiden, I shall not have you subjected to tortures."

"Mahpiyasapa is merciful," said a man.

"Our women will not be pleased," said another man.

"You will be treated with the dignity of free women," said Mahpiyasapa.

"Let the sentence be passed," said Kahintokapa, he of the Casmu Kaiila, he of the Yellow-Kaiila Riders.

Bloketu put down her head.

"Proceed," said Iwoso. "Pass your sentence! I do not fear slavery!"

"In the morning," said Mahpiyasapa, "take them to the summit of the trail, where we had placed the barricade. There, then, from that place, let them be flung to the rocks below."

Bloketu looked at him, aghast.

"No," cried Iwoso. "No! No!"

50

WHAT OCCURRED AT THE SUMMIT OF THE TRAIL

The wind was cool at the summit of the trail, near where the barricade had been placed.

It was shortly after dawn.

The two prisoners were brought forth, stripped, their hands tied behind their back. The hair of both, now, was unbound. They seemed ashen. They seemed numb. It seemed they could scarcely stand. They were brought forth, slowly. Cuwignaka conducted Bloketu by the arm. Iwoso's arm was in the grip of Hci.

"Let their ankles be tied," said Mahpiyasapa.

Bloketu and Iwoso stood while Cuwignaka and Hci, crouching down, looped thongs about their ankles. They tied their ankles together in the fashion characteristic of close hobbles, the ankles not crossed but parallel to one another. In this way the girls, though well secured, could remain standing.

"Are the prisoners present?" asked Mahpiyasapa.

"Yes," said Cuwignaka.

"Yes," said Hci.

"Are their wrists tied?" asked Mahpiyasapa.

"Yes," said Cuwignaka.

"Yes," said Hci.

"Are their ankles tied?" asked Mahpiyasapa.

"Yes," said Cuwignaka.

"Yes," said Hci.

"Let the sentence be carried out," said Mahpiyasapa. Behind him, and standing about, as well, were the members of the council. Others, too, stood about.

Cuwignaka seized Bloketu from behind by the arms. "No, no!" she cried, wildly, throwing her head back. Cuwignaka forced her inexorably, implacably, to the edge. "I beg the alternative!" screamed Bloketu. "I beg the alternative!" screamed Bloketu. "I beg the alternative!"

Cuwignaka looked at Mahpiyasapa.

"What alternative?" cried Iwoso, wildly.

Mahpiyasapa made a sign and Cuwignaka, at the very edge of the surface, released Bloketu. She fell to her knees and scrambled back from the edge, her knees abraded on the rock. She, kneeling, her hands tied behind her, her ankles thonged, wildly, faced Mahpiyasapa. "I beg the alternative," she wept, hysterically, "Master!"

"Master?" asked Mahpiyasapa.

"Yes, 'Master'! " she cried. "As a slave I must address all free men as 'Master.' "

"You are not a slave," said Mahpiyasapa. "You are a free woman."

"No, Master!" she cried. "I am a slave! I am a slave! I pronounce myself a slave! I have been a slave for years, a secret slave. I now confess my deception, acknowledging that I am, and have been, a slave, only a slave, for years! Forgive me, Masters!"

"Look at her knees!" said a man.

The girl looked down, startled. Her knees, without her even having thought of it, widely spread, were in slave position. It had been done inadvertently, unpremeditatively, naturally, unconsciously. Such things can betray a woman. But she did not, then, draw her knees together. She remained, agonized, frightened, in the shameful position.

"Slave!" cried more than one man, scornfully.

"Are you a white female?" inquired a man.

"We are all sisters," she said. "I am no more than they."

"You have pronounced yourself a slave," said Mahpiyasapa, wonderingly.

"Yes, Master," she said.

"Now," said Mahpiyasapa, "you are a slave, even if you were not before."

"Yes, Master," she said.

"What is your name?" asked Mahpiyasapa.

"I have no name," she said.

"This being a slave," said Mahpiyasapa to the members of the council, standing about him, "clearly it is not fitting that she be subjected to the honorable death of a free woman."

The members of the council nodded their agreement.

"Later, shameless slave," said Mahpiyasapa to she who had been Bloketu, "you who had the insolence, the punishable audacity, to pretend to be a free woman, it will be decided what is to be done with you."

The slave, trembling, put down her head.

"This one, at least," said Hci, seizing Iwoso from behind by the arms, "is a free woman."

"Then," said Mahpiyasapa, angrily, "let the sentence, as passed, be carried out in her case!"

"No!" cried Iwoso, helpless as a doll in Hci's merciless grip. "I beg permission to kneel!"

Hci looked at Mahpiyasapa. Then he let Iwoso fall to her knees. She was weeping. "I, too, am a slave," she wept. "I, too, am a slave!"

She threw her soft body to the rock at Mahpiyasapa's feet. Lying on her belly before him, her hands bound behind her back, her ankles thonged, she pressed her lips, again and again, helplessly, to his moccasins, covering them with kisses. "I, too, am a slave!" she wept.

"On your knees," he sternly ordered her.

She struggled up to her knees. She noticed, startled, that her knees were spread widely. But then, no more than the other girl, did she close them.

"Speak!" ordered Mahpiyasapa.

"I pronounce myself slave," she said. "I, too, I confess, have been a secret slave, one masquerading for years as a free woman!"

"Is this true?" asked Mahpiyasapa.

"Yes, Master," she said.

"She lies merely to avoid the rocks," said a man, sneeringly.

"She may think she is lying," said Mahpiyasapa, "but recourse to such a lie would be had only by one who is truly a slave."

"That is true," said the man, musingly.

"In any event," said a man, "she has now pronounced herself a slave."

"Yes," said another man.

"You understand, do you not," asked Mahpiyasapa of the girl, "that the words alone were sufficient, that in speaking them you became a slave, even if you were not a slave before?"

"Yes, Master," she said. Matters such as intention, as I have earlier indicated, are in such cases irrelevant to the legal enactments involved.

"What is your name?" asked Mahpiyasapa.

"I have no name," she said.

"These women are slaves," said Mahpiyasapa, turning to the council. "No longer is it fitting that they be subjected to the honorable death of free women."

The council grunted its agreement.

"The sentence then," said Mahpiyasapa, "is rescinded."

The girls looked up at him, elated.

"Now give them to the women," said a man.

"They will be pleased to get them," said another.

"That should have been done in the first place," said another.

"Please, no," begged she who had been Bloketu.

"As slaves," said Mahpiyasapa to the girls, "you may now be subjected to lengthy and insidious tortures, and not even necessarily for crimes, at so little as the whim of a master."

The girls looked at him, trembling, their eyes wide with terror.

"Give them to the women," laughed a man.

"Take us as slaves," begged she who had been Bloketu.

"Please, Masters!" wept she who had once been the proud Iwoso.

"I do not accept you as slaves of the Kaiila," said Mahpiyasapa.

The girls shuddered, rejected.

"Is there any here," asked Mahpiyasapa, "who would accept these slaves?"

No one spoke.

"Give them to the women," said a man.

"Give them to the women!" cried several of the men.

"Please, Master," cried she who had been Bloketu, suddenly, turning and throwing herself to her shoulder, and then to her belly, before Cuwignaka. She kissed his moccasins fervently, lying bound on her belly before him. "Please, Master," she begged, weeping, "please accept me as a slave!"

Iwoso threw herself on her belly, on the rock, before Hci. "I am a slave!" she wept. "Please, Master, do not let them give me to the women!" Her tears flowed copiously, staining the rock and his moccasins. Her body trembled. Her small wrists moved helplessly behind her, confined in their tight thongs. Her lips pressed again and again to his moccasins, covering them with pleading, desperate kisses. "I beg you, Master!" she wept. "Please, please accept me as a slave!"

He crouched down, and turned her to her side, that she might look up at him. "You said you would rather die than be my slave," he said.

"I lied," she said. "I lied! I am a slave! You may punish me for such things!"

"I often wondered," said Hci, "if you might not have been a slave."

"You see now it is true, Master!" she said.

He regarded her.

"But not only am I a slave," she said. "I am your slave!"

"My slave?" he asked.

"For years," she said, "I have known that I was your slave. Surely, too, you, when you looked upon me, must have known that you were my master!"

Hci said nothing.

"These things were confirmed at the post," she said, "when you taught me my sex, and your power!"

Hci regarded her, not speaking. His face was expressionless.

"I ask only," she said, "the opportunity to prove to you that I am worthy of being owned."

He stood up, his arms folded. He was lean and strong, in the breechclout.

"Give them to the women!" cried a man.

"Give them to the women!" cried men.

"No," said Cuwignaka.

The men were suddenly silent, startled.

"I accept this woman," he said, indicating she who had been Bloketu, "as my slave."

She who had been Bloketu laid her cheek on the rock beside his moccasins, shuddering.

"Give that one to the women!" cried a man, indicating she who had been Iwoso.

"No," said Hci, his arms folded, surveying the men. "She is my slave."

"So be it," said Mahpiyasapa. "The matter is done." He, then, and the others, began to disperse.

Iwoso lay shuddering at Hci's feet, helpless.

"You are Cespu," said Cuwignaka to she who had been Bloketu.

"Yes, my master," she said. In Kaiila, the word 'cespu' means "wart."

"You are Cesli," said Hci to she who had been Iwoso.

"Yes, my master," she said, named. The word 'cesli' in Kaiila means "dung," that of either men or animals. Among the Kaiila such names as Cespu and Cesli are not uncommon for slaves.

I looked about. Cuwignaka and Cespu, and Hci and Cesli, and I, were alone at the trail summit. I decided that perhaps it was time to take my leave, as well.

Cuwignaka, gently, was untying the ankles of Cespu.

"A slave begs a boon," said Cesli to Hci.

"Yes?" asked Hci.

"Please untie my ankles, Master," she said.

"Why?" he asked.

"That I may serve my master," she said.

I withdrew from the summit of the trail and, in a few moments, stood high on the escarpment, looking over the plains. The horizons in the Barrens are vast and beautiful.

I looked down, once again, to where the barricade had been previously placed. There, near the trail's summit, about a hundred feet to my right and a few feet below me, on the ascendant, sloping, exposed surface of the trail, the cliff on one side, the wall on the other, slaves were in the arms of their masters.

I looked again then on the breadth of the Barrens, surveying them from the height of Council Rock, returning thereafter to my lodge.

51

THE FLEER BRING A VISITOR TO CAMP

"They found it on the prairie," said a man, "the Fleer did. They have brought it here."

Two stout ropes were on its neck, each slung to the saddle of a kaiila, on its opposite sides. Men with lances rode behind it. The creature was weak, and had been much bled. Its upper body was almost covered with ropes, binding its arms tightly to its sides. A heavy branch, about eighteen inches long and three inches thick, had been thrust between its jaws, and its jaws tied shut about it. The claws had been torn out of its feet.

"What is it?" asked a man.

"It is one like those who were with the Yellow Knives," said a man, "those defeated on the trail."

This was the Kur I had come to think of as the eighth Kur. It had been apparently separated from its companions at the time of the massacre of the wagon train and the fight between the soldiers and the savages. I had met it once before, when it had returned to the field to feed. It was that Kur which had been threatening the Waniyanpi, and whose attack I had frustrated. As we had not been similarly armed, it alone, afoot, and I with Grunt, he with an armed crossbow, and as it had not rushed upon me, I had not contested its withdrawal from the field. Such had seemed in accordance with codes to which I had once subscribed, codes which I had never forgotten. I had later learned from he who was then Pumpkin, then one of the Waniyanpi, that nine bodies of beasts had been found on the field. These had not been buried but had been dragged away, into the fields, by the red savages. Thus I had been unable at that time to determine whether or not Kog and Sardak had been among the Kur survivors of the attack. There had been seventeen wagons with the mercenary column which I had conjectured had contained one Kur apiece, given the irritability and territoriality of such beasts. Subtracting the nine beasts which had been slain in the fighting, probably mostly by Fleer, who seemed to have less apprehension concerning their appearance than several of the other tribes, I had arrived at a probable figure of eight Kur survivors.

When Cuwignaka and I had spied on the victory celebration of the Yellow Knives and soldiers at the summer camp we had counted only seven Kurii there, including Kog and Sardak. The eighth Kur, then, as I thought of him, seemed clearly to have been separated from his fellows. I had conjectured that he had perhaps perished on the prairie. Now, however, he had apparently been taken by Fleer, and within the general vicinity. This was, I suspected, no accident. He had probably been following the warriors, conjecturing perhaps that the movements of such large numbers of men might have to do, in one way or another, with the projects of his peers, with whom, doubtless, he had hoped to resume contact.

"What shall we do with him?" asked a man. "The Fleer do not want him. Too, some Fleer are uneasy concerning the killing of such a creature."

"Tell them," I said, "to take him to the lodge of the dark guest."

The man then turned to the Fleer. He pointed to the Kur, and then, with a sweeping gesture, indicated a direction. He then crossed the index fingers of his right and left hand, like lodge poles. He then lifted his head and opened his mouth, as though baring fangs, and lifted at the same time his right hand, the fingers crooked like claws, in a threatening gesture.

The Fleer in charge of the captive nodded and, with a movement of his hand, indicated that his companions, the Kur in their charge, should follow him.

My eyes and those of the Kur met. He, too, I think, recalled our previous encounter.

He was then, shuffling in the dust with bloody feet, from which the claws had been extracted, bound helplessly, dragged on ropes and prodded with the butts of lances, conducted toward the lodge of Zarendargar.

52

A BOON

"Take up your sword, I beg you," said Alfred. He had already seized up his sword from the low, flat rock in the midst of the encircling savages, Kaiila, Dust Legs, Fleer and Sleen. I looked at the sword, lying on the rock. I had little taste for what must be done.

"I do not think you are my match," I told him.

"If you do not," he said, "they will strip me, and put bells on me, and run me for boys on kaiila, as sport for their lances!"

Of the soldiers there had been only five survivors from the fray, Alfred, and four of his officers. Only the four officers had been permitted to draw lots. Of these three would be run for the boys, in the grasses, stripped and belled for lance sport. The other would be returned west of the Ihanke, that an account might be rendered of what had occurred in the Barrens.

"Please!" begged Alfred.

"They respect you as a commander," I said, "else they would not permit you this option."

"Please," he said.

I did not wish to see Alfred, belled as though he might be a slave girl, running, cut and bleeding under the lances. Circles are painted on the body. Points are scored. The least vulnerable areas, of course, are the first targets. The boys can make such a game last as long as an Ahn.

"You are of the Warriors, are you not?" asked Alfred.

"Yes," I said. My collar had been removed yesterday. I was now free.

"Please," he said.

I took up the sword from the flat rock.

It was soon finished.

I had then wiped the blade.

53

THE RED-HAIRED SLAVE GIRL

The naked, large-bosomed, red-haired slave licked and kissed at me and then, when I wished, unable to help herself, cried out her yielding to me.

She was still muchly covered with mud and had been somewhat beaten.

I had acquired her as a portion of my share of the loot from the Yellow Knives.

It seemed that when she had come to my lodge she had thought that her life with me, I being white, might be easier than it would be with a red master.

She had then spent the night outside the lodge, naked, in the rain, her hands tied behind her back, her neck tied to a stake.

She lay beneath me in the mud. I had freed her hands, but her neck was still fastened to the stake.

"Master," she gasped. "Master!"

I contented her for a bit, and then stood up. She looked up at me, helplessly.

"Master!" she whispered.

"Cespu, Mira!" I called. The girls came running, summoned slaves.

I indicated the large-bosomed redhead at my feet.

"Free her of the stake," I said, "and then clean and comb her. Make her sparkle."

"Yes, Master," said Mira.

"Then take her to Grunt, as a present," I said. "He will know what to do with her."

"Yes, Master," said Cespu.

"Yes, Master," said Mira.

54

I RETURN TO MY LODGE

"'Where is this one called Cuwignaka?'" translated the young, light-skinned, muscular fellow.

The warrior who had spoken was Fleer. This could be told at a glance from the hair, which was worn in a high, combed-back pompadour. He carried a feathered lance, with a long iron point, a trade point, socketed, fastened to the lance shaft with two rivets. His kaiila had a notched right ear. It bore various coup marks and exploit markings. Among these, on the flanks, on each flank, there was a society marking, a flat black line, a semicircular, curved blue line above it, the line of the earth, the overarching blue dome of the sky above it. He was a member of the Blue-Sky Riders. Grunt and I had seen him once before, long ago, in the vicinity of the field of a massacre, where a wagon train had been destroyed. Only recently had we learned that he was a war chief of the Fleer.

"I am Cuwignaka," said Cuwignaka, stepping forward. He now wore a breechclout. Yet, still, the shreds of the white dress clung about his upper body. Cuwignaka's words were translated by the light-skinned, muscular lad.

"I had thought," Grunt had told me yesterday, "that I was dead, but I discovered that I was not dead. I had a son, among the Dust Legs."

Grunt had found the lad in visiting the Dust Legs after the massacre of the summer camp. It had been largely through Grunt's influence that Dust Legs had made the long journey to Council Rock, to aid the Kaiila. The lad's mother, long ago, had loved Grunt. It was said she still lived. The lad had something of Grunt's facility with languages and his father's shrewdness and good sense in trading. He had been one of the few Dust Legs who was permitted in Fleer encampments, and had lived with them. He, originally conversing in sign, had subsequently learned their language.

Dust Leg and Kaiila, as I have earlier indicated, are closely related languages. Kaiila is commonly, interestingly, regarded as a dialectical version of Dust Leg. Dust Leg and Fleer are also related, but much more distantly. Commonly Dust Legs and Fleer, when they meet in peace, communicate in the *lingua franca* of the plains, sign. The lad, it was said, had children of his own.

The lad and Grunt had decided to go into partnership, this being thought to be to the advantage of both. Grunt could speak Gorean and the lad was fluent not only in Dust Leg and Kaiila, but Fleer as well. I had little doubt they would become famous on the plains. This winter, instead of returning west of the Ihanke, Grunt had told me that he planned to winter with the Dust Legs. There was a woman there, for whom he had once cared. He was eager to see her again. It seemed she had not forgotten him.

The Fleer warrior regarded Cuwignaka. His kaiila moved under him, restless with its energy.

" 'I have heard of you,' " translated the light-skinned lad. " 'It is well known on the plains that there is one among the Kaiila whose name is Cuwignaka, Woman's Dress, who has no quarrel with the Fleer.' "

Cuwignaka, standing, his arms folded, regarded the Fleer warrior. He said nothing.

"It is because of you," said the Fleer warrior, "that we came to Council Rock."

Cuwignaka looked puzzled.

"Do you know," asked the Fleer warrior, "why we came to Council Rock, and, because of us, the Sleen came?"

"No," said Cuwignaka. The Fleer and Sleen are allies.

"Because," laughed the warrior, "we have no quarrel with Cuwignaka!"

He then turned his kaiila about, by its jaw rope, and rode away.

"There will be peace, I think," I said, "between the Kaiila, and the Fleer and Sleen."

"No," said Canka, standing nearby, "I do not think so. It is only, rather, that it was a noble warrior's gesture."

"I did not think they were capable of such," said a man.

"Of course they are," said Hci, with us. "They are fine enemies."

"Canka does not think there will be peace," I said.

"Let us hope not," said Hci.

"I do not understand," I said.

"Ah, Tatankasa, Mitakola," said Hci, "I fear you will never understand us, or folk such as the Fleer or Sleen."

"Perhaps not," I said.

"War is part of our life," he said. "It is what makes us

what we are. I do not think the Kaiila could be the Kaiila without the Fleer, or the Fleer the Fleer, without the Kaiila."

"Good friends are priceless," said a man. "So, too, are fine enemies."

"Great enemies," said a man, "make great peoples."

"Do not be concerned, Mitakola," said Cuwignaka. "I do not think I understand them either. They are my people, and I love them, but I, too, may never understand them."

I watched the Fleer riding away. "That is reassuring," I said.

"You are now a warrior, my friend," said Hci to Cuwignaka. "What name will you take? Have you chosen one?"

"Will you take again your old name?" asked Canka. "Petuspe?" 'Petuspe', in Kaiila, means "Fire-Brand."

"No," said Cuwignaka. "And I have chosen my name."

"What will it be?" asked Hci.

"Cuwignaka," smiled Cuwignaka.

Hci smiled. "You have made it a warrior's name," he said. "Others, too, might now take it as such."

"What of you, Hci, my friend?" asked Cuwignaka. "Long ago you were known as Ihdazicaka. Will you take again that name?" 'Idazicaka', in Kaiila, means "One-Who-Counts-Himself-Rich."

"No," smiled Hci. "Now, although I feel I am one who may truly account himself rich, I shall keep the name Hci. It is a name of which I have become proud. In the time that I have worn that name I have taken my highest coups. More importantly, in the time that I have worn that name, I have, for the first time in my life, found friends."

Canka, Cuwignaka and Hci clasped hands.

A few hundred feet away, I saw some Dust Legs, a party of them, returning to their own country.

Among them, stripped naked, his hands tied behind him, riding backwards on a kaiila, his ankles bound together on a long strap, it running between them under the belly of the kaiila, rode the officer who had won the draw. He was a blond, slim young man. He had been the youngest of the officers. At the edge of the Ihanke, when it was reached, some weeks from now, he would be tied and beaten with switches, as though he might be a slave girl. Then, still stripped, and his hands tied then behind him, he would be released, to make his way as he could to Kailiauk, that white settlement closest to the Ihanke.

I saw a white slave girl staggering past, bent over. She was stripped. She carried a great bundle of sticks, tied together, on her back. She was pretty. The sticks would doubtless serve as fuel. She was doubtless on her way to the lodge of her master.

The Yellow Knives had been defeated ten days ago.

We were now in a great victory camp, near water, within sight of Council Rock, some seven or eight pasangs in the distance. In this camp there were Fleer, Sleen, Dust Legs and Kaiila. There had been dances and feasts. There had been much loot to divide, taken from Yellow-Knife encampments, and there had been much exchanging of gifts, even between hereditary, inveterate enemies such as the Fleer and Kaiila. Women, too, even free women, of these peoples, of those bands within trekking distance, had journeyed to the encampment. Such times of celebration, of festivals and peace, particularly among diverse tribes, are rare and precious. This was now Wayuksapiwi, in the calendar of the Dust Legs, the Corn-Harvest Moon, or, as it is spoken of in the reckoning of the Kaiila, Canwapekasnawi, the moon when the wind shakes off the leaves.

Only too clearly did the browning grass and the cool winds presage the turning of the seasons, and the advent of the gray skies and long nights of the bitter moons, Waniyetuwi, called the Winter Moon; Wanicokanwi, called the Mid-Winter Moon; Witehi, the Hard Moon; and Wicatawi, the Urt Moon. The vernal equinox occurs in Istawicayazanwi, the Sore-Eye Moon. Grunt and I had originally come to the Barrens, it now seemed long ago, in Magaksicaagliwi, the Moon of the Returning Giants. Already various groups, in small numbers, had begun to withdraw from the victory camp.

I, too, I thought, must soon be on my way. I must soon take my leave of the Barrens. I must begin the long journey back to the Ihanke, and thence to the Thentis Mountains, and the Vosk, and the Tamber Gulf and Port Kar.

I turned my steps toward my lodge, that which I shared with Cuwignaka, and his slave, Cespu, and with she who was now my own slave, she to whom I now held full legal title, lovely, obedient blond Mira. Cuwignaka had wished to give her to me but I had insisted on paying five hides for her. Grinning, he had accepted. She was a slave. Why should she not be bought and sold? She was now mine, totally.

I stopped before a quartet of stripped, kneeling white slaves, neck tethered, with their hands bound behind their back. They were the four girls who had been taken from

Grunt long ago by Yellow Knives, near the scene of the massacre of the wagon train, and the battle between the soldiers and the coalition of red savages, Lois, Inez, Corinne and Priscilla. They had been returned to Grunt after the defeat of the Yellow Knives, as a part of his portion of the booty. I examined them. They were lovely flesh loot. Priscilla bore a mark in black paint on her left breast. She had been sold for four hides to Akihoka, a friend of Canka, and also a member of the All Comrades. Corinne, the French girl, also bore a mark in black paint on her left breast, a different mark. Grunt had sold her to Keglezela, another of Canka's friends, also for four hides. Keglezela was also a member of the All Comrades. Neither Akihoka nor Keglezela had yet taken delivery on the women.

Lois and Inez had not been sold. They would serve as burden bearers for Grunt, on his way back to the Dust-Leg country. Then, if he had not sold them in the meantime, presumably they would accompany him back to Kailiauk in the spring, whence, after selling his goods and making his profits, and restocking his stores, he would presumably return once more, trading, to the Barrens, this time presumably in the company of the light-skinned young man he had met amongst the Dust Legs but weeks ago, his son.

I pulled Lois' head up by the hair. "You gave the alarm," I said, "when I, and two friends, stole tarns from Kinyanpi at a Yellow-Knife camp."

She shuddered with terror, held.

"Did you know that it was I with them?" I asked. "Did you recognize me?"

She trembled. "Yes, Master," she whispered, terrified.

"You did well," I said.

She looked at me, startled.

"What are you?" I asked.

"A slave girl," she whispered.

"See that you serve your new masters even better," I said.

"Yes, Master," she said.

I then released her, and turned about. Inez's neck, too, I had noted, looked well in its leather bond.

Others, too, there were, whose fate I had learned, Max and Kyle Hobart, and the two former Earth girls, Ginger and Evelyn, who had been slaves in Kailiauk. The Hobarts, with men, had pursued Grunt into the Barrens. Dust Legs, friends of Grunt, had attacked them. Grunt, retracing his steps, had located the scene of the attack. There he had found them, the only survivors, stripped and put in leg stretchers, as though they might be slave girls, lying in the grass, awaiting his attentions. He had not killed them. He had chained them in his coffle. They, though strong men, had been forbidden to so much as touch any of the scantily clad beauties who, neck-chained, as they, preceded them in the coffle.

Near the field of the massacre and near the place where the soldiers and red savages had fought they, with two girls, Ginger and Evelyn, whom they had muchly desired, as long ago as Kailiauk, were taken from Grunt by Sleen warriors. This was done at the same time as Yellow Knives had been appropriating Lois and three others of her sisters in bondage, Priscilla, Corinne and Inez. The Sleen had taken the Hobarts to serve as boys, performing lowly tasks and doing such things as watching kaiila. The girls they had taken for the common purposes for which luscious white females are employed by red masters.

During their time with the Sleen apparently Max and Kyle Hobart, unable to help themselves any longer, and finding the girls staked out, naked, in a desolate place, presumably for punishment, had raped them. Shortly after this the slaves had begun to meet. These meetings were typical of the clandestine trysts of slaves. They took place in the shadows, behind lodges and at places marked in the high grass, where they might tie in one another's arms, if only fearfully and briefly, fearing the step of a master, the shadow of a whip.

It was in these days, and in these meetings, so different from the alcoves of Kailiauk, that the girls learned that they were the slaves of the Hobarts and the Hobarts learned to their joy that they, though themselves collared, owned slaves. The relationship of the Hobarts and the girls, I am sure, had not escaped the attention of the Sleen. I think it quite likely that the Sleen, in their kindness, and recognizing the need of strong men, such as the Hobarts, for women, had taken this fashion of rewarding them for good service. I am sure that it was no accident that the Hobarts had been sent on an errand near the place where the two beauties had been staked out. Similarly, there is little, I suspect, which transpires between slaves which is not known to masters. It is usually only a question as to whether the masters wish to take action or not. This hypothesis is further confirmed by the fact that the Sleen, in trading with Grunt, Grunt making use of booties acquired from the Yellow Knives, offered him, in effect, the package containing both the Hobarts and their lovers.

The Hobarts, with whom I later discussed these things, now share my suspicions in this matter. Grunt, incidentally, has freed the Hobarts, and put them temporarily in his employ. They will accompany him to the country of the Dust Legs, helping him in the transportation of goods to that point, and will then, before the winter, continue on to Kailiauk, there to arrange buyers for Grunt's hides, to be delivered in the spring. They will then, presumably, return to their ranch, outside of Kailiauk. In payment for these services each will receive a female slave.

I saw two lovers riding by, the woman behind the man, on his kaiila. Their names were Witantanka and Akamda.

"Master!" cried the slave girl, desisting for the moment from following her master, and kneeling swiftly before me, and kissing my feet.

"Greetings, Oiputake," I said.

She looked up at me. "I thank you," she said, "for the most precious gift a man can give a woman."

"What is that?" I asked.

"Herself," she said.

"It is nothing," I said.

"Howo, Oiputake," called her red master, turning about. He was Wapike, "One-Who-Is-Fortunate," of the Isanna.

"Ho, Itancanka!" she cried, springing to her feet, joyfully, and running to follow him.

Two hunters I saw returning, friends; one was Cotanka, "Love Flute," of the Wismahi, and the other was Wayuhahaka, "One-Who-Possessess-Much," who had elected to remain with the Isbu. Once he had been Squash, a lad of the Waniyanpi. Across the back of the kaiila, before the lad, lay a tabuk. I was reminded that the Kaiila, in spite of the stores acquired from the Yellow Knives, much of which had been their own, from the summer camp, must still do hunting for the winter.

Hurrying at the flank of Cotanka's kaiila, welcoming him back to camp, was a blonde, barefoot, collared and wearing a brief shirtdress. It was she who had functioned, in effect, as a "lure girl" in one of the actions at the summer camp. She now belonged to him. A thousandfold and more, doubtless, had Cotanka seen that she had repaid him for her part in the duplicity which had endangered him before permitting her to lapse into the stringencies of a more common slavery, that of the absolute and uncompromising bondage in which female slaves are typically, and without a second thought, held on Gor.

The hunters and the slave were met at the entrance to Wayuhahaka's lodge by another slave, a blond, barefoot girl in a brief, tightly-belted tunic of Waniyanpi cloth. She greeted her master radiantly. She lowered her head and knelt, crossing her arms over her breast. This, in effect, was a mixture of sign and Gorean convention. Crossing the arms over the breast indicates love in sign. That she had done this kneeling and lowering her head, then, signified submission, love and that she was a slave. She sprang to her feet at a command from Wayuhahaka. The name 'Strawberry' was still being kept upon her. This seemed a suitable name for a slave. The tabuk was then slid from the back of the kaiila into the girls' arms. They staggered under its weight as it was, for such a beast, a large one. While the women worked the men would sit before the entrance to the lodge and talk.

"Wasnapohdi!" I called, seeing her passing by, a roll of kailiauk hide on her shoulder.

She, delighted, ran to me and knelt before me.

"Are you pleased with your new master?" I asked.

"Oh," she cried, breathlessly, rapturously, "he is my master! He is my master! For years, in my heart, I have known I belonged to him! Now, at last, I am his legal slave! He is so strong with me, and perfect! I am so happy!"

Her new master was a lad of the Napoktan, some two years her senior, Waiyeyeca, "One-Who-Finds-Much," who, long ago, had once owned her when they were both children. He was now a fine young warrior and she a needful, curvaceous slave. One who found Wasnapohdi in his arms, I thought to myself, would indeed be one who had found much.

"I was so fearful that he would not buy me," she said. "I was fearfully overpriced by Grunt, my former master!"

"What did you bring?" I asked. I already knew, of course.

"Four hides of the yellow kailiauk!" she said.

I whistled, softly, as though astonished.

"Can you believe it?" she asked.

"I think so," I said. "You are, after all, a property not without certain charms."

"And Grunt, my master, would not even bargain," she said. "The price was put on me as a fixed price."

"I see," I said. This was unusual in the Barrens, and unusual, too, even in the cities.

"And I," she said, "only a white female and a slave!"

"Grunt is a shrewd trader," I said. "Doubtless he was sure of his buyer."

"My master was not pleased to pay so much," she said. "When he took me to his lodge he was angry and beat me. Then he made lengthy love to me, and I was his."

"I see," I said. Grunt had doubtless priced Wasnapohdi as high as he did in order that the young man might never again be tempted to lightly dispose of such a property. Yet I think this precaution was not truly necessary on Grunt's part. I did not think that Waiyeyeca, now having come again into the ownership of his former childhood slave, would ever be likely to let her go again.

"I shall miss my former master, though," said the girl. "Though he was strict with me, as is fitting, for I am a slave, he, too, was very kind to me."

"He saved your life at the summer camp," I said, "putting you on a tether and enforcing slave sanctions upon you, to lead you to safety."

"I know," she said.

"Doubtless, Slave," I said, "you are on an errand. That you not be whipped for dallying I permit you to be on your way."

She put down her head and, tenderly, kissed my feet. Then, with a smile, shouldering again the roll of kailiauk hide she was carrying, she leapt up, and sped on her way. She was going toward the lodge of Waiyeyeca. Something, I supposed, had been exchanged for the hide. Perhaps it would be used to repair one of the skins in Waiyeyeca's lodge. He had a woman now to attend to such matters. He had recently purchased her.

I continued on, then, toward my own lodge.

"Hurry, hurry, lazy slave!" I heard. I heard then the hiss of a switch and a girl, carrying two skins of water, cry out in pain. She was a white female slave. She was naked, collared, red-haired and large-bosomed. She belonged to Mahpiyasapa. One of Mahpiyasapa's wives, with a switch in her gnarled, mutilated hand, the woman with whom I had once spoken outside of his lodge before the attack on the summer camp, was supervising her in her duties.

The large-bosomed, red-haired girl looked at me. My face was expressionless. Then, crying out, she hurried on, struck twice more by the switch. She was now called Natusa. 'Natu' designates corn silk, or the tassel on the maize plant; it can also stand for the hair on the side of the head. These things, of course, are all silky and smooth to the touch. 'Sa' stands for red. The name, accordingly, has no precise translation into either Gorean or English. "Red Silk" will not do as a translation because corn silk, or the hair at the side of the head, is quite different from silk, the cloth. Similarly, the expression "red silk," in Gorean, tends to be used as a category in slaving, and also, outside the slaving context, as an expression in vulgar discourse, indicating that the woman is no longer a virgin, or, as the Goreans say, at least vulgarly of slaves, that her body has been opened by men. Its contrasting term is "white silk," usually used of slaves who are still virgins, or, equivalently, slaves whose bodies have not yet been opened by men. Needless to say, slaves seldom spend a great deal of time in the "white-silk" category. It is common not to dally in initiating a slave into the realities of her condition. The translation "Red Corn Silk," too, does not seem felicitous. The best translation is perhaps "Red Tassel," the tassel being understood as that of the maize plant, prized by the red savages. The connotation in all these cases, with which the red savage, in the fluency and depth with which he understands his own language, is fully cognizant, and to which he responds, is that of something red which is pleasant to feel, something that is soft and smooth to the touch.

It was no mistake or coincidence that the red-haired, large-bosomed Natusa had come into the ownership of Mahpiyasapa. Canka, as a portion of his loot from the Yellow Knives, had taken five hides of the yellow kailiauk. These he had given to Mahpiyasapa, as a gift, in a sense, but also, in a way, as a payment for his earlier acquisition of Winyela, whom Grunt had brought originally into the Barrens as a property for Mahpiyasapa. In taking these five hides Mahpiyasapa, in effect, forgave Canka for his exercise of the warrior rights which had brought Winyela's pretty neck into his beaded collar.

I had then, luckily, among Yellow-Knife slaves, discovered she who was now called Natusa. Upon my expression of interest she had been given to me as a part of my portion of the loot. I had kept her for a bit, subjecting her to discipline and use, and then I had given her to Grunt. Grunt, happily, of course, sold her to Mahpiyasapa for the five hides of the yellow kailiauk which Mahpiyasapa had received from Canka. Canka, thus, cleared his accounts, so to speak, with his chief and acquired, thereby, a clear moral as well as legal title to Winyela. Grunt, of course, received his five hides and

Mahpiyasapa received the rare, red-haired woman he had, in effect, ordered from Grunt last year. Mahpiyasapa, incidentally, was more than pleased with these developments. It had been no secret in the camp that he had regarded Winyela's breasts, at least for his tastes, as too small. Red savages often, like many men of the Tahari, tend to find a special attractiveness in large-breasted women.

On the way back to my lodge I passed a bargaining place, an open area serving for trading and exchanges, not unusual in an intertribal camp. There I saw Seibar, who had once been Pumpkin, of the Waniyanpi, trading, in sign, with a Dust-Leg warrior. Seibar was offering a netted sack of maize. The Dust Leg was bidding sheaves of dried kailiauk meat. No longer must those who had been Waniyanpi content themselves with the consumption of their own produce and deliver surpluses without recompense into the hands of masters.

The community was now, in effect, a small freehold in the Barrens, and yet, strictly, in the letter of the law, stood to the Kaiila as a leased tenancy. Not a square hort would the Kaiila surrender, truly, of their tribal lands. Yet the rent for the tenancy had been set at one ear of maize per year, to be delivered to the reigning chieftain of the Isbu Kaiila. Yesterday this ear of maize had been delivered, with suitable ceremonies, to Mahpiyasapa. The tenancy was subject to certain conditions, recorded suitably on two hides, each bearing the marks of the appropriate signatories. One of these hides remained with the Isbu; the other went to the leased tenancy. The two major conditions specified on the hides were that the tenancy was subject to review, to be followed by revocation or renewal, every tenth winter, and that the numbers of individuals in the tenancy were to be strictly limited, any excess in population to be removed by emigration to the lands west of the Ihanke. The red savages did not wish to countenance increasing white populations within their territories.

Thus, first, those who had been Waniyanpi were now no longer slaves of the Kaiila and, second, they now maintained what amounted, for most practical purposes, to a small free state within the Barrens. These things were given to them as gifts by the Kaiila, in appreciation for the services rendered during the time of the war with the Yellow Knives and soldiers, for providing us with a tarn base within striking distance of Council Rock, and sheltering and supporting our men during the period of their training.

The community of those who had been Waniyanpi, of

course, was not identified with a particular area of land, and certainly not with a territory occupied under the conditions of a leased tenancy. It now, in the Gorean fashion, for the first time, tended to be identified with a Home Stone. The community could now, if it wished, the Home Stone moving, even migrate to new lands. In Gorean law allegiances to a Home Stone, and not physical structures and locations, tend to define communities.

Seibar had wished to call the small community New Ar, but had abandoned this proposal in the face of an unfavorable reception by his fellows. Ar was not as popular with some of his fellows as it was with him, and that redoubtable municipality, the largest city in the Gorean north, was unfamiliar to many of them, even in hearsay. After much discussion it was decided to call the tiny community Seibar's Holding, this being a manifestation of the respect and affection they bore their leader. The only reservations pertaining to this name seemed to be held by Seibar himself who, to the end, remained the stubborn champion of "New Ar."

The red savages, themselves, incidentally, have their own names for the new, small community. In Kaiila it is called "Anpao" or, sometimes, "Anptaniya." The expression 'Anpao' means "Dawn" or "Daylight." The expression 'Anptaniya' has a more complex meaning in translation. It means, rather literally, "the breath of day." It is used to refer, for example, to the first, lovely glimmerings of morning. The expression is related, of course, to the vapors raised by the sun in the early morning, these perhaps, poetically and beautifully, as is often the case in the languages of the red savages, suggesting "the breath of day." In both expressions, of course, the connotations are rather clear, that darkness is over, that a new day is at hand.

I did not call myself to the attention of Seibar. Last night we had feasted. I did not wish to renew the bitterness of farewells.

I had soon, then, returned to the vicinity of my lodge. I was met there by Mira. She knelt before me and put her head to my feet. Then she lifted her head. "Word has come from the lodge of the dark guest," she said, "brought by Akihoka. The dark guest has pointed to the translator."

"I understand," I said. The translator was programmed in Kur and Gorean.

"I think the dark guest would speak with you," she said.

"Yes," I said.

"But, why, Master?" she asked. "What have you to do with the dark guest? And how is it that among your things there was a translator?"

I smiled.

"Who is it, to whom I belong?" she asked.

"Curiosity," I said, "is not becoming in a Kajira."

"Forgive me, Master," she said, putting her head down. I decided I would not, this time, whip her.

"I am going to the lodge of the dark guest," I said. "We will speak together."

"But what, Master, am I to do?" she asked.

"Surely you have woman's work to attend to," I said.

"Yes, Master," she said.

"Attend to it," I said.

"Yes, Master," she said.

55

THE COMMINGLINGS OF BLOOD

Cuwignaka's knife moved on his own forearm, and then on mine, and then on Hci's.

"You cannot be a member of the Sleen Soldiers of the All Comrades," had said Hci, "for you are not Kaiila, and you do not know our dances and mysteries, the contents of our medicine bundles."

"There is another thing," had said Cuwignaka, "which can be done."

"Do it," had said Hci.

Cuwignaka held his arm to mine, and then I held my arm to that of Hci, and then Hci, in turn, held his arm to that of Cuwignaka. Thus was the circle of blood closed.

"It is done," said Cuwignaka.

"Brothers," I said.

"Brothers," said Hci.

"Brothers," said Cuwignaka.

56

I TAKE MY LEAVE FROM THE CAMP

I tied Mira's hands together before her body.

"When we reach civilization," I told her, "I will have you properly collared and branded."

"I am a slave," she said, "I shall look forward to my collaring and branding."

"That will confirm your status upon you," I said, "legally, and in the eyes of all."

"Yes, Master," she said.

I looked down upon her.

"Do you think that I will be slain in Port Kar?" she asked.

"I do not think so," I said, "but I would speak freely, and in great detail, if I were you."

She shuddered. "I will do so," she said.

The house of Samos in Port Kar was famous for its methods of interrogation. They would be used without reservation, of course, in the case of mere slaves.

"You are not as terrified now," I said, "as last night." It had been last night when I, after returning the translator to my things, had bound her hand and foot, and then informed her of the identity of her master. She had squirmed in misery and terror at my feet, her worst suspicions having been confirmed. She, a former agent of Kurii, had fallen into the hands of one who had done service for Priest-Kings, one who had doings with Samos of Port Kar, one who was known to some as Tarl Cabot, to others as Bosk of Port Kar.

"If you are perfectly cooperative," I had told the terrorized girl, "you many, afterward, be permitted to live as a woman—and a slave."

"I will be perfectly cooperative," she had whispered, "—Master."

I smiled at her.

"No, Master," she said, "I am not as terrified as I was last night."

"Good," I said.

I hoisted her to the back of a kaiila and she, to keep her balance, momentarily frightened, clutched at its mane, fastening her fingers in it. I took a long strap and tied it about her right ankle and then, drawing it tight under the belly of the kaiila, looped it twice about her left ankle. I then jerked the entire arrangement tight again and fastened her left ankle in place. Her thighs were then tied tightly about the great chest of the kaiila; they were held, bound as she was, flattened against, and pressed deeply into, the body of the animal; I saw them move with its breathing; on their interiors, later, would be found the marks of the beast's warm, silken coat and oil from its hide.

The beast did not have reins but a neck rope. I took this neck rope, a long one, and slung it about the pommel of my saddle.

"Master has not seen fit to permit me clothing," she said.

"That is true," I said. I had taken from her even the insignificant rags I had permitted her to wear, weeks ago, in what was then the compound of the Waniyanpi.

"I shall be brought back from the Barrens, then," she said, "as a naked slave."

"Yes," I said. This seemed fitting for one who had entered them as a proud free woman, and an agent of Kurii.

We were on a rise near the victory camp. It was near dawn.

I could see some folk making their way towards our position.

Farewells were rapidly spoken.

I then slung some supplies on the kaiila on which the girl, tied, was mounted. These I put both before her and behind her. Among those behind her, in saddle sacks, balanced by sheaves of meat, was a translator.

I mounted.

I then made my way, slowly, down from the rise, moving in a westward direction.

I did not take with me the tarn I had captured in the tarn country. I thought it preferable that it, a trained bird, be left with the Kaiila. Tarns were precious to them, particularly in connection with acquiring new tarns. They would need every tarn, I conjectured, which they could obtain. Indeed, I suspected that they would soon attempt to obtain them even through the channels of trade. As the appearance of kaiila in the Barrens, long ago, had wrought a social and cultural revolution among the tribes, so, too, I suspected, now might the tarn. The tarn, as the kaiila before it, might now bring about a transformation on the prairies. I was apprehensive when I thought of the skills of red savages on the kaiila. How fearsome might they then become astride the mighty tarn. Yet, it seemed to me that the mastery of the tarn, in its way, was perhaps the key to assuring the continued stability of the Barrens. If tribes without tarns could not hold their own against those who had them, then these other tribes would presumably be forced from their lands and into westward migrations. These, in turn, might displace others. In a generation or so, it seemed clear that the integrity of the Ihanke itself might be threatened. Too often in the histories of worlds had the displacements of peoples become the prelude to lengthy and bloody wars. Stability's key, in the paradoxes of martial reality, is commonly combative parity.

I stopped the kaiila and turned about, to look back. Many of my friends were on the rise near the camp.

Zarendargar was not among them.

Two days ago I had been summoned to his lodge. There, with Zarendargar, was the eighth Kur, unbound.

This Kur, according to its own account, had been contacted in its wanderings in the Barrens by a ship of Kurii.

The sentence of death, according to the beast, had been rescinded against Zarendargar.

He was now to be recalled to the Steel Worlds.

"Surely you do not believe this?" I asked Zarendargar, Half-Ear, through the translator.

"It was for this reason that my comrade sought me here, at great risk," he said.

"Do you believe that?" I asked.

"Yes," said Zarendargar. "It is true."

"How do you know?" I asked.

"He has sworn it, by the rings," said Zarendargar.

"You will go with him?" I asked.

"Yes," said Zarendargar. "A rendezvous with the ship has been arranged."

"When will you leave?" I asked.

"Tomorrow," said Zarendargar. "The rendezvous is distant. The trek will be long."

"Why has this sentence been rescinded?" I asked.

"A shift in political power has taken place in the Cliffs," he said. "Now, too, once again, it seems my services are desired."

"To what end?" I asked.

The lips of that great shaggy face curled back, revealing the fangs. It was a Kur smile. "I do not feel that it would be appropriate to say," came from the translator.

"I suppose," I said, "as one who has upon occasion espoused the cause of Priest-Kings, I should attempt to slay you."

"Surely it was not for that reason that you came to the Barrens," he said.

"No," I smiled.

"Nor was it for that reason that I had the story hide transmitted to the west."

"You did that deliberately?" I asked.

"Yes," he said. "In this fashion I sought to draw the Death Squad into the Barrens where they might be dealt with and sought, too, to enlist your aid in my battle with them."

"I do not understand," I said.

"I assumed," he said, "they would attempt to enlist the aid of men in what, from their point of view, would seem to be a project of interest to men, my apprehension and destruction. Surely they would attempt to contact Samos of Port Kar and, in this, would presumably be apprising you, too, of their plans."

"We rendered them no assistance," I said. "They had to make other arrangements, with mercenaries."

"That is what I thought would happen," said Zarendargar. "I was a better judge of men, I think, than they."

"Perhaps," I said.

"You would come to the Barrens," he said. "I was sure of it."

"You were correct," I smiled.

"They did not expect you to come to the Barrens," he said.

"Of course not," I said.

"That was a serious miscalculation on their part," he said. "But perhaps they could not be blamed for it. They could not know something which I knew."

"What is that?" I asked.

"That once, long ago," he said, "we shared paga."

Yesterday, early, Zarendargar and his companion had left the victory camp. I did not, of course, attempt to follow them.

I continued to look back to the rise behind me. I lifted my hand to the folk gathered there.

Mahpiyasapa, civil chieftain of the Isbu Kaiila, was there, and his friend, Kahintokapa, of the Casmu, he of the Yellow-Kaiila Riders. His shield still bore the visage of Zarendargar. Grunt was there, too, and his son, by the Dust-Leg woman. With him, as well, was his friend, Wagmezahu, Corn

Stalks, of the Fleer, who had come with the Fleer to Council Rock. Tomorrow Grunt and his son, with the Hobarts, and various slaves, would set forth for the Dust-Leg country, where he would winter. I saw Canka and Winyela, and Wasnapohdi and Waiyeyeca; and Oiputake, with her master, Wapike. Many others were there, too, come out from the camp, men such as Akihoka and Keglezela. Too, prominent among those on the rise were two I had known even to the pledge and testimony of the knife, even to the touchings of wounds, even to the comminglings of blood, my friends, my brothers, Hci and Cuwignaka.

I then turned away, again, and again, slowly, took my way westward, toward the Ihanke.

Toward noon I did look upward once, and behind me. In the sky there was a great black tarn.

I lifted my hand and arm to it, the palm of my hand facing inward, in Gorean salute. It turned then, taking its way eastward. I watched it until it disappeared, a distant speck in the blue skies over the vastness of the Barrens.

I then continued on my way, the neck tether of the kaiila behind me looped about the pommel of my saddle.